The Love Season

"In a juicy peach of a summer tome, Hilderbrand again alchemizes her three favorite elements—food, love, and Nantucket—with eminently readable results. . . . *Season* is so gratifying."
—*Entertainment Weekly* (Grade: A–)

"Summer fare that's a cut above the usual beach provisions . . . Hilderbrand, who wrote 2002's *Nantucket Nights*, serves up a mouthwatering menu, keeps the Veuve Clicquot flowing, and tops it all with a dollop of mystery that will have even drowsy sunbathers turning pages until the very satisfying end."
—*People* (four stars)

"Hilderbrand's fifth book is a fulfilling tale of familial excavation and self-exploration. . . . It's a refreshing, resonant summertime treat." —*Publishers Weekly*

"Hilderbrand's sensitive portrayal of a young motherless woman on a journey of self-discovery, and her guilt-ridden godmother's attempt to find the courage to confront the past, is very moving."
—*Booklist*

"A good page-turner." —*Library Journal*

"As a storyteller, Hilderbrand ranks among the best, and she has ingeniously constructed this foray into the past around a meal. . . . This is a don't-miss novel." —*The Star-Ledger* (Newark)

The Blue Bistro

"A perfectly enjoyable beach book." —*Publishers Weekly*

"Hilderbrand keeps things moving briskly in between sumptuous descriptions of food, drink, and tableware, throwing in an in-depth lesson on the restaurant business for good measure. Fun, stylish, and absorbing vacation reading." —*Booklist*

"A wonderful, wonderful love story . . . the kind that you read, then recommend to many, many friends—and so, I recommend it to you. Highly." —James Patterson, bestselling author of *Suzanne's Diary for Nicholas*

"A wonderfully poignant behind-the-scenes journey into the world of high-end restaurants, island life, and the inner workings of the human heart. A great summer story." —Lolly Winston, *New York Times* bestselling author of *Good Grief*

"Hilderbrand adds depth to the novel with her multifaceted characters. The restaurant comes alive with believable conflicts between the staff and patrons. But the love story between Adrienne and Thatcher is the jewel of the novel. Together they discover the meaning of devotion and the rarity of real love." —*RT Book Reviews*

"This brand-new book is sure to become a summer favorite." —*ReadersDigest.com* (chosen as their #1 Unforgettable Beach Read)

Nantucket Nights

"Things get more twisted at every turn with enough lies and betrayals to fuel a whole season of soap operas. . . . Readers will be hooked." —*Publishers Weekly*

"What a perfect summer pleasure Elin Hilderbrand provides in *Nantucket Nights*, mixing the complexities of family life and friendship with suspense, romance, and moonlit Nantucket nights." —Nancy Thayer, author of *Custody*

"Dips deep into *Peyton Place* country." —*Kirkus Reviews*

"Ms. Hilderbrand paints a picture of idyllic Nantucket life that slowly starts to unravel as the ugly underbelly is revealed. Hidden secrets, a mysterious disappearance, and the pain of betrayal form the basis for this haunting read." —*RT Book Reviews*

"The novel is fast paced and suspenseful enough to keep readers interested. A likely candidate for summer-vacation reading." —*Booklist*

The Beach Club

"Surprisingly touching . . . a work of fiction you're likely to think about long after you've put it down." —*People*

"A strong, emotional pull . . . readers will remain absorbed until the surprising denouement." —*Publishers Weekly*

"A feisty novel . . . lively enough to keep a sunbather awake." —*Kirkus Reviews*

"A charming, easygoing story about the tangled lives and loves of the summer crew and guests at a hotel and beach club." —*The Boston Globe*

"A steamy tale." —*Boston Herald*

Also by Elin Hilderbrand

❧

Winter Stroll

The Rumor

Winter Street

The Matchmaker

Beautiful Day

Summerland

Silver Girl

The Island

The Castaways

A Summer Affair

Barefoot

The Love Season

The Blue Bistro

Nantucket Nights

Elin Hilderbrand

High Tide

The Beach Club
&
Summer People

St. Martin's Griffin ☙ New York

HIGH TIDE: THE BEACH CLUB. Copyright © 2000 by Elin Hilderbrand. SUMMER PEOPLE. Copyright © 2003 by Elin Hilderbrand. "New York City, June 2016" copyright © 2016 by Elin Hilderbrand. All rights reserved. Printed in the United States of America. For information, address St. Martin's Press, 175 Fifth Avenue, New York, N.Y. 10010.

www.stmartins.com

The Beach Club designed by Victoria Kuskowski
Summer People designed by Kathryn Parise

The Library of Congress Cataloging-in-Publication Data
is available upon request.

ISBN 978-1-250-10489-2 (trade paperback)

Our books may be purchased in bulk for promotional, educational, or business use. Please contact your local bookseller or the Macmillan Corporate and Premium Sales Department at 1-800-221-7945, extension 5442, or by e-mail at MacmillanSpecialMarkets@macmillan.com.

First Edition: May 2016

10 9 8 7 6 5 4 3 2 1

THE BEACH CLUB

FOR CHIP,

WHO GAVE ME ENOUGH LOVE EACH DAY

TO LAST LIFETIMES,

AND WHO NEVER ONCE STOPPED BELIEVING

Acknowledgments

My warmest and most sincere thanks to the following people:

Michael Carlisle, my agent and fellow Nantucketer, for making this dream come true.

My entire family.

My "Nantucket family," whose essence is in this book: Rob, Nickie, Eric, Margie, Ginny, John, Jeff, Richard and Amanda, Jeffrey and Sue, Suki, Justin and Forest, the "G" and the "D", Vanessa, Keith, Misha, Sally, Brooks and Parker, John and Kelly, Martha, Glenn, J.L.N., and the great Mary Baker.

For their enormous kindnesses and friendship, thanks to John and Nancy, Paul, Rita and Palmer, Tal, Jonnie, Pat and Doris, Fred, Irene, Jim, Barbie and the rest of the "porch night" crew, and Tim and Mary.

Thanks to Richard and Teena for giving me the best part-time job on the island.

Special thanks to Heather, whose insight and criticism were invaluable.

My love for Nantucket Island is powerful and unlimited, but in the end, there is only one reason why I stayed. His name is Chip Cunningham, he is my husband and my hero, and this book is for him.

The Opening

May 1

Dear Bill,

Another summer season is about to begin on beautiful Nantucket Island. I have just returned from my winter retreat—Nevis, Vail, Saipan—it's your guess where I've been. The important thing is that I'm back, and I am prepared to sweeten my offer to buy the hotel. I know you have some crazy idea about family loyalty and passing the business on to your daughter, but things don't always work out the way we want them to. Alas, I have learned this the hard way. So as you start this season of sun and sand, consider my offer: twenty-two million. That's a pretty good deal, and if you don't mind my saying so, you're not getting any younger.

    Feel free to write to me at the usual P.O. box downtown. I'll be waiting to hear from you.

As ever,

S.B.T.

ON THE FIRST OF May, Mack Petersen swung his Jeep into the parking lot of the Nantucket Beach Club and Hotel for the start of his twelfth summer season as manager, the Almost Head Honcho. Twelve was an important number, Mack decided, with its own name. A dozen. Mack's dozen years of working at the hotel were like eggs, all in one basket, like the Boston cream doughnuts served at the hotel's Continental breakfast, one practically indistinguishable from the next. There were twelve months in a year, twelve signs in the Zodiac, twelve hours of A.M. and P.M. Twelve was a full cycle, a cycle completed.

Maybe Maribel was right, then. Maybe this was the year things would change.

Mack walked across the parking lot to look at Nantucket's most picturesque beach. Over the winter, northeasterly winds blew the sand into smooth, rounded dunes, in some places six and eight feet high. Mack trudged to the top of one of the dunes and gazed out over the water. The Beach Club sat on the north shore of the island, on Nantucket Sound, where the water was as flat and placid as a fishing pond. The white sand was clean and wide, although they lost beach to erosion, some years as much as twenty-five feet. Last year they had gained beach and the owner of the hotel, Bill Elliott, was so happy that he had thrown his arm around Mack's shoulder, and said, "See there? We're not going to lose her after all." As though the Beach Club and Hotel belonged to them both. Which, of course, was not the case.

Mack had stayed on Nantucket through the winter with his girlfriend Maribel, but he hadn't checked on the hotel even once. It was a rule he'd created over the years: *I won't think about the hotel in winter*. Were the shingles falling off? Was the paint peeling? Were they losing beach? Those were questions for Bill and his wife, Therese, but they spent their winters skiing in Aspen, and if anyone were going to check on the place, it would be Mack. But he never did. He knew that if he let it, the hotel would obsess him, drive him crazy.

The most photographed part of the hotel was the pavilion—a covered deck with five blue Adirondack chairs facing the water. All summer, guests sat in the low, wide chairs with their feet up on the railing, drinking coffee, reading the paper. This picture of summer bliss made it into the Nantucket chamber of commerce guide year after year.

The lobby of the hotel was its own freestanding building with a row of windows that looked over the pavilion and the beach. The hotel rooms began outside the back door of the lobby: twenty single-story, cedar-shingled rooms formed a giant L. Ten rooms ran down toward the water and ten rooms faced the water. All the rooms had small decks, and thus the rooms were distinguished by the names, "side deck" and "front deck." Therese had further nicknamed the front deck rooms the "Gold Coast," because they were so expensive.

Twenty rooms might not seem like a lot at first, but the beach also hosted a private Beach Club: One hundred members paid annual dues to sit under umbrellas for the ten weeks of summer. They could have saved themselves the money and gone to Steps Beach to the west, or Jetties Beach to the east, but year after year membership of the Beach Club was full. Mack's primary job was to treat the guests and the Beach Club members like royalty. He arranged dinner reservations and the delivery of flowers, wine, steamed lobsters, birthday cakes. He had a key to every door, and knew the location of every extension cord, vacuum cleaner bag, feather pillow. He hired and fired the staff and created the weekly work schedule. He knew every Beach Club member's name by heart and the names of all the children. Mack ran the place. Bill and Therese had owned the Beach Club and Hotel for twenty years but Mack understood its ins and outs, its cracks, sore spots, and hideaways better than anyone. It had been his course of study now for twelve years.

A thousand guests would walk into the lobby over the next six months. Some had been coming to the hotel as long as Mack had worked there. The baseball managers (in July, over the all-star break), Leo Hearn, a lawyer from Chicago (Memorial Day), Mrs. Ford, a widow who came for the month of September and smoked a pack of cigarettes in her room each day.

Then there would be Andrea Krane, a woman Mack thought he might be in love with. Andrea arrived in June and stayed for three weeks with her autistic son, James. Mack imagined her long, honey-colored hair twisted into a bun or a braid. Smiling a rare smile, because when she arrived at the Beach Club she was happy. She had three weeks stretched in front of her, twenty-one days sparkling like diamonds on a tennis bracelet.

Mack watched the ferry approach in the distance. It was full of people coming to work for the season—waiters and waitresses, ice cream scoopers, lifeguards, landscapers, nannies, chambermaids, bellmen. Twelve years ago it had been Mack on that boat—his first time on the ocean—and when he stepped off at Steamship Wharf his life changed. Nantucket had saved him.

• • •

TWELVE YEARS AGO, MACK was eighteen, a farm boy. Born and raised in Swisher, Iowa, where his father owned a 530-acre farm—corn and soybeans, hogs and chickens. The farm had originally belonged to Mack's grandfather, then his father, and Mack grew up understanding that it would one day be his. School felt like a waste of time, except that it was a place to socialize. Mack loved to talk—the bonus for spending hours on a combine by himself was that his father took him to The Alibi for a greasy ham-and-egg breakfast, or to the feed store— and there was always lots of talk.

Mack's mother worked part-time at an antique store in Swisher—a quiet job of crystal figurines and classical music. Mack's parents belonged to Swisher Presbyterian, but they weren't strict about going to church, nor were they prescriptive about what Mack should believe. In fact, his mother once told him she didn't believe in heaven.

"I just don't believe in it," she said as she scrubbed potatoes at the sink and Mack puzzled over his trigonometry homework at the long oak harvest table. "I believe that when you die, you die, and you're back to where you were before you were born. Oblivion, I guess you'd call it."

Two months before Mack's high school graduation, his parents went out for their Saturday night dinner date. On their way home on Route 380, a tractor trailer sideswiped their car and they crashed into the guardrail and died. There hadn't been foul weather—no rain, no ice. Only carelessness on the part of the truck driver, and possibly, on the part of Mack's father, who should have hit the brakes harder when the truck pulled in front of him. (Had his father been drinking? A cocktail before dinner, wine?) It didn't matter to Mack; it didn't change the fact that two good people were dead. Mack was left orphaned, although *orphaned* wasn't a word anyone used, and nei- ther was it a word Mack thought of often. He was, after all, eighteen. An adult.

Mack left the farm to his father's lawyer, David Pringle, and his father's sidekick Wendell, and the farmhands who worked there. He picked up his high school diploma, caught a bus east and took it as far as it would go, a romantic idea, one his mother would have liked. When the bus stopped in Hyannis, Massachusetts, Mack thought he would find a small apartment and a job, but then he caught his first glimpse of the ocean and he learned there was a boat that would take him even farther east, to an island. Nantucket Island.

Mack found his job at the Beach Club by accident. When the ferry pulled in to Steamship Wharf, Bill Elliott stood waiting on the dock, and when Mack stepped off the boat, Bill tapped his shoulder.

"Are you here for the job at the Beach Club?" Bill asked.

Mack didn't even think about it. "Yes, sir, I am."

He followed Bill to an olive-colored Jeep. Bill hoisted Mack's duffel into the back and they drove off the wharf and down North Beach Road without another word. When they pulled into the parking lot of the hotel, Mack saw the view of the water—he was still not used to so much water—and then he heard a hum. *Hum. Hum.*

"What's that noise?" Mack asked.

"The seagulls?" Bill said. "They can be pretty loud. Where did you come from?"

"Iowa," Mack said.

Bill's forehead wrinkled. "I thought you were coming from New Jersey."

It confirmed Mack's fear: there was some kid from New Jersey standing on the wharf, waiting for Bill to pick him up.

"No, sir, I came from Swisher, Iowa." He heard the noise again. *Hum. Hum.* Home—it sounded like a voice saying *"Home."* "You don't hear that?" Mack asked.

Bill smiled. "I guess you didn't have too many gulls out in Iowa. I guess this is all brand-new."

"Yes, sir," Mack said. A voice was saying *"Home, home."* Mack could hear it as plain as day. He extended his hand. "I'm Mack Petersen."

Bill frowned. "Mack Petersen wasn't who I was picking up."

"I know," Mack said. "But you asked if I was here for a job, and I am."

"Do you know anything about hotels?" Bill asked.

"I will soon, I guess," Mack said. And he heard it again; it was the funniest thing. *Home.*

Mack didn't believe in spiritual guides, past lives, fortune-tellers, tarot cards, or crystal balls. He believed in God and in a heaven, despite what his mother told him. But what Mack heard wasn't the voice of God. The voice wasn't coming from the sky, it was coming from the land beneath his feet.

Mack had heard the voice at other times over the past twelve years, too many now to count. He read about phenomena like this—the Taos Hum, the Whisper of Carmel—but never on Nantucket. Mack once found the courage to ask Maribel, "Do you ever hear things on this island? *From* this island? Do you ever hear a voice?" Maribel blinked her blue eyes, and said, "I do think the island has a voice. It's the waves, the birds, the whisper of the dune grass."

Mack never mentioned the voice to anyone again.

MACK LISTENED FOR THE voice now as he lingered on the dune. Just four days earlier, he'd received a phone call from David Pringle, the lawyer who'd supervised the farm in Iowa for all the years since Mack left. David called every now and then urging Mack to rent out the farmhouse, or to apprise him of profits and loss, taxes, weather. But he had never sounded as serious as he did four days ago.

"Wendell gave his notice," David said. "He's retiring after harvest."

"Yeah?" Mack said. Wendell, Mack's father's right-hand man, had been in charge since Mack left.

"I told you this was in the future, Mack. I told you to do some thinking."

"You did," Mack said. "You surely did."

"But you haven't done the thinking."

"No," Mack said. "Not really." When had Mack last talked to David? Last November after harvest? A Christmas card? Mack couldn't remember. He only vaguely recalled a conversation about Wendell getting ready to leave.

"We need someone to run things," David said.

"Hire one of the other hands to do it," Mack said. "I trust your judgment, David."

David sighed into the phone. He was a good person, and less like a lawyer than anybody Mack had met on the East Coast, where even men who weren't lawyers acted like lawyers. "Since the Oral B plant opened, we've lost a lot of help," David said. "We haven't had a hand here longer than six months. You want me to put a transient like that in charge of your father's farm?"

"Are they all transients? Aren't there a couple of hardworking kids, looking for a chance?"

"Wendell and I don't think so," David said. "We've talked about it. If your little love affair with that island isn't over, Mack, I mean, if you're going to stick it out in the East, then Wendell and I agree it's time to put the farm up."

"For sale, you mean?"

David hummed into the phone. "Mmmm-hmm."

"I don't think I can do that," Mack said.

"You have the summer to think it over," David said. "If you're not going to sell it, then you ought to come home and do the job yourself. You've been out there a long time."

"Twelve years," Mack said.

"Twelve years." Mack could practically see David shaking his head in disbelief. "Your decision, but this is what your father left you. I'd rather see you sell it than let it fall to pieces."

"Okay," Mack said. "So I'll talk to you in a couple of months, then?"

"I'll be in touch," David said.

MACK COULDN'T IMAGINE SELLING his family's farm but neither could he imagine leaving Nantucket. The farm was the last place he'd kissed his mother's cheek, he was born and raised there, and worked side by side

with his father. Sell the farm? Leave Nantucket? An impossible decision. Twelve years later, Mack didn't know where his home was. And
so, as he stood on top of the dune, he listened; he wanted the voice to
tell him what to do.

MAY FIRST WAS BILL Elliott's least favorite day of the year; it was one of
the few mornings that he didn't make love to his wife, Therese. May
first was Therese's day to sleep in undisturbed while Bill tried not to
panic. The doctor told him panic was bad for his heart; stress of any
kind could take months off his life. (Bill noted the use of that word,
"months," and it terrified him. His life had been pared down to incre-
ments of thirty days.)

At dawn, he left his house for a walk along Hulbert Avenue. The
summer homes on Hulbert were boarded up, Bill was relieved to see;
it looked as if the houses were sleeping. So there was still plenty of
time to whip the hotel into shape. The reservation book filled up by
the Ides of March, but taking reservations was the easy part. The hard
part was now, this morning, thinking about all the work that had to be
done. The enormous, rounded dunes of the beach. Twenty rooms
with furniture piled on top of the beds, draped with white sheets.
Dusty, disorganized.

Bill reached home, wheezing. He was sixty years old and because
of his weak heart, already an old man. This past winter in Aspen, he
hadn't been able to ski the black diamonds, nor the blues; he had been
embarrassingly limited to the gentle green slopes of Buttermilk Mountain. His hair was the color of nickels and dimes, his knees ached in
the evenings, and he needed good light for reading. Last week on the
flight back from Aspen, he used the lavatory four times. But the kicker
was this: Just after the New Year, he and Therese were out at Guido's
with another couple, a doctor (though not Bill's doctor) and his wife,
eating cheese fondue when Bill felt pressure in his chest, a squeezing,
as though his heart were a balloon ready to pop. The doctor at the
table took charge of calling an ambulance. There was talk of chopper-
ing Bill to Denver, but thankfully, that wasn't necessary, and in the

end, Bill was okay. It hadn't been a heart attack, just angina, heart muscle pain, a warning. The doctor recommended retirement. A few years ago, last year even, this would have been unthinkable, but now it sounded tempting. Bill's daughter, Cecily, would be graduating from high school in a couple of weeks and she'd already passed her eighteenth birthday. So it was only a matter of time before he could leave the running of the hotel to Cecily.

As Bill opened his front door, a white envelope fluttered to his feet. The letters had begun! Bill tore the envelope open and read the letter—as ever, from the mysterious S.B.T., an offer to buy the hotel out from under Bill's feet. Good old S.B.T. had been writing letters for several years now trying to convince Bill to sell. Twenty-two million? *Don't tempt me today, S.B.T.,* Bill thought. Bill occasionally wrote back to the post office box—he'd never met the man (or woman) and they wouldn't offer a name at the post office when Bill inquired. There weren't any S. B. T's in the phone book; for all Bill knew, the initials were fabricated. The mysteriousness of it was both frustrating and intriguing, like having a secret suitor. A suitor, at his age! Bill crumpled the letter and deposited it into the trash can at the side of his house. *Are you watching, S.B.T.? Are you watching?*

When Bill reached the kitchen and poured his first cup of decaf, he heard a car pull into the parking lot, and the tightness in his chest alleviated a bit. *Mack.* Bill was so happy that he wanted to shout to Therese, *Honey, Mack's here!* He interrupted more than a few of her May first slumbers this way. But this time Bill was quiet. He closed his eyes and recited "Stopping by Woods on a Snowy Evening" to himself, like a prayer. *And miles to go before I sleep.* It was amazing the way the words came to him. After the episode at the restaurant, Bill had retreated into poetry, into the words of an old man, a New Englander. Never mind that Frost's Vermont was a far cry from this island (there wasn't a single tree on Bill's whole property). Never mind that. For reasons unexplainable, Frost's poetry helped; it was a balm, a salve. It eased Bill's aging soul.

Mack looked exactly the same: the ruddy, smiling face and that bushy

head of light brown hair. Bill knew Mack as well as he might have
known a son. Bill shook Mack's hand and he couldn't stop himself
from hugging him too.

"So," Bill said, "you decided to come back." This was their long-
standing joke. Mack never said he would return in May, and Bill never
asked. But every May first Mack appeared in the parking lot and each
time, Bill greeted him this way. Bill wanted to say something else; he
wanted to say "Thank you for coming back," but he didn't. It would
embarrass Mack, and it might be better if Mack didn't know how
much Bill needed him. "How was your winter?"

"Not bad. I worked for Casey Miller on a huge project in Cisco. It
snowed twice and both times I got the day off and went sledding."

"How's Maribel?" Bill asked.

"The same," Mack said. "They love her at the library. And at the
post office and the bank, and Stop & Shop. She knows everyone. It's
like walking around with the mayor."

"She's hankering to get married?" Bill asked.

"I can hardly blame her," Mack said. "We've been together a long
time."

"So is this it, then? Is this the year Mack gets married?"

Mack shrugged. Bill could see he was embarrassed now, by just
this. Bill clapped him on the shoulder. "How about we give this place
the once-over, for starters?"

Mack looked relieved. "Okay," he said.

THERE WAS NO WAY Bill Elliott could look at his hotel objectively; it was
as familiar to him and well loved as the face of his wife. Always on May
first the hotel looked formidable and tough, boarded up like an old
western ghost town, and today was no exception. The hotel had gray
cedar shingles like nearly every building on Nantucket. Plywood had
been fastened over her doors and windows, paint peeled from her
frames. Bill pictured the hotel at the height of summer; it was the only
way he could keep his blood pressure from skyrocketing. Her trim
would be as white as fresh eggs, her windows sparkling, Therese's

geraniums and impatiens in full bloom—red, white, pink. The water temperature at sixty-eight degrees, the skies clear with a light southwesterly wind that would barely flutter the scalloped edges of the beach umbrellas. Who could complain then? Still, even today, Bill was in love with what he saw. Despite the shutters and the peeling paint and the undulating beach, she was the most beautiful hotel in the world. He would no sooner sell it than cut out his own heart.

Bill and Mack walked along the side deck rooms and took a left by the front deck rooms. Room 21 through room 1, skipping a room 13, of course. All present and accounted for, although Bill had nightmares during the winter of the rooms flying away in a northeaster like something from *The Wizard of Oz*. Bill stepped up onto each deck and stamped his feet to check for rotting boards. Mack perused the roof for missing shingles and inspected the shutters for leaks. "She's tight," Mack said. They headed back across the beach to the parking lot and Bill took keys out of his pocket. He unlocked the doors to the lobby and they stepped in.

"Home, sweet home," Bill said.

"Oh, brother," Mack said.

"Are you ready?" Bill said. He wished Mack looked more confident, more eager. Maybe this winter had taken a toll. "I'm going to shower and change," he said. "And you can get started. We have a hotel to run."

THE BEACH CLUB WAS Therese Elliott's canvas, her block of clay. Every May presented the same challenge—to make the hotel look more glorious than the year before. Therese had embarked on the quest for beauty when she was a girl growing up on Long Island—in Bilbo, perhaps the most unattractive town in all of America. Therese's family lived in one of the first subdivisions, on a cul-de-sac where the houses were built in three styles: ranch, split-level, and bastardized saltbox. Her parents' house (from the age of ten she referred to it as her parents' house, never her own) was a ranch with plasterboard walls, white Formica countertops threaded with gold, and veneered kitchen cabinets. The house had a swatch of green lawn and a chain-link fence that marked the property line along the sides and the back.

Now that Therese was in the hotel business, she compared the neighborhood where she grew up to a Holiday Inn—every living space alike in its absolute sterility, in its absence of charm. As an adolescent she felt bewildered walking home from school past the identical houses and identical yards, realizing that for some reason people *chose* to live like this—without distinction, without beauty. Her neighborhood couldn't even be called *ugly*, because ugly might at least have been interesting. The best word to describe the neighborhood of Therese's childhood was *unliterary*. She couldn't imagine anything noteworthy or romantic happening among the white-and-black, gold-threaded Formica-ness of the place.

And so, at eighteen, she left.

For Manhattan, with its color and confusion, beauty and ugliness side by side. She flunked out of Hunter College after two semesters, because instead of studying she spent hours walking through Chinatown, Chelsea, Clinton, Sutton Place, the Upper West Side, Harlem. When her parents received her poor grades, they insisted she return to Bilbo and enroll at Katie Gibbs, but she refused. She found a job waitressing at a German restaurant on Eighty-sixth and York, where fat old men admired the color of her hair and gave her generous tips. She saved enough money to leave the city for the summer with a girlfriend whose family had a beach house on Nantucket.

Nantucket cornered the market on beauty—the tumbling south shore waves, blue herons standing one-legged in Coskata Pond, Great Point Lighthouse at sunset. Therese took a job as a chambermaid at the Jared Coffin House in town, and when summer turned into fall and her girlfriend returned to the city, Therese stayed. More than thirty years later, she loved it still. She had married a local boy, given birth to two children, one who died and one who lived, and she and Bill transformed the Beach Club into a hotel. A beautiful place where love flourished.

Bill and Therese lived on one edge of the hotel property, in an upside-down house. The first floor had two spacious bedrooms—one for their daughter, Cecily, and one for the baby that died. The second floor had a rounded bay window that overlooked the hotel, the beach, and the sound. Therese stood at the window on this first day of May, but all she could see was a reflection of herself. It was a bad, vain habit, catching glances of herself in mirrors and windows, in the glass of picture frames, but she couldn't keep from looking. What did she see? At the age of fifty-eight, she still fit into a silk skirt she bought before Cecily was born. Her hair was the color of ripe peaches, with one streak of pure white in front that appeared after she gave birth to her dead baby. Her mark of strength and wisdom, of Motherhood.

Above anything, Therese was a Wife and a Mother. But now her family was in danger of falling apart. Her husband suffered from heart problems and her daughter was graduating from high school and headed for college. Suddenly, Therese pictured herself abandoned, alone. Bill dying, Cecily going away, until there would be nothing in her life except her own reflection.

She had to force herself away from the window and down into the hotel lobby. When she flung open the doors, her spirits lifted. Mack crawled around on the exposed beams of the lobby, wiping them down with a damp rag. Mack in the rafters: it was a sure sign of spring.

"You got to work before I could hug and kiss you," she said. "You got to work before I could tell you what to do."

Mack swung around and sat with his legs dangling. "I already know what to do," he said. "I'm not exactly new here."

Therese flopped onto a sofa that was covered with one of the hotel's sheets and put her feet on a dusty sea captain's chest. "You could run this place alone, I suppose. The rest of us are only getting in your way." She had known Mack for twelve years and he was closer to her than anyone except for Bill and Cecily. She could tell him just about anything.

"You sound so melancholy," Mack said. "Where's the uptight woman I know and love? What happened to the never-ending pursuit of cleanliness?"

"I'm worried about Bill," she said. "He had heart problems this winter. Did he tell you?"

"No," Mack said. "What kind of problems?"

It was comforting to hear a voice from above. "Problems that happen when people get older," Therese said. "His doctor told him he could only ski the baby slopes. It wasn't a good winter for Bill."

"He looks okay," Mack said. "A little pale, maybe, but okay. And his spirit's up."

"You think so?" Therese was concerned about Bill's preoccupation with Robert Frost—he'd taken it up the way a dying person might take up religion—although the reading and reciting seemed to help him.

"How's Cecily doing?" Mack asked.

"She doesn't know about her father's heart," Therese said. "That's one nice thing about having her away at school. She doesn't have to worry. And since she's not worrying, she's doing quite well."

"She wrote a letter at Christmas telling me about some Brazilian guy she met and I haven't heard from her since," Mack said. "Is she going to graduate or did she run away to Rio?"

The Brazilian boyfriend, Gabriel, another stumbling block. But Cecily had barely mentioned him the last two times she called home, and Therese hoped that with the end of the school year in sight, her infatuation was petering out. "Believe it or not, she's going to graduate."

"And college?" Mack asked.

"The University of Virginia. Hard enough to get into that she impressed her friends, and reasonably priced enough to impress her father. We're thrilled."

"She'll be on the front desk this summer? She's *more* than capable, Therese. If she's going to run the hotel someday she needs to learn it."

"Not the desk," Therese said firmly. Mack rolled his eyes. He could think what he wanted, that Therese babied her daughter, but Cecily was still a child. She didn't need a job that could drive even a mature, well-adjusted adult insane. "Bill hired a woman to work the day desk, someone he met at the gym in Aspen. Her name is Love."

"Love?"

"Yes," said Therese. "We need more love around here. Speaking of which, you noticed I haven't asked about your girlfriend."

"I didn't expect you to," Mack said.

"I can't resist. How are things? Are you still together? Still happy?"

"Yes."

"Still happy, but you're not going to marry her?"

"We have no plans to get married, no," he said.

"Wait until you see Cecily," Therese said. "All grown up. A woman. And so gorgeous. Vibrant. Irresistible." And headstrong, opinionated, difficult, her Cecily. Therese lifted her feet from the dusty chest and stood up. "If you marry Cecily this will all be yours. Bill would be so relieved. He loves you like a son, you know. He really does."

"You make it sound like we're living in a fairy tale," Mack said. "If I marry the fair daughter, I get the whole kingdom."

"You could rule the Beach Club kingdom."

"I'm not marrying Cecily, Therese."

"Well, you're not marrying Maribel." Therese and Mack had this same conversation every year, and she knew it irked Mack, but Therese couldn't help herself. To her, only one course of events made any sense—Mack marrying Cecily and the two of them taking over where Bill and Therese left off. She also knew that people rarely did what made sense.

"I haven't decided about marriage at all yet," Mack said. "But I can tell you, if and when I do get married, it won't be to Cecily. And if you don't believe me, ask her. She'd rather eat glass, direct quote."

"I won't give up," Therese said. She caught her reflection in a tarnished mirror, and then she pulled out her artist's tools from the utility closet—vacuum, bucket, cleanser, and her feather duster—and started to work.

MARIBEL COX KNEW SHE was the subject of gossip—among her mother's friends at the Christian Calendar Factory, among her colleagues at the

library, among Mack's co-workers and Bill and Therese down at the
Beach Club. She knew they were all whispering, "When are Mack
and Maribel going to do the *right thing*? When are they going to get
married?"

The truth of the matter was this: Maribel wanted to get married
with a raging, fiery passion, but the only person who knew it was Maribel's mother, Tina. Every Wednesday night, Maribel called Tina and
every Wednesday night, Tina said, "Well?" Meaning: well, did Mack
finally say those five little words, "*Maribel, will you marry me?*" Every
Wednesday night, Maribel said, "Well, nothing." And her mother
said, "Keep the faith."

Maribel and Mack had been dating for six years, living together for
three. Maribel had found a man Afraid to Commit.

"Like mother, like daughter," Tina said. Maribel pictured her
mother: twenty pounds overweight, permed hair, smoking a cigarette
as she talked on the phone. Tina herself had never been married. She
met Maribel's father at an outdoor concert, and Maribel was conceived in the woods nearby, up against a tree. Her mother never saw
the man again; she'd only known him for one day.

"If he's anything like you," Tina was fond of saying, "he must be a
great guy."

Maribel loved her mother dearly, although this love was tinged
with shame and pity. Tina worked as a supervisor at the Christian calendar factory in Unadilla, New York. Her mother didn't belong to a
church, and yet spending all day around Christian calendars, she
picked up certain phrases: "Keep the faith," and "Godspeed," and
"We are all His little lambs." It had always been just Tina and Maribel;
there was never anyone to help them out, no man in Maribel's life
growing up. Mack lost his parents in a car accident and Maribel tried
to believe this was the same thing as her not having a father, but in fact,
it was vastly different. When Maribel thought of her father, there was
no one to picture. She was left with an empty spot inside, a part of her
missing. A hole.

When Maribel was thirteen, she begged Tina to describe her father.

"Remember, Mama, remember everything you can." Tina sucked on her cigarette and closed her eyes: *His name was Stephen, he had sweet, chocolaty breath and a pencil-line scar above his eyebrow. I remember the scratch of bark against my back. It was getting dark, the sky turning pink and lavender through the trees. I didn't know your father real well. But when I was with him, I had a feeling something good would come of it.*

Maribel wanted to get married for two people—herself and her mother. She wanted Mack to take care of them, the way Stephen might have. Mack made just as many comments about the future as Maribel did, if not more. There was no doubt in Maribel's mind that Mack wanted to spend the rest of his life with her. He loved her.

So what, then, was the problem?

After years of taking self-help books off the shelves at the library, Maribel drew a conclusion: Mack was afraid to grow up. The phone call he received from David Pringle last week proved it. Mack owned a huge farm in Iowa, but he didn't want to go back and run it and he didn't want to sell it. Both options involved too much commitment, too much responsibility. It was as though he wanted the farm to exist on its own, magically, a farm from a dream, while he stayed on Nantucket and ran the stupid hotel. At any minute, Bill Elliott could drop dead and the hotel would go to Cecily, and Mack would be out of luck. But Mack loved his job at the hotel—six months on, six months off, never telling Bill if he were coming back or not—because it gave him freedom. Because he didn't have to take it—or anything else—too seriously.

In Maribel's opinion, Mack needed to ask Bill Elliott to profit-share. Thirty percent of the hotel's profit should go to Mack each year. Many of the guests who took Mack and Maribel out to dinner admitted (after a few cocktails) that should Mack ever leave his job, they would stop coming. The hotel was lovely, they said (but expensive, and the rates went up every year); it was the *service* that kept them coming back. It was walking into the lobby and having Mack there with his cheerful, booming voice, "*Hel-lo*, Mr. Page! Welcome back. How was your winter?" It was Mack who picked up the Page children and swung them around while he complimented Mrs. Page on her new haircut. And that was what people paid for. They wanted to be coddled; they wanted to be courted.

Maribel was convinced profit sharing was the answer. If Mack profit-shared, he would take his job seriously. He would take his life seriously. He could afford to hire someone really qualified to run the farm. His house would be in order. He would propose. And the empty spot inside of Maribel would shrivel, shrink, disappear.

ON MAY FIRST, MARIBEL and Mack had just moved into their "summer place"—a basement apartment in the middle of the island. It was the only housing they could afford in the summer, when island rents doubled and tripled. In winter, things were different; in the winter, they lived on Sunset Hill, next to Nantucket's Oldest House. The house on Sunset Hill was just a cottage, but Maribel and Mack called it the Palace. They loved the Palace—its low doorways and slanted ceilings and floors. In the quiet, cold, gray mornings of January, they lit a fire in the kitchen and Maribel made Mack cinnamon toast and oatmeal before he went out to bang nails. In the evenings, they walked into town through the deserted streets, past houses closed for the winter, sometimes not seeing another soul. They loved the Palace and it was sad every year to pack up their belongings and move to mid-island.

Maribel waited to broach the topic of profit sharing until Mack had worked at the Beach Club for three days. By then he'd gotten a taste of all the work the hotel needed and he'd had a chance to reflect on the crazy summer ahead of him. Then, on the fourth morning, Maribel made Mack scrambled eggs with fresh herbs. They sat at the dining table surrounded by stacks of unpacked boxes and duffel bags. Moving in went slowly.

"I've been thinking about money," she said. "And the housing."

"I know you hate this place," Mack said. "But every year you get used to it."

"I had an idea, Mack." She curled her bare toes into the fibers of the shag carpet. "I think you should ask Bill to profit-share."

There was a long silence, Mack eating. "You've been talking to your mother?" Mack said. "You've been reading one of those Men Live on Mars books?"

"You need to secure yourself a future at the club. It's been twelve years. It's time to ask Bill to profit-share." She spread her painted-pink fingernails out on the dining table and counted off twelve years, then she counted off six years of Mack and her together.

"I can't," he said.

"Why not?"

"Because I can be replaced. If I ask to profit-share, Bill can say no, and fire me. He can hire someone else."

Maribel clasped her hands and leaned forward. She wasn't eating. Too nervous. "He would never fire you. He loves you. And you say he's not doing well. Don't you think he wants to know that you'll be there to take care of the hotel after he's gone?"

"The hotel will be Cecily's," Mack said, his mouth full.

"She's a child."

"She's eighteen. She'll figure it out."

"What about you, then?" Maribel said. "Us? What do we do when Bill dies? I know it's not something you want to think about. . . ."

"You're right, it's not. He's not on death's door, Maribel. He's just a little frail."

"He's never been well. Now he's just one year closer."

Mack finished his eggs and buttered a piece of toast. Maribel brought him a jar of Concord grape jam. Then he said, "I don't want to ask."

"Why not?" Maribel said. She dipped a finger into the jam and tasted it.

"Because it's his business to pass on to Cecily. My father left me a business. I understand how it works. I'm not going to put Bill in the awkward position of having to relinquish part of his profits to keep me happy."

"You could use the money to hire someone to run the farm," Maribel said. Mack slathered the jam over his toast. Maribel watched his every move; he was a mystery to her. "And it's not as though you're asking him to hand over the business. You'd simply be asking for part of the profits. Don't you think you influence those profits?"

"Of course," Mack said. "But I'm not going to ask him. I've worked for Bill for a long time. It would embarrass us both."

"Okay, then," Maribel said. "If you don't want to ask Bill, let's move to Iowa. Let's run the farm ourselves."

"You don't want to move to Iowa," Mack said.

"Yes, I do," Maribel said. This wasn't a lie, exactly. If it would take moving to Iowa to get Mack to marry her, she would do it. She thought of her mother's life—twenty-eight Christian calendar years of being alone. That would not be Maribel's life.

"But I love Nantucket," Mack said. "I'm happy here."

"So you're going to sell the farm then?" Maribel said. "You've decided?"

"No," Mack said. Maribel felt a twinge of guilt, because he did look completely at a loss. He wiped his plate with the crust of his toast. "Why do I have to decide now?"

"Because you're thirty years old, Mack. Because you want more money, more respect. Don't you want things to change?"

"I guess," he said.

Maribel reached across the table and touched his hand. He trusted her; he knew that her thinking was for both of them. "Ask Bill to profit-share. If he says no we can leave for Iowa."

Mack took his empty plate to the sink. He turned the faucet on, then off, then on, and he poured a glass of water and drank it slowly and deliberately, in a way that made Maribel want to scream. He was always making her wait!

"Let me think about it," he said.

"Don't you think it's time we took the next step? Don't you think it's time you got what you deserved?"

"Yes?" Mack said.

"Okay, then," Maribel said.

Maribel watched from the living room window as Mack walked out to the Jeep and drove away. *I want you to feel good about yourself,* she thought. *I want you to ask me to marry you!*

THE FIRST THING JEM Crandall thought when he arrived at the Beach Club to interview for the bellman's position was that it was like a scene from a movie—the ocean, the sand, and then the leading man—strong handshake, sailing-instructor suntan, who called himself Mack, and said Why don't we interview on the pavilion? The pavilion! Nantucket was the fanciest place Jem had ever been, and he'd certainly never been interviewed on a pavilion before.

The pavilion turned out to be a covered deck with blue Adirondack chairs that faced the ocean.

"This is like a little porch," Jem said, taking one of the chairs.

"What do you think?" Mack said. He half sat, half leaned on the railing with his back to the water, so he could look at Jem. Jem stared at Mack's ankle, swinging back and forth like a pendulum. He was wearing deck shoes without any socks.

"It's fucking gorgeous," Jem said. He shut his eyes. What had he just said? *Fucking?* Swearing, in a job interview! "Excuse my French," he said. "I just meant . . ."

"I know what you meant," Mack said. He scribbled something down on his clipboard, probably, *Low-class, not right at all for the job.* Jem sat up straighter in the chair, but it was hard to achieve really perfect posture because of the way the back of the chair was slung.

"Sorry," Jem said.

Mack checked his Ironman sportswatch. He was dressed like a J. Crew model—navy cotton sweater, khakis, a Helly Hansen Gore-Tex vest lined with fleece. Jem tried to keep from fixating on Mack's swinging ankle.

"So you want to be a bellman," Mack said. "I have two questions. How long can you stay and do you have a place to live?"

Jem arranged his thoughts. In career counseling at William and Mary, he learned that the key to a good job interview was to tell the truth, and not what he thought the interviewer wanted to hear. "I can stay until closing," Jem said. "I graduated from college, like, last week."

"Where'd you go to college?" Mack asked.

"The College of William and Mary."

"Okay, so you graduated. And you don't have another job to start in the fall?"

"Not lined up, no."

"What are you planning to do?"

Jem tried to sit up. "I'm going to California. I want to be an agent." An agent: that was the first time he'd said the words out loud. It sounded okay. *I want to be an agent.* Jem was afraid to tell his parents about his plans because they would reject the words "Los Angeles" right away. They would argue it was too far from home. Jem's parents lived in Falls Church, Virginia; they were small-town people. They had to pull out the atlas to locate Nantucket.

"An agent?" Mack said.

"Yeah," Jem said. His feet itched and he wondered if he'd gotten sand in his socks. He stared at Mack's bare ankle, then tore his eyes away. "An agent for actors."

"Do you act?"

"I'm not very good. I modeled a little in college, though. I was Mr. November in the college calendar." Mr. November: It was a good, handsome picture—Jem in jeans, sitting on a split-rail fence in historic Williamsburg. But now Mr. November sounded ridiculous. Things that seemed okay in college didn't always translate to the real world. Jem should have kept his mouth shut. From now on, he was just going to answer the questions.

Mack pinched his lips together in a line, as if he were trying not to laugh. "What about a place to live?"

"I have a place to live," Jem said. Jem rented a room through a college friend's aunt who had a house on North Liberty Street. The room was fine, but it didn't have kitchen privileges. When Jem asked the friend's aunt how he was going to eat, she said, "I usually rent to people in the restaurant business." Jem's father owned a bar in Falls

Church—an English-style pub called the Locked Tower; if he'd wanted to wait tables, he would have stayed at home. "The room's decent," he told Mack. "But it doesn't have a kitchen. And I need to save money to go to California." He straightened his spine. "I'm on the lookout for free food in a big way. What I really need is a girlfriend who likes to cook."

"My girlfriend likes to cook," Mack said. "And look what it got me." He patted his gut. "Love handles."

Jem smiled politely.

"Are you handy?" Mack asked. "Can you change a lightbulb? Set an alarm clock? Do you know what a circuit breaker is? If a guest calls the front desk and says his electricity is out, could you fix it?"

"Probably. I can change a lightbulb and set an alarm clock. I know my way around a fuse box."

"You'd be surprised how many people can't set an alarm clock," Mack said.

"Well, I can," Jem said. "Like I said, I just graduated from college." He laughed. Mack scribbled down something else.

"Hopefully, you'll remember to set your own," Mack said. "The day bellman needs to be here at eight A.M."

"Do I have the job, then?"

"I need someone for three day shifts and three night shifts, one day off. There isn't a lot of sitting around. If you're not stripping the rooms for the chambermaids or helping a guest with bags, then you'll be doing projects, assigned by me. Small maintenance jobs, watering the plants, cleaning the exercise room, sweeping up shells in the parking lot. And part of the deal is helping to open the place, from now until Memorial Day. That's eight to four every day but Sunday. I can offer you ten bucks an hour, plus tips. Do you *want* the job?"

Tips. A world-class beach resort. Contacts waiting to be made. Jem could have kissed the guy. "Yes, I do. Absolutely."

Mack offered his hand and Jem tried for a nice, firm handshake that showed he meant what he said.

"You have the job," Mack said. "Welcome to the Nantucket Beach Club and Hotel. You'll work with a bellman named Vance Robbins who's been here twelve years, just as long as I have. Vance will show you the ropes. Come tomorrow at eight, ready to shovel."

Jem jumped to his feet. "I'll be here," he said. He probably sounded way too eager, but it was exciting—getting a job, spending the summer on this island. He couldn't wait to write to his parents and tell them. But first he had to find a grocery store and buy some bread and a jar of peanut butter and hope it didn't draw ants.

Mack led him to the front porch of the lobby. "We'll see you tomorrow," Mack said.

"Do you own this place?" Jem asked. A seagull dropped a shell onto the asphalt of the parking lot and then swooped down to eat whatever was inside.

"No," Mack said. He tugged at his vest defensively.

"Oh," Jem said. "Well, it is gorgeous."

"Fucking gorgeous," Mack said. "You're right. It is."

VANCE ROBBINS STOOD SIX feet and one half inch tall, which was the same height as Mack Petersen. He turned thirty years old on March 22, and so did Mack Petersen. They were exactly the same height and exactly the same age.

"Like twins," Maribel once made the mistake of saying. Vance and Mack were not twins. First of all, Vance was black and Mack was white. Secondly, Vance was a bellman and Mack was the manager.

Vance had hated Mack for twelve years. Twelve years ago, Vance was a high school graduate on his way to Fairleigh Dickinson in the fall, and he lined up a summer managerial position at the Beach Club with Bill Elliott over the phone. Bill was supposed to be waiting when Vance got off the ferry, but Mack cut in and replaced him. It was pure dumb luck—Mack got off the boat first and he was the right age, he had the right look, and Bill took him to the hotel instead of Vance. It wasn't until an hour later that Bill returned to the wharf to get Vance—and by then Mack had infiltrated the joint. Bill claimed Mack had better experience because he'd worked on a farm—a *farm*, for God's sake—and he wasn't leaving for school in September, and so Mack got the manager's job. Vance was Mack's equal in height and age, but returning to the Beach Club in the spring and seeing Mack made Vance only too aware of how they weren't equal. Vance was a black sheep, an evil twin, a kid who got off the boat thirty seconds too late. A bellman.

"Hey, Vance! Good to see you, man! How was your winter?" Here was Mack now, clapping Vance on the back, pumping his hand. Mack ran his palm over Vance's smooth skull. "You shaved your head . . . it looks great. You look, I don't know, intimidating."

"Thanks," Vance said. He couldn't help smiling. He expected Mack to say shaved heads weren't acceptable at the Beach Club. Vance caught himself and tried to scowl. This was how it happened every year. He spent all winter despising Mack and then when he showed up in the spring, Mack was disarmingly nice, *cool* even, and Vance was forced to abandon his hatred. But not this year. This year Vance was going to hang on to his hatred with both hands.

"Man, how was your winter?" Mack asked. "How was Thailand? Did you get laid?"

"Of course," Vance said, and again, he couldn't help smiling. When he pictured himself on the beach at Koh Samui or under the capable massaging hands of Pan, a nineteen-year-old Thai girl with long, shiny black hair, he wanted to give up every detail. Mack, he knew, had spent all winter on this gloomy rock. "Thailand kicked ass. I rented a bungalow on the beach for six bucks a night." He nodded toward the hotel. "Closer to the water than room eleven and a hundredth the price. I got massages that lasted well into the night. I ate banana pancakes and grilled fish every day."

A young guy with dark curly hair holding a shovel approached them. "That sounds like paradise," he said. "Where were you, California?"

"Thailand," Mack and Vance said at the same time. Their voices were indistinguishable. Vance shook his head.

"Thailand," Vance said again, on his own. The familiar acidity of hatred filled his chest, and he popped two Rolaids. In the summer, when Mack was around, Vance ate hundreds of them.

"Vance, this is Jem. I hired Jem yesterday. Jem, Vance Robbins, the head bellman."

Vance took another look at the kid as he ground the chalk between his molars. He was too handsome but probably impressionable. Easy to boss around.

"Jem, like in *To Kill a Mockingbird?*" Vance asked.

Jem nodded. "Not many people get the reference."

Vance stuck out his hand. "Pleasure," he said.

Mack ran his palms over Vance's noggin again. "I missed you, man. How come you didn't send me a postcard?"

Vance shrugged. Why the hell did Mack like him so much? Why couldn't he take a hint?

VANCE AND JEM STARTED digging out the snow fence. The sun was shining and it was actually kind of warm. By noon they would probably be able to work without shirts. Vance liked opening and closing work best because it was quiet work, and honest. He'd started jogging in Thailand, and doing sit-ups and push-ups. He'd swum every afternoon. He was bigger now in the arms and across the shoulders. Sometime this summer he was going to beat up Mack—beat him to a pulp, just once, so that Mack would know Vance hadn't forgiven him for horning in, for stealing away the job that should rightfully have been his.

Vance and Jem worked side by side peacefully with Jem only looking up once to ask, "Hey, do they buy you lunch around here? I'm starving."

Vance checked his watch; it was ten-thirty.

"Sometimes the boss will spring for subs," Vance said. "Bill Elliott, the owner. Have you met him yet?"

"No."

"It's always good to remember that Mack isn't *really* the boss. Bill is."

"So Bill buys us subs?" Jem asked.

"If we put in a hard morning he sometimes will," Vance said. "But not every day."

"Does this place serve breakfast?" Jem asked.

"Continental breakfast, eight-thirty to ten. You'll be in charge of setting it up and taking it down when you work the day shift. Didn't Mack tell you that?" Vance was annoyed; Mack was lax about explaining duties to new workers. It always fell to Vance to explain the whole truth and sometimes the new bellman got bristly, thinking Vance was creating more work for him. But this kid, Jem, just beamed.

"No," Jem said, "he didn't say anything about breakfast. That's great!"

Vance heard his name being called, and Maribel jogged onto the beach. She was wearing shorts and a red sports bra, and she had a windbreaker tied around her waist. Blond hair in a ponytail. She threw her arms around Vance's neck and kissed him on the cheek. As much as Vance hated Mack, he couldn't bring himself to feel anything but dumbstruck infatuation for Maribel.

"You look divine!" she said. "Positively exotic. I love men without hair. You look like Michael Jordan. How was Thailand?"

"Good," he said. He couldn't figure out what Maribel saw in him either. Every time she spoke to him he had trouble stringing together a sentence.

"You've got this incredible bod. This is the year you get a girl then, huh?"

Vance clenched the handle of his shovel, hoping she would see his forearm muscles ripple. He was glad he'd removed his shirt. Before Vance could answer, Jem said, "We haven't met. I'm Jem Crandall."

"Jem?" Maribel said. She shook Jem's hand and Vance felt a familiar sense of dread. Jem had his shirt off as well, and he was using some lady-killer smile that showed all his teeth. "Jem, like in *To Kill a Mockingbird*?"

"Exactly," Jem said. "Not many people get the reference. Vance did, though."

Maribel turned to Vance. "Well, of course. Vance is our literary lion."

Vance shrugged. Maribel called him that because he graduated from FDU with a degree in American lit, and he once had a story entitled "The Downward Spiral" published in a small magazine.

"I'm Maribel Cox. Mack is my boyfriend." She paused to let this information sink in. It was as though she were telling Jem, *I'm important, I'm with Mack.*

"Maribel works at the library," Vance said.

"Explains why you know about books," Jem said.

"Are you just starting here today?" Maribel asked.

"Yeah," Jem said. He leaned on his shovel with crossed arms. "They've got me digging ditches already."

Maribel turned back to Vance. "You guys should come over for dinner tonight. I'll roast a chicken, do those real French *pomme frites* that you like."

"I can't," Vance said. One of the rules he had set for himself was No More Socializing with Mack.

"I can," Jem said eagerly, but Maribel ignored him.

"Maybe next week then," she said. "Is Mack around?"

"Look out back," Vance said. "Or in the office. He might be in the office with Bill."

"Okay," Maribel said. She touched Vance's flexing forearm. "Hey, you, good to see you." She jogged toward the hotel. "And nice meeting you, Jem!"

When she was out of earshot, Jem said, "That girl is a knockout. And she cooks!"

"Taken," Vance said. He spoke in a way that might be construed as protecting Mack. But Vance just wanted Jem Mockingbird to realize that if Vance couldn't have Maribel, no one else could either.

LOVE O'DONNELL ARRIVED ON the island by high-speed ferry. Even though it was mid-May, the weather was gray and drizzly. And cold. Love stood on the bow of the boat, her Polar Fleece wrapped tightly around her. She wanted to watch the ferry approach Nantucket. She wanted to feel sea mist on her face. As it was, she wasn't sure if the moisture she felt on her face was sea mist or rain, and through the dense blanket of fog she couldn't see Nantucket at all until just before they reached the harbor. Then she caught a glimpse of the red beam of Brant Point Lighthouse and behind, the gray-shingled buildings of town, and the white steeple of the Congregational church she'd seen in pictures. The Beach Club, where she would be working, was to the west someplace and the cottage she had rented for the season was mid-island, where the locals lived.

Love wasn't a person who went places on impulse. This trip qualified as the most impulsive thing she'd ever done. She'd lived in Aspen for the past seven years working at a popular outdoor magazine. But then she met Bill Elliott at the gym. They were lying side by side on the mats, using the Abdominizers. Love sneaked a look at Bill in the mirror, because that was what one did at gyms in Aspen—inspected the opposite sex. Especially Love. Ever since her fortieth birthday, Love had been looking for a man to father her baby.

She smiled at Bill in the mirror. "Sometimes I wonder if these things actually work," she said, indicating the Abdominizer.

Bill laughed. "I figure everyone using them looks pretty good."

Love crunched twice more, then said, "Do you live here in Aspen?"

"Just for the winter," Bill said. "How about you?"

"Local," Love said. "Where do you live in the summer?"

"Nantucket," Bill said. He finished with his Abdominizer and stood up. Love stood as well and followed Bill to the StairMasters. An out-of-towner was a requirement in Love's search for a father for her baby, because she wanted a baby but absolutely did not want a husband.

"What do you do in Nantucket?" Love asked. She punched her weight, one hundred pounds even, into the console of the StairMaster.

"My wife and I own a hotel," he said.

"Oh, you're married," Love said. This was not necessarily an obstacle; after seven years in Aspen, Love knew he could still be thinking of an affair.

"Yes, and I have an eighteen-year-old daughter at boarding school.

Finishing up." Love pumped up and down on the stairs. She was so delighted to hear that Bill already had a child that she felt almost guilty. Out of town, previous reproductive success, a business owner—Love ran down her mental checklist, and glanced around the gym. There were two noticeably pregnant women using free weights, and who knew how many others not yet showing. Many of Love's friends, co-workers, and acquaintances were now, in their late thirties and early forties, starting families. In the past eighteen months, Love had taken a crash course on new millennium parenthood: seven-grain zwieback crackers, strollers with all-terrain mountain bike tires. She saw women in the gym and on the cross-country paths with healthy, swollen bellies. Love's desire to be a mother was a physical, painful hunger. Since her fortieth birthday, she could think of nothing else. Love wanted a baby, flesh and blood that would be connected to her for the rest of her life, and she wanted to raise her child alone. There was a group in Aspen called Single Mothers by Choice; Love saw their flyer posted in the health food store. When she finally got pregnant, she would join.

At the end of the workout she smiled at Bill, and said, "You're in good shape."

Bill winked. "Just doing what the doctor says: I get plenty of exercise, and I make love to my wife. Good for the spirit!"

Love's hopes fell down around her feet like a couple of sagging ankle weights. It was okay with her if a man wanted to admit he was married, but talking about his sex life was taboo. She hoped her disappointment didn't show. But then, on their way out of the gym, Bill offered to buy Love something from the juice bar. While Love sipped a carrot-raspberry juice, Bill told her about the hotel on Nantucket.

"She started out as a Beach Club in 1924. Men wore silk suits and top hats, and women carried parasols. There were over four hundred wooden changing rooms, rented twice a day to meet the demand. My father bought the place in 1952 and I built hotel rooms on the property when he retired twenty years ago."

"It sounds wonderful," Love said. "I've always wanted to see New England."

"Well, then, I'd like to make a proposition," Bill said.

Love's thighs tensed. "What's that?" she said.

"Why don't you come work for me this summer? We need a full-time person on the front desk. She's a beautiful hotel, I promise." Love was familiar with his tone of voice; she heard it all the time. He was setting her up on a blind date. Still, it might be the perfect plan. Leave Aspen for the summer and return in the fall, pregnant.

She finished the last of her juice, licking her teeth clean of raspberry seeds. "I already have a job," she said. "But it's a thought."

BILL OFFERED LOVE THE job every time he saw her at the gym. "What would you miss in six months?" he asked her. "Would you be leaving someone behind?"

This question offended her. She was certain Bill knew the answer was no. No one and nothing to leave behind. Not even a dog, like so many other athletic, unmarried Aspen women. Dogs made her sneeze.

"No," she said.

"Listen," Bill said, "I'm going to be retiring soon, whether I like it or not. I'd like to have a good summer. If you think you want to be part of it, I'd love to have you work for us."

His liver-spotted hands trembled at his sides, and despite all his exercise, his skin had a grayish tint. But his eyes sought her eagerly, as though he believed there really was a talented front-desk person somewhere inside of her. And so, at the beginning of April, with the closing of the ski slopes imminent, Love agreed to take the job. A summer at the beach, then, on Nantucket.

The ferry sounded its foghorn. Here she was.

LOVE O'DONNELL WAS ORGANIZED. She had three maps, and a book called *Vintage Nantucket* which she had read cover to cover. She disembarked onto Straight Wharf and picked up her luggage: a North Face duffel bag and her Cannondale M1000. (She never went anywhere without her mountain bike.) She inhaled the ocean air. It smelled of salt and fish, as she expected. What she did not expect was how rich it was, how luxurious; it was air pregnant with oxygen. If nothing else, she would be happy to live here all summer and breathe this air.

Love's taxi driver was a tall, thin girl with dyed-black hair, a nose ring, and seven or eight earrings in each ear.

"Where you headed?" the girl asked. Her T-shirt said Piping Plovers Taste Like Chicken.

"Hooper Farm Road. But I'd like to see a little first, if you don't mind. What's your name?"

"Tracey," the girl said. "And I'm no tour guide."

"Do you live on the island?" Love asked.

The girl glanced behind her at the line of cabs. She threw Love's bike in the back of her station wagon, got into the driver's seat and waited for Love to climb in, then she pulled away. "I'm here for the summer," she said.

"Your first summer?" Love asked.

Tracey nodded. They drove slowly up the cobblestones of Main Street.

"Mine, too," Love said. Her voice jumbled and bounced with the tires. "Did you know these cobblestones were brought here by the early settlers as ballast on their ships?"

Tracey didn't respond. Love looked out the window at the names of the shops and restaurants: Murray's Liquors, Espresso Café, Congdon's Pharmacy, Mitchell's Book Corner. Then they reached a brick building with stately white columns: Pacific National Bank.

Love tapped on the glass. "They call this the *Pacific* Bank because the Nantucket whaling ships had to sail to the Pacific Ocean to hunt whales. They went all the way down around Cape Horn. Sometimes ships were gone for five years. But that's where the money came from, the Pacific Ocean."

"You're a regular encyclopedia," Tracey said.

Love ignored the sarcasm. She didn't want her first interaction on Nantucket to be a negative one. She studied her map. "Let's keep going to the top of Main Street."

They crept up on the Greek Revival Hadwen House, which Love intended to tour in the next few days. "This big white place on the left has an upstairs ballroom," Love said. "The ballroom was built with a retractable roof, so people could dance under the stars."

"Really?" Tracey said. She slowed down. "You mean, the roof rolls back?"

"It's such a romantic idea, dancing under the stars," Love said. She leaned back in her seat. "I've got something to confess, Tracey. I came to this island to get pregnant."

"Whoa, lady, that's more information than I need to know," Tracey said. "If you want to tell me stuff about the history that's fine, that's stuff I might use again on somebody else, but don't tell me personal stuff, please. They don't pay me enough."

Love laughed. "Everybody comes to Nantucket for a reason. Some people came to hunt whales and the Quakers came to escape religious persecution. And I came to get pregnant. It feels good to tell you that I came here to have a baby. Now that someone knows, I feel like I'm responsible for it."

"You're not responsible to me," Tracey said. "Believe me, you're not."

"Would you look at me?" Love asked.

"What?" Tracey said.

"Would you turn around and look at me?"

Slowly, Tracey turned. Her brow twisted in extreme discomfort.

"I came to the island to get pregnant," Love said. "I will get pregnant."

"Okay, so now what do you want me to do? Say 'Amen'?"

"No, just watching me say it is enough." Love checked her map. "Let's go to the Old Mill," she said. "I know the way."

The next day, Love skated to the Beach Club. A pleasant-looking, sandy-haired man was standing on a stepladder, fiddling with the lamppost. Love swung in a half-circle near the ladder and came to an easy stop.

"I'm Love O'Donnell," she said. "You Mack?"

"Yep." He screwed the glass bulb back into the lamppost and patted it. "Hope this works." He stepped down from the ladder and shook Love's hand. "It's nice to meet you."

"Likewise," she said. He had nice blue eyes, and Love judged him to be in his early thirties. Too young.

"I need to wash my hands and then we'll get started," Mack said. "Feel free to look around. Those are the doors to the lobby." He pointed across the parking lot. "I'll meet you there in a few minutes."

Love skated across the parking lot. Bill had explained the hotel as an L, and that's what Love saw: plain, gray-shingled rooms, some running down toward the water and some facing the water. Nothing special about them from the outside except that they were all built in the sand and looked out over the ocean, which today was slate gray. Love felt a wave of disappointment. She was expecting world-class, something grandiose. What had Bill said he charged? Six hundred dollars a night?

Love skated over to the steps that led into the lobby. She removed her Rollerblades thinking she would go in and talk to this guy Mack, but if it didn't work out she could probably get a job in town. At the Jared Coffin House maybe, or another place with a bit more character.

The lobby, however, was a pleasant surprise. In fact, Love decided after about thirty seconds that it was the most attractive room she'd ever seen. The first thing she noticed were six quilts that hung from the exposed beams so that they resembled sheets billowing on a clothesline. The floors were polished wood and hunter green carpet that sank under Love's stocking feet. There was a brick fireplace against one wall and the opposite wall had giant windows that faced the beach. The room was decorated with white wicker furniture, plants and trees, a black grand piano, and toys: miniature bicycles, tiny Adirondack chairs, a rocking horse. Love approached the front desk, which was made of the same shiny, honey-colored wood as the floor. She picked up a tiny brass bell and gave it a tentative swing. Mack appeared from the back.

"Come around," he said.

He showed Love the door that led to the office. The office was a cramped, cluttered room with a stereo, a fax, and a horribly messy desk, although it had the same million-dollar view of the water. Then Love saw a cracked door and noticed there was another office behind it. Bill's office? Love knocked timidly and pushed the door a bit. Bill sat at a huge, lovely desk, reading.

"Hi, Bill," Love said.

Bill looked up. He fumbled with his book and it fell to his feet.

"Oh, hi," he said. "Hello. You're here. You came."

"Yes, of course," she said. Would it be presumptuous to imagine that her presence flustered him? "I told you I'd be here."

Bill picked the book up from underneath his desk.

"Well, okay," he said. "Good. What do you think?"

"The lobby's pretty," she said. "I haven't seen the rooms."

"They're not quite ready yet," Bill said. He flipped through the pages of his book and they made a ruffling noise, like a bird's wings flapping. "Mack will show you the ropes. But it's good to see you here. I guess I'll see a lot more of you."

"Yes," Love said. "I guess you will."

"THE KEY TO YOUR job as a front desk person is to dot your *i*'s and cross your *t*'s," Mack said. "Write everything down. A guest wants dinner reservations: write it down. A guest receives a fax: log it into the fax log book. A guest needs a cab to the airport at six A.M.: write it down for Tiny. Tiny works the night desk. She'll call the cab the night before, and make sure the guest has paid his bill. Never fails, once a summer a guest walks out of here without paying his bill because some desk person forgot to write it down. Not a good thing."

Love produced a notebook from the front pocket of her anorak, and scribbled things as Mack spoke. "Tiny," Love said.

"Tiny doesn't answer personal questions, so don't ask her any. She's probably the smartest one of us all. She doesn't air her dirty laundry. The rest of us, well, we work together so much, sometimes we can't help it. We're kind of like a family."

"Family," Love wrote.

"You brought a notebook," Mack said. "I like that. I've trained at least fifteen desk people over the years. There've been good ones and bad ones. Good desk people are detail oriented. They pay attention. They listen. They use discretion."

"Discretion." Big letters. Underlined.

"A lot of our clientele are very wealthy," Mack said. "They're used to having certain things done for them. For example, some people won't want to take a cab into town. They'll expect a ride."

"What do I tell them?" Love asked.

"Explain that it's not our policy to give rides but that you'd be more than happy to call them a cab."

"Common sense," Love said.

"There will be guests who say they don't like the fruit at breakfast. They'll want peaches instead of bananas. If someone asks for peaches, write it down. I buy the breakfast and I've been known to honor requests for peaches. We don't offer room service so we try to do the best we can on the breakfast."

"No room service," Love repeated. She wrote it down.

"You'll be working every day from eight to five, except Tuesday, your day off. That's a lot of time on the desk. In July and August it can get pretty hectic. You'll be bombarded with requests, questions, people checking out, people checking in. If it gets to be too much, let me know. Let Therese know, let Bill know. Don't try to tackle everyone's problems at once. It won't work."

"I took a magazine to deadline each month," Love said. "I can handle the pressure of twenty hotel rooms."

"Mid-June, of course, the Beach Club starts," Mack said. "We have a hundred members who pay dues to use the beach. They each have a locker. They each have a key. They all need chairs and towels. The kids want buckets and shovels. On a hot day in August when you have thirteen check-outs and twelve check-ins and twenty-five kids running through the lobby with sandy feet and a guest in room twelve telling you his toilet is overflowing and old Mrs. Stanford has lost the key to her Beach Club locker, *then* you will know the meaning of pressure."

Clearly he was trying to scare her. "I guess so," Love said.

Mack lowered his voice. "I did want to say a little more about the guests. What I've learned in twelve years is that it's common to experience feelings of . . . resentment." He looked around the lobby as though there might be a guest or two hiding behind the wicker sofas. "The people who stay here, the people who use the beach, all have a lot of money. And they look to you not as an equal but as someone who works for them. Listen, a guy comes from New York, he has two weeks off a year and he's spending that precious time and a boatload of money here at the hotel. He wants things perfect. You see what I mean? It gets tricky, dealing with egos. There's a lot of financial muscle flexing going on here."

Love smiled. Didn't he know she had come from *Aspen*? "I get your point."

"But what I've learned is that wealthy people are frequently sad people," Mack said.

"I've found that to be true as well," Love said. "Money can only get you so much. It can't cure your cancer or get you love. It can't make you fertile."

Mack smiled. "Fertile?"

Love blushed. Her personal life was slipping already, showing like a bra strap. "Yeah, you know, money can't get you a child. Your own child."

"Exactly," he said. "You're going to do a fantastic job. I can tell."

AFTER LOVE FINISHED HER lesson about the phones and the fax and the credit card machine, and after she impressed Mack with her knowledge of the island, he left to take care of a lock in one of the rooms. Love drummed her fingers on the polished wood of the desk, stared down at the phone console, gazed out at the lobby, and thought, *This is where I'm going to meet the father of my child.*

She heard a voice in the back office. She tiptoed through Mack's messy office and listened at Bill's door, which was still ajar.

Love held her breath and knocked. Bill cleared his throat, then said, "Come in!"

He was the only one in the office. "I heard you talking," she said. She smiled at him. "Do you always talk to yourself? I do."

"I was reciting Robert Frost," he said. " 'One could do worse than be a swinger of birches' and all that. I didn't realize anyone was still here."

"Sorry I startled you," Love said. "The poem you were reciting, is that a favorite of yours?"

"They're all favorites," Bill said, thumping the cover of his book. "This one is called 'Devotion.' I just stumbled across it."

Love moved farther into the office. There were two wicker chairs by the windows. Love sat down. "Read it to me," she said. "I don't read nearly enough poetry."

Bill closed his eyes and leaned back in his creamy leather chair. He was so thin his wrist bones protruded like knobs. " 'The heart can think of no devotion, greater than being shore to the ocean, holding the curve of one position, counting endless repetition.' " He opened his eyes. "You know what that means, don't you?"

My first day of work, a man reads poetry aloud to me. "What does it mean?" she asked.

"He's talking about love," Bill said. "He's saying the greatest demonstration of love is devotion, being there with your beloved day in and day out. Have you ever been married?"

"No," Love said.

"I've been married thirty years, and I love my wife more now than ever. It's like all those days, even the really boring, awful days, have added up. Each day I love her yet more." He closed the book. "So I guess I'm what Frost would call devoted."

"Sounds like it," Love said. Her feelings a bit crushed.

"How about you? Are you devoted to anything?" Bill asked. "Anyone?"

"I'm devoted to having a baby," Love said. "I'm devoted to finding someone to father my baby."

Bill's eyebrows arched, his mouth formed a silent O. Love's personal life was a woman popping out of a cake, *Surprise!*

"A baby is certainly a noble devotion," he said.

Love put her hands on her thighs and stood up. "Too bad *you* can't help me," she said.

Bill laughed nervously. "Endless devotion." As Love walked by his desk to leave, he held out his hand. It was a frail hand, but warm and sincere. "Someone is going to be very lucky," he said.

MACK HAD BEEN RUNNING the Beach Club for twelve years, Bill had owned it outright for twenty, but it was Lacey Gardner, the Grande Dame of Beacon Hill and Nantucket, who had true bragging rights. She had joined the Beach Club in the summer of 1945—fifty-three years ago—did she need to say it? Seven years before Bill's father, Big Bill Elliott, even bought the place. Lacey had been around longer than anybody.

At eighty-eight, she was the oldest living graduate of Radcliffe College and that earned her a permanent seat in the front row at Harvard's commencement. Every year on the day following commencement she drove from her apartment in Boston to Hyannis and put her car on the 9:45 ferry to Nantucket.

Lacey's tenure on Nantucket seemed to her like many different lifetimes. Her parents had brought her over to the island in 1920, when she was ten years old. She remembered the ferry docking and the hoteliers standing on the wharf calling out the names of their establishments: Sea Cliff Inn, Beach House, Point Breeze. Years later, she came to Nantucket for weekends with her chums from Radcliffe. On summer evenings they danced on the open porch at the Moby Dick in 'Sconset. Back then, 'Sconset was a refuge for actors and actresses when Broadway closed for the summer; Lacey still remembered productions of *Our Town, Candida*, and *The Bride the Sun Shines On* out at the 'Sconset Casino. Dancing on the porch, lobster and chicken dinners for a dollar fifty a plate, cabaret fashion shows—this was the lively, carefree summertime Nantucket of Lacey's youth. And she was the only one left to remember it.

In 1941, her gentleman friend Maximilian Gardner proposed to her on the beach in Madaket. Lacey was thirty-one years old and still not married. She worked for the Massachusetts Board of Health. Men called her feisty and independent, and women called her a career girl and a snob. But she loved Maximilian Gardner. At first he was just one of the young men in her fun-loving crowd, but then she noticed the way he looked at her. It was when Maximilian Gardner looked at her that Lacey felt most like a woman.

Lacey and Max were married by a justice of the peace on Madaket Beach, in November 1941, a month before the bomb fell on Pearl Harbor, a week before Max left for basic training. When he came home from the war three years later, they had a church wedding, but by then Lacey was thirty-four, and too old to start having children.

Lacey and Maximilian became permanent fixtures in Nantucket in the summer. They joined the Beach Club—and the Yacht Club and Sankaty Golf Club—and Lacey opened a hat shop on Main Street, called simply Lacey's. She and Max bought a house on Cliff Road, and they split time between this house and their town house on Beacon Hill. They were married for forty-five years, and they held hands every night as they fell asleep. Lacey was holding Max's hand on February 14, 1986, the night he died. She had never been a sentimental woman, and yet her heart was broken on Valentine's Day.

This was how her life on Nantucket seemed like a life divided: her life before Max, her life with Max, her life after Max. After Max, she sold the house on the Cliff and the town house in Boston. She rented an apartment in Boston, and asked Big Bill Elliott for a permanent room at the hotel.

"Don't forget," she told him, "I've been here longer than you have."

Big Bill didn't forget. He gave Lacey her own cottage, behind the lobby of the hotel. The view wasn't great—it looked out at the laundry room and the back of the parking lot—but it had three bedrooms and most importantly, it was her own place—Lacey Gardner's—bought and paid for with pure longevity. In Big Bill's last will and testament, he left the cottage to Lacey; it was hers to pass on when she died.

Well, she wasn't dead yet. She was alive enough to drive her new Buick off the ferry. Always, this thrilled her. She loved shooting down the ramp and feeling her tires hit Steamship Wharf. From the wharf, it was one mile exactly to the Beach Club.

When she pulled into the parking lot, she saw Mack standing on the tiny deck of her cottage, waiting for her with the same smile he wore in the photograph she kept on her refrigerator all winter. The first summer Mack worked at the Beach Club he had knocked on Lacey's door to introduce himself. This was the summer after Maximilian had passed away, a mere four months later. When the boy said his name, "Hi, I'm Mack," Lacey nearly tumbled out of her chair. Because of course, what she heard was "Hi, I'm Max," as though her husband had returned to her in the form of this boy. Now she knew better, but she believed in divine intervention; she believed that somehow, Maximilian had sent her Mack.

Lacey beeped the horn with abandon. She reached for the power window switch and suddenly Lacey and Mack were face to face. He kissed her through the open window before she could even pull into her parking space.

"Hey, Gardner," he said. "Welcome home."

Tears rose and she shooed Mack's face away. Pulled the car into her spot and put up the window and took a deep breath. Mack opened the door, gave her his gentleman's hand.

"You look wonderful, Lacey. I swear you're getting younger."

"Nonsense," she said. But she took Mack's face in her hands and gave him a kiss for saying so. Truth was she felt as alive and vital as ever. "Eighty-eight and still kicking."

"New car?" Mack asked, as he lifted her suitcases out of the trunk.

Lacey nodded. "They were hesitant to give me a loan down at the bank. I told them I'd pay it off in two years. That did the trick. So I'll be out of debt by age ninety."

Mack laughed and walked with Lacey toward the cottage. "Everyone's back. We have a new woman at the front desk and a new bellman. The bellman is very handsome, Lacey, so watch out. He's on his way to California."

"Don't tell me there's been another Gold Rush? See there, if you live long enough, everything will start to repeat itself."

"Vance is back. He went to Thailand and shaved his head. I'm warning you in advance so you don't make some kind of comment. You know Vance is sensitive."

"Goodness, yes," Lacey said.

"Bill and Therese are fine," Mack said. "Cecily got into the University of Virginia, but she has a Brazilian boyfriend, so who knows." Mack swung the door to her cottage open.

"Here we are," Lacey said. The place had a familiar smell, a mingling of Pine Sol and her scented talcum powder. She put down her pocketbook and looked around—her Spode on the kitchen shelves, her Maggie Meredith prints. The original sign from her hat shop hanging jauntily over the leather sofa seemed to announce her arrival: Lacey's. "Pour us a drink. Oh, wait, I forgot—there's a case of Dewar's in the trunk of the car."

"Be right back," Mack said.

Lacey wobbled down the hall to her bedroom. She touched her pillowcase, crisp and white. It was disturbing to look at the bed, however. She couldn't look at it without thinking, *This could be the bed I die in.* She supposed this was true for everyone; her odds were just greater.

MACK MIXED A DEWAR'S and water and poured himself a Coke while Lacey took a seat in her armchair.

"The cottage looks marvelous, dear," Lacey said.

"The new chambermaids tried to clean the place, but they didn't know that in Therese's vocabulary, *clean* is an absolute—like truth, or peace. I had to go in behind them and finish the job myself."

"That makes me feel all the better," Lacey said. She tried to straighten her dress hem around her knees. That was the darnedest thing about sitting down as an old woman—getting comfortable and looking good were nearly impossible. "You've given me an earful about everybody else, but I haven't heard about you. How, Mack Petersen, are *you* doing?"

Mack handed her the drink and settled himself on the sofa. There was something he wanted to tell her, she could tell right away. Lacey was a confidante to Mack, and to practically everybody else on the property for that matter. She joked about hanging a shingle, but secretly she liked imparting her wisdom. What good was she if she couldn't share with people what she'd learned? She had eighty-eight years of experience stored inside her like volumes of an encyclopedia.

"Is there something wrong?" she asked.

"I'm fine," he said, but he didn't meet her eyes. He wasn't ready to tell her what it was just yet, but she could wait. They had all summer.

THE DAY BEFORE THE first guests arrived, Mack took some time off and went for a drive in his Jeep with the top down. He bumped along the cobblestone streets of town, looking at the historic homes: red geraniums in the window boxes, antique onion lamps, flags snapping in the wind. Painters hung off the sides of houses, and landscapers planted hydrangeas. The air was rich with the almost-Iowa smell of freshly cut grass, and Mack's Jeep with the top off was an almost-tractor. Growing up in Iowa, he'd learned to appreciate the seasons, and spring on Nantucket was the equivalent of planting time. Getting the land ready, laying seed, and waiting for growth.

He twisted through the narrow streets until he reached the top of Main Street, then he headed west toward Madaket. He hit the gas and sped up, enjoying the wind and sun on his face. He thought about what Maribel said about profit sharing. Asking Bill to profit-share made Mack anxious. What if Bill thought Mack was anticipating his death? What if Bill died thinking Mack wasn't grateful for all Bill had done for him already? Worse still, what if Bill said no? Bill, his almost-father. But not his father. Mack was thirty years old and he supposed the time had come to expect more from himself. If he weren't brave enough to ask Bill to profit share, if he weren't brave enough to make Nantucket his own, then he should return to his five hundred and thirty acres in Iowa.

When Mack reached Madaket, he stopped at the wooden bridge named for Madaket Millie. A sliver of blue ocean showed beyond the dune grass to his left, and Madaket Harbor, with sailboats bobbing on their bright red moorings, was to his right. *Speak to me*, he thought. *Speak to me now.* But it didn't work this way. He never asked to hear the voice, it just presented itself the way it had his first day on Nantucket. Mack listened, hoping. He needed help—anyone could see that. But Nantucket was quiet. All Mack heard was the wind in his ears.

Memorial Day

May 25

Dear S.B.T.,

So, we're at it once again this year! While it's true I'm not getting any younger, I still have no interest in selling the hotel. My staff is in place, Mack is back running the show, and my wife, Therese, is sitting next to me at the helm. The hotel has been buffed and polished and we look forward to a stellar season. As ever, you are invited to reveal your identity to me and come sit in my office, take in the view and talk. I feel we would have a great deal in common, and maybe after an hour or two of face time you will understand why my response to your offer has to be no, thank you. We're doing fine.

Cordially,

Bill Elliott

THERESE ELLIOTT WAS ONLY interested in the unhappy people who stayed at her hotel. She, like Tolstoy, found happy people all alike; they were boring, dullards, plukes. And so, Mack dealt with the happy guests (except for Andrea, the woman with the autistic son, but Therese sensed this was a different matter altogether) and he left Therese with the damaged and wounded, the guests who suffered despite their money. They had lost a wife, or a child, or their leg or their breasts to cancer. They assumed responsibility for a parent with Alzheimer's. They were divorced, widowed, married but alone. They had been abused. They fought suicide, depression, alcoholism.

Therese worked the reservation phone over the winter in Aspen and she heard all kinds of stories as she booked the rooms. She vividly remembered the day she spoke to Leo Hearn—February 6—it snowed eleven inches the night before, fresh powder, and Bill left the house at nine-thirty for Buttermilk Mountain. Therese's daughter, Cecily, called at ten—noon on the East Coast where she went to boarding school—to say she had the flu and was puking her guts up. Therese felt both upset and angry—upset that Cecily was sick and so far away, and angry that Bill wasn't home to worry with Therese because he was too busy skiing the green slopes. It was horribly sad to think of Bill, who had once raced down Jackpot with the best of them, limited to skiing with awkward beginners. *Why don't you stay home with me?* Therese had asked. *We'll play cards, go shopping.* But Bill got a thrill out of feeling his skis cut through the snow, just a few sweet turns. Therese imagined Bill falling, his body shattering like a teacup. She would be a widow, left to raise a headstrong teenage daughter and run the hotel all alone. Tragic possibilities always lurked near the front of Therese's mind, just behind her common sense.

At one o'clock, Leo Hearn called.

Leo Hearn wasn't a new client. He'd been coming to the hotel for four or five years and he'd always been Mack's domain—he was hale, robust, a Man's Man. He had started a second family in his late fifties: a young wife, two small children. He was a lawyer. In other words, someone who held very little interest for Therese, until this phone call.

She noticed something new in his voice right away. A softening, a surprising deference.

"Hello, I'd like to make a reservation for Memorial Day weekend, please," he said. "I might be too late, but, oh, heck, I hope not. This is Leo Hearn calling from Chicago."

"Leo *Hearn?*" Therese said. The man whose voice boomed through the lobby, making the staff cringe? The man who broke one of Mack's fingers with his crushing handshake? "Leo, this is Therese Elliott." She flipped through the reservation book to May, Memorial

Day. "I'm looking at Memorial Day right now and it's wide open. What do you need?"

"I need a better shrink and a better nanny," he said. "In fact, I think what I really need is to start over. You know, with my life."

Therese looked out her floor-to-ceiling window at the back of Aspen Mountain. "I see."

"My wife is gone," Leo said. "You remember Kelly? She left me. And I mean *left*. She left without any money and she left without the kids."

"The babies?" Therese asked.

"Whitney is ten months and Cole is almost four," he said. "She left them."

Therese's throat soured as she thought of Cecily, puking into a plastic bucket in some awful dorm room two thousand miles away. That was bad enough. She couldn't imagine a mother abandoning her children, her babies, forever.

"My doctor said I should keep everything as normal as possible. So that's why I'm calling. I want to bring the kids to the island. All my kids. I have two older boys too, did you know that? Boys, ha!" Leo said. "They're grown men. Of course I fouled everything up with them in the eighties when I divorced their mother. But they say they'll come to Nantucket. Humoring me, probably. I think my oldest son is gay. He's an attorney and he works on gay rights and the kid's never had a girlfriend that I've known about. My other son, Fred, is a third-year at Harvard Law, but Fred is tricky, see, because Fred's still angry with me from what happened with his mother. I was hoping if the kids spent time with their older brothers maybe they would stop crying." He paused, and Therese wondered if Leo Hearn weren't so boring after all. "I just want my children to stop crying."

Therese gazed out at the mountain, thinking, *Please, Bill, come home.* "I understand."

Leo cleared his throat. "Do you have three rooms available?"

• • •

THERESE WAS PUTTERING AROUND the lobby on the Friday of Memorial Day, perfecting it for opening weekend, when Leo Hearn and his children arrived.

"Leo," she said, walking over. "I'm glad you got here safely."

"Therese," Leo said. He hugged her and kissed her cheek awkwardly. He turned to his family. "Meet the gang. You know Cole and the baby. This is our nanny, Chantal, and my sons Bart and Fred. We're quite the entourage."

Entourage indeed. An attractive blonde held the baby girl. Then the sons: the one named Bart, tall and thin, dressed in a suit, and the one named Fred a younger replica of Leo Hearn himself—broad shouldered and stocky. Weaving between everyone's legs was the little boy, Cole. Therese crouched down, and said, "Hello, Cole. Welcome back."

Cole stopped a second and looked at her, his brown eyes suspicious. Then he went back to his aimless weaving. An unhappy child was the sign of an unhappy family; no one could convince Therese differently.

"Come here, Cole," Leo said. Cole ran and hid under the piano. Leo shrugged. He looked at his other two sons and rubbed his hands together. "So, what do you say, guys, should we play some tennis this afternoon?"

"I don't know," Fred, the young Leo, said. "We just got here. Maybe we could relax."

"Maybe," Leo said. "Or maybe we could play tennis like I suggested. You want to play, don't you, Bart?" he asked the son in the suit.

Bart loosened his tie. "Sure, Dad, I'll play."

"Well, then, we need a fourth," Leo said.

Slow down, Leo, stop trying so hard. Therese's mother instincts kicked in like adrenaline. She went back to watering her plants.

"We need a fourth," Leo repeated. His eyes scanned the lobby as though someone might magically materialize.

"I don't have to play," Fred said. "I'd really rather relax. You can play with Bart."

"This is a family weekend," Leo said. "I'd like to play tennis with both of you. We just need a fourth."

"I was third seed singles at Bilbo High School in 1958," Therese said. "But you probably don't want to play with an old woman."

Leo smiled. "No, that's great, that's perfect. We'd love to have you join us, Therese. Wouldn't we, guys?"

Fred and Bart rustled around and made gestures that looked sort of like nods.

"Shall we say four o'clock?" Leo asked.

"That gives you time to relax," Therese said. "Why don't you check in and Vance can show you to your rooms." She set her watering can down on the piano. Cole was stretched out on the carpet underneath, pretending to be asleep. Therese whispered to him, "When you wake up I have some beach toys you might like." She waited a few seconds and Cole raised his head.

"What kind of toys?" he asked.

"Toys for building castles," she said. "Want to see?"

"I want my mom back," Cole said. "She's not coming back." He had thick black eyelashes, the kind grown women envied.

"I know you want to see your mom," Therese said. "But what I have are beach toys. Do you want to see the beach toys?"

Cole nodded.

Therese held out her hand. "Come with me."

AFTER THERESE GAVE COLE a bucket, shovel, and a large inflatable lobster, and delivered him safely to his room, she went into Bill's office and collapsed in one of the wicker chairs by the window. Bill typed at his computer.

"The Hearns are here," she said. "Remember I told you the wife vanished and left mister with those two tiny children? Plus a couple of grown sons from the first marriage?" Out the window, she was glad to see both Bart and Fred spreading beach towels under an umbrella. "Remember I told you? Well, I'm playing tennis with them this afternoon."

Bill stopped typing. "Call me crazy, but it sounds like you're meddling, Therese. Or getting ready to meddle."

Cole and the nanny trudged onto the beach. Cole ran for the edge of the water with his pail and shovel. Just a normal little boy. Therese's mother instincts whistled like a tea kettle. She looked at Bill, and at the volume of Robert Frost poems on his desk. The two of them had known so much pain. Therese's way of dealing with it was to sniff out other people's sore spots, wanting to make them better. Bill's way was to read his poetry.

"I am meddling," she said. "But they needed a fourth."

"Be careful," Bill said. "These are people's lives you're dealing with. Not lab animals set up for one of your psychology experiments."

Therese stood up, smoothed the folds of her silk skirt. "I take great offense at that."

"I know you do," he said. "But will you please be careful?"

"I'm always careful," she said.

"When have you been careful?" Bill asked. "I have never met anyone more willing to get involved in the jumble of other people's lives. It's your insatiable need to clean everything up, to create order, to make things lovely again. You can't stand to see a mess."

"I want to help," Therese said. "I've never done anything except try to help."

"What about Mrs. Ling leaving her husband last year at the end of her stay? Are you going to tell me that wasn't any of your doing? What about convincing the Avermans that they should send their son to military school? What about arranging the wedding in the lobby for the woman who was dying of lupus?"

"She wanted to get married!" Therese said. "I helped make that woman's life complete. And Mrs. Ling is happier without her husband—you read the card she sent during the holidays."

Bill held up his palms. "Therese, I'm only asking you to think about pulling back a little this year. To begin with, think about letting Leo Hearn deal with his family problems on his own. What do you say to that?"

Therese put her hands on her hips. She and Bill were opposites: Bill liked numbers, and the cool, lofty images he found in poetry—

and not just any poetry but the poetry of Robert Frost, who wrote about the woods, lakes, paths, leaves. Frost: the man's very name dripped icicles. Bill wasn't equipped to deal with the guests—happy or miserable.

"Tennis is at four," she said. "So if anyone's looking for me, that's where I'll be."

"Be careful!" Bill said.

NANTUCKET IN MAY WAS funny as far as the weather was concerned. It had been fair and breezy all day but at four o'clock fog rolled in. Therese changed into her whites and she was standing on the front porch of the lobby when Fred popped out of the gray mist.

"Dad and Bart are going to be a minute," he said. "They were the ones who wanted to play and now they're not even ready."

Therese bounced her racket off her knee; she still used a wooden racket, with a frame. "So, have you been to Nantucket before?" she asked.

"No," Fred said. "Nantucket was a place where Dad brought his new family. We only got invited this year because the crisis hit."

"The crisis?"

"Dad's wife, Kelly, left him and the kids high and dry. I hate to say it but that's what you get for marrying someone twenty-five years younger than yourself. Dad deserved it. What goes around comes around and all that." Anger lifted off Fred like a bad smell.

"What do you do, Fred?" Therese asked.

"Me? I just finished law school. I'm studying for the bar."

"So you're going to be a lawyer," Therese said.

Fred shoved his hands in the pockets of his white shorts and bowed his head. "I don't know," he said. He looked at her. "Have you ever met a lawyer you liked?"

Therese laughed. "What a question. If I didn't like lawyers, I'd be out of business."

"I don't like lawyers," Fred said. "Actually, my brother's okay and he's a lawyer. But he's different." He swung around to look at the lobby. "Hey, do you own this place?"

"My husband and I do."

"Man, it must be a gold mine."

"It is," Therese said. Fred smiled as she hoped he would. And then Leo and Bart came around the corner with Chantal, Cole, and the baby.

"The kids are going to come with us," Leo said. "I thought I'd make this a real family affair. Cole can chase the balls."

Cole started to cry. "I was having fun on the beach," he said.

Fred kicked a hermit crab shell across the parking lot. "Great," he said. "Just great."

THEY REACHED THE COURTS at four-fifteen. The fog was thickening.

"Is this even worth it?" Fred asked. "In a few minutes we won't be able to see the ball."

Leo opened a can of balls and whacked one across the net at Fred's feet. "You need to change your attitude, Buster."

Chantal sat in the grass near the net while the baby toddled around her. Cole was crying.

"This is spectacular," Fred said. He turned to Therese. "Have you ever seen such a happy family?"

"Would you like to be on my team?" she asked.

"Okay," he said. He yelled across the net. "Hey, Dad, we're going to play mixed doubles. Me and Therese against you and Bart."

"Fuck you, Fred," Bart said.

"Watch your language," Leo said.

"That was uncalled for, Fred," Bart said.

"I was only kidding," Fred said. "I was only trying to add some levity to this little affair, this pathetic attempt at family bonding. Sorry if I offended you."

"Dad's right," Bart said. "You need to lighten up."

"Why are you kissing Dad's ass, Bart?" Fred said.

Leo raised his voice. "I *said* watch your language. We have the children here."

Then Bart turned to his father. "Why do you call *them* 'the children'? Fred and I are also your children."

"It's an age thing," Leo said.

"So now that I'm twenty-eight years old I'm no longer your child? I've become, what, your colleague?"

Chantal stood up. "I can't take this," she said. Therese hadn't even realized the girl spoke English. Chantal, wasn't that a French name? The girl had a flat, Midwestern accent. "This low-level ground fire is driving me nuts. You people don't need to be playing tennis. You need to be dealing with your issues. I'm going back to the hotel." She picked up Whitney and took Cole by the arm. He protested, and Chantal said, "Fine, you want to stay, stay." She marched off.

Therese watched her go. She should probably leave as well. Bill believed that the only people who could fix family problems were the family members themselves. But Therese worried about Cole. The skin around his eyes was red and mottled from so much crying. He wore a little white polo shirt and little tennis shoes. He sat in the grass with his feet out in front of him, his arms crossed.

"I should go, too," Therese said. "I don't belong here."

"Please stay, Therese." This from Fred. "I don't think any of us can handle it if another woman walks out."

"Yes," Leo echoed. "Please stay. We'll behave, won't we, guys?"

"Okay," Therese said. "I'll stay." She winked at Cole. He hiccuped.

THERESE CONCENTRATED ON HER tennis—the green ball and her old-fashioned racket—but she couldn't help noticing the silence that settled over them like the fog. The men barely grunted out the score. Was this their idea of good behavior? If you have nothing nice to say, say nothing at all? Didn't they know it was unhealthy to hold feelings in?

A little before five o'clock, they were tied at six games apiece.

"Shall we have a tiebreaker to see who gets the set?" Leo asked.

"I agree under one condition," Therese said. "You men have to talk to one another."

"Talk?" Fred said.

"Yes, you know, talk to one another, like normal people," Therese said. "Chantal was right. You need to communicate."

Fred got ready to serve. "Okay," he said. "I have something I'd like to talk about. I've decided I don't want to be a lawyer." He slammed the ball and it whizzed past Leo.

"What?" Leo said. "What did you say?"

Fred and Therese switched sides and Fred took another ball from his pocket. He tossed it up and caught it, and looked at his father. "I don't want to be a lawyer."

"You just graduated from Harvard Law School and now you don't want to be a lawyer? Ninety thousand dollars later and you've suddenly had a change of heart?"

"It's about more than ninety thousand dollars," Fred said. "It's about my life."

"Well, I'm gay," Bart said.

"Wait a minute," Leo said, wiping his forehead with the sleeve of his shirt. "One bombshell at a time. You don't want to be a lawyer?"

"Don't ignore what I said, Dad," Bart said. "Don't pretend like the fact that I'm gay doesn't exist."

"No," Fred said, "I don't want to be a lawyer."

The fog was so thick Therese could barely make out Cole at the edge of the court. But he sat there, listening.

Leo looked at Bart. "You're gay. I don't know what I'm supposed to do with that. Say great? That's wonderful? I'm so happy for you? What's appropriate?"

"How about, 'Thank you for telling me'?"

"Okay," Leo said. "Thank you for telling me. And, Fred, if you don't want to be a lawyer, then what *do* you want to be?"

"I don't know," Fred said. "A motorcycle cop. An independent filmmaker. A house husband."

Bart looked at his watch. "Our time's up," he said. "We have to be off the court."

"And nobody won," Fred said.

The fog made it look as though the afternoon were going up in smoke. Therese's fault, for meddling. As they walked back to the hotel, Cole took her hand.

"I want my mom," he whispered.

Therese squeezed him to her side. "I know," she said. "I know."

THE NEXT MORNING, THERESE followed behind the chambermaids with her checklist, inspecting their cleaning jobs. Was the toilet working? Was the temperature of the water in the toilet bowl correct? Did the tile floor in the entryway need scrubbing? Were the lightbulbs working? Therese had twenty-four items on her checklist. In all the years that the hotel had been open, no one had ever complained of a dirty room. Not once.

Therese watched one of her new chambermaids—a girl from Darien named Elizabeth—as she started on the bathroom in room 7.

"Check under the mirror for grime," Therese said. "Dirt has favorite hiding places and that's one of them."

Elizabeth wiped her forehead with the back of her rubber-gloved hand. "Okay," she said. She went back to scouring the top of the toilet, then she turned to Therese. "But do I really have to check the temperature of the water in the toilet bowl?"

"We need to make sure the mixing valves are working correctly. If the water's too hot the toilet will whistle, and the guests will be up all night listening to it. If the water's too cold . . . well, have you ever sat on a toilet filled with ice cold water?"

Elizabeth shook her head.

"It's no fun," Therese said. "Just take your gloves off and stick your finger in the water. See if it feels comfortable."

Elizabeth got two very distinct worry lines in her forehead. "But people *poop* in that water."

"By now the poop is hundreds of yards away. It's clean water, I assure you." Therese watched Elizabeth pull at her rubber glove one finger at a time and gingerly dip the end of her pinky into the water.

"It's comfortable," Elizabeth said.

"For goodness' sake." She nudged Elizabeth aside and dragged her own hand through the water. "You're right," Therese said.

Therese moved on to room 8, knowing that Elizabeth was rolling her eyes in frustration and would no doubt write a letter home to her mother complaining about her boss who made her test the toilet bowl water. Half the chambermaids Therese hired quit, but the ones who stayed became the world's best housekeepers.

In room 8, sitting on the unmade queen-sized bed, was Leo Hearn. Therese checked her clipboard.

"This isn't your room," she said. "What are you doing in here? You don't belong in here."

"I was waiting for you," he said.

"I'm working," Therese said. "Why aren't you with your children?"

"My children hate me," Leo said. "I can't get anything right. The nanny hates me and she's not even related to me. No wonder my wife left."

"Your kids don't hate you," Therese said. "You're just having a difficult time."

"I'll say it's difficult. One kid is a lawyer in a good practice but he's gay. He likes men. The other kid is straight but he doesn't want to be a lawyer. He wants to be a *house husband*. I told them if I took the lawyer part of Bart and joined it with the heterosexual part of Fred, they'd make the perfect son."

"Oh, Leo," Therese said.

"I let that pearl slip after four Stoli tonics at dinner last night. Now neither one of them is speaking to me. It's like I don't exist."

"You hurt them," Therese said. "You need to apologize."

"At the time, I thought maybe they'd take it as a compliment. They each got it half right."

"No," Therese said. "Because you're telling them that they only equal half a person in your eyes. You're not accepting their choices."

"I don't know what to do," Leo said, his broad shoulders slumping.

Therese sat next to him. "You want a piece of advice from an old woman?"

"You're no older than me," he said. "But you're right. I feel old."

Therese caught her reflection in the mirror over the dresser. If Bill were watching her now, he'd cringe. He'd tell her to pat Leo Hearn on the hand and wish him good luck. But Therese wanted to help. "Twenty-eight years ago, I lost a child. A son. Born dead." Therese felt Leo shift slightly away from her on the mattress. "And I would give anything to have just one of your three sons. They are strong, healthy, smart, good people and it's your responsibility to love them. That's all, Leo, just love them."

"I'm sorry you lost your son," Leo said.

"I'm sorry, too," she said. "But I'm even sorrier to see someone like you with four beautiful children acting like an ass."

"I am an ass," Leo said. "I am just a really big ass. No wonder my wife left me."

"Stop thinking about yourself, Leo. Parents aren't allowed to think about themselves."

"Do you have some kind of instruction manual that I don't have?" he asked.

"My instruction manual has been twenty-eight years of pain for my son. And it makes me grateful for what I do have, my husband, my daughter Cecily." Therese misted up. She waved her hand. "Go find your kids," she said.

Leo left the room and Therese watched him go. Then she eyed her checklist. At that moment it seemed so silly she wanted to pitch it out the window. Therese let a couple of tears drip down her cheeks, then she heard a knock on the door. It was Elizabeth.

"Are you okay?" Elizabeth asked.

Therese wiped her face and looked in the mirror. The white streak in her orange hair stood out like a scream in a nursery, something wrong, something amiss. Her baby boy dead. How shocked she'd been to look at herself in the mirror after thirteen grueling hours of labor and find that she'd turned into an old woman, with white hair. White hair that couldn't be dyed, that wouldn't hold color. So she wouldn't couldn't forget.

ON SUNDAY, LEO APPROACHED Therese during breakfast. He lowered his voice. "Things are better," he said. "I took your suggestion and recanted the statement about the perfect son."

"Good for you," Therese said.

Leo checked his watch. "Cole hasn't cried in twenty hours. A new record. But I still feel like I'm balancing a tray of expensive china on my head."

"That's known in the parents' manual as the balancing-expensive-china feeling," Therese said. "All parents feel that way sometimes."

"I'm taking Bart and Fred out alone tonight," Leo said. "A men's night out, you know, big, juicy steaks, red wine, cigars, the whole bit."

"Just love them, Leo," Therese said.

"I'm leaving Chantal with the kids and ordering them take-out shrimp and fried clams. But would you check on them? In case Cole starts to cry. I know he likes you."

"I'd be happy to check on them if it makes you feel better."

Leo spun his coffee cup in his hands. "You know, I've been thinking about what you said and I really am sorry about your son."

"I didn't tell you that story to get your sympathy, Leo," Therese said.

"I know." Leo turned red and looked down at the carpet. "I just wanted you to know it made me think."

"Good." It made him think, but he would never know what it felt like to hold a dead baby. Lucky, lucky man. "I'll keep an eye on your kids," she said. "Don't worry about a thing."

LATER, THERESE WOULD RECALL certain images: the Hearn men dressed in navy blazers and white shirts and bright summer ties standing on the front porch of the lobby while Chantal snapped their picture, their arms wound around each other, looking not so much like father and sons as like fraternity brothers, team members, friends. Then, another picture with Leo holding Cole, and Bart and Fred holding the baby girl. Therese watched all this from the bay window of her house, and she felt pride at that moment. Pride! She had helped! Therese noted the arrival of the young delivery man from Meals on Keels who showed up with Styrofoam cartons of food. She thought, "I'll check on them after they eat." Therese searched her empty kitchen cabinets for something that might qualify as dinner. She was a great housekeeper but a terrible cook and she thought guiltily of all the times Cecily had complained growing up, "There's nothing to eat in this house!" Therese fixed two cucumber and cream cheese sandwiches and a handful of pretzels. She poured herself a glass of Chardonnay and a cranberry juice for Bill. She took the glasses first and then the plates to the bedroom where Bill was lying in the near dark with a washcloth over his eyes, snoring. It was seven o'clock.

Then the phone rang and Therese left the plates of food on the bed next to Bill's sleeping body as she went to answer the phone. She remembered hoping it was Cecily.

But it was Tiny, her normally serene voice high-pitched, like the very top of a guitar string. "We have a situation down here. I've called an ambulance."

Therese flew down the stairs, out of her house, and across the parking lot, her long skirt billowing behind her. There had been no sense asking what or who. Her mother instinct shrieked like a siren. It was the Hearn children.

Chantal stood in the lobby holding Cole. His arms and legs were pink and swollen, his face a red, angry balloon.

Chantal was shaking. "He's not choking, I checked. I know how to do the Heimlich but he's not choking. I don't know what's happening."

Therese took Cole from her; he was heavier than she expected. "Go get the baby."

Therese put her ear to Cole's mouth. Cole's breathing was hoarse and wheezy. His eyes were swollen shut. "Can you hear me?" Therese asked him. "Are you awake?" Then Therese heard sirens. "Call a cab for the girl," Therese said to Tiny. "And call Leo Hearn at the Club Car. I'll go with the boy to the hospital."

Therese hurried out the front of the lobby to meet the ambulance. Cole's body went limp in her arms. The paramedic jumped out and took Cole from her.

"He fainted," Therese said. Cole's skin was turning scarlet; he looked like a boiled lobster. "Is he going to die?"

The ambulance driver flung the doors of the ambulance open, put Cole on a stretcher and loaded him in. "You coming with us?" he asked Therese. "You the boy's grandmother?"

"No," she said. Heart breaking at the word "grandmother" though she was certainly old enough. *Mother. Mother.* "But I am going with you." Therese hiked her skirt and climbed into the back of the ambulance. The siren sounded and they sped off down North Beach Road.

The paramedic lifted Cole's eyelids. "The kid's in shock," he said. He put a blanket over Cole, then took his blood pressure. He produced a needle from his bag and stuck it into Cole's arm.

"What are you doing?" Therese asked. "I said I'm not the boy's mother, or grandmother. Don't you have to ask permission or something?"

"We have a little anaphylactic reaction here," the paramedic said. "A severe allergic swelling accompanied by hives, low blood pressure, fainting. And the kid's having problems breathing because his throat is swelling shut. Has he been eating nuts maybe? Or shellfish?"

"Clams, I think," Therese said. She wondered if saying "a little anaphylactic reaction" was like saying "a little cancer" or "a little heart attack." Low blood pressure, shock, fainting—all that sounded so serious. "He's allergic, then?"

"Look at him," the paramedic said. "This is more than indigestion."

"Is he going to die?" Therese asked again. She might fend off the worst kind of news if she faced it head on. *Was the child going to die?* Less than six months before, she rode in another ambulance, when it was Bill on the stretcher, his face pale and shiny with sweat. The paramedics then talked about flying Bill to Denver in a helicopter that Therese suspected they saved for dying people. She had been too afraid then even to speak the words. But now she saw it was easier to start with the worst possibility; she might outsmart death by pretending she wasn't afraid.

The paramedic had red hair like Cecily and he was young, perhaps only a few years older than Cecily. He smiled and patted Therese's shoulder.

"No," he said, "he's not going to die."

AT THE HOSPITAL, THEY took Cole away on a gurney and the nurse tried to hand Therese forms to fill out, but she said, "I'm not his mother, I'm not his grandmother. I'm not related at all. I don't know his date of birth or anything. His father will be here soon."

A minute later, Chantal ran into the waiting room. She held the baby, who was asleep.

"I'm sure to get fired now," she said.

Therese took the baby from Chantal and nodded for her to sit down. Therese kissed the sweet, fragrant top of the baby's head. She remembered Cecily at this age: the tiny, solid weight of her. The smell of a baby, the softness of a baby. *Baby, baby.*

She whispered to Chantal, "It's not your fault, dear. Cole was allergic to what you ate. Did you have clams?"

Chantal sniffled. "Clams and shrimp. And then he swelled up like a piece of bubble gum. This whole trip has been a nightmare."

Leo stormed into the waiting room with Bart and Fred behind him. Tie loose, eyes bloodshot, smelling like smoke.

"What happened?" he said. "Where's Cole? I want to see my son."

Therese put a finger to her lips. "Cole had an allergic reaction to the clams. You need to speak to the nurse. She wants you to fill out some forms."

"I don't want to fill out any goddamned forms! I want to see my son! I get a call at the goddamned restaurant telling me my child has been rushed to the emergency room, and I'd like to see him." Leo glared at Therese, as though she were responsible. How could she blame him? She had given Leo permission to love his children, without warning him that as soon as you allowed yourself to love them fully, you left yourself open to this kind of hurt, this kind of incredible fear. Leo started in on the nurse at the desk.

"What happened?" Fred asked.

"It was an allergic reaction to the clams, they think," Therese said. She uneasily recalled that emergencies were like this: you repeated what little information you had again and again until finally you received more information. "He turned bright pink and puffy, and right before the ambulance arrived he fainted in my arms. The paramedic gave him a shot. The paramedic seemed to think Cole was going to be fine."

Leo returned from the desk with a clipboard. "They won't let me see him yet," he said. "They said the doctor will be out shortly, whatever that means. Cole had an allergic reaction to the shellfish." Leo looked at Fred. "Did you know he was allergic to shellfish?"

Fred shook his head.

"Bart, did you know Cole was allergic to shellfish?"

"No, Dad, I didn't."

"I didn't know either," Chantal offered up. "Otherwise I wouldn't have let him eat the clams. But he said he *wanted* some. I just gave them to him without thinking."

"I didn't know he was allergic," Leo said. "I'm the boy's father and I did not know he was allergic to shellfish." He collapsed into a molded plastic chair.

Bart patted him on the back. "It's okay, Dad."

"It's not okay," Leo said. "Because I'm sure his mother knew he was allergic, and his mother's not here. She took that important piece of information with her, just like she took all of the other important pieces of information. I didn't know Cole was allergic, I don't know how to make Cole stop crying, and I certainly don't know how to care for a baby girl. I only had boys, and I don't know much about them either."

They were all quiet for a while and then Fred cleared his throat. "Is it possible that this is the first time Cole's ever eaten shellfish and that nobody knew he was allergic because he'd never tried it before?"

"It's possible," Chantal said. "I've never seen Cole eat anything but hot dogs and pasta."

Fred tousled his father's gray hair. "So that means if Kelly were here, she wouldn't have known Cole was allergic either."

"Thinking like a lawyer," Bart said. "Harvard isn't wasted after all."

A bald man in a blue jogging suit came out into the waiting room. "Mr. Hearn? Mrs. Hearn?"

"Are you the doctor?" Leo asked.

"Dr. Maniscalco," he said, offering his hand. "Nice to meet you. Cole is going to be fine. He had an allergic reaction to some clams he ate but we gave him a shot of epinephrine, and some corticosteroids to reduce the swelling. That should take care of it. He can never eat any kind of shellfish again. He shouldn't be in a room where clams are steaming, he shouldn't even pick up a clam on the beach. If you hadn't gotten him here in time, there could have been some serious complications."

"But he's okay, right, Doctor?" Leo asked. "Can we take him home?"

The doctor nodded and Leo followed after him down the hall. He returned several minutes later holding Cole, whose brown eyes were wide open, thick lashes blinking; he was sucking his thumb. Therese felt the cool wind of relief. She watched her reflection in the sliding glass doors as she swayed the baby back and forth. It seemed so natural, holding a baby.

• • •

BILL WAS WAITING UP when she got home.

"What I want to know is," he said, "are we going to get sued?"

"No," Therese said.

"Good," Bill said. "It's the family of lawyers we're dealing with so I was nervous. I woke up and found the sandwiches and I wondered why I was eating alone, and so I called Tiny. I guess I slept through the sirens." He took Therese's hand and she sat on the floor in front of his chair so he could rub her shoulders. "Was it awful?" he asked.

"I've seen worse," Therese said. "But I was scared there for a while. In the end, though, the little boy's okay, and I think the family is going to make it as well."

"They survived the meddling of Therese Elliott," Bill said.

What Therese wanted more than anything else at that moment was for Cecily to come home. She wanted to look at her own child and know that she was safe. And she wanted a good night's sleep.

"We have fourteen check-outs tomorrow," Therese said. "And only three chambermaids. And if that's not bad enough, tomorrow is Memorial Day."

BILL ELLIOTT NEVER FORGOT Memorial Day. In the morning, he made love to Therese as sweetly and tenderly as he knew how. He kissed her eyelids and they leaked tears. Therese clung to him, and when Bill entered her, her sobs quieted. Therese had been his wife for thirty years and still, Bill could not believe the love that overcame him. This Memorial Day morning, the love and sadness mixed together.

"I love you," Bill said.

"I know."

One hour in bed and they relived the full weight of a pain that had assaulted them so long ago. Though perhaps Bill was the only one who felt the full brunt of the pain; perhaps for Therese, the pain had faded over the years. He hoped for her sake that it had.

Twenty-eight years ago, Therese was thirty and Bill was thirty-two. Therese was eight months pregnant with their first child, and Bill worked for his father at the Beach Club. The hotel rooms had not yet been built, although Bill and Therese planned to see an architect and approach Big Bill with the idea—a Beach Club and a *hotel*. Rooms facing the water. It was thrilling to think of handing something so concrete to their new child. Thrilling to think about passing the hotel on to a son.

No one was ever able to explain what went wrong. Therese had sharp pains one day while shopping in town. She called the doctor from the lunch counter at Congdon's Pharmacy and he jokingly told her not to drive the Jeep over the cobblestones. That night Therese asked Bill to feel her belly. Was the baby kicking? *Tell me you feel the baby kicking.* Bill spread both hands over Therese's naked belly, his fingers splayed, and rubbed it as though it were a crystal ball. He thought he felt a distant pounding, but then he realized it was Therese's frantic heartbeat. No, he felt nothing.

Therese called the doctor in the middle of the night, and he agreed to meet them at the hospital. Bill remembered the ride to the hospital—no ambulance, no sirens—just the quiet, dark minutes in the Jeep with Bill imagining how he would apologize to Dr. Stevenson for dragging him out of bed for no reason. *It's our first time*, he'd say. *We're just a little nervous.*

But an apology wasn't necessary: The baby was dead. Dr. Stevenson induced labor and for thirteen hours Therese pushed—Bill at her side—both of them crying, Therese screaming out, *It isn't fair!* Bill was thinking and maybe Therese too (Bill would never know), *What if the doctor is mistaken? What if the baby is alive?* Therese flung her arms against the metal rails of the bed, trying to hurt herself. *It isn't fair*, she screamed, and no one—not Bill, not the nurses, not Dr. Stevenson—told her she was wrong.

The baby was a boy. A perfectly shaped, normal-seeming little boy, except his skin was gray and when Bill held him he was cool to the touch, like a baby made of porcelain. The nurse left them alone in the room with the baby; she told Bill they should hold the baby for as long as they wanted. "It makes the grieving easier," she said. "Most couples who miscarry never get a chance to hold their baby." Bill and Therese both held the baby. They held him separately; they held him together—for a few minutes, a complete family.

Bill found it impossible to believe that holding his son made his grieving easier. Even now, twenty-eight years later with his wife in his arms, in their warm bed, he could remember what it felt like to hold his dead son. They named him W.T. Elliott—William Therese Elliott—and buried him in a plot in the cemetery on Somerset Road, even though everyone in Bill's family had always been cremated. But cremating the baby was unthinkable. What would he amount to? A handful of ashes that they would fling out into the sea? It would be too horrible to watch the ashes float away; it would be too much as if he never existed.

After they buried the baby, Bill vowed to make love to Therese in the mornings. At first he had to make himself go through the motions. He was afraid of getting Therese pregnant again—and he was afraid of not getting her pregnant. But making love to Therese was the best way he knew to show his devotion, and it became as natural for him as waking up, opening his eyes.

Ten years later when Therese was forty and Bill was forty-two, and Bill, at least, had given up hope of a child, Therese got pregnant again. It was impossible to feel joyful about this pregnancy—it was, Bill remembered, nine months of unspoken fear. But in the end, they had Cecily, who came out of the womb with red hair like her mother. She was kicking and screaming, undeniably alive.

AFTER THEIR LOVEMAKING, THERESE rose from the bed, blew her nose into a Kleenex and said, "I love him. This is Memorial Day. I remember him."

Bill said, "I know. Me too."

He lay in bed a few minutes longer, listening to the sound of his wife in the shower, and he said, in a whisper,

" 'They cannot scare me with their empty spaces
Between stars—on stars where no human race is
I have it in me so much nearer home
To scare myself with my own desert places.' "

"My own desert places." Bill loved his wife and daughter until his heart and lungs and liver and brain stretched and ached and pressed at their boundaries. But he had one desert place: he wanted a son. Sometimes Bill heard Mack's voice or saw Mack throw his head back and laugh, and he thought, *My son would be almost this age. This could be my son fixing the lamppost, driving the Jeep. This could be my son. Why couldn't this be my son?*

MACK DIDN'T HAVE AN hour or even fifteen minutes on Memorial Day to meditate about his parents, but he thought of them more than usual. Maribel had asked him late one night, "If you could have your parents back for an hour, would you do it?" The question upset him so much, he turned away from her in the dark. Mack wanted to pluck his parents out of Oblivion and tell them, face to face, *I miss you, every day I miss you, and I love you.* Who wouldn't want that? But even if it were possible, he would never do it. To have his parents back for an hour meant giving them up after an hour, and that was a loss from which he would never recover. He couldn't stand the thought of losing them again.

Maribel was the only one to ever ask questions about the night of the accident. Mack had been out with friends, seeing a movie. When his friend Josh Pavel pulled down the long dirt road that led through cornfields to the Petersens' farmhouse, Mack saw the sheriff's car in his driveway. There were no flashing lights, nothing like you saw on TV, only the sheriff, a man Mack knew from school assemblies, sitting on the front porch steps, his hat resting on his knees. The sheriff stood up, put his hands on Mack's shoulders, and said, "Your mother and dad are gone. They've been killed."

"And how did you feel at that moment?" Maribel asked him.

Mack stared at her blankly. "What moment?"

"The moment you learned they were gone."

He swallowed. "I don't know. I can't remember the exact moment. It's nothing I think about. It was the worst moment of my life. I don't want to reexamine it."

"You've blocked it out," she said.

"I remember I threw up, he said. I vomited into my mother's rhododendrons. I remember being embarrassed about that, in front of the sheriff."

"Did you cry?" Maribel asked.

"I don't know."

"You must have cried."

"I don't know if I cried right then. I'm telling you, I can't remember much. I remember the sheriff waiting for me on the porch, his hat on his knees."

Ever since David Pringle's phone call, Mack found himself thinking about the farm—the smell of the soil, the barn, the hog pen. The rough, hairy skin of a sow's back, and the way the pigs squealed like children. To this day, Mack's house had been left just as it was—Mack's bedroom with his Iowa Hawkeyes pennants and his 1985 *Sports Illustrated* swimsuit calendar hanging on the wall. A valentine from Michele Waikowski thumbtacked to his bulletin board.

His parents' room too had been left as it was—his father's Carhartt overalls in the closet, and his mother's dresses. His mother's pale hair still in her hairbrush. The food in the kitchen had been cleaned out, except for Mack's mother's refrigerator pickles. "Leave the refrigerator pickles," Mack told David Pringle. His mother used to say they would last forever.

Mack knew it was odd to keep things as they were, crazy even. He supposed the farm hands gossiped about the house, along with the people in Swisher, along with people simply passing through Swisher; by now, it was legend. *The farmhouse, untouched since the couple was killed in a car crash twelve years ago. Haunted? The woman's hair still in her hairbrush.* For years, David Pringle had been urging Mack to clean out the house and rent it, but Mack refused. Mack's life with his parents was, in fact, frozen. The house was a museum of sorts, a museum Mack could visit if he ever found the desire, or the courage, to return.

Because it was Memorial Day, Mack let Love go home early—she'd been swamped all weekend—and he took over behind the front desk and imagined his parents standing there with him. *Here is the lobby*, the quilts Mack hung every year. *Look out at the ocean,* the ferry taking a crowd of people back to the mainland. *Listen to this couple here checking out.* They were sunburned across their cheeks, bike helmets tucked into their duffel bags.

"We had a great time," the man said, handing over his American Express card. (Mack would *not* want his parents to know how much the room cost.) "Thank you very much."

"Yes, and thank you for recommending the bike ride to Altar Rock," the woman chimed in. "It was spectacular."

The couple went to meet their cab, touching a few of Therese's wooden toys on the way out, as if for luck.

See? I made them happy. I made them smile. But when Mack turned around, of course, no one was there.

MEMORIAL DAY: A DAY for remembering. Still, Lacey Gardner had better days for remembering Maximilian—his birthday, August 18, or their wedding anniversary, November 11, even Valentine's Day, because that, sadly, was the day Maximilian had died. Besides, Memorial Day was for veterans, wasn't it? Or was Veterans' Day for veterans and Memorial Day for the rest of God's people? Darn it, Lacey couldn't remember and didn't much care except that she had invited the new bellman in for a drink and he was asking her all kinds of questions about Maximilian, practically forcing Lacey to remember him.

"What did your husband do for a living?" Jeremy asked. (He introduced himself as Jem, but Jem wasn't a real name in Lacey's opinion and she told him so. She would call him Jeremy.)

"Banker," Lacey said. The boy agreed to a scotch, a point in his favor. Lacey poured two drinks and brought them over to the coffee table. Jeremy sat on the sofa looking at a photograph of Maximilian taken the summer before he died. He was tan and healthy-looking in that picture, standing on the deck of their house on Cliff Road.

"Is this him here?" Jeremy asked.

"Indeed," Lacey answered. "That's Maximilian Percy Gardner." She walked back to the kitchen—although in this tiny cottage, living room, dining room, and kitchen were one and the same—and fished through her refrigerator for cheese. She put some brie on a plate with a few Carr's water crackers. Then there was a knock at the screen door. It was Vance with her bucket of ice. Goodness gracious, she forgot to put ice in the cocktails and hadn't even noticed.

"The iceman cometh," Lacey said. Vance didn't smile—his face remained clenched in the same tight scowl he always wore. It would do the young man a world of good to smile every now and again, but she'd been telling him that for years, and to no avail. Now Vance had shaved his head. What on earth for? Lacey asked him. Some kind of gang? For freedom, Vance told her. He liked to feel the cool breeze against his scalp.

Vance peered into the living room, took in Jeremy sitting on the sofa.

"I'd ask you to join us," Lacey said quickly, "but I know you're on duty. There's nothing like work to ruin a cocktail hour."

"That's okay," Vance said. He set the bucket of ice down on the counter. "See ya."

"Thank you, Vance!" Lacey called. She took the cheese and crackers to the table and went back for the ice. Having company meant a lot of dashing about. If she'd kept her mouth shut, she would be sitting in her chair, watching Dan Rather.

By the time Lacey reached the coffee table with the bucket of ice, Jeremy had dug into the cheese. Lacey was able to drop into her chair and relax just a minute while he finished chewing. She noticed he left the picture of Maximilian facedown on the sofa. This was quite definitely a strike against him.

"Let's hear about you," Lacey said. "Where do you come from? Your family?"

"I grew up in Falls Church, Virginia," he said. "My father owns a bar."

"A bar, really?" Lacey said. "Do you have siblings?"

Jem fixed himself another cracker. "A younger sister," he said. "She's bulimic. My parents go with her to counseling. You know what bulimia is, right? She stuffs her face with food and then she pukes it all up." Jeremy popped the cracker into his mouth.

Lacey sipped her drink. The photograph snagged Jeremy's interest again. "So this is your husband. He looks like Douglas Fairbanks, the old actor. How long were you married?"

"Forty-five years," Lacey said. "I married late in life. I was thirty-one years old. I had a career, you see, and many people, my father included, thought that was like hammering the final pegs into the coffin of my spinsterhood. But Maximilian married me anyway."

"So you were married for forty-five years," Jeremy said. "How many children do you have?"

Lacey wondered if there were a formula for determining how many questions a person would ask before finding the exact wrong question, the question that brought a second too long of silence, the question that caused the voice of heartache to answer. Jeremy had found it early on; Lacey hated to answer this question.

"No children," she said. "As I told you, we married late."

Jeremy fixed himself another cracker. "You said you were thirty-one. That's not too old to have children."

"It was for us," Lacey said. She had always blamed her barrenness on her advanced age—thirty-four by the time Maximilian returned from the war—although now she saw programs on TV about childless couples and she realized it could have been the result of any number of complications. The fact was, she hadn't gotten pregnant and she'd wanted to adopt. But Maximilian refused—it was the only time in forty-five years they had argued. They would not adopt! He was so stubborn about this, Lacey could hardly believe he was the same man

she had married. By way of explanation, Maximilian told her he once
had a chum who adopted a baby, and it turned out the baby was one-
quarter Japanese. Who cared if the baby were one-quarter Japanese—
or full-blooded Japanese for that matter? Lacey asked. She hadn't
been in the war, Maximilian said. True, this was true; Lacey hadn't
been in the war. But that had little to do with the matter at hand. Lacey
had simply wanted a baby.

She looked at the photograph of Maximilian, which Jeremy
returned to its upright position. She and Maximilian had a good life—
a rich and varied life filled with work, travel, erudite people. But Maximilian didn't stick it out with her the way he promised. He died in his
sleep. He wasn't even sick; it was as though he were just too tired to
keep on living. Too tired! They fell asleep together, holding hands,
but Lacey woke up alone. Clearly, when Maximilian made his decision about adoption he hadn't realized how alone she would be.

"Would you like another drink?" Lacey asked.

"I can fix them," Jeremy said.

"Good," she said, settling into her chair. "Because I'm getting
comfortable."

Jeremy made the drinks and when he handed Lacey hers, she
tasted it. "Very nice. Now tell me, Jeremy, about your career plans. I
hear Nantucket is merely a resting stop for you, on your way to Hollywood."

Jeremy nodded. "That's right. I'm headed west in the fall. I want to
be an agent."

Agent, Lacey thought, like the FBI? No, that couldn't be right.
There was that old term, agency man; what had that meant? Or maybe
not agent but aged, like herself.

"Agent?" she said.

"I used to think I wanted to act," Jem said. "I tried in college and it
didn't work out so well. But I like business, so I figure I'll go out to
L.A. and help people who can act. Represent them. Make them
money. Be their friend."

The world had surely deteriorated if one now got paid for being a
friend. "That sounds lovely," Lacey said.

Jeremy fixed himself yet another cracker. Well, he'd worked all day—it was understandable the boy would be hungry. Lacey was going to heat up a swordfish potpie for her dinner. She contemplated asking Jeremy to stay, but that seemed like too much.

"What do your parents think of all this?" Lacey asked.

A piece of cracker stuck in Jeremy's throat and he coughed. Perhaps she had stumbled upon Jeremy's sore spot. Perhaps the bulimic sister was a much safer topic than his parents.

"They don't know about California," he said. "My parents want me close to home, especially with my sister all messed up. They want me to find an internship in D.C. or something. So they don't know about California yet. Do you think that's bad?"

"To be honest, I've never understood why children feel they need their parents' approval," Lacey said. "I believe the earlier you stop hoping for that, the happier you'll be. Look at me—my father went to all kinds of trouble to send me to Radcliffe, but then he sniffed when I pursued a career. But I didn't let that stop me. I had a career that I adored and a husband, too."

Jeremy's face brightened. "Yeah, I figure they might not like the idea at first but once I make it, they'll be fine with the whole thing."

"You might be better off not worrying what your parents think at all. Ever."

"They *are* my parents," Jeremy said. "They did raise me."

"All a parent can do is hope for the best," Lacey said. This was the philosophy she always believed she would have followed with a child. Raise them as well as you can and then let them go. Jeremy looked at her strangely. Maybe he didn't understand how much eighty-eight years of life could teach a person. She was relieved when he stood up.

"I should be going," he said. He leaned over and kissed Lacey's cheek, another point in his favor. "Thanks for the drink and the cheese and stuff."

"You're welcome, my dear," she said. "Come again."

Jeremy left the cottage, closing the screen door quietly behind him. Lacey stayed in her chair. She could reach for the remote control and turn on Dan Rather, or she could stand up and retrieve the swordfish potpie from the freezer. But for a moment she did neither. She was paralyzed with loneliness, and anger about that loneliness. She kicked the coffee table and the picture of Maximilian fell over with a clatter. This pleased her for an instant and then she felt irritated. Surely there were better days to get angrier than hell at her dear, departed Maximilian than this, Memorial Day.

The Gold Coast

June 5

Dear Bill,

I don't know why you insist on torturing yourself by continuing to run the hotel. Just imagine—with the money I'm offering you, you could buy a huge home here on Nantucket—right next door!—and a house in Aspen as well—and enjoy life for a change. I have no evil intentions in buying the hotel; I am only trying to right the wrongs I've done in my life.

I've caught a glimpse or two of you over the past three weeks and I must say, you look harried. Carrying that heavy book with you everywhere! What is that book, anyway, Bill, the Bible? Don't turn to religion, Bill—turn to me. My offer stands.

S.B.T.

LOVE COULDN'T BE CERTAIN, but she thought Mr. Beebe, in room 8, was interested in her. He and his wife arrived on Nantucket in their own plane. This wasn't a big deal—Love knew people in Aspen who owned jets, and some of them were just regular people that she saw in line at all-you-can-eat taco night at La Cocina. But Mr. Beebe *called* from his jet. To Love, this indicated a blatant disregard for the value of money. She felt the same way about people who used the phones on regular planes. It seemed ludicrous to pay so much money for something so transient. So while Love didn't begrudge Mr. Beebe his jet, a part of her was annoyed by the phone call.

Mr. Beebe's question: Would there be a car at the airport to pick him up?

"I'm sorry, sir," she said, loudly (the reception was poor.) "You'll have to take a taxi. There's a taxi stand in front of the terminal, and always plenty of taxis waiting."

"I'm arriving in my own plane," Mr. Beebe said.

Love agreed with the Beach Club's policy. All of the guests were important, but no one was important enough to get picked up at the airport. Not Michael Jackson, not George Bush, and not this man, Mr. Beebe.

"Yes, sir, I understand," she said. "We look forward to your arrival."

Mr. Beebe was a very handsome man. He stood well over six feet tall and had wonderfully broad shoulders, and his dark hair was going gray in the front. He wore white slacks, a crisp blue Façonnable shirt, a navy blazer, Gucci loafers. Mrs. Beebe was frosted blond and already deeply tanned. She wore a hot pink linen dress and about thirty gold bangle bracelets that jingled as she walked. They were a stunning couple.

Mr. Beebe smiled broadly as he approached the desk.

"Are you the young lady I spoke to on the phone?" he asked.

Love fought off the desire to snarl at him. She was *hardly* a young lady. The wealthy often assumed that anyone not as rich as they were was also inferior in other ways—younger, shorter, less intelligent. It drove Love nuts. "Yes, I am," she said. "My name is Love O'Donnell."

"Love," Mr. Beebe said. "What a beautiful name. Love."

"You're the Beebes?" Love asked. She pronounced the name like the gun. "You're in room eight, on the Gold Coast."

"The Gold Coast," Mr. Beebe said. "That's us."

Mrs. Beebe gave a shrill laugh. Love looked at her, startled.

"My wife's nervous," Mr. Beebe said. "In general, but now specifically. New place and everything."

Love called the laundry room, where she knew Vance would be sitting on one of the dryers, reading. "Check-in," she said.

Mrs. Beebe laughed again. Her laugh was almost inhuman; it sounded like the mating call of some exotic bird. Then she spoke. "That plane really did me in."

"Will you be needing dinner reservations?" Love asked.

"Yes," Mr. Beebe said. "I'll come back a little later and we'll talk. Right now I need to get my wife to the beach."

Vance appeared and took the Beebes' bags. When Mrs. Beebe saw Vance, she erupted again in laughter, and it sent shivers through Love. Was Mrs. Beebe laughing at Vance because he was black? Because of his shaved head? Oh, she hoped not.

A few minutes later, Vance returned to the desk, and said, "That lady was drunk in case you were wondering. Well, drunk or high. Rich people have access to drugs we can only dream about. Anyway, mister gave me a fifty and he said he'll talk with you in an hour or so."

Exactly an hour later, Mr. Beebe appeared again at the desk. He'd shed his blazer, and rolled up the sleeves of his shirt. He came into the lobby without shoes. His feet were pale and vulnerable looking.

He leaned on the desk with his arms crossed in a surprisingly casual and intimate way. "My wife is happily ensconced on the beach," he said.

"Good," Love said. In the hour he was gone, she'd looked through the files for a copy of his confirmation letter. There was no address on the letter, only a fax number in area code 212: Manhattan. A copy of Mr. Beebe's personal check was stapled to the letter, but that showed no address either, only the name—Arthur Beebe. Arthur. Love wondered if he went by Art or Artie. "Did you want to discuss dinner reservations?" she asked.

"Yes," he said. "We're here for six nights."

"Twenty-one Federal is a must. And American Seasons. You'll want to eat out in 'Sconset one night, perhaps at the Chanticleer. Do you like classic French?"

"No," he said, "I don't." He leaned forward. "How trustworthy are you, Love?"

"Oh, I don't know," Love said quickly. How trustworthy was she? She hoped to God he wasn't about to confide something in her. Mr. Beebe's eyes were an intense green, and she wondered if maybe he were drunk or high also. Maybe he and his wife had indulged in a little cocaine on the plane. And who cared if they did? It certainly wasn't Love's place to judge, just as long as Mr. Beebe didn't disclose where he got the drugs—or worse, tell her some private information about his wife. "I'd say I'm pretty trustworthy."

Mr. Beebe let his eyes drift down the length of Love's body at the speed that a feather floats through the air. "You look like you're in good shape," he said. "Will you go jogging with me tomorrow morning?"

"Jogging?" Love said. She should turn him down, of course. Mack said there was to be No Dating the Guests, although surely going running with a married man wouldn't qualify as a date. It sounded like a date to Love, however, because she always met the important men in her life while exercising.

"I need a jogging partner," Mr. Beebe said. "We could go before you start work, maybe?"

Tomorrow before work. Love's mind zipped around in a crazy pattern, like a balloon losing air. She had to be on the desk by eight-thirty. She could conceivably bring a change of clothes and shower in the bathhouses. If she got here by seven, that would all be possible. But what if someone saw her? Mack? Bill? Another guest? Could jogging with someone be considered a special service? If she jogged with Mr. Beebe tomorrow would she then be required to jog with any guest who asked? What would Mrs. Beebe think? Would it seem like just another concierge duty, this jogging? And what was all that about Love being trustworthy? If such a simple request brought up so many questions, then maybe the request wasn't so simple after all. What could *not* enter Love's decision making was the fact that she *wanted* to go jogging with Mr. Beebe. She wanted to spend an hour with him alone, their heart rates accelerating, their legs pumping. Love's own desire worried her. Her answer should definitely be no.

"Thanks for the offer but I don't think I can," Love said. "With work and everything, it would be too much, I'm afraid."

"Oh, come on," Mr. Beebe said. "Come on, Love. What about after work then?"

Love wished someone else would come into the lobby. Mack was at lunch. Bill was in his office with the door closed. Love felt both flattered and uncomfortable. Who was this man to insist Love go out of her way *on personal time* for him?

"I'm sorry," Love said, in what she hoped was a definitive way. "Now, what about the dinner reservations? Did you want to try American Seasons, or—"

Mr. Beebe straightened up and sliced his hand through the air. "You make them," he snapped. "Surprise me. But no classic French. Say, do you ever get a day off?"

"Tuesday," Love said. "My day off is Tuesday. But—"

"On Monday I'll come in and we'll make plans for Tuesday. How does that sound?"

"I'll have to see," Love said. "I mean, I'll check. Maybe. I don't know."

"I'm beginning to think you don't like me," he said. "I'm starting to take offense here."

"Please don't take offense," Love said. She liked his green eyes and his salt-and-pepper hair. She had an urge to use his name, Arthur, Art, but enough! She lowered her eyes. "I'll start on those dinner reservations." She picked up the phone to show Mr. Beebe that she was serious, and to get him to go away, which he did—Love heard the whisper of his bare feet sauntering off down the hall. When the reservationist at 21 Federal answered, Love's throat was dry, and it took her a second to think of what it was she had wanted to say.

LOVE THOUGHT ABOUT ARTHUR Beebe all afternoon and into the evening. There was no denying her attraction to him. He was sexy. She couldn't say what made him sexy—maybe his green eyes, maybe his friendly, almost cozy manner with her at the desk. Maybe his airplane. Or maybe, Love thought, she was simply impatient. Finding a father for her child made Love feel like a sniper, an assassin. Centering her crosshairs on every man she saw. But she'd been working the desk for two weeks now and not a single eligible gentleman her age had wandered into the lobby. Of course, Arthur Beebe wasn't an eligible gentleman. He only acted like one.

After work, Love skated home to her rented house on Hooper Farm Road. She lived with two other people. Randy and Alison were a couple in their twenties and they both worked at 21 Federal. Alison worked the reservation book and so it'd been easy for Love to get the Beebes a table there for tonight, even though it was last-minute. Alison always encouraged Love to stop by the restaurant for a drink. *You can't meet people if you don't go out!* she said.

Love enjoyed having the house to herself, although she was lonely at times. Their house was small, but it had a nice grassy yard with a picnic table out back. After Love got home from work, she tried to nap, but today she couldn't sleep. She was thinking of Arthur Beebe. Ridiculous, pathetic even, but true. She made herself lie still for twenty minutes, then she put on exercise tights and rode her Cannondale out to Madaket. She liked to exercise right around dusk, and then come home and fix herself dinner and eat outside if it was nice, read her book and fall asleep. It was a pleasant routine, if unexciting. But tonight when Love returned from her bike ride, she was antsy. She felt as though she might jump out of her skin. She showered, put on her short black skirt and called a taxi, which delivered her to 21 Federal.

Alison greeted her at the door.

"Love!" she said. "Good for you. Are you here for a cocktail or dinner?"

"Cocktail," Love said. She was afraid to turn her head and look around the restaurant. "Can you join me?"

Alison checked her watch. "I can join you in half an hour," she said. "Have a seat at the bar. I'll meet you there."

The bar at 21 was clubby, with a lot of brass and dark wood. Love chose a seat that faced the dining room. She ordered Champagne from the bartender. As Love brought the flute to her lips, she caught Mr. Beebe looking at her from his table in the dining room. Love pretended not to see him. She crossed her legs, wishing that she smoked cigarettes so that she'd have something to do with her hands other than idly twirl her Champagne flute. Usually when she went to restaurants alone, she took along a book or *Time* magazine. But really, wasn't that frumpy of her? Wasn't that shutting other people out? Love watched the bartender dunk highball glasses into soapy water, and she sneaked looks at the Beebes' table. Mrs. Beebe had her back to Love. She appeared to be doing most of the talking; Arthur Beebe said very little. He nodded every once in a while and ate his food. Love recrossed her legs. She felt Arthur staring at her. She flagged down the bartender.

"I'd like to see a menu," she said.

Love felt a tap on her shoulder and turned around, expecting to find Alison, but instead she saw Vance.

"Vance!" she said. "What are you doing here?" He was wearing jeans, a tweed sportscoat, and aviator sunglasses. His bald head gleamed like polished wood.

Vance took the stool next to her. "I come here all the time," he said. "Are you going to order something?"

Why was he wearing sunglasses inside? At night? Obviously he had emotional and possibly even psychological baggage. Love didn't want him to stay and eat with her. Arthur Beebe had seen her and Vance together at the Beach Club. If he saw them eating together tonight, he might think they were dating.

"I don't know," she said, putting the menu down. "I'm not that hungry."

"Get the portobello mushroom," Vance said. "It's outstanding. In fact, let me treat you to your first Twenty-one portobello. I promise you will never forget it."

"That's not necessary," she said. It was funny, though—she did love portobellos, almost better than anything in the world.

"I insist," Vance said. He waved at the bartender. "I'll have a Dewar's straight up, and we'd like two portobellos."

"And I guess I'll have another champagne," Love said. She peeked over at the Beebes, and accidentally locked eyes with Arthur. Love raised her eyebrows and Arthur winked. The wink nearly knocked her off her barstool.

Vance turned around. "I see the druggies are here," he said.

"Who?" Love said.

"You know, the people who checked into room eight this afternoon. The woman with the horrible laugh."

Love sipped her Champagne. "My roommate works here," she said. She swung around on her stool, still reeling from the wink, and searched for Alison. Alison was standing at the hostess station; she pointed to Vance and gave the thumbs-up.

Love rolled her eyes. Even Alison thought Vance was her date! How was it she only knew a handful of people on this island and they all converged here?

Vance leaned in close, and said, "There's something I want to know."

Love backed up. "Me too. Why are you wearing those sunglasses?"

"Traveling incognito," Vance said, pushing them up his nose. "Guests are crawling all over this place. I don't want them to recognize me."

The first thing someone would notice about Vance was that he was a large African American man with a shaved head, and no pair of sunglasses could hide that. "Why not?" she asked.

"Mixing business and pleasure makes me uneasy," he said.

"Oh," Love said. "Well, what did you want to know?"

"I want to know what you think of Mack."

"If you don't like mixing work and pleasure, then why are you asking about Mack?"

"Forget about work," Vance said. "What do you think about Mack as a person?"

"I don't really know him as a person," Love said. "He seems fine. He has that great Midwestern, apple-pie personality. He's a good boss. He has a pretty girlfriend. I guess you could say I like him as a person."

Vance shook his head. "So you've been taken in too."

"Taken in by what?"

"By the facade that is Mack," Vance said. "No one in the world is that happy all the time. That fucking pleasant. His whole attitude of not having an attitude. I'm surprised you don't see past that."

"I'm sorry," Love said. "I don't." Across the room, the Beebes got their check, and then a few minutes later, they stood up. Arthur Beebe took his wife's arm and left the restaurant. He didn't look her way once. Love experienced familiar pain. Really, this was absurd! How

could Arthur Beebe, whom she had just met that day, matter to her
enough to cause this crazy longing?

The portobellos arrived and thankfully, Vance seemed less interested in talking and more interested in eating. Love took a bite of her
mushroom. It was delicious. At least there was that.

THE BREAKFAST HOUR WAS the busiest part of Love's day. By the time
she reached work, Jem had set up the buffet table: the coffee and hot
water thermoses, the carafes of orange and cranberry juice sitting in a
tub of ice, the glass canisters of granola, Cheerios and All-Bran, the
milk, sugar, butter, cream cheese, silverware, plates, bowls, napkins.
Then at eight-thirty, Mack entered with the day's doughnuts, the
bagels, the muffins and five loaves of Something Natural bread. A few
people loitered while Jem set up; these were the people who needed
their coffee. Mack's arrival indicated the Official Start of Breakfast,
and the lobby filled with guests pretending to wait patiently for their
choice of doughnut. It never ceased to amaze Love what waiting to eat
did to people. They became completely irrational.

Arthur Beebe balanced three doughnuts on his plate and poured
himself a glass of orange juice. Mrs. Beebe only drank coffee. They
moved with their food to one of the wicker sofas. Some guests liked to
take their food out onto the pavilion, and some liked to eat in their
rooms. But thankfully, Arthur Beebe was a lobby eater. He set his
plate and glass down on the carpet and then went in search of a desirable section of the newspaper.

The newspaper frenzy followed directly after the doughnut frenzy.
The hotel provided complimentary editions of *The New York Times,*
the *Boston Globe*, the *Wall Street Journal*, and *USA Today*. But everyone wanted *The New York Times*, and of course, being from Manhattan, Arthur Beebe was a *Times* reader. Love watched him as he read.
She wanted him to look at her! She'd worn her sexiest dress—a short,
flowered sundress with spaghetti straps. Then, finally, she got her
wish. Mrs. Beebe finished her third cup of coffee, said in her shrill

voice, "I'm going to *bathe*, Arthur," and left the lobby. A few seconds later, Arthur Beebe put down the paper and cha-chaed his way to the desk.

"The funniest thing just happened," he said.

Love surveyed the lobby. There were still a few stragglers refilling their coffee cups, but for the most part the guests had returned to their rooms.

"What's that?" she said.

"This morning I wanted a coconut doughnut. And I noticed only one coconut doughnut on the buffet table. So I reached for it. But another man snapped it up first."

"That's been known to happen," Love said.

"So I give this guy a dirty look to let him know he's taken my doughnut. Then I pick up the *Times* and who do you think is on the front page of the business section? The very same guy." Arthur Beebe held up the paper. Love squinted at the picture. The grainy photograph was of Mr. Songttha, room 17.

"You're right," Love said. "Well, if it makes you feel any better, that man's not even staying on the Gold Coast. He's only in a side deck room."

As soon as she said this, a human noise came from the back office: Mack clearing his throat. Love hadn't realized he was sitting back there. Giving out information about other guests was prohibited. Especially when Love was insinuating that Mr. Songttha hadn't paid as much for his room as Mr. Beebe. Love bounced on the balls of her feet nervously. What kind of effect was Arthur Beebe having on her? Her good judgment had totally vanished. She was so busy chastising herself that she didn't catch what Arthur Beebe said next.

"I'm sorry?"

"I asked if you had a good time last night at the restaurant."

"I stopped by for a drink and I bumped into a co-worker," Love said. This was her rehearsed line—getting across that she and Vance were *co-workers*, and that they hadn't *planned* to meet—but it didn't exactly answer his question. "How about you and Mrs. Beebe? Did you like your meal?"

"It was marvelous," he said. He put his hand over Love's. For an instant they were holding hands. Then Mr. Beebe gave her the wink. "Keep up the good work."

Love watched him leave the lobby. She took a few deep breaths, scribbled a note on a piece of paper, and wandered back into the office where Mack sat at his messy desk.

"I made a mistake out there," Love said. "I'm sorry."

"At least you recognized it yourself," Mack said. "It's important to be discreet. Don't discuss the guests at all, especially not with other guests."

Love thought of what Vance had said the night before. Was Mack a phony? Now that Love thought about it, it was a bit disconcerting to have him behind her, listening in like Big Brother.

"I need to make a request," she said.

"What's that?" Mack asked.

"More coconut doughnuts," she said. She handed him the slip of paper; it was amazing how doing this one small thing for Arthur Beebe delighted her. "Here, I've written it down."

ARTHUR BEEBE WALKED INTO the lobby that afternoon, wearing swimming trunks and a crisp white polo shirt. Love was perched on her high stool, reading *The Prince of Tides*.

He leaned on the desk, arms crossed, the face of his Tag Heuer flashing. "Hello there, Love. How are you?"

Love slipped a hotel brochure into her book to mark her page, and smiled. Arthur stared at her, and Love stared back, unembarrassed. Then the phone rang, catching them both off guard.

It was Mario Cuomo, calling for Mr. Songttha. Love tightened her grip on the receiver and said in her most professional voice, "Let me put you through to his room." She patched the call and laid the receiver down quietly. Arthur was smiling at her. She wished she could tell him that she'd just spoken to Mario Cuomo, but she'd learned her lesson that morning. She was attracted to Arthur Beebe but she wasn't prepared to lose her job for him.

"Did you need something special?" Love asked. "Beach towels or something?"

"No, no, nothing like that," Arthur Beebe said. "My wife is busy sitting in the sun. I can only take it for an hour or so before I get bored. I came in here to talk."

To talk. To her. He sought her out. The phone rang again. Love looked at the console and saw it was the same call—Mario Cuomo— bouncing back to her.

"I'm sorry, sir, Mr. Songttha's not in his room. Would you like to leave a message?" She wrote down Mario Cuomo's name and number, shielding the notepad with her body. She hung up and put the message in the slot for room 17.

"Songttha? That's the guy from the newspaper, right?" Arthur asked. "Who called for him, Alan Greenspan?"

Love laughed as though she found this preposterous. "No, no, not Alan Greenspan." She had to change the subject away from Mr. Songttha! She climbed back onto her stool. "So, Mr. Beebe, what do you do for a living?"

"Oh, a little of this and a little of that. I wish I could say I worked the front desk at this hotel. I'd probably be much happier."

"It has its ups and downs," Love said. "Did you go running this morning?"

"I did," Arthur said. "I ran through town."

"You should try the bike path," Love said. "Less traffic, and prettier."

"You can show me the way yourself when we go on Tuesday," Arthur said. "You promised, remember? Your day off, Tuesday."

Love knew she very specifically had *not* promised to run on Tuesday. She couldn't remember her exact words, but she was pretty sure she hadn't even agreed. It was just like the wealthy to assume everything would go just as they wanted. And what if Arthur Beebe didn't even work for his money? What if he were an example of the idle rich, flying his plane, sitting on beaches? Love knew this should make him far less attractive in her mind. But it didn't.

"Okay," she said. "Tuesday."

"It's a date," Arthur said. "So, where are we eating tonight?"

Love checked her notebook, although she already knew the answer. "Ships Inn," she said. "Eight o'clock."

"And will we see you there?" Arthur asked.

Love hesitated a second. Did Arthur Beebe think Love had intentionally followed him to 21 Federal the night before?

"No," she said. "Tonight is a stay-at-home night."

Arthur Beebe straightened up. "That's too bad," he said.

BUT, IN FACT, LOVE couldn't keep herself away from Ships Inn. After a fish burrito at home, Love told herself she would go for a walk through town, window shop, get an ice cream cone. She did just this. She spent half an hour in Mitchell's Book Corner before purchasing *What to Expect When You're Expecting*. She spent forty-five minutes in Top Drawer looking at lingerie, and bought a lacy white bra and panty set after realizing that all the underwear she owned was athletic and functional. She went to the Juice Bar and ordered a kiddy cup of Almond Joy ice cream, because she too loved coconut.

And at ten o'clock, she found herself walking home via Fair Street, where she lingered outside Ships Inn. She crossed the street to St. Paul's Episcopal Church and read last week's program, even though she was a nonpracticing Roman Catholic. Then she heard the freakish, high-pitched warble laugh. Mrs. Beebe. Love saw the Beebes standing in front of the restaurant waiting for a cab. It was unlikely that they would be able to pick Love out in the dark, and so she sat on the steps of the church and watched. She watched Arthur standing with his hands in his pockets while Mrs. Beebe did a tap dance around him. She was drunk, and happy.

Love watched them until the cab came. Arthur helped Mrs. Beebe into the cab. He hesitated before he got in himself. It seemed to Love he was looking at her. Love sat clutching her package in her lap as Arthur Beebe blew her a kiss.

• • •

THE NEXT MORNING, ARTHUR Beebe said, "That was you last night? In front of the church?"

Love had debated all night about how to answer this question. "Yes," she said.

"Good," Arthur said. He lowered his voice. "I didn't want to blow a kiss to a stranger."

"Don't worry, you didn't," she said.

"That's right," he said. "I blew one to you."

Love blushed. She was glad Mack was outside washing his Jeep.

"Well, thank you," Love said.

"I thought you said last night was a stay-at-home night."

"I went shopping," Love said. "I bought a book." She hesitated. "And some lingerie."

Arthur narrowed his eyes. "You know what I've always wanted to do?"

"What?" Love said.

"Fly my plane to Antarctica. What do you think of that? My wife thinks it would be too cold. Do you think it would be too cold?"

"Depends who you're with," she said. Desire shot through her. Her thighs ached. "I'd like to go to Antarctica."

"Yes, I thought so," Arthur said. "I thought you seemed like a woman in search of some adventure. So maybe Tuesday, then? A little adventure?"

"Adventure," Love said.

That night, the Beebes were eating at the Summer House out in 'Sconset, and thankfully Love managed to stay away. Instead, she rode her Cannondale to the airport. She inspected the private jets, wondering which one belonged to Arthur Beebe. She decided on a gray plane with a red racing stripe. The body of the plane was long and phallic. Love imagined herself boarding this plane for Antarctica, or places unknown.

Love's conversations with Arthur Beebe worked on her like aphrodisiacs. Arthur Beebe putting his hand over hers, and saying, "Keep up the good work!" Arthur Beebe asking to see her book so he would have an excuse to touch her fingers or the inside of her arm, Arthur

Beebe asking if she'd bought any more lingerie. Arthur Beebe reminding Love about Tuesday. Their running date Tuesday. Their date Tuesday. Tuesday, her day off. It became the world's biggest euphemism. Tuesday, to Love, meant only one thing: she was going to have sex with Arthur Beebe.

And how did Love feel about this? At certain times—the few heady moments after Arthur left the lobby, for example—it thrilled her. She envisioned herself and Arthur jogging along Cliff Road, Love inhaling deep breaths of the oxygen-rich air. At home, she could offer Arthur lemonade, a mimosa, a refreshing shower. Randy and Alison announced they would be off-island on Tuesday, which only convinced Love further that sex with Arthur was destined to happen. They would have the house to themselves. It would be fervent, Love supposed, maybe even rushed. He would have to get back to the hotel. Charged, delicious, secret—these were words Love associated with sex with Arthur Beebe.

But sometimes, other words popped into Love's mind. Foolish, irresponsible, not to mention *immoral*. How could she sleep with Arthur Beebe? He was a married man, and a hotel guest. She might ruin his marriage, jeopardize her job. The Beebes were leaving on Wednesday, paying their bill, boarding the jet plane, and flying back to Manhattan. Checking out. Would Arthur leave her a *tip*? It was too horrible to imagine.

On Monday afternoon, Love and Arthur confirmed their plans. They would meet in front of the lobby at 7:45 the following morning and start their run.

"We'll go where the day takes us," Arthur said with a wink.

Go where the day takes us. That seemed like a good way of looking at it. Love always operated with a plan, but why? Why not go with the flow, follow their noses, fly by the seats of their pants? No reason why Love had to decide in advance about having sex with Arthur Beebe. She needed to take it easy. Relax. At five o'clock, after work, Love walked home past the Hadwen House. The Hadwen House with its ballroom under the stars. Its dreams of romance.

• • •

TUESDAY MORNING, A TAXI dropped Love off at the Beach Club at 7:35. She liked being early. It gave her a few minutes to stretch her legs and look at the ocean. The 6:30 ferry was a white speck on the horizon. Love watched the seagulls drop hermit crab shells onto the parking lot. She glanced at Bill and Therese's house and figured they were probably in bed making love, but today Love didn't feel jealous. Today she would just be one of many lovers on Nantucket. That was all she wanted—to be another person's focus, if only for a day, if only for a few hours. Love was honest enough with herself to realize that unless a baby was conceived, this would be the best part of the whole affair: the sweet, exquisite anticipation.

But after another ten, twelve minutes, her anticipation became tinged with nerves. Her multipurpose sports watch said 7:48. Then 7:50, and then 7:53. Love jogged back and forth in front of the hotel; she peeked in the windows of the lobby, thinking perhaps Arthur was waiting for her inside. But the inside of the lobby was dark, deserted.

At 8:00, Mack pulled into the parking lot. He was early! She hid around the corner of the lobby and waited until he unloaded the cartons of that day's breakfast and carried them into the lobby. Then she sneaked behind the pavilion, and down the side deck rooms to the water. She jogged past the Gold Coast. A few of the guests were out on their decks reading, a woman sat on a mat doing yoga. Love ran by room 10, room 9, room 8. The door to room 8 was closed, the deck uninhabited. Love ran all the way down to room 1 and then cut behind the Gold Coast rooms. The back door to room 8 was also closed. Love returned to the front of the lobby in case she had missed Arthur somehow. She consulted her watch. It was 8:06. She shielded her eyes and peered into the lobby. Jem and Mack set up the breakfast, the coffee loiterers loitered. Tiny stood behind the front desk. But no Arthur Beebe.

A minute later, the front doors of the lobby opened. Mack lugged Therese's plants out onto the front porch. There was no time to hide again; Mack saw her.

"Hey, Love, what are you doing here?" he said.

"I was just . . . running," she said. Although she wanted to, there was no way she could ask Mack if he'd seen Arthur Beebe.

"Nice day for it," Mack said. He was in client mode: chipper, chatty, ready to skate across any topic of conversation. She could be in tears and he wouldn't notice.

"I'm off," she said.

Love ran home as fast as she could. She pushed herself to go faster, faster, faster than her fastest mile split (a 5:49 in the Boulder 10k, 1988). She arrived at home winded and sweaty, her heart pounding in her throat and her face. At first she was glad Randy and Alison were away, because she certainly didn't want anyone to witness her humiliation. But the empty house was awful too—the way the wind blew right through it—and she wished for some company.

Love waited until ten o'clock, the usual time for her first conversation with Arthur Beebe, and then she called the front desk.

Tiny answered. "Good morning, Nantucket Beach Club."

Love cleared her throat. "Yes, is Arthur Beebe in, please?"

"I'm sorry," Tiny said. "The Beebes are no longer staying with us."

"No, no," Love said. "Tiny, it's me, Love. I think you've got the wrong room. The Beebes are in room eight. They're not checking out until tomorrow."

"Oh, Love," Tiny said. "The chambermaids went in to clean about forty minutes ago and noticed all the Beebes' stuff was gone. So I called the airport. The Beebes' jet left at five o'clock this morning. They skipped out on their bill—two grand." She gave an amused little laugh. "Happens every year. I'm always suspicious of people who don't use a credit card, but you figure someone with his own plane is going to be able to foot the bill. But not these folks—they snuck out of here in the middle of the night, like they were on the lam or something. What's the deal? Did you know these people? What did you want with them anyway?"

Antarctica, Love thought. Would he have been so cruel as to dash his wife off to Antarctica? She hoped not, despite the fact that right now she wanted Arthur Beebe as far away from her as possible. At five o'clock this morning, Love had been lying in bed, listening to the birds, thinking about Arthur Beebe. Had she heard a plane flying overhead? No, just the birds.

"Oh, nothing," Love said. "I didn't want them for anything."

BY THE NEXT MORNING, Love had convinced herself that she was the reason Arthur Beebe had left the hotel in the predawn hours. Perhaps his feelings for her escalated, perhaps he was frightened by their intensity. Perhaps last night at dinner (Straight Wharf), he told Mrs. Beebe about his running date with Love—and maybe she was the one responsible for their early departure. There were many excuses Love could make for the man, but it didn't change the fact that Arthur had disappeared, literally, into thin air, taking her hopes for a child with him.

Love was folding hotel brochures, thinking of how she might surprise Arthur Beebe someday in New York when Vance poked his head out from Mack's office.

"Come here," he said. "I want to show you something."

The lobby was empty and so she slipped back into Mack's office. Mack was in the laundry room fixing a dryer.

"What?" she said.

"You know the people in room eight, the druggies? The ones who skipped their bill?" Vance said.

"The Beebes?" Love said. The name tasted funny on her tongue.

"I stripped their room yesterday and look what I found," he said. "This ain't no BB." He brought his hands out from behind his back and showed Love a gun.

"You found it in their room?" Love asked. It was a handgun, shiny and silver. She tried to picture it in Arthur Beebe's hand; she tried to picture him pointing it at someone.

"I told you they were drug dealers. Their own plane? Taking off in the middle of the night? And then I find this baby tucked in between the mattress and box spring? Come on, Love, we're not stupid here."

A little of this, a little of that. "What should we do?" Love asked. "Should we call them?" A part of Love wanted to speak to Arthur

Beebe again. He'd left her feeling empty. Angry and humiliated, yes, but mostly empty.

"They never left a *phone number*. Tiny searched for it yesterday, but when Bill made the reservation, all he wrote down was a fax," Vance said. "And guess what? We can't fax a gun."

"We could send a fax telling them we have the gun," Love suggested. She wanted to fax herself to Arthur Beebe.

"Tiny faxed them about their bill, and we haven't heard back. If we had the address, we could send the gun through the mail, although you can't send the clip and the gun together," Vance said. Love didn't ask how he knew this. Vance pointed the gun out the window. "Pow," he said softly. "Listen, I'll take care of the gun. Let me know if Beebe calls asking for it."

"Okay," she said. It was scary watching Vance point the gun. *Pow!*

Love went back to the desk. The gun created possibilities Love hadn't even considered. If Arthur Beebe were a drug dealer, if he did use his plane to fly back and forth between countries transporting illegal substances, then she should be glad nothing had happened between them. She should be *relieved* Arthur left. But she wasn't.

JEM CRANDALL WAS MAKING mistakes. He supposed his mistakes were standard, run-of-the-mill mistakes that any freshman on the job would make. What he couldn't figure out was how to stop them from happening before he got fired. If he got fired, he might not be able to find another job. It was June already and the college students had arrived in force. If Jem couldn't find another job, he would have to return to Virginia and work at his father's bar, the Locked Tower, and deal with his nutty sister, Gwennie, and her bulimia. He wrote himself a note— soap on the bathroom mirror—No More Mistakes! When he shaved, it was tattooed across his forehead.

Jem's first mistake was also the most embarrassing: Mrs. Worley. The Worleys were a heavy-set couple from Atlanta. He noticed them each morning hovering around the breakfast buffet while he tried to clear it. Once, mister followed Jem into the galley kitchen when Jem left with the platter of muffins. Mr. Worley selected the last two mixed-berry muffins, and Jem, who understood unreasonable hunger, said, "Yeah, those are my favorite, too."

Several days later, when mister was paying his bill, Love said, "Jem, room ten is ready to be stripped. The Worleys are checking out."

Jem licked his fingers clean of powdered sugar (he was allowed to eat the leftovers from breakfast), and said, "Okay, I'm going."

Stripping the rooms was Jem's least favorite part of the job. The chambermaids cracked jokes about "love stains" when they made the beds, and although Jem laughed at the term, it didn't make him feel any better about having to gather the sheets up in his arms. And love stains weren't as offensive as some of the things people left in the sheets. He'd seen blood, urine, used condoms, and food—globs of guacamole, a lobster claw. He was responsible for taking out the trash, and he tried not to look at what the guests threw away. One horrifying day, he found a Styrofoam head covered with a stringy brown toupee sitting on a dresser. He also collected the soiled towels, bathmat, and bathrobes from the bathroom. Another lovely task, but at least it was better than swabbing nests of hair out of the bottom of the shower.

Jem went to work on the Worleys' room. The TV was on—ESPN SportsCenter—and Jem watched the highlights, waiting for a score on the Orioles' game as he did his work. He threw the quilt and the blanket off the bed and stripped the sheets, trying not to think of the rotund Worleys rolling around in them. He removed the plastic bag from the trash can, twisted it and tied it. The TV announcer finally showed a clip of the Orioles' game—and Jem thought of his father, who had a collection of Orioles memorabilia hanging behind the bar at the Tower.

Jem checked the closets for items left behind. He checked the drawers. He'd heard Vance whispering about some great thing he found in one of the rooms. Jem guessed it was lingerie, or a dirty magazine. These closets and drawers were empty, thank God.

Jem swung open the door to the bathroom and heard a loud gasp. Mrs. Worley was sitting on the toilet, reading the TV Guide. She looked at him with wide brown eyes, her mouth agape. All Jem could think at that moment was *Please don't stand up.* But it was too late. Mrs. Worley stood, and Jem couldn't help but look. His eyes were drawn to her lower half: her shorts drooping around her ankles, her stomach hanging like so much bread dough over her . . .

"Get . . . get!" Mrs. Worley stuttered. Her face was bright pink.

"I'm sorry, ma'am," Jem said. "They said you were checking—" Mrs. Worley lunged, slammed the door in his face. A second later, he heard Mrs. Worley crying. Jem hurried out the door, leaving the trash and the pile of dirty sheets behind. He stumbled into the sunshine, feeling exposed and ashamed. He wanted to run for the safety of his rented room, lock the door, jump into his bed and hide under the covers. Instead, he sought refuge in the coolness of the laundry room, which had the soothing, clean smell of detergent. He stayed there for nearly half an hour, wondering if Mrs. Worley would report him. Jem buried his face in a pile of green fluffy towels and tried to think of other things, pleasant things—going to the Muse and drinking a cold beer, talking to a pretty girl in a sundress—but he couldn't shake the image of Mrs. Worley, her thighs, white and dimpled like cottage cheese. It was far, far worse than even the Styrofoam head and toupee. Jem felt sick to his stomach. Then the phone rang in the laundry room. It was Mack.

When Jem walked into Mack's office, he was still shaking. "Are they gone?" he asked.

Mack nodded, his face grim. "You're lucky she wasn't thinking sexual harassment, or attempted rape."

The picture of Mrs. Worley standing up from the toilet presented itself again in Jem's mind, as he feared it would for the rest of his life. "No way," he said, "not in a million years."

"A smart thing to do when you see a closed door is to *knock,*" Mack said. "Otherwise we leave ourselves open to those kinds of allegations. You don't want that, do you?"

Jem shook his head. Mack's face twisted, and then he burst out laughing. "You poor kid," Mack said. "You should see yourself."

"It was so embarrassing," Jem said. He watched Mack laugh, and wished for some laughter from himself, a warm release, but none came. It *was* funny, in a way, wasn't it? Jem waltzed into the bathroom with every intention of collecting the towels until—whammo! Mrs. Worley, front and center. Of course, Mack hadn't heard Mrs. Worley scream, and he hadn't heard her crying.

Mack sobered up and wiped his eyes. "I'm not angry," he said. "But I am serious. Always knock before you strip the rooms. Do you hear me?"

"I hear you," Jem said.

"You'll have to write Mrs. Worley a note of apology. It was your mistake."

Jem wondered what he could possibly say to Mrs. Worley—*I'm sorry for the very awkward moment? I'm sorry to have barged in on you in the john?* He almost smiled until he heard Mack use the word "mistake." It was then the train of thought first materialized: getting fired, working at the Locked Tower, his sister, Gwennie.

"Okay," Jem said. "I will."

Three days later, a very famous man checked into room 6. The man was so famous that when Jem saw him at the front desk he had a hard time keeping a straight face. Why didn't Mack warn them people like this were coming? Jem might have worn a cleaner shirt. But the Beach Club showed no one favoritism, and so Jem led this famous man, a major player, a mogul (for if anyone in the world could be called a mogul this man was it) to room 6, as though he were anyone else. Jem could only think of the man as Mr. G. This was what he was called in the media, the same way that Donald Trump was called "the Donald." Mr. G had brought a briefcase, and a small black Samsonite suitcase. Jem took the Samsonite. It was so light that Jem wondered if it were empty. He walked just in front of Mr. G, reciting his spiel about the chambermaids, the ice machine, the Continental breakfast from eight-thirty to ten.

"I won't be here for breakfast," Mr. G said. "I'm only staying overnight. I have an extremely important meeting tomorrow in Washington."

"Just overnight?" Jem said. "At least you have a nice day for it." It was true: the sun was shining, the ocean a glorious blue. Jem walked along the boardwalk, then up the three steps to the deck of room 6, and paused for a minute, searching his pocket for the key. He couldn't believe he was about to unlock a door for Mr. G.

Mr. G cleared his throat and Jem fumbled with the keys. *Get the door open, you idiot!* he thought. *This is Mr. G!* Jem opened the door. "Here you go," he said. He waited until Mr. G stepped in and put down his briefcase. "My name is Jeremy Crandall. Just let me know if you need anything."

"I'd like a wake-up call for six-fifteen." Mr. G said. "And I need you to show me how this phone works."

Jem picked up the receiver of the phone. "The phone works just like a regular phone, sir," Jem said. Did this sound snide? He needed to get a grip. "Except you have to dial nine to get an outside line. If you want the front desk, you dial zero." He set the receiver down, then moved quickly to the alarm clock. "Is there anything else?"

Mr. G smiled. Jem smiled back. He and Mr. G were smiling at each other.

"No," Mr. G said. "Thanks for your help." He reached into his pocket but all he brought out were a few pennies and a dime. "I'll get you later."

Jem waved his hand. "Don't worry about it. It's a pleasure to help and meeting you. I mean it was nice meeting you. Exciting." Jem backed out of the room onto the deck. He waved to Mr. G. "Let me know if you need anything."

Mack wasn't in the office, but through the crack in the door, Jem saw Bill reading at his desk. Bill was a poetry buff, and half the time he sat in his office he wasn't even working; he was reading poems, then closing his eyes and trying to recite them from memory. It amazed Jem that Bill didn't seem at all flustered by Mr. G's arrival. Perhaps he didn't even know.

Jem tapped on Bill's door. "Bill? I just wanted to let you know Mr. G—is here and I've shown him to his room."

Bill knit his eyebrows. "Okay," he said. "Thanks for the update."

Love came into the office. "He's been on the phone since he got here," she whispered. Her cheeks were pink. Love was always talking about the big shots she saw in Aspen—Ed Bradley, Sean Connery, Elle McPherson. But even Love was impressed by Mr. G. She put her hands on her hips. "This doesn't seem like much of a vacation," she said. "He's here for the afternoon, dinner with friends, and then he leaves first thing tomorrow, poor thing." Love was returning to her normal self, acting like everybody's aunt. "I wonder if he brought his bathing suit. That's something I'd like to see. Mr. G—in a pair of trunks."

The fax machine beeped and churned out a few pages. Love checked it. "For Mr. G, naturally," she said. She wrote the fax information in her notebook then handed the pages to Jem. "Care to do the honors?"

Jem walked to room 6, the fax pages fluttering in his hands. He wondered what would happen if he let the pages go. What if he were responsible for tossing Mr. G's fax to the wind? It was torturous to consider. He wanted to read the fax, but it was good discipline to respect the man's privacy, to resist peeking at the masthead.

Jem knocked on the door. "Jeremy Crandall here," he said in a strong voice.

The door opened. Mr. G had the phone to his ear; he was still in his suit. He looked at Jem quizzically, and Jem held out the fax pages. Mr. G took the fax, glanced at it, and reached into his pants pocket. He pulled out the same few coins then shook his head, and handed the coins to Jem.

"Thanks," Jem said. When he returned to the lobby, he checked in his pocket. Mr. G had given him thirteen cents.

THAT NIGHT, JEM ATE three peanut butter sandwiches and drank two cans of warm Sprite, and he wrote his first letter home to his parents. Jem's father was a famous man in Falls Church. The owner of the Locked Tower, a member of Rotary, and Kiwanis. A model citizen. Jem could have this kind of fame too. But, he was ashamed to say, he wanted something bigger. He was cursed with aspirations.

"My job is going well," Jem wrote, "and guess who checked into the hotel today? Mr. G!" Jem wanted to show his parents that he could live away from home, hold a job, use good judgment. "He tipped me thirteen cents." If Jem gave his father news to share at the Tower—and surely Mr. G was news—maybe his parents wouldn't object quite so much when he brought up California. Lacey Gardner told Jem to disregard what his parents thought, and though he found this extreme, one thing was true: he was going to California whether his parents liked it or not.

Then Jem thought of his sister, Gwennie. She ate his mother's baked chicken, grilled steaks, chocolate cake, and then after dinner she disappeared into the upstairs bathroom or outside—no matter how closely Jem's parents watched her—and she puked it all up. And Gwennie had reinvented the laws of perpetual motion. When she was on the phone with her girlfriends, she paced the house. She went jogging in the middle of the night while their parents slept. She ate standing up, and if she had to eat sitting down, she scissored her legs back and forth under the table. Just thinking about it made Jem exhausted, and sad.

"All in all, I'm doing well," he wrote. "I think this summer is going to be quite a learning experience." His mother would appreciate that. "I miss you! Love, Jem."

JEM MAILED THE LETTER on his way to work the next morning. He still had the thirteen cents in his pocket. He might just carry that thirteen cents all summer, for luck. As Jem approached the Club, he saw Mr. G standing on the front steps of the lobby. Jem checked his watch. It was five of eight. Mack stood next to Mr. G, holding a carton of doughnuts.

"Jem!" Mack called out.

Jem ran to the front porch of the lobby. But something wasn't right. Both Mack and Mr. G looked upset.

"Did you set the alarm clock for Mr. G—yesterday afternoon?" Mack asked.

Jem's mind swam through murky water to yesterday afternoon. He had set it, hadn't he? Oh, God, his life was over. But he distinctly remembered sitting on the side of the bed and pressing the plastic buttons. Setting the alarm for six-fifteen. Mr. G had said six-fifteen, hadn't he?

"It didn't go off," Mr. G said quietly. He looked up into the sky. "Needless to say I had to call and cancel with the president."

The president? Of the United States? Jem clenched his stomach. "Oh, sir," Jem said. "I'm sorry."

"Sorry, of course, doesn't put me on my plane an hour ago," Mr. G said. "Sorry doesn't make it up to the president."

A cab pulled up to the front of the hotel. Jem reached for Mr. G's Samsonite, but Mack snapped it up first. "I've got it," Mack said. "Go wait for me in my office."

A FEW MINUTES LATER, Jem shuffled through the sand, following Mack to room 6.

"I asked you in the interview if you could set an alarm clock," Mack said. "And you assured me that you could. Do you remember?"

"Yes," Jem said glumly. He thought of the letter to his parents and wished he hadn't sent it. Jem imagined his mother at the Giant, pushing her cart through the produce section, telling everyone she knew that Jem had met Mr. G. What she wouldn't know was that Jem had screwed up royally, that Jem had single-handedly fouled up Mr. G's meeting with the president of the United States.

In room 6, Mack checked the alarm clock.

"It's set for six-fifteen," Mack said, and for a second Jem felt the sweet wash of vindication. Then Mack said, "Six-fifteen in the evening. See this P.M. thing here, P.M. means—"

"I know what it means," Jem said.

"The alarm must have gone off while Mr. G—was at dinner."

"I'll write a letter of apology," Jem said. "I'll sit down and write it now."

"Don't write a letter," Mack said. "I don't want you to waste any more of that man's time. Okay, Jem? But see if you can use your head.

See if you can make me feel like less an idiot for hiring you. Now, go do your job."

JEM SAT ON A bench outside the Stop & Shop eating half a roasted chicken. It was Monday, his day off, and he'd had another miserable weekend. The incident with Mr. G depressed him so much that he didn't feel like going out. It was the fifteenth of June and Jem hadn't seen the inside of a bar since he and Vance had shot pool at the Chicken Box back in May, before the hotel opened. He supposed if he went out he would meet some girls at least, but he was shy about going to the bars alone. His father always said that a person who goes into a bar alone goes to drink, *and you know what that means.*

Was that any different from sitting outside the grocery store alone, eating chicken alone, or going to the beach alone, which was where Jem was headed next? He felt like a loser—he kept messing up at his simple job, and after five weeks on the island, he still had no friends. If this was what happened to him on Nantucket, what the hell would California be like?

The Stop & Shop parking lot was jam-packed: cars lined up at the entrance, snaking onto Pleasant Street. These were the Summer People, Jem supposed, coming to refill their cupboards with watermelons, hamburger buns, Popsicles.

Jem gnawed on a chicken leg and watched a woman roll a shopping cart with about fifty shopping bags and a baby girl up to her Isuzu Trooper. She loaded in her groceries, which probably cost as much money as Jem made in a week. The shopping cart with the baby rolled backward just as a couple of college chicks in a red Cherokee rounded the corner. Jem ran out in front of the Cherokee. The car jerked to a stop. Jem pushed the shopping cart closer to the Isuzu, although he was chagrined to see the cart hadn't really been in the way.

"Watch where you're going," he said to the girls. "And slow down."

The girl driving said, "For your information, I was watching where I was going. I wasn't even close to hitting it."

The baby's mother turned and saw Jem holding the cart.

"I'm sorry?" she said. Her eyes locked on Jem's fingers gripping the handle of the cart. Jem started to sweat. It was about a hundred degrees out and his face and hands were shiny with chicken grease. He pictured a scenario where he grabbed the shopping cart and it slipped from his greasy grasp and rolled right in front of the Cherokee, making him not a baby snatcher but a baby murderer. He needed to be more aware. Awareness, how did one acquire it?

"I'm sorry," he said. "Those girls almost hit your cart. Your baby."

The woman looked at him blankly and Jem experienced the uncomfortable feeling he got when he was waiting for a tip from one of the hotel guests. He walked away.

Jem returned to his bench and found Maribel sitting next to his messy pile of napkins and chicken bones.

"Busy saving the world?" she asked.

"Wait a minute," Jem said. This was exactly what he meant about being more aware. Where had Maribel come from? "You saw that?"

"Brave and valiant. This damsel's impressed." She shifted a backpack at her feet. "So, what are you doing here?"

"It's my day off," Jem said. "I'm headed for the beach."

"Me too," Maribel said. "The library is closed on Mondays."

Maribel was in a pair of jeans shorts and a yellow flowered bikini top. Her blond hair was in a bun. Jem saw faint yellow hairs on the tops of her thighs.

"Do you act?" he asked. "Sing? Dance? Juggle?"

Maribel laughed. "No, why? Do you only sit on benches with people if they have special talent?"

"I just thought you could be my first client," Jem said. "You know, I thought maybe you needed an agent."

"I'm a librarian," Maribel said. "In fact, I'm not even a librarian. I'm not brainy or organized enough to be a librarian. I'm a fund-raiser. I ask people for money, and when I get the money I think of ways to spend it. Now, do I need an agent? Yes, I do. A beach agent."

"I'm actually a very good beach agent," Jem said.

"Meaning you can guarantee me a fun time while I'm there?" Maribel asked. "What's your cut?"

"Fifty percent," Jem said. "Of the fun time."

"Okay," Maribel said, slinging her backpack over her shoulder. "Let's go."

MARIBEL DROVE A JEEP Wrangler just like Mack's, but newer. It was black and the inside was roasting hot. Jem's legs stuck to the vinyl seats.

Maribel pulled out of the parking lot, and said, "So, do I dare ask? How's work?"

"It's great," Jem said, trying to sound upbeat. Usually Jem felt comfortable with women, but with Maribel he was going to have to watch what he said. Talking to her was as good as talking to Mack.

"You like Bill and Therese?" Maribel asked.

"I almost never see them," Jem said. "Bill sits in his office reading and Therese is busy chasing the chambermaids around. She rides those girls hard."

"Therese is a renowned slave driver," Maribel said. "I suppose you've heard she hates me."

"No," Jem said, "I hadn't heard."

"Things used to be okay between us, but ever since Cecily got to high school—Cecily's their daughter, you know—Therese has been dead set on pushing Cecily and Mack together. An he's twelve years older than she is! It's ridiculous."

"Do you ever think maybe Mack will give in? You know, to get a piece of the Beach Club and all?"

"No," Maribel said sharply, "I don't."

"Sorry," Jem said. He should just keep his mouth shut! "I didn't mean I thought he should. Hell, no. You two make a great couple. How long have you been together?"

"Six years," Maribel said.

"Are you planning on getting married?"

"No," Maribel said. "We have no plans to get married." She paused. "You know what the funny thing is about Cecily? She and I are good friends. Everything would be so nice if Therese just backed off."

"Oh," Jem said.

"Never mind," Maribel said. "It's just politics. You're smart to stay out of it." They turned left by the high school. "So tell me, do you have a girlfriend?"

"Me?" Jem said. "No, not right now."

"Haven't met anyone on the island, a handsome guy like you? Mr. November?"

He'd opened his mouth during his job interview, and it would haunt him forever. "I haven't been out much," he said.

"Cecily's coming home next week," Maribel said. "Maybe you'll like her."

"I don't know," Jem said. "I hate being set up."

Maribel patted his knee. Jem felt a sort of thrill when she touched him, and instantly he began to worry. What was he doing with his boss's girlfriend? Maribel turned onto a sand road. The Jeep started bouncing up and down in whoop-dee-dos.

"Where are we going?" he asked.

"Miacomet," she said. "The pond's coming up on the left."

Jem looked out Maribel's window. Cattails and dune grass bordered the pond, and there were a few wild irises. A red-winged blackbird.

"This is one of my favorite spots," she said. "And the beach is terrific too—very peaceful. It's a nude beach."

Jem took a deep breath. *Nude beach?* "Wait a minute, I'm the beach agent here. I don't know if that's in the contract."

"Does it make you uncomfortable?" Maribel asked. "Because we can go someplace else." But she made no move to slow down the car.

"Well . . ."

"You can keep your suit on," she said. "I sometimes do. Tell you what, I will today, how about that?"

Now Jem felt like a child. What was wrong with a nude beach, really?

"Whatever you want," he said.

Maribel shrugged. "Okay."

Maribel drove the Jeep over the dunes onto the beach. She was right—it was peaceful. The beach was a long stretch of practically deserted sand—way down to the left Jem saw the mob of folks at Surf-side, where he usually went. The waves here were giant and rolling, and the water bottle green. Behind them, all Jem could see was blue sky and dune grass. This was the real Gold Coast. He started to relax.

"This is nice," he said.

Maribel spread out a blanket, stripped off her shorts, and sat down. She waved Jem over. "Join me," she said. "I brought lunch."

Jem sat tentatively on the edge of her blanket. He removed his shirt and looked down at his abs. He did a hundred sit-ups before he went to bed each night and it was paying off. "Thanks, but I already ate some chicken."

"I packed enough for about sixty people," Maribel said. "And I'm a good cook in case you haven't heard." She unwrapped a sandwich and handed Jem half. "Here, this is Saga, prosciutto, and fig."

The sandwich was delicious, the kind of delicious Jem had never tasted before.

"You like it?" Maribel asked.

He finished chewing. "It's the best sandwich I've ever eaten."

"You can be my sandwich agent."

"Definitely," Jem said. "Definitely your sandwich agent." An old woman walked by, naked. She smiled at Maribel and Jem and wandered off down the beach.

"See, it's no big deal. This is a free and easy place." Maribel pulled more food out of her backpack: homemade potato chips, clusters of tiny purple grapes, thick chocolate brownies.

"Nothing at all like the chicken at Stop and Shop," he said. "And no exhaust. Where did you learn to cook like this?"

"I taught myself," Maribel said. She threw a scrap of bread to the seagulls. "My mother worked full-time and when she got home she was too tired to do much of anything. I liked having dinner ready for her. I cleaned the house and did the laundry, too. My mother called me her housewife. And I thought of it as practical training."

"Training?"

"For when I get married myself," Maribel said.

"So you do want to get married," Jem said.

"What's that supposed to mean?" she asked.

Jem had stepped in mud and he hadn't even seen it. "Nothing. It meant nothing. I'm sorry." Where was safe ground? He finished his sandwich and licked his fingers, and then, before he could stop, he thought about being married to Maribel himself, and how awesome that would be, awesome beyond his wildest dreams.

"You know when you asked me about work before?" Jem said. "I was just wondering, does Mack ever say how I'm doing?"

"Not really. He did tell me about Mr. G."

"He did?"

"Yeah, and I don't see what the big deal is. So the guy was an hour late. So he had to cancel with the president. Shit happens. I'll bet by noon he'd forgotten all about it."

"There was this other thing that happened, too," Jem said. "This woman Mrs. Worley. I walked in on her in the bathroom and she started to cry."

Jem was expecting Maribel to laugh the way Mack had, but she didn't.

"When I was a little girl, I walked into the men's room at a restaurant and I saw the men standing next to urinals. I didn't know men peed standing up. I don't have any brothers and my father wasn't around, and I just didn't know. Now, *that* was a shocker."

"So it was just you and your mother then?" Jem asked.

"My mom was only nineteen when she had me. It's just the two of us." Maribel fell back onto the blanket. "Nap time." She rolled onto her side and propped her head up with one arm. "I'm going to take my top off, if that's okay with you."

"Wait a second. You said—"

She put her hand on his arm, and again he felt a thrill.

"We don't have to tell Mack we met up," she said.

"We don't?" He didn't like where this was headed: lying, secrecy, a secret from his boss. But Jem was happy sitting next to Maribel—so astonishingly happy whereas just an hour before he'd been so miserable—that he didn't care. "Go ahead then," he said.

Maribel untied her bikini and slipped it over her head. Jem looked at her breasts; he knew she wanted him to look at them, and admire them the way he'd admired the food. They were just like the rest of Maribel—sunny, perky, gorgeous. They were the size of teacups with a pale pink nipple. She took a bottle of Coppertone from her bag and rubbed herself with lotion. In a minute, Jem had an aching erection pushing through his swim trunks. He flipped onto his stomach.

"Nap time," he said.

He closed his eyes and tried to think about other things, things that were not Maribel related, things that were not Maribel's breasts and their impossibly pink softness. He surprised himself by falling asleep. When he woke up, it felt as though he were emerging from a hot, dark tunnel. He raised his head. Maribel was lying on her stomach, reading. She still had her top off.

"What are you reading?" Jem asked.

She flashed him the cover. "*The Collected Stories of John Cheever*," she said. "And there's a whole lot of cheating going on."

"Really?" Jem said. What was *that* supposed to mean? "Hey, want to go for a swim?"

"Sure," she said. He was thankful that she put her top on, tying the strings tightly. When Jem felt ready, he dashed to the water. Maribel chased after him. The water was freezing but that was okay. He needed to cool down. Maribel went under and when she popped back up, she shrieked.

"This is great," Jem called out. A wave rolled over him.

"Next stop, Portugal," Maribel said. She went under again and surfaced right next to him. "The rip current is bad here," she said. "I don't want to get too far away from you."

"I don't want you too far away," Jem said. He touched Maribel's

forehead. Her hair was sleek. God, she was pretty. If she were anybody else, he might playfully untie her bikini. He might go under and
pop up with her on his back. He might simply hold her and let her
rock in his arms as the waves passed over them. But it wasn't anybody
else. It was Maribel.

"Would you like to come over for dinner some Sunday?" Maribel
asked.

Here was the dinner invitation Jem had been waiting for, and yet
now he felt uncomfortable. "Sunday is the day Mack eats with Lacey,"
he said.

Maribel squinted her eyes toward shore. "Yep."

"So it would just be us?" Jem asked.

"You're more than welcome to bring a date," Maribel said.

"I couldn't find a date," he said. "Would you tell Mack I was coming for dinner?"

"Would you want me to?"

He took a mouthful of salty green water and spouted it through his
teeth. "I don't know."

"What do you say we call this a friendship," Maribel said. "Unless
you're still determined to be my agent, in which case it's a business
arrangement. Would that make you feel better?"

"Yeah," Jem said, "it would."

"So you'll come for dinner sometime?" she asked.

"Okay," Jem said.

"Great," she said. She rode the next wave all the way to shore,
where she washed up on her hands and knees. Jem watched as she
picked herself up, cleaned the sand from her legs, and headed back to
the blanket. At that moment, Jem hoped she didn't tell Mack about
their day together. It had been Jem's best day on Nantucket by leaps
and bounds—good enough to wipe away all the nonsense that had
preceded it, and Jem wanted the memory of it all to himself.

Summer Solstice

June 20

Dear S.B.T.,

At the risk of sounding ridiculously proud, I will tell you that on June 18, Therese and I traveled to Concord, Mass., where we watched our daughter, Cecily, graduate from Middlesex. She strolled across the manicured lawn like her other classmates, but she stood out, a shining star, a flashing beacon. Cecily is already a young woman, far more mature and sophisticated than her peers. She is our pride and joy and I know you will understand that it is for her sake that I will never sell the Beach Club.

Do you have children, S. B. T.? You have never mentioned any. I would be interested to know the answer to that question, if you are willing to disclose it.

Cordially,

Bill Elliott

ON THE TWENTY-FIRST OF June, summer officially arrived. The sun stayed out longer, the restaurants opened seven nights a week, and the bars were full of college girls who, Vance noticed, favored blue toenail polish and tattoos this year. The weekly edition of the *Inquirer and Mirror* printed its first five-section paper of the season. The Stop & Shop was such a madhouse that management kept the store open twenty-four hours, which meant Vance could pick up his Cheerios and lunch meat at 3:00 A.M. if he wanted. The cobblestone streets of town were clogged with cars coming off the ferry, bicyclists, and pedestrians, people holding their maps, crossing the street without looking. Who

were all these people? The island became inundated with Range
Rovers from Connecticut (that sounded like a stereotype, but Vance
swore it was true; that morning on Main Street he counted no less
than three Range Rovers, all with the telltale blue license plate). The
Steamship Authority ran six boats a day in each direction and the
Nantucket airport was busier than Logan in Boston. The climbing
roses and hydrangeas bloomed, causing more slowdowns; through
his open window, Vance heard women cooing, "Look at the pretty
flowers!"

It was popular to complain about the tourists and so Vance decided
to take the opposite approach. He embraced the tourists. He waved to
people in the long lines outside the Juice Bar and the Brotherhood, he
gave directions to a family on bicycles—the man turning his map every
which way, while the mother, with a baby jammed in a booster seat on
the back of her Schwinn and three kids behind her, said, "Honey, why
don't you just ask someone if we're headed toward a beach? Here, ask
this nice man." Tourists, to Vance, meant one thing: money. Vance
had been raking in sweet tips from the hotel guests, especially since
Jem was constantly screwing up, making Vance look good.

June 21, summer solstice, was also the day the Beach Club opened.
This meant that a hundred Beach Club members would now be crawling over the property like ants on a picnic. The members wanted *their*
specific umbrella in *their* specific spot on the beach. Some members
had been sitting in the same spot for forty or fifty years. (Vance did the
math: if a person came to the Beach Club four times a week and stayed
for six hours a day during the ten weeks of summer over fifty years that
meant they had spent *twelve thousand hours* sitting in the same place.)

One of the good things about the Beach Club opening was that
Vance had two more lackeys to boss around. Mack hired beach boys
named Kevin and Bruce who looked just like all the other beach boys
Vance had seen over the years—pimply, sarcastic prep school kids
who somehow lucked into the cushiest job on the island. That morning, Vance wanted to scare the kids so they would not only respect
him but shudder a little when they saw him coming. They waited in
front of the lobby at eight o'clock sharp, a good sign. Vance parked his

Datsun 300ZX, and the two boys looked it over appreciatively, another good sign. As he stepped out of the car, they nervously eyed his shaved head. Excellent. Vance bit his tongue to keep himself from grinning.

"You the beach boys?" he asked.

"Man, could you call us something else?" the taller, skinnier kid asked. "I don't want to be associated with some washed-up sixties band." This kid wore a South Carolina Cocks hat, another popular item at the bars this summer. With a lightning-quick motion, Vance hit the bill of the cap and flipped it off the boy's head. The boy flinched and stepped back; his hair was matted as though he hadn't even run a comb through it that morning.

"Are you Kevin or Bruce?" Vance asked.

"Bruce."

"Bruce, let me tell you something. Beach boys have been called beach boys since the Club opened in 1924. And guess what, buddy? We're not changing it for you. Got that?"

Bruce bent down to pick up his hat while Kevin, who was chubbier with more pimples, stared wide-eyed at Vance. They were off to a good start.

VANCE TOOK THE BOYS past Lacey Gardner's cottage to the umbrella room.

"These are the beach umbrellas," he said. "They cost a hundred sixteen dollars apiece. If you break an umbrella because you're negligent, you get docked that much plus the amount it costs to ship these babies back to the south of France where they were made." This wasn't true but Vance found that saying this led to fewer broken umbrellas. "The umbrellas come in kelly green, royal blue, and canary yellow. Sometimes members want a certain color. You're going to have to memorize who those people are and their umbrella color. I'm not taking any crap from a pissed-off member because they got royal instead of canary. *Capiche?*"

Kevin picked at his chin. "How will we know which ones?"

"I'll teach you," Vance said. He hefted seven umbrellas onto his shoulder. "Follow me."

THE SUN WAS OUT and already hot. Vance raised his face. He'd picked up some kind of crazy sun addiction in Thailand; he couldn't get enough of it. But practically speaking, a warm, sunny summer solstice was bad news. The Beach Club would be packed, and because the beach boys were brand-new that meant Vance would have to set up all one-hundred umbrellas by himself.

"Now," Vance said, "this is how you set up an umbrella. Watch carefully." He held up the spike, as long as a Louisville Slugger. "This is the bottom of the umbrella, the part that gets driven into the sand. It's sharp, as you can see, and for this reason you have to make sure you drive it deep. I don't want to tell you about umbrellas I've seen that got loose in the wind because some beach boy did a half-ass plant job. Can you imagine catching this spike in the face?" He lowered his voice. "Or the balls?"

Bruce curled his lip, Kevin looked like he was about to lose his breakfast. Vance bit his tongue again. Then he raised the spike in his arms and blasted it into the sand.

"Pretend the sand is your ex-girlfriend," he said. "Or hell, pretend it's me." Plenty of times, Vance imagined the sand was Mack. "Then wag the spike back and forth until it goes even deeper. When you feel there's no possibility of it getting loose even in gale force winds, pack sand around it like this. Then you're ready to put up an umbrella." Vance slid the umbrella pole over the spike and locked it in. He opened the umbrella triumphantly; it bloomed like a big royal blue flower. "There," Vance said. "That's how it's done."

"Not bad for a bellman," a voice said.

Mack walked toward them through the sand. *Not bad for a bellman?* What the hell kind of comment was that? All of Vance's good work at getting these Romper Roomers to respect him was down the drain with that remark.

Mack shook hands with the two kids and then he put his arm

around Vance's shoulders. Vance tensed, like Mack's arm was one of the cobras he'd seen at the Snake Farm in Bangkok.

"Vance was a beach boy himself once upon a time," Mack said. "So maybe someday you too will be a bellman."

Bruce scoffed. Vance wanted to flip the kid's hat off again and make him eat it. Vance had half a mind to quit right then and there, and as long as he was at it, he might as well beat Mack to a pulp in front of these two clowns. If the money weren't so damn good, he would do it.

Vance picked up another spike. He threw it to Bruce, point first. "Here," Vance said. "You try."

Bruce lifted the spike the way Vance had done and brought it down with an "Ooomph!" The spike grazed the sand and shot between Bruce's legs, like he was hiking a football. Kevin giggled.

"Unbelievable," Vance said.

Mack clapped Vance on the back. "Keep up the good work, Professor," he said. "By the way, there's a twelve-knot west-southwest wind."

Vance thought briefly about how sweet it would be to set all the umbrellas facing east northeast just so he could watch them pop out of the ground and fly down the beach. He thought of the Beach Club members lying impaled and bloody in the sand. But why should he punish the members when the person he was after was Mack? Vance crunched two Rolaids between his teeth. Then he picked up the spike and tossed it to Bruce.

"Try again," he said.

BY NINE-THIRTY ALL THE umbrellas were up and Vance's arms ached. Bruce was the crappiest umbrella planter Vance had ever seen, although Kevin wasn't bad, just a little shallow. Vance showed the boys where the Sleepy Hollow chairs were kept and instructed them on how to properly open and close the chair without snapping their fingers off. He left them out on the beach, practicing opening and closing the chairs like the amateurs they were.

When Vance got back to the office, Mack was in the lobby schmoozing with the guests. Vance went into the utility closet and shoved past the stand of vacuum cleaners. There, in the back of the closet, sat Vance's locked toolbox. Vance found the key on his ring and opened the box. Inside was his hammer, various nails and screws, a set of adjustable wrenches, a ratty, torn-up copy of "The Downward Spiral," Vance's published short story, and Mr. Beebe's handgun. It was a .38. Vance held it straight out in his arms. Mack was lucky Vance didn't have the gun when he made his cutesy remark. Mack was lucky Vance didn't feel like going to jail, otherwise he would be Vance's first target, no question about it.

"Not bad for a bellman," Vance said softly. "Pow."

WITHIN TWENTY-FOUR HOURS of summer solstice, two important women in Mack's life arrived on the island: Andrea Krane and Cecily Elliott. Cecily arrived first, at ten o'clock on Sunday night. Mack was watching TV with Maribel asleep in his lap when the phone rang.

"I'm home. Mom and Dad said I should call. Hope I didn't wake you up."

"Cecily?" Mack said. Maribel blinked her eyes. "How are you, kid?"

"Butt tired. I partied until seven o'clock this morning, then spent the day trying to get my dorm room clean enough so they would give Dad his security deposit back."

"Are you happy to be home? We missed you, kid."

"I'm not a kid. I'm eighteen years old, Mack."

"I know. How was graduation?"

"Boring. Hot. I was hungover for that, too."

"How's the boyfriend?"

"I'll fill you in tomorrow," Cecily said. "Can I please talk to Maribel?"

Mack covered the receiver. "It's Cecily. She wants to talk to you."

"Of course," Maribel said. She took the phone from Mack. "Cecily? Hey, girlfriend, how are you? No, you didn't hurt his feelings. He understands there are some things that can only pass between the lips of women. Now, tell me everything." Maribel disappeared into the bedroom.

Mack listened to Maribel's muffled laughter through the wall. The friendship between Maribel and Cecily surprised him. For the past several years, Therese had been trying to light a fire between him and Cecily, insisting that if they got married, the Beach Club would go to them both. Mack loved Cecily like a sister and he supposed Cecily reciprocated, although she was frequently sarcastic with him, and sullen. She'd had a crush on him when she was eleven or twelve, but as soon as the crush faded it seemed as if he'd disappointed her, fallen short of her expectations. This made him feel like doing a better job, so he tried to stay updated about her boyfriends and school, but everything she told him sounded suspiciously like old news, or a lie.

Cecily adored Maribel, and for good reason: Maribel was beautiful, friendly, intelligent, genuine, and all despite the fact that she'd been raised by a single working mother in rural New York. Mack had met Maribel during her first summer on the island, when North Beach Road was part of her daily running route. Mack found himself waiting for her to show up, the blond runner. He volunteered to sweep the parking lot around ten o'clock, hoping she would take off her headphones and talk to him, but she never stopped, except for a brief moment, to drink in the sight of the ocean. One day Mack waited in the middle of the road with a bottle of Evian. She waved him away, but her eyes lingered on the bottle; it was, thankfully, a very hot day, and she gave in. She poured half the bottle down her front and inhaled the other half sloppily, letting it drip down her chin. She gasped, "Thanks," and was about to run off when he said, "Can I call you?" She readjusted her headphones, and said, "Library, in the afternoons." Mack remembered his first time walking into the Atheneum, its intimidating white columns, its intimidating quietness. He found Maribel in the stacks, reading a paperback romance, licking her finger as she turned each page. He tapped her on the shoulder and she whipped her head around, narrowed her blue eyes. She couldn't place him. He said, "I manage the Beach Club. I see you running." She reddened and quickly replaced the book on the shelf. "You like romances?" he said. "No," she answered sternly. "I don't."

But she did. Her job at the library was a summer position, and when the fall came, she stayed. And stayed, for six years.

This past Christmas Eve, Maribel had the stomach flu and yet she insisted on going to the midnight service at the Unitarian church. No sooner had the choir filed in singing "Oh, Come All Ye Faithful," then she had to be sick. Mack escorted her out and she threw up all over Orange Street. They sat on the steps in the cold still night, with the clock tower above them as they listened to the faint singing from inside. "The most beautiful night of the year," Maribel said. "And I ruined it." Mack almost proposed right then, and what a story it would have been, but no, he didn't have the courage, if courage was what he was missing. In the end he just held Maribel's hand, and when she felt well enough, they walked home. After six years, Maribel didn't pester him about marriage, but he wasn't stupid. He knew he had to make a decision soon. First, he had to decide about the farm and the Beach Club, and then he had to decide about Maribel.

An hour later, Mack went into bed. He found Maribel fast asleep in her clothes, holding the receiver of the phone to her chest. Her lips parted and she gave a sudden kick.

"Jump-starting your motorcycle," Mack said softly. He kissed her forehead. "Sweet dreams."

Maribel's eyes flew open. "What am I doing?" she asked.

"Running in place," he said. He wasn't sure if she was awake or not. "What did you and Cecily talk about?"

"Nothing," Maribel said. Her eyes fell closed again. "Love."

MACK SAW CECILY THE next morning after breakfast. He was standing on the front porch of the lobby when she popped out of her house. She was in bare feet, wearing baggy Umbro shorts and a Middlesex Field Hockey T-shirt. Cecily was tall and lanky and had long red curls, two shades darker than her mother. She walked toward Mack gingerly, over the asphalt and the broken hermit crab shells.

"You need to toughen your feet," Mack said.

"I liked being in a place that had grass, you know. Don't you ever miss grass, Mack?"

"If we had grass, I'd be mowing it," he said. He met Cecily on the first step and hugged her. "I missed you, though. And hey, congrats on getting into UVA. We have a bellman here from Virginia."

Cecily lifted her leg to inspect the sole of her foot. "I know. Mom told me."

"So when do you leave for college?"

"Geez, Mack. I just got here. Can't you let a person relax for a minute? College isn't exactly an exciting prospect for me. I just spent four years in a dorm, okay? We're talking about more of the same."

"Sorry," Mack said. "I thought college was pretty cool and I was only on the Cape."

"College is college," Cecily said. She squinted at him. "I can't believe you haven't proposed yet."

"How rude of me." He dropped to one knee. "Cecily, will you marry me?"

Cecily slouched, hip thrown out. "I don't know how Maribel puts up with you."

"That makes two of us," Mack said. "I'm impossible."

"Not an excuse," Cecily said. "When are you going to ask her?"

"I don't know," Mack said. "Maybe around the time you graduate from college."

"You are impossible," Cecily said.

"So," Mack said, "tell me about the boyfriend."

"He's smarter than you and much better looking," Cecily said. "But you're changing the subject. When are you going to ask Maribel to marry you?"

"Did Maribel send you out as her scout?" Mack said.

"No." Cecily avoided his eyes by inspecting her other foot. "We just want to know."

"Who's 'we'?" Mack asked.

"The world," Cecily said. "When are you going to marry her, Mack?"

"I don't know," Mack said. "One of the things you'll learn as you grow up is that sometimes 'I don't know' is the only answer you're going to get."

"Please spare me the growing-up bullshit," Cecily said. She looked past him into the lobby. "Can you believe Mom and Dad won't let me work the front desk? Dad's putting me on the beach. At least I'll get a tan. Who's that working?"

"Love O'Donnell," Mack said. "She's nice. You'll like her."

"I'll have to like her later. I'm going back to bed."

"The Beach Club opens today, Cecily. That makes this your first day of work."

She waved at him and headed back through the minefield of shells to her house. "I'm the owner's daughter," she said. "I do what I want."

ANDREA KRANE AND HER fifteen-year-old son, James, arrived on the late ferry, which docked at 10:30 P.M. Mack was working the desk, giving Tiny the night off, and he let Jem go home early. The lobby was quiet. From the front porch, Mack watched the lights of the ferry approach the island. Andrea was on that boat, standing on the upper deck trying to pick out the lights of the hotel from off the dark coast.

I'm right here where you left me. Last July he watched her boat leave from this very spot. It was morning then and Mack waved his arms, although he knew she couldn't see him.

When the ferry headed around Brant Point and Mack heard the long, low horn announcing the boat's arrival, he went back inside and sat behind the desk. Twenty minutes later, Andrea walked in the door. She was in sweatpants and a navy blue windbreaker, her hair pulled back in a ponytail. She carried a huge duffel across her back and a suitcase in each hand. Mack scrambled to help her.

"I got it," she said irritably when he reached for her bags. "If you help, you'll throw me off balance." She made it to the front desk and let everything drop. "Here I am." She took a deep breath and looked at the quilts, the wicker chairs, the fireplace, the plants. "God, I love this place. I'd like to buy this place. Do you think Bill and Therese would sell it to me? No, don't say anything. Just let me take this all in. In a minute, it's going to feel like I never left."

Mack hadn't seen Andrea in eleven months, he hadn't heard her voice or smelled her scent, and yet here she was in front of him, exactly as she had been when he last kissed her.

"Okay," she said. "I'm ready."

Mack kissed her.

"Do that again," she said.

Mack kissed her with more intensity, although still not the way he wanted to kiss her. If it weren't in violation of her rules, he would carry her back to room 18 and make love to her right then and there. Instead, he stepped back.

"How was your trip?" he asked. "And where's James?"

"He's in the truck, rocking," she said. "That should give you some indication of how the trip went. As soon as he gets out of his routine, he starts to panic. I bought him a book about airplanes to keep him occupied. His new thing is planes. We've been getting up at six o'clock each morning and driving to BWI to watch them take off."

"Let's go get him," Mack said. "I have his room all set up with the bedspread. That might make him feel better."

"You're a doll," she said. "And remember, don't let him upset you."

Mack had known James since he was five years old when he was afraid of toilet seats and he held his hands over his ears and screamed in a strangled voice. Every year Mack hoped James would become cured of his autism. Dealing with James was frustrating and even a little scary. Mack felt a familiar dread as he followed Andrea out to her truck.

James sat in the passenger side of Andrea's green Ford Explorer with his head bent, rocking back and forth. Andrea opened the door, but the rocking continued. James's rocking blocked out all other stimuli; it was his way of keeping himself under control.

"Climb out of the truck, James," Andrea said. She waited a few seconds. "Climb out."

James stopped rocking and got out of the truck like an automaton. He was such a handsome kid, with Andrea's honey-colored hair and gray-green eyes. Puberty had come to James this year—he was taller, with faint whiskers above his lip.

"Say hi to Mack," Andrea prompted.

"Hi, Mack," James said.

"Hi, James. I'm glad you got here safely." Mack looked at Andrea. "Are there other bags?"

"I'll get them," she said. "You take James to his room."

"Follow me, James," Mack said. He took the boy's arm but James pulled away. James opened the door to the truck and Mack thought he was going to climb back in and start rocking again but all he did was pick up a book.

"*Understanding Aeronautics,*" James said. "Three hundred twenty-five pages, illustrated, heavy stock laminate paper. Copyright 1990. Reprinted 1992, 1994. This copy belongs to James Christopher Krane." He tucked the book under his arm and followed Mack through the lobby, out the back door and along the boardwalk to room 17.

Mack stepped into the room and James followed. "This is your room, James."

James sat immediately down on the bed and started stroking the bedspread. "James's blanket," he said.

"That's your blanket," Mack said. "Nobody uses it but you." It was a green chenille bedspread, the kind the hotel rooms had ten years ago. Now all the rooms had hand-stitched quilts, but Mack stored one chenille bedspread in the utility closet for James.

Andrea opened the door that connected with room 18. "Mom's room is right here, remember, James?"

James turned on the TV.

"James, please put your clothes in the dresser," Andrea said. "We're going to be here for three weeks."

"Twenty-one days," James said.

"That's right. Twenty-one days just like always. Let me show you where the bathroom is." Andrea turned on the bathroom light. "It's right here. And Mack took off the toilet seat. There's no toilet seat in here, okay, buddy?"

James stared at the TV. "No toilet seat," he said.

"That's right, no toilet seat. No reason to be afraid. You've stayed in this room many times before. Do you feel comfortable?"

James stared at the TV.

"James, I asked if you felt comfortable here."

"Are we going to the airport in the morning?" James asked.

"Yes, we are, we're going to the Nantucket airport."

"Okay," James said.

"Okay. Mom is going to unpack and then go to sleep. Knock on my door if you need anything."

Andrea beckoned Mack into her room.

"Good night, James," Andrea said.

"Good night, James," Mack said.

"Good night," James said. "Good night."

Andrea shut the door and fell back onto the bed. "What an exhausting day. Every day with James is exhausting but travel really drains me." She unzipped her windbreaker. Underneath she wore a red T-shirt. "Do you notice a difference in him?" she asked.

"That's not fair," Mack said, plunging into the leather chair. "You know him much better than I do."

"I'm so close to him that I can't notice any changes. Tell me what's different from a year ago. Maybe I shouldn't ask you until tomorrow. He wasn't exactly the best version of himself tonight."

"Well," Mack said. He wasn't thinking of James, but of the lobby, which he had left open, and of the phone, which he left unattended. "Let me use your phone." Mack forwarded the hotel's calls to Andrea's room. Then he sat back down in the chair. "He's taller," Mack said. "He's getting a beard in, have you noticed that?"

"I've been ignoring it," Andrea said. She hugged her knees to her chest. "Really, as if it weren't difficult enough for me to raise a special-needs child on my own, now I have to raise a man? I have parents asking me questions all the time, about toilet training and school and what kinds of vitamins their kids should take, and I give them answers but I feel like such an impostor. Because meanwhile I'm watching James grow up and I don't know what to do about it. I don't know what to tell him about shaving, or about girls and sex. He loves to masturbate, and every time I find him doing it, I hide in my walk-in closet and cry. In a couple of years, I'm going to have to help him find a job and another place to live. There are hurdles in front of me and I can't even see how high they are."

"Do you hear from Raymond?" Mack asked.

"I heard his wife just had her third baby. He sends me large sums of money, really enormous sums that I'm simply socking away. But he won't see James, nothing's changed there. It's like the kid doesn't exist for Raymond, except as some kind of charity case to throw money at. Being rejected by your father is enough to break a normal kid. I don't know how it's affecting James."

"I can teach James to shave," Mack said. "Later in the week, once he's gotten used to me again."

Andrea flashed her green-grays at him and then she started to cry. "Thank you," she said. "I was hoping you'd offer. It's so horrible of me to depend on you, but you know what? I like having three weeks out of fifty-two when I know there's someone I can count on. It's nice to know I'm not completely alone."

"You're not alone," Mack said. He sat next to Andrea on the bed. He put his arms around her and she pressed her wet face into his chest. Mack closed his eyes and inhaled the scent of her hair. He loved Andrea's sadness. Her sadness was about the inscrutable mixed-up messages in her son's brain, and about being left to bring him up by herself, but Andrea's sadness was generous enough to encompass everything, including an eighteen-year-old Iowa farm boy losing both his parents in a single moment. And somehow she managed to make sadness, her own and everyone else's, seem necessary, right.

"I love you," Mack said.

She sniffled. "I know."

They had never made love. This was Andrea's rule from the beginning—it would make things too complicated, she said, and there was also the issue of logistics, because of James. There was always James—and long ago Mack suspected that after the ferocity with which Andrea loved James, there was little left over for anyone else. Andrea never told Mack she loved him—always she responded by saying "I know." She let him hug and kiss her and once or twice a summer when James was asleep in the other room they fell back on the bed groping for one another and Mack ground against her, sweating, crazy, aching. But she never gave in, she never let go.

The phone rang and Mack stood to answer it.

"Who could be calling me?" Andrea asked.

"It's Maribel," he said. He checked his watch. "It's almost midnight." He picked up the phone. "Nantucket Beach Club."

"Mack," Maribel said, "it's late."

"I know," he said. "I had a late check-in. I'll be home in a little while."

"I might be asleep."

"Okay," Mack said. He paused before he hung up, thinking about Maribel the night before as she lay asleep with the phone on her chest; he thought about the little kicks and twists she made in the night. He knew her so well. She was like another part of him. As Mack replaced the receiver he thought, *I love them both.* It happened, he supposed; he was just glad he didn't have to choose between them, not tonight, anyway.

"I should go," he said to Andrea.

"When are you going to marry her, Mack?"

"I don't know," Mack said. "I kind of wish people would quit asking me that."

Andrea smiled. "Would you like to come to the airport with James and me tomorrow? Normally we leave at six but since I'm on my much-needed vacation, we won't leave until seven. Want to join us for an hour?"

"Sure," Mack said. "I'll meet you in the parking lot, how's that?" He kissed Andrea, and stepped out onto the deck. "Good night."

Andrea closed the door behind him, and Mack walked over the

boardwalk into the sand. He looked at the stars and listened to the waves rushing onto the beach. He wondered if his parents could see him, and if they could see him, he wondered what they were thinking.

NOT ONLY WAS MARIBEL asleep when Mack got home, she was asleep when he rose at six-thirty the next morning. He considered waking her to let her know he was leaving early, but she looked peaceful, a strand of blond hair caught in the corner of her mouth, flutters underneath her eyelids.

"What are you dreaming about?" he whispered. But she didn't waken, and Mack got up to shower. Before he left the apartment, he picked a yellow zinnia from the flowerbed and put it on his pillow, where she would see it when she opened her eyes.

WHEN MACK GOT TO the hotel, Andrea was already behind the wheel of the Explorer with James in the passenger seat, reading his book. Mack hopped in the backseat.

"I hope I'm not late," he said.

Andrea smiled wearily. "Old habits die hard," she said. "We've been waiting since six."

"Since six," James said.

On the way to the airport, Andrea said, "James, the planes at this airport are going to be smaller than the ones we're used to seeing in Baltimore." She looked over the seat at Mack. "I don't want him to be disappointed."

"Maybe we'll get lucky and see a jet," Mack said.

"I see jets every day," James said. He paged through his book. "Boeing 747, 767, DC-10. Is there a tower at this airport?"

"I don't know," Mack said. "I can't remember."

James laughed. "*All* airports have a tower. It's where the air traffic controller sits so there are no crashes." James made an exploding noise and smacked his hands together.

Once they reached the airport, Andrea parked at the far edge of the field so they could watch the planes land. She turned off the ignition, leaned her head against the headrest, and closed her eyes. James, however, became extremely alert and animated; he was a different kid from the one Mack had seen the night before sitting in front of the TV.

"Here comes one!" James shouted. He riffled madly through the pages of his book.

Mack leaned over the front seat. He massaged Andrea's shoulder with one hand and looked through the windshield. "What kind is it?"

"I can't tell yet," James said. The sun was bright and James squinted. Mack offered James his sunglasses and James happily put them on.

"Mom, look!" James said.

Andrea opened her eyes for a second and smiled. "Very handsome," she said.

The plane landed, its wheels skidding and smoking on the runway. James clapped.

"Turboprop," he said. "Gets most of its thrust through the propellers."

"Have we seen those in Baltimore?" Andrea asked.

"Yes, Mom," James said. Something in James's tone of voice— ("*Yes, Mom, of course, Mom, don't be silly*")—sounded like a typical teenager. This was what made James so frustrating. He could be so normal—and at other times so impenetrable. Andrea once told Mack that the messages in James's brain were a code she could only crack randomly, with luck. A code without a key.

"Here comes one!" James said. The plane landed right in front of them, like an actor taking a bow, and James applauded. "Safe landing!"

They watched planes land and take off for forty minutes. James applauded for both occasions and during the lulls he paged through his book, reciting facts about planes for Mack.

"Planes are heavier than air," he said. "They need wings in order to fly. Planes have three kinds of motion: yaw, roll and pitch." He moved his hand through the air and made a noise with his lips.

"You sure know a lot about planes," Mack said.

"Yeah," James said. "I know it all."

Andrea was quiet, and finally she turned the key in the ignition. James's spine stiffened. "Is it time?" he asked.

"It's time," she said.

James pointed to the blue numbers of the digital clock. "It's *not* time," he said. "We have until eight o'clock. This says seven-forty-five. Right here, Mom, see?"

"We have a visitor," Andrea said. "And Mack has to get the doughnuts so the rest of the people staying at the hotel will have their breakfast." She pulled away.

"Get the doughnuts," James said. "Getthedoughnutsgetthedoughnutsgetthedoughnuts." He rocked back and forth.

"James," Andrea said sternly, "we're coming back tomorrow. And tomorrow we'll stay until eight. Please don't get upset."

"Getthedoughnutsgetthedoughnutsgetthedoughnuts," James said.

Mack leaned forward. "Thank you for letting me come with you today."

"Getthedoughnuts," James said. "Airport, then shower."

"We have to get back to the hotel first, James," Andrea said. "There's no shower in the car."

"Airport, then shower," James said.

"That's right, James. When we get to the hotel, you can take a shower."

James rocked back and forth, saying under his breath, "Doughnuts, shower, doughnuts." Mack caught Andrea's face in the side-view mirror. She smiled weakly and shook her head.

When Andrea pulled into the Beach Club parking lot, she said, "Thank you, Mack, for coming with us. James, would you thank Mack?"

"Airport," James said. "Then shower. Thank you."

"Sounds like somebody wants to get in the shower," Mack said,

"How could you tell?" Andrea said. She got out of the car. James was already headed for his room. Mack looked up at Bill and Therese's house but saw no sign of stirrings and figured they were still in bed. Vance hadn't arrived yet, nor Love, nor the new beach boys. Mack followed Andrea to her room. Andrea unlocked James's door and James stripped his clothes on the way to the bathroom, including Mack's sunglasses, which fell to the floor.

"I thought you had to get the doughnuts," Andrea said. "Don't make a liar out of me. James, close the door, please!"

The door closed and the water came on.

"I do," Mack said. "But I feel bad for throwing off your routine."

"Flexibility isn't James's strong suit," Andrea said. "I should have thought of that before I invited you."

"And you were quiet in the car," Mack said. "Is everything all right?"

She picked up Mack's sunglasses and fingered them idly. "Going to the airport is good for James but it sure is lousy for me," she said. "I can't help thinking that James will never be able to just choose a place off the map and take a trip there. He's not safe in the world, Mack, and he's never going to be. I'm the only person who's going to love him enough."

Mack hugged her. "You don't know that."

"For a while taking care of him was getting easier," she said. "Now it's getting harder. And seeing you makes everything worse."

Mack held her at arm's length. "Worse? Why's that?"

"Because you make me remember that I'm not just a mother but a woman, with needs."

"You're not saying . . ."

"No," she said. "I haven't changed my mind about that." She sighed. "I'm having a hard time switching into my vacation mode. I promise I'm going to try and relax, okay? I'm going to sit under my cool blue beach umbrella and read my trashy novels and watch James as he decides if it's okay to go in the water. I'm going to order a couple of cheeseburgers from Joe's Broad Street Grill and have one of the darling college boys deliver them right to my umbrella. I'm going to try and have fun, dammit." She raised her face. "Do I say this every year?"

"Yes," Mack said. "And every year you succeed." He kissed her. If Maribel were a yellow zinnia, what would Andrea be? A red rose maybe, something a little more somber, a little more serious. "I'll see you later." He slipped from James's room out the back door and looked both ways. No one was around. It took him a split second to remember about the doughnuts, to remember that he had a hotel to run.

THE REASON MACK FORBADE his staff to date the guests was this: It was distracting. It was distracting to work in the same place that the object of your affection lay in the sun, swam, showered, ate breakfast, and slept. Because you wanted to join them, because you wanted to check on them every ten minutes, because you wanted to have fun with them—slip under their umbrella, join them for a nap, share a bagel. But you couldn't; you were at work. And so, Mack told his staff there would be No Dating the Guests. I'm making your life easier, he said. Trust me.

After all the years with Andrea, Mack had his distractions under control. She and James ate breakfast on their deck and Andrea, true to her word, rarely moved from her place on the beach, so Mack never wondered what she was up to. He did take a few more night shifts on the front desk from Tiny than usual, but he did this every June and Tiny never asked why.

Mack tried, most especially, to pay enough attention to Maribel. Nights he was home he took her out for dinner, he drove her down the beach to see the sunset, he made love to her with the windows open and the sounds of crickets floating around their dark bedroom. He tried not to think of Andrea while he was with Maribel, he tried not to think of Andrea's sad gray-green eyes, but it was impossible. He wondered if he were acting like someone with a guilty conscience.

One night as Mack and Maribel had dinner at Le Languedoc, Maribel reached over and took Mack's hand.

"I want to ask you something," she said.

Instantly, Mack started to sweat. "What's that?"

Maribel leaned in closer. "It's less than two weeks until the Fourth of July. The summer is flying by. And I want to know if you've thought any more about the profit sharing."

Mack blew out a stream of air. His body felt cool and tight. "Hmmmm." Under other circumstances, he might have been angry with Maribel for pushing this issue, but now there was Andrea. Mack had told Andrea about the phone call from David Pringle, and about the farm. He told her he might ask Bill to profit-share and Andrea said, "I'm surprised he hasn't offered it to you." Mack felt the same way: that Bill should *offer* him part of the profits.

"I haven't asked Bill yet," he said. "I'm still thinking it through."

"You have to give David an answer about the farm, Mack."

"I'm aware of that, Maribel," Mack said. "It's my farm. I have until fall anyway."

"Asking Bill about the profit sharing should make your decision clear. If he says yes, you sell the farm. If he says no, you run the farm."

"Nothing is clear," Mack said, although he realized it would seem that way to Maribel, or to anybody else for that matter. "I don't know if I want to run the farm. And I don't know if I want to sell it."

Maribel retracted her hand. "King of the I-don't-knows," she said.

She was baiting him, but Mack wouldn't argue. She was right. He didn't know a lot of things. For example, he didn't know how he could possibly be in love with two women. Had he felt this way last year? The year before that? Why was it hitting him so squarely in the jaw this year? Was it part of being thirty? Mack supposed he could confide in Bill, but for Bill, there had only been Therese, and no matter how much poetry Bill read, he wouldn't understand when Mack said, "I love them both."

AT THE END OF Andrea's first week, Mack had his usual Sunday night dinner with Lacey Gardner.

"What do you want to drink, dear?" Lacey asked him. "Dewar's or a Michelob?"

"I love them both," Mack said.

Lacey looked at him as though he'd just burped the alphabet. "Would you like me to pour you one of each, then, and you can drink them side by side?"

"I'm sorry," Mack said. "Michelob. Actually, better make that a Dewar's."

"Uh-oh," Lacey said. "Do we have a problem?"

"A couple of them," Mack said, taking a seat on the couch. The Sunday dinners weren't formal; Mack and Lacey each had about nine cocktails apiece and then if they remembered, they ate a sandwich, some cold meatloaf, or Lacey heated up a swordfish potpie.

"How big are these problems?" Lacey asked.

"The biggest," Mack said. "Love and work."

"Those aren't the biggest," Lacey said. "Health is the biggest. If we have our health, we're okay. Agreed?"

"Agreed," Mack said, thinking of James. "Agreed. But are love and money the second and third biggest?"

"Definitely top ten," Lacey said, bringing Mack his drink. She settled into her favorite leather armchair. She always dressed up for the Sunday dinners that weren't really dinners—tonight in a bright blue pantsuit with a gold Nantucket basket pin on her lapel. She'd been to the hairdresser and her white hair was fluffed and styled.

"You look great tonight, Gardner," Mack said. "Have I told you that already?"

Lacey waved at him. "You know why I invite you over here, don't you? Good for the ego. So, where shall we start?"

Mack sipped his drink. All Dewar's and no water. "I'm thinking of asking Bill to profit-share."

"You're speaking to the oldest of women," Lacey said. "What does that mean, profit-share? It sounds like one of those horrible terms from the 1980s."

"It just means that I get a portion of the bottom line. So my salary would depend on how well the hotel does. And we know the hotel does very well."

Lacey nodded. "What does Bill get in return for giving you his profits?"

"He keeps me happy," Mack said. "I stay."

"You're not happy?" Lacey asked. "That's news to me. And it'll be news to a lot of other people, I assure you."

"I'm happy and I'm not. I'm thirty years old, Lacey."

"And I'm eighty-eight," Lacey said. She pointed a manicured fingernail at him and smiled. "Gotcha there, didn't I?"

"Some things are happening back home," Mack said. "In Iowa. The boss on my father's farm is retiring and my lawyer wants me to sell the farm or go back and run it myself."

"I thought you were all finished with Iowa," Lacey said.

"There's five hundred acres with my name on it. I have to go back sometime."

"That's the argument for Iowa," Lacey said. "What's the argument for Nantucket?"

"I love it here."

"I concur. Where is better than Nantucket in the summer?" Lacey asked. "If there's a place more desirable than where you already are, Mack, do tell me about it."

"If I profit-share with Bill it would be easier to stay. I'd feel like the Beach Club is at least partially mine. I'll feel responsible for it."

"I thought you liked not feeling responsible for it," Lacey said.

"I have to grow up sometime."

"If you want to ask Bill for part of the hotel's profits, go ahead. Keep in mind that he'll have a reason for answering just as you have a reason for asking."

Mack had already given a lot of thought to what Bill might say. Bill might react as Mack hoped, and say, "Of course we can profit-share, I should have thought of that myself." Or he could simply say no. Or he could say, "Let me think it over. I'll run some numbers and get back to you." The worst thing would be if Bill said nothing, if he wrinkled his brow and retreated into himself, hurt that Mack had even asked for a piece of his business.

"We'll see," Mack said.

"Now, what about love?" Lacey asked. "But perhaps it's time for another drink?"

Mack spun the ice in his glass. "I'll make them," he said. He took the glasses to the kitchen and fixed two more drinks, adding a healthy dose of water to his own. "My problem is . . . Andrea's here."

"With James?" Lacey asked. "Is he any better?"

"A little bit," Mack said. That morning, Mack had helped James shave for the first time. Mack started the lesson by cutting his finger and letting the blood bloom to show James how sharp and dangerous the razor could be. Mack lathered up his face and then James's face. When James saw himself in the mirror, he giggled uncontrollably.

"Santa Claus," James said, touching his fingers to the shaving cream and tasting them. He grimaced and spat into the sink.

"That's right," Mack said. "When you lather up, you'll look like Santa Claus."

"Lather up, lather up!" James said.

Mack shaved a path from his own cheek down to his chin. Then he rinsed the razor. He put his arms around James from behind and said, "Now I'm going to do the same to you." But James raised his hands to his face and sidled away screaming, "Blood! Blood!"

"No," Mack said. Andrea was in the next room listening. "There isn't going to be any blood because I'm going to show you how to do it the right way." Mack knew that if he nicked James even a little bit, the lesson would be over. But Mack shaved smoothly and James giggled.

"It tickles," he said.

"Give me your hand." Mack guided James's hand with the razor along his face until he was completely shaved.

"No cuts this time," Mack said. "But sometimes there are cuts. And that's okay because they're little cuts." Mack finished shaving himself and then he showed James how to splash his face with water, and apply lotion.

"Some people use aftershave," Mack said. "But not me."

"Yeah," James said, "not me either."

"Look in the mirror, buddy, you're all shaved."

"All shaved," James repeated. He touched his face. His faint mustache was gone.

"We'll do it again in a couple days," Mack said. "Would you like that?"

James nodded.

"Do you want to show your mom?"

James burst out of the bathroom. "All shaved, Mom," he said. "No cuts this time."

Andrea, who had been sitting on the bed pretending to read a magazine, stood up. "You look so handsome," she said. She touched James's face. "Did Mack teach you how to shave?"

James nodded proudly, perhaps he was so proud that he lost language, because he said nothing. He let his mother hug him and then James turned and kissed Mack on the lips.

"HE'S BETTER," MACK SAID to Lacey. "And Andrea is great."

"So you're back to two women," Lacey said.

"I love them both," Mack said.

"Call me crazy, but I don't think you love either one," Lacey said.

"Of course I do," Mack said. "I definitely love Maribel. And with Andrea—well, Andrea is special. I love Andrea. There's no other word for it, although I feel differently about Andrea than I do about Maribel. But they both feel like love, Lacey."

"If you were going to marry Maribel you would have done it already. But you haven't. And who can blame you? You're already enjoying the party. Now, do I think you're going to marry Andrea? No! You've been fiddling around with her longer than Maribel."

"That's not fair," Mack said. He sometimes thought of showing up in Baltimore to live with Andrea, marry her, shoulder half her burden, and be like a father, or an uncle, to James. But wasn't Lacey right? Wasn't that just idle thinking on his part? Still, he couldn't imagine a life without Andrea, although if he married Maribel he would have to let Andrea go. "The reason it's a *problem*, Lacey, is that I don't know what to do."

"I stand by my word. You don't love either one," Lacey said. "When I spent time with Maximilian I knew I was with the only man for me. There was never another man, Mack, not even when Maximilian was away at the war."

Mack ran a hand through his hair. "I know," he said. Maximilian and Lacey had a storybook marriage, like his parents, like Bill and

Therese. Meant for each other, born to be together, holding hands every night before they went to sleep—it drove Mack nuts. Imagine being content every hour for forty-five years—surely Lacey was exaggerating. "Maybe you're right. Maybe I don't love either of them." When he said this, though, it sounded like a lie. He knew he loved them both.

THAT NIGHT WHEN MACK left Lacey's, he checked in at the front desk of the hotel with Tiny.

"Anything going on?" he asked.

Tiny looked up from her book, *One Hundred Years of Solitude*. This was the perfect title of a book for Tiny, who always seemed to be alone in her thoughts. She got her nickname because of her small voice, although her voice wasn't small so much as distant, as though she were talking to everyone from a faraway place, another dimension that she alone had reached.

"The couple in room four had a row and both room three and room five called to complain."

"What did you tell them?"

"What could I tell them?" Tiny said. "I can't be held accountable for other people's bad behavior."

"You must have told them something."

"I told them if it continued, I would call the manager and have him take care of it." She smiled a rare smile. "That would be you."

"Okay," Mack said. Vance poked his head out of the back office and made a face. "I'll check it out. Then I'm going home."

Mack tiptoed down the boardwalk with every intention of checking on room 4 but when he passed Andrea's room, the temptation was too great, and he knocked lightly on the door. A few seconds later, she let him in. The room was dark; Andrea had been asleep. She was wearing a white cotton T-shirt and white panties and her hair was loose around her shoulders.

"It's late," she said, putting her arms around his neck. She kissed him.

"Only ten o'clock," he said. He became aroused by the feel of her body through the T-shirt. She was still warm from bed. He sat on the bed and pulled her into his lap, and kissed her. Normally, this was when she pulled away, but tonight she responded with her tongue. She wiggled deliciously in his lap and ran her hands under his shirt. Mack rolled her onto the bed.

"I've been wanting this since the second you got here," he said.

Andrea ran her hand lightly over his erection. Mack groaned and sucked on her neck. He climbed on top of Andrea and rocked gently into her soft thigh. He was going crazy holding back, but he didn't want to scare her; he could feel himself sweating and he pulled off his shirt. He ran his hands under Andrea's T-shirt and caressed her full breasts. He lowered his mouth to her nipple and it hardened. Andrea pressed her hips into him.

"Will you let me inside you?" Mack asked. He cupped Andrea's ass inside her panties. "Will you?" If she said yes, he would go home and tell Maribel tonight, he swore it.

"No," Andrea said, breathing into his ear. "I can't."

"You can," Mack said. "Please?"

"I'm sorry, Mack," Andrea said. She pulled away and snapped on a light. "I got carried away. Sorry, sorry, sorry."

Mack squinted from the sudden brightness. He flopped onto his back, his erection pushing through his chinos. "Sorry?" he said, trying not to get angry. He lay there for a second, catching his breath. The room spun. Mack reached for Andrea's hand. "This actually hurts."

"Shame on you for showing up unannounced," she said.

Mack looked to the window and saw that Andrea's shades were up. A figure stopped at the window, then slunk away.

"Turn off the light," he said. He went to the window and dropped the shades, then he put his shirt back on. "I have to get out of here. I'll see you tomorrow."

"Give me a kiss good night," she said.

Mack kissed her. "I love you."

"I know," she said.

• • •

MACK STEPPED OFF ANDREA'S deck onto the boardwalk. He heard the sound of water rushing onto shore, and then, faintly, a woman crying. At first, he tried to convince himself it was a gull, but as he listened closer, he heard breathy sobs, definitely a woman crying. *Maribel.* Mack ran around the corner to the Gold Coast, trying to imagine what someone would have seen through the window: him lying on his back, shirtless, holding Andrea's hand, his erection straining through his pants. *Oh, God, Maribel.*

A blond woman sat on the deck of room 4. Mack cleared his throat and she looked up—it was difficult to see in the dark, but Mack knew instantly it wasn't Maribel. This woman's face was streaked with makeup; Mack recognized her from breakfast.

"Mrs. Fourchet?" Mack said. From Quebec, Mack recalled, where her husband owned a Porsche dealership.

"My husband hates me," she said in a defiant voice.

Another loud voice came from inside room 4. "I do not hate you, Meredith. Now will you please get inside?"

"We're paying to see the ocean, Jean-Marc," the woman squawked.

"It's too dark to see anything," the man said. "Now get in here."

"Folks, I'm going to have to ask you to pipe down," Mack said. He was so relieved that he smiled as he said this. "Could you please be a little quieter?"

The door to room 4 opened and Mr. Fourchet stepped onto the deck. "I paid six hundred bucks for this room. I'll have a brass band on this deck if I so choose."

Mack had to wipe the grin off his face. "A brass band?" Mack said. "Ask me in the morning and I'll see what I can do. Do you like the tuba?"

Mr. Fourchet looked at Mack strangely, then he shrugged and said in a softer voice to his wife, "Come in, Meredith, please?"

"I'm *not coming in!*" Mrs. Fourchet shrieked. "And if this fellow wants to call the police then so be it! The Nantucket Police Force can take me away. Ha! The Nantucket Police Force, I'm sure *that's* an intimidating group."

"Meredith, stop giving him a hard time," Mr. Fourchet said. "Will you come inside?"

"No!" Mrs. Fourchet said. "I'm not going anywhere until I see the Nantucket Police Force drive their dune buggy up the beach."

The door to room 3 opened: Janet Kava, wearing a pair of thick glasses, stepped onto her deck. Janet was a mathematics professor at the University of Pennsylvania. She and her partner, Eleanor, had brought along their new adopted baby.

"Mack," Janet said. "Thank God you're here. These people have been screaming at each other for half an hour."

Mrs. Fourchet shot Janet a withering look. "Dyke," she said.

"*Excuse* me?" Janet Kava said. She poked at the bridge of her glasses with a purposeful finger. "*What* did you say?"

"Your baby cries all night long, but that's okay, I suppose," Mrs. Fourchet said. "That's okay because she is the *love child* of you and your lesbian friend."

"That's right," Janet Kava said. "Eleanor and I love each other. We love each other emotionally and physically just like you and your brutish husband love each other. But we don't have squabbles for all the world to hear."

"I think I'm going to be sick," Mrs. Fourchet said.

"Meredith," Mr. Fourchet said.

"Ladies, please," Mack said.

"We are *women,* Mack," Janet Kava said. "Not ladies. Especially not one of us."

"I'll say," Mrs. Fourchet said. "The ladies I know like men."

"I'm ten seconds away from coming over there and demanding an apology," Janet said. "And it won't be very ladylike, I assure you."

Mrs. Fourchet wiped under her eyes. "I must look a mess," she said innocently. She stood up. "I think you're right, Jean-Marc, I think it's time to come in."

Janet Kava glared at Mrs. Fourchet until she disappeared, then she slammed her own screen door shut.

"Good night," Mack said.

Mack ran past the side deck rooms. He looked in Andrea's window but it was dark; she was probably already asleep. All of the lights on the side deck rooms were out and it was difficult to see as he made his way down the boardwalk toward the lobby. When he reached for the back door, he felt a strong hand on his shoulder. Mack swung around. Vance.

"How're you doing, man?" Mack asked. "I had a few words with the people in four. They seem to be settling down."

Vance's expression was strained, as though he were lifting a heavy weight.

"Are you all right?" Mack asked.

"I need to talk to you a minute," Vance said. His hand rested firmly on Mack's shoulder.

"Okay," Mack said. Vance was acting even stranger than normal, but this sometimes happened. Lots of little things bothered Vance and they built up once a summer to the point that he exploded and Mack had to placate him with an extra day off or a small cash bonus.

"I need to talk about you and room eighteen," Vance said. "I saw you in there just now, man. Pretty incriminating."

Mack's relief at finding Mrs. Fourchet instead of Maribel drained away. The four drinks he'd had at Lacey's kicked in; his head swam. "I know it probably looked bad, man, but it's not what you think."

"If it's not what I think, then what is it?"

"We're friends," Mack said. "I've known that lady a long time."

"I've known her just as long as you have, but you don't see me lying on her bed with my shirt off, now do you?" Vance asked. His fingertips dug into Mack's shoulder blade. "How do you explain holding this woman's hand and she's not wearing very many clothes herself?"

Mack took a deep breath. He tried to shrug Vance off. "I wish you'd just forget about it, okay? It's perfectly innocent."

Vance's nostrils flared. "You are so full of shit."

Then Vance raised his hand. He was holding a gun.

Mack's shoulders froze, except for the spot where Vance's hand rested, that spot was very hot and bright. "What are you doing?" Mack said.

Vance poked Mack in the chest with the gun. Mack couldn't move, his knees were locked. Mack was sweating; he felt the cold breeze coming off the water.

"You're going to tell Maribel," Vance said. His voice gurgled. "You're going to tell Maribel what you've been doing or I'll tell her for you."

"You don't know the first thing about it," Mack said.

"I know what I saw," Vance said. "I know what it looked like."

"I already told you, that's not how it is," Mack said.

"You're going to tell Maribel," Vance said. He pressed the gun deeper into Mack's chest. In the dim light, Vance's skin looked purplish. "You are such an idiot. You have a gorgeous, perfect woman like Maribel and you screw around on her. Total fucking idiot."

The nose of the gun stuck into Mack's chest. He thought about the hot, sharp pain of taking a bullet to his heart. His heart would explode and bits and pieces of Maribel and Andrea would splatter everywhere. He *was* an idiot, thinking idiot thoughts.

"I could fire you," Mack said.

"I could fire *you*," Vance said. "No dating the guests, remember? Not only breaking the rules, but showing yourself to be the hypocrite I always knew you were."

"But you have a gun," Mack said.

"That's right," Vance said. "I have a gun. And so I have a choice. I can fire you or I can kill you. Or I can hope you act smart and go home and tell Maribel that you've been in another woman's bed tonight."

Mack's mouth was dry. "Why are you threatening me? We work together. We've worked together since the beginning. We're, I don't know, buddies. Aren't we?"

Vance laughed, a sharp bark. "You have no idea how much I hate you. You really have no idea. Unbelievable. You step off the boat thirty fucking seconds sooner than I do and all of a sudden you're the white prince and you assume everyone loves you. Maribel loves you, room eighteen loves you, Bill and Therese and all the guests whose asses you kiss love you. No such luck, buddy. You push me right to the edge, Petersen, to where I can see myself doing something like this. I can see myself taking you out and saying it was an accident, say-

ing I found the gun in a room and was fooling around and oops, it
went off. So they send me to Walpole for a year or two. So what? It
might be worth it, brother man."

"You're crazy," Mack whispered.

"Are you going to tell Maribel?" Vance asked. "That's all I'm really
concerned about in the here and now. Are you going to tell her?"

Mack nodded. "Yes."

"Okay," Vance said. He took the gun away from Mack's chest and
studied it. Mack exhaled and the muscles in his legs tingled. "This
baby is fully loaded, ready to go. But if you tell a soul, I'm just going to
say I was playing a joke on you."

"For Christ's sake, Vance."

"Hey," Vance said, pointing the gun in Mack's face. "I'm serious
about Maribel. Either you tell her what's going on with you and room
eighteen or I'll tell her what I saw. Which was you lying on that
woman's bed, and the woman half-naked and you grabbing at her."

"I wasn't *grabbing* at her," Mack said.

"Tell Maribel," Vance said. He lowered the gun. "I *would* shoot
you if I thought I could get away with it."

"Why do you hate me?" Mack asked. "I apologized for taking your
job back when it happened. It had nothing to do with our skin color
and you know it. Besides, Vance, that was another lifetime ago." Mack
reached behind him for the doorknob to the lobby. He wanted to be in
the warm, bright lobby with Tiny, although for all Mack knew she
could be hiding around a corner waiting to club him with a tire iron.

Vance spat at the ground near Mack's feet. "Get out of here," he
said.

BY THE TIME MACK pulled into the driveway, Maribel had finished drying the dishes and putting them away. She had changed out of her
white shorts and soft beige half sweater and into a T-shirt and boxers.
She had washed her face and her neck with Noxema. By the time
Mack walked in the door at midnight—which was late even for a Lacey

Gardner night—Maribel was pretty sure she had eliminated all clues that Jem Crandall had been there for dinner.

Or *sinner*, which was what she started calling it as soon as they arranged the time and the place. Her sinner with Jem. A small, intimate sinner party.

Having Jem over had been the result of two things. The first was that Maribel kept thinking back to the day she spent with Jem at the beach. It felt like they were somehow *meant* to have run into each other in the parking lot of Stop & Shop. And Maribel instinctively took Jem to the nude beach in Miacomet. Why? They could just as easily have gone to Cisco. But Maribel had *wanted* to show herself to Jem. And show herself she did—all look and no touch—but the looks Maribel was unable to forget.

Secondly was the fact that, in the past week or so, Mack had pulled out his old Iowa church-social manners. He constantly asked how she was feeling, was she okay? Then at Le Languedoc, he balked when she asked about the profit sharing. Mack had no intention of asking Bill to profit-share, and no intention of marrying her, and this kindness was just a front, just a way of letting her down easy. More than anything, Mack hated when things actually *happened*—moments like the one when the sheriff told him his parents had been killed. And so he wouldn't ask Bill to profit-share but he wouldn't tell Maribel that. He would just keep on saying please and thank you and I don't know, sweetheart, I just don't know—forever.

The combination of these two things led Maribel to call Jem and invite him over.

"For Sunday," she said. She was in her quiet, safe, book-lined office at the Atheneum, with the door locked. "Dinner at my house. Seven-thirty?"

"Sunday?" Jem said. A twinge of uncertainty in his voice. "Sunday, you mean, while Mack's at Lacey's?"

"That's right," Maribel said.

Dead air. Maribel heard the soft murmur of library patrons' voices on the other side of her door.

"You're putting me in a bad place," Jem said. "You're asking me to lie to my boss."

"I'm asking you to dinner," Maribel said. "Mack won't be there. I won't tell him you're coming over unless you want me to. But really, Jem, it's no big deal. I frequently have people over, friends, you know. They . . . drop by."

"Yeah, well, this is more than me dropping by," Jem said. "This is you calling in advance. And the way my luck has been going, you'll tell Mack and I'll end up fired."

"I'll take that as a no, then," Maribel said. "Maybe another time."

"No," Jem said. "Not another time. Sunday's fine. I'll be there Sunday."

Maribel's hands were sweating; she rubbed her palm on the receiver and it made a squeaking noise. "Sunday," she said, "seven-thirty. For sinner, I mean, dinner. Dinner at seven-thirty. Do you know where I live?" It felt strange to say "I" instead of "we." "I live at ninety-five Pheasant Road, the basement apartment around back."

"I'll find it," Jem said.

WHEN MACK CAME HOME at five on Sunday evening before going to Lacey's, Maribel nearly confessed to her dinner plans. Mack was in the apartment for about an hour, and Maribel shadowed him from room to room. First, she lay next to him in bed while he napped. Mack was the kind of person who could fall asleep at will, like he was letting go the string of a kite, and this always amazed Maribel. Really, did he have no nagging thoughts? Was his mind such an easy friend that it just set him free? Apparently so. Maribel lay next to him, studying his sandy hair, his sunburned face and sun-cracked lips, her own eyes wide open, unblinking. Thinking, *I'll tell him when he wakes up. I'll tell him I'm being a good Samaritan, feeding a hungry kid. If he makes the slightest fuss, I'll call Jem and cancel.*

When Mack was in the shower, Maribel sat on the fuzzy toilet seat cover in the steam and thought, *I'll tell him when he gets out.* Mack turned off the water, pulled back the shower curtain and Maribel handed him a towel. He dried his face, and scruffed the towel over his head, he dried his chest, his arms, his balls, and stepped onto the bathmat, wrapped the towel around his waist. Mack never concerned himself with how he looked. He was perfectly comfortable in his own body, as though he knew he could drive Maribel absolutely mad by just existing.

Before he left the house, Mack popped open a beer, took a long swallow, kissed Maribel, and said, "Don't wait up tonight, I might be late," and he jogged out the door to his Jeep. It was obvious he trusted her implicitly. Maribel felt guilty for a second, but then she wondered if he were suffering from plain indifference. He hadn't asked what she was doing at all.

As soon as the rumble of the Jeep's engine faded, Maribel called her mother. Sundays her mother slept late, puttered in her tiny vegetable garden, and then sat on the screened-in porch with her friend Rita Ramone and drank vodka gimlets. Maribel knew Rita would be languishing on the chaise longue next to her mother, listening to every word, but Maribel called anyway.

"My little girl!" Tina cried out. "What a surprise! Do you have news for your mama?"

Maribel guessed Tina was on her third or fourth gimlet. "No," she said.

"Mack's off at Lacey's?" Tina asked. "Are you lonely, sweetie pie?"

"Not really," Maribel said. "I'm having someone for dinner."

"Well, I hope they taste good!" Tina said. She laughed with abandon and Maribel could hear Rita in the background asking, "What's so funny?"

"It's a guy I'm having over," Maribel said. "A cute guy."

Tina was still laughing. "How cute?"

"He was Mr. November in some calendar," Maribel said.

"Not the Christian calendar," Tina said. "Although a cute guy or two might boost sales."

"Mack doesn't know a thing about it, either," Maribel said.

Tina's voice sobered. "Oh, my." The phone was muffled: Tina relayed this news to Rita Ramone. Then she said, "Rita thinks the only way to get a man is to play hard to get. Is that what you're doing, sweetie? Playing hard to get?"

"I don't know what I'm doing," Maribel said.

"Well, that makes three of us," Tina said. "Here, now I'm going into the house so we can talk serious." In the background, a door closed. "Okay, tell me what you're thinking."

"I'm thinking Mack is a lost cause," Maribel said.

"You've thought that many times before," Tina said. "Is this time any different?"

"I suggested the profit sharing, but he hasn't said anything to Bill."

"Maybe he's waiting for the right time," Tina said.

"Maybe," Maribel said. "Or maybe he thinks it's okay to string me along forever. But it's not okay. There are other men in this world who find me attractive, and I just happened to invite one of them to dinner on a night when Mack's out. That's not a crime, is it?"

"You know I'm terrible at figuring out men," Tina said. "I wouldn't exactly call myself Queen of the Successful Relationship."

"Mama," Maribel said. Her mother's Sunday afternoons with Rita Ramone were half girl talk and half wallowing in self-pity. "Do you think it's okay that I invited this person for dinner?"

"Yes," Tina said definitively. "What's his name?"

"Jem," Love said. "Jem Crandall."

"Jem Crandall," Tina said. "God has blessed Jem Crandall. You know I love you?"

"Yes," Maribel said.

"Have fun and we'll talk on Wednesday. I have to get back to Rita before she burns the house down."

"Okay, Mama."

"Godspeed, Maribel."

AT EXACTLY SEVEN-THIRTY, JEM appeared at the door with a bottle of Chardonnay, looking as nervous as Maribel felt. His dark hair was wet and he was wearing a blue chambray shirt and navy shorts. Birkenstocks. He was so handsome. He was tall and broad-shouldered and strong and young and he had wavy dark hair and that beautiful smile and not an ounce of self-congratulation. It was perfectly normal to be attracted to people other than your partner, Maribel reasoned. She was indulging a crush. Flushing it out of her system.

"You brought wine," Maribel said, taking the bottle from Jem carefully, as though it were a baby. "That was very thoughtful."

"I know about wine," Jem said. "My father owns a bar." He put his hand on Maribel's arm and bent over and kissed her. The kiss was brief; Maribel was still holding the wine to her chest, but it threw the whole room into disarray.

"Oh," she said. They looked at each other. Jem had blue eyes that matched his shirt. He was ridiculously, absurdly handsome, and Maribel looked into his blue eyes until it was like too much chocolate cake, and she knew looking another second wouldn't be good for her. She shifted her gaze.

"I can give you the nickel tour of the place from right here," she said. "Kitchen, dining room, living room. The powder room is this door here and then the bedroom." Maribel paused after the word "bedroom."

"It's nice," Jem said. "I rent a room in some old house. I'd kill for my own kitchen."

"I made some munchies," Maribel said. "Let's sit down."

"Okay," Jem said. He bounced on the balls of his feet and rubbed his hands together. "Want to open the wine? I could use a drink. I have to tell you, I'm a little nervous."

"Nervous?" Maribel said. "About what?"

"Not about what you think," Jem said.

"What do I think?"

"I'm not worried that Mack is going to come home and find me here."

"Good," Maribel said. She knew Mack wouldn't show up before ten-thirty or eleven, even though right now a part of her wanted him to.

"I'm nervous just being around you," Jem said. "I want everything to go right. That day at the beach . . ."

"The day at the beach was lovely," Maribel said. She took the mushroom caps stuffed with Boursin cheese out of the oven and moved them onto a platter with a spatula.

"It was better than lovely," Jem said. "It changed my whole view of the island. Before that day, I hated it here. But after that day, things got a lot better. It was weird, the way that happened, like you have magic powers."

Maribel took the shrimp cocktail out of the fridge. "I wish," she said. She almost added, *If I did, I'd start by using them on Mack.* She handed the shrimp to Jem. "You can take these to the coffee table. We'll sit on the sofa."

They arranged the food on the coffee table and Jem poured the wine. Maribel lifted her glass.

"Cheers," she said. "Here's to being nervous."

They sipped their wine. "Really nervous," Jem said.

"Eat something," Maribel said. "You'll feel better."

Jem picked up a peachy pink shrimp and dragged it through the cocktail sauce. Maribel watched the muscles in his jaw working as he chewed.

"Delicious," he said. He sampled a few mushrooms.

"How old are you?" Maribel asked.

"Twenty-three," he said. "I'm basically still a work in progress."

"There's no better place to be a work in progress than Nantucket."

"I guess," Jem said, "but I feel like I'm just biding my time here. I feel like this is a resting point for me before my real life begins."

"Your real life?"

"California," Jem said. "I can't be your beach agent forever, you know." He drained his glass of wine and fell back into the cushions of the sofa. "I'm leaving for the West Coast in the fall. You should come with me." He picked up Maribel's hand and kissed her palm.

Maribel closed her eyes, thinking, *How refreshing, a man who's not afraid to admit he's nervous, not afraid of being a work in progress, not afraid to commit.*

"Thanks for the offer," she said.

"I'm serious," he said. "I want you to come with me."

Maribel gently reclaimed her hand. "I hardly even know you, Jem."

"We can fix that," he said. "I'll tell you everything. My father owns a bar, my mother stays at home, and my sister is a whacko with an eating disorder. I graduated from college with a three-point-one GPA, and I was Theta Chi. I played lacrosse in high school. I love going to the movies. And you know who you remind me of? Meg Ryan. I thought that the first time I saw you."

"Thanks," Maribel said. "I guess."

"When I was six years old, my parents belonged to a swim club. One day my sister and I were sitting on the edge of the pool while my parents did laps and when they were both at the other end of the pool, I pushed my sister in. She was only three or four at the time, and she sank to the bottom like a lead weight."

"Oh, God," Maribel said.

"A lifeguard noticed Gwennie and he saved her. Nobody ever knew I pushed her, they thought she fell. And Gwennie was too young to understand. Except when she went to therapy for her bulimia, she told the shrink I pushed her."

"But they don't think that caused her bulimia?" Maribel asked.

"It made me feel pretty bad anyway," he said. "But relieved, too, you know, because for a lot of years I was the only one who knew I almost drowned my sister. The worst thing I've ever done, by far. So now you know that about me. What's the worst thing you've ever done?"

Maribel frowned. She thought about getting drunk in high school, a white mouse she bought at a pet store and took to a slumber party to put in Ursula Cavanaugh's sleeping bag, cohabiting with Mack. This, her sinner with Jem.

"I guess the worst thing I've done isn't something I've done, it's something I've felt." She thought of Tina, who would be sacked out in front of *The X Files* by now. "There are times when I'm ashamed of my mother."

"Oh," Jem said. "Uh-oh."

"My mother was never married. She was a hippie, I guess, and she had sex with some guy she didn't know and never saw again and I was born."

"Wow," Jem said. His eyebrows shot up. "And she never remarried or anything?"

"She dated some, when I was younger, but there was no one serious and then she lost interest and gave up." Maribel sipped her wine. "She works in a calendar factory. A *Christian* calendar factory."

"Does she like it?" Jem asked.

"Yeah," Maribel said, "she does. She's in charge there. But it's not exactly the life she dreamed up for herself and it's not any kind of life I would want. She lives her life through me, she has all these hopes for me."

"That's nothing to be ashamed of," Jem said.

"I just wish she wanted something for herself," Maribel said. "But she doesn't. And that makes me angry, and even embarrassed. I feel like such a bad daughter, but I can't help it. Every once in a while, I think, *This woman cannot be my mother.*"

"I feel that way about my sister sometimes," Jem said. "My parents say my sister is giving us all lessons in love and acceptance."

"I need some of those lessons," Maribel said.

"We all do," Jem said. He kissed her hand again.

DINNER WAS GRILLED SALMON, cold herbed potato salad, some greens dressed with balsamic vinegar. They finished the bottle of wine and Maribel pulled out chocolate mousse, and one of Mack's beers for Jem. He was telling her stories about the Beach Club. For years, Maribel had been hearing stories about the Beach Club and never once had she enjoyed them. Mack took his job at the hotel so seriously that Maribel hadn't realized what a funny place it could be.

"There's one guest, Mr. Feeney," Jem said, "and he's staying at the hotel for a week. Every day Mr. Feeney calls the front desk to complain about his toilet."

Maribel giggled. "His toilet?"

Jem took a swallow of beer. "His toilet." He burped. "Excuse me. So anyway, Mr. Feeney calls up every day. The tank's not filling quickly enough, it's making noises that keep him and the missus up at night, every day something different. So each morning I check it out, jiggle the handle, not knowing what I'm doing, but Mr. Feeney doesn't realize that. He's crowding into the bathroom with me, just so damn pleased that someone is taking his toilet problems seriously. And I want to say to him, 'Mr. Feeney, you might enjoy your vacation more if you stopped worrying about your toilet and started sitting with your wife on the beach, dabble your feet into the ocean, enjoy the salt air.' But around the fourth day or so, I realize something very profound. You know what that is?"

"What?" Maribel said.

"Some people don't like being happy. They're much more comfortable when they have a problem. And such is the case with Mr. Feeney. The guy is on vacation with his wife, in a world-class hotel, but that's not good enough. He *likes* worrying about his toilet. It gives him pleasure. It's like a hobby for him."

"Mr. Feeney and his toilet hobby," Maribel said.

"Exactly. And I'm Mr. Feeney's toilet agent, as you might have guessed. So then, the last day of this guy's stay, he calls me. And I say, 'What's wrong with your toilet today, Mr. Feeney?' And he says, 'Well, Jem, it won't flush.' So I check it out and it's true—it won't flush. We jiggle the handle, we toy around with the floater, nothing. The toilet won't flush, it won't gurgle, nothing. I ask him, has he done anything special, anything out of the ordinary? He says no, and I can tell he's enjoying every second of this because now his toilet really is broken."

"So what do you do?" Maribel asked.

"Mack shows up and we try the plunger and it's clear something is clogging the john, something big, but the plunger isn't helping. So we lift the john right off the floor. Take it outside where we can maneuver it better and look inside and what do you think we find?"

"I don't know," Maribel said.

Jem motioned for Maribel to lean in close to him. She put her elbows on her knees and held her face in her hands and Jem did the same. Their noses were practically touching and Maribel could smell his tangy breath.

"What did you find?" she whispered.

"Cantaloupe rinds," he said. He scooted forward an inch and kissed Maribel once, very lightly. "We found cantaloupe rinds." He kissed Maribel again, he parted her lips and tasted her. He tasted her like a boy who had been living all summer without a kitchen, he tasted her like someone who wasn't just hungry but starving. Maribel thought, *This feels good, I feel good, I feel delicious. This boy is young, unfinished, he is so handsome and sweet.* She thought, *What would I do if Mack walked in right now, how would I explain this, Good Samaritan?* She thought, *Wasn't this what I was hoping for when I called him? But it's innocent, just kissing, a crush.* She thought, *How cantaloupe rinds? Why cantaloupe rinds?* She thought, *Is this the worst thing I've ever done or just the beginning of the worst thing?*

Finally, Jem separated from her and his eyes scanned the clock on the wall behind her. "I should go," he said. "I don't want to, but I should."

Maribel walked him to the door. She turned on the outside light and moths beat themselves against the screen.

"What does this mean?" Jem asked. "The whole time I was kissing you I was wondering what this could mean."

"I don't know," Maribel said, and at that moment she felt like Mack. Mack and his infuriating "I don't knows." But it was true; she didn't know what the kissing meant.

"Is this an affair?" he asked. He laughed sarcastically. "God, I'm having an affair with my boss's girlfriend. This is just great."

"Jem," Maribel said, "it isn't an affair. We just kissed. That's all we're talking about."

"We kissed," Jem said. "And I'd like to kiss you again sometime. In fact, I'd like to do more than kiss you. How about that?"

"Jem," Maribel said, "let's wait and see, okay? Let's play things by ear."

"I hope to God you're not a tease," Jem said. "I hope to God you didn't invite me for dinner and tell me all that stuff about your mother and kiss me for so long only to get Mack's goat. I hope you're not catching me up in the middle of something, Maribel. Because that would hurt my feelings. I do have feelings about you, you know."

Maribel nodded.

"Thanks for dinner," he said huskily. He opened the screen door and stepped out; his blue eyes and blue shirt disappeared into the dark night.

Maribel's lips felt stretched and blurred. "You're welcome," she said.

MARIBEL COVERED HER TRACKS in every way she could think of, but when Mack walked in the door of the apartment, he looked confused and uncomfortable. *He knows,* Maribel thought. She was curled up on the sofa, but when Mack came in, she sat up.

"What's wrong?" she said.

Mack sat next to Maribel and bent his head, ran his hands through his hair.

"Mari," he said.

"What is it?" She put her arms around his shoulders and kissed his cheek. "What's wrong?"

"I have to tell you something and I don't want you to get upset. Just hear me out."

"What is it?" she said.

"I mean it. I want you to let me say what I have to say."

"Okay," Maribel said. "I'll listen. You tell me."

Mack cleared his throat. "After Lacey's tonight I stopped by one of the rooms to see Andrea Krane. You remember Andrea? And her son James?"

"I remember Andrea," Maribel said. Andrea was a pretty older woman, and James, in the few times Maribel saw him, had tugged at her heart. A young boy with autism, whose whole life was a foggy day.

Mack said, "Well, I went to see Andrea and things happened."

"What kind of things?" Maribel asked. She thought of James flapping his arms and shrieking, she thought about his incessant rocking.

"I kissed her," Mack said. "I was in her room sitting on her bed and I kissed her."

Maribel was befuddled; this was some strange, cruel reversal. Was Mack telling her *he* kissed someone else? The back of her throat soured. He kissed Andrea, James's mother? Thoughts of Jem were suddenly crowded out of the room; Maribel's secret guilt and pleasure about Jem were spirited away, gone, replaced by horror, shock. Tears sprang to Maribel's eyes. *I'm a hypocrite,* she thought. *Mack did nothing worse than what I did tonight.* Nothing worse except to speak the truth out loud and that did make it seem a hundred times worse.

Mack stood up and came back with a box of Kleenex. He wiped at Maribel's face. "I'm sorry, Mari. I've known her a long time, longer than I've even known you. There's always been something between us. But this year, I don't know why, that something just got bigger. I think I love her."

"Love her?" Maribel repeated. She gathered her breath to speak, to match his brutal blow, but when she tried to find the words to tell him about Jem, she gagged. Maribel didn't love Jem. This wasn't a fair trade at all. *Oh, God,* she thought, *what is he doing to me?* Love *Andrea?* A guest? Six years later and it wasn't the farm or his job or Cecily at all, it was *Andrea Krane?* Maribel thought of Tina, and how this news would break her heart. It was over, a relationship over, just the way Mack had lost his parents. Boom. Over.

"You have to leave," Maribel said. "You have to move out, down to the hotel. I don't want you here."

"No," Mack said. "No, wait please, Mari. Maribel, hold on. I know you're upset. But please don't throw me out. I have to try and explain."

"You love Andrea," Maribel said. "What else is there to explain?"

"It's this summer, something is happening. The world wants me to grow up. You want me to grow up. And I don't want to grow up. I feel so childish. I love Andrea, but I love you, too, Maribel. You know I do. Andrea is vulnerable, and her life is difficult, much more difficult than you or I could ever imagine. I feel for that, Maribel. I feel for that and for the fact that she doesn't give up. I love her for that."

"Her life is difficult?" Maribel said. "*My* life is difficult! My life is very, very difficult. Have you forgotten that? Have you forgotten what I've gone through to get here, Mack?"

"That's different, Maribel. I'm not taking anything away from you. But you're not dealing with what Andrea is dealing with."

"Go to her then," Maribel said. Thinking, hatefully, *Go to her and her fucked-up son.* "Get out of here."

"But I love you, too," Mack said.

"Tough shit," Maribel said.

"I don't want to leave," Mack said.

"What *do* you want?" Maribel asked. "Do you have any idea? Do you want to sell the farm? Do you want to manage that blasted hotel your whole life? You don't know. Do you want to get married and have kids? You don't know. You don't know anything except that you love us both. You want me here at home and Andrea down at the hotel. I'm sorry, Mack. I am so, so sorry." Maribel was hysterical now, her breathing ragged, her tears hot and salty; her eyes stung. She plucked a Kleenex and tried to blow her nose but she was blocked up, stuck. She thought of the broken toilet. Her life was a toilet.

"I'm going to do something for you," Mack said.

"The only thing you can do for me is to get out of here," Maribel said. Her voice was small and nasal.

"I'm going to ask Bill to profit-share. I'm going to ask him right after the Fourth. I swear it, Maribel."

Maribel tried to snort, but her nose was stuffed up. Her snort sounded like a bleat. "Ha! Why now, Mack? So you can give James and Andrea a good life? So you can show them how important you are? Go ahead and ask Bill for the profits. I hope he turns you down. I hope he fires you and you leave this island."

"But I'm doing it for you, Maribel," Mack said. "I'm doing it because you want me to."

"I want you to *marry me*!" Maribel screamed. She couldn't believe how angry, how upset she was. Never in her life would she have predicted the relationship would crumble like this, so suddenly, in one night. "I want you to marry me! I thought the problem was with *you*. I thought you were just not *grown* yet, I thought you still had issues with your parents, the farm. And I thought if you asked Bill to profit-share you'd feel better about yourself, you'd feel established, you'd feel *ready*. What I didn't realize is that the problem isn't with you, Mack, it's with *me*. I'm not the woman you want."

"You are the woman I want," Mack said.

"Then *ask me to marry you*," Maribel said.

Mack reached for her again and she surrendered. She buried her face in his chest and cried even harder. His shirt, his smell, her Mack, she loved him so much. He was all she wanted, all she needed to fill the empty space where her father should have been. But she waited five minutes, ten minutes, and he said nothing. He was shushing into her hair, but he wasn't asking her to marry him. Suddenly her head was heavy, a sandbag, her mouth was dry and scratchy from the wine and the tears.

"You have to go," Maribel said. Unsteadily, she stood and pointed in the direction of the door. "I'm sorry."

"Mari, you don't mean that."

"I do," she said. She walked into the bedroom and fell onto the bed. Her eyes closed the second she heard Mack's Jeep pull away.

MACK SPENT THE REST of the night in the Jeep in the Beach Club parking lot. He considered sneaking into Lacey Gardner's cottage and crashing on her couch, but he didn't want to frighten her. And so, Mack wrapped himself in his Polar Fleece, put the seat back as far as it would go, and closed his eyes.

He woke to the sound of talking. He sat up and looked around—it was still dark. He didn't see anyone near the lobby or on the beach. Mack climbed out of the Jeep, quietly, and he made out the figure of Cecily sitting on the front step of her parents' house, talking on the portable phone. Mack checked his watch; it was three-thirty.

"I love you," she was saying. "I can't stand it here without you. I'm dying of love for you."

Please, Cecily, Mack thought. *Do not fall in love.* But from the sounds of it, it was too late. He climbed back into his car.

"I love you, Gabriel." Cecily's voice was sweet, pleading. "Can you hear me? I love you."

What seemed like only minutes later, Mack heard the sound of tapping on the window of the Jeep. He opened his eyes. It was Andrea and James. The sun was up. Mack checked his watch; it was six o'clock. He opened the door.

"Why do I get the feeling you're not here to go with us to the airport?" Andrea said.

"Is Mack coming to the airport?" James asked. "Are we shaving today, Mack?"

"How're you doing, buddy?" Mack asked. He looked at Andrea. "I told Maribel."

"Told her what?" Andrea asked. Her green-gray eyes widened. "About us? Why? Oh, Mack, what did you say?" She turned to James. "Get in the car, James. Mom will be there in five minutes."

"It's six-oh-three, Mom. We're late already."

"Five minutes," Andrea said.

"Five minutes." James tapped the face of his watch. "Mom will be there at six-oh-eight."

Andrea waited until James climbed into the Explorer, then she said, "What happened?"

"I had to tell her," Mack said. He thought of Vance, pointing the gun at him like it was some kind of toy. But when he got right down to it, Mack hadn't told Maribel because of Vance; he told her because it was time. He told her because he couldn't stand lying anymore. Vance was just a manifestation of Mack's own conscience, like something out of fucking Shakespeare. "I told her I loved you."

"No," Andrea said. She put her hand over her heart. "She must be devastated. The poor girl. Ouch."

"What about me?" Mack said. "She threw me out. I spent the

night here in the parking lot." His mouth felt as if it were lined with flannel, he stank with the four scotches he'd had at Lacey's, his head ached and his legs would cramp up as soon as he stepped out of the Jeep. He needed five more hours' sleep, a hot shower, some clean clothes.

"You're a man, Mack," Andrea said. "Men will always survive."

Mack touched Andrea's hair. "You might see me surviving this winter in Baltimore."

"Mack," Andrea said, shaking her head sadly.

"What?" Mack said. "I could help you with James. I could give you the help you need."

"Go home and take it all back," she said.

"You don't want me in Baltimore?"

"Just go home," she said. "I'm not coming between you and Maribel. She's much better for you than I am."

"But I love you," Mack said. "That's how I ended up here. I love you."

"Maybe," Andrea said. "Or maybe you feel sorry for me. The point is, you should be with Maribel. I'm just a friend, Mack, a summer friend. You have no idea what my life is like the rest of the year. You have no idea what happens once I return to America."

"I know I don't. What I'm saying is, I want to find out."

"I should stop coming here. I've depended on you too much, and I made you feel like you can help me. But you can't help me, Mack. Nobody can help me. James is my lot in life—he's my blessing, he's my albatross." She tried to smile. "Anyway, I hear the Vineyard is nice too. Maybe next year we'll go there."

"No," Mack said. This was too much: to lose them both in one night. "No way."

Andrea picked up Mack's wrist and checked his watch. "My five minutes is up," she said. "Go home." He listened to her footsteps crunch across the shells and the loose gravel. He heard the soft dinging of her open car door and James saying, "You're one minute late, Mom." Then Andrea started the car and drove away, but he didn't turn to watch her go.

Mack sat back in his seat and looked at the water. Maybe he should just drive into the sound. Then he heard a voice, a low thrumming voice. *Home.* He bowed his head. *Home.*

"I can't believe this," Mack said. He closed his eyes.

5

Independence Day

July 2

Dear Bill,

The answer to your question is yes, I am a parent. You do not need to know how many children I have, or if they are sons or daughters—it isn't relevant and it's too painful for me to discuss anyway, even in a letter. I know your daughter is quite young—seventeen? eighteen?—and I know she lives away from you a good part of the year. I wonder, Bill, if you have any idea what goes on in your daughter's heart and mind. Does she want what you want? Does she see herself continuing with the family business? Does she love the hotel the way you do, Bill? Have you ever asked her? Maybe before you turn my offer down, you should.

Sincerely,

S. B .T.

CECILY'S JOB THIS SUMMER was to watch the beach, keeping her eyes peeled for people who blatantly ignored the signs saying Nantucket Beach Club: Private Property. After four years at Middlesex—tens of thousands of dollars spent on her education—this was the job her parents gave her. Lookout. Policewoman. Head scout of the Nantucket Beach Club patrol.

Cecily sat on the steps of the pavilion with a clipboard and a computer generated list of the Beach Club members. If she saw people on the beach she didn't recognize, she had to ask their names. If their name appeared on the list, she smiled and repeated their name, "Why *hello*, Mrs. Papale!" as though she had recognized them all along. That was what a club was about: Being recognized, belonging.

If their names didn't appear on the list, she had to ask them, politely, to leave. Cecily's father was too chicken to do this job himself, although he claimed he wasn't afraid, but rather, too busy, doing financial things and reading from his volume of Robert Frost.

On one very hot and crowded day just before *the* major holiday of summer, Cecily encountered her first squatters. She was sitting with her legs stretched out in the sun when an unlikely couple wandered in from the right. What made them "unlikely" was exactly the thing that Cecily hated about her job: they looked poor. The price to sit on a swatch of her father's beach under one of the umbrellas her mother ordered from the south of France was five thousand dollars for the summer. It was too much money for almost anybody to afford—and definitely too much money for the couple spreading their towels (short white towels, the kind one might find in a Holiday Inn) under a royal blue umbrella.

The couple looked like Jack Sprat and wife. The man was skinny and pale, wearing a black T-shirt and cut-off jeans, and the woman wore an enormous turquoise muumuu. The woman carried a red Playmate cooler, which she plunked down at the foot of the towels.

Cecily heard a clicking noise behind her. She turned to see her father tapping with his pen on the window of his office. He pointed at the couple.

Reluctantly, Cecily stood up. She trudged through the hot sand, savoring the torturous burning on the soles of her feet. The man turned his head from left to right, checking, literally, to see if the coast were clear. The woman plucked a green bottle out of the cooler: a Heineken. The beer of choice at Middlesex. The man offered the woman a penknife from the front pocket of his jeans shorts and the woman flipped the top off the bottle and let it land in the sand.

"Excuse me," Cecily said. The man's head whipped around. He hadn't thought to look behind him. "I just need to check your name off our list."

The man stood up. The front of his T-shirt had a mandala on it. He had long dirty blonde hair and a mustache. He touched his mustache when Cecily spoke.

"The name's Cadillac," he said. "Joe Cadillac."

Joe Cadillac. It was a good try: maybe he thought it made him sound rich. Cecily checked her list. She could feel her father's eyes boring into her back. The burning of her feet became unbearable and she moved to stand in the shade of the royal blue umbrella.

"Cadillac, hmmmm. Like the car, Cadillac?"

The man cleared his throat. "That's right."

"I don't see it here," Cecily said. She didn't meet the man's eyes.

"Are you sure you're spelling it right?" he asked. "Cadillac, with a 'C?' With two 'C's?' "

"Yes," Cecily said, "I'm sure."

The man shoved his threadbare towel under one arm. "Okay," he said, "we'll go then."

The woman let out a long, shrill laugh, like a hand trickling down piano keys. "Heavens, *Joe*," she said. She had curly blond hair and wore red lipstick. "Would you please let us stay, sweetie?" she asked. "Just for today? I'm afraid in this sun I'll positively fry up." The woman had a stripe of bad sunburn already—across the tops of her round cheeks and the bridge of her nose.

"I can't let you stay," Cecily said. She felt horrible; she felt like a child or an angry neighbor saying "Get off of my property!"

The woman held out the beer. "Would you like a swig?" she asked. "It's ice cold."

Cecily eyed the sweating bottle. How she wanted to take it, and force her father to watch her making her own choices.

"Debra, let's go," the man said.

The woman beamed at Cecily. Mrs. Sprat, Mrs. Cadillac. Cecily tore her eyes away. She looked, instead, at Nantucket Sound, lapping lightly onto her father's beach.

"I'm sorry," she said.

CECILY WAS ALSO MAÎTRE D' of the beach, the goodwill ambassador. She chatted with the Beach Club members, and made sure everyone was happy. Once she got to know the members by name and learn a little bit about them, the list would become unnecessary. Cecily hated chatting, she even hated the word *chatting*. She could never think of what to say that would sufficiently mask her real question. *Why are you spending your money this way? Haven't you heard of world hunger? Don't you have a conscience?* The Beach Club had existed since 1924. Back then, the club cost a quarter a day and was open to the public. Her father had sepia-tone pictures of men and women in old-fashioned bathing suits sitting under crazily striped and polka-dotted sunshades, drinking bottles of sarsaparilla. This was how Cecily preferred to think of it. She'd kept one of those pictures, framed, in her dorm room at school.

The number of people on the beach peaked on the Fourth of July, and this year, it was sunny and hot. On the south shore, Cecily knew there would be radios blaring, volleyball games, picnics, kegs, Frisbee, dogs. But here at the Beach Club, things were as much f un as a pile of wet bathing suits, as exciting as a handful of sand. Mr. Conroy, who had a glass eye and a pair of saggy old-man breasts, sported his star-spangled swim trunks. That was it in the way of excitement.

Cecily stood in her father's office. "Total hell," she said, looking out the window at the beach.

"Someday it's going to be yours," he said.

"What if I don't want it?" Cecily said.

"What's not to want?" Bill said. "Now get out there and show 'em who's boss."

"You're the boss," Cecily said. "*You* get out there."

Bill laughed, then his voice got serious. "Go," he said, "and don't forget to wish everyone a happy Fourth of July."

TO START HER ROUNDS, Cecily had to walk past Kevin and Bruce, the beach boys.

"Hey, sexy!" Bruce called out. Bruce was skinny with pimples and glasses, and he thought he was a hot shit because he was going to Yale in the fall.

Cecily gave him the finger. Kevin never said anything. He just sat next to Bruce and giggled. The beach boys were exactly that—boys. They set up the umbrellas in the morning and then plunked themselves in the sand like a couple of ugly frogs, and when a member needed help with chairs or towels, the boys reluctantly got to their feet. They had an even cushier job than her own.

Cecily walked by Mr. and Mrs. Spoonacre, Mr. and Mrs. Patterson, and stopped at the kelly green umbrella closest to the water where Major Crawley sat. Always the same spot closest to the water, always a kelly green umbrella, and always alone—because Mrs. Crawley was allergic to the beach. Major Crawley had retired from the army before Cecily was born, but he still looked like a major. He wore army green trunks, aviator sunglasses, and his gray-silver hair was clipped in a crew cut.

"Hello there, lady friend," the major said.

Cecily crouched in the sand next to the major's Sleepy Hollow chair. They had a short conversation every day. Cecily's father told her the major deserved extra attention. He'd been a Beach Club member for almost fifty years. "Hello, Major. Happy Fourth of July."

"Let me tell you a little something," the major said.

Major Crawley loved to tell Cecily stories about her grandfather. Sometimes, if Cecily was lucky, he would talk instead about his days on the last mounted cavalry in Germany, riding through the forest, looking for runaway Nazis.

"Your grandfather, Big Bill Elliott—and we all called him Big Bill— asked me for advice when he bought this Beach Club. You know what I told him?"

"Complimentary towels," Cecily said.

"That's right. Do you know why?"

"It's the small courtesies that make a place stand out," she said.

"Someday all this is going to be yours, and you're going to have to see that the place is run with integrity. I might not be around to prod you."

Cecily had heard the same speech dozens of times. She wanted to tell the major that she had no intention of running the Beach Club, because deeper, more exotic voices called her name. Other countries, other cultures. "Tell me about Germany again."

"Germany?" the major said. "My time in the hills, you mean? Riding Liebchen? That was a good horse. A mare. Mares don't frighten easily, and that's why we all rode mares. Because we were looking at some scary stuff there in the hills."

"Nazis," Cecily said. "The murderers."

"Had one of them Nazis hold a gun to my head," the major said. "Thought I was dead. Only eighteen years old. And do you know what I was thinking about, right at that second?"

"Mrs. Crawley?"

The major's aviator sunglasses slid to the end of his nose. "Hadn't met Mrs. Crawley yet. She came later."

"Your parents?"

"Nope." He poked at his sunglasses. "Thought about cigarettes and beer. Those were the two most important things in my life. All I wanted to do was smoke Luckies and drink Miller High-Life. And I thought how sad it was that all my smoking and drinking potential was about to fall facedown in the mud with a bullet shot through it."

"So then what happened?"

"The slimy German had the gun to my temple, pressed right into my brain and I could smell him. He stank like a pig. He had me on my knees and my eyes were level with his crotch and then I saw that the stinking bastard was wetting himself, he was so afraid. I knocked the gun out of his hand and that kid ran off. Someone in my company found him later and shot him dead." Major Crawley took off his sunglasses and lay back in his Sleepy Hollow chair. "I often wonder if maybe that weren't such a bad kid. Anyway, we killed him. Couldn't have mercy on someone who agreed to stand behind all that murdering of the Jews."

"There was a kid at my school who's a Nazi," Cecily said.

The major shook his head. "No, lady friend, not possible. We got them all." The major's words grew low and grumbly. "Today's the

Fourth of July and I'm happy to say you're in a safe place. No Nazis here." He nodded off to sleep in his chair. Cecily pulled his complimentary beach towel over his legs, so they wouldn't burn.

CECILY THREADED HER WAY between the umbrellas in the front row, past Mrs. Minella, the Papales, and the Hayeses, the only African American Beach Club members. She heard someone call to her.

"Miss! Miss!" A man under one of the canary yellow umbrellas gestured to her. Cecily walked slowly toward him and his wife, skimming her eyes over the list. These were new members this year—the Curtains? The Kershners? The man was balding but made up for it with a perfectly trimmed goatee. The woman had red hair like Cecily, only she had millions of freckles, whereas Cecily tanned.

Cecily smiled. "Hi, how can I help you?"

"We need you to settle an argument," the man said.

"Douglas!" the woman said. She folded her arms across the sheer top of her Chanel bathing suit.

Douglas and Mary Beth Kershner. Cecily found their names on the list.

"What you need to understand is that my wife is a *giving* person," Douglas Kershner said. "Charity woman *supreme.*"

"Douglas," Mrs. Kershner snapped.

"And under the guise of the Church, she has planted a garden for the poor, so that the less fortunate citizens of Groton, Connecticut, can enjoy fresh produce," Douglas Kershner said.

There were tiny wrinkles in the corners of Mrs. Kershner's mouth.

"I didn't know there were any poor people in Groton," Cecily said. She'd only been to Groton once, for a field hockey game.

"There are poor people everywhere," Mrs. Kershner said.

"But now, in Groton, Connecticut, the poor can enjoy arugula, raddichio, and tarragon," Mr. Kershner said. "Tarragon for the poor!" He raised his hands above his head in a gesture of mock political triumph, giving Cecily a view of his hairy armpits. "Have you ever heard of anything so absurd?"

"Douglas!" Mrs. Kershner said.

"Why don't you plant corn?" Cecily asked. "Or tomatoes?"

"Or potatoes," Mr. Kershner added. "Something of substance."

Mrs. Kershner sniffled. Behind her black cat's-eye sunglasses, she was crying.

"You don't respect me, Douglas," she said. "You ridicule everything I even attempt. And you drag in complete strangers to throw rocks at my spirit."

Cecily took a step back. She hadn't meant to throw rocks at anyone's spirit. Gardens for the poor was a good idea. She thought about tending a plot of land, harvesting tomatoes and corn and shiny green peppers. Putting the produce in a basket and distributing it around Nantucket's public housing development, to the single mothers who drove a taxi or worked at the Stop & Shop. She wondered what her father would think about this. Cecily drifted away from the Kershners, but she couldn't help herself from turning around to look at them one last time. Mrs. Kershner packed her things to leave the beach, while Mr. Kershner continued speaking, waving his arms at the water.

AT THE VERY EDGE of the property Cecily found Maribel asleep facedown with the straps of her bathing suit untied. Her blond hair was caught up in a messy bun and her back was brown and slick with oil. Cecily sat carefully next to Maribel's towel and looked to her left at all the umbrellas neatly lined up in rows and columns. It was like an obstacle course she had to complete in order to get to this safe place, this good place, next to Maribel. With Maribel, Cecily could be herself; with Maribel, Cecily could talk about love.

Cecily had been in love for almost a year with Gabriel da Silva, a Brazilian who lived in the dorm across the quad from Cecily at school. Gabriel was a year older than the other boys, and taller, more muscular, more sophisticated. He spoke three languages—English, Spanish, and the beautiful Carioca Portuguese—and unlike the other boys, Gabriel had a soul. He told Cecily about the favelas in Rio, where children starved. Gabriel had adopted a family in the favelas—a mother and three sons. He gave them money and he watched the little boys while the mother, Magrite, sold coconut ice cream at a stand on Copacabana Beach. Gabriel would like the idea of a garden for the poor. Cecily pictured Gabriel without a shirt, standing under the brilliant Brazilian sun, his dark skin tanning to the color of tree bark, as he shoveled the rich, black earth—*a garden in the* favelas.

Thinking about Gabriel made Cecily impatient. She traced her pinky finger down Maribel's spine. If Cecily weren't in love with Gabriel, she would probably be in love with Maribel.

Maribel woke with a shiver and lifted her head. Her cheek was dusted with sand.

"Geez, Cecily," Maribel said. "You scared me."

"Sorry, lady friend," Cecily said. "I'm surprised to see you here. Have you talked to Mack?"

"I don't want to talk to Mack."

"You do so," Cecily said. "Otherwise you'd be at the beach somewhere else."

"It's the Fourth," Maribel said. "The other beaches are too crowded."

"Do you miss him?" Cecily asked.

"Of course I miss him," Maribel said.

"I miss Gabriel," Cecily said. They had made love exactly ten times the week before school let out, (discovered once, by the school's cleaning lady). By the time Cecily's parents showed up for graduation, the insides of her thighs were rubbed raw.

"It's not the same thing," Maribel said. "You and Gabriel are still together."

"I know," Cecily said. Cecily didn't know what was going on between Mack and Maribel. Some stupid, fucked-up *thing* that made them both miserable. "I have something to tell you."

"Tell me Andrea Krane has checked out," Maribel said. "Tell me she's *gone home*."

"Next week," Cecily said. "But don't worry, Mack is sleeping at Lacey's."

Maribel hid her face in her hands. "I don't even want to think about where Mack's sleeping. It makes me sick."

"What I have to tell you is . . ." Cecily waited until she had Maribel's full attention, or as much of her full attention as she could hope to get with Mack lurking around. "What I have to tell you is that I'm not going to college in September."

Maribel groaned. "Yes, you are, Cecily."

"No," Cecily said. "I'm not. I'm deferring a year. I've already signed the form saying I'm deferring. I'm eighteen, I can do that."

"And next you're going to tell me that you're flying to Brazil."

"And Argentina, and Ecuador and Venezuela. I'm traveling with Gabriel."

Maribel regathered her bun so that it stuck off the top of her head like a knob. "Everyone's lost their mind," she said. "Have you told your parents this?"

"No," Cecily said. "But I've been saving my money. It's ridiculous how much I make doing this stupid job." She knew she had to tell her parents soon, although she indulged a fantasy of boarding the plane for Charlottesville and simply continuing south, without telling them at all. If she called regularly, her parents might never know the difference. "They'll probably disown me. But that would be good for you. The club could go to Mack."

"What do I care now?" Maribel said. "It's over with Mack, I told you."

"You'll get back together," Cecily said. Then she heard someone calling her name.

"Miss Elliott." The voice was low and rich. "Excuse me, Miss Elliott."

Mrs. John Higgens stood on the pavilion with her cane out in front of her. She was wearing a blue one-piece bathing suit with a tissue tucked into her bosom. Cecily stood up, wiped off her hands, and jogged over.

"Can I help you, Mrs. Higgens?" Cecily asked. Sometimes older women needed an arm to hold on to in order to make it through the sand.

"Yes, my dear, I hope so." Mrs. Higgens was another person, like Major Crawley, who had belonged to the Beach Club for a hundred million years. "I certainly hope so. Stand with me here if you will and look at the beach. Do you see what's wrong?"

The edges of the umbrellas fluttered in the wind. Mr. Conroy, in his patriotic trunks, inched his way toward the water.

"No, Mrs. Higgens, I don't." It could be anything: children throwing sand, the return of Joe Cadillac, the wrong colored umbrella. "What's wrong?"

"There are two *black* people on the beach, my dear," Mrs. Higgens said. "That's what's wrong."

Cecily's bowels twisted. Not the wrong color umbrella, then, but the wrong color person. She watched Mr. Hayes step out of the ocean. Mrs. Hayes handed him a complimentary beach towel and he dried his face and arms.

"Yes, Mrs. Higgens. Those are the Hayeses," Cecily said. "They've been members since 1995." The Hayeses were quiet, normal people who respected one another. Mr. Hayes owned an office furniture business in New Jersey and Mrs. Hayes was an admissions officer at Princeton. They had three grown sons.

"I've seen the black young man who works here, what's his name? Vance? He puts up my umbrella, and that's fine. But working here and *belonging* here are two different things," Mrs. Higgens said. "Don't forget, young lady, I knew your grandfather. There were no *black members* when he was in charge."

Cecily wondered what would happen if she gave old Mrs. Higgens the shock of her lifetime. *For your information, Mrs. Higgens, my boyfriend is black. I make love with a black man and it is the kind of wonderful I'm sure you have never felt.*

"We want you to be happy, Mrs. Higgens," Cecily said. This was her father talking, the exact words he would say if she sent Mrs. Higgens into the office, which was what she should probably do: let *him* deal with it. But if she was going to start her life as an adult, she was going to have to be brave. "However, if you're not comfortable with people of other races on the beach, then I guess you'll have to find another beach club."

Cecily heard a pained gasp, as though she had stepped on Mrs. Higgens's foot with a heavy shoe, but Cecily didn't look back. She marched through the sand the way she imagined Major Crawley marched through Germany looking for Nazis—proudly, and with something to believe in. *We got them all.* She sat back down next to Maribel's towel.

"What did the old lady want?" Maribel asked.

"Nothing," Cecily said. She stared out at the cool blue water. Her face burned. "I'll tell my parents tonight. But right now, let's talk about love."

LOVE, IT WAS ALL so complicated. That was probably why you didn't get to the good kind of love until you were a teenager. Cecily's love for Maribel was the best shade of blue sky and blue water. Her love for Gabriel was a herd of wild horses galloping out of control. And her love for her parents was a nagging toothache, impossible to ignore and forget.

"YOU DID ABSOLUTELY THE right thing, sweetie," Therese said, her mouth full of tomato sandwich. "I hope we never see the woman again."

"It's five thousand dollars down the tubes," Bill said. He cleared his throat. "But of course when you get to my age, you understand that you can't put a price on human decency."

"The woman is a racist pig," Cecily said. "Who knows how many more of the members are like that deep down?"

"Hopefully none," Therese said. "But if we hear anyone else making comments like that, we'll set them straight."

Cecily looked at her dinner: a tomato sandwich on white bread, and some blue corn chips. A red, white, and blue dinner for the Fourth of

July, had her mother's idea of funny. Cecily couldn't bring herself to eat. She told her parents what happened with Mrs. Higgens, thinking they would be *angry* at the way she handled it. Then it would be easy for Cecily to be indignant, and to tell them she was leaving. But her parents, much to her dismay, were being supportive; they were being *cool*.

"You don't remember what this country went through in the sixties," Therese said. "But it was quite something. Mrs. Higgens is right about one thing, there weren't any black Beach Club members back then, were there, Bill?"

"I'm embarrassed to say, the Hayeses are the first black Beach Club members *ever*. Wait, that's not true. The Krupinskis, they were black."

"Well, *she* was black, he was Polish, remember?" Therese said. "They belonged to the club in, what, '83 and '84? They had that gorgeous café au lait child, the daughter."

"For God's sake," Cecily said. "Café au lait? You're talking about them like they're something exotic off the menu. You're as bad as Mrs. Higgens."

Therese gave her a strange look. "It's an expression, darling. Okay? My, you're touchy. And why aren't you eating?"

"This whole situation has got me really upset, okay?" Cecily said.

Bill frowned. "You're still so young," he said. "You have no idea how rotten people can be, but you'll learn."

"Bill, that's depressing," Therese said.

Cecily walked into the living room, to the bay window that overlooked the Beach Club. It was getting dark and the hotel guests emerged from their rooms to sit on the beach so they could watch the fireworks. Every year, Cecily and her parents watched the fireworks from the widow's walk. It was amazing to watch from that high up, with nothing separating you and the sky. Cecily turned around. Her parents were eating their sandwiches, munching on the chips.

"I have some news," Cecily said.

"More news?" Therese said. "More news aside from the Mrs. John Higgens news?"

"We're proud of the job you've been doing, by the way," Bill said, his voice getting dangerously sappy. "You handled this Mrs. Higgens situation with aplomb."

"Thanks," Cecily said flatly. Wishing her parents would stop being so nice. "Okay—here goes—bombs away. My news, you're ready?"

She was terrified: like jumping off the high dive at the indoor pool at school, like the first time Gabriel unwrapped a condom. She prayed to God, and to her dead brother, W.T., and to Gabriel. *Please let them understand.*

"I've decided to defer a year before I go to college, because I want to do some traveling. So I'm not going to UVA in September. I'm flying to Rio instead."

Cecily shifted her attention to the parking lot: two BMWs, one Rover, one Jag. Mack's Jeep. Lacey's Buick. The thousand scattered pieces of broken shell, the million grains of sand. When she felt confident enough to turn back around, her parents were both staring at her. Her mother had mayonnaise in the corner of her mouth. "Honey, I'm sorry, I don't understand what you're telling us."

"I've sent a slip to the admissions office at the University of Virginia, telling them I'm deferring a year. I'm traveling through South America with Gabriel instead. Which part don't you understand?"

Therese turned to Bill. "Bill?" Tears in her voice.

Bill took Therese's hand. "Cecily, wait a minute. Can you just wait a minute, please? Why are you telling us this? Are you trying to hurt us?"

"It's not about you guys," Cecily said. "It's about me. I need to break away."

"But you have college," Therese said. "That's what Middlesex was for. That's what prep school *means*—college preparatory."

"What about you, Mom? You never finished college." Cecily's mouth had an acidic tomato taste. "You never graduated from Hunter."

"I'm ashamed of that," Therese said. "I didn't have the smarts for school that you do."

"Don't pick on your mother, Cecily," Bill said. "That won't help you."

"Lots of people take a year off," Cecily said. "Why do you think UVA even has such a thing as a deferral form? Because it happens all the time. Everyone does it."

"Everyone does *not* do it," Bill said. "You know I hate hyperbole."

"Well, you know I hate it when you use words like hyperbole," Cecily said.

"If you want to go to South America, we can take you over Christmas break," Therese said. "It'll be fun!" She tittered. "I've always wanted to go to Iguazu Falls."

"I've always wanted to meet the girl from Ipanema," Bill said.

"I'm going with Gabriel," Cecily said. "He's a very nice person. You have no way of knowing that because he wasn't at graduation. He had to fly back early. But trust me, he's nice. We love each other. We've been in love for a while now."

"You can't go away with some boy, some *foreign* boy we've never met. You're a child, Cecily. So you can forget that idea right now," Therese said. She lifted her dinner plate, and Cecily's untouched plate of food. "I'm sorry."

"I'm counting on you taking over the hotel, Cecily," Bill said. "Your mother and I haven't told you everything that's been going on, but I need to retire soon. You can't just go running off to another continent. Being a part of this family comes with responsibility."

"I don't want the hotel," Cecily said. "I'm sorry to say it, Daddy, but I'm not interested."

"That's absurd. You can't be not interested. It was Grandpa Bill's, it's mine, it's going to be yours."

"Give it to Mack," Cecily said. "He wants it, I don't."

"It doesn't work like that. I can't give it to Mack."

"Why not?" Cecily asked. "He'd do a better job than me. Besides, when Grandpa Bill died, you *wanted* the club, you wanted to build hotel rooms. I don't want that. You can't make me want that."

Bill put his hand over his heart. "Oh, God."

Therese stood behind him. "Your father is sick, Cecily. We didn't want you to worry, but he's sick. You can't tell him things like this or he's going to have a heart attack."

Cecily rolled her eyes. "You guys are too much. Giving me a *guilt trip*, telling me Daddy's *sick*? You should have had more children. You should have had more than just me."

Therese winced. "How can you say that? You know about W.T.! For years we tried to have children, *for ten years*, and finally there was you. I'm sorry you don't like it, but some of us are not as fortunate as you, my dear, picking and choosing the way we'd like our lives to go. Most of us just have to take what life deals us, but I am *not* going to stand here and deal with you telling your father you don't want to be a part of the family tradition that has *sustained* you and given you a *good life*. I am not going to listen to you tell me where you are going with what strange boy." Therese wound her white streak of hair around her finger. A Mom trick, to make Cecily feel guilty. "Have you slept with this boy?"

Cecily laughed, looked back out the window. She remembered the startled expression on the cleaning lady's face. "Mother."

"Mother, what? Was I supposed to assume my fifteen-year-old was away at school having sex?"

"I'm eighteen, Mother, okay? Can we establish that fact?"

"You're not going to Brazil," Bill said.

Cecily held out her arms. "Put handcuffs on me, then," she said. "Put handcuffs on and lock me in the house, because that's what it's going to take to keep me here."

Therese started to cry. "I can't believe you're doing this to us," she said. "I can't believe that after what I had to endure before, I now have to endure this."

"It's not like I'm dying," Cecily said. She calculated in her head: if she had to leave tonight, could she do it? She'd cashed all her graduation checks plus two paychecks so far from her father. But it still wasn't enough. She'd have to stay a while longer. "I'm just going away for a year, okay. How about that? A year abroad. I'll be back next summer."

"You're not going anywhere," Bill said. "I'm sorry, honey."

Suddenly, there was a noise, a tremendous boom, so loud it rattled the window. Cecily looked outside in time to see the first fireworks, a brilliant spray of red and yellow and white. Then there was another boom—silver sparkles.

"Happy Independence Day," she said. She stomped down the stairs and left the house, slamming the door behind her.

JEM CRANDALL WATCHED THE fireworks from Jetties Beach with thousands of other people. Kids waved sparklers, parents nodded off to sleep in beach chairs, a group of college students sat in a circle singing the theme song from the Partridge Family. There was no reason for Jem to be amidst all this chaos when he could be down at the Beach Club enjoying peace and quiet, except that here, at Jetties, he was with Maribel. She sat beside him on a beach towel wearing a Nantucket red miniskirt, a white T-shirt, a navy blue cardigan sweater, her blond hair in a ponytail, her tan legs tucked neatly beneath her.

"Are you okay?" Jem asked her. She was quietly picking onions out of her sub sandwich, and tossing them into the sand. (When he called to suggest a picnic, he hoped she would cook, but she told him that now that Mack had left, she would never cook again, hence the sandwiches, and he ordered hers, stupidly, with onions.)

Maribel bit into her sandwich. He put his hand on her knee.

"What's wrong?" he asked. But, of course, he knew what was wrong: it had been a week since Mack moved out. At first, when Jem saw that Mack had moved into Lacey's, he thought Mack had found out about his date with Maribel. Jem asked Vance—carefully, casually—did he know what happened?

"Lover boy blew it with his babe," Vance said. "Screwed around with her on room eighteen."

Jem called Maribel immediately and she confirmed this. Mack was having some kind of relationship with Mrs. Krane, in room 18.

"I don't want to see you, Jem," Maribel said. "I'm a wreck. My life is a disaster area. I'm just sifting through the rubble."

She didn't want to see him but Jem called every day—sometimes she just cried into the phone and Jem held the receiver, helpless. Only with his sister, Gwennie, and her bulimia had he ever felt this helpless. But finally, Maribel agreed to see him—tonight, the Fourth of July, but only if they came to this beach and hid amongst all these people. She didn't want Mack to see them together.

Maribel turned to him. "The past six Fourth of Julys Mack kissed me when the fireworks started." Her eyes were glassy; she pulled a tissue from her skirt pocket. "I've lost a part of my life, Jem."

"I know," Jem said.

"Do you know?" she asked. "Have you ever been hurt like this? Have you ever experienced loss like this?"

"No," he admitted. He had never been in love. He'd never cared about someone more than himself. Jem did have real feelings for Maribel, though, scary feelings, lurking in a dark, unexplored place inside of him. He could feel them gathering strength. He wanted Maribel to be happy she was sitting with him this Fourth of July, but she treated him like the runner-up, the silver medallist, a stand-in.

A thunderclap, and the sky lit up with color. There was a collective "Oooooh, aaaaah!" Some clapping. A burning smell. The fireworks had begun. Jem looked at Maribel: even crying, she was still so pretty. He moved his face closer to hers. Her hand shot up, as if she might slap him.

"Don't," she said. "Please."

"I just want to hold your hand," he said. He wiped a tear from under her eye with his thumb. "Can I do that?"

Maribel surrendered. Jem held her hand all through the fireworks. Her lifeless, clammy hand that was clearly not excited about being held by Jem's hand. He was a mannequin, a crash-test dummy, a Band-Aid. But he didn't care.

LOVE GOT STUCK WORKING the front desk because Tiny wanted the night free. Free for what? Love wondered. Tiny didn't strike Love as a patriotic person.

"Are you going to watch the fireworks?" Love asked.

"No."

"What are you going to do?" Love said. She spent fifteen minutes every day with Tiny during their shift change, and yet Love knew absolutely nothing about her; nor, it seemed, did anyone else.

"That sounds like a personal question," Tiny said. "And I don't answer personal questions. But since you're so curious, I'll tell you that I'm avoiding the fireworks. I don't want anything to do with them."

By seven-thirty Love understood why. The fireworks were being set off from Jetties Beach down the way, but stragglers wandered into the lobby.

"Do you have a bathroom my daughter can use? She swears she's going to whiz herself. Hey . . . these are pretty quilts. This is a nice place. Where are we?"

At first Love was solicitous—she let fourteen people use the bathroom and then she locked not only the bathroom door but the door to the lobby as well. No one else was coming in! But then the Beach Club members arrived, knocking, waving, mouthing "It's me, it's me." They wanted their umbrellas set up, they wanted Sleepy Hollow chairs.

"I paid five thousand dollars for my membership," Mr. Cavendish said. "I will sit in comfort and watch the fireworks."

Mack materialized out of nowhere. That was one good thing about his breakup with Maribel—now he was always around.

"We can do chairs," Mack said. "I'll meet you out at the beach."

Love put Tchaikovsky's *1812 Overture* on the stereo for mood. Vance walked into the office.

"The fireworks are about to start," he said. "I came to show you how to get to the roof."

"The roof?"

"You want to see the fireworks, don't you?" Vance asked. "Come on, follow me."

"I can't leave the desk," Love said. "What if somebody needs something? What if somebody calls?"

Vance reached around Love and busied out the phones. His hand grazed Love's waist and she flinched.

"Relax," Vance said. He wheeled her through Mack's office and into the utility closet, his arm around her. The utility closet was dark and Vance reached for the string to the light, but he couldn't find it.

"What are we doing in the closet?" Love asked. She laughed nervously. This reminded her of stupid kissing games she had played at parties twenty-five years ago. Go into the closet with a boy and stay there until something happens.

"This is the way to get to the roof," Vance said. "There's an escape hatch, and I have a ladder. We climb up and pop out."

"Won't someone see us?" Love asked.

"I've been doing this for years," Vance said. "Do you trust me?" His voice was closer than Love expected.

"Yes," Love said.

"We just need to find the light is all," Vance said. He stumbled over something. "I should have brought my flashlight. Wait, here it is." Vance clicked on the light. They were standing among vacuum cleaners, mops, pails, extension cords, and huge boxes of toilet paper. "Before we go up, I want to show you something." Vance opened a toolbox and brought out some crinkled papers. "It's a short story I wrote that got published in *Slam!* Have you ever heard of *Slam!?*"

"No," Love said.

"I always see you reading so I thought you might want to take a look at it."

"Sure," Love said. The story was entitled "The Downward Spiral." Exactly the kind of gloomy title she expected from Vance. Still, she was touched he showed it to her. The paper was mildewed at the edges; it had obviously been sitting in that box a long time. "I'd be happy to read it. A published story! I'm impressed. I didn't know you were a writer."

Vance shrugged. "I thought since you used to work at a magazine . . . just read it and tell me what you think."

He set up the ladder. "You go first," he said. "I'll follow behind you."

Love climbed the ladder and Vance followed. She felt his breath on the backs of her knees, and she worried he could see up her skirt.

"Look above you," Vance said. "See the hatch?"

Planted in the dusty boards of the ceiling was a metal door, sealed with rubber like a refrigerator. It made a sucking noise as Love opened it to the night sky. She hoisted herself out onto the roof and Vance popped up beside her.

Love raised her arms to the cool air of the dark blue sky. "Much better than being stuck in the lobby." Below, hotel guests and Beach Club members arranged their chairs and blankets. Love could see all the way down to the mob of people at Jetties.

"Be careful," Vance said. He sat on the sloping roof. "Come here."

"But the ocean!" Love said. The water was a shimmering blue, one shade lighter than the sky. A ferry floated toward the island. "This is gorgeous. Thank you for bringing me here."

"I'd feel better if you sat down," Vance said.

"What's wrong, am I making you nervous?" She edged down to the lip of the sloping roof. It was just like skiing a double fault line.

"Love," Vance said. "Please come here."

She pretended she was at the Hadwen House, dancing under the stars. Love waltzed across the shingles to where Vance sat. He pulled her down so close to him that their shoulders brushed. And then, suddenly, Vance put his arm around her and kissed her cheek. Love stiffened. What was he doing? He kissed her mouth. Love wasn't sure what she expected from a kiss from Vance, but she certainly didn't expect it to be so soft, so warm, so tender.

There was a pop, like a giant balloon exploding, and then a shower of red, gold, white. Fireworks. Love closed her eyes and Vance kissed her again. Then she pulled away.

"Vance," she said. "What's going on?"

Vance's profile was cool as a coin.

"I like you," he said.

"You like me?" She stared across the roof of the hotel. There it was: a giant *L,* for Like.

"Yeah," he said. "I do. Is that some kind of crime?"

"No," Love said. "I'm just surprised." It was so odd—he was so odd, so sullen and grouchy, always lurking in the shadows, bad-mouthing Mack, peeling out of the parking lot in his Datsun. He seemed better suited for someone like . . . well, like Tiny. In fact, Love suspected from the beginning that Vance and Tiny were conducting a little romance. But no, Vance liked Love. She couldn't help but feel flattered.

"I'm much older than you," she said. "Do you know that?"

"Not that much older."

"Ten years older," she said. "You're thirty, right?"

Vance picked up her hand and held it. "I don't care how old you are. I think you look great," he said. "I think you look hot." He kissed her again.

He was a terrific kisser, that was for damn sure. He had a strong, fit body, and he might have a handsome face if he ever smiled. Love shuffled her expectations, rearranged her plans. Could this work? Could she have a fling with *Vance*?

"Let me ask you something," she said. "What do you think about children?"

Vance raised his eyebrows. "Children? What do you mean?"

"Do you want children?"

"Children?" Vance said. "Children? Hell, no. I just want to kiss you, Love."

Love felt if she walked to the edge of the roof she could pluck a star out of the sky and take a bite. Her dream getting closer: a child that would be hers, and hers alone.

"So kiss me," she said.

FOR MACK, THE FOURTH of July was the busiest day of the season. Still, each of the past six years, he sneaked away five minutes before the fireworks started to watch them with Maribel. Tonight, Maribel didn't show. It had been a week since he told her about Andrea. He'd returned to the basement apartment only once—in the middle of the day when he knew Maribel would be at work—to get some clothes and his toothbrush. Everything was where it belonged, and Mack didn't take too much. On his way back to the hotel he drove by the house on Sunset Hill, their Palace. They were so happy in the Palace. Mack idled his Jeep out front until another car pulled up behind him. He didn't know what to do.

THIS YEAR, FOR THE first time, he watched the fireworks with Andrea and James. They sat on the steps of their deck, Andrea drinking a glass of red wine.

"Mind if I join you?" Mack said. He sat between them. "How're you doing, James?"

"He has cotton in his ears," Andrea said. "The fireworks scare him. Too loud."

"Really?" Mack said.

"Of course, you'd have to be his mother to know that."

"Well, now I know and I'm not his mother," Mack said.

"You're not his father either," Andrea said.

Mack looked at her. He'd stopped by to help James shave again that morning, but Andrea was reading and barely looked up when he walked into the room. Now her honey-colored hair was wet and pulled severely into a bun. She slugged back her wine. "What do you mean by that?" he asked. "Are you angry with me?"

"I don't want to talk about it right now," Andrea said.

"Why not? James can't hear us."

"He'll intuit something is wrong."

"Is something wrong?"

"Oh, Mack," she said. "I don't know why you told Maribel."

"I had to tell her."

"You didn't have to tell her. The last six summers it wasn't a problem. You and I had our friendship and then you went home to Maribel. And James and I went home to Baltimore. But now it's ruined, my dear. The bubble's burst. The spell is broken. It's not fantasy anymore, it's reality, and someone got hurt. You're sleeping in an old woman's cottage, and I'm scared to death you're going to show up on our doorstep this winter."

"You made it clear you don't want that," Mack said.

"I don't want it and you don't want it either," Andrea said. She set down her wineglass and took his hand. "You're confused. You have to make a decision about your father's farm and your job here at the Beach Club, but you did *not* have to choose between me and Maribel. There was no decision to make."

"Because you don't love me," he said.

"It's not just me, it's you. You love Maribel. It's written all over you."

"I know," Mack said.

The sky crackled and caught on fire. James took Mack's other hand.

"Red," James said. "Silver. Purple. Green and purple."

"Here we go," Andrea said. "The Recitation of the Colors."

"Blue and gold. Silver only. Pink, purple, green."

Andrea sighed. "All I want is for him to grow up knowing I loved him. That I put him first. Do you think he'll ever know that?"

"Pink and gold. White squiggles."

Mack squeezed James's hand. "Of course he'll know you love him. He knows it now, he counts on it, he lives for it. I am *jealous* of James. He's cornered the market on your love. None left for anybody else."

"That's not fair," Andrea said.

"None left for me, then," Mack said.

"Silver and green," James said. "Blue and purple."

"Will you still help James shave?" Andrea asked. "Will you still wave good-bye to us when we pull out of the parking lot?"

"You know damn well I'll do whatever you ask me," Mack said.

"I want you to get back together with Maribel," Andrea said. "Please? I won't be able to leave until you patch this up."

"It's not that easy," Mack said. "I didn't leave Maribel, she kicked me out. I'm not sure she wants me back."

"Of course she wants you back," Andrea said. "You're Mack Petersen. Everybody wants a piece of you."

"Red and blue and white. Red, white, and blue, Mom!" James exclaimed.

"Everybody wants a piece of me except for you."

"Now you sound pitiful," Andrea said.

"When you leave, will that be the last time I ever see you?" Mack said. "Are you coming back next year?"

"I don't know," Andrea said. The fireworks lit up her face, and then it darkened again. "Are you?"

AT SEVEN-THIRTY THE NEXT morning, Mack knocked on the Elliotts' front door, something he'd never done before. If he had business at Bill and Therese's house, which was rare, he always just let himself in. But today, he knocked.

Therese opened the door. Her eyes were puffy. "Mack," she said. "What's wrong? I can't hear about a hotel emergency today. I just can't. I want to pretend the hotel doesn't exist. I was going to have Elizabeth check the rooms."

"Yeah?" Mack said. Something was wrong, but Therese was funny about telling other people her problems. "I came to talk to Bill."

Therese swung the door open. "He's upstairs. Go on up. He needs cheering."

"Okay," Mack said. His hands were numb. *I should leave,* he thought. *Now isn't the right time.* But Maribel would never take him back if he didn't at least *ask. This is going to go well,* he thought. *This is going to be the answer to the chaos in my head.*

He climbed the stairs and saw Bill sitting at the kitchen table with his book of Frost poems open in front of him. "Hey, boss," Mack said.

Bill looked up. "Mack," he said. "What's wrong?"

"Nothing's wrong. I need to talk to you about something. But if now's a bad time . . ."

"No, no, it's fine," Bill said. His face was pale and the translucent skin under his eyes was mapped with tiny red and blue lines. "Do you want coffee?"

"Maybe, yeah," Mack said. He took a mug of coffee from Bill and sat down at the table. He looked at the upside-down book of poems, and wondered if there were any clues in that book about how to live.

"What is it?" Bill said. "Is it about Maribel?"

"No," Mack said. "I want to explore a possibility with you."

Bill was quiet.

"You know, I've worked here twelve seasons, and I'd like to . . . well, I'd like to stay." Mack blew on his coffee but when he tasted it, it was lukewarm. "I was wondering if you'd be open to profit-sharing with me."

"Profit-sharing?"

Therese came into the kitchen. "You want what?"

Mack spun in his chair. "It was just an idea I had."

"What was?" Bill asked.

"Profit-sharing. You know, me getting paid based on how well the hotel does. Taking thirty percent or whatever."

"Thirty percent." Bill's face was expressionless.

"Does that sound outrageous?" Mack asked. "Maybe it is, but I do a fair amount of work around here. And you see, what's happened is my parents' lawyer has called and I have to make up my mind about the farm, do I want to live there, or do I want to sell it."

"So you're telling me you're leaving?" Bill said.

"No," Mack said. "I'm just exploring my options. It seems like this is a good time to discuss my future. And I'd like to profit-share."

Therese laughed, not happily. "Are we wearing bull's-eyes painted over our hearts, Bill? Is that what's happening? Everyone we love feels free to take a shot at us?"

"I'm not taking a shot at you," Mack said. "I just need to think about my future. You guys are like my . . . my family. You know Maribel and I are having problems. I need to *do* something to make her happy." He could feel Therese's instant disapproval. Why had he brought up Maribel? Was it easier to make it sound like this was *her* idea? "But it's for me, too. I have to decide about my family's farm. Either I sell it, which I don't want to do, or I go out there and run it, which I don't want to do. It's an impossible decision."

"Are you telling us that if we don't agree to profit-share, you'll leave?" Bill asked.

"I don't know," Mack said. "If you agree to profit-share, it'll be easier to decide."

Bill looked at his open book. "I see the difficulty of your position," he said. He traced his finger along the lines of the page, as though he were reading aloud. "You're a young man who has to make a choice. I can remember myself at your age. Should I take a risk and build the hotel rooms? But I was lucky. I had a wife who supported me."

"We can't profit-share," Therese said. She sat down at the table. Her orange hair hung in strings around her face and her white streak was tinged with gray, like dirty snow. "We can't profit-share, because of Cecily."

"I'm not asking to own a part of the hotel, Therese. I'm only asking for part of the profits."

Therese lowered her voice. "Cecily has threatened to leave," she said. "She informed us last night that she wants to travel through South America with the boyfriend."

Mack remembered Cecily on the phone in the middle of the night. *"I'm dying of love for you."* "Really?" he said.

"She *wants* us to give you the hotel," Therese said. "She said it herself. If we profit-share, she'll be *relieved*. She'll think, 'Okay, I'm free to go. Mack's in charge.' She'll think we've given up." Therese tapped the counter with her fingernail. "I'm *not* giving up. I already lost one child. I'm not about to lose number two. She might not go if she thinks we need her. I stayed up all night thinking it through. Cecily's weak spot is that she loves us. But if she knows we have some new, official arrangement with you, she'll leave."

"You don't know that," Mack said.

"Therese is right," Bill said. "I'm sorry, Mack. Under other circumstances I would consider it . . . but no, I'm sorry."

I'm sorry: Maribel was sorry but she had to kick him out; Andrea was sorry but she didn't love him; Bill and Therese were sorry but they wouldn't profit-share. *Sorry, Mack, but there's no room for you.* The summer was turning into a big cauldron of sorry stew.

Therese said, "You could always marry Cecily."

Mack was too angry and hurt for any words except the most mundane. "I have to get the doughnuts."

Bill dropped his elbows onto the table, folded his hands, and bowed his head. "Does this mean you're going to leave us, Mack?"

Mack shrugged. "We'll have to see."

The Boys of Summer

July 10

Dear S.B.T.,

If we are to continue in this strange correspondence, I want some answers. Who are you? What do you do for a living? Why do you want this hotel? What could it possibly mean to you? And, most crucially, what right do you have telling me what my own daughter wants or doesn't want? What do you know about me, really? You know only what I've told you in letters and what you might observe from the street. Isn't that right?

Or are you someone on the inside? Are you a Beach Club member, a hotel guest, someone who walks the property every day? Answer me!

Bill Elliott

MACK SPENT THE DAYS following the Fourth of July questioning his future. His sweat equity had turned out to be nothing but sweat—salty water—and at the Beach Club, there was more than enough of that to go around. He'd been threatened with a gun by one of his employees, his girlfriend had kicked him out, and the woman he loved didn't love him back. Running the farm in Iowa was looking better and better. It might not be so bad—climbing up into a combine again and knowing that as far as his eyes could see, the land belonged to him. He had half a mind to call David Pringle and tell him to hire a cleaning lady because Mack Petersen was moving back. He heard the eerie, haunting voice of Nantucket calling out *Home,* but Mack didn't know what that meant anymore. He always assumed it meant Nantucket was his home, but the other night it seemed just as feasible that the voice was telling him to go home to Iowa. It might feel good to return, Mack thought. It might feel as good as it had felt to leave.

But then, just as Mack had almost made up his mind, the Boys of Summer arrived.

"How-Baby" Comatis always made Mack feel better, because when Mack saw How-Baby, he thought about hot dogs and cold beer, dugouts, organ music, extra innings, home plate. He thought about baseball: the word that defined summertime for the rest of America. Howard Comatis was president of the Texas Rangers, and he stayed at the Beach Club every July during the all-star break. He came with his wife, Tonya, and his two baseball buddies—Roy Silverstein (VP of marketing for the California Angels) and Dominic Saint-Jean (president of the Montreal Expos) and their wives. How-Baby was in every way the group's leader—he was a tall, muscular Greek with a full head of black hair and a bushy mustache. His wife, Tonya, called everyone baby, and she always called Howard How-Baby, whether she was speaking to him or about him, and the name stuck. Mack had a hard time thinking of Howard Comatis as anything but How-Baby.

Mack first saw How-Baby when he opened the door of Lacey Gardner's cottage at seven-thirty in the morning. How-Baby was standing on Lacey's tiny porch.

"Howard," Mack said, startled. "Good morning. Welcome back."

How-Baby held out a Texas Rangers hat. "Put this on," he said. "We have fifty bucks riding on who could get you to wear their hat first. The other two bozos are waiting by the lobby. They have no detective skills whatsoever."

Mack took the hat. He had three like it at home from previous years, but he'd left them in the apartment with Maribel. He creased the brim, and tried it on: a good, snug fit. "All right," Mack said. "Thanks."

How-Baby put his arm around Mack's shoulder. "You're a good kid. Come with me. I want to show you off."

Sure enough, Roy Silverstein stood on the front porch of the lobby holding a California Angels cap and Dominic St. Jean was stationed out by the Nantucket Beach Club and Hotel sign, holding an Expos cap.

"Damn," Roy said, when Mack and How-Baby rounded the corner. "I thought for sure Dom was going to get Mack when he pulled in. Where'd you find him, How-Baby?"

"None of your business," How-Baby said. "Now pay up."

Roy was short, bald and skinny. He wore a pair of madras swim trunks cinched at the waist. He reached into his pocket and pulled out twenty-five dollars. "Hey, Dom," Roy said. "How-Baby got to Mack first. Don't ask me how."

Dominic crunched across the parking lot. Dominic was the most elegant of the three men. Because he was Canadian, he sometimes lapsed into speaking French, and he was the best dressed—this morning in creased navy slacks, a lemon yellow polo, and tasseled loafers.

"*Merde,*" Dominic said. He spun the cap around his index finger, then he tossed the cap to Mack. "Wear it tomorrow."

"No, wear mine tomorrow," Roy said.

"You stick with the front runner, Mack," How-Baby said. "Stick with the Rangers."

Tonya Comatis popped her head out the lobby door, her auburn beehive hair-do spun high like cotton candy. "Boys, get back to your rooms. I won't have you competing with each other all week." Her face brightened when she saw Mack. "Mack, baby," she said. She kissed his cheek, leaving, Mack was sure, a ruby red lipstick mark. "Why, you look ex-haus-taid!"

"It's early," Mack said.

"No, I mean, you look really *tired.* You look tired to your bones."

"Give the kid a break, Tonya," How-Baby said. "Now, Mack, can you find us the plastic bat and a few of those Wiffle balls for this afternoon? I'm going to teach these clowns a thing or two."

"You'd think they'd want to get away from baseball," Tonya said. "You'd think they'd want to forget all about it. But no. They love it. They absolutely love it."

"If baseball were a woman," How-Baby said, "I'd marry her."

"I'd marry her first," Roy said.

"She wouldn't marry either of you," Dominic said. "You're both too ugly."

• • •

THAT AFTERNOON AT FIVE o'clock when the beach boys took the umbrellas down for the day, the beach became a playing field. How-Baby and Roy marked the bases and the fair/foul line in the sand. Tonya and the other two wives—Dominic's wife was a quiet blonde named Genevieve, and Roy's wife this year wore ponytails and looked just about eighteen—pulled shorts on over their bikinis and brought out bottles of cold Evian. The teams were co-ed—usually How-Baby and the two wives versus Roy, Dominic, and Tonya, but sometimes it was How-Baby and Tonya against everyone else. One thing stayed the same: How-Baby's team always won. He clobbered the wiffle ball into the ocean every time he was up. The first two balls were lost out at sea. "That would have been a home run at Wrigley," How-Baby said, as he rounded the bases. "That would have been a homer at Candlestick." Then Tonya made a rule that hitting the ball into the water constituted an automatic home run.

"I know you, How-Baby," she said. "You'll try for the upper decks at Yankee Stadium next, and we'll lose the only ball we have left."

How-Baby was amazing in the field, too. He pitched so fast the ball was a white blur. He had Roy and Dominic and the ladies swinging at air, and if they did hit the ball it was usually a crazy-spinning pop-up that fell right into How-Baby's hands. There was a magic to the man, a magnetism that neither Bill nor Mack's father had taught him.

Nine innings with How-Baby took about an hour. Then, the players came in from the field, Roy wiping his bald head with a handkerchief.

"The bastard doesn't even cheat," Roy said to Mack. "If he cheated, at least I could hate him."

"I hate him anyway," Dominic said. He swatted How-Baby's behind.

"Join us for a cocktail," How-Baby said. He wasn't sweating or winded; he was as cool as the breeze off the water.

"Okay," Mack said. It was after six and he'd planned to spend the evening with Andrea—it was her final night on the island and he was supposed to help James shave. Then he hoped to walk with Andrea and James up the beach, but suddenly that seemed depressing. Mack might find a perfect scallop shell or a sand dollar and he would give it to Andrea as something to remember him by, knowing full well that by the time she reached Baltimore, it would be broken or lost. Better to spend time with people who made him feel good.

Mack followed How-Baby to room 1. (How-Baby always booked room 1—there was no question how the man felt about being first.) They sat in the deck chairs. Tonya appeared with two sweating beers, and How-Baby drank half of his in one long swallow. The man lived with gusto.

"So, Mack, tell me, how was your winter?"

"It was good," Mack said. A pale, unenthusiastic answer, but it was all he could muster—and it wasn't a lie. The winter *had* been good; it was only since May that things had started to spin out of his control. "Maribel and I lived on Sunset Hill again, next to the Oldest House."

How-Baby stroked his mustache. "I wanted to ask you about Maribel. I got worried when I heard you were living out in back of the hotel with an old lady. Because you know Tonya and I think you're a marquis player, but we like Maribel a whole bunch too."

"Everyone likes Maribel," Mack said.

Tonya stepped onto the deck. "So we'll see her, then?" she asked. "We'd like to take you kids out to dinner."

"I know you're busy," How-Baby said. "But there's something I want to ask you. Something big."

Tonya swatted How-Baby on the arm. "Now you're teasing," she said. "Just tell him what it is, How-Baby. Tell him right now."

"You don't have to tell me right now," Mack said. "Because, you see, with Maribel. . . ."

"Okay, I will tell him right now," How-Baby said. He finished his beer in a second swallow, then let out a strong, healthy belch. "I have a job for you."

"A job?"

"A job, working for me, working for the Rangers. When this job opened up, I thought to myself, 'I know exactly who I want this job to go to. Mack Petersen, that's who.' "

Mack laughed. "As you know, Howard, I already have a job."

How-Baby turned to Tonya and chuckled. "Didn't I tell you that's exactly what Mack was going to say?"

"You sure did, How-Baby. Now tell him the rest."

How-Baby leaned forward. "Son, I know you like your job here at the hotel. And the job I'm offering you is hotel-related. This job is you setting up travel plans for the team—flights, hotel rooms, restaurants. It means a lot of interaction with the players, it means seeing the rest of the country." He paused dramatically. "It means I will triple your salary. But you'll still have your winters off, just like you do here. You're free in the winter and in the summer you're traveling, fraternizing with the biggest names in the sport, and you're making money." How-Baby settled back in his chair. "How can you pass that up?"

The first word that popped into Mack's mind was *ridiculous*. The second word was *why? Why was it ridiculous?*

"It sounds tempting," Mack admitted.

"But you have doubts," How-Baby said. "You have doubts because I'm asking you to make a major league switcheroo here. I understand that. And so I want you to think it over. I want you to discuss it with your pretty Maribel and see what she has to say."

"We know she's going to love the idea," Tonya said.

"We know she's going to love the idea because that young lady has a good head on her shoulders. She knows a winner when she sees one. After all," How-Baby said, clapping Mack on the back, "she picked you, didn't she?"

"Sort of," Mack said. He felt stupid admitting the truth to How-Baby. How-Baby wasn't interested in what Mack had lost; he was interested in winning. "Maribel kicked me out of the apartment. I made a mistake."

Tonya tugged on her earlobe. "Another woman?" she whispered.

Mack's neck grew warm. "Something like that."

How-Baby slapped his leg. "I knew it," he said. He nudged Tonya.

"Didn't I tell you Mack was in the doghouse and that's why he was living out back? I knew it."

"It's worse than just the doghouse," Mack said. "It's complicated."

How-Baby put his hands behind his head and leaned back in his chair. "Of course it's complicated," he said. "It's love. Love is the greatest thing in the world. And you're talking to a man who's been married twenty-seven years."

"That's right," Tonya said. She kissed How-Baby's forehead, leaving two red lips behind. "But love is hard work too."

"Harder than pitching a no-hitter with four fingers," How-Baby said. "Harder than playing centerfield in a hundred-degree heat. It's damn hard."

"Yeah," Mack said.

"Let me ask you something," How-Baby said. "Do you love Maribel? Do you really love her?"

Mack nodded. "Yes."

"Well, then, let's hear you tell the world. Go on and say it."

"I love her," Mack said.

"Say it louder," How-Baby said.

"I love her," Mack said.

How-Baby scooted to the edge of his chair. "Say it louder."

Mack hesitated; this must be the way How-Baby motivated his players, by getting them to release their testosterone. "I love her!" Mack said.

"Say it louder," How-Baby said.

Tonya whispered. "Louder, Mack baby, louder."

"I love her!" Mack said.

How-Baby stood up. "Say it louder!" How-Baby screamed. "Say it as loud as you can. Stand up and say it from your guts."

Mack faced the water. There were still a few stragglers on the beach, but so what?

"I love her!!!" he shouted. "I . . . love . . . her!"

How-Baby applauded. "That's right," he said. "You love her. I believe you. I believe you love her."

Roy Silverstein came out onto the deck of room 2.

"I see How-Baby's doing his Baptist preacher routine again," he said.

Mack collapsed in his chair. For the first time in weeks, he really laughed. Was it crazy to even consider taking this job? He was so locked into his choice between Nantucket and Iowa, he had never even thought there might be a third option. He'd been sitting around waiting for Nantucket to speak to him—and maybe that's what had just happened. Maybe How-Baby was the voice he was waiting for. Mack wondered what the water looked like down in Texas. If he could get Maribel back, he would find out.

SOON THEREAFTER, MACK LEFT the deck, shaking hands with How-Baby, kissing Tonya on the cheek, and telling them he would consider their offer.

"Worry about the girl, first," How-Baby said. "That's what's important."

Mack rounded the corner to the side deck rooms. He knocked at room 18. Andrea opened the door. Behind her, Mack saw her half-packed suitcase, but he didn't feel as sad as he'd expected.

"I'm here to help James shave," he said. "I promised him."

She looked him over. "I *am* going to miss you, you know."

"Is James here?" Mack asked. He called into the room. "James, buddy, it's Mack. I'm here to help you shave."

"Hey," Andrea said. "I *said* I was going to miss you."

"You don't have to miss me," Mack said. "You're choosing to. Is James here?"

"Of course he's here. Where else would he be?" Andrea turned. "James, come here, please."

A few seconds later James skulked into the room.

"I'm here to help you shave," Mack said.

James spun on his heels and headed for the bathroom without a word. Mack followed him. James stood in front of the mirror, and Mack sat on the toilet.

"This is a graduation of sorts," Mack said. "Because you're leaving tomorrow." He wondered if Andrea had gone over all this with James already. He wondered if it would matter, if James had any concept, really, of what was going on around him.

"Time for shaving," James said.

"I'm going to watch you," Mack said. "You go ahead. Tell me what's first."

"I don't know," James said.

"Lather your face with shaving cream," Mack said. "Like Santa Claus, remember?"

James sprayed the foam onto his fingers and dabbed it onto his cheeks.

"And now what?" Mack said. "What comes next?"

James said nothing. How did How-Baby do it? How did he make people respond with exactly what he wanted to hear? "Pick up the razor," Mack said. "We've done this three times already. Now I want you to shave yourself, James."

"I don't know," James said.

"You don't know what?"

James stared into the mirror. Mack's heart deflated as he looked at the fifteen-year-old kid with a foamy white beard. He felt for Andrea, who would have to watch tomorrow, and next week, and maybe even next year, until James could get comfortable with the routine, until he could divide the task into steps. She was right, of course: nobody else would love James enough to have that kind of patience and that kind of stamina without losing their temper, without becoming frustrated enough to leave, as her husband had. Not even Mack.

Mack stood behind James and took the razor. He began to shave him gently.

"Do you like baseball, James?" Mack asked.

"Yes," James said, automatically.

"Do you hate baseball?" Mack asked.

"Yes," James said.

"You can't like it *and* hate it," Mack said. "You can't do both. Do you understand that, James? You can't like baseball and hate it."

"I like it in person," James said. "I hate it on TV."

Mack smiled as he shaved under the curve of James's chin. "Maybe I can get you some tickets to see the Orioles," he said. "How would you like that?"

"Yes," James said.

Mack shaved James's upper lip. "When you do this on your own, you have to be careful of your lip. You don't want to cut your lip or you'll bleed for hours. There, you're all done." Mack stepped back. "I want you to rinse your face," Mack said.

James turned on the water, splashed his face and dried it with a towel.

"What do we do after we rinse, James, can you remember?"

James stared into the mirror.

Mack picked up the lotion and squirted some into James's palm. "Rub this into your face. We don't use aftershave, do we, James?"

"No," James said.

"You're going to have to remind your mom of that. No aftershave, just lotion. And stand up for yourself. I'd hate to think of you walking around smelling funny."

James rubbed in the lotion. "All shaved," he said.

"All shaved. You're ready to go, then." Mack reached for the latch on the bathroom door, but then stopped short. "Do you like me, James?" he asked.

"No," James said. His green-gray eyes were a blank slate. "I love you."

BEFORE MACK LEFT THE room, he watched Andrea pack. "Your son's smooth faced again," he said. "But I don't think I taught him a thing. I'm sorry."

Andrea held a sweater under her chin and folded in the sleeves. "Don't worry about it," she said.

"Okay, then, I'm going," Mack said.

"I'm afraid I don't have the energy for a big emotional good-bye," she said.

"Me either," he said.

Andrea narrowed her eyes. "You aren't beholden to me or anyone else, Mack. You're your own person. A good person. But will you think about what I said, about Maribel?"

"I already have," Mack said.

Andrea slid one of James's flip-flops onto each of her hands. "I guess it's ridiculous to think I'll never see you again."

"I'm beginning to believe nothing is ridiculous," Mack said. "Let's just say so long for a while. You might see me again, but it won't be where you think."

"You're leaving here?"

"I promise I won't show up on your doorstep," he said.

"You're really leaving here?" Andrea said.

Mack gave her a squeeze. "Safe travels tomorrow." He inhaled the smell of her hair, but again, he wasn't as sad as he expected. He made a point of not saying "I love you," but Andrea seemed to hear it anyway.

"I know," she said.

MACK DROVE TO THE basement apartment. He knocked tentatively on the door, but heard nothing. Then, he knocked a little louder. After a second, Maribel swung the door open.

"Oh, God," she said. Her tan face went pale, as though she were going to be sick.

"Mari, I'm sorry, I have to talk to you."

"Talk?" she said.

"Can I come in?" Mack asked.

The skin above her eye twitched. "I guess," she said.

She pushed the screen door open for him and he stepped into the apartment. Jem Crandall was sitting at the dining table eating pizza from a box. He, too, looked sick when he saw Mack. He stood up.

"Jem," Mack said. "Hi."

"I'm going," Jem said. "I'm out of here."

Mack tried to hide his surprise. It was hard enough to see Maribel, but then to have one of his bellmen sitting at the dining table eating pizza?

"I don't get it," Mack said. "What are you doing here?"

"We're friends," Maribel said. "Get over your surprise. You don't know what my life is like anymore."

"No," Mack said. "Obviously I don't."

Jem moved toward the door, taking the piece of pizza he was eating with him. "I'll let you two hash this out," he said. Then he turned around. "But if you hurt her, Petersen, if you lay a hand on her or you make her cry with something you say, I'll kill you."

"Great," Mack said. Now both his bellmen wanted to kill him.

"I mean it," Jem said. "And I'm saying this despite the fact that you've been pretty cool to me. But you did a bad thing to Maribel, and if you do anything else, you're in trouble."

"Okay," Mack said. He repressed the urge to smile. "I'll keep that in mind."

Jem bit into his pizza. "Yeah," he said, his mouth full. "Do that."

After Jem left, Maribel sat at the dining table. "So, you've reclaimed your turf," she said. "Why don't you tell me what you want. You want closure? I figured as much, but I'd hoped you'd call first."

Mack looked around the apartment. He missed it. Even the shag carpet and the moldy, old-sponge smell. "I love you," he said.

"You don't cheat on someone you love. You don't perpetuate a lie for six years with someone you love. Okay, Mack? Do you see how your credibility has worn thin?"

"Yes," Mack said, "but I do love you."

"Ha."

"I asked Bill to profit-share," he said.

Maribel raised her eyebrows. "Really?"

"He turned me down," Mack said. "He and Therese both. They said . . . well, do you know what's going on with Cecily?"

"That she's deferring a year from school you mean? To be with the boyfriend?"

"It has them really upset. And they won't profit-share with me because they think if they do Cecily will be more likely to leave. They think she'll be glad I'm taking care of the hotel for them, and she'll feel free to go."

"They're absolutely right," Maribel said. "Cecily's said as much. So it sounds like you're out of luck."

Mack looked at his hands. "I did ask, though."

Maribel fidgeted with the corner of the pizza box. "You're too late, Mack."

"We only broke up two weeks ago. How can I be too late? And another thing I'd like to know is what Crandall was doing here."

"He likes me," Maribel said. "I could go out on a limb and say he's in love with me."

"Great," Mack said. "He's too young for you, you know."

Maribel snorted. "That isn't for you to decide."

"So you're an item, then? You've fallen for Mr. *November*?"

"I don't know what I'm doing, Mack," Maribel said. Her voice was sad now, not angry, not sarcastic. "I'm thinking of leaving the island."

"Why?" he said.

"Because I'm finished here. I gave it a shot and it didn't work. Six years ago, you and I had a summer romance and I decided to stay. But it was always a summer romance, wasn't it? The kind of romance that's so thrilling because you know it's going to end." She flashed her blue eyes at him. "And guess what? Our summer is finally over."

"I agree. Our summer is over."

"Plus, I think people who live on islands . . . well, I'm beginning to think there's something wrong with them. It's like they're *hiding* from something. It's like they're afraid of the rest of the world and so they *isolate* themselves, surrounded by all this water."

"What are we hiding from?" Mack asked. "What are we afraid of?"

Maribel tore the pizza box into tiny pieces. "I don't know," she said. "I'm afraid that you don't love me enough. You're afraid that I love you too much. Or maybe we're each just afraid of ourselves." She started to cry.

Mack reached across the table and took her hand. "I got a job offer today," he said. "And if you agree to come with me, I'm going to take it."

"What kind of offer?" she said.

"Working for How-Baby," Mack said. "For the Texas Rangers. Setting up hotel rooms, restaurants, flights. It would mean traveling around the States. It would mean the winters off. It would mean more money."

Maribel went to the sink, ripped a paper towel off the roll and blew her nose. "How-Baby," she said. "I always liked that man."

"He and Tonya want to see you," Mack said. "They can hardly wait. And How-Baby said he would triple my salary, Maribel. Triple it."

"What are you going to do about the farm?" Maribel asked.

Mack thought about that for a minute. He still didn't know what to do about the farm. "We'll figure it out," he said. "Maybe I'll wait a year to see how I like this job. I'll have Pringle hire someone for one harvest, and if the job works out, maybe I'll sell the farm. The thing is, we'll be able to do it, you and me, I know we will."

"You'll have to do it alone," Maribel said, bunching the paper towel in her hand. "I'm not going with you."

"You have to come with me."

Maribel paced the kitchen floor so that the soles of her running shoes squeaked against the linoleum. "You just don't *get it*, do you?"

Mack took a deep breath. He felt as though he were falling, in a dream. "You don't get it," he said. "I'm asking you to marry me."

For the first time in their relationship, he'd surprised her. Well, maybe the second time, because he knew finding out about Andrea had surprised her too. Just watching her gave Mack a rush. She was wearing a pale pink T-shirt, jean shorts, her running shoes. Her hair was in a bun held together by a pencil. At that moment, Mack wanted to *be* Maribel—she was getting something she'd wanted for so long.

"You're asking me to marry you?" Maribel said.

I should sink to one knee, he thought. It seemed silly, there in the dampness of their rented apartment, but Mack made himself do it. He knelt.

"Will you marry me? Will you be my wife?" The words came right out; it was easy. He would say them over and again; he would scream them out. "Will you please marry me?"

Maribel stared over the top of his head as though his thoughts were suspended in a balloon. *Answer me!* the balloon would say. And then for a second it occurred to him she might say no, and that was like peeking into a dark hole with no bottom.

"Maribel, will you marry me?" Mack asked a little louder.

She looked at his face as though she were surprised to find him there, on one knee, his eyes level with her tan legs.

"Of course," she said. "Of course I'll marry you."

LACEY GARDNER COULDN'T BELIEVE it. For twelve years she'd watched Mack grow up: She watched him run the hotel, graduate from the community college on the Cape, grieve for his parents; she watched him take girls on dates. And she watched him, especially carefully, with Maribel. But never in a million years would she have predicted this—and Lacey was old enough now to have very few things shock her. But this, yes. Mack brought her usual cup of coffee and the *Boston Globe* from the lobby, and before she even scanned the headlines, there was this news.

"I've asked Maribel to marry me and she said yes."

His tone of voice was barely repressed joy, pride, awe, and Lacey supposed that was as it should be. Lacey experienced first surprise and next, sadness. Mack, then, lost to her forever, in a way.

"And all this time, I thought you were saving yourself for me."

Mack hugged her across the shoulders so that she nearly spilled coffee in her lap. His energy astounded her—maybe he was in love with the girl after all. "You're the best, Gardner. The absolute best. You're the first person I've told."

"You'll be moving out, then?" Lacey said. She eyed the leather sofa where Mack had slept the last two weeks. Usually, he came in after she fell asleep and was up before she awoke, but for two weeks there was another human being under her roof, and that felt good. She sometimes heard Mack's footsteps or the toilet flush in the middle of the night, and once, when she couldn't sleep, she tiptoed out to the living room and saw his figure under the blankets and she wished he would never leave, that he would simply stay with her until she died.

"I'll be moving back to the apartment," he said. "But we'll still have our Sunday night dinners. I told Maribel that was part of the deal. Sunday nights are for you, Lacey."

"Well, good," she said.

Mack was getting married.

Lacey remembered back to September of 1941 when she and Maximilian drove Sam Archibald's dune buggy out to Madaket. Sam Archibald wasn't on Nantucket that summer because he'd enlisted in the army and was at training camp in Mississippi. Maximilian received a postcard from him that said, "*Half the gents here have never seen the Atlantic, much less played croquet in 'Sconset. Take the old girl around in the bug and have a good time for me.*" On September 16, that's what they were doing—driving to Madaket. The mood between Lacey and Maximilian was more serious than normal, because of the war. Everyone sat by their radios listening for word on Hitler. The military used Tom Nevers Field as a training ground for landing in the fog; the coast guard patrolled the beach, looking for U-boats. There were piles of sandbags in the streets of town and all around them, men enlisting in the service. Lacey supposed it wouldn't be long before Maximilian went away also. Then she would be left to drive the dune buggy to the beach alone.

When they reached Madaket, Lacey and Maximilian walked through the sand barefoot.

Maximilian said, "I brought you out here for a reason."

Lacey laughed, but it was so windy her laughter was carried away. "You brought me out here because Sam wrote and said you should. You men, always sticking together!"

Maximilian's necktie lifted in the breeze. "No, Lacey, that's not it."

And then, of course, she thought he was telling her that he was off for the war as well. *You men,* she thought, *always sticking together.* No wonder the armed forces worked. Men loved each other's company; they loved a group, the bigger the better. And she thought, *If Maximilian is going, I'll enlist too. I won't be left behind with the women, I just won't.*

But Maximilian said, "Lacey, I brought you here to ask for your hand in marriage, both hands, and the rest of you, for that matter, if you'll have me. I promise to provide you with a home, and to give you the life you're accustomed to as well as I possibly can—"

Lacey interrupted him by putting her fingers to his lips. She remembered that too, the way his warm lips felt under her fingertips. "Yes," she said. "The answer is yes."

She held tight to that memory, and to the flood of happiness it brought her, even though two months later Maximilian did join the service and was gone from her for three years. Those were days when love meant something because it stood side by side with life and death. Those who survived had a reason to be nostalgic, and she, Lacey, had survived.

Mack waited for her to speak. What could she say? Things were so different these days she could hardly understand them. "You're doing the right thing," she said finally.

Relief crossed his face like a ray of light.

"Thank you," he said. "I was hoping we'd have your blessing."

"You always have my blessing, Mack Petersen," Lacey said. And that much, at least, was the truth.

WHEN CECILY FOUND OUT Mack and Maribel were getting married, she experienced envy like a slap across the face. She heard the news from Maribel, over the phone.

"He's going to marry me! Mack and I are getting married! Can you believe it? Married, married, *married*!"

Cecily stared at herself in the mirror, a bad habit of her mother's. "You're so fucking lucky," she whispered. But Maribel blabbered something about a church and flowers, and didn't hear. Cecily quietly hung up the phone and took it off the hook. Then she fell facedown on her bed and cried. She should be *happy*; she had wanted this for both Mack and Maribel. But the truth was, she liked it better when Mack and Maribel were miserable. She liked it better when she was the one lucky in love. Now Mack and Maribel were beyond lucky; they'd hit the jackpot. *Married!* Cecily cried bitter, jealous tears. She knew Maribel would be trying to call back, but she didn't care. She couldn't talk to Maribel, and she couldn't face Mack. It was completely irrational—their good news didn't mean bad news for Cecily. Lots of people could fall in love and get married at one time. But that thought didn't make anything better, not with Gabriel thousands of miles away and Cecily stranded here, on this dinky, go-nowhere island.

Could it be she was so upset because *she* wanted to marry Mack? When Cecily was younger she'd had a terrible crush on him. Every day she wrote in her journal what Mack said to her: "Hey, there, Sunshine, whatcha up to?" "Cecily, babe, let's see you turn a cartwheel." She wrote down every time he pulled her curls or flung her over his shoulder like a sack of flour. Nights when he went on dates she stayed in her room without turning on the radio or TV, convinced that if she was having a miserable time, he was, too. Then the next day she pestered him for the name of the girl, what she looked like, what they did on their date. Dinner? Movie? Dancing? And then shyly, Cecily would ask, "Did you kiss her, Mack?" And Mack would either say, "Sure did, Sunshine," or "Nope, not that one, too ugly." Cecily always prayed for the latter answer. She prayed that all of Mack's dates had a faint mustache, or bad breath. She hoped he would realize no girl was as pretty as Cecily.

By the time Cecily was old enough to go on dates herself and Therese grabbed hold of the idea that Mack and Cecily should be together, Cecily was N.I.—Not Interested. By that time too, Maribel was in the picture, and Cecily fell for Maribel almost as hard as she'd fallen for Mack. Cecily imitated the way Maribel talked, the way she wore her hair, the way she dressed. From the beginning, Maribel treated Cecily like an equal, and it worked like magic. Cecily was hooked.

Was Cecily so upset because she was in love with Mack, or Maribel? She'd read Freud and other dead European males at Middlesex, and some would say she wanted to be married to both of them. Gobbledy-gook. She wanted to be married to Gabriel, that was all there was to it. But Mack and Maribel had separated themselves from her. *We're getting married. You're staying single.*

For the time being.

Cecily opened the drawer of her bedside table and counted her money. She was getting closer, but still not close enough. She snuffled, blew her nose, and went into the bathroom to splash water on her face. She was due on the beach in half an hour and as much as she wanted to stay hidden in her room, missing a day's work meant missing a day's salary, and money was the only thing keeping her from Gabriel.

She stomped upstairs to the living room and found her father staring out the bay window at the activity below. This was his quiet time, while Cecily's mother was busy with the chambermaids, and Cecily never interrupted. Plus, whenever Cecily talked to either of her parents now, they clung to her words as though she might never speak again. They must have thought if they paid her more attention, she wouldn't leave, but that was completely fucking erroneous on their part.

Cecily cleared her throat. Her father snapped to attention.

"Good morning," he said. "How are you this morning?"

"Mack and Maribel are getting married," Cecily said. The inside of her mouth was dry and chalky.

"I'm sorry?"

"They're getting married." Saying it aloud was the worst kind of pain—worse than menstrual cramps, worse than falling down and skinning her palms. "Maa—reed."

"They're getting married?" Bill said. "You know this for a fact?"

Cecily couldn't bring herself to say anything further. And if her father made a big, happy deal over it, she would leave immediately, tonight, today. But thankfully, he didn't. He took the news quietly and then seemed reflective, but not in a glad or happy way.

"Well," he said. "How about that?"

BILL ELLIOTT KNEW THE instant he heard the news about Mack and Maribel getting married that Mack was going to leave. Part of Bill cheered Mack on—*Good for you getting married, good for you return-*

ing to the land that's yours, good for you! But then the reality of the situation hit and Bill felt a familiar tightness in his chest. He left Cecily
banging cabinets, muttering, "There's never any fucking food in this
house," and went into his bedroom to lie down. Mack leaving spelled
disaster for the Beach Club. He was the manager and he managed like
nobody else. Kids loved him, adults loved him, the crotchety old
ladies of the Beach Club loved him. Most importantly, Bill loved him,
and if it weren't for the fact that he had a daughter of his own, Bill
would not only have profit-shared with Mack, he would have left the
hotel to him without a second thought. He lay on his bed, and
thought, *I have survived worse. I survived losing my son.* But thinking
about Mack leaving gave Bill an oddly similar feeling— empty, sad,
hopeless. He closed his eyes. Why not sell the hotel then? Cecily
didn't want it and how could Bill run it without Mack? S.B.T.'s face
appeared to him, a demon.

Later, his fears were confirmed. Mack was talking with a guest in
the lobby and Bill touched him on the elbow, and said, "When you get
a second."

Then Bill sat at his desk and looked out the window. The most
beautiful beach in the world—the blue water, the white sails in the distance, the brightly colored umbrellas in the sand. It was glorious here.

Mack knocked lightly, pushed open the door. "I guess you
heard?"

"Why don't you tell me yourself," Bill said.

Mack stuffed his hands in the pockets of his khaki shorts. "I'm
going to marry her."

"Getting married was the best thing I ever did," Bill said. "By far
the best thing."

Mack jingled his key ring. "I know you feel that way. You and
Therese have had a big influence on me. I really appreciate that.
You've been role models."

"That sounds like a good-bye," Bill said. "Is that a good-bye?"

"Did someone tell you I was leaving?"

"No one needed to," Bill said.

Mack looked out the window and Bill followed his gaze, willing him to see how beautiful it was, hoping he would understand that the rest of the world was not this beautiful.

"I'll stay through the season," Mack said. "I would never strand you midseason."

"But next year? . . ."

"Next year, no. This will be my last year. This is it."

The demon face of S.B.T. shimmered on the horizon. "I just can't picture you as a farmer," Bill said. "But I want you to know I understand why you're going back. In the end, you have to protect what belongs to you and your family."

Mack's lower lip dropped. "Oh . . . no. Whoops." He laughed. "Well, you got it half right anyway. I'm leaving, but I'm not going back to Iowa."

"You're not?" Bill said.

"No," Mack said. "I'm going to work for Howard Comatis. For the Texas Rangers. It's a baseball team."

"A baseball team?"

"Howard Comatis, room one. He's president of the Texas Rangers. He offered me a job yesterday. And I thought about what you said, about wanting to give the hotel to Cecily. So anyway, it just seemed right. And I'll still have winters off. So it's not as if I'll never see you again. We can visit you in Aspen. You can finally teach me to ski."

"Howard Comatis?" Bill said. "The big hairy guy? The loud obnoxious guy?"

"That's him."

"You're going to work for *him*?" Bill asked. This news affronted him. Mack working on his family farm was one thing, but a guest snatching him away was another. Guests had been trying to hire Mack away for years, but he'd always turned them down. "What will you be doing?"

"Hotel rooms, dinner reservations, travel plans. Getting the team from place to place, that kind of thing."

"How much is he paying you?" Bill asked.

"A lot," Mack said. "We haven't talked actual numbers but it'll be a lot."

Bill nodded. It must have been a lot for Mack to give up Nantucket. "I'd do anything to keep you here, Mack," Bill said. "I'll give you a raise right now."

Mack put his keys back in his pocket. "Not this kind of raise. Besides, you made it clear that your first concern is Cecily, and that's okay." He knocked on Bill's desk. "Bill, that's okay."

Bill rubbed his forehead. "If Cecily weren't threatening to leave, if Therese and I hadn't already lost a child, all that, things would be different."

"But they aren't different," Mack said.

"I don't know what I'm going to do without you," Bill said.

"We don't have to say good-bye right now," Mack said. "It's only July. We still have lots of time."

Bill looked back out at the beach. Dutifully, Cecily started to circulate among the umbrellas; a ferry approached on the horizon.

"We have time," Bill said. "Okay, you're right. We have time." He stood up and stuck out his hand and when Mack shook it, Bill embraced him. "Congratulations," he said.

FOUR BRIDESMAIDS IN ROOM 19 destroyed the place. Therese put down her clipboard. Empty diet Coke bottles rolled around on the floor, potato chips were ground into powder in the carpet, three wet bikini bottoms sat in soggy clumps on the bathroom tile. The top bedsheet had been ripped in half, hair spray scum covered the mirror, a nail polish spill pooled like blood on the dresser. These girls had requested extra towels. Extra towels! They were lucky they were here in the name of love. Therese had half a mind to kick them out.

Elizabeth appeared in the doorway with her cleaning cart and her vacuum. "Gross."

"Gross, you're not kidding," Therese said. A pair of stockings fluttered over the brass reading lamp by the bed, a swollen tampon floated in the toilet. "This is the most disgusting room I have ever seen."

"Really?" Elizabeth asked. She seemed encouraged by this news. "This is the worst?"

"You don't have to clean this room," Therese said. "I'll do it."

"*You're* going to clean it?" Elizabeth said. She peered into the room. "They sure did drink a lot of diet Coke."

"Go on to eighteen," Therese said. "But leave me your vacuum."

Elizabeth left and Therese furiously unwound the cord for the vacuum. Mack appeared in the doorway. "Geez," he said. "What a mess. Here, let me help you." He started to pick up the bottles and put them in an empty Lion's Paw bag.

"Leave them be," Therese said. "Anyone who makes this much of a mess deserves to live with their own filth."

"But I want to help," Mack said. "What can I do to help?"

Therese looked him dead in the eye. "I'm not changing my mind about the profit sharing," she said. "You know I love you, Mack, but I can't do it. I have a teenage daughter to think of. When you have a teenager of your own, you'll understand. Boy, will you ever."

"It's not the profit sharing," he said. "I have something else to talk to you about."

Therese spied a bra dangling from the ceiling fan. She switched on the vacuum and swathed a path only where the floor was clear—around the cans, around the chips, around the clothes. It took her thirty seconds. She shut the vacuum off. "So what is it?" she said.

"I'm getting married."

Married. The word took her so by surprise that she closed her eyes. When she opened them again, she caught her reflection in the scummy mirror. She looked fuzzy, as if someone were trying to erase her. "You're getting *married*?"

"I asked Maribel and she said yes."

"I thought you two were on the rocks," Therese said. The room went out of focus. It looked like a wedding that had been through the blender. "I thought she threw you out."

"We've worked through that," Mack said. "I'm going to marry her, Therese."

"I don't believe it," she said. She didn't want to believe it. Her dream of Cecily marrying Mack, a dream for the trash. She stood on the bed and unhooked the bra from the fan and threw it on the floor with the rest of the girls' clothes, although what did it matter now? What did a messy room matter now that everything else was collapsing? Therese found a notepad. *"The proprietress has cleaned your room!"* she wrote. She left it amid the clutter on the nightstand and wondered if they would even see it, if they would even notice. Mack sat on the dresser, tapping his fingers on the top drawer.

I know what's best for you. Therese thought. *Nobody believes it, but I do.*

SHOTGUN WEDDING. HANDGUN WEDDING. However you phrased it, Vance had Influence. His stunt with the gun had brought about Mack and Maribel's breakup, and then Mack's proposal. Vance might have been jealous—Mack marrying someone as perfect as Maribel—but instead he felt a grand satisfaction. He snagged control from Mack's hands. He had made something happen. And oddly enough, it was something good.

It inspired Vance to go after Love. She was older than he was, but she was pretty and athletic and organized. He liked the way she spoke to guests; he liked the way she listened. He liked the way she didn't wear makeup or hairspray. She was a natural Colorado outdoor beauty. She smelled like a pine cone. A refreshing change from the girls Vance usually brought home from the bars. She made him want to lighten up. She made him want to laugh. So he would have his own summer romance for once. And who knew, maybe someday he'd be the one getting married. Vance. Vance Romance.

MARIBEL WONDERED IF SHE'D ever be this happy again. Hearing Mack finally propose was an answer to her daily prayers. Just when she'd given up hope, just when she thought she would have to somehow endeavor to move on, he asked. He asked and she said yes. More than anyone, Maribel wanted to tell her father. A man who didn't exist, except for in her mind. *See there, someone wants me. Someone wants to marry me!*

Maribel called Cecily, and then her mother, and after relaying the news to a teary, elated Tina ("God bless you, Maribel. God bless you and Mack"), Maribel called Jem. She called early in the morning—during the bracket of time when Mack had left for work but Jem would still be at home.

He answered sleepily. "Hello?"

"Jem, it's Maribel."

"Maribel?" He sounded confused, then alarmed. "Did Mack hurt you?"

Maribel felt a flurry of guilt. "He didn't hurt me," she said. "He proposed."

Silence. Then, quietly, "You're kidding."

Maribel winced. "No."

"Oh, God," Jem said. "Wow. He asked you to *marry* him? The nerve of that guy." More silence. "But you said no, right? I mean, this is a guy who left you in the dust for another woman. This is a guy who cheated on you."

"Jem . . ."

"You said no, didn't you?"

"I said yes."

"You said yes."

"It's complicated," Maribel said. "We've been together for six years. You understand that."

"Not really," Jem said. "Not really at all."

"Jem," Maribel said, "I'm sorry. You'll have to trust that I know I'm doing the right thing."

"Because you're in love?" Jem said.

"Yes," Maribel said.

"And what does being in love feel like?" Jem asked. "Does it feel like when you're with the person you're the best version of yourself and when you're not with the person your insides hurt?"

"I don't know, Jem," Maribel said gently. "It's different for everyone."

"And does that person become the only person who matters, and no matter what you can't stop thinking about her. Is that what it's like, Maribel?"

"Jem . . ."

"Is being in love finally realizing why we were put on this earth? Is it when everything starts to make sense?"

"Jem," Maribel said. What could she possibly say? He was right. "Yes, Jem."

"Yes," Jem said, "I thought so."

"You're not in love with me, Jem."

There was huff on the other end of the line. "I wish you were right," Jem said. "I really wish you were."

"Jem . . ."

"I have to go," Jem said. "I have to get to work." And with that, he hung up, and Maribel, who thought nothing could squelch her happiness, stared at the dead receiver. She closed her eyes and wished his pain away. She knew just how he felt.

THE NEXT EVENING, MACK and Maribel went to dinner with How-Baby and Tonya at Kendrick's, on Centre Street. How-Baby reserved the back room for just the four of them; a magnum of Dom Perignon chilled on the table. Mack had been very careful not to say anything to How-Baby about his engagement to Maribel or his decision about the job, but from the looks of things, How-Baby already knew. Or maybe this was just his superconfidence shining through: live as though everything was going to go your way. When Mack took his seat, though, he started to enjoy it: the private, candlelit room, the waiter pouring him a glass of Champagne. There was already the sense that things had changed.

How-Baby raised his glass. "I'd like to make a toast," he said. "To you charming young people. Maribel, you are positively glowing, and Mack, that makes you one lucky man." How-Baby winked.

They all clinked glasses and sipped the Champagne. Maribel *was* glowing—she hadn't stopped smiling since Mack proposed. When they were home alone, she talked about nothing but the wedding. Mack was tickled to see her so excited, although the idea of a wedding disheartened him. He had no family to speak of; he would invite Bill and Therese and Cecily and Lacey Gardner. He felt a pang of guilt. The people he loved best, the people he would soon be leaving. He looked across the table at How-Baby and Tonya. His future.

"I have a toast as well," he said. How-Baby raised his bushy eyebrows. The man knew, he just *knew.* "First of all, I'm proud to announce that Maribel and I are getting married."

Tonya squealed and grabbed How-Baby's arm. "You darlings!" Her beehive tipping dangerously close to the candle flame. "That is brilliant! We're so happy. Aren't we, How-Baby?"

How-Baby clapped his hands. "Congratulations! Maribel, my sources tell me you just landed the most eligible bachelor on the island."

"I sure did," Maribel said. "He's the answer to my prayers."

Mack laid his hands on either side of his dinner plate. "And I've thought about your proposition, Howard."

"Have you, now?" How-Baby said.

"I have," Mack said. He wondered what it would be like working for a guy who always sat on top of the world. Did the man ever falter, ever have a bad day? The Rangers had lost both halves of a double-header that very afternoon, but How-Baby was as smooth as ever.

"What did you decide?" How-Baby asked. "Did you decide to join the team? Or will you remain loyal to the Beach Club?"

"I've decided to join the team," Mack said.

Tonya squealed again. How-Baby rounded the table to shake Mack's hand.

"Good for you, Mack! I promise you won't be disappointed. You'll be our new travel and hospitality manager, answering directly to me. Tomorrow you show me your W-two from this year, and I will triple your salary." He grabbed a fistful of Mack's shoulder. "Welcome to the big league."

"It was a hard decision to make," Mack said, reaching for Maribel's hand under the table. "My job at the Beach Club is the only job I've ever had, unless you count some construction work or helping on my father's farm."

"That's right," How-Baby said. "I forgot about you coming from the heartland. Where is it? Indiana?"

"Iowa," Mack said.

"Do your parents still farm, Mack?" Tonya asked.

Mack paused. A new job meant starting over, explaining his circumstances, letting other people know him. He wished he could just say yes.

"My parents were killed in a car crash when I was eighteen," he said.

Silence. Always, when Mack told this part, there was silence. He longed for Bill and Therese, because with them there wasn't a need to explain.

How-Baby looked up from his menu. "Did you have a good relationship with your father?"

"I did," Mack said. "We had a very good relationship."

How-Baby nodded. "I can tell. Know why? Because you're a good kid. A team player. If I should be so fortunate as to meet your father someday in heaven, I'll tell him he raised a fine young man."

Mack looked at Maribel; her eyes were shining.

"Thanks," Mack said.

"Did you consider what your father would have thought about changing jobs?" How-Baby asked. "Did you maybe even have a conversation with him about it?"

"I figured he would tell me to do what was going to make me happy, and to go where I was wanted."

"You're wanted in Texas," How-Baby said. "We're going to take good care of you."

The Eight Weeks of August

August 1

Dear Bill,

Suffice it to say, I am someone who has made mistakes, and in buy-ing the hotel, I am trying to remedy them. You may think I intend to raze the hotel and build trophy homes instead, or condominiums. Although that would be most lucrative, that's not what I propose. I want to keep the hotel as it is.

From what I gather of recent developments, you're going to have a real shake-up in personnel. I hate to capitalize on another man's misfortune, but in this case, I can't help myself. I raise my offer to 25 million, along with the promise that the Beach Club and Hotel will remain intact.

Don't be daft, Bill. Take the money.

S.B.T.

NOTE SCRIBBLED IN FRONT DESK NOTEBOOK (TINY'S HANDWRITING)
Beware the eight weeks of August!

LOVE AND VANCE LAY next to each other in Love's twin bed, naked. They had just made love for the eleventh time. Late last night, Love took her temperature and checked it against her temperature from earlier in the week. It had risen three degrees; she was ovulating. Now she propped her legs on the footboard of the bed. The conception books recom-mended fifteen minutes of repose to give the sperm a fighting chance.

Love and Vance had been dating for four weeks, ever since sitting on the roof of the hotel on the Fourth of July. Their first real date was a few days later. Vance borrowed Mack's Jeep and took Love to Eel Point to go clamming. Vance made his own clammer out of a piece of PVC pipe. It had handles and two holes punched into the sealed end. He chose a spot in the wet sand near the water's edge, and sank in the open end of the pipe. He put his thumbs over the holes and pulled up. When he released his thumbs, a column of sand fell from the pipe, along with four cherrystone clams. Love picked the clams up, rinsed them, and put them in the clamming bucket. She felt as if they'd struck gold.

"Can I try?" she asked.

"Sure," Vance said. They moved farther down the shore. It was the perfect Nantucket summer evening—light breeze, piping plovers and oystercatchers, the sinking sun.

Vance wrapped his arms around Love from behind and spoke softly into her ear. "Hold your hands like this and push down. There you go, push." His lips grazed her ear, sending a warm buzz through her body.

Love brought up six clams.

"Show me again," she said. She loved the feel of his arms around her.

They collected a bucket of clams, and then Vance laid a blanket out in the sand. He showed Love how to hold the clam knife, how to slide it between the tight halves of the clam to pry it open. *Unlock the clam.* They ate the sweet, salty clams right out of the shell, drank a bottle of wine, and watched the sunset.

The more Love discovered about Vance, the more he impressed her. Around work, he skulked and moped and bristled with negative energy. But away from work he was sincere, kind. He had interests: he clammed and fished, and scalloped in the fall; he could play rag tunes on the piano. He'd traveled all through Southeast Asia and he knew fifty Thai words. He taught Love to say hello, *sawadee kah!*

The first two weeks there was No Sex, because Love was ambivalent about entering a relationship. Vance told her he didn't want children, but Love had hoped for a complete and total stranger—someone like Arthur Beebe—who would impregnate her and be gone. Relationships could get sticky.

The night she gave in, they were sitting in the driveway of Love's house on Hooper Farm Road after an evening at Mitchell's Book Corner (Vance loved to read; he kept a list of books and checked them off when he finished, something Love did as well). Before Love got out of the car, Vance asked her to touch his head.

"You always look at my head like you're afraid of it. So I want you to touch it." He dipped his chin, and the bare, brown expanse of his skull pointed at her, a blank face. Love hesitated; Vance's head did scare her.

"You want me to touch your head?" she said.

"Yes."

She expected it to be cool and smooth, like a marble. But it was warm, and she felt the beginnings of stubble. She ran her hands over it the way one might rub a pregnant woman's belly: what was in there? Something mysterious, unknowable.

Love invited Vance inside.

NOW, TWO MORE WEEKS had passed and they'd made love eleven times. Vance frequently spent the night at Love's place; they developed a routine, a way of being together.

Love was lying with her feet on the headboard dreaming of a tiny brown baby when Vance asked her to read his published short story.

"Come on," he said. "I want to know what you think."

"Okay," Love said. "I'll read it." There was still time before they had to go to work, and the story had been on her nightstand since the Fourth of July. Love was wary, however. Her job at the magazine in Aspen taught her all about writers and their hypersensitivity to anything that might be construed as criticism.

"Thank you." Vance whipped the story off the nightstand and handed it to Love. A ring from her water glass marked the first page.

"Are you going to watch me while I read it?"

"I'm not going to *watch* you," Vance said. "I'll read, too." He picked an *Atlantic Monthly* off the floor.

"Fine," Love said.

"Fine," Vance said.

"The Downward Spiral" by Vance Robbins

There was little hope left for Jerome. His life was closing in on him like the walls of a cramped tunnel. Jerome needed to break out before the walls crushed him, but he knew that wouldn't happen. He was filled with hate.

Jerome's life of misery began when his mother, Lula, threw his father out of the house when Jerome was in kindergarten. His father had just lost his seventh job in a row. Lula herself had had the same job since before Jerome was born. She was a car mechanic. Fiats and MGs were her speciality.

Love looked up from the story. Vance flipped through the pages of the *Atlantic*. He caught her eye over the top of the magazine, like a spy at a bus stop.

"What do you think so far?" he asked.

"It's good," Love said. "I like how the mother is a car mechanic. Is *your* mother a car mechanic?" Here was one thing about their newly established routine that baffled Love: Vance never talked about his family or his home. He seemed to be without a past. When Love asked where he grew up, he said, "Here and there. The East mostly." He had majored in American literature at Fairleigh Dickinson University in New Jersey, which he called "Fairly Ridiculous." But there was no mention of parents, siblings, or a hometown; the one time she'd been over to his cottage, she saw a picture of two people she thought might be Vance's parents standing arm in arm in front of a split-level house with aluminum siding. When she asked him. "Are these your folks?" he didn't answer.

Vance didn't answer the question about his mother either. No surprise there.

"Keep going," Vance said. "A lot happens."

He went back to the *Atlantic* and Love continued reading.

Lula worked at Hal Duare's Garage until six in the evening, and then she stopped at JD's Lounge for a bloody Mary or two before she made her way home, smelling of motor oil and Tabasco sauce. Jerome was in charge of making dinner—bologna sandwiches mostly—and he fell asleep in front of the TV. Some mornings he woke up still in his clothes, his back stiff from the floorboards. Jerome always brought home A's from school, but Lula wasn't impressed. She glanced at his papers briefly before letting them waft into the trash can.

Love looked up. "I can't believe the way some people parent."

"Tell me about it," Vance said.

Love laid the pages over her bare breasts. "Parenting is such a daunting job," she said. She pictured her egg: a girl waiting for a date.

Vance closed his magazine. "I imagine it will be."

"Will be?" Love said. "But not for you. You don't want children."

"I never said that."

"Yes, you did," Love said. "I asked you when we were on the roof on the Fourth of July, did you want children, and you said no."

Vance maneuvered his arms around Love so he was holding her. He had muscular arms and nice hands with blossom pink palms. He kissed the corner of her eye. "You know I'm crazy about you."

Love's skin itched, as if she were about to break out in a rash. "I thought you definitely didn't want children. You hate all the children at the Beach Club."

"That's an act," Vance said. "My reputation as a grump must be upheld."

"So all this time I thought you hated children, you secretly wanted some of your own."

"I could see having a kid someday," he said.

"You've changed your mind, then. I can't believe this. Men aren't *allowed* to change their minds."

"I think it might be nice to have a kid someday."

"You think it might be *nice*," Love said. "Having children isn't *nice*, Vance. It's an enormous responsibility that lasts for the rest of your life."

"I know," Vance said. "Listen, I'm not saying I want to have a baby in nine months."

"You *don't* want to have a baby in nine months," Love said. "Of course not. Ridiculous thought." Her voice was reaching its upper registers, its screechy tones. She wondered if he thought this was a pleasant surprise, like the ragtime piano. *Surprise, I love children!*

"I said *someday*, Love. Someday is a word that women don't understand. It means, *possibly*, in the *future*. Women always want to know when, when, when. But all I'm saying here is someday. Someday I'd like to get married, someday I'd like to have children. Look at Mack. He told Maribel 'someday' for six years, and now they're going to tie the knot. So, you see, someday really exists."

"You want a child someday, but not anytime soon," Love said. She waited a beat. "And maybe not at all."

"I wouldn't go so far as to say not at all. I would like a child someday. And I just defined someday. Why are we having this conversation?"

"What conversation?" Love said. She was officially perspiring. She couldn't tell him what was happening in her body; he thought she was on the pill. She wanted a baby more than she wanted to tell the truth. "Back to the story," she said.

When Jerome grew older, he became attracted to women who reminded him of Lula. Women who worked hard and drank hard, women who mistreated him. First, there was Nan. Jerome met Nan when he was fourteen and she was twelve. She would tongue kiss him one minute and the next minute she would punch his thigh and call him a fag. It wasn't long before Jerome was in love with Nan.

After Nan came Delilah, who, like the biblical Delilah, insisted Jerome cut his hair. Jerome was so crazy for Delilah, he not only cut his hair, he shaved his head.

"Wait a minute," Love said. "Our hero just shaved his head for some woman named Delilah. Does any of this ring true? Did you shave your head for a woman?"

"I told you why I shaved my head," Vance said. "I like to feel the sun."

"Jerome shaves his head for a woman named Delilah."

"That's Jerome," Vance said. "He's a fic-tion-al character."

"Would you shave your head for me?" Love asked.

"I think the question is, would I grow my hair for you," Vance said. "And the answer is yes. I'd do anything for you."

"Anything?"

"Anything," Vance said. "In fact, I've been wanting to ask what you think about me coming out to Aspen this winter."

"Aspen?" Love said. This was getting out of hand. "What about going back to Thailand? I thought that was a definite."

"That was before I met you," he said.

"Okay, wait," Love said. "Wait, wait. This is all moving so fast."

"Don't you want to give this a fighting chance?" Vance said.

"I'm not coming back to Nantucket next summer," Love said. "*This* is a once-in-a-lifetime type of thing."

"I'm not stuck here either, you know," Vance said. "If Mack can leave, I can too."

"I thought you wanted to work here without Mack. I thought that was the goal of the last twelve years. You'll finally be in charge."

"Let me put it to you this way," Vance said. "I wouldn't be opposed to moving to Colorado."

Moving to Colorado? Love froze up with fear. *Moving to Colorado?*

"Let me finish your story," she said.

"I should shower," Vance said. "How are you getting to work?"

"Blading," Love said. Vance had to be at work earlier than Love so he could supervise the beach boys. As part of their routine, he'd been driving her home in the evenings, but as far as Love could tell, no one at the Beach Club knew she and Vance were seeing each other. Everyone was absorbed with the craziness of their own lives. Jem even caught Vance and Love standing in the utility closet—they were kissing when he opened the door looking for some bleach—and he didn't seem to think finding them in the dark closet together was strange. He just stood there and said glumly, "I need bleach," and after Love handed it to him, he closed the door.

While Vance was in the shower, Love tried to finish the story, but she found herself sucked back to those terrifying words, *moving to Colorado*. She closed her eyes and saw sperm shooting through her, racing for her waiting egg. She felt dizzy. *Wait! Stop!* she wanted to say. *He wants to move to Colorado! Stop!*

Love tried not to think about it. She read somewhere that 70 percent of conception was will, a positive attitude, and so she would fight her body with her mind. She would think negative thoughts, ugly, sad thoughts. She picked up Vance's story and skimmed through the pages to the end.

Jerome goes to college and gets a degree in hotel and restaurant management. He falls in love with an Italian girl named Mia, and marries her in a big, opulent wedding with lots of uncles and homemade gnocchi and finger kissing. Jerome and Mia open an Italian restaurant called Mamma Mia's. It's a very successful venture until some of the customers start getting sick and dying. Turns out Mia is putting poison in the red sauce.

Love reread that part. Could that be right? Mia, *poisoning* the red sauce?

Jerome gets sued and the business goes belly up. Mia is indicted and Jerome spends all the money he has left on her lawyer, a man (suspiciously) named Mark Paterson, with whom Mia falls immediately in love. She wants a divorce from Jerome so she can marry Mark when she gets out of jail. She's sentenced to thirty years.

Broke and without his wife, Jerome returns to his hometown and finds his mother sitting on a barstool at JD's Lounge drinking a bloody Mary, but when he approaches her she pretends she doesn't know who he is, and when he starts to repeat, "I'm your son. It's me, Mom, Jerome," she has the bouncer throw him out.

The story ends with Jerome buying a bottle of Courvoisier and setting out to drive his Datsun into the side of the Browning Elementary School. Without question, a downward spiral.

Love lowered her feet from the footboard and stood up. She jumped on the balls of her feet. A stream of warm semen trickled down the inside of her thigh. She was shaking from head to toe when Vance came out of the bathroom, a towel wrapped around his waist.

"What's wrong?" he asked.

I've conceived. We've conceived. How easily this too could become a downward spiral. Vance suing for custody and taking away the child that was meant to be hers alone. Stealing her dream.

"I read your story," Love said, and she burst into tears.

Vance put his arms around her. He kissed the top of her head. "It's just a piece of fiction." He ran his hands down her bare back, which, much to her dismay, aroused her.

She knocked his hands away. "You have to leave," she said.

"Come on," he said. "I can be a little late. The boys know what they're doing."

"You have to *leave!*" Love was so disappointed with herself, letting this get out of hand. First he wanted to visit Colorado, then move there, and the next thing she knew he would be asking her to marry him, he would be interested in fathering the child that was only minutes old inside of her. "Get out!" she said, pointing to the door.

"You hated the story," Vance said. "You thought it was trash."

"That's not it," Love said. "Your stupid story has nothing to do with it."

"It's not a stupid story," Vance said. "It is a published story. My only published story."

"Listen, I need some space, okay?" Love said. "I see you every day at work, and I see you every night. Can you give me some space for a couple of days? Please?"

Vance dropped his towel and angrily stepped into his boxer shorts. "You hated my story. And the irony is, I let you read it because I thought you would understand. Ha! I should have known that I, Vance Robbins, am utterly un-understandable. Story of my life." He slid on his red shorts and pulled a shirt over his head backward. When she touched his arm, he shrugged her off. "I'm leaving," he said, twisting the shirt around his body. "Enjoy your space."

AS IF THAT WEREN'T bad enough, it started to rain, which immediately presented the problem of how to get to work, because Love wouldn't be able to use Rollerblades, or ride her bike. She called a cab, and as she waited for it to show up, she imagined taking an EPT and having it turn out positive. Her stomach flippety-flopped. Damn Vance! He'd ruined it. Thinking about pregnancy was supposed to make her feel elated, not apprehensive.

Love's cab was thirteen minutes late. She huffed as she climbed into the backseat.

"I said eight-fifteen." She looked at the cab driver. The short black hair, the seven silver hoop earrings. It was Tracey, the girl who had picked Love up from the ferry her first day on the island.

"It's raining, lady," Tracey said. "You're not the only person on the island who wants a cab this morning."

"I know you," Love said, leaning forward. "You're Tracey. You gave me a ride in May, remember? I showed you the Hadwen House and the Old Mill."

Tracey blinked into the rearview. "Oh, yeah." She laughed. "You're the woman who wants a baby. So what happened? Did you get knocked up?"

"This morning, I think," Love said.

"Wow," Tracey said. "Congrats. You don't seem too happy about it. What's wrong, did you boink somebody ugly?"

The girl should write a book on how to be indelicate, Love thought. "No," she said. "Worse. I boinked someone who now claims he wants a child."

Tracey backed out of the driveway. "Okay, so what?"

"I want to be a single parent. I want the baby for myself."

Tracey turned down the radio. "You'll excuse me for saying so, but that's fucked up."

"I don't expect you to understand," Love said. "You're too young."

Tracey lifted her hands from the steering wheel and held them palm-up as if to say, *I am what I am.* "Are you going to tell the guy you're pregnant?"

"I might not be pregnant," Love said. "I just think I am."

"If you were thinking for the kid, you'd tell him," Tracey said. "Every kid should have a shot at two parents. To deny the kid that is wrong. That's my take on it. If you care."

"Well, I don't care," Love snapped. Immediately, she was embarrassed. First she yelled at Vance and now at Tracey, an innocent cab driver.

Tracey was quiet for the rest of the ride. When she reached the Beach Club, Love gave her a five-dollar tip, even though this was an ugly gesture in her book: act rude and then try to make up for it with money. But what else could she do?

"I'm sorry I was short," Love said. "Thanks for the ride."

"Tell him," Tracey said.

BECAUSE OF THE WEATHER, the lobby looked like a second grade classroom without a teacher. Guests were eating their muffins and bagels and doughnuts, leaving trails of powdered sugar and smears of cream cheese on everything they touched. Someone had spilled coffee on the green carpet, and sections of the newspaper were scattered about as though the whole pile had been dropped from the rafters. Kids ran around screaming, and the phone was ringing. Vance stood behind the desk, his lips puckered.

"You're late," he said.

"Vance, listen, I'm sorry," Love said.

He raised a hand. "I don't want to hear it."

"It wasn't about your story," Love said. "I liked your story."

"Love, the damage is done, okay? Don't insult me further by trying to backpedal."

The phone rang again. Vance made no move to answer it. Love hurried through the office, hanging her wet jacket on the handle of a vacuum. She popped out to the front desk and Vance disappeared. Vanishing Vance. The phone nagged at her like a crying baby.

"Nantucket Beach Club and Hotel," Love said.

"Do you have any rooms available for this weekend?" a woman asked. "The lady at Visitor Services told us you were located on the beach."

"We're fully booked, ma'am," Love said. "We've been fully booked since early spring."

"Can you check to see if someone has canceled?" the woman said.

"Just a moment, please." Love poked her head into the office. Vance sat at Mack's desk, staring out the window. Why did they have to work together today of all days? Why couldn't he be Jem? "Vance, do you know where Mack is? I have a reservation call."

Vance said nothing.

"Vance?" Love said.

Nothing.

"Okay, *fine*," she said. She picked up the phone. "No cancellations, ma'am. Sorry."

A man with horn-rimmed glasses stood at the desk. He had a muffin crumb in his mustache. "Do you know when the sky is going to clear?" he asked.

"Do I know when the sky is going to clear?" Love said. "No, sir, I don't. You have a TV in your room. You could check the weather channel."

The man wiped the crumb off his lip and Love relaxed a little. "My wife has forbidden me to turn on the TV," he said. "This is a no-TV vacation. Which is really going to be trying if the rain persists, you see what I mean?"

"I'm sorry," Love said.

A line formed at the front desk. This had never happened before—it was as though everyone thought of a question for Love at the same time.

An older woman with two children stepped up. "I'm Ruthie Soldier, room seven," she said. "What is there to do with kids when it rains?"

"There's the Whaling Museum," Love said. "That's only down the street. There's the Peter Folger Museum. There's the Hadwen House."

"Is there anything to do that will be fun for these kids?" Ruthie Soldier said. "I don't want to bore them with history."

"Thank you, Gramma," the older child, a girl wearing multicolored braces, said. "We have to go back to school in a few weeks anyway."

"You could go out for ice-cream sundaes," Love said.

"We just ate bagels," Mrs. Soldier said. "Is there a movie house with matinees?"

"No," Love said. The phone rang. She eyed the console's blinking red light.

"What about bowling?"

"No bowling."

"Do you have any board games?"

Love tried to block out the ringing phone. "Let me check," she said. She thought she'd seen an old, mildewed Parcheesi in one of the closets. In the office, Vance was still lounging at Mack's desk.

"Vance, do we have any board games?" Love asked. "These people want something to do with their kids."

Vance smiled meanly. He was his back-at-work creepy self. Someone whom Love would not date, not sleep with, and certainly never parent with.

The phone continued to ring. Love ran back to the desk to answer it. The people standing in line crossed their arms and shifted their weight. A man still in his pajamas tapped his bony, bare foot impatiently. Where was Mack?

"Nantucket Beach Club and Hotel," Love said.

"This is Mrs. Russo. I'm calling to see if the Beach Club is open today."

Love looked out the window. The peaked roof of the pavilion created a minifalls. "It's raining, Mrs. Russo. No Beach Club today."

"That's a shame," Mrs. Russo said. "We paid so much money."

Love hung up. The line of people swarmed and blurred in front of her hand and then she remembered Mrs. Soldier. "No games," Love said. "Would you like a VCR?"

"That would be lovely," Mrs. Soldier said.

Love went back to Vance. "Room seven wants a VCR."

"They're all signed out," he said.

Love returned to the desk. "The VCRs are all signed out," Love said. The man in the pajamas raised his hand. She was the second grade teacher.

"Yes?" Love said.

"You're out of coffee," he said.

"You're kidding," Love said. Several people in line sadly shook their heads. Normally, they didn't run out of coffee until midafternoon and by then things were quiet enough that Love could make more. She poked her head into the back office again. "Vance," she said, in her most pleasant, ass-kissing voice, "we're out of coffee. Could you be a doll and make some more?"

"That's your job," he said.

"I know," she said. "But I have a line of people out here who need help. Really, a line."

Vance smiled at her again. He hated her. "I wouldn't want to *infringe* on your *space*."

"Oh, God," Love said. "Please help me."

Vance had the crossword puzzle from the *Boston Globe* in front of him. Love thought she might cry. She stepped out to the desk. "The coffee is going to be a minute," she said.

The man in the pajamas pointed a bony finger at her. He was a health-class skeleton with skin. "We pay a lot of money for these rooms," he said. He looked to the person behind him in line, as though he wanted to organize some kind of group revolt. "I heard you say there are no more VCRs. Why not? Why doesn't every room have a VCR?"

"I don't know," Love said. "It's not my hotel."

The phone rang. Love's hand itched to answer it, but she was afraid that if she did, the guests would storm the desk. The rain had turned the normally well-heeled guests into a class of emotionally needy students, into a band of ruby red Communists. Where was Mack?

An elegant-looking gentleman in an Armani suit was next in line. Love remembered checking him in: Mr. Juarez, room 12. "I have a flight to New York at ten-thirty this morning. Would you be so kind as to call and see if it's going to be delayed?"

"I'd be happy to," Love said. This man, at least, was pleasant. She liked his tone of voice. She liked his calm demeanor. She wanted to shake his hand. Gold star student.

Love called the airport and found it was closed temporarily, due to lightning.

"I'm sorry, Mr. Juarez," she said. "The airport is closed. No one is flying."

"I have a lunch meeting at one o'clock that can't be missed," he said.

"The man at the airport said 'temporarily,' " Love said. "So perhaps they'll resume flying in a little while."

"Will you call again when you get a chance?" Mr. Juarez asked. He slid a fifty-dollar bill across the desk. Love hesitated. Everyone behind Mr. Juarez was watching.

"I'm sorry," she said softly. "I can't accept that."

Mr. Juarez slipped the bill into his coat pocket. "It's yours if you get me on a flight."

The honeymooners from room 20 stepped up; behind them, the room was a carnival. "We'd like lunch reservations," the wife said. "Somewhere in town. Where do you suggest?"

Sit in your room and feed each other grapes, Love thought. *There's a big bowl of them over there*—but when Love looked at the breakfast buffet, she saw the grapes were all gone.

"Why don't you go into town and try your luck?" Love said. "I can lend you an umbrella."

"Okay," the husband said.

"We'd like a reservation," the wife said. "We'd rather not waste our time."

The husband nodded along. "That's right."

"The Chanticleer serves lunch," Love said. "So does the Wauwinet. Which would you prefer?"

"I'd prefer coffee," the skeleton in the pajamas called out. "I'd really like a steaming mug of coffee to drink on this dreary day."

Back by the piano, two boys were yelling at each other. Love looked over in time to see them hit the floor. "Whose children are those?" she asked. No one answered. "Well, they must belong to somebody." Still no one. They pulled each other's hair and started slapping and punching. "Boys!" she said. "Stop it!" Her maternal instincts rose in her like a fever. "Boys!" No one in the line made a move to stop them. Love hoisted herself over the desk, and ran to where the boys were rolling around. They were stuck together, one had a death grip on the other's hair. Love physically wedged herself between the two boys. Then, perhaps realizing that there would be no more coffee or lunch reservations until this was taken care of, the honeymooners came to help Love hold the boys away from one another. The honeymooners smiled at each other, as if to say, *Isn't this cute, a fight?* One of the kids started to cry, and the other's nose bled all over the carpet. The husband took out a handkerchief and gave it to Mr. Bleeding.

"Are you two brothers?" Love asked.

Mr. Crying shook his head. He was pudgy and sweet looking, and now he had two raised red scratches under his eye. "No. We're not brothers. We're friends."

"I'm not your friend," Mr. Bleeding said. The handkerchief bloomed with red. "Not anymore."

Love herded both boys toward the office. She didn't make eye contact with anyone in line. At Mack's desk, Vance diligently counted squares on his crossword.

"You can help these two cowboys find their parents," Love said.

"Cowboys?" Mr. Bleeding said. "We are *not* cowboys."

"You're monsters," Vance said. He meant it to be derogatory, of course. Love had never heard Mr. I Want a Child Someday call children anything but monsters, but both boys brightened up.

"We're monsters," Mr. Crying said. He stopped crying, and nudged Mr. Bleeding.

"Yeah, we're monsters," Mr. Bleeding said. He gave Love a withering look. "But we're not cowboys."

"Whatever," Love said.

Reluctantly, Vance stood up. Love returned to the desk, and she heard Vance telling the boys a joke as they moved down the hallway.

Back at the desk, Love saw the skeleton in the pajamas shaking his head.

"What's your name, sir?" she asked him.

He straightened up and crossed his arms against his chest. "Michael Klutch."

Mr. Klutch! The man who had booked rooms 4, 5, and 6 all for himself. He was staying in room 5, and the other two rooms were "buffer rooms," so he didn't have to hear his neighbors shutting their dresser drawers or flushing their toilets.

"We're going to make a list," Love said. "Put your name on the list and I'll get to you as soon as I can. I am now going to make some coffee." Love walked back into Mack's office, and the phone rang. Love tried to walk past it, but the receiver was a magnet.

"Front desk," Love said.

"This is Audrey Cohn, room seventeen. My son just came in with blood all over his face! I'd like you to call an ambulance right away. There's blood everywhere."

"It's a bloody nose," Love said. "He was out here in the lobby unsupervised and he got into a fight. All he needs is a wet washcloth."

"*Please* call an ambulance," Audrey Cohn said.

Love was glad it had come to this—sirens and flashing lights—because maybe *that* would get Mack's attention. When Love stepped out into the hallway, she bumped into Mr. Juarez.

"I didn't sign the list," he said, "because you were helping me before." He removed the fifty-dollar bill from his pocket and wound it through his slender, tan fingers. "I was hoping you'd be so kind as to call the airport again."

"Mr. Juarez," Love said. "I have to make the coffee. Please sign the list." She hurried into the galley kitchen and closed the door. There, taped to the cabinets, was a piece of paper that had been ripped from the front desk notebook, and on it, a note in Tiny's handwriting. "Beware the eight weeks of August."

Love got the coffeemaker chugging and walked back into the lobby. The guests were still standing in a line. Love slowly made her way behind the desk.

"Now," she said. "Who's next?"

Before anyone could answer, Love heard the sirens and saw red lights whip around the lobby walls. A paramedic stormed in the lobby doors, black uniformed, self-important, his walkie-talkie alive with raspy static.

"Who's hurt?" he said.

Love called room 17. "Your ambulance is here."

Audrey Cohn laughed. "Jared is fine," she said. "We cleaned him up and it turns out it was just a bloody nose. No ambulance needed."

Love retreated into the office and sat in Mack's chair. The front of her dress was sticking to her. She heard a commotion in the lobby, everyone talking at once. Then, Vance walked in.

"What's with the ambulance?" he said.

"Room seventeen had me call it for the kid with the bloody nose. Now she doesn't want it. What should I tell the paramedic?"

"Tell him you're sorry," Vance said.

"I've told everybody I'm sorry this morning," Love said. "I'm sorry it's raining, I'm sorry the airport is closed. I'm sorry we don't have VCRs, nor do we have coffee. I am very sorry!"

"And don't forget you're sorry you asked me to leave this morning," Vance said. "You're sorry you hurt my feelings."

"Of course I am," Love said. She caught his eye. "Vance, I *am*."

"I won't come to Colorado this winter," he said. "Because you only want a summer romance, is that it? No strings attached?"

"Yes," Love said. Was her egg still waiting for a date? For a mate? "Is that okay?"

Vance rubbed the top of his head. Love knew what it felt like, warm and stubbly, alive, growing in. "Sure," he said. He gave her a hug; her feet weren't touching the ground when the paramedic stormed into the office.

"Is there a problem here or *not?*" he asked.

"No, bud, no problem here," Vance said.

The paramedic spun on his heels and left the office, slamming the door behind him. Love and Vance kissed a long making-up kiss, and then she returned to the desk—but the line had dispersed, all except for Mr. Juarez, who stood patiently with his hands folded in front of him.

Love called the airport and found it had opened. "You're all set," Love said. "Let me call you a cab." She thought uneasily of Tracey. *Tell him.*

Mr. Juarez gave Love the fifty, which she tucked into her pocket. Then she poured herself a cup of coffee. Outside, the rain slowed to a drizzle; the clouds were breaking up. Love heard piano music, bright and jangly, a rag tune. Across the lobby, Vance, her summer-romance man, played her a song.

JEM WAS GLAD WHEN August arrived because that meant he was one month closer to being finished with Nantucket. As soon as he heard Maribel and Mack were getting married, he wanted to pack his stuff, buy a ferry ticket, and leave. But Jem stayed. He needed the money, but more than that, he couldn't bring himself to leave the island because of Maribel. She came to the hotel almost every day now that she and Mack were engaged, and it was pure hell to see her. The last time, she showed off her diamond ring. It was a single round stone, simple and sparkling, like Maribel herself. It nearly killed Jem to look at the diamond. It was physical proof that she was Mack's. Time to start accepting it.

As painful as it was to see Maribel, Jem was certain that not seeing her would be much, much worse. And so, when she showed up around the hotel, he was both miserable and elated; he couldn't keep from talking to her. How's work at the library? How's your mother? How's the running? In turn, Maribel would ask, How's work going? Have you been to the beach much? Been out? Met anyone? She wanted him to find a girlfriend. But he wouldn't give her the satisfaction. If he made her feel guilty, so be it; at least he made her feel something.

"No," he answered. "Haven't been out. Haven't met anyone."

NEIL ROSENBLUM WAS THE first guest to snag Jem's interest in a long time. He looked like Stephen Spielberg. He had shoulder-length gray hair and tiny frameless glasses. He wore a Hawaiian shirt open at the neck, a pair of jeans, espadrilles. He was staying in room 5, alone, for three nights. He brought a knapsack and a garment bag, and when Jem tried to help him with these, he raised a hand, and said, "I never pack more than I can carry myself. But why don't you show me the way?"

Jem led Neil Rosenblum down the beach to his room, giving the usual spiel about the chambermaids, the ice machine, the Continental breakfast. Neil wasn't listening. He stared out over the beach, shaking his head. Jem climbed the three steps to the front deck of room 5 and unlocked the door.

"Here you go, sir," Jem said.

Neil Rosenblum walked past Jem into the room. Jem waited just a minute—the Tip Linger. Neil dropped his backpack and laid his garment bag across the leather chair.

"Let me know if you need anything," Jem said, backing up. The No-Tip Retreat.

Neil Rosenblum swung around. "Wait a minute," he said. "What's your name?"

"Jem Crandall."

Neil Rosenblum stuck out his hand. "I'm Neil," he said. "It's nice to meet you."

Jem shook his hand. "Likewise."

Neil Rosenblum looked around his room. "I have to tell you, Jem, this place is just what a guy like me needs. A place to let it dangle for a few days."

"Yes, sir, I know just what you mean."

"Call me Neil." Neil unzipped his backpack and took out a couple of folded shirts, a bathing suit, a pair of flip-flops, a disposable camera, a bottle of Ketel One vodka and a plastic baggie full of weed. He held the baggie up.

"Do you smoke, Jem?" Neil asked.

Jem tried not to show his surprise. "No, Neil, not really."

Neil opened the baggie and sniffed its contents. "Too bad." He held up the Ketel One. "Do you drink?"

Jem shifted his weight and looked at the room's digital clock radio. It was only 2:45. "I have to work until five o'clock."

"But you do drink?" Neil asked.

"Yes."

"I own Rosenblum Travel. Ever heard of it? Ever seen the commercials?"

"I don't think so."

"We're out of New York—Manhattan, New Jersey, Connecticut. It's a huge business. Huge! And it's killing me." Neil sat down on the bed. "Do you know why I'm here, Jem?"

"No," Jem said.

Neil kicked off his espadrilles. "I'm here to smoke dope, drink vodka cranberries, and sit in the sun. I'm here to dabble my feet at the ocean's edge. I'm here to do things I enjoy. I am not here to talk on the phone, read faxes, listen to voice mail, or send wealthy Mrs. Tolstoy or Mrs. Dostoevsky on a luxury cruise to Leningrad. I'm leaving Tuesday morning, at which time I'll take my suit out of this garment bag and put it on. But until then, I don't want any phone calls. No messages. If you knock on my door, it should be because you want to drink with Neil Rosenblum or help me smoke some of this weed."

"Okay," Jem said. "I understand."

"He understands, he says. I hope so. I really do." Neil pulled a bill out of his jeans and handed it to Jem. Tip Success. "Come back at five o'clock and we'll have a drink. See if you can round me up some tonic, a couple of limes, a little Ocean Spray. How does that sound?"

"Tonic, limes, Ocean Spray," Jem repeated. As he left Neil Rosenblum's room, he looked at the bill. It was a hundred dollars.

AT FIVE-TEN, JEM STEPPED onto the deck of room 5 with a paper bag containing two bottles of tonic, two of cranberry cocktail, and six limes. The door to room 5 was closed. Jem knocked, and waited. Neil opened the door. His hair was disheveled and he was wearing his Hawaiian shirt and his bathing suit but not his glasses. His eyes were red. He looked confused when he saw Jem. "Yes?" he said.

Jem held the bag out. "I brought you some tonic, the things you asked for. . . ."

"Oh, right, right. God, I fell asleep. Come on in, have a seat. I was on my way to the beach, but I guess I never made it." He picked up the baggie of dope. "The guy who gave this to me is a professional."

Jem sat on the edge of the bed. He couldn't help but notice the indented place where Neil had slept.

"Do I have glasses?" Neil asked.

"You were wearing some this afternoon," Jem said.

Neil rubbed his eyes and laughed. "My eyeglasses, yes. Thank you for reminding me. I meant do I have drinking glasses? Highballs? Martinis?"

"Glasses are on top of the fridge," Jem said.

Neil made the drinks. "Shall we go onto the deck?" he asked.

"Sure," Jem said. He felt awkward, as if this were a first date. Jem accepted one of the vodka cranberries from Neil and walked out onto the deck. Jem sank into one of the deck chairs. It had been a long time since he'd had a mixed drink; at the bars, he could only afford beer. Neil sat in the other deck chair, his eyeglasses in place. It was beautiful: the water, the sun, the cold cocktail, the surprisingly comfortable deck chair. A sliver of beautiful life.

"So, Jem, tell me," Neil said. "How did you find your way to this island?"

"I just picked it off the map," Jem said. "I knew kids in college whose families had homes here and I thought I could make money."

"Are you making money?" Neil asked.

"Well, yeah," Jem said. The hundred-dollar tip rested deep in his pocket. "I guess."

"And what are your plans after Nantucket?" Neil asked.

"I'm going to L.A.," Jem said. "I want to be an agent."

Neil Rosenblum threw his shaggy gray head back and laughed. "Oh, Christ," he said. "That's just gorgeous. He wants to be an agent. He's heading to L.A. You kill me, kid."

"Why?" Jem said. He didn't love being laughed at.

"Going to Hollywood to break into the business? I didn't think people did that anymore. Just like no one goes to Paris to become a writer; it's been done. Overdone. I can tell you what's going to happen. You're going to get to Cali and work at the Bel Air or Spago until you get fed up, and then you know what you're going to do?"

"What?" Jem asked.

"I don't know," Neil said. "I don't know what you're going to do. Come back East? Get hooked up with some pretty older lady like Nicole Simpson and have her jealous ex-husband hack you into tiny bits? Join a cult and participate in group suicide? I don't know."

Jem finished his drink. Neil said, "Do you want another?"

Jem shrugged. "Are you going to quit making fun of me?"

"Ooooh," Neil said. "I hurt his feelings. I'm sorry." He disappeared into the room, leaving Jem to stare at the water. Then he reappeared with fresh drinks. "You know what I was doing when I was your age? I was backpacking through Southeast Asia. Kathmandu, Bangkok, Koh Samui, Singapore, two months on Bali. I spent a penny a night in the teahouses in the Himalayas. Four bucks a night for a room in Thailand plus all the *paad thai* I could eat. I didn't shower for a month and when I finally saw a mirror I barely recognized myself. And guess what? I was the happiest I've ever been. Now look at me. I assume you know how much I'm paying for this room—more than I spent on my entire trip through Asia! And I'm no fucking happier than

I was watching the sun go down on Kuta Beach, drinking Bintang beer. That's the truth."

Jem chewed on a piece of ice. "I've worked hard for my money this summer," he said. "I'm not going to waste it traveling."

"Waste it!" Neil said. "You wouldn't be wasting it, my friend. You'd be giving yourself something you can take to the grave. And I'm not feeding you a sales pitch. You couldn't afford my tours and you wouldn't enjoy them. I'm saying you should go on your own, while you're young. See the Taj Mahal, the Nile River, the Raffles Hotel."

"My parents are going to be upset enough about California," Jem said. "Never mind Timbuktu."

Neil looked at Jem over his glasses. "Surely you don't still listen to your parents."

"I don't want to piss them off," Jem said. "Probably sounds childish to you, but that's how I feel." Jem watched the sun sink behind a bank of clouds. "I should go," he said.

"He should go, he says. Yes, by all means, go home. Get away from the old geezer who's putting ideas in your head."

THE NEXT MORNING, JEM was standing outside watering the roses when Maribel jogged over, her body glistening with sweat.

"Hit me with the hose," she said.

Jem sprayed a light mist in her direction.

"I'm hot, Jem," she said. "I mean it. Get me wet."

"Okay," Jem said. He pulled the trigger of the hose and the water hit her chest, her bare stomach, her legs. She turned around and he hosed off her shoulders, her back, her ass, until she was soaked and Jem had an erection.

"What if I wanted to take you on a trip through Southeast Asia?" he said. "Would you go with me? We could stay at the Raffles Hotel."

Water dripped off the end of Maribel's ponytail. "You're sweet," she said. "Thanks for the shower." She jogged away. Maribel probably didn't mean to tease him, but each time he saw her inspired hope, and then the hope was shot down. It was just like his sister, Gwennie. She ate a meal, and helped Jem's mother with the dishes, drying the plates with a tea towel and nesting them away. But then she retreated to the upstairs bathroom, turning on the noisy exhaust fan. "Putting on my makeup," she'd say. When she emerged, ten, fifteen minutes later, the bathroom smelled too piney, freshener fresh.

Jem gathered up the hose and went into the lobby. Love said, "You have a message. I can't believe this. There's finally a handsome, single man staying in the hotel alone, and he's after you." She handed Jem a pink message slip that said:"Happy hour? NR." "And since you're going over there, you might as well tell him he has two messages. I put his blinker on a long time ago but he hasn't responded."

"He doesn't want any messages," Jem said. "But, whatever, I'll take them."

Love handed two message slips to Jem, and he shoved them in his pants pocket. Then he popped out the side door and read them. It was like reading someone's mail, but Jem wanted to know a little more about the guy before he had drinks with him again. The first message said, "Your girlfriend called. 11:05 A.M." and the box that said "Please call" was checked. The second message was from a Dr. Kenton. Dr. Kenton was probably his psychiatrist. Since coming to Nantucket, Jem learned that everyone in New York saw a psychiatrist. Or Dr. Kenton could be a client who wanted Neil to set up a golf vacation in Tahiti. Jem crumpled both messages and put them back in his pocket.

After work, Jem knocked on the door of room 5. This time Neil was awake, smoking a joint.

"You wanna smoke?" Neil asked.

"Sure," Jem said. First, though, he sat in the leather chair. He'd stripped this room at least twenty times, and every time he wanted to sink into the chair. It felt like a giant hand. He pinched the joint between his thumb and index finger and inhaled. He held the smoke for as long as he could, and then he passed the joint back.

"Have you given any more thought to traveling?" Neil asked. "Because I was thinking about it after you left yesterday. If you're set on Cali, that's fine, but you should travel first."

"What do you care?" Jem said. "I mean, not to be rude, but what difference does it make to you if I go or not? You said I couldn't afford your tours and I'm sure you're right."

"I care as a fellow human being," Neil said. "When I look at you I see a young person with his whole life ahead of him, and I say to myself, 'Man, if I had it to do over, I'd go back. That trip is one thing I don't regret.' "

"So because you don't regret it, I have to go?" Jem said.

Neil smoked the joint down. "If you went, I promise you'd thank me. Guaranteed."

"Do you mind if I ask you a question?" Jem said. He went over to the dresser, which had become a makeshift bar, and poured himself a Ketel One.

"Go right ahead," Neil said.

"Why did you come on vacation alone? Obviously it's not to be by yourself otherwise you wouldn't keep inviting me here."

"Why did I come alone? Why do I keep inviting you here?" Neil threw his hands over his head, fell back onto the bed and addressed the rafters. "I have problems. A few small ones and a big one and I came here to think them through. Now, sometimes you want to think things through alone, but sometimes you want another input. An impartial input. You don't know me. I don't know you. You don't have to sit here and drink with me, but you've agreed to. Maybe that's because you want another hundred-dollar tip. Maybe you're doing this out of altruism. I don't know the reason why you're here. I asked you here because I need a disinterested third party. Do you know the difference between disinterested and uninterested?"

Jem shook his head. "Doesn't matter. I'm interested."

"He's interested, he says. Okay, fine. Do you think I'm married?"

"No," Jem said. He remembered the crumpled message slip in his pocket. *Your girlfriend.* Now would be the time to pull the message out and show it to Neil, but he didn't.

"Why not?"

"You don't strike me as the marrying type," Jem said. "You seem too free-wheeling."

"I'm not married," Neil said. "I live with a woman in New York. Her name is Desirée. Desirée, desire, that whole thing. If my life were a play, it'd be called 'A Girlfriend Named Desire.' Whoa!" He wobbled a little as he stood to fix himself a drink. "We have a baby together, a little girl."

"That's nice," Jem said. He laughed, although nothing was funny.

"Desirée isn't Jewish and she doesn't want to convert. This means my daughter, my only child, won't be raised Jewish."

"Is that the big problem?" Jem asked.

"That's a little problem," Neil said. "Another little problem is whether or not I should marry Desirée. I desire her, yes, but do I love her? Do I love her enough to make her my wife? Or, do I get married for my daughter's sake?"

Jem was receiving hazy messages, mixed-up messages that weren't making it from his brain to his tongue. He couldn't speak. He remembered Maribel that afternoon, *You're sweet*. And then he realized that she came into the parking lot and left without seeing Mack. "I love a woman named Maribel," Jem said. "I love her like crazy. But she's engaged to someone else. She's engaged to my fucking *boss*."

"You love her?" Neil said. "When you wake up she's the first thing on your mind?"

"She's before the first thing," Jem said. "I dated her for two weeks. I kissed her and held her hand, and I've seen her breasts." He leaned his head back against the chair. "This woman *infiltrated*."

"I'm going to roll another joint," Neil said. He found a station with jazz music on the clock radio. "The first thing on my mind when I wake up is an image of my favorite place—Pangboche, Nepal—in the Himalayas. That place defines peace, man. That's what I expect heaven to look like." Neil rolled the joint, licked it, lit it. Jem couldn't smoke anything else. He waved the joint away. Neil took a drag and talked in a pinched voice while he held his breath. "Second thing on my mind is my little girl, Zoe." He exhaled. "There's nothing better than having a woman-child. I'm forty-two years old and I've had my problems with women just like everybody else. And then I find myself the father of a woman-child. Finally, a woman who loves me unconditionally. It's a grand feeling." Neil took another hit off the joint; Jem's head reeled just watching him. "Third or fourth thing on my mind is maybe Desirée, if I'm lucky. If you've found a woman who's your first thing, man, you should go after her."

"I've tried," Jem said.

"Have you tried ignoring her?" Neil asked. "That works like a dream."

"I can't ignore her," Jem said. "It would be impossible."

"You must do it!" Neil said. "If you want her, you must shun her."

"She wants me to shun her," Jem said. "Because she's engaged to someone else. She has a diamond ring."

"Engagements get broken every day," Neil said. "Rings get returned."

"It'll never happen," Jem said.

"You have to ignore her," Neil said. "Starting right now." He gently pressed the joint into the sole of his flip-flop. "Let's go."

They walked the mile into town, and Neil devised a simple plan: they would start drinking at the bars closest to the harbor and work their way up Main Street. And so they went: a beer at Rope Walk, a goombay smash at Straight Wharf, a Cap'n Cooler at the Bamboo Bar, vodka cranberries at the Club Car. Neil brought his disposable camera, and at each bar, he took a picture of himself and Jem by holding the camera out and pushing the button. Jem wished he wasn't wearing his clownish uniform; he didn't exactly want to be remembered as looking like he worked on the Love Boat.

When they stepped out of the Club Car, it was dark. Jem had told Neil about his fuck-up with Mr. G and he told the Mr. Feeney toilet story. He was bone-dry on funny stories, except for the Mrs. Worley story, which only now, after five drinks, seemed even remotely funny. They walked over to the Boarding House for martinis and Jem told Neil about Mrs. Worley, about the moment of shock and horror when he opened the door and found her there, shorts sagging around her ankles, the desperate expression on her face as she reached for the door. They laughed until they were bent over on their barstools, hiccuping.

"We need food," Neil said.

At Languedoc, they ordered steaks, and by the time Jem's food arrived, he realized he'd barely thought of Maribel all night.

"Here's what I think you should do about Desirée," Jem said. He was so drunk he didn't know what he was going to say next. It sounded like he was about to give Neil Rosenblum advice about his woman problem, something he was ridiculously unqualified to do. "I think you should ask her to raise Zoe Jewish—ask her nicely—and if she refuses, then I think you should raise Zoe Jewish yourself."

"I can't do it," Neil said. "The mother has to be Jewish. That's how it works."

"Oh," Jem said. "That sucks."

"Yeah," Neil said. "I'd really like to resolve this. You want to know your kids are going to be okay." He got a serious look on his face, and Jem sensed the evening about to cave in, as though all the drinking and smoking might wash over them in an unpleasant way. But then Neil rebounded. He smiled. "Let's go dancing," he said.

They caught a cab on Water Street and went to the Muse, a dark, smoky club bar with live music. As soon as they stepped in the door, Jem spotted a group of women his age. Neil nudged him. "Here we go," he said. "*Good-bye, Maribel.*"

The girls were all looking at Jem. He picked out the prettiest one—a brunette who was wearing a baseball hat backward, a man's plain white T-shirt, jeans, and Birkenstocks. Jem approached her. "I need a glass of water," he said. "How about you? Can I buy you a glass of water?"

"I'm drinking Rolling Rock," she said, holding her bottle up.

"I need a glass of water," he said. "The inside of my mouth feels like a fur coat."

The girl smiled wanly, took a swig of her beer, and mouthed something to one of her girlfriends. Probably, *Help me!* Neil talked to two blondes, both wearing black dresses. Or maybe Jem was seeing double. Neil leaned across the bar waving a twenty, then he picked up three beers and handed one to each of the blondes. Definitely two girls there. Jem suddenly felt alone. He put his hand on the brunette's shoulder.

"What's your name?" he asked.

"Dee Dee."

"I'm Jem. Do you want to dance?"

"No, I want to sit and talk."

Jem stared at his shoes. They were covered with bar sludge. He wondered what people would think at work tomorrow.

Dee Dee put her beer down. "I'm only kidding," she said. "I want to dance."

They threaded their way through the crowd. The band was loud, funky—it was music without words. That was fine; Jem was suffering from sensory overload as it was. All these people! He wedged in close to Dee Dee and started to move his arms and legs. He was dancing, he thought. Soon Neil was dancing next to him with the blondes and he snapped a picture of Jem and Dee Dee with his disposable camera.

Good-bye, Maribel, Jem thought. He wanted worse than anything to be out of this bar and at Maribel's house. He just wanted to look at her.

He shouted into Dee Dee's ear, "I have to go." He stumbled off the dance floor and out into the parking lot, where throngs of people slouched and smoked, slurred their words. A police officer waited in a car across the street.

Don't do anything stupid, Jem told himself. He found ten bucks in the pocket of his Nantucket red shorts: another tip success. That would be enough to get him to Maribel's house or to his own, but not both.

A driver for Atlantic Cab idled in front of the bar, smoking a cigarette, reading the *Inquirer & Mirror.*

"I'm going to see her no matter what you say," Jem told the driver. "Ninety-five Pheasant."

"Hey, man, I won't stop you," the driver said. "Hop in." He nuzzled his radio. "I'm at the Muse, headed for Ninety-five Pheasant. One passenger."

"Two passengers."

Jem turned around. Neil was standing next to him.

"Two passengers," the driver said. "Let's go."

They climbed in and the cab pulled out of the parking lot.

"What was wrong with the young lady in the baseball hat?" Neil asked.

Jem slumped against the cab seat. "I'm going to see Maribel. I have to see her, man."

"No, you're not," Neil said. He handed some money to the cab driver. "Take us to the Nantucket Beach Club, please."

"We're going to see Maribel," Jem said. He was going to be sick. He raised his voice. "Driver, can you pull over?"

He must have had the sound of vomit in his voice, because the cab driver responded right away. "Pulling over."

Jem puked onto the side of the road. Gravel, a little grass, his chunky vomit.

"Are you okay, buddy?" Neil asked, patting him on the back.

"Happens every night," the cab driver said. "Believe me when I say, this is better than some. Had a chick last week blow chow into the back of my head."

Neil pulled Jem back into the cab. "You can't see Maribel tonight, my friend. You're a mess. I'm going to take you back to the Club. You need a swim. You need to cool off."

"Okay," Jem said. Sour mouth, pasty mouth. Water sounded good.

JEM STRIPPED TO HIS boxers and waded into the cool water of Nantucket Sound. Water he couldn't drink. What was that rhyme? Rub-a-dub-dub? He plunged all the way in, and the water lit up around him, a pale, glowing green. It was like magic; he had an aura, a body halo.

"Phosphorescence," Neil said. He waded in behind Jem and dove into the shallow water. The water lit up around him like a force field. Neil surfaced. "There are living organisms in the water, and when we disturb them, they glow. There's great phosphorescence off the coast of Puerto Rico. I send hundreds of people to see it every year."

Jem floated on his back and looked up at the sky, the stars, the moon. His stomach relaxed, his shoulders loosened. Everything was going to be okay, he told himself. He pictured himself pounding on

Maribel's door until he woke up both her and Mack. Jem would have said something stupid and sappy to Maribel and he would have punched Mack in the face, thereby losing his job. And for my finale, lady and gentleman—vomit all over the step.

Jem found his feet and stood on the sandy bottom. Neil was off about twenty yards, waving his hands through the water like fins, watching them glow.

"Thanks for bringing me back here," Jem said. "You kept me from embarrassing myself."

"I don't know about that," Neil said. He went under and surfaced closer to Jem. He looked like a different person with his hair wet, and without his glasses. "You stranded a pretty girl on the dance floor of the Muse, and you hurled all over Prospect Street."

"Yeah, but you didn't let me see Maribel. Thank you."

"You love her," Neil said. "Your dead-drunk behavior proves it. You love her. True love always wins. That sounds like total bullshit, but I happen to believe it. You'll get her."

"You've smoked too much dope," Jem said.

Neil kicked up his feet and floated on his back. "When I told you the man who gave me the weed is a professional, I meant it," he said. "He's a doctor."

"A doctor?" Jem said.

"I have pancreatic cancer," Neil said. "I'm dying." He said this the way one might announce he's a vegetarian, or a conscientious objector; he said it as though he wholeheartedly believed in it.

The water grew cold, and Jem started to shake. He swam to shore on one breath. He crawled onto the sand and cut his toe on something sharp. He flipped onto his ass and inspected the damage in the moonlight. There was a gash just below his toenail. He was bleeding.

"I cut myself," he said softly. Tears sprang to his eyes. He felt amazingly sad, and thirsty. He needed water. He wiped a drop of blood from his toe and tasted it—ringing, metallic, sweet. Was that disgusting, tasting your own blood? He gazed out at the water; Neil floated on his back. "Hey, fuck you!" Jem said. "Fuck you for messing with me like that." He was shouting but he didn't care. He didn't care if he woke up the whole hotel. "Fuck you for kidding around like that."

Jem heard a splash and seconds later, Neil was sitting next to him on the beach. He was kind of thin, now that Jem noticed, but he didn't look sick; he didn't look like a dying person.

"I'm not messing with you," Neil said. "I'm not kidding around."

Jem wiped at his tears angrily. Why the fuck was he crying? He'd only met Neil yesterday, for God's sake. He barely knew the guy. So he was dying, so what? They were all going to die, every single person, no one would escape it. Jem was going to die, Maribel, Mack, the girl Jem left at the Muse, the cab driver, Jem's parents, Gwennie, Mr. G, Mrs. Worley. Everyone. So why the tears? Maybe because life felt good—even though Jem was miserable about Maribel, it felt good to hurt, to yearn, to want. It felt good to drink twelve drinks in one night, it felt good to empty his stomach on the side of the road, it felt good to submerge his body in the cool water and watch it shine and sparkle around him.

"This is the big problem, then?" Jem asked. "It better be, because if you have one bigger than this, I don't want to hear about it."

"This is it."

"Okay," Jem said. He dug his wounded toe into the sand, and reached for his white shirt, pulled it over his head. It smelled like smoke. He looked around for his shorts, and when he found them, he said, "You had two messages, and I didn't give them to you because you said you didn't want them. But one was from Dr. Kenton. I should have told you."

"No, you obeyed my wishes. Dr. Kenton was calling to tell me I'm not getting better."

"You don't know that," Jem said.

"I do," Neil said. "Who was the other message from?"

"Desirée."

"My girlfriend full of desire. I guess she'll be the next one to find out."

"Man, don't tell me I'm the only person who knows."

"You and Dr. Kenton."

Jem needed a tall glass of water, with ice. "Why me?"

"Have you told anyone else how you feel about Maribel?"

"I told Maribel. But that's it," Jem said.

"Well, then, why me?" Neil asked.

"Because you were there," Jem said.

"Exactly," Neil said.

Jem sat quietly for a little while, watching the water lap onto the beach. He turned around; every light in the hotel was off. Tiny had gone home long ago. He tried to picture Neil dead, closed up in a box, buried in a hole in the ground, or burned into ashes. It was impossible. After Neil left the hotel, Jem would never see him again—but that was true of all the guests who stayed at the hotel. Jem knew them for a time, and then they left, and if and when they returned next summer, Jem would be gone. That was the depressing thing about working at a hotel. No one ever stayed. How did Mack and Vance do it year after year, getting to know people and then having them leave, sometimes never to be seen again?

"I think you should marry Desirée," Jem said. "For your daughter's sake. Maybe when she finds out you're . . . you know, sick, she'll convert to Judaism."

"Maybe it doesn't matter," Neil said. "I'll know soon enough."

Soon enough. Jem wondered what kind of time Neil was looking at. Months? Weeks? More tears fell, and Jem let them go.

"You really think I can get Maribel?" Jem asked.

"No," Neil said. "Yes. I don't know."

Jem fell back into the sand; he could go to sleep right there. "I should get home," he said. He felt bad abandoning Neil, but he had to make it back to his tiny rented room. He had to drink some water. He managed to stand up and Neil stood as well and they looked at each other through the darkness. Then, as though they were meeting for the first time, Neil stuck out his hand, and Jem shook it.

WALKING TO WORK THE next day, Jem thought, *I am alive.* He could move his feet, swing his arms, hear the sound of his own voice, *Hello.*

I'm alive. He'd put some Mycitracin and a Band-Aid on his toe, and it throbbed as he walked. *I'm alive.*

Jem half expected Neil to be gone when he got to the hotel. Or maybe that's what Jem hoped for—that Neil had disappeared in the night. Jem looked for him at breakfast, but he didn't show. Then Jem got caught up in his daily duties—stripping the rooms, sweeping up shells in the parking lot, trying to clean the bar sludge from his shoes. He bought two bottles of Gatorade from the soda machine and drank them straight down, thinking it would help his hangover. He ate a bagel with cream cheese left over from breakfast, and then he asked Love, "Has Neil Rosenblum checked out?"

"No," Love said. She consulted her notebook in that authoritative way she had, as though she were consulting the Bible. "He checks out tomorrow. You should know that, he's your friend. Did you two have fun last night?"

"Yeah," Jem said. "We did."

At noon, Jem knocked on Neil's door, but there was no answer. Jem scanned the beach: No Neil. Maybe he went to town, or maybe he was still asleep. Jem went back to the front desk.

"Are you *sure* Neil Rosenblum hasn't checked out?" he asked Love. "Did the chambermaids clean his room? Did they say his stuff was still there?"

"He's here," she said. "I just saw him out in the parking lot."

Jem hurried through the lobby and peered out the front doors. Sure enough, there was Neil standing between a Mercedes and a Range Rover, talking to a blonde. One of the girls from the Muse. Jem strolled over, and much to his horror realized the blonde was Maribel. Jem hesitated; he wanted to run away, but Maribel saw him and waved. Slowly, Jem approached. Neil could be telling Maribel anything—what did he care if he fiddled with Jem's relationship? He probably thought that dying gave him license to say or do whatever he pleased.

"Here's our boy now," Maribel said. Jem smiled weakly. "Mr. Rosenblum was just telling me how he was going to invest in your business in California. He says he's never seen anyone with more promise."

Neil fingered his glasses thoughtfully.

"I can't believe how lucky everyone is this summer," Maribel said. "First, Mack gets a job with the Texas Rangers, and now you're starting your own business in California. Aren't you excited, Jem?"

Neil pounded Jem on the back. "Of course he's excited. We're both excited. This is the kind of guy you run across once in a lifetime."

Maribel turned pink and nodded emphatically. "I agree."

"Whoever lands this fellow is lucky. Lucky!" Neil looked at Maribel. "You should have *seen* the women after him last night at the bars."

Jem glared at the pavement; he kicked a hermit crab shell into the tire of the Rover. "There weren't any women after me."

"I'll bet there were," Maribel said. Jem raised his eyes and let himself feast on her for just a few seconds. She was wearing crisp linen pants and a white tank sweater. Her toenails were painted silver; they glinted like chips of mica.

"Did you come from work?" he asked her.

"Actually," she said, "I came down to see if you wanted to go to lunch."

"Me?" Jem said. "What about Mack?"

"It's August," Maribel said. "He's busy. Do you want to go?"

"We already have lunch plans," Neil said. "Two of those women I was talking about are waiting for us in town."

Jem narrowed his eyes at Neil. *Shut up! She's asking me to lunch!*

Maribel's smiled drooped. "You're meeting women for lunch?"

"No, we're not," Jem said. "At least, I'm not."

"You are," Neil said. "These women aren't interested in me. I'm old enough to be their grandfather. They're after you, buddy. They'll be crushed if you don't come."

"You'd better go then," Maribel said. She caught Jem's eye and he almost melted in a puddle on the pavement. *I love you, Maribel!* He called out silently. *I really love you!* Maribel turned to go. "See you later, Jem. It was nice meeting you, Mr. Rosenblum."

"It was nice meeting *you*, Maribel," Neil said. He put his arm around Jem and wheeled him toward the lobby. "I know this hurts, buddy, but it's for your own good. Did you see how crestfallen she was when she heard you already had a date? I know a jealous woman, and believe me, she was jealous."

"You're an ass," Jem said. "I could be at lunch with Maribel right now."

"But you're here with me," Neil said. "And your time with me is limited. You have the rest of your life to spend with Maribel."

"And what was that about you investing in my *business*," Jem said. "That was a lie."

"Absolutely," Neil said. "I was trying to help."

"Stop trying, please."

"Do you want to come to my room for a drink?" Neil asked.

Jem plucked his shirt away from his body. "I'm working, as you can see."

"Come on," Neil said. "Take a lunch break."

"I could've taken a lunch break with Maribel," Jem said. "But you ruined it."

"I hope I'm still alive when it's time for you to thank me," Neil said.

THAT EVENING, NEIL CALLED Desirée and proposed. He did it while Jem sat on the deck, and Jem could hear the happy screams coming all the way from New York City. Neil held the phone away from his ear. "She says yes," he whispered. Jem couldn't help but feel sorry for Desirée, for the moment when her joy became shock and horror. It seemed unfair that Jem should know what was in store for her, when she didn't even know herself.

Jem didn't have the heart to drink much, and neither did Neil. He smoked his joint. It turned his pain into background music. Without the dope, he said, the pain was like someone banging on the front door with a brick.

They ordered lobsters for dinner, and baked potatoes and corn and coleslaw and biscuits. It was Jem's first—and probably only—lobster of the summer, but he couldn't help thinking of death row and how a prisoner chose his last meal. They ate on Neil's deck and watched the sun go down. It was so nice out and so delicious, it seemed like just that, an ending.

"Tomorrow I get back into the suit," Neil said. "I'll get married, set up a trust fund for my daughter, fly to Nepal and die."

"Fly to Nepal?"

"Once things get really bad, I'm going to Pangboche. I'm going to stay in one of the teahouses until the end. The Nepalese will cremate me right away and scatter me in the mountains."

Jem tore the claws off his lobster. "You know what pisses me off?"

"What?" Neil poked a fork into his baked potato. "They didn't give us any sour cream."

"You're giving up. And that sucks. You don't care about anyone else, do you? You don't care about your daughter, or Desirée, or me. If you cared, you wouldn't give in."

Neil didn't look up from his dinner, but his voice was low and serious. "I have cancer, Jem. It's all through me. I don't have a choice here, buddy boy."

Jem stood suddenly, and drawn butter dripped down his leg. "You're not upset enough. You've accepted the fact that you're going to die and that's fine with you. But what if it's not fine with the rest of us?"

"Sit down and enjoy your lobster," Neil said. "And let's have another drink. I am getting married, you know. Let's have a toast."

Jem stormed into Neil's room. The garment bag had been opened and Neil's suit was laid neatly out on the bed. It was spooky almost, prescient, the empty suit. Jem picked up the bottle of vodka and drank from it straight. He gasped for air. Horrible burning, a big fat mistake. *I'm not giving up*, Jem thought. *I will fight for Maribel until the end.* He slumped in the leather chair.

After a while, Neil came in, pushed the suit aside, and sat on the bed. He removed his glasses, breathed on them, wiped them on his shirt, and put them back on. His face had changed; it was stripped of all confidence. It was a human face, a scared face.

"What would you have me do?" Neil asked.

"Stay alive," Jem said.

"Stay alive," Neil said, as though he had never considered it before. "Stay alive."

JEM ALMOST CALLED IN sick the next day. He woke up with his hand on his erection, thinking of Maribel. Then he remembered Neil, and his insides filled with a heavy sadness. He could barely get out of bed. Neil's flight left at nine, and Jem knew he had to get down to the hotel on time to say good-bye.

Jem put on his red shorts, his last clean white shirt, his messed-up shoes, and left the house. Normally he liked the walk down North Liberty Street—it was shady, the houses were kept-after, he passed blackberry bushes, and now that the berries were finally ripe, he picked a handful and ate them. He started down Cobblestone Road. Usually, this was where he considered his day: would anything interesting happen? What would be left after breakfast? Would he see Maribel? Today he thought about Neil, and how after only three days, Neil had become his friend.

Just before Jem turned onto North Beach Road and walked the last hundred yards to the Beach Club, he heard a car horn. Jem saw Neil, wearing a suit, sticking his whole torso out the window of a cab, but the cab didn't slow down. Neil was leaving.

"Hold on!" Jem said. "Wait!"

Neil cupped his hands around his mouth and called out, "I'm on my way, buddy!" Neil's tie waved good-bye in the breeze, and the cab disappeared around the bend. Just like that.

Jem stopped. He listened to the gulls. North Beach Road was sunny and still. *Okay,* Jem thought, *so it's over. He's gone.* Jem expected the devastation to hit him any second; he took tiny steps forward, waiting for it. He thought about taking a cab out to the airport, or even asking Mack if he could borrow the Jeep and drive out there himself to say good-bye. But the road was still and sunny, the gulls cried out. Neil was gone, and for a second, Jem felt something he thought might be peace.

THERE WAS AN ENVELOPE at the front desk with his name on it.

"That man was *so* handsome," Love said. "Especially in his suit. He was single, right?"

"Engaged," Jem said. He held the envelope up to the light of the window. Definitely not cash in there. It was probably a letter. Jem thought of Neil dressed in his suit, heading back to New York to get married and settle matters for his daughter—it made Jem happy. He didn't want to read any letter that might ruin this feeling.

Jem ate two mixed-berry muffins and a chocolate doughnut and then he threw the envelope into the trash and covered it with dirty napkins and banana peels and half-eaten pieces of wheat toast, just to be sure he wasn't tempted to pull it back out. It was a very manly thing to do, he decided, throwing the letter away. A woman would never throw away an envelope unopened.

JEM SAW MARIBEL RIGHT before quitting time. She was in her yellow bikini top and her jean shorts—the exact outfit she wore on their first date to Miacomet Beach. Jem watered Therese's plants on the lobby porch and Maribel slogged up the three steps in her flip-flops, her damp beach towel slung over her shoulder.

"Too much of a good thing today," she said. "The sun in August. How was your lunch date yesterday?"

Jem was on the verge of saying, "I didn't go. It was all made-up." But he didn't want to be disloyal to Neil. "It was fun," he said.

"Yeah?" Maribel said. Jem studied her. Did she seem jealous? "Mr. Rosenblum was so nice. Is he still around?"

"Left today."

"He really seemed to like you," Maribel said. "He seemed to believe in you."

Jem stopped watering and looked at Maribel. "He did like me. He did believe in me."

"Jem, what's wrong?"

"What do you mean?"

"You look strange," she said. "You look upset. Are you all right?"

"Now that you mention it," he said, "I'm not sure." He put down the watering can, walked past Maribel, through the lobby and into the galley kitchen. He held his breath and dug around in the trash until he pulled out the envelope. It was stained with coffee, smeared with strawberry jam.

Inside was a check for fifteen thousand dollars and two one-way tickets from Nantucket to Los Angeles, courtesy of Rosenblum Travel. The note attached said: "Get her. NR."

Heat Wave

August 14 (not sent)

Dear S.B.T.,

I have notified the authorities about your harassment by mail. Your letters—all of which I've saved—insinuate that you've been stalking me, spying on me, spying on the hotel. The police will uncover your identity and your pursuit of me and of the hotel will be put to an end. Leave me alone!

Bill Elliott

August 15 (sent)

Dear S.B.T.,

Do you read poetry?

Bill Elliott

IN THE MIDDLE OF August, a heat wave hit Nantucket like none Lacey Gardner could remember, and she had been on the island for close to a century of summers. In general, Nantucket was a place to escape the heat because of the sea breeze. It could be in the nineties in Boston and New York, and Nantucket would be a comfortable seventy-seven. Lacey had only noticed the heat once before—in 1975, on the day islanders called Hot Saturday, when the thermometer hit one hundred degrees. Lacey and Maximilian had stayed inside, running the fans at full blast, playing cards in the guest bedroom of their house on Cliff Road, because that room stayed dark most of the day. They drank three pitchers of lemonade and at four o'clock started with Mount Gay

and tonics, heavy on the ice. Lacey felt as though she were on vacation—staying in the one room of the house she never used, sliding aces
and queens across the quilted company bedspread. When it grew
dark, she and Maximilian slipped into their bathing suits and walked
to Steps Beach for an evening swim. They felt like teenagers, sneaking
around in the night, although even in 1975, they were senior citizens,
and had to grip the railing tightly as they descended the stairs to the
sand.

When they arrived at the beach, it was as crowded as midday. A
patchwork of towels and blankets covered the beach, citronella candles flickered, and in the moonlight, Lacey saw men with sideburns
holding hands with topless girls. A radio played the Beatles' "The
Long and Winding Road." Some of the kids brought picnics—summer sausages, cheese, chicken salad, and cold beer. Max and Lacey ate
and drank and splashed around in the water as though they were forty
years younger. Lacey watched Maximilian smoke marijuana for the
first time with a man named Cedar. She studied all the young people
as their lean bodies floated through the hot night, and she wished
again for children. She decided to say something to Max walking
home. It was almost midnight, Hot Saturday turning into Sultry Sunday. She said, "Maximilian do you ever wish we'd had children?"

Max didn't answer. Maybe it was the marijuana getting to his brain,
or maybe it was his same old stubbornness on the topic. His determi-
nation never to admit he might have been wrong.

THIS AUGUST WAS THE worst heat of all. In the sun it was broiling, in the
shade it was difficult to breathe. The flag out in front of the Beach
Club drooped like an old nylon stocking. The first hot night, Lacey
tossed in bed, kicked off the sheets, flipped her pillow. Finally she
struggled for the lamp and made her way over to the air-conditioner
and turned it up as high as it would go. That sufficed for the night, but
when morning came and Lacey ventured into the hallway, she nearly
gagged. The air was thick, syrupy, a steaming Turkish bath. She
opened all of her windows and switched on her two ancient fans. She

kept her bedroom door closed and cranked the air-conditioning, thinking that if worse came to worst, she could lie in bed and read her mystery novel all day, refusing to step out.

Mack appeared as usual. Instead of coffee, he brought her an icy Coca-Cola.

"Bless you, Mack Petersen," she said. It was eight-thirty, and already Mack's sandy hair was wet around his ears and he had the smell of a man who'd worked all day.

"It's eighty-two degrees right now," he said. "Radio said it would top ninety by ten o'clock."

Lacey took a sip of her cola. It was so cold and crisp, it stung the back of her throat and her eyes watered. She coughed.

"Be careful in this heat," Mack said. "I want you to promise me you won't exert yourself."

"Because this kind of weather kills old ladies, is that what you mean?" Lacey said. "Well, it won't kill me. I've lived through worse than this. But just to be safe, I'm going back to the bedroom where it's cool. Knock at the end of the day to see if I'm okay, would you, dear? But just knock. I have half a mind to sit in there naked."

Mack laughed. "You got it, Lacey."

He left with a wave, and Lacey took another swallow of cola and let out a healthy belch.

"What am I going to do when you're gone?" she said out loud. "Who will take care of me?" She sounded more plaintive than she meant to, but it was a fair question. What would she do when the handsome messenger that Maximilian sent, left her? She guessed either another boy would come, or her time with substitutes would finally be over, and she would join Maximilian in whatever came next. Dying wasn't quite as scary when she thought of it this way—as the place where Maximilian was waiting.

IT WAS SO HOT that Mack and Maribel slept nude under one thin sheet. Maribel made cool things for dinner—chilled cucumber soup, Caesar salad, melon balls. She recited cool words: silver, glass, mint, shade, green, blue, drink, flute, ice, a bed of ice, a world of ice. She pulled F. Scott Fitzgerald's "The Ice Palace" off the shelf at the library, and then "The Snows of Kilimanjaro," Ann Beattie's *Chilly Scenes of Winter*, David Guterson's *Snow Falling on Cedars,* and even Richard Russo's *The Risk Pool.* She stacked the books on her desk, looking at them every so often to repeat their cool titles in her head.

Maribel and Mack fought almost every night. Because of the heat, and the crazy things it did to the hotel staff and guests, Mack shut down. He came home, took off his clothes, ate what Maribel put in front of him, and sat in a sweaty heap in front of the TV until bedtime. If he and Maribel talked at all, they snapped at one another.

Mack never mentioned getting married anymore. They didn't talk about a wedding, they made no plans. Now Maribel feared she might end up one of these women who were engaged for fifteen years. One night, she asked Mack about it.

"Are we going to get married on the island this fall? Because if we are, we need to make plans."

"I don't know," he said, his eyes glued to the baseball scores. "I can't think."

"You can't think?" she said. "I'm asking you about our *wedding* and you can't think?"

"It's hot, Maribel," he said. "All day at work I have people complaining. The beach is hot, the sand is hot, the water is too warm. We had a beach boy get sunstroke today and off he goes to the hospital. I check on Lacey every two hours because I'm afraid she's going to wilt. I caught Jem with his ass in the ice machine. He was *sitting* in the ice machine. I don't have time to think about a wedding."

"Fine," Maribel said. "Maybe we won't get married then."

"Don't play games with me, Maribel," Mack said. "Because right now nothing is funny. Including that comment."

Maribel felt tears rising and she went into the bedroom where at least the fan was on. She lay across the bed and swept every strand of hair from her neck, tucked them into a bun. She moved so that the air from the fan hit her bare neck. She had never been able to enjoy happiness because she always wondered, *When will it end? When will something bad happen?* She wanted to call her mother, but the phone was in the other room. Besides, what would she tell Tina? That right now she hated Mack? That right now the thought of a whole life with him was dreary and depressing? That maybe, just maybe, she wanted to get married so badly that she made certain compromises. Compromises like the fact that she agreed to marry Mack when only weeks before he confessed he loved another woman. Maribel tried to forget about that, she decided to believe that when Andrea Krane left the island, Mack's feelings for her vanished as well. And since Mack planned on leaving his job at the hotel there was no danger of him seeing Andrea again. But did he still have feelings for her? Maribel was so thrilled, first with the proposal and then with the ring, that she hadn't allowed this question into her thoughts. But now, Maribel realized that of course Mack loved Andrea. You didn't stop loving someone in a matter of weeks. Mack had probably proposed to Andrea first, and when she said no, he came to Maribel. She was his second choice. No *wonder* Mack couldn't think about the wedding. He didn't want to marry her at all. That scene a few weeks ago with him all sincerity and sweet promises had been a lie.

Maribel marched out to the living room. Moths threw themselves against the screen door with reckless abandon.

"Do you still love Andrea?" Maribel asked.

"What?" Mack said. He wore only his boxer shorts. Twelve years ago he had left Iowa, but he still looked like a farmer: tan neck and arms, pasty white torso. "What did you just ask me?"

"Do you still love Andrea Krane? I want to know."

"You're ridiculous," Mack said. "I just spent a small fortune putting a diamond on your finger and you have the nerve to ask me that. What's gotten into you?"

"You're not answering my question," Maribel said.

"Your question is obnoxious," Mack said. "I asked you to marry me and you said yes. I gave you a ring. Now, why would I do that if I still loved Andrea?"

Maribel winced at the word "still" because it admitted one fact: he had loved her. "That sounds like an answer to my question, but it's not. You're not telling me you don't love her."

"What's wrong with you?" Mack was yelling now, standing up. Sweat dripped down his face. The temperature in the room rose; the room was boiling over. Maribel took a deep breath, trying to remember the stack of books on her desk, the chilly titles. What were they? All she could think of was *The Risk Pool*. A pool of risk, that's where she was right now, swimming in it. The moths batted themselves against the screen. If it weren't so abusively hot Maribel would have shut the door, to block out the horrible sound.

"Do you want to marry Andrea?" Maribel asked.

Mack's blue eyes were on fire. "I don't want to marry anybody," he said.

There was a split second of silence, enough time for only a single thought. *Oh, God.*

Mack said, "But you."

Except by then it was too late because in that speck of silence, Mack had told the truth. A silence so short, so small, an infinitesimal silence, exposed him. *I don't want to marry anybody.*

He came toward Maribel, cooling off, ticking like a car engine, and he put his arms around her gently so as not to smother her. "I don't want to marry anybody but you."

He could say whatever he wanted now, she supposed, because he'd told her the truth. For one glimmering instant, the truth was free, and Maribel recognized it. She had known it all along: Mack didn't want to marry anybody.

She bent her chin to her chest, and Mack kissed her forehead.

"Are you okay?" he asked.

She pulled away. "I'm just hot," she said. "I'm sorry."

She retreated into the bedroom, threw herself on the bed face down and cried. She didn't have the genius for love—if that was what love required—genius, like one had for painting, or the piano. Genius for love didn't run in her family. And so Maribel had relied on persistence, she gritted her teeth and dug in her heels and butted her head

THE BEACH CLUB 261

against the brick wall until it surrendered. Her tears cooled on her cheeks. Sore head, she thought, sore heart.

CECILY WAS IN THE office with her father when he discovered his big mistake. It was too hot for her to be out on the beach; walking on the sand would have blistered the soles of her feet. The heat freed her from chatting and schmoozing, thank God, but her father insisted she join him in the office so she could better understand how he ran the hotel. Because he wouldn't live forever, he said, and she might be in charge sooner than she thought.

Bill swiveled in his chair. "I can't believe it," he said. He shuffled some papers, ran his fingertips over one page, then another. He wiped his forehead with a handkerchief. "It must be this heat," he said. "In twenty years, I have never done this. Never!"

"Done what?" Cecily said. The mercury routinely rose to ninety-seven degrees in Rio. Soon, Cecily would be sweating next to Gabriel in bed. She only needed five hundred more dollars before she could escape. Her father had called UVA trying to reverse her deferral, but ha!—it was too late. Now her parents wanted her to come to Aspen, where they would ski with her, and teach her about the hotel. It was as if they were blind, deaf, stupid. "What'd you do?" she asked.

"I can't believe it," Bill repeated. He flipped through his book of Robert Frost poems. He did it again and again until Cecily realized he was having some kind of panic attack.

She sat up straight in her chair; in this heat, even that took effort. "Dad, what'd you do?"

"I double-booked a room," he said. "I have a confirmation letter here for a family of four, the Reeses, for room fourteen, August twenty-four through August twenty-seven. And I have a confirmation letter for a Mrs. Jane Hassiter for that same room for the same dates."

Cecily fell back in her chair. "Move somebody."

He opened the reservation book and Cecily peered at it. The whole month was highlighted in fluorescent green.

"We're full," he said.

• • •

THAT WAS HOW MRS. Jane Hassiter ended up staying in Cecily's house during the heat wave. First, though, Cecily and her father called every guest house and B and B in the phone book. No vacancy. There wasn't room on the island for even one more person, a lonely widow. That's how Cecily's mother described Mrs. Hassiter, a lonely widow. Cecily's father prayed for a cancellation, but none came. Her mother tried to calm him.

"Mrs. Hassiter can stay in our house," she said. "We have the extra room, don't forget."

"The extra room" was on the first floor in the front of the house, with a window looking over the parking lot at the beach. It even had its own bathroom. But in Cecily's eighteen years, no one had ever stayed in that room. It was meant to be the bedroom for Cecily's dead brother, W.T., but he'd never slept in it. W.T. didn't make it home from the hospital; he was born dead. Cecily's parents preserved the room, though, for the ghost baby, their dead son.

"I don't think that's a good idea," Bill said.

Cecily rolled her eyes. Her parents were outrageously predictable.

"*You* double-booked the room, Bill," Therese said. "Mrs. Hassiter is on her way. There isn't any space on the island. We don't have a choice. We made a mistake, we have to pay up."

"It'll be fine, Dad," Cecily said. Both her parents looked at her as if she'd spoken Portuguese. Those were the nicest words she'd said since the Fourth of July.

Bill exhaled; his shoulders loosened. "I hope you're right," he said.

CECILY WAS STANDING AT the front desk talking to Love when Jane Hassiter walked in. Hotel guests were a mixed bag, but they had one thing in common—they all looked rich. Their watches gave them away, their Italian shoes, their haircuts. Rarely did someone step into the lobby looking like Jane Hassiter.

It was terrible to say—horrendous, awful—but Mrs. Hassiter immediately reminded Cecily of the woman who cleaned her dormitory at Middlesex. Mrs. Hassiter walked into the lobby in the same way that woman skulked around the students' rooms—as though she didn't belong in a place so fancy and nice. And then, as Mrs. Hassiter got closer, Cecily zeroed in on her tight, steel gray pin curls, her watery blue eyes, and she filled with warm dread. Mrs. Hassiter *was* the woman who cleaned at Middlesex; she was the housekeeper, the custodian, right here in the lobby of the hotel. Jane—yes, her name was Jane. Cecily had said, "Good morning, Jane," when she swept the halls with her wide broom, and "Thank you, Jane," when she cleaned the bathroom and emptied the trash. The girls on Cecily's hall bought Jane a Christmas present every year—a silk flower wreath, a subscription to *Reader's Digest.*

Cecily shivered despite the heat. The last week of school, Jane unlocked the door to Cecily's room with her giant ring of keys, and walked in on Cecily and Gabriel making love. Cecily was sitting in Gabriel's lap, facing him, her legs wrapped around his back as he lifted her up and down on his beautiful penis. They were supposed to be at breakfast, but they had skipped so that they could make love yet again. Cecily heard the jangle of Jane's keys, and before she could move, Jane stepped in, ogled them. Cecily pulled Gabriel's face into her chest as though he were a child that needed protecting and she shrieked, "Get out! Get out of here, Jane!"

Jane, what could Jane have thought? She looked hurt, Cecily remembered. She said, softly, "I'm sorry. So sorry." And closed the door.

Cecily climbed off Gabriel and cried. She cried because Gabriel was leaving for Brazil and one of their last times making love had been ruined. She cried because now there was danger of being expelled, right before graduation. And she cried because she had yelled at Jane, frightened her, hurt her. Nobody yelled at Jane. No one except Cecily.

Jane didn't report them. Of course not, Gabriel said, who was she anyway? An old woman cleaning up after a bunch of teenagers. Cecily made herself forget about the incident; she concentrated instead on the vodka parties, graduation, making a scrapbook for Gabriel. Cecily cast her eyes down when she passed Jane in the hall.

It was the world's worst coincidence that Jane, the cleaning woman, whom Cecily hoped never to see again, was the only guest in the history of the hotel ever to stay in Cecily's house. Cecily had half a mind to hide in the back office. But this was the behavior of the old Cecily. The new Cecily, the one headed for South America, faced adversity when it walked in the door.

Jane wore a plaid blouse, a pair of men's denim overalls cuffed at the ankles, and shiny AirMax running shoes. Jane walked with her head down, every once in a while allowing herself to glimpse a quilt or a painting, when she gave a tiny gasp. She looked so painfully out of place that Cecily wanted to apologize a hundred times.

Vance came in the door behind Jane carrying two brown paper bags, like the kind they used at Stop & Shop. He set them down at the front desk, practically at Cecily's feet. *Those are her bags,* Cecily thought. *This is her luggage.* She wanted to weep. They occasionally saw people like Jane Hassiter over the years, but Cecily was too young then to care or understand: Men and women who saved up their whole lives to splurge like this, just once.

"I'm Jane Hassiter," she said to Love. "I have a reservation." It was Jane's voice. *I'm sorry. So sorry.*

"Indeed, Mrs. Hassiter," Love said. "You requested a side deck room, but I'm pleased to inform you we've upgraded your room, free of charge. You're going to be staying in the proprietor's suite."

"The proprietor's suite?" Jane said. She looked at her shoes. "That's wonderful."

"Vance will show you to your room," Love said.

"I'll do it," Cecily piped up.

"Okay," Love said. "Mrs. Hassiter, Cecily here, the owner's daughter, will show you to your room."

Jane raised her head and looked at Cecily. Cecily's cheeks burned. Jane smiled shyly. "It's nice to meet you, Cecily."

She was pretending. Cecily felt both relief and disappointment. In the last five minutes, Cecily's guilt swelled like a blister that needed to be popped with sharp words of accusation. *You little slut! You ungrateful, spoiled child!*

When Cecily found her voice, it was very small. "Welcome to Nantucket."

"Thank you," Jane said. "This place, it's yours? You lucky girl."

Cecily would gladly have signed the deed over to Jane that instant. *I don't want this place. I don't want it at all.* "It belongs to my parents," she said. She picked up the paper bags and allowed herself a peek at the contents. One bag held clothes and one held a second paper bag, twisted at the neck. Cecily made her way slowly through the lobby so Jane could enjoy it. The lobby was air-conditioned, but waves of heat rose from the asphalt out in the parking lot. It was a griddle. She let Jane through the lobby doors. "We're going to the big house over there."

"Forgive my asking," Jane said, "but what did I do to deserve this? The proprietor's suite, my God!"

"It's just the way things worked out," Cecily said. Her father was posted at the upstairs window, watching them swim through the waves of heat to the house. Earlier that day, he'd read Jane's confirmation letter out loud. " 'We look forward to having you stay with us.' Ha! Little did we know what we meant by that."

Cecily didn't enter the extra room very often. There was just a double bed, an empty dresser, a regular bathroom. When Cecily swung the door open, she saw her mother had fixed it up for Jane—a quilt on the bed, two of those idiotic miniature bicycles on the dresser, fresh flowers, and a box of chocolates from Sweet Inspirations, which were probably all melted together by now. A fluffy white robe hung in the empty closet.

Cecily closed the door in case her father should come wandering down. Now that they were alone, Cecily wanted to say something. She was about to burst.

"This is just lovely," Jane said. "So lovely. I can't believe my good fortune."

"Jane," Cecily said. "Mrs. Hassiter, Jane—"

Then there was a knock at the door and Therese stepped in.

"Hello, Mrs. Hassiter, welcome."

Jane shook hands with Therese. "Thank you. This room is so fine."

"I'm glad you like it," Therese said.

"It's my dead brother's room," Cecily said. Both her mother and Jane stared. Cecily wanted to kill herself. Why had she said that?

"Cecily," Therese said.

"Your dead brother?" Jane said. "I'm sorry to hear it."

Therese cleared her throat. "Go find your father," she said. "Go right now while I talk to Mrs. Hassiter."

Cecily stomped up the stairs to where her father was standing by the bay window watching Beach Club members pull up in their Range Rovers and unload beach bags, buckets and shovels, picnic lunches.

"I think we should let Mrs. Hassiter stay for free," Cecily said. "She's not even in the real hotel. Her room isn't on the beach."

"Has she complained?" Bill asked.

"No, she's happy. But you can't charge her. It wouldn't be fair." Cecily lowered her voice. "Besides, I don't think she has much money."

"We have fifty percent in a deposit," he said. "I'd be happy to leave it at that."

"No," Cecily said. "You should return it all."

"That's what you'd do if you were running the hotel?" Bill asked.

The obvious trap. Cecily sniffed. "I'm just saying what I think you should do, as a decent person."

"Decent person, huh?" her father said. He focused back out the window. "I can't believe this heat. It's like nothing I've ever seen."

"Dad?" Cecily said.

"Okay, we won't charge her," he said. "We'll just pretend like she's an old friend."

CECILY TRIED TO GET a minute alone with Jane—to apologize, and offer this up—her stay at the Beach Club free of charge. But Jane didn't emerge from her room, and Cecily was too timid to knock. Cecily spent an hour on the beach talking with Major Crawley, the Hayeses, and Mrs. Papale, who was turning herself into a human crouton. Cecily eyed the front door of her house for Jane, but Jane didn't materialize. Perhaps she hadn't brought a bathing suit. Cecily cursed guilt, the worst of all emotions, worse than hate and heartbreak put together. Cecily not only felt guilty about yelling at Jane and having sex with Gabriel when she should have been in the dining hall, but now she felt guilty about telling Jane she was staying in a dead boy's room. It wasn't even true, technically.

AT ELEVEN O'CLOCK THAT night, Cecily's usual hour to call Gabriel, she resisted picking up the phone. She had been lying on her bed for two hours, listening for any activity that might be going on in Jane's room. She heard the water (a shower), the water (teeth brushing) and two toilet flushes. Every fifteen minutes, Cecily checked down the hall to see if Jane's light was still on. If the light was on at midnight, Cecily was going down there. It would be impossible to sleep with this guilt hanging around her neck like a medieval shackle. Cecily replayed the awful moment in her room at Middlesex again and again in her mind, wishing she could somehow change the ending, change it so that it was not Jane who caught her *screwing* during breakfast, change it so that at the very least Cecily hadn't screamed *Get out of here!* and hadn't used Jane's name, *Get out of here, Jane!*

And then, at last, Cecily heard Jane's door open, she heard footsteps in the hallway. Cecily leaped from bed and opened her bedroom door. Jane stood in front of her in a high-collared nightgown.

"I think your brother is trying to contact me," Jane said.

"Excuse me?" Cecily said.

"He's trying to contact me. He's making noise."

Cecily followed Jane down the hall and into the extra room. Sure enough, there was a light tapping on the window.

"Turn off the light," Cecily said. She went to the window and peered out into the darkness to see if the wind was knocking a branch against the pane. But there was no wind; the American flag sagged in the spotlight, impotent. No one was outside, and yet Cecily heard the tapping, so light, so faint, it was all she could do to keep from imagining a baby's fist, the size of an egg, tapping the glass, demanding to be let in. "I need to get out of this place," she said.

"This room is haunted," Jane said.

Cecily sat on the edge of Jane's bed. "It could be. No one has ever slept in here before."

"Why me?"

"My father overbooked," Cecily admitted. She forgot about the ghostly tapping and became excited that at last she had gotten a chance to apologize to Jane. "Listen, I know you recognize me. Cecily Elliott, room two-seventeen, Darwin House. You saw me and my boyfriend . . . and I yelled when I shouldn't have. I feel terrible about it, but I love him so much. It's the kind of love that hurts whenever I breathe, practically, because he's living in South America, and I've been saving my money to go see him."

"I do know you," Jane said. "You're a hard person to forget. And your boyfriend, so handsome!"

"Yes," Cecily said. Longing for Gabriel rose in her throat, like a song she couldn't sing. "Anyway, I wanted you to know I was sorry. Also, I spoke with my father and he's not going to charge you for the room."

"Oh, please, dear," Jane said. "I want him to charge me."

"What?"

The tapping started again, and Cecily wondered if this were all just a very bizarre dream, caused by the unrelenting heat, a mirage.

"I want him to charge me," Jane said. "I have to get rid of my money." She opened the top drawer of the dresser and pulled out the paper bag that was twisted closed. She turned the bag upside down on the bed.

Money fell out of the bag, money the way it appeared in the movies, in neat stacks the size of bricks. Cecily gasped: hundreds and fifties and twenties.

"Where did you get that money?" Cecily asked. She almost asked Jane, *Did you steal it?* Jane, the cleaning woman, was filthy rich.

"It was my husband's money. He owned apartment buildings in

Lawrence, and this is twenty years of rent right here. It was supposed to go to my son but he refused to take it. My son thought Jerry was prejudiced because he wouldn't rent to blacks or Puerto Ricans."

"*Was* he prejudiced?" Cecily asked.

"Yes," Jane said, sadly. "Someone with dark skin, like your boyfriend, wouldn't have been able to rent from Jerry."

"That's really shitty," Cecily said. "I told off a woman this summer because she didn't want black people on our beach."

Jane wrung her wrinkly hands. "I can't excuse what Jerry did. But I don't want the money to go to waste."

"Why did you come here?" Cecily asked. "Why did you pick our hotel?"

"I found this," Jane said. She opened the second drawer where she had put her clothes. She pulled out a Nantucket Beach Club and Hotel brochure with the picture of the pavilion and the five blue Adirondack chairs, and handed it to Cecily. "I found it when I was doing the final clean at school."

"You found it in my room?" Cecily said.

"Must have been," Jane said. "I was pretty sure I'd recognize someone around here, but I didn't know it'd be you." Jane patted Cecily's hand. "I'm glad it was."

"Me too," Cecily said.

"How much money do you need to see your young man?" Jane asked.

"Five hundred dollars," Cecily said.

Jane counted out ten fifties and pressed them into Cecily's palm. "There you go," she said, "a little graduation present from old Jane."

Again, the tapping. Cecily closed her eyes and listened. Maybe it wasn't W.T. at all. Maybe it was Gabriel knocking, beckoning to her from far away.

"I can't take this," Cecily said. "I really want to but I can't."

Jane frowned. "You feel like my son, then? Won't take the money because it's tainted?"

"Sort of, yeah." Cecily thought of Mrs. John Higgens, and let the bills flutter to the bed.

Jane walked back to the dresser and pulled out her wallet. "I have four hundred and eighty-six dollars here from my last paycheck from Middlesex," she said. "Will you take this?"

Jane's paycheck, that she earned by cleaning up after Cecily and her classmates? It seemed strange to take that money, too, but at least it wouldn't be unethical. Cecily could fly to New York first thing in the morning, and she'd be on her way to Rio before her parents even realized she was gone. It was thrilling, and positively terrifying. Terrifying! She couldn't do it. But then Cecily thought of Gabriel, the way he cupped her face when he kissed her, the way his smile spread slowly across his face like a sunrise.

"Thank you, Jane," Cecily said.

"Where are you headed again?" Jane asked.

"Rio de Janeiro," Cecily said.

And with those words, she was free.

THERESE KNEW THE SECOND her baby boy died inside of her, and she knew as soon as her feet hit the ground in the morning that Cecily was gone. The house sounded hollow beneath her feet; it sounded like a house without children. She didn't let herself panic until she checked Cecily's bedroom, however, because in this heat, her instincts could be wrong. Therese tiptoed down the stairs so as not to wake their guest, Mrs. Hassiter. Knocking lightly on Cecily's door, Therese said, "Honey, are you in there?"

No answer, but that didn't mean anything. Cecily was probably still asleep; she didn't have to be on the beach until ten.

Therese was halfway up the stairs when she caught her reflection in the mirror. *Fooling yourself*, her reflection said. She marched back down to Cecily's room and opened the door.

Cecily's bed was made, the room neat and clean. It was a teenager's dream room: queen-size bed, TV, stereo, built-in bookshelves that held Cecily's schoolbooks and her field hockey trophies. There was a spartan desk—built to Cecily's specifications—an old hotel door sitting on two filing cabinets. A framed black-and-white photograph of the Beach Club circa 1928 hung over Cecily's bed. On the nightstand was a hotel envelope, the kind guests left tips in for the chambermaids. On the front, in Cecily's youthful hand, it said, "Mom and Dad."

Therese sat on Cecily's bed, picked up the envelope, and held it in her lap. Her hands trembled.

Therese knew all about running away. She'd practically done the same thing on her eighteenth birthday when she took the Long Island Railroad from Bilbo to Grand Central Station, her father's World War II army bag slung over her shoulder. She was only sixty miles from home, but it might as well have been another continent— her orderly, cookie-cutter neighborhood left behind for Manhattan. She would never admit it to Bill, but she understood why Cecily wanted more. Cecily was her mother's daughter. Forty years ago, Therese had gone searching for beauty, and found love. Cecily searched now for love—maybe she would be lucky enough to find beauty. Maybe: if she didn't get killed or end up in jail or contract some appalling disease.

Therese opened the envelope.

Dear Mom and Dad,

I'm sure you two are pissed like never before, and I'm sorry. You are great parents and I understand why you didn't want me to go. But I had to chase this feeling because it's the best feeling I've ever had. You two love each other, think of life without that and you'll understand why I left. I'll call to let you know I'm okay, but don't come after me because it will be an impossible search. I love you both and I'm sure you think leaving is easy for me, but trust me, it isn't.

Love, Cecily

Therese scanned Cecily's bookshelves for her yearbook, and when she brought it down, the book fell right open to Gabriel's picture.

Gabriel da Silva: He was filed under *S*. Therese studied his picture with a dissonant, high-pitched whine in her ears, like something caught in a vacuum cleaner. Gabriel was astonishingly handsome. Toasty brown skin, black hair, a diamond stud in his left ear. Perfect straight white teeth in the kind of smile that singed the page. He'd signed the yearbook next to his picture—something in another language, Portuguese?—and then: "I love every inch of you. Gabriel da Silva." Therese stared at the words. I love every inch of you. The words of a lover, forcing Therese to imagine the secret, soft inches of Cecily that Gabriel loved. But then, after that intimacy, he signed his full name. Therese held the book open and put the words and the picture together. *I love every inch of you. Gabriel da Silva.*

THERESE DIDN'T TELL BILL where she was going—he was in the kitchen eating his cereal. She left the house with a wave, and said, "I have to run a quick errand. Back soon." Mrs. Hassiter hadn't stirred and Therese was relieved; she didn't feel like explaining anything yet.

Outside, the air was thick as chowder. Therese cranked the air-conditioner in her car and opened all the windows on the way to the airport. She couldn't remember the last time she had left the property on a summer morning; always, her first concerns were the rooms, the chambermaids, and guests with problems more pressing than her own. But now Therese appreciated the morning, even though it was hot, and the lawns were turning brown and the hydrangeas had dried up into crisp little heads. It was nice to be off property. A lone jogger dripping with sweat plodded down North Beach Road. It was Maribel. Therese wanted to stop and ask, "Have you seen Cecily?"—but she flipped down the eye shade and accelerated.

At the airport, Therese searched for Cecily in the ladies' room, the gift shop, the restaurant. Not there. Then Therese surveyed the local carriers. When she asked at Colgan—Any young redheads on a plane to New York this morning?—the perky attendant bit as though Therese was holding out an apple. "You *must* be her mother, you two are, like, identical twins! I mean, gosh, you have the same hair. I guess people tell you that all the time."

"So she made her plane then?" Therese said. "Good. What time did it leave?"

The girl checked the board behind her. "She was on the first plane. The six-oh-five. It was early, I remember that!"

"And that was to New York?"

The girl bobbed her head. "La Guardia. I think she had a transfer to JFK, though."

"Thanks for your help," Therese said.

"Where was she headed, anyway?" the girl asked. "In the end, her final destination?"

Her final destination? Therese swallowed. "Brazil," she said.

Therese ordered breakfast in the restaurant. As she ate her eggs, she considered taking a poll of other mothers. *Do I get on a plane and go after her, or do I let her go?* Therese thought back to all the guests she had advised with their personal problems, guests like Leo Hearn. *No, Leo,* she thought, *there is no instruction manual for parents. I made it all up.* She bit off the corner of her toast and saw Cecily at a year and a half, toddling by herself through the sand, falling over onto her hands. Cecily at thirteen, the night of her first kiss, climbing into bed with Therese to tell her all about it. They were so close, identical twins, motherdaughter. And yet in only a couple of hours, so much distance between them. Where was Cecily? In another country, sleeping with the dark prince.

Out the window, a small propeller plane got ready for takeoff. The props spun, there was a lurch, and then the plane rolled forward, picked up speed, until just barely lifting its nose and soaring, soaring. There were a million metaphors for childhood, and here was one of them right outside the window. What could Therese do but hope that somewhere, Cecily was soaring?

"ARE YOU KIDDING ME?" Bill shouted. They were upstairs in the living room, and as far as Therese could tell, Mrs. Hassiter hadn't stirred.

Bill waved the letter in the air. His face was bright red and his hair glittered from silver to white; he was aging in front of her eyes.

"Your heart," Therese said. "Bill, please. I can't lose you, too."

"Why do you look so calm?" he said. Suspicion flickered across his face. "You knew, didn't you? She's your daughter, Therese. She's always been your daughter. She confided in you and you let her go."

"Not true," Therese said. But she did feel preternaturally calm, as though someone had drugged her. *I love every inch of you.* Therese never kept secrets from Bill, but she didn't show him the yearbook. "I had no idea! I just went to the airport to see if I could catch her."

Bill checked his watch. "We're going back right now. There's no way she's made it out of New York yet. International flights leave at night. We have all day to turn JFK upside down."

"You're thinking of west-east flights," Therese said. "Those leave in the evening. North-south flights leave in the morning." She had no idea if this were true; she didn't even know where the thought had come from.

"We'll go anyway," he said. "We're irresponsible parents if we don't. I'm sure she wants us to come after her."

"Bill, come here and sit down." Therese led him to the couch and he sat down despondently, his hands in his lap. Then, with a sudden burst of energy, he bounced up again.

"There isn't time to sit down," he said.

"We're not going to New York," Therese said.

"Cecily is *expecting* us," Bill said. "She's probably lingering at her gate, waiting for us to march down the concourse. This isn't the kind of thing you hope to get away with at the age of eighteen."

"There's only one person she wants to see," Therese said sadly. "And it's not you, and it's not me."

"I can't even *think* about that boy," Bill said. "If I think about that boy, I'm going to lose my mind."

"She's living her life, Bill."

"You're in cahoots with her," he said.

"No, it's just . . ." How to explain this feeling? Therese was worried, but seeing the picture of Gabriel da Silva excited her, too. And she hadn't expected to feel excited. Her daughter was alive and *living*. When Therese left home, wonderful things happened. She ended up here. "I thought Cecily leaving would kill me. But I feel okay. It's like anticipating her leaving was ten times worse than her actual leaving. She's *gone*, Bill. We're through worrying about how to keep her here. We're *liberated*, in a way."

"You're nuts," he said. "Cecily hasn't gone to overnight camp, my dear. She hasn't left for college, or another relatively safe place where we can get a hold of her. She has flown to *Brazil* to sleep with a boy we've never even met."

"I guess what I'm saying is that I know she's coming back," Therese said. "Unlike W.T., Cecily is coming back."

Bill collapsed on the sofa. "Oh, God," he said.

Therese heard soft footsteps on the stairs and Mrs. Hassiter popped into the living room. She looked at Therese expectantly.

"Breakfast is in the hotel lobby, Mrs. Hassiter," Therese said. "It's our compliments. Just go on over and help yourself."

"I already had breakfast," Mrs. Hassiter said. "I want to talk to you about something else."

So she'd overheard them. "We're having a bit of a family situation," Therese said. "Things might be rather hectic. I apologize."

"I understand," Mrs. Hassiter said. She looked at her hands. "I understand because I have a child of my own."

Therese got a funny twitching in her stomach. "Did you see my daughter this morning, Mrs. Hassiter? Did you see her last night?"

Mrs. Hassiter's pale blue eyes sought Therese's, then Bill's, helplessly. *Oh, dear God,* Therese thought. *She has some part in this.* But before Mrs. Hassiter could answer, Bill pointed his finger; his voice was tight and sharp.

"Do you know where our daughter is?" he asked. "Do you?"

Mrs. Hassiter nodded slowly. "I wasn't thinking as a parent last night. But these kids seem so grown-up. Much older than my own son at that age."

"What did you do?" Bill asked. Therese dug her fingernails into the buttery leather of the couch. "What did you do to Cecily?"

Mrs. Hassiter took a deep breath. "I gave her the money to go."

Therese felt all her previous calm fly from her, like her soul leaving her body. Gave Cecily the money! They let the woman into their home and she interfered with the delicate balance they had worked so hard to achieve. She tipped the scales in favor of Cecily and off Cecily went—with a stranger's money in her pocket—to Brazil.

Bill spoke first. "The nerve of you," he said. "You had no place doing that."

"I know," Mrs. Hassiter said. "I realized that this morning. I should have just let things be. But I was possessed by pride."

"By pride, Mrs. Hassiter?" Bill said. "What is *that* supposed to mean?"

Mrs. Hassiter looked at both of them, then her eyes took in the rest of the room: the leather couch, the Turkish rug. "I'm a janitor at your daughter's private school," she said. "At Middlesex. I clean the rooms. I've been doing it for twenty-one years."

"You know Cecily from Middlesex?" Therese asked.

"We didn't know each other well," Mrs. Hassiter said. "And I didn't know you folks owned this hotel. But when I saw your daughter here, I couldn't help myself. Those kids never thought much of me. They were always polite, but they thought of me as the cleaning woman. And they were all so young and beautiful and well-to-do. I wanted to prove I was good for something other than changing your daughter's linen and cleaning the toilets. So I gave her four hundred and eighty-six dollars. It was money I earned."

"Well, I hope you're *happy*!" Bill shouted. "Because here we sit without our daughter. We've been stripped of all our options, Mrs. Hassiter, thanks to you."

"I'm sorry," Mrs. Hassiter said.

"That doesn't fix a goddamned thing!" Bill said.

"Bill," Therese said. She squeezed his hand; she had never seen him this angry before. Therese looked at Mrs. Hassiter—her shoulders slumping, her feet bright and unlikely in a pair of fancy sneakers.

The thought that a woman this age felt she had to prove something to Cecily broke Therese's heart. She tried not to let herself soften toward Mrs. Hassiter, but she couldn't help it. The woman gave Cecily the money; in the end, she only expedited the inevitable. "There's nothing wrong with being a cleaning woman," Therese said. "I'm one myself. It's a job I respect."

Mrs. Hassiter looked at her hands again, as though she were ashamed of them. "It's not the same. You own this beautiful place."

"It is the same," Therese said. "In fact, you can do me a favor."

"What is it?" Mrs. Hassiter asked.

"I need you to supervise my chambermaids this morning while I take my husband out. Then you'll see how much our jobs are alike. And just so you know, I would only trust my job to a professional."

Mrs. Hassiter pushed up her sleeves. "I'd be glad to," she said. "I'll go right now."

THERESE SAID NOTHING TO Bill until they were both in the car and Mrs. Hassiter had safely reached the lobby. Therese turned the key in the ignition, set the air-conditioning, and adjusted the vents so that they blew directly onto herself and Bill. "I know you're mad at me," she said, backing out of the parking lot. "But I won't let myself blame that poor woman."

"I don't blame the woman," Bill said. "I blame myself for double-booking the room. There's a reason why we don't let strangers sleep in our home, Therese. They don't belong."

"Don't be angry with Mrs. Hassiter."

"She tells a sob story and that's all you need to hear. She's a saint now and a martyr."

"I feel for people, Bill," she said.

"If you're going to feel for people," Bill said, "how about starting with Cecily and me?"

"I have always put you first," Therese said. "Every day for thirty years I've put you first, and you know that." She turned onto Main Street, which was bustling with activity, and she was grateful for the distraction. "I can't remember the last time you and I were on Main Street on a summer day," she said. She pointed out the Bartlett Farm truck, its sectioned bed bursting with red and yellow tomatoes, zucchini and squash, string beans, lettuce, and a colorful array of flowers, which bloomed despite the heat. "Look over there. Bountiful summer."

"My summer hasn't been bountiful," Bill said. "First I lose Mack, then my only child."

Therese gripped the wheel with both hands as they rumbled over the cobblestones. "She's coming back."

"Where are we going?" Bill asked. "I see you're not driving to the airport."

"No," she said. "I'm not."

They reached the Somerset Road Cemetery and Therese wound her way through the sandy paths until they came to W.T.'s grave. Bill gave a little groan and smacked his head back against the seat. "You're trying to torture me."

"No," she said. "I just want to remind you what real loss feels like."

They stood together on the patch of dry grass in front of the headstone. Therese read the inscription aloud. "W.T. Elliott, beloved son, April seventh, 1970.' " Then, as if she had given them permission, they both started to cry. Bill pulled out his handkerchief and held it to his nose as his body wracked with sobs. Therese cried into the crook of Bill's arm. At one point, she gained a moment of clarity, enough to wonder what they must look like: two middle-aged people standing in the hottest Nantucket sun on record, crying for someone who died such a long time ago, someone they had never even known.

After a while, Therese let Bill go. She plucked her blouse away from her sweat-soaked body and flapped her arms as if she were a bird, as if she could fly. Then she took a tentative step toward the car. Sweat rolled down her back, and the edges of her mind were blurry with the tears, the grief, and from standing still for too long in the heat. Blurry from wondering—*would* Cecily be back? Or would they be left to cry in graveyards. Nobody's parents.

"You know what I want more than anything else?" Therese said.

"What?" Bill said.

"Rain," she said.

IT WAS SO HOT in Love's Hooper Farm Road house that she had to try the early pregnancy test three times. At dawn, she peed into a plastic cup, and then got ready to dunk the test strip to see if it changed color. The first strip stuck to her sweaty fingers like flypaper, and when she tried to unstick it, it ripped in half.

"Good thing they give you more than one chance," Love said. She'd been talking to herself since she woke up that morning. She treated her second test strip more delicately. It was supposed to turn pink (positive) or blue (negative) when she dipped it in the urine. But the second strip turned green as soon as she picked it up. Green! She dipped it gingerly into the urine, hoping the green would magically change, a frog turning into a prince. But no—it stayed a disappointing, sickly green.

Love hopped on her Cannondale and rode back to the Stop & Shop—the only place carrying early pregnancy tests that was open at six thirty in the morning—and she plucked another test off the shelf. Unfortunately, the sole cashier was the same young man Love went to an hour before, when she bought her first test.

"That's right," she said. "I need another one."

The cashier might have looked at her with understanding, or he might have made a gagging face, as if to say, *Too much information, ma'am;* Love couldn't meet his eyes to find out. *I could be pregnant!* she almost said. But, of course, he would realize that. Love managed to keep her mouth shut until she paid another eighteen dollars and hurried from the store.

BEFORE SHE DIPPED THE third strip, Love washed her hands and dried them thoroughly. Then she pinched the strip between her fingernails and dunked it like a doughnut. She laid it on the little resting pad provided. Now she had to wait—five minutes, the instructions said.

She had to wait.

Love walked out into the hallway, through the kitchen, to the small living room that faced the road. She sat on the dingy sofa and stared at the blank wall in front of her. Her roommates, Randy and Alison, were still asleep.

"I've never actually sat in this room before," Love whispered. "Probably a good thing." The room was perfect for waiting because of the innocuous rentedness of it—an ugly sofa with two rock-hard cushions, a braided rug, a TV with nonfunctional, rabbit-ear antenna. It was as sterile as a doctor's waiting room—nothing to excite or agitate, perfect for thinking.

Love had missed her last period. At first she thought she was just late, normal for her because she exercised so much. After a week, late became a miss. But Love wouldn't let herself get excited until she knew for sure. Her other symptoms could easily have been caused by the heat. She went to the bathroom more frequently—but she also drank water all day to keep from dehydrating. She felt dizzy and tired, but who wouldn't after skating in ninety-five-degree heat, 100 percent humidity? She vomited once—but that was after eating sushi, and in this heat the fish was probably spoiled. Love couldn't tell if she was pregnant, or just hot, like everyone else.

She checked her watch. Four minutes, twenty-six seconds. She made herself stand up.

"Good-bye living room," she said.

Then something caught her eye. On the wall behind the sofa was a picture the size of a baseball card. Love stepped closer to take a look, then recoiled. It was a photograph of an Indian swami, a brown-skinned man wearing a white turban, his hands in front of him in prayer, a mean-looking snake around his neck. Underneath the picture it said, *"Pray with Swami Jeff."*

Swami Jeff? Maybe Alison or Randy tacked the card to the wall as some sort of joke. The man's dark eyes penetrated Love and she shivered. He frightened her. She took the picture off the wall and held it in her hands. She wanted to throw it away. But instead Love raised the picture in front of her face and kissed Swami Jeff right on the lips. *You want me to pray with you, I will. I want a baby, Swami Jeff. Please, I want a baby!* She put the picture of Swami Jeff facedown in a kitchen drawer with the can opener and measuring spoons, and then bravely she walked into her room.

The strip was pink. *P* for pink, *P* for positive.

Love snatched up the resting pad. The strip was bright pink, lively pink, the pink of a healthy internal organ. There was no doubt about it. Love was *P* for pregnant.

She wanted to scream and shout and dance. She wanted to wake up Randy and Alison and tell them the good news. And what, *what* could be better news than this: another person coming into the world! A goal accomplished. A dream come true. She was pregnant!

Then, for just a second, Love experienced sheer terror. What made her think she was remotely qualified to be a mother? Or ready? So she was forty years old, so what? A person would have to be fifty or sixty to have the knowledge to raise another human being. It was an irrevocable thing she had just done. There was no going back.

She sat on her bed, and thought of Vance, who often slept with her there. Last night he'd declined because of the heat. What was she going to do about Vance? Love went back into the kitchen. She opened the drawer where she'd put the picture of Swami Jeff. Her knees buckled and she sucked in her breath. Through the holes of the cheese grater, Love saw Swami Jeff's intense black eyes; the picture was *face up* in the drawer. She nudged the cheese grater aside. Swami Jeff stared at her. Love shut the drawer. She was *positive* she'd put the picture in facedown. (*Positive,* she thought, *I'm positive.*) Love opened the drawer again and picked up the picture. She took Swami Jeff into the bedroom.

Okay, Swami, what am I going to do about Vance? Shall I tell him or not? She stared at Swami Jeff's face and tried to ignore the snake curled around his neck, baring fangs. She closed her eyes and pressed the picture to her forehead.

What was she expecting to see? A vision, maybe—a scene from the future, like a film clip—Love walking down Durant Street in Aspen pushing a stroller. Was Vance in the picture? That was what she wanted to know. But there was no scene, no vision at all. Love held the picture of Swami Jeff in front of her and neatly ripped the card down the middle, slicing him between the eyes.

Vance met Love in the parking lot of the Beach Club as she was locking up her bike.

"How was your night last night?" he asked. "I was thinking of you."

"Uneventful," Love said. "An absolute bore. A hot bore."

"I have some news," Vance said. "Big news."

"Big news?" Love asked. She hoped he wasn't about to propose coming to Colorado again. She hoped he wasn't about to propose anything. She shut her eyes, but saw nothing. "What is it?"

"Cecily's gone," Vance said. "She got on a plane and flew to Brazil without telling a soul. Bill said he and Therese woke up yesterday—and boom, Cecily was gone. She left them a note. The guy is really bumming."

"Poor Bill," Love said.

Vance shrugged. "I think it's only natural," he said. "You have kids and then at some point they leave the nest. What can you do?"

Instinctively, Love touched her abdomen. "You might feel differently if you had your own child," she said.

"My kids are going to be out of the house by eighteen," Vance said. He took out a navy bandanna and wiped his head. "But, listen, I don't want to talk about having kids right now."

I don't want to talk about having kids right now.

Love made a decision: She would tell Vance about the baby if she went home and found the picture of Swami Jeff restored to a whole.

"Me either," she said.

ON HER WAY TO the front desk, Love peeked into Bill's office. He sat at his desk with his eyes closed, his hands folded in front of him. The volume of Robert Frost was nowhere to be seen. *We are at the two ends of parenthood,* she thought. *I have just started to hold on, and Bill is letting go.* She wondered what that kind of pain must feel like. She couldn't imagine.

• • •

WHEN MACK HEARD CECILY was gone, his hand itched to call How-Baby and turn down his brand-new job. Bill was bereft, a man lost at sea, his heart floating on a refugee raft somewhere between Nantucket and Rio de Janeiro. Bill, his almost-father. Mack admired Cecily's courage for leaving. He'd run away once, twelve years before, but then Mack had run from emptiness. Cecily ran from a home where people loved her. When his turn came, Mack wondered, would he be brave enough to go?

JEM CALLED MARIBEL AT the library.

"If you don't want to go to Southeast Asia, how about Brazil?"

THE FUNNY THING WAS, Maribel had just scoured the shelves for novels about Brazil, and finally found one by Jorge Amado called *Gabriela, Cinnamon and Cloves*. She hid in the stacks and read several passages, thinking, *This doesn't sound bad. This doesn't sound bad at all.*

"IT'S HOTTER IN BRAZIL than it is here!" Lacey exclaimed, when Mack told her of Cecily's escape. "What was the dear girl thinking?"

Secretly, Lacey was elated. She was all for chasing a dream; she was all for chasing love.

BILL PUT HIS VOLUME of Robert Frost back on the shelf in his bedroom; it had done him no good. His daughter was gone, Mack was leaving, Bill's health was slipping away, and what did his wife want more than anything else? Rain. In the end, Bill decided, it was very Frost-like of Therese. To stare in the face of all this emotional anguish and want nothing more than a simple rain.

9

September

September 4

Dear Bill,

I am not one to say 'I told you so,' however, I do believe the abrupt departure of your daughter should send you a clear message. She isn't interested in the hotel, as I suspected. She has deserted it, and you. Your manager, Mack, is in line to leave next if you don't do something about it. The time has never been better for you to sell. What are you waiting for? A sign from God?

S.B.T.

SEPTEMBER: IT USED TO be Bill's favorite month of the year. After Labor Day weekend, the Beach Club closed and the property quieted down; it gained serenity. But Bill couldn't enjoy September without Cecily. He couldn't stomach listening to one more back-to-school-sale commercial on the radio, knowing that Cecily wasn't matriculating at the University of Virginia that fall. Bill didn't know where Cecily was or what she was doing. He had a horrible, recurring image: Cecily wandering through the streets of Rio, trailed by a gang of brown-skinned Brazilian boys wearing gray camouflage, carrying switchblades and razors, intent on raping and killing her.

He read and reread his latest letter from S.B.T. Who the hell was this guy, some kind of spy? That ass Comatis who had hired away Mack? Bill ran through the list of Beach Club members, but he came up empty. One thing was for sure: the letters from S.B.T. were eating at him. *What are you waiting for? A sign from God?* Yes, he thought. Exactly.

Bill had lost all his energy, and worse, his chest pain returned, a dull ache around his heart. He missed his daughter and he feared for the future of his hotel. The only thing he could do with ease was lie in bed with the remote control, flipping between channels to make sure there were no news stories about young American girls raped and killed abroad. It was far easier to watch TV than it was to read poetry. TV was colorful, silly, full of laughter and melodrama. TV made Robert Frost seem as exciting as a pile of dry twigs. Mornings after Cecily had left, Bill let himself get sucked into the TV.

That was how he first heard about Freida.

September 8, the Tuesday after Labor Day, Freida was born in the West Indies. The National Hurricane Center in Miami posted a bulletin: She was a mean storm. The newscasters on the weather channel showed fancy graphics—Freida, a swirling, multicolored eye, 210 miles wide with sustained winds of 93 miles an hour, moving up the eastern seaboard. They expected her to make landfall around Cape Hatteras, but the following areas could expect trouble from Freida as well: the Chesapeake Bay, Long Island Sound, Nantucket. *Nantucket.* The newscaster said the name of the island and Bill felt a surge of recognition, as though his own name were being spoken aloud on national TV. He wondered if Cecily was listening.

"Nantucket?" Bill said.

"Of course the storm may miss Nantucket altogether and head northeast out to sea," the newscaster said.

BY THE TIME BILL made it down to the lobby, everyone was abuzz about Freida's arrival. Love talked to a couple about where the experts tracked Freida, and how she might move along, or might lose energy and scatter, dissipate. They discussed Freida as though she were a person. Was she organized? Did she have weak spots?

Mack waited in Bill's office, tensed, pumped up, ready to pounce. "Did you hear?" he said. "We're going to get creamed."

Out the window, it was the perfect September day, though still hot at eighty-five degrees. The sky was blue, the water flat. No clouds.

"We'll see. They said it might veer off into the North Atlantic. That's what they usually do. This island hasn't seen a bona fide hurricane since 1954."

"What's our plan of attack?" Mack asked.

A wave of exhaustion swept over Bill. It was ten-thirty and he wanted to put his head on the desk and sleep. "We're not going to do anything."

"What do you mean?" Mack said. "We have to board up. We have to bring everything inside. It's a hurricane, Bill."

Bill took a deep breath and closed his eyes. The Brazilian boys were gaining ground on Cecily, getting closer. They were after his daughter. Somehow, Bill had to flush that image.

"Bill?" Mack said. "Freida is going to hit the island from the west. She's two hundred miles wide. Do you realize how big that is?"

"It sounds like you *want* this hurricane to come," Bill said. "It sounds like maybe you want to watch the place get flooded. That would be fun for you, wouldn't it? Watch the place wash away and then take off for Fenway Park."

"You've got to be kidding me," Mack said. "I don't *want* the hurricane to come. But I'd like to be ready. There are people sitting in the rooms, facing the water."

"What do you care if the hotel gets wrecked? You're leaving at the end of the season." Bill was short of breath. "Tell me," he said. "I'd really like to know. What do you care?"

"I care," Mack said. "I've worked here for twelve years. Believe me, I care."

"Obviously not enough," Bill said. His chest was on fire. "Get out." He pointed to the door. "I don't want to talk about the storm. Now get out!"

Mack's eyes widened. He pressed his lips together and left the office.

Bill leaned back in his swivel chair and tried to take several deep breaths. In, out. In, out. His heart thrummed in his ears. He picked up the picture of Cecily that he kept on his desk. Cecily at fifteen, wearing her Middlesex Field Hockey T-shirt over her bathing suit, sitting in an

Adirondack chair, on the pavilion, her bare legs tucked underneath her (scab on one knee), her red hair crazy and curly around her face. An heiress sitting on her throne. *Where was she?*

By Thursday, Freida had wreaked havoc in the Bahamas, and she moved along the eastern coast of Florida where she hooked up with a local low-pressure system and increased in size and speed. Class four, 230 miles across, sustained winds of 101 miles per hour. The newscaster hadn't said "Nantucket" in twenty-four hours. Instead they showed clips of the Caribbean: palm trees with their heads ripped off, washed-out bridges, whole houses floating away. Every hour at fifty past, they flashed the international forecast. Rio was sunny, thirty-three degrees Centigrade.

Bill lugged his body out of bed and walked straight down to the beach. People lounged under the umbrellas, a man was swimming. No hurricane here. Then Bill heard someone coughing and he turned to see Clarissa Ford standing on the deck of room 7, smoking. She waved to him. He waved back. She waved *at* him, beckoning. Bill groaned inwardly. Clarissa was seventy years old, a widow, her very wealthy husband killed years ago by half a million cigarettes, and yet Clarissa continued to smoke. She stayed at the hotel for the whole month of September, spending over sixteen thousand dollars. A year's worth of the college tuition that Bill would not be paying to the University of Virginia. He slogged through the sand until he was a few feet from her deck.

"Bill," she said. Clarissa Ford's face was tan and wrinkled; she looked like dried tobacco. "Bill, how are you, my dear?"

"I'm okay, Clarissa, how are you?"

"Fine, dear, wonderful." She inhaled on her cigarette. "You see I've been obeying the little rule your wife set up for me this year. I've not smoked in the room once."

"I find that hard to believe, Clarissa," Bill said. Last year they had to air the room for three days after she left. And still room 7 had the faint smell of an ashtray.

"It's *true*," she said. "I've been out here morning, noon, and night."

"Thank you," Bill said. "We appreciate it."

Clarissa ashed into the sand just off the deck. There was a gray spot the size of a saucer already. "How's my darling Cecily?"

Bill looked out over the water. A ferry approached from Hyannis. "I don't know," Bill said. "She ran off to South America."

Clarissa's laugh sounded like wagon wheels rolling over gravel. It sounded like someone balling up a cellophane bag. "Tell her to come over and visit me when she gets a free second," Clarissa said. "I haven't seen her in eons. She must be all grown up! Is she ready for college?"

"I told you, Clarissa. She's run off to South America."

"Honestly, Bill. Will you send her over? I have some valuable wisdom to impart."

"Impart it to me," Bill said. "I could use it."

"You take yourself so seriously, Bill, dear," Clarissa said. She waved her cigarette like a magic wand. "Lighten up!"

"You know we're getting a hurricane?" Bill said. "The hotel could wash away."

Clarissa crushed her cigarette out on the railing of the deck. Bill winced. "Pshaw!" she said. "That's exactly what I mean by too seriously, Bill. It won't be a hurricane! It'll just be a little rain here in paradise."

ON FRIDAY, A PHONE call came to the house. It was Nantucket's fire chief, Anthony Mazzaco.

"We're going to get some weather here, Bill. It's not a pretty picture. You need me to send someone down to help ya? Mack tells me you haven't made a move. Now, you got people in those rooms, Bill, you have to make a move."

"Look outside, Tony," Bill said. "Do you see rain? Do you see a storm?"

"She's coming," Tony Mazzaco said. He, too, sounded excited. "She's coming."

• • •

ON SATURDAY, FREIDA MADE landfall in Norfolk, Virginia. The newscaster on the weather channel drew a yellow arrow off the coast of Long Island, heading out toward the North Atlantic. *Good*, Bill thought, *let Long Island take the hit.* But for some reason, the man said, "Nantucket is in a position to catch Freida's wrath. Nantucket is in her way." Nantucket again. Bill sat up, and saw how, as Freida moved for the chilly North Atlantic waters, she would sideswipe Nantucket. She was huge, two hundred plus miles wide. The island was thirteen by four. Freida could gobble them up.

Freida, the mean woman. Only in Bill's mind, Freida was a girl with crazy red hair—she was an angry teenager throwing a tantrum. The room blurred.

He sat in bed, trying to focus. He hadn't showered in two days. The bedsheets had a smell. Bill tried to care about the storm, about the hotel, about himself. He tried to care, but he couldn't. He would let her come.

IT WAS ALL OVER the TV and radio; everyone in town was talking about it. Tourists booked flights and hopped on the steamship. Stop & Shop's parking lot overflowed with people buying bottled water, bread, candles, Duraflame logs. Boats came out of the water, houses were shuttered, deck furniture stored. The Nantucket police and the fire station answered worried phone calls. There was a small-craft advisory and as of Sunday morning, the ferries were canceled. A hurricane watch and coastal flood warning were issued by the National Hurricane Center for the island of Nantucket. Hurricane watch became hurricane warning.

And Bill would do nothing about it. Mack had never seen him act like this. Since Cecily left, the guy had crumbled, caved in. He accused Mack of wanting this storm, *wanting* it! But nothing could be further from the truth. Mack loved the hotel and he would do whatever he could to protect it.

Even if it meant going over Bill's head.

Mack found Therese bringing her plants in from the front porch. A good sign—maybe she believed in Freida even if Bill didn't.

Mack kicked a hermit crab shell across the parking lot. "I'm going to gather Vance and Jem and start shuttering this place if that's all right with you."

Therese ran her hand through her pale orange hair. She looked tired, and sad. "What does Bill say?"

"He says don't do it. He doesn't seem to care what kind of hit we take."

"You're right," Therese said. "He doesn't care. Why should he care?"

"When Cecily comes back, Therese, it might be nice if there was a hotel left to pass on."

She touched the leaves of her geraniums. "I wish you'd asked her to marry you . . . just *asked* her, you know?"

"Therese," Mack said. "Can I please do my work?"

"Go ahead," she said. "Do what you have to do."

MACK BEGAN THE TIME-CONSUMING task of screwing wooden shutters over every window. It only took two or three minutes to put up a shutter—but there were so many windows. He raced to finish the lobby and office before it grew too dark to work. He hauled the wooden shutters out of storage, grabbed fistfuls of screws and kept two or three pinched between his lips as he worked. Just as he was finishing the windows of the lobby that faced the water, he smelled smoke. He looked around. Clarissa Ford stood behind him in the sand, the ubiquitous cigarette dangling between her fingers.

"You're not going to shutter my room, are you?" she asked.

"Tomorrow," he said. "Not tonight."

"Not tomorrow," Clarissa said.

"Yes, tomorrow. I'm sorry, but there's a storm coming."

"I don't want you to shutter my windows. And certainly not my door."

"I'll leave the back door alone," Mack said. "I don't want to trap you in there. But I'm sealing up the front. Especially your room, Mrs. Ford. Your room faces the water."

"I don't want you to do it. I'll sign whatever I have to, a release for my safety."

"Your safety's important to us, Mrs. Ford," Mack said. He wiggled his feet in his boots; talking to her was slowing him down. "But we're also concerned about the hotel room."

"I'll talk to Bill," Clarissa said. "He'll say to leave my room alone, I guarantee you."

Mack shrugged. "You're right," he said. He turned back to the shutter in his hand. "Fine, then. You'll go without."

AT DUSK, JEM AND Vance came off the beach, sweating. They'd put up snow fencing, and stored the deck furniture from every room. Mack finished with the lobby windows and called it a day. He looked over at Bill and Therese's house before he pulled out of the parking lot. It was dark and still, as though nobody lived there anymore.

AT HOME, MARIBEL COOKED a huge lasagna. "We can eat it for dinner over the next few days," she said.

"I may have to stay down at the hotel tomorrow night," Mack said.

"*Stay* at the hotel?" she said. "Are you kidding?"

"As it is, I left forty windows facing the water totally exposed. One of them could shatter. Someone could get hurt. I probably shouldn't have left tonight. I should have stayed down there."

"And worked in the *dark*?" Maribel said. She took a bite of lasagna. She'd been argumentative lately, like she didn't believe a word he said about anything anymore. "If you're staying at the club, I am, too."

"You'll be safer here," Mack said.

She stabbed a piece of lettuce. "I'm not staying here without you."

"Maribel, you'll be safer here. That's the only good thing about living mid-island. Away from the water you should be okay."

"Okay?" Maribel put her fork down with a clang and stared at him. "I should be *okay* here alone during the biggest storm this island has seen in forty years? What if a tree falls down? What if we lose power?"

"You probably will lose power," Mack said. "But you have candles and a flashlight."

"Great. So I spend three days in the dark by myself. We're *engaged*, Mack." She flashed her diamond in his face. "See this? It means we're part of a team. And I'm coming to the hotel with you."

"No, you're not."

"You don't want me around," she said. "You don't want anything to do with me."

"I'm thinking of your safety."

"You're thinking of yourself. As always."

"What's that supposed to mean?" he said.

"What do you *think* it means?" she asked. Her mouth twisted in an ugly way. "It means you only think about yourself and your stupid fucking job."

Mack tried to keep his voice steady. "You're not staying at the hotel, Maribel," he said. "Now stop acting like a five-year-old."

Maribel stood up. She pushed Mack's shoulders back, and then she moved to hit him. He raised his hands to shield his face. "What are you doing?" She clawed his arm so ferociously that he started to bleed. "What's *wrong* with you?" he asked. He went to the kitchen sink and washed his arm. Maribel collapsed in her chair, crying. Mack was afraid to look at her; he examined the marks on his arm. Then he heard a clatter, and he saw Maribel put her bare elbows in her food as she cried into her hands.

"Maribel, what's going on?"

She picked up her plate and threw it across the room. It crashed against the coffee table. The plate broke; lasagna and salad went everywhere. "What is wrong with you?" Mack said. "You scratched me. Do you see this? You made me bleed. Are you crazy?"

She nodded; her elbows were greasy with red sauce and salad dressing. "You don't love me," she said. "You've never loved me."

"I do love you," Mack said. "I asked you to marry me. That was what you wanted, wasn't it? I gave you what you wanted."

When Maribel stood up, she knocked her chair over. "I want *you* to want it!" she said. "I want you to want it as badly as I do. But you don't."

Mack tried to get a hold of her, but she smacked him out of the way. Her face was purple, she cried so hard he couldn't even see her eyes. "Maribel, people are different. I can't feel the way you do because I'm not you. I'm me. And I'm doing the best I can."

"It's not good enough!" she screamed. "You don't love me enough!" She hit herself in the face with her open palms. "There's something wrong with me! You don't love me enough. You don't! You don't love me enough."

Mack grabbed her arms, and she fought him. She snarled and cried in his face and he smelled her warm, garlicky breath. He held her by the wrists.

"I do love you enough," he said. A red mark surfaced where she'd hit herself. A red mark on her pretty face. How could he love her enough when she always wanted more?

"You're hurting me!" she said. Mack let go of her wrists. He'd gripped them so tightly, he left white marks. She darted into the bedroom, slamming the door behind her and locking it. Mack knocked on the door. "Maribel? Please open up. Mari, I don't know what's happening." He heard nothing from the other side of the door but her muffled crying. Her brokenhearted crying. Even with his best intentions, the best he could give, he'd somehow failed. Mack listened for a minute, and then he cleaned up the shattered plate and the thrown food, wrapped the tray of lasagna with foil, put it in the fridge. He washed his bloody scratch marks and held a clean dishtowel against them. He knocked on the door again. "Mari, please. Tell me what's wrong."

"You're what's wrong!" she screamed. "I'm what's wrong. This whole thing is wrong."

"Maribel, open the door, please. Please?"

"Leave me *alone*!" she shouted.

He tried the doorknob. Locked. He could jimmy it with something from the utensil drawer, but why? What was the point? *This whole thing is wrong.*

Mack went to the sofa to watch the weather channel.

Freida was off the Jersey Shore.

LACEY GARDNER COULDN'T CONCENTRATE on the storm because something else was bothering her. She had forgotten what Maximilian looked like. It was the oddest thing. She closed her eyes and concentrated on the things Max used to do—reading in his chair, making a tricky putt in golf. But she couldn't picture him at all. She couldn't imagine him in her mind.

She collected all her photographs of Maximilian and spread them out on the coffee table. Twenty-one pictures of Max—from the age of thirty-three in his military uniform to the photo of Max on the porch of the Cliff Road house during his last summer. Lacey studied each picture, and then she leaned back on the sofa and shut her eyes.

Nothing.

He had vanished. She could think his name, think of a hundred thousand moments with him, right up until the moment in bed the last night when he took her hand. But she couldn't see his face in her mind. She opened her eyes and there were twenty-one images of Maximilian smiling at her. Then she closed her eyes, and there was darkness.

Lacey started to weep. It might be a passing phase, brought on by all the stress, the heat, the impending storm. Or it might be that now, at age eighty-eight, she was slipping away. The best part of her—the part that remembered Maximilian and kept him alive—was gone.

There was a knock at the door. Lacey wiped her face quickly with her handkerchief, but not before Mack saw her.

"You're crying," he said.

"No, I'm not."

Mack waited a minute, then he said, "If something's bothering you,

you can tell me. You don't have to be everyone's pillar of strength and wisdom all the time."

"Nothing's bothering me," she said. She nodded at the coffee table. "I'm just looking at old pictures."

Mack surveyed the table. "Maximilian was a handsome man." He pointed to the picture of Max in uniform. "He looks like me in this picture, don't you think?"

"Yes," Lacey whispered. Her Max, her Mack. She took Mack's hand. "I love you. Do you know that? Have I ever told you that? I love you."

Mack knelt beside her. "Lacey, what's wrong?"

The tears started up again, out of her control. "I miss him," she said.

"I know, Lacey," Mack said. "I know you do."

She cried more tears, tears she thought had dried up long ago. Mack held her hand, saying nothing. After several minutes, she snuffled into her handkerchief, and blew her nose. "I'm okay now," she said. She noticed a bandage on Mack's arm. "What happened to you?"

"Rough night at home," he said. "Actually, I came to ask you a favor. I'd like to stay here tonight, if I could."

Relief flooded Lacey, replacing, almost, the emptiness, the blankness. "For Pete's sake, of course. Stay here, please."

Mack squeezed her hand. "Okay, I will. Thank you."

She wouldn't have to be alone, then. Maximilian was missing, but Mack would be here instead to help her fend off the horrible darkness. For one night more, at least.

MONDAY BEGAN AS A mild, sunny day, and Mack made headway on the remaining eighty shutters. Around noon, the wind shifted from southwest to due west and by the time the chambermaids finished cleaning the rooms at one o'clock, the sky was low and gunmetal gray.

Again, Bill didn't show up in the office. Therese fluttered around behind the chambermaids, but when they finished their work, she retreated to her house. Mack shuttered away. When the wind picked up, sand pelted the side of his face and the back of his neck, a thousand tiny needles. A gust lifted his Texas Rangers hat off his head. His hands were busy with shutter and drill gun, and all he could do was turn and watch his hat blow down the beach. It was eerie in a way; suddenly the beach was deserted. Bill and Therese had dropped the future of the hotel in Mack's hands.

By three o'clock, waves pounded the beach so that Mack felt the vibrations through the soles of his work boots as he rushed to finish shuttering. He skipped room 7, Clarissa Ford's room, and when he made it down to room 2, she stepped onto her deck with a lit cigarette. The wind plucked the cigarette from her fingers immediately; it was halfway to Jetties Beach before she even realized it was gone.

At 3:45, the first drops of rain fell. Mack screwed in the final shutters. The wind moaned; Mack's right ear filled with sand. Then the rain picked up. Sand blew in drifts halfway up the snow fence. Mack held his drill inside his jacket, raised his arm to shield his eyes, and ran for the back door of the lobby. By the time he reached the back door, he was soaked and his boots were filled with sand. He stood under the eaves and looked at the roiled, black sea. Mack thought of Maribel, at home on the sofa reading, her feet bundled in an afghan. She hadn't said a word to him when he left that morning. No apology, no explanation—nothing but the silent assurance that whatever he was doing, it wasn't enough. Mack watched the waves crest and crash. One came halfway up the beach. The next one even farther. He didn't understand her.

Inside, Vance and Love played gin rummy at the front desk. Jem was slumped in one of the wicker chairs, asleep.

"You can all go home," Mack said. "I'm staying at Lacey's tonight. I'll take care of things until this bitch passes." He shook Jem's shoulder. "You can leave, Jem. Why don't you take my Jeep? You can't walk home in this."

Jem opened his eyes. "The Jeep? What will you drive?"

"I'm not going home tonight." And then, before he could think better of it, he said, "Take the Jeep and check on Maribel. She's all by herself. I'm sure she wants company."

Jem sat upright in the chair. "Is that supposed to be some kind of joke?"

Mack's stomach prickled with jealousy, and with fear. He pictured Maribel crying, he pictured his fingers gripping her wrists, leaving behind white bracelets. "It's no joke, man. I can't get home tonight. You'd be doing me a favor if you checked on her."

"I'd be doing you a *favor*? Really?" Jem said.

"Just go," Mack said. He flipped Jem his keys.

Jem didn't hesitate. He took the keys and ran, following Vance and Love out the door. Because the windows were shuttered, Mack couldn't watch them drive away. And that kept him from yelling after Jem, and telling him it was all a mistake.

AS SOON AS THE rain started, Bill got out of bed and ran to the living room window. The ocean was huge, the waves bigger than any Bill could remember. The lobby was shuttered, and so were the rooms—Mack's doing. Bill couldn't bring himself to feel one way or another. He couldn't feel anything except this crazy longing, this crazy sadness.

Therese came up the stairs. "You're up," she said. She stood with him at the window. "Our kingdom. I hope it doesn't get washed away."

"What does it matter?" Bill said.

"Bill," Therese said, "she's coming back."

"She's not coming back!" Bill said. "Stop saying that, Therese. Cecily *isn't coming back!*"

Therese said quietly, "She is."

"She's not," Bill said. The Brazilian boys chased Cecily now. One boy—Gabriel—grabbed Cecily's bright red hair. He held a razor to her neck.

Bill went to the closet and put a slicker on over his pajamas. "I'm going up to the widow's walk."

"What?" Therese said. She collapsed on the leather sofa. "You've lost your mind."

"What does it matter?" Bill said. He marched through the bedroom and opened the door to the attic. In the attic was a flight of stairs leading to a hatch that popped up onto the widow's walk. Bill had trouble opening the hatch door; he pressed his hands flat against it and pushed with all his might. Then the door flipped open and the wind and the rain nearly knocked Bill down the stairs. He knelt on the stairs and clenched the railing. He would get up there, and sit on the widow's walk. It might kill him, but what did it matter? He was the father of two children: one dead, one missing.

Then he heard a voice, footsteps. Therese climbed up after him.

"I'm coming up there with you," she said. She was five or ten feet away, but it sounded as though she were calling to him from the end of a long tunnel. The wind lifted her pale orange hair; she looked like a ghost or a witch, but she looked beautiful, too—his bride, the woman he loved.

Bill gripped the railing with one hand and reached for her with the other. The wind was impossibly strong. Poetically strong—if they did manage to climb onto the widow's walk, maybe the wind would pick them up and carry them away, to their son, their daughter.

Rain drove through the hatch. Bill was soaked to the skin. He was in bare feet.

"Come on," he said. He raised his head through the opening. The sky screamed in his ears, the world rained down on him. All he could see was white. Bill tried to look around, but he couldn't find the sea, he couldn't find the hotel. The sky was blank, the color of wind. Wind filled his eyes, his ears, his nose—he was drowning in the wind. *What are you waiting for? A sign from God?* "You can have it!" Bill screamed to the sky. He was sure that somehow S.B.T. could hear him. "You . . . can . . . have . . . it!" He lost his balance and faltered in his footing, but Therese steadied him. He brought his head back inside. The stairs were wet and slippery; Therese's blouse stuck to her skin. Mascara ran down her face, her orange hair was wet, the color of a pumpkin.

"He can have it," Bill said. "I give up. He can have it."

Therese held on to him. "Who can have what?" she asked. "What are you talking about? Who are you screaming at?"

Bill had lost his hope. He didn't have the stuff in him; beneath his skin and bones and cartilage, he was dry, an empty gourd. He managed to close the hatch door, spurred on by what was now his hatred of this storm. Once the hatch was closed and locked, Bill followed Therese into the bathroom. He vomited into the toilet. He vomited up the Brazilian boys with their razor blades, and Cecily screaming with fear. He vomited up S.B.T. taking the Beach Club from him. He vomited up Dead and Missing. He vomited until it was all gone, and the inside of his mouth was puckered and sour.

Therese drew him a bath, and he gingerly lowered himself into the warm water. Therese sat next to him on the floor. He was the owner of a beach hotel waiting out a hurricane. Helpless. He was the father of a teenage daughter. Hopeless.

MARIBEL WAS ON THE phone with Tina when the power went out and the phone died in her hand. Maybe it was just as well. Tina had started to cry almost as soon as Maribel spoke.

"Mama, I'm going to break the engagement."

"What?"

"It's not meant to be, Mama. It's not going to work." Maribel had replayed the night before a hundred times in her mind. Something had broken inside her, and she lost control. She'd hurt Mack, she made him bleed. And he'd nearly snapped her hands off. They were finding new ways to hurt each other. It had to stop.

Tina hit full-blown snuffles, sobs. "You're just angry, Mari. You're angry at Mack now and you've been angry at him before. You'll get past it."

"I'm not angry anymore, Mama. I'm beyond angry. We don't make each other happy. We don't want the same things."

"Why are you giving up?" Tina said. "Why after so long?"

Maribel heard the desperate note in her mother's voice and she squeezed her eyes shut against it. *I want this for her,* Maribel thought. *I want to get married because I know it will make her happy. It will take away the demons of her loneliness, to know that I, at least, won't have to spend my life alone.*

"Will you love me anyway?" Maribel asked. "Will you love me even without Mack?"

More sobbing. "You know I love you best of anyone in the world. You know you're my number-one prize. If you made this decision, then it must be God's will."

"It's my will," Maribel said. "Mama, it's my will."

And then the power went out.

Maribel had candles and matches ready, and in seconds the apartment glowed with candlelight. She went into the bathroom and splashed water on her face, and then she opened a bottle of red wine.

Maribel toasted the air. "Fuck you, Freida," she said. She sipped her wine. She would get good and drunk.

There were headlights in her window. Maribel saw the Jeep swing into the driveway. Her heart stood up. Mack hadn't left her alone after all. He'd come home. Maribel's mind stumbled over words for an apology.

Oddly, there was a knock at the door. A knock? Maribel flung the door open, and there, standing in the rain, was Jem.

AS JEM DROVE THE Jeep to Maribel's apartment, he thought about the two words Neil Rosenblum had left him with: *Get her.* The wind was blowing so hard that Jem had to grip the steering wheel with both hands just to keep the Jeep on the road. The wipers flew back and forth, and at every low point, Jem drove through deep puddles that sloshed over the hood of the car. The rain was ridiculous, and Jem probably would have crashed if there had been other cars on the road. But from the look of things, Jem was the only one out. On his way to see Maribel, with Mack's permission.

Jem pulled into Maribel's driveway and switched off the ignition. The trees in Maribel's backyard bowed in the wind, and a carpet of fallen leaves covered the grass. A heavy branch crashed to the ground. Jem ran like hell down the sloping side yard to the apartment. The gas grill lay on its side. Jem knocked on the door. *Be home,* he thought. Maybe this was all a joke—maybe Maribel was off-island.

But then she opened the door. The apartment was lit by candles.

"Jem," she said. "I thought you were Mack."

Jem's heart sagged. Here he was standing out in the middle of a hurricane, and what did she say? *I thought you were Mack.*

"Mack's at the hotel," he said. "He sent me here to keep you company. Listen, can I come in?"

"He *sent* you here?" Maribel said. Her brow creased into lines that looked like an *M. M* for Maribel. Or more likely, an angry *M* for Mack. It occurred to Jem then that Maribel might not enjoy being handed off like a baton.

"Can I come in?" Jem pleaded. His shoes filled with water. The wind blew sideways. Another branch fell in the yard.

"For a minute," she said. She ushered him in and slammed the door behind him. "So Mack sent you here. He *sent* you here."

"Sort of." Jem was afraid to move anywhere in the room. He dripped onto the welcome mat. "Can I take my shoes off?"

"You're only staying as long as it takes you to tell me exactly what Mack said."

Jem looked around, stalling for time. "You lost power," he said. He needed to think. He felt hesitant to get Mack into trouble, since Mack was the one who gave him the okay to come. But that was the whole point. Mack was a creep. He was giving away his girlfriend.

"What did Mack say?" Maribel picked a glass of wine up off the coffee table.

"He said, uh . . . he said you'd be alone and that I should keep you company. And he gave me the keys to the Jeep."

Maribel slugged back some wine. "So he's pimping me out."

"Excuse me?" Jem didn't like the sound of that word anywhere near Maribel.

"He sent you over here because he wants us to have sex. That's his way out of the relationship." She finished her glass of wine and then she ripped her cardigan sweater right down the middle, so that the buttons popped off and disappeared into the shag carpet. Underneath the sweater, she wore a shiny blue bra, which she unhooked and flung onto the sofa. Jem was confused, but he couldn't keep from looking at her breasts. They seemed fuller than they had at the beach that day.

"What are you doing?" he asked.

She unbuttoned her jean shorts and let them fall to her ankles. She slid her hands inside her flowered panties and slipped these off as well. She stood before him, completely nude in the candlelight. Jem thought he might faint.

"You can take your shoes off," she said. "And the rest of your clothes, for that matter."

"What's going on?" he said. His body screamed out for her. Her ass, the curve under her chin, the backs of her knees. But something was wrong. She was steaming like a tea kettle, and it wasn't from desire for him.

"You're angry at Mack," he said.

"You're damn right I'm angry!" she said. "He set all this up. I'm sure he thinks he's doing us both a favor! But he's manipulating our feelings. And guess what? I don't care. He wants us to have sex, we'll have sex."

Just hearing Maribel say the words almost knocked Jem out. The front of his shorts was pitched like a tent. But this was wrong, everything about it was wrong.

"I love you, Maribel," Jem said. "And I've never been in love with anyone before, but I don't want you to sleep with me because you're angry with Mack. I'm going home." He opened the door, afraid to turn around and see what she was doing. He thought he heard her pour another glass of wine. He geared himself up to make a run for the Jeep, thinking if he timed it right he could run between gusts of wind.

Another branch fell, and Jem took that as his sign. He ran from Maribel's house as quickly as he could.

Once he was safely inside the Jeep, he thought it might be okay to cry, or yell, or do something to release all his haywire, fucked-up emotions. The rain pounded on the top of the Jeep; it was like sitting inside a tin can. He turned the key in the ignition, praying he hadn't ruined the engine by taking on those giant puddles. Fortunately, the engine started and Jem backed out of the driveway. He couldn't see where he was going, but that mattered very little. He pulled onto what looked like the road and hit the gas.

He made it about a hundred yards when he saw red and blue flashing lights—a police car blocked Bartlett Road, the road that led to everywhere else. A policeman in a fluorescent orange raincoat waved his arms at Jem. Jem rolled down the window.

"All the roads are closed," the policeman shouted. "You'll have to go back to wherever you came from."

"I can't," Jem said.

The officer shrugged. "I can't let you on the roads. You'll have to."

"I can't go back," Jem said. "I live on Liberty Street."

All Jem could see of the officer was his light blue eyes and his nose and his lips, which were scrunched together by his tightly drawn hood. "You can't go on the roads."

"Will you put me in jail if I try?" Jem asked. Jail was far preferable to returning to Maribel's.

"No, I won't put you in jail!" the officer said. "What I'm saying is, you can't pass. I'm sorry. Now turn around!"

Jem managed to turn the Jeep around and head back down Pheasant Road. He considered pulling into a random driveway and spending the night there. Spending the night in his wet clothes in a chilly, wet car without food or water when the woman he loved was a hundred yards away? Jem pictured Neil Rosenblum shouting at him. *Get her!*

Jem drove back to Maribel's and sat in the Jeep, thinking of what he might say. Then he raced to the house and knocked once again on the door.

Maribel had put her clothes back on, although her cardigan hung open.

"I love you," he said.

"Will you hold me?" she asked.

He nodded, and stepped inside.

• • •

MACK STAYED AT THE desk by himself. At seven o'clock, when the power went out, he ran along the back of the hotel, knocking on the rooms' back doors to make sure everyone was all right. Spirits were high. The guests lit candles, drank wine, ate sandwiches, read novels. When Mack was certain everyone was surviving, he returned to the desk. He sat by the light of three votive candles and listened. The wind was an opera—a baritone rumble and soprano whistle singing simultaneously. Mack heard sand hit the wall of the lobby, but not water. Not yet.

Mack wondered what was happening with Jem and Maribel. He wanted to race home and stop whatever was going on, but after the scene the night before, he knew he had no choice but to let Maribel go. *Let her go?* He gently removed the bandage from his arm and inspected his wound. He couldn't believe she'd scratched him like that, he couldn't believe he'd made her that unhappy. *This whole thing is wrong.* A six-year mistake.

By ten o'clock, Mack was tired of thinking. He stepped out the side door, and ran through a gust of sandy wind to Lacey's.

SHE WAS SITTING IN her armchair with ivory beeswax candles burning and a Dewar's on the table next to her. She wore her nightgown, a pink silk bathrobe, pink terry cloth slippers. The pictures of Maximilian had been collected into a neat pile.

"Max?" she said when he walked in. "Maximilian?"

Mack shook off water like a dog. "It's me, Lacey, Mack."

Lacey jumped. He wondered if he'd woken her. "Mack, dear, hello. How goes it?"

"Nothing's flooding. That's what's important. There's ankle-deep sand in the parking lot, but sand can be shoveled. Do you feel like talking?"

"Heavens, yes," Lacey said. "You know me, I always feel like talking."

Mack collapsed on the sofa. "What should we talk about?"

"Let's talk about your wedding," she said. "I want to buy a new dress. A bright red dress. I want people to call me a harlot!" She kicked her feet in their pink slippers. "You know, Maximilian and I actually got married twice. Have I told you that? We married the first time in November of '41, just before Max went off to the war. Judge Alcott performed the ceremony on Madaket Beach and Isabel and Ed Tolliver witnessed. After the ceremony, the four of us went to the Skipper for lunch. Max left for Maryland ten days later for basic training. Then, a few months later, Max was shipped to the Philippines. Those were gruesome times, because the Japanese had bombed Pearl Harbor, and there was Maximilian, practically in Japan himself. While Max was in the Philippines, our friend Sam Archibald died over in Europe, and I had to write to Max and tell him that." Lacey sipped her drink and stared into the candles. "Where was I headed with this story? Oh, yes, our two weddings. We had a church wedding when Maximilian returned. That was a waste of my father's money. We were already married!" Lacey finished her drink. "Let's talk about your wedding," she said. "I only want to talk about things that are in our future. I spend far too much time talking about the past. And I'm stopping, right here, right now. Here's to the future!" She raised her empty glass to him.

"I'm not going to marry Maribel," he said.

"You're not?" she said.

"No."

"Have you told Maribel this?" Lacey asked.

"Not in so many words," Mack said. Just thinking about Jem touching Maribel made him queasy. "But I think she has an idea. I don't know how to explain it. I just can't marry her."

"You don't have to explain it to me," Lacey said. "I have long lived by the expression, 'Nobody knows where it comes from, and nobody knows where it goes.' Love doesn't make sense most of the time and that's what's so wonderful about it."

They were both quiet. Freida calmed down, too, but only for a second.

Lacey pushed herself up from the chair and took a few steps toward Mack. "Some days I think I'm old and wise, and other days just old. I'm going to bed. You'll be in and out tonight, I suppose?"

"I'll try to be quiet."

"Don't worry about it. Just make sure you blow the candles out. We wouldn't want to burn down the cottage Big Bill left me."

Mack hugged Lacey around the shoulders. "So you don't think I'm crazy? Breaking my engagement?"

Lacey put her cool hands on his face. "What you must realize, Mack, dear, is that I will love you whatever you decide. That's the definition of love." She picked up a candle and teetered off down the dark hall. Mack stayed to make sure she reached her bedroom door safely. Before she opened it, she turned to him. The candle lit up her smile.

"You're my boy," she said.

WHEN MACK RETURNED TO the lobby, it was nearly eleven. Freida shook the hotel like a gambler shaking a cup of dice, as if she were trying to lift the hotel off its foundation. Mack pulled an extra pillow and blanket out of the utility closet and drifted to sleep lying on the floor behind the front desk. A loud crash woke him. He shined his flashlight around the walls of the lobby. Then he heard another crash. He walked out to the middle of the room and listened. Another crash, rhythmic crashing. Waves.

There was a knock on the back door of the lobby. Norris Williams, room 3.

"There's water on the decks," he said. He was wearing his white hotel robe; his hair was soaking wet, as though he'd just stepped out of the shower. "I can hear the waves crashing."

"Is there water coming into your room?" Mack asked. He didn't know what he was supposed to do. Where could the guests go? To Bill and Therese's? To Lacey's?

"Not yet," Mr. Williams said. He was the bookish type, with soft hands, an estate-planning lawyer. The type that wasn't good with emergencies of the physical kind. "My wife and I would like to come into the lobby, if you don't mind. We'd feel safer."

"That's fine," Mack said. No sooner had Mr. Williams left than there was another knock at the back door. Mrs. Frammer, from Denmark, room 6.

"The water's coming in. The carpet by the front door is wet," she said. "Are we supposed to stay on this ship until it goes down? I saw *Titanic*. We all did."

"You can come into the lobby," Mack said. He zipped up his jacket. Rain pelleted through the open door like machine-gun fire. Mrs. Frammer scooted past him inside and Mack dashed into the rain and pounded on back doors. "Come into the lobby!" he cried out.

The guests grabbed jackets and their flashlights and ran past Mack toward the lobby. Mack knocked on every door, and all the guests got ready to leave immediately, except for Clarissa Ford. She came to the back door, saw everyone running, and said, "God help us."

"I'm not kidding around this time, Clarissa. It's time to get out."

"I already told you, Mack, I'm not going anywhere."

Mack nudged past Clarissa into her room. A window was cracked. Mack grabbed the knob of the front door with both hands and yanked it open.

The waves crashed over the steps of the front decks. A wave ran right over Mack's feet onto the green carpet. But the carpet might be the least of their worries. The Gold Coast could break off and wash away altogether. Mack slammed the door shut and dead-bolted it. He jammed two bath towels into the crack at the bottom of the door.

He took Clarissa by the arm. "We have to get out of here," he said.

She pulled her arm away; Mack thought of Maribel. "I already said, I'm not going."

In the distance, over the screaming wind, Mack heard sirens.

"Fine," he said.

A fire engine and two vans pulled up on North Beach Road. The parking lot was so clogged with sand that they couldn't pull in. But it didn't matter; Mack was relieved to see help of any kind.

Four men in fluorescent orange coats entered the side door of the lobby. "Someone called on a cell phone and said you needed evacuation," one of the officers said. He was block shouldered and capable looking, the type who flourished in physical emergencies. "So we're here to take everybody to the high school. They have a generator running. They have food, water, and bedding."

"I was the one who called," Norris Williams said, brandishing his phone as though it were a winning lottery ticket. He was still in his bathrobe. "I'm ready to go. Lead the way."

Mack stationed himself at the side door and ushered the guests outside, handed them off to the block-shouldered officer, who helped them climb over the dunes to the vans. Mack counted heads. Mr. Sikahama from Hawaii, room 14, said he wasn't paying six hundred dollars to spend the night in the hallway outside of geometry class, and he hoped he was getting a full refund. Mrs. Frammer kissed Mack on the cheek, as though she expected never to see him again. After everyone was delivered to the van, the officer came back to Mack. "Is that everybody?"

"Just about," Mack said. "I'm staying here."

"And is there anyone else?"

Mack saw the beam of a flashlight coming from Bill and Therese's doorway. "Wait a minute," he said. The beam bounced and jiggled, and then Mack saw Therese, wearing Cecily's Middlesex Field Hockey windbreaker over her nightgown. Bare feet.

"I'm going with those people," she said. "I think someone should go with them, and Bill refuses to leave."

"Okay," he said. "Go."

"Lacey's already in the van?" Therese asked.

"Lacey," Mack said. He ran for Lacey's cottage, flung open the door and charged down the hall to her bedroom. He knocked on her door.

"Gardner?"

He heard a muffled noise, a grizzled breathing. He cracked the door. Lacey was asleep, snoring softly. "Gardner," Mack said. "Wake up."

Lacey's face was ghostly white in the beam of his flashlight. Mack toggled her shoulder. "Lacey, it's me."

Her eyelids fluttered. "Max?" She blinked.

"We're evacuating the hotel, Lacey," he said. "It's time to go."

"I knew it would be soon," she said. "But I'm not ready."

"Lacey, we're going to the high school. The firemen are here."

She opened her eyes. Blue eyes, sharply focused. "High school?"

"Water's hitting the decks. It's time to get everybody out."

"It'll take more than a little water to move me," Lacey said. "Are you going to the high school?"

"No," he said. "I'm staying here."

"Me, too," she said. "If we drown, we drown." She sank her head deeper into her feather pillow. "Wake me when it's morning, if you please. If you please."

THE SAND IN THE parking lot was sculpted into dunes, some of which held water. The wind thrummed and shrieked. Mack clambered over hills of sand to the lobby porch. He positioned himself behind one of the porch columns to keep out of the blowing sand. He shined his flashlight onto the beach.

The waves crashed over the pavilion as though it weren't there, and broke about ten feet shy of the lobby—ten feet, the length of a compact car. Mack was paralyzed, watching Nantucket Sound gone berserk. Attacking.

Mack heard someone call his name and he saw the beacon of a flashlight from Bill's doorway. Mack spotted Bill climbing over the sand dunes, around puddles the size of a child's swimming pool. He clenched a yellow slicker at the neck; underneath, he wore pajamas and a pair of galoshes.

"What's happening?" Bill yelled.

Mack couldn't speak; he was furious. *What's happening?* Mack pointed his flashlight at the beach. *What's happening is called a hurricane. A natural disaster. A state of fucking emergency.*

What Mack said was, "Everyone's out except for Clarissa and Lacey."

"How bad's the water?" Bill asked.

"It's pretty bad," Mack said. As angry as Mack was, he didn't want to have to break the news: water in the rooms, Bill's ship going down.

Bill switched off his flashlight and Mack did the same. They stood together in darkness. All Mack could see was the white foam getting closer and closer to the lobby.

Bill took Mack's hand and held it.

He's terrified, Mack thought. *First he loses me, then his daughter, then his hotel.* Mack wasn't sure what he'd do if Bill started to cry. Mack sneaked a sideways look at him. Bill was smiling. *The guy's lost his mind,* Mack thought. *He's gone insane.*

"I'm selling it," Bill said.

"What?" Mack said.

"I'm selling the hotel for twenty-five million dollars. I have a buyer, and I've decided to sell it."

Mack switched on his flashlight and aimed it at the water's edge. A wave crested and broke and the white foam danced up the beach.

"I don't believe you," Mack said.

"What's not to believe?" Bill said. "Cecily's gone, you're leaving, my baby son is dead. For me the hotel was never just the building, Mack. It was the people inside the building."

Mack kept his flashlight on the water, mentally marking the water line. He marked wave after wave after wave, until he fell into a kind of stupor. The waves kept rolling and crashing, Mack's eyelids drooped. In his standing dream-sleep, each wave that washed over him had a name. David Pringle, *If you're going to stick it out there in the East;* Vance and his snarling lip; Maribel in a sheen of sweat, begging, pleading, *Why did she always want?* Lacey wearing pink fuzzy slippers, *You're my boy.* Andrea and James, with their matching green-gray eyes. Therese, a dead-child white streak in her hair. Too-handsome Jem, Mr. November, running out the lobby door with his embarrassed happiness. Cecily crying into the phone, *I love you, Gabriel, I really love you.* Mack's parents, in Oblivion. As if none of this mattered. The waves lulled Mack back to May, to before May, before Andrea and How-Baby and David Pringle's phone call, back when things were normal, when things were easy. What had made him happy? The hotel—the front desk, the ringing phone, the beach. The guests, the staff. Bill, Therese, Cecily, Lacey. The Beach Club made him happy. Of course the hotel was more than just a building. For Mack it was a way of life. Even in the middle of a raging hurricane, this was where he wanted to be. Right here.

Mack snapped to attention; his legs were numb. The wind howled like a woman giving birth, but the water wasn't getting any closer. Mack looked to his right; he was surprised to see Bill still standing there, his lips moving. Reciting poetry. Praying.

"You can't sell the hotel," Mack said. "You've put your whole life into it."

"I can start a new life," Bill said. "Take Therese and move to Hawaii, or Saipan, wherever that is."

"Bill, you can't sell the hotel. I won't let you."

"You can't stop me," Bill said.

"I can stop you," Mack said.

"How?"

"I can stay."

Bill nodded slowly.

"Am I right?" Mack said. "Will that stop you?"

"Will you stay?"

"Will that stop you?"

Bill turned to him. "Is it you who's been writing me letters?" he asked. "Are *you* S.B.T.?"

"No," Mack said.

Bill shook his head. "No," he said. "I didn't think so."

"I'll stay," Mack said.

"Okay," Bill said. He shined his flashlight over the parking lot and Mack followed the beam—a Toyota 4-Runner was up to the tops of its tires in sand, and the bikes in the bicycle rack were buried to their handlebars. The wind wasn't letting up.

Then Mack heard a noise, a voice. The voice. *Home. Home.* It was the hum, loud and distinct over the scream of the wind. *Home.* Mack reached for Bill's arm. "Do you hear that?"

"What?" Bill said.

"That voice. The voice saying 'Home.' Do you hear it? Please tell me you hear it. Do you? There—there it is again. Home. Just tell me you hear it."

Bill climbed over a mound of sand, headed for the safety of his house. "I don't know what you're talking about," he said.

WHAT WOKE MACK UP first was the smell of coffee, and the promise of light. Mack feared opening his eyes; he didn't want to be disappointed. Then he heard whispers—giggles, laughing. Mack let himself rise to the surface of his sleep, enough to realize that his back ached, his arms ached, his feet ached. He opened his eyes. Vance and Love stood over him. Vance held two cartons of Hostess doughnuts and Love carried a cardboard tray of coffees.

Mack raised his head an inch. "Is it over?"

"It's over," Vance said. "But it's not pretty. Get up and see for yourself."

Mack managed to sit up on his own and with a hand from Vance, he stood. Light peeked in around the shutters all over the lobby.

"I can't believe it," Mack said. "That looks like sun."

"Maybe you'd better wait a while before you look outside," Vance said. "I'll give you a hint. I had to park the Datsun a quarter-mile up North Beach Road."

"We walked over the sand," Love said. "Thanks to my cross-country skiing experience, I got the coffee here without spilling a drop."

Vance threw his arm around Love's neck and kissed her. "That's my girl."

Mack thought of Maribel. Suddenly, more than his body ached. "Anybody seen Jem?" he asked hopefully. "Or my Jeep?"

Vance and Love shook their heads; Love looked at the ground.

"Have some coffee," Vance said. He handed Mack a cup. "Were you up all night?"

"Just about," Mack said. "Do we have power?"

"Not yet," Vance said.

"We evacuated all the guests," Mack said. "The fire trucks took everyone to the high school. I didn't want to leave the hotel."

"You're so loyal," Love said.

"He's crazy," Vance said. "You sure you're ready to go outside? Brace yourself, man. I'm warning you."

"I'm ready," Mack said. "It was pretty bad last night."

"Let's go," Vance said. "I want to see your face."

Mack and Vance walked out the side door. What struck Mack first was this: it was a beautiful day. The heat and humidity of the previous weeks were gone. It was crisp, and the sky was a brilliant, spectacular blue.

The Beach Club looked like the Sahara Desert. The sand in the parking lot was chest high in places. The front porch of the lobby where Bill and Mack stood the night before was buried—there were drifts of sand halfway up the lobby doors. The pavilion was entirely buried, with the exception of the peaked roof, which stuck out—a head with no body. The beach was strewn with seaweed, dead seagulls, rocks.

The hotel was still standing, although the decks were buried under sand. Mack and Vance walked around and entered the back door of each room. All the front deck rooms had saturated carpets—Mack's shoes squished as he walked. The bottoms of the bedskirts were wet, some of the dressers had water marks.

"If we take up all the carpets and cut a big hole in the floor, we might drain these rooms someday," Vance said.

"The carpet definitely has to be replaced," Mack said. "That'll be a big job."

"I'll bet you're glad you're leaving," Vance said. "You picked the right time to get out."

Mack didn't say anything.

He headed down to room 7. Clarissa Ford stood in the back doorway, smoking.

"You survived," Mack said. "How's your room?"

"Demolished," she said. She lowered her eyes. "I spent all night in the bathtub." Mack looked into room 7. Clarissa had piled all her clothes on top of the bed, but they were soaked. The lamps had shattered, the TV set was smashed, the leather chair ruined.

"Oh, God," Mack said. "It's amazing you lived."

Clarissa exhaled a stream of smoke. "I'll pay for it all, needless to say. I wonder if Therese will let me help her redecorate. Then when I come back next September it will really feel like home."

"Don't count on it," Mack said. "Anyway, what's important is that you're safe. It was quite a night."

"Oh, darling," Clarissa said. "I was part of it."

MACK NUDGED VANCE'S ELBOW before they reached the back door of the lobby. "Listen, will you call my house? If Jem's there, tell him to get his ass down here."

"I can't believe what you did yesterday," Vance said. "You gave her away, man. Why the hell did you do that?"

"I have my reasons," Mack said. He rubbed his hands over Vance's shaved head. "Will you call for me, man?"

Vance swatted Mack's hands away. "I'll call as long as you stop touching me. I don't love you, you know, Petersen."

"I know," Mack said. "Thanks."

WHEN MACK WALKED AROUND front, a school bus pulled up on North Beach Road and the hotel guests disembarked: Mrs. Frammer, Mr. Sikahama, Mr. Williams in his bathrobe. They climbed over the dunes toward the lobby. Therese, with Cecily's windbreaker zipped up to her throat, crawled toward Mack wearily, a soldier returning from war. She shielded her eyes from the sun.

"How was it?" Mack asked.

"Did Cecily call?" Therese said.

He hated the desperate note in her voice. She'd only been away eight hours. "Not that I know of. The phones were down all night."

"I was thinking if she watched the news or anything . . ." She dug her toe in the sand. "Our kingdom is destroyed. I thought maybe if she knew that, she'd call."

"Not destroyed, Therese. We were lucky. Only room seven is gone. The rest of the front deck rooms have carpet damage and some other minor stuff. Vance is going over them with the Shop Vac. They'll be okay for the guests by this afternoon."

Therese squinted. "Really?"

"Not great, but okay."

"Not ruined?"

"Not ruined."

"The guests can sit on the beach until then. We ate breakfast at the school. Have you seen Bill?"

"Not since last night," Mack said.

Therese glanced up at the bay window. "He's probably up there watching. If he hasn't keeled over from a heart attack. I don't even want to tell you what he went through last night."

"I saw him just before he went to bed," Mack said. "He looked all right."

Therese's eyes watered and she blinked tears. Mack couldn't remember ever seeing Therese cry. She looked like a child in her nightgown, the ill-fitting windbreaker, bare feet, her peach-colored hair tucked behind her tiny ears. He'd seen Cecily show an uncanny resemblance to Therese over the years, and now he witnessed the opposite: Therese slouched before him looking for all the world like her teenage daughter.

She sniffled and straightened up. "I'd better go see Bill," she said. "Let me know when Vance is finished and I'll send the chambermaids over."

"Will do," Mack said.

Therese turned back before she entered her house. "How's Lacey?" she asked.

MACK TOOK A CUP of coffee to Lacey's cottage. Her apartment was dim, light entered around the edges of the shutters, throwing stripes across the Oriental rug. "Gardner?" he called out. Mack tiptoed down to Lacey's bedroom and tapped on her door. "Lacey, it's safe to get up. The evil Freida has passed."

He listened, but heard nothing. She was still asleep. She'd asked him to wake her when morning came. *If you please.* Mack opened Lacey's bedroom door and peeked in.

Lacey's eyes were closed. One hand was clenched in a fist over her heart, and her other arm dangled off the edge of the bed. On the floor was a beeswax candle, broken in half. Had that been there last night? He couldn't remember.

"Lacey?" Mack said. He listened for her breath, for her soft snore. He listened, waiting for her eyes to snap open. Waiting for her to mistake him once again for Maximilian. He waited until he couldn't wait anymore, and then he touched her cheek—it was cold.

Lacey was dead.

MARIBEL KNEW THE POWER was back on when she heard the phone ring. She opened her eyes and was instantly aware of Jem's arm draped over her waist. She didn't rise to answer the phone. It was either Mack or Tina, and she didn't want to talk to either of them. The phone rang four times, but no message played—the tape must have been erased with the power outage.

Maribel rolled toward Jem. He lay facedown in Mack's pillow. His young, strong shoulders were bare, he had one arm folded under his head and one touching Maribel's side. Maribel felt a wave of desire. She lifted the covers. Jem wore only his boxer shorts.

She lay back, weighing her options. She could slip off Jem's boxers and make love to him, or she could let him be. Maribel looked out the tiny bedroom window. She saw actual sunlight, a good sign if ever there was one.

Before Maribel moved a muscle, she explained things to Mack in her mind. *I am not doing this because I'm angry. I'm not angry. I'm hurt and disappointed because I loved you in as many ways as I knew how and in the end, those weren't the right ways. So here I am now, about to do this thing because I think it will help me to be happy, if only temporarily. Although I'm coming to learn that all happiness is temporary.*

Maribel pressed her lips to Jem's shoulder. She moved her mouth a fraction of an inch lower, and kissed him again. She waited, but he didn't stir. She picked a spot on the curve that ran from the side of his neck to his shoulder and she kissed him there, a ripe, wet kiss.

The phone rang again. Maribel counted the rings in her head. She looked hopefully at Jem. He breathed heavily, oblivious. What was it with men and their love affair with sleep? Maribel slid out of bed and hurried into the living room for the ringing phone.

"Maribel?" It was a man's voice, but not Mack's.

"Yes?"

"It's me, Vance."

"Hi, Vance," Maribel said. "Mack's not here. I thought he was down at the hotel."

"He's here," Vance said. "I'm, uh . . . I'm actually looking for Jem. Is he there?"

Maribel dropped onto the sofa. "What makes you think he's here?" she asked. Her heart thudded like heavy, scary footsteps. "Did Mack say he was here?"

"Mack wanted Jem to check on you last night. But I'm glad he didn't. He shouldn't have been out in the weather. I'll tell you what, I'll try Jem at home."

"Don't bother," Maribel said. "He's here."

"He is?"

"Yes," Maribel said. "What do you need him for?"

"Uh . . ." There was a pause. "We need him to come down and work."

"I'll tell him," Maribel said. "I'll send him down when he wakes up."

"Okay," Vance said, though she could tell from the sound of his voice that he thought it was anything but okay. "Thanks, Maribel."

"You bet," she said.

• • •

MARIBEL REPLACED THE PHONE and stepped outside to inspect the damage. The backyard was a disaster area. The trees were stripped of leaves and branches. The detritus was all over the yard—twigs the size of pencils, branches the size of a man's arm. A huge bough had fallen into Maribel's garden and crushed the zinnias and impatiens. There were standing puddles in the lawn, ankle deep. But the sun was shining and it felt good on Maribel's arms and bare legs.

She closed the door and went back into the bedroom. Jem was awake, sitting up. His dark hair was mussed and he had sleep marks on his face from the pillow. Maribel sat next to him on the edge of the bed.

"Who was on the phone?" he asked.

She placed a finger on his lips and chose a spot just below his collarbone, and kissed it. If there were going to be rumors, she thought, they might as well be true.

THE PHONE RANG FIVE more times while Maribel and Jem made love, although Jem didn't seem to notice. He concentrated on kissing her, caressing her. He was strong and young and sexy and he loved her. He said it over and over, "I love you, Maribel. I love you." When he came, he cried out. He was overwhelmed with love, and Maribel knew just how he felt. Here was a flower where all the petals said the same thing, *He loves me.*

Jem hugged her close and kissed her hair. "I want you to come to California with me."

"Oh, Jem."

"I do. I really do. I asked you before, when I came for dinner. Remember?"

"I remember," she said. The phone rang again—and again, Jem didn't seem to hear it. "I don't know what to say. I'm not sure I want to go to California."

"Where do you want to go?" Jem asked. "Tell me where and I'll take you."

Maribel smiled. "I want to go to Unadilla." She wanted to see her mother. She wanted to rock in Tina's arms.

"I'll go to Unadilla. I'll go, I swear it," he said.

It wasn't hard at all, to be loved this much. This was the kind of love Maribel needed—unconditional, blind, devoted; it was the love she had missed in a father.

Later, when Jem was in the shower, the phone rang again, and Maribel answered it. *I've made my decision,* she thought, *and whoever's on the other end is going to have to hear about it.*

"Hello?" she said.

"Mari?" It was Mack, but he sounded upset. It sounded like he was crying.

"What's wrong?" she said. He sobbed into the phone. Maribel narrowed her eyes. Had she done this to him? "Mack, what's wrong?"

"Lacey's dead," he said.

The words dropped in Maribel, like coins in a well. "Lacey's dead," she repeated. Lacey was dead. "Oh, God, Mack. I'm sorry. I'm so, so sorry."

He cried into the phone like a little boy. He cried, Maribel admitted, the way she wanted him to cry over her.

"She was my best friend," Mack said.

"I know," Maribel said, and she felt a stab of pain. Lacey Gardner had filled the role of best friend while Maribel had tried so desperately to fill the role of wife. Maribel had missed what was most important. She listened to Mack cry, shushing him every once in a while, marveling at how her love for him was like something she held underwater—as soon as she let go, it bobbed to the surface. She wanted to repeat over and over, "I'll be your friend, Mack, I'll be your friend," but she wondered if it was too late for that. Lacey was dead. The world as they knew it was ending.

BILL THANKED GOD FOR Therese. People in distress were her specialty, her domain. No sooner had she returned to the hotel with the guests than Mack pounded on the door to tell them the news about Lacey.

Therese brought Mack inside and gave him a glass of water, she sat next to him on the sofa and held his hand. She cried with him a little, and said, "Lacey's where she wants to be, Mack. She's with her husband, finally."

"But what if that's bullshit," Mack said. "What if there is no meeting place in the sky."

Bill waited to hear what Therese would say. He wondered this himself—every time he had chest pains, and last winter when the ambulance rushed him to the hospital—*what came next?* It was a question without an answer. Nobody knew, not even Robert Frost. Bill had always believed in something bigger; for twenty-eight years, since W.T. died, *something bigger* planted itself in Bill's mind. A reason. Lacey Gardner, here yesterday, gone today. Why?

Therese said to Mack, "We have to hope. When I'm dying and ready to go, you know what I'm going to do? I'm going to hope with all my heart. And then I'm going to let go. Hope I don't disappear. Hope I land somewhere safely."

The ends of Bill's fingers tingled. He loved his wife. When he was dying and ready to go, he would hope, too. He would hope that death did not separate them.

THERESE SENT FOR THE undertaker, and personally cleaned Lacey's cottage from top to bottom. It was Therese who found Lacey's will. Therese called the paper and put in the obituary. Therese contacted Father Eckerly at St. Mary's and arranged for the service, to be held on Friday.

That night as she and Bill lay in bed, Therese said, "I read Lacey's will before I sent it to her lawyer. She left Mack her cottage, you know."

"She did?"

"You didn't think she'd do otherwise?"

"I never gave it any thought at all," Bill said. That was the truth: Therese had fussed over Mack and the rest of the staff who were upset—Vance, Jem, Love—but no one asked Bill how he felt. And he had known Lacey Gardner longer than anyone. He met Lacey when he was eight years old, an ornery, sullen little boy. Lacey and her husband, Maximilian, were Beach Club members and they were on property every day of the summer after the war ended. Lacey used to shake Bill's hand like an adult, and say, "How do you do?" Bill would cross his arms across his chest and give her a withering look. Then Lacey promised she'd give him two pennies if he would smile. "Nope," he said. "I don't smile for money." Bill could remember what Lacey looked like as a young woman (blond hair in a chignon, dresses that cinched at the waist)—throwing her head back and laughing, wiping the corner of her eye with an embroidered handkerchief. She reminded him of that moment many times in the years that followed; it was their shared punch line. *I don't smile for money.* He supposed he meant his affections couldn't be bought; they had to be earned. And Lacey Gardner had earned them.

He never thought of Lacey dying—she seemed superhuman, the one member of his parents' generation who was going to live forever. But now she was dead. Not only was Bill deeply saddened by the loss but he knew what this meant: he was next.

"So she left her cottage to Mack," Bill said. He recalled his conversation with Mack during the storm. "He promised he'd stay." He took his wife in his arms and spoke into her sweet hair. "I just want someone to stay."

MACK MOVED HIS THINGS out of the basement apartment while Maribel was at work. He threw his clothes into garbage bags and sorted through the CDs. He packed his pay stubs and pictures of his parents. The TV was his, but he let Maribel keep it; the kitchen stuff was all hers, except for a bottle opener shaped like a whale that had belonged to Maximilian. Mack took that. They'd bought the gas grill together, but he let it be. He packed all his belongings into the back of the Jeep, and then he sat in the driveway. He considered leaving a note. A note saying what?

Back at the club, there was no shortage of work. Mack shoveled sand—it was like eating a giant plate of spaghetti—he couldn't seem to make any headway. It kept his body busy and hurting; he tried to concentrate on the physical pain and not his other pain. Lacey gone. Maribel gone.

After work, Mack carried his bags into Lacey's cottage. He dug out the whale bottle opener and popped the top off a Michelob. He settled down in Lacey's chair. He had two phone calls to make.

The first was to How-Baby.

A sugar-voiced, southern secretary answered the phone. "Is this *the* Mack Petersen, as in, our new vice president of travel and hospitality?"

"Yeah," Mack said weakly. "Can I speak to Howard, please?"

How-Baby came on the line, voice booming as though he were sitting three feet away. "I was worried about you!" he said. "We saw you take a real beating from Freida. Watched it on national news. How's the hotel?"

"She'll be okay," Mack said. "But there's a lot of work to be done."

"So it doesn't look like you'll be getting out of there easily," How-Baby said.

"I'm not getting out of here at all," Mack said. "That's why I called."

How-Baby was quiet.

"I'm calling to turn down your offer, Howard," Mack said. "I have to stay here. It's not personal and it has nothing to do with money. Believe me, everything you offered is top-notch. It's just what my gut is telling me."

Still How-Baby was quiet.

"Howard, are you there?"

How-Baby coughed; Mack tried to imagine him upset, agitated, thrown off guard. Caught unaware. It didn't seem possible.

"I'm here," How-Baby said. "You know, just last night Tonya asked what we were going to do next summer when we came to Nantucket and you weren't there. She said she couldn't imagine it."

"She won't have to imagine it," Mack said. *New job gone.*

"No," How-Baby said. "I guess she won't."

• • •

THE SECOND PHONE CALL was to David Pringle. Mack took a long swallow of his beer before dialing.

"David, it's Mack. Mack Petersen."

David chuckled. "It's only September, Mack. I was figuring you'd put off this phone call for at least another month."

"Nope!"

"What's happening?" David asked. "You had all summer to think about it. Come to any conclusions?"

"Has Wendell changed his mind?" Mack asked.

David whistled. Mack pictured him leaning back in his leather chair, shirt sleeves rolled up. "No, he hasn't changed his mind. He's rented a hall for his retirement party."

"Oh."

"You're going to sell, then?"

"No one else has shown any promise?" Mack asked. "This summer, no one . . ."

"Mack, I told you how things were. Nobody will put forth the effort on a farm that's not their own. Wendell did it out of love for your father, simple as that. There's no one else."

"Okay," Mack said. "Sell." *Farm gone.*

"I'll put it up first thing in the morning," David said. "We're not going to get rich from this, you know."

"I know."

"What should I do about the house?"

"Don't do anything," Mack said. "I'm coming back. I'll clean it out myself."

"You're coming back?"

"After the hotel closes, I'll drive out. Take a week or two."

"Call me when you get here," David said. "You can sign some papers. And, well . . . I'd like to see you, Mack. I'll bet you're all grown up."

"I am," he said.

• • •

THE NEXT DAY, MACK stood on the front steps of St. Mary's Church on Federal Street in gray pinstriped pants that belonged to a suit he never wore, greeting the people who came to Lacey's memorial service. This was no different from his job at the hotel, really—greeting people and making them feel welcome. Concierge of the funeral. Manager of grief. Vance and Love and Bill and Therese milled around the aisles of the church, seating people, but Mack didn't want to be inside any longer than he had to. He had "hired" Clarissa Ford to work at the front desk of the hotel and answer the phone. (She showed up wearing a bright blue suit, smelling like lilies of the valley. "There's no smoking in the lobby," he said. "It's okay," she said. "I'm quitting.")

Tiny arrived at the church, and with a man no less, a young man with a ponytail and a mustache.

"Mack," Tiny said, "this is Stephen Rook." She looked at Stephen. "This is Mack."

Mack shook Stephen Rook's hand. He wondered if this were Tiny's boyfriend.

Tiny said, "Stephen is my husband."

"Your husband?" Mack said. "I didn't know you were married, Tiny." He smiled apologetically at Stephen Rook. "She never tells us anything about her personal life."

Stephen Rook raised his hand as if to say, *Hey, that's cool,* and Tiny said, "Stephen is deaf, Mack."

"Whoops. I'm sorry. Tell him I'm sorry."

"He reads lips," she said.

"Thanks for coming," Mack said.

Stephen raised his hand again, and escorted Tiny into the church.

Many of the people at the service were elderly friends of Lacey from back in the day. They shook Mack's hand, explaining how they knew Lacey from Sankaty, or the Yacht Club, or how they used to shop in Lacey's hat store. Lacey's doctor and dentist came from Boston, and so did the Iranian doorman from her Boston apartment building, a slight, dark-skinned man named Rom. Rom whipped out a Polaroid of Lacey standing with his children in front of the Charles River. "She always said she loved Nantucket best," Rom said. "Now I'm here, I see why."

The current class president from Radcliffe arrived with a female friend—Meaghan and Meredith—Mack couldn't tell them apart once they introduced themselves. They called Lacey "Ms. Gardner" and said they were planning a fund-raising drive to start the Lacey Gardner Scholarship Fund for young women business owners. Mack was amazed. Here he was certain he knew Lacey better than anyone else, and yet he hadn't met half these people.

Then, just as Mack was about to head inside, Jem and Maribel walked up. Maribel wore a black linen dress, her blond hair pulled back in a clip, no makeup. She looked beautiful. Jem had on a navy blue double-breasted blazer, like something a sea captain would wear.

"Mack," Maribel said. She smiled sadly and hugged him, and Mack shut his eyes and squeezed her, thinking how if things were different, she might be coming to this church to marry him.

"I'm sorry," he whispered in her ear. "I'm sorry."

When they separated, her eyes were red; the crying had begun. "Me too," she said.

Mack shook Jem's hand. Mack wanted to thank him, and he wanted to toss him off the church steps. But before he could decide between the two, the church bells rang, and the three of them stepped into the sanctuary.

MACK HATED ORGAN MUSIC, he hated the cloying smell of funeral flowers. He hated coffins and pallbearers, although if Lacey had asked him, he would have carried her coffin on his back. Fortunately, though, Lacey had requested cremation, and Therese kept the urn of Lacey's ashes tucked under her arm next to her pocketbook. After the service, they were going to scatter the ashes at Altar Rock.

Mack sat in the front row of the church next to Bill and Therese. Behind him, he could hear people crying. The priest, Father Eckerly, spoke of Lacey's life: her years at Radcliffe, her tenure working for the

State Health Department, her marriage to Maximilian, her shop on Main Street. Her model life as a Catholic, and as a working woman who was also a devoted wife.

"Lacey provided us with many lessons about how to live," Father Eckerly said.

Mack shifted in his seat. He hated funerals because they all reminded him of the funeral service for his mother and father. His parents were rolled down the aisle of Swisher Presbyterian in matching coffins. Wendell gave the eulogy. He spoke of what a tragedy it was, how unfair, Mack, only eighteen, robbed of his parents. The church was packed with people—family, friends, neighbors, kids from school, farmers from as far away as Davenport and Katonah. They were there to pay their respects, but somehow the tragedy overshadowed his parents' simple, good-hearted natures. Somehow, his parents got lost in all the sadness.

After the ceremony, they buried Mack's parents in the cemetery behind the church. Mack watched stone-faced as they lowered his parents into the ground. When the minister threw a handful of dirt onto the coffins, Mack cut through the crowd and walked back to his house, which was over a mile away. He sat alone in his bedroom until his uncle came and fetched him. "They want to see you at the luncheon," his uncle said. "You're all that's left of this family and people want to see you." Mack went to his aunt's house, where everyone said it was the saddest thing they'd ever known to happen, it was the saddest funeral they'd ever attended.

The problem with funerals, Mack decided, was that they never did a person justice. Father Eckerly could drone all day about Lacey's balancing act of career and home—a woman before her time—but that didn't get at the real Lacey. The real Lacey drank Dewar's from the stroke of five o'clock until bedtime, she listened for hours without judging, she defended love and the strength of the human spirit.

Mack closed his eyes. He didn't know what he would do without her.

• • •

BY THE TIME THEY made it to Altar Rock, Mack felt better. He drove Love and Vance in his Jeep, Bill and Therese and Tiny and Stephen followed in the Cherokee, and Rom and the two Radcliffe women wanted to come along as well—so Mack suggested they take Lacey's Buick. The three cars twisted through the moors, which were just starting to turn red. Autumn was less than a week away. Mack ascended the steep hill to Altar Rock—the highest point on the island. He parked, picked the urn of Lacey's ashes off the front seat (Therese gave the urn to him after the ceremony, saying, "I think Lacey would want to ride with you"), and climbed out of the car.

When Mack first read Lacey's will, he wondered why she wanted her ashes scattered at Altar Rock—why not scatter them into the water at the Beach Club? But as soon as he stepped out of the car, he understood why. The panorama was spectacular—from here he could see Sankaty Lighthouse, Nantucket Harbor, and in the distance, Great Point Light. If they scattered Lacey's ashes at the Beach Club, the water might carry her away. But when they scattered her ashes here, she would become one with Nantucket.

Mack waited until the group gathered into a semicircle, then he opened the urn. He expected ashes, like from a cigarette—he thought fleetingly of Clarissa Ford—but these ashes were chunky and hard, like pieces of coral. He took a handful and passed the urn to his left, to Bill. Bill took a handful and passed the urn to Therese, and so on, until the urn reached Rom and Rom had to turn the urn upside down so that the last few pieces of Lacey's remains came loose in his palm.

Mack turned to Bill. "Do you want to recite a poem?" Mack whispered. "Or should we, I don't know . . . should we all say something?"

Therese leaned over. "Why don't we each pick a spot and say something privately before we scatter?"

Mack raised his voice. "Okay, uh . . . everyone can pick a spot and say something privately and then, I don't know . . . bombs away, I guess."

Love and Vance faced Sankaty Light, Bill and Therese faced south toward the airport, the Radcliffe women turned to the harbor. Tiny and Stephen Rook tossed their ashes out over the moors. Rom threw his into the air like a baseball.

Mack held his ashes. His hands were sweating and the ashes left a white, chalky residue. He stood next to the stone marker for Altar Rock, wondering what he could possibly say to Lacey, or to God. Lacey had no grandchildren, Bill and Therese had no son, Cecily had no brother, Maribel had no father, Andrea had no husband—and Mack had set himself down among these people like a piece in a jigsaw puzzle. He filled their gaps and they filled his. But now some of the pieces had disappeared, leaving Mack exposed. Lacey was gone. Whatever Mack held in his hand—the ashes of her bone, her heart, her brain—he wanted to keep, in a jar, or a sugar bowl somewhere. He wanted to keep this last little part of her with him.

Gradually he became aware that everyone else was finishing up, and while no one stared at him, he got the distinct feeling they were waiting. He couldn't shove Lacey's ashes in his pants pocket now.

He squeezed his eyes shut. *I love you, too, Gardner,* he said. *Thanks for being my friend.*

He let Lacey go.

THE GROUP STOOD AROUND Altar Rock a few moments longer in silence. Then Stephen Rook said something in sign language.

"It is a beautiful day," Tiny repeated.

Everyone nodded in agreement, and drifted toward their cars. They were going back to Lacey's cottage for some lunch. After everyone went home, Mack wanted to sit in Lacey's armchair, in Lacey's cottage—now his armchair in his cottage—and drink a stiff Dewar's.

He climbed into the Jeep and Love and Vance piled into the back, even though Lacey's ashes were no longer up front. The empty urn rolled around on the floor.

"I feel like your chauffeur," Mack said.

"We want to be together," Love said.

"Yeah," Vance said. In the rearview mirror, Mack watched him put his arm around Love's shoulders. Mack thought of Maribel, and he wondered if the feeling of being the stupidest person in the world would pass.

Mack led the caravan back down the hill into the thick of the moors. He was deep in thought—about Lacey, about his parents, and about Maribel—but he did notice when Love abruptly cleared her throat.

"I'm pregnant," she said.

10

Windshift

October 3

Dear S.B.T.,

I almost gave in to you. I almost let myself relinquish the hotel—not for the love of money—but out of frustration. My daughter is gone, that much is true. I don't know if or when she'll be back. Her disappearance has left me with a hole inside. After much thought, I realized that you, also, must have a hole inside—because what else drives one man's desire for what another man has? I hope that you find something to fill the void within yourself—but it will not be my hotel.

   I have indulged this correspondence mostly for fun—it has been a piece of detective work, trying to discover your identity. I suspected everyone from Mack to Therese to my old, good friend Lacey Gardner, God rest her soul. I suspected hotel guests and Beach Club members. But now I would guess you are someone else entirely—someone on the outside looking in—possibly even a trickster without a penny to your name. It doesn't matter, S.B.T. I want to thank you for showing me how valuable the hotel is—worth much, much more than $25 million. You can't put a price on love.

   And so, with this letter, I officially end our correspondence. I wish you luck in whatever else you pursue.

Yours truly,

Bill Elliott

NOW THAT AUTUMN HAD arrived, the front desk was a peaceful place to work. Love kept the woodstove fired throughout the day and a mug of warm herbal tea by the phone. She wore bulky sweaters and the fleeces she hadn't touched since early May. Normally, wearing winter clothes and lighting fires got Love excited for winter. Love had a plane ticket back to Aspen leaving after the hotel closed on Columbus Day, and although she was going to use it, she wasn't staying in Aspen. It was amazing, really, how her life had changed in less than six months. Not just the circumstances of her life but her way of thinking as well. Her whole life before coming to this island had been charted, graphed, strategized. What she realized now was that it was much more fun to let Life tell her how things were going to be.

Look at the way she announced her pregnancy. She'd resolved to keep it a secret, but then Lacey died, and although Love didn't know Lacey that well, she felt something up on Altar Rock, some sort of movement, a rush, what Vance would call a "gut feeling" that Lacey's death and her child's conception were not unrelated. They were part of a cycle, they were part of how the big picture worked. And descending into the moors—the breathtaking green-red-gold moors of Nantucket, Love blurted out the news.

She stunned Vance and Mack, that was for sure. Vance's expression remained unchanged for a split second, then his mouth opened and he laughed. Not a funny laugh, but a happy laugh. He hugged and kissed her and he laughed. He clapped Mack on the shoulder and Mack let go of the stick shift long enough to grab Vance's hand.

"That's terrific, you guys," Mack said. "Man, is that great. Congratulations."

"I'm going to be a dad," Vance said. His voice was filled with awe, Love supposed, and fear maybe too, but no hesitancy. "I'm going to be a father." The words didn't frighten her at all; driving down the bumpy, sandy road she knew she loved Vance. He was totally wrong for her—ten years too young, too sullen and moody and utterly mysterious—and yet she loved him. She wanted to be with him, she wanted to know him and she wanted him to father her child, in every sense. Standing on Altar Rock, she felt her heart open up to include other people; she felt her life grow beyond just herself. This was a gift she had never expected from pregnancy, or wanted, but here it was. She was forty years old and she was growing up.

Love and Vance talked about what they were going to do. First they considered Vance moving to Aspen. He could get a job at the Hotel Jerome, or the Little Nell. After the baby was born in May, they could return to Nantucket. This plan had its appeal, but when Love thought about it, she realized she didn't want to live in Aspen any longer. "Can we stay here?" she asked him. "Can we stay on Nantucket?"

He smiled. She wasn't used to this—him smiling all the time now. "Sure," he said.

Vance discovered that the house Mack and Maribel usually rented for the winter would be empty. So the house on Sunset Hill—the house Mack called the Palace—would be theirs. It was a house that fell out of the pages of Love's book, *Vintage Nantucket*. The uneven wooden floors might throw her pregnant body off-balance, but the ceilings and the doorways were low enough that she had plenty of places to brace herself.

And so, they would stay on Nantucket, and this seemed the final piece of Love's happiness. She was pregnant, she was in love with Vance, and over the past five months she had fallen in love with Nantucket. She was staying.

A COUPLE WEARING SWEATERS and gloves and hiking boots walked into the lobby, their cheeks bright with the cold. It was room 15, the Hendersons. They were young and laid back, the kind of couple Mack had promised would show up in the fall.

"We just walked the trails at Sanford Farm," Mrs. Henderson said. She had gray eyes and thick black eyelashes. "This place is so gorgeous. It's like make-believe. The houses in town, the shops, the restaurants. And then when you get out of town, the natural beauty is astounding."

"The island is magical," Love agreed.

Mr. Henderson approached the desk, one hand in his front jeans pocket, and one hand wrapped around a mug of coffee. "We're school-teachers in Vermont," he said. "And Vermont is beautiful. But not like this. It must have something to do with being on an island, all that water, you know." He looked at Love. "Do you live here?"

Here—Nantucket—the land of stars and clams, oxygen-rich air and romance?

"Yes," she said.

JEM CALLED HIS PARENTS from the phone in Maribel's apartment. He knew his family was waiting to hear from him. Waiting for him to come home.

His sister, Gwennie, answered the phone.

"It's me," he said. "Mom and Dad there?"

"That's just great," Gwennie said. "We don't hear from you in six months, and then you can't even say hello like a normal person? That's just great, Jem."

"Gwen, are Mom and Dad there, please? This is costing money."

"Don't you want to know how I am?"

"Sure," he said.

"I'm more blood than flesh," she said. "But I've gained six pounds."

"Excellent," he said. "No more puking?"

"Not as much. When are you coming home?"

"I need to talk to Mom or Dad," Jem said. "Put on whoever's in the vicinity."

Gwennie didn't bother to cover the receiver. "*Mom! Dad!*" she screamed. "*Jem's on the phone!*"

His mother got on. "Jem! Thank you for calling, honey."

"Hi, Mom."

"How are you?"

"I'm great. It's been quite a summer."

"It sounds like it. I photocopied your letters for my bridge club. You don't mind, do you? If it said something private, I blocked it out. But you really didn't say anything too private. Everyone wanted to know about the people you were meeting. It sounds like that island is really something."

"It is." He imagined his letters being passed around the bridge table like a cut-glass bowl of nuts.

"When are you coming home? Daddy and I want to pick you up at the airport."

Jem's father picked up the other phone. "Hey, boy! We miss you down here. Feels like you've been away forever."

"What's going on, Dad?"

"I'm watching the Redskins lose and your mother's making chili."

"Gwennie's just starting to get better," his mother whispered. "She's not purging nearly as often."

"She said she gained six pounds," Jem said. "That's great."

"I talked to Bob Beller about getting you an internship at Brookings," his father said. "How about that? The Brookings Institution—now, there's a high-powered place."

Jem took a deep breath. Hearing his parents' voices made him miss them—he pictured his house, the kitchen with the copper pots hanging, his bed and goose-down pillows, the den with the pool table and the organ that Gwennie hadn't touched since she was nine years old. He missed it—and he wondered if maybe that was what kept him from calling all summer. He didn't want to miss them too much.

"I'm not coming home," Jem said. "I'm going to New York State for a couple of weeks, and then I'm going to California." He coughed. "Actually, I'm moving to California."

Gwennie must have been listening on a third phone because she yelled out, "He's not coming home! I told you he wasn't coming home and I was right!"

"You're not moving anywhere," his father said.

"Paul," Jem's mother said. "We can't clip his wings." She sweetened her voice. "Why do you want to move to California, Jem? That's so far away."

"I want to be an agent," he said. "I want to open my own talent agency."

"You need capital to open a business," his father said. "Opening a business is not just something you do the year after you graduate from college."

"I know," Jem said. "I'll work for someone else first, and save my money." He thought about the fifteen thousand dollars sitting in Nantucket Bank with his name on it. He had *not* written home about that—his parents would think accepting Neil's money was wrong. They would wonder what he'd done to earn it. "Anyway, I have to be in California to break into the business."

"I was right!" Gwennie shouted. "I told you so!"

"What did you learn up there this summer?" his father asked. "That you don't need your family anymore?"

"Did you meet a girl?" his mother asked. "Did you . . . did you get some girl in trouble?"

With the exception of Gwennie's bulimia, his family was like something from the wrong decade. *Did you get some girl in trouble?* His mother couldn't even say the word *pregnant.*

"No," he said. "No one's in trouble."

"Except you," his father said. "If you don't get yourself home by the end of the month."

"I don't want to work at Brookings, Dad," Jem said. "And I don't want to tend bar at the Tower." The Locked Tower: now the very name of the place gave him the shivers.

"You're not going to California," his father said. "I forbid it."

"Paul!" Jem's mother said. "We talked about this. If Jem wants to go to California, what can we do to stop him? He's twenty-three years old."

"I am not pleased, Jeremy," his father said. "And I'm not sending you any money, so I hope you earned plenty up there. I'm going to call Bob and tell him to forget about the internship. Is that what you want me to do?"

"Yes," Jem said.

"Okay, then." His father hung up.

"Mom, are you still there?" Jem asked.

"Yes," she said.

"Her name is Maribel Cox," Jem said. "She's blond and pretty and nice and incredibly smart. She works at the library and she runs and she's a terrific cook. I love her, Mom."

"You love who?"

"Maribel Cox," he said. "You should be happy for me because this is, like, the best thing that's ever happened to me aside from being born."

"You love Maribel Cox." His mother sighed. "It probably shouldn't surprise me, but it does. You've always been so levelheaded about girls."

"I'm being levelheaded now," Jem said. "I swear."

"Will you call us when you get to California? Will you tell us where you're living?"

"Do you think Dad will ever speak to me again?"

"He's disappointed, and I have to tell you, I'm disappointed, too, crushed, really. So when you hang up you tell Maribel Cox, whoever she is, that you hurt your mother's feelings."

"I'll call you and tell you where I am," he said. "I'm sorry about everything. I'm glad Gwennie's getting better, and—"

"That's enough, Jeremy," his mother said. "We love you."

She hung up.

"Whoa," Jem said. He punched off the portable phone and fell back into the sofa cushions. "Whoa." He thought back to what Lacey Gardner had told him, about how children should stop hoping for their parents' approval and just live their lives. This fortified him for a minute, but then he realized that just because Lacey was dead didn't mean she was right.

Maribel came into the living room. "How was it?" she asked softly.

"We're going," he said.

OF ALL THE GUESTS who stayed at the hotel, Cal West was Therese's favorite. She didn't know him particularly well; he wasn't what she would call a friend. He wasn't handsome or charming, and he didn't have any egregious personal problems for her to work out—no divorce, no untimely deaths, no emotional or psychological conditions. Nothing about Cal West stood out. He was boring.

Cal West came from Ohio, a place Therese imagined to be even more dull and orderly and monochromatic than the town she grew up in on Long Island. Ohio—the name of the state was deceptively rounded; what Therese pictured was a square of dun-colored carpeting, flat, unattractive. What did people do in Ohio? Cal West worked in the provost's office at Ohio State University. He processed papers having something to do with collegiate life.

Cal West had a triangular face—his forehead was wide and his chin narrow and the planes of his cheeks were straight edges. He had wispy brown hair which he combed down with water, a few faint acne scars, brown eyes. He stood five eight, wore sweater vests and loafers.

He'd started coming to the hotel six or seven years earlier for Columbus Day weekend. Therese might never have noticed him at all except the first year a strange thing happened. When she went in to clean Cal West's room, the place was immaculate. The bathroom sparkled, the bed was made with perfect corners. At first, Therese thought she'd entered a vacant room, but Cal West's suitcase was in the closet and his shirts and pants hung neatly on hangers. Therese checked the room the next day, and the next. His room was pristine. Therese could have gone through the motions of vacuuming the carpet and remaking the bed, but why? She had finally discovered a person as clean as she was.

Cal West spent hours reading in the lobby in front of the woodstove. One year he read the Bible, one year Shakespeare, one year every book that had won the Pulitzer Prize, in chronological order. In the evenings Cal removed his reading glasses, leaned back in the rocker, and listened to the music—Haydn, Schubert, Billie Holiday. Cal West seemed to have a quiet, contented life, and Therese envied that. She thought Cal West must be very wise. He'd done something right.

This year when Cal West walked into the lobby, he was as calm and unassuming as ever. He brought one plain black suitcase with a matching garment bag. He wore a maroon argyle sweater vest and a tweed jacket.

"Therese," Cal said. "Hello." He shook her hand. Always, with Cal, there was a warm handshake when he arrived and when he left. No more, no less.

"Hello, Cal," Therese said. "Welcome home."

Cal nodded; he took everything seriously. "Thank you," he said. "It's good to be home."

"How was your year?" Therese asked.

"Fine, just fine."

Just fine: The typical Cal West answer. But this year Therese wanted to know more. Surely there was something noisy, confusing, or messy in his life.

"How's work?" she asked.

"Fine," he said.

"What do you do again?" she asked. "You work for a university, but what do you *do*?"

"I work in the provost's office," he said. "I process complaints."

"Really?" Therese said. "What kind of complaints?"

"Professors complain about funding, and students complain about professors."

"Do you have a lot of student contact?" Therese asked.

"A little bit," Cal said. He shifted his weight; he was still holding both pieces of luggage. To put them down might anchor him permanently in this conversation with Therese—something he clearly didn't want. "I process written complaints only." He laughed. "My God, if I accepted verbal complaints, my job . . . well, it would be chaos."

Therese smiled at his sweater vest. "Any special women in your life, Cal?"

"No." The answer was taut and clipped. He nodded toward the front desk. "I think I'll check in now."

Cal moved for the front desk as though it were home base, a place where he'd be safe. Therese puttered around her plants, checking the leaves for waxiness, checking the soil for moisture. She looked at Cal West's back as he stood at the desk. What would it be like to be married to Cal West? To have life unfold evenly, without stumbling blocks, without unpleasant surprises like having a baby die inside you or waking up and finding your teenage daughter has disappeared? Therese would never know. She chose Nantucket, and the hotel, where things were always changing; she chose Bill. Bill, who climbed up on a widow's walk during the worst storm in forty years out of devotion to their daughter.

Before Cal headed down the hall and outside to his room, Therese called to him. "Cal!"

Cal turned around. The expression on his face was both fearful and annoyed.

"Let me walk you to your room," she said.

He stood, unmoving, until she was alongside him. She thought crazily, cruelly, of following Cal into his room and trying to seduce him. The idea of it was so completely out of the question that Therese laughed to keep from hating herself. She liked Cal West; what was her problem? Why did she have the urge to shake him up?

"You know," she said as they moved toward the back door of the lobby, "I have a complaint to file. Or maybe it's my daughter who's filed the complaint. She's run away."

"Really?" Cal said. "Run away?"

"She ran away to Brazil," Therese said. "After a very handsome boy." They stepped out onto the boardwalk. Cal West always rented room 20, which was only one room away from the lobby. As soon as they stepped outside, they were at his deck.

"I'm sorry to hear that," Cal said.

"Never mind," Therese said. Cal gripped his key tightly in his right hand; no doubt he wanted her to be on her merry way so that he could enjoy the hotel. "No, not never mind. I'm curious, Cal. I'm curious to know what you think about it. You work with young people. What do you think about an eighteen-year-old running away?"

"We don't get many kids running away from college," Cal said. "Especially not Ohio State. The kids love it. It's paradise for them."

"So you're saying no one runs away."

"No one I know of." He pointed his key at the door of his room.

"But I process complaints about grades and things. Bad food in the dining hall. Sorry I can't help."

"Okay. Look at it this way. What would you do if your daughter—your only child—ran away to another country for some boy?"

Cal licked his lips nervously and stared at his feet. She was torturing him by asking him such a question, by making him imagine such a thing could happen to him.

"I . . . I don't have any children. I really don't know what I would do."

"What if you did have children?" Therese asked.

"Well, then, I'd be quite a different person."

"Cal," Therese said—her voice was growing belligerent, she could hear it. She was verbally abusing her favorite guest, her fellow clean freak—but she yearned for an answer. "What do you think I should do?"

"I don't know, Therese. You're asking me a question that's impossible to answer."

Therese touched his shoulder. "You know, Cal," she said. "Sometimes I wish I could be you for a few days."

He nodded. "I feel the same way about you."

"You do?" Therese said.

"Of course," Cal said. He unlocked the door to room 20 and somehow managed to get himself and his bags inside and turn around so that he stood on the other side of the door, as though he were bidding her good-bye. "You took the risk."

"The risk?"

"The greatest risk there is. The risk of parenthood. You're a mother. And who am I? I'm a nobody."

"You're not a nobody, Cal. You're a man with a peaceful life."

He smiled wanly and closed the door, leaving Therese standing on the steps of his deck, thinking that maybe this was why Cal West was her favorite guest—not because he was the cleanest guest or the quietest, or even the last guest but because something about his calm, safe life made her feel loud and daring and brave. Like a mother.

VANCE CLEANED HIS HOUSE, literally and figuratively. He'd lived all summer in a rental cottage behind a giant house owned by Frank Purdue's
chief financial officer. The house was called the Chicken and Vance's
cottage was called the Egg. This fact alone had been enough to keep
Vance from telling people where he lived. He didn't want to hear jokes
about being an egghead or laying an egg or egg on his face, or which
came first, the chicken or the egg—or any other stupid reference that
people like Mack and Jem might come up with. Love had been to the
cottage, but only a few times, and not for very long. It wasn't a good
place to bring women. Vance didn't straighten often and so the cottage
collected a jumble of CDs and books and tools.

That would all change now that Vance was going to be a father.
Finally, after twelve years, Vance had two things that Mack didn't—a
woman and a child-on-the-way. Finally, after twelve years, Vance was
released from whatever evil spell Mack cast on him. He was set free
with this new life, as a lover and a father.

Carefully, Vance went through everything in his cottage. He packed
his books neatly in boxes, he folded his clean clothes and made a pile
for laundry. He threw away his poster of Vanessa Williams, his car
magazines, he threw away beer bottles and wrappers from frozen burri-
tos. In two weeks, he and Love were moving into the house on Sunset
Hill—it was a chance to start over with everything clean and in order.

It was while going through his kitchen cabinets—tossing out any
dishes that had chips or hairline cracks—that Vance found Mr. Beebe's
gun. The night after Vance pulled the gun on Mack, he brought it
home and hid it inside a ceramic pitcher. As Vance lowered the pitcher
from the shelf, he heard a rattling and instantly remembered the gun, a
nickel-plated .38. Vance held it in his palm, marveling at himself. How
had he ever summoned the guts to point this at someone? It was disgusting, and criminal, and Vance felt ashamed, stereotypical: a black
guy with a gun. He'd held the gun to Mack's head, he poked it into his
chest. What made Vance feel even worse was that Love had no idea
he'd kept the gun; she thought he sent it back to that creep, Mr. Beebe.

Vance had to get rid of the gun.

It wasn't the kind of thing he could throw away in a plastic garbage bag with the flawed dishes. What if someone found it and traced the dishes back to him? No, it couldn't simply be *thrown away*; he had to dispose of it.

Vance wrapped the gun in a pair of his ratty old underwear and climbed into his Datsun. He drove to the beach known as Fat Ladies' Beach, which could only be reached by unpaved roads. Vance pulled up to the edge of the beach (the only problem with his Datsun was that he couldn't drive it in the sand). He picked up his underwear and got out of the car.

It was gray and foggy, and gray waves smacked the beach. Vance trudged through the sand to the water's edge. He looked to the left and the right to be sure no one was surf casting or digging for clams. When he was sure that he was all alone, he wiped the gun with his underwear to remove fingerprints and chucked the gun out into the water. He stuffed his dingy underwear into his jacket pocket and sat on the hood of his car for a minute to make sure the gun didn't wash up on shore.

OCTOBER WAS A GREAT month. He could sit on this strip of beach all day and not see another soul. Vance liked fog, he liked the cool, damp, drizzly weather, especially now that he had Love. This winter, he would bring her to see the ocean every day.

Vance climbed into his car and backed up. He turned to look at the water one last time—and he saw something shiny wash up on the beach. Vance squinted; he felt the beginnings of heartburn and he reached into the console for a Rolaid. Then he pulled his brake and ran out onto the beach. The gun lay there, shiny and wet.

He picked up the gun, wrapped it in his underwear, and ran to his car. He drove away from Fat Ladies' Beach, wondering what to do.

He drove to the dump.

The dump was crowded with end-of-the-season dumpers with

their end-of-the-season rubbish. People hauled bloated, shiny black bags of trash, milk crates of bottles and cans, and decrepit furniture to the dumpsters and recycling center. The gun wrapped in underwear lay on the passenger seat, an unwanted passenger. And now Vance wished he'd brought a bag of some kind to hide the gun instead of his underwear. A pair of white BVD's, with the telltale striped waistband. More gray than white.

Vance studied his choices for the gun. He could either toss it into a dumpster the size of a mobile home meant for household trash, or he could recycle the gun under metals. Vance decided immediately against household trash. A gun didn't qualify.

He recycled the gun.

Or tried to. Shoving the swaddled gun under his arm, he walked, head down, for the recycling shoot.

"Vance?"

Vance raised his eyes. Pale orange hair. The white streak. Like a skunk, Vance always thought.

"Hi, Therese."

She seemed upset, like maybe she'd been crying. Since Cecily had left, she cried a lot.

"I came to throw away some of Lacey's old things," she said. "Things nobody wanted."

"That's too bad," Vance said.

"A life lived fully and so much ends up here at the dump." Therese's billowing skirt was too exotic for the dump. For the disposal of life rubbish.

"Yeah," Vance said. "Well, see you."

But Therese had eyes like no one else. Dirt-seeking eyes.

She tugged at the crotch of the underwear that was sticking out from under his arm.

"What's this?" she asked.

"Old underwear."

"You came to throw away a pair of old underwear?"

"Yeah."

She smiled. "You men are so funny. I'll tell you what. Give your underwear to me. I'll use them as rags. That's what I do with Bill's underwear."

Vance tightened his crab claw on the gun. "Sorry. No can do."

Therese tugged at the crotch of his underwear. "Come on."

"Nope." Vance backed up until he felt the Datsun's hood against his legs. He opened the door and slid in, the gun pinched against him. Therese regarded him in a way he was used to—weirdo, oddity, freak. Little did she know he was trying to mend his ways.

VANCE DROVE INTO TOWN and parked at Steamship Wharf. The noon boat was barely visible on the horizon. The steamship workers took their lunch break. Vance walked behind the ticket office where a couple of benches overlooked the harbor, for tourists with enough ingenuity to find them. Some scallopers rigged their boats, but for the most part, the wharf and harbor were deserted. Vance stood on the very edge of the wharf and gazed down into the water. It looked deep, and still. Vance pulled out the underwear, wiped the gun and dropped it into the water. It made a satisfying plunk and disappeared.

Vance steadied his breathing. No cop approached to write him a ticket for littering, the steamship wasn't cruising into its slip holding seven hundred eyewitnesses to what he'd done. It was October, Vance was the father of a living being, and he was getting his house in order.

He waited a few minutes more to make certain the damn gun didn't come bobbing to the surface, and when he was confident the gun was gone forever, he walked back to his car.

Steamship Wharf: the place where twelve years before, he'd stepped off the boat thirty seconds behind Mack, thirty seconds too late. He'd spent a fair amount of time over those years bemoaning this fact. But now, he realized, it didn't matter. He was going to be a father. A father! Vance climbed into his car and drove off the wharf, and it was as close to a fresh start as he'd ever hoped to have.

• • •

DURING HER LAST WEEK on the island, Maribel ran. That was how she wanted to say good-bye—by running, fast and long. It was true autumn now, high autumn, the best season on Nantucket. Colors were vibrant—the dark reds of the bayberry in the moors, the red-orange of flaming bush, the ambers of the dune grass. Some days she was glad to be leaving Nantucket when it was most beautiful; she could always remember it like this. Other days she asked herself, *How can I possibly go?*

Maribel ran through the streets of town. Not only Main and Federal and Centre and the streets the tourists knew, but the narrow, twisting back streets as well—Fair and School and Darling and Farmer and Pine, South Mill, Angola. She studied the antique homes, the postage-stamp gardens and friendship stairs, the screened-in porches and widow's walks and transom windows. She loved the names of the houses—Fair Isle, Left Bank, A Separate Peace, Captain's Daughter, Beach Plum, Aloft, Nana-tucket, Molly's Folly, Hunky Dory, Independence Day, Life Savour. *Good-bye.*

Maribel ran to Surfside Beach and through the State Forest to the airport. She ran Polpis Road to Shimmo, Quaise, Quidnet. She ran out Cliff Road past the old golf course at Tupancy Links, down Eel Point Road by the truly huge summer homes on Dionis Beach. She ran to Madaket Harbor.

She ran to Miacomet on a perfect autumn morning—fifty degrees, bright sunshine, brilliant blue sky. She ran down Miacomet Road sheltered on both sides by pines, until the land opened up by the pond. Mallards paddled just off the banks, and three swans glided through the water. Three white swans like something out of a fairy tale, graciously curved necks, and white tufted feathers at their hind ends, fluffed like tulle. The swans looked like women in fancy dresses. They looked like women in wedding dresses.

At the end of Miacomet Pond, where she could see the ocean peeking over the dunes, Maribel stopped running. She sat down on the marshy bank of the pond and she cried. In the weeks since the hurricane, Maribel told herself that the turn of events was inevitable. Breaking up with Mack, getting together with Jem, leaving the island—all part of some larger plan for her life. But it wasn't easy. She remembered the rides she'd taken with Mack in the Jeep with the top down, all the walks through town in the winter, holding hands. Mack and Nantucket were interchangeable, one and the same, and that was why she had to leave.

She didn't want to chase love anymore, she didn't want to pursue a futile dream. She couldn't make Mack love her any more than she could make her father, whoever he was, wherever he was, love her. She wondered why God had created this kind of exquisite pain, a pain so awful and so complicated, it had its own word—unrequited. She was trading in unrequited for requited, for the opportunity to *be* loved, to be held and cherished the way she deserved. With Jem, she told herself, she would be loved more, she would hurt less.

And, too, Maribel felt the only way she might ever get Mack was to leave him. She didn't think he'd change his mind immediately—but maybe someday. Maybe someday when she was a school librarian in some Los Angeles suburb, a huge bouquet of yellow zinnias would arrive with a card from Mack. Or maybe she'd have to wait until she was as old as Lacey Gardner. She imagined sitting on a porch in rocking chairs and talking with Mack in fifty years—not about what went wrong with their relationship, because by then they would have forgotten what went wrong. No, they would remember happiness. Living in the Palace, seeing the seals at Cisco Beach, listening to Christmas carols from outside the Unitarian church. They would remember all the things that were good about being young and healthy and together on Nantucket. If Mack asked her to marry him when they were in their eighties, she would say yes. And the wait would be worth it.

THE DAY BEFORE SHE and Jem were scheduled to leave, Maribel found herself running down the familiar road to the hotel. She told herself she was headed down there to see Jem—he had to work right up until the very end, carrying bags for the last guest, stripping the last room. But she knew she was really running toward the Beach Club to see

Mack. Six years earlier, this was how they met. He waited for her every morning in the parking lot, pretending to sweep, and then one day he gathered the courage to offer her some water. She couldn't help but wonder, *What if I hadn't accepted it? What if I'd changed my course and never met Mack at all?* Her life would be a different shape, different colors. Many hours could be wasted this way: pondering the way things might have been.

Mack must have sensed her because he was out front by himself, taking down the Nantucket Beach Club and Hotel sign. He turned as soon as he heard footsteps, and when he saw her his face brightened, but only momentarily.

Maribel was terrified, her heart kept on its eight-minute-mile pace even after she stopped to talk to him. She was having difficulty catching her breath. This was ridiculous! she wanted to shout. How could they say good-bye?

Mack spoke first. "What boat are you on tomorrow?" he asked.

She swallowed. "Noon."

He held the unwieldy wooden sign out in front of him. "Another season almost over," he said. "Only Cal West is left."

"You're staying the winter?" she asked. "And next year?"

"Yeah," he said. "I called How-Baby and turned down the job. I think you were right about me. I think I'm stuck here."

She looked out across the beach at the water, at the ferry headed for Hyannis. Tomorrow, it would be her ferry. "You could be stuck worse places," she said.

"Do you want me to see you off tomorrow?" he asked.

"Would you?" she said.

He kicked a hermit crab shell across the road. "I'll be there."

Maribel bit her lip; she was going to cry, but he didn't have to know about it. She waved, turned toward home, and ran like hell.

BILL HAD SURVIVED ANOTHER season. Barely. And not without profound loss. His daughter was gone, and the hotel needed colossal amounts of work—the floors and carpets on the Gold Coast had to be relaid, sections of the roof had to be repaired, and Clarissa Ford's room—Lucky number 7—had to be totally renovated. Bill was leaving those projects until the spring, when he hoped he would feel more enthusiastic than he did now.

Bill couldn't run the hotel without Mack's help, that was for sure. Bill watched from his bay window as Mack walked into Lacey Gardner's. Mack would stay there over the winter—he'd already agreed to pay Bill for the cost of heating.

Bill went over to Lacey's. The cottage had a spare look to it inside, although the sign for Lacey's hat shop still hung, and her Radcliffe diploma. But the Spode was down and the flowery Nantucket prints. It looked less like an old lady's house and more like a monastery.

Mack came down the hallway carrying two empty boxes.

"You need some stuff for the walls," Bill said. "I'm sure Therese can spare a few things from the hotel."

"All the prints in our apartment were Maribel's," Mack said. "She's taking them. But that's okay. I'm going to bring some things from home."

"From home?" Bill said.

"I'm going back to Iowa at the end of the month," Mack said. "For Harvest."

"You're going to Iowa?"

"I'm selling the farm," Mack said. "I need to meet with my lawyer. I need to clean out my parents' house. So I figure I'll put a trailer on the back of the Jeep and haul it all back here."

"That's a big step," Bill said. "Selling your farm." Bill felt ashamed. With all the other excitement, he'd forgotten Mack had to make this decision about his farm. If he'd paid attention, there might have been a way he could have helped. But maybe not.

Mack threw the empty boxes down. "I haven't managed to make it back to Iowa in the last twelve years, I don't see myself moving back there in the next twelve. This is my home."

"Well, I've been rethinking your proposition about the profit sharing," Bill said.

"Forget about it," Mack said. "That was Maribel's idea, not mine."

"I want to give you something," Bill said. "I want to thank you for staying." An idea came to Bill then—an idea so crazy, so luminous that Bill flushed, his heart moved in his chest as though it were trying to escape. Where did the idea come from? From losing W.T., then Cecily, from Mack cleaning out his parent's house, from standing here in Lacey's cottage. It came from all of those places, and from the desert place inside of him. He should talk to Therese first, of course, they should think long and hard about this idea, they should have time to embrace it, shun it, and embrace it again. But Bill couldn't wait. Mack stood in front of him, sandy haired, ruddy faced, handsome, saying he would stay. The son Bill had always wanted.

Mack shoved his hands in his jeans pockets. "You don't have to give me anything," he said. "You've given me plenty already."

"I'd like to adopt you," Bill said.

"Adopt me?" Mack's brow folded and Bill felt like a fool. Just because he yearned for a son didn't mean Mack wanted parents. He'd had two perfectly good parents—that was obvious from who the boy grew up to be. "You want to adopt me?" Mack asked.

Bill nodded, and then he was overcome with the fear that Mack would say yes.

Mack smiled. "I'm flattered, Bill. I'm . . . I'm touched. But I don't know about that."

Bill exhaled; he hadn't realized he was holding his breath. "I don't know either," Bill said. "It was just an idea. You mean a lot to Therese and me. We want to do something for you."

"How about a raise?" Mack said. "I am saving to buy a piece of land."

"I'd be happy to give you a raise," Bill said. "A big raise."

"And full control next time there's a storm?"

"You got it," Bill said.

"And one afternoon off a week," Mack said. "If I ever get another girlfriend, I want to be able to spend some time with her."

"Agreed," Bill said. "Do you want this all in writing?"

"No," Mack said. "I trust you . . . Dad." Mack grinned, then laughed, then reached out to shake Bill's hand, and Bill embraced him. *Dad.* So it would be a joke between them from now on, that was fine. But Bill couldn't help wishing that sometime in the next twelve years Mack would take him up on his offer, and become his son.

When Bill returned to his house, Therese was on the phone with the realtor from Aspen, setting up arrangements for their winter house.

"We'll be there December fourth," Therese said.

After she hung up, Bill said, "Maybe we shouldn't go back to Aspen this year. After all, I can't ski anymore, really. Maybe we should go to . . . Hawaii."

Therese flashed him a disgusted look. "We can't go to Hawaii."

"Why not? It'll be warm. We'll get a condo with maid service and a cook. We can walk on the beach—"

Therese cut him off. "We can't go to Hawaii because Cecily won't know to look for us there. The only place she'll look for us is at the house in Aspen."

"Oh," Bill said. Two good ideas shot down in one day.

"Don't you see how it's going to work?" Therese said. "One morning we'll be sitting on the sofa drinking coffee and staring out at the back of the mountain, and we'll see a bright spot. Cecily's hair. She'll be trudging up the road from town with her backpack, and we'll see her beautiful hair. That's how it's going to work. That's how it's going to be."

Therese spoke adamantly. She was nuts, of course, as delusional as Bill had been during the storm. They were taking turns being crazy. *That's how it's going to be.* Bill admired her confidence. He closed his eyes and hazily saw the scenario she painted. The cool, sharp evergreens that bordered the road to Independence Pass, the snowdrifts three feet high—and sticking out so that they couldn't miss it, Cecily's red hair. He guessed it wasn't impossible. Maybe if they went through the motions of sitting on the sofa with their coffee every morning, God would recognize their pain, and more importantly, their devotion, the two of them sitting there like a kind of prayer, and He would let this wish come true. Okay, then, they would go to

Aspen and look out the window and wait for their daughter to come home.

Bill nodded to let Therese know that he agreed, and then he took her hand and led her into the bedroom. She was alive and warm and she was staying, had always stayed and always would. She was his wife of thirty years. Bill made love to Therese, even though it was three o'clock in the afternoon.

WHEN MACK WAS HALFWAY to Steamship Wharf, he wondered why he'd offered to see Maribel off. He supposed he owed it to her—you dated a woman for six years and lived with her for three and it felt suspiciously like a piece of you was getting on the boat and leaving. Mack wished he owned a dog; he could talk things over with a dog without worrying about a response. He needed someone to bounce ideas off; he was sick of himself. In Iowa, he would pick up a Labrador or a German shepherd from a large farm litter. A new best friend.

Mack occupied his mind with thoughts of his new dog until he reached the steamship parking lot. It was ten to twelve; Maribel's Jeep wasn't in the lot. He missed the statement she'd made, then, officially driving off Nantucket. Mack swung his Jeep into a space and hopped out. There were tourists dragging suitcases on wheels, and there were the usual stout Steamship Authority workers in their Day-Glo vests. But no Maribel. She probably decided to forgo the good-bye; she probably found it too difficult.

Then Mack felt a tap on his shoulder, and there she was.

"Jem drove the car on," she said. "I told him I was waiting for you."

"You've spent a lot of time waiting for me," he said.

She teared up immediately, and pulled a Kleenex out of her suede jacket. "I came prepared," she said, wiping her eyes.

"You'll be happier without me," Mack said. "That's why I did what I did."

"You gave up," she said.

"You deserve better."

"It doesn't help to hear you say that," she said. "Because I love you and I believe in you."

"I know," he said. He opened his arms and took her in. He'd seen enough movies to understand that there were two kinds of endings— the kind where Maribel decided at the last minute to stay with him despite everything, and the kind where she got on the boat and left. Mack didn't know which ending he was pulling for, a sign in and of itself. Maybe he had a warped sense of what love should be, but he thought that in love everything would be clear—instead of the muddy, confused, back-and-forths he'd had with Maribel. Still, as he held her, as she cried into his sweater, he thought, I will never watch her run in her sleep again. I will never see her jog toward me, ponytail swinging. I will never make her smile. It was his job now to play the uncaring ogre, so that she could leave and find happiness elsewhere. He owed her that much. But what about his own happiness? Where would he find that? Where would he even look if Maribel left?

Over the loudspeaker came the fuzzy announcement that the noon boat for Hyannis was ready to depart. Maribel lifted her face from his chest, her mascara ran and her upper lip quivered. But she said nothing. It was Mack's turn to speak.

"I can't believe this is happening," he said. "Will I ever see you again?"

"Does it matter?"

"Of course it matters," he said. "Maribel, I love you."

"You love me?" she said.

"Yes." He was sure that hearing this hurt worse than anything else he could have said, but what could he do? It was the truth.

Maribel blinked her blue eyes, more tears fell.

"I want you to stay," he said. "Please stay."

She smiled, and for a second Mack saw her as she was when it all began: Maribel standing in the stacks of the Nantucket Atheneum secretly reading a paperback romance. Six years younger and full of hope.

"I want you to stay," he said.

"You're lying," she said. "But thank you." Then, she turned and ran from him.

A Kleenex fell from her pocket and blew toward Mack. He picked it up—it was wet and stained with black splotches. He put it in his pocket and climbed into his Jeep. If he had a dog in the seat next to him, he might be able to watch the boat pull out of its slip and listen to its lonely moan of a horn. But he couldn't do it alone, so he drove away.

BACK AT THE HOTEL, things were quiet. The wind sang a bit, and Mack heard the thock of a gull dropping a hermit crab shell onto the asphalt. This was a taste of what the winter would be like—after Bill and Therese left for Aspen and it was just him, living alone in Lacey's cottage. He hoped he'd learn to appreciate his solitude. That was what Mack wanted—to hear this quiet and be able to call it peace.

A man jogged into the parking lot. He was in his early fifties, with thick blond hair, wearing a Nantucket sweatshirt and navy nylon shorts. His legs were red with the cold. He looked familiar and Mack ran through the summer's faces. Beach Club member? Hotel guest?

"You're Mack," the man said.

Mack smiled. Concierge to the very end. "That's right. Can I help you?"

The man trotted up to Mack. Sweat dripped down his temples. He had clear blue eyes. "I've been wanting to introduce myself for a long time," he said. "My name is Stephen Bigelow Tyler." He said the name in such a way that Mack felt he should recognize it. Stephen Bigelow Tyler? The guy looked familiar, but nothing clicked.

Mack stuck out his hand. "Pleasure."

Stephen Tyler glanced up at Bill and Therese's house. "I run down here all the time. Usually at dawn when it's quiet, but sometimes after dark."

"It's a beautiful spot," Mack said.

"I've been trying to buy the hotel from your boss for years," Tyler said, and he laughed, wiping his forehead against his shoulder. "Stubborn man you work for, he won't sell. Though I guess I should be glad. I offered him twenty-five million for it."

"You're the one who's been trying to buy the Beach Club?" Mack said.

"Quite unsuccessfully," Tyler said. "Which is too bad because I wanted to give it to you."

"Give what to me?"

"The hotel. I wanted to buy the hotel and give it to you."

"Give me the hotel?" Mack backed up a step. Any crazy person could come down here now that it was off-season. This guy didn't seem particularly dangerous—what seemed dangerous was that Mack felt he was telling the truth. Tyler wanted to give *him* the Beach Club? Mack thought of How-Baby, David Pringle, Vance pulling a gun on him in the middle of the night. Who was behind this?

"Who are you?" Mack said.

"I'm Maribel's father," he said.

A combination of fear and excitement spread through Mack as he stared at the man's ruddy legs, his neat white socks, his Nike AirMax running shoes, the same brand that Maribel wore. Maribel's father. Her *father*, for God's sake. Then Mack's eyes traveled back to the man's face. There was no doubt. The hair, the eyes, and something unnameable in his face that Mack had seen in another face every day for the past six years.

"Does she know you're here?" Mack asked. "Does she even know you exist?"

Tyler shook his head. "I found her years ago, by accident, when I spotted her with her mother at a shopping mall I was developing in upstate New York. I recognized her mother, and when I got a look at Maribel I had someone do a little research. I kept track of her all these years, although I never told her who I was. Because I have other children, and a wife, in Wellesley. I didn't want to complicate things for myself or for her or for her mother." He took a deep breath. "I just wanted to give her something wonderful, something huge, so that she would have a happy life."

"And you're telling me now because she's gone."

Tyler pushed up the sleeves of his sweatshirt, like he was getting ready to fight, but then his shoulders sagged. "I watched you two a few minutes ago, at the boat. I thought of introducing myself then, to give Maribel a reason to stay. But like I said, I didn't want to complicate her life, I wanted to make it easier. So now she's gone and she doesn't know. It's better that way."

Mack disliked the thought of someone watching his last minutes with Maribel. "Maybe," he said angrily. "Though I don't see how it could be. I know far too much about absent parents. If she ever calls me or comes back here, I'm going to tell her."

Tyler frowned. "I hate to say it, son, but I don't think she's coming back." He kicked at some gravel. "We both lost her. But hey, maybe I'm wrong. In any case, let me give you my card. I think I can help you sell your farm."

"My farm? You know about my farm? What are you, some kind of spy?"

Tyler shrugged. "I'm her father is all," he said. "I've been watching out for her." He took a business card from his shorts pocket, handed it to Mack, and before Mack could even read the scripted print: *S.B.T. Enterprises, Boston, Nevis, Nantucket*, Tyler jogged away.

Mack stood in the wind until Tyler disappeared down North Beach Road, taking Mack's dream with him. Owning the Beach Club, running it with Maribel. Now it was nothing more than a great story to tell.

But to whom?

MACK WALKED INTO THE office. A mistake, he realized, because out the window, he saw the ferry disappearing on the horizon.

The phone rang and it startled him, although it comforted him, too, the familiar sound, the reminder that summer's end was temporary, and not a true end. Someone always wanted to book for *next* July or August.

Mack picked it up. "Nantucket Beach Club and Hotel," he said.

"Mack?"

A female voice, distant-sounding, like someone calling from the other side of a long tunnel. Mack glanced back out the window, and fingered the Kleenex in his pocket. Maribel, calling from the ferry? It didn't sound like Maribel; it sounded more like a woman who expected him to be excited to hear from her. Andrea, in Baltimore?

"Yes," Mack said.

"Mack, it's me," the voice said. "Come on, I haven't been gone *that* long."

"Cecily?" Mack said. He plugged his other ear. "Cecily, where are you?"

"In Rio," she said. "At the airport."

"Are you coming home, kid? God, your parents are sick with worry."

"I'm coming home."

"What happened?" Mack asked. "Is everything all right?"

"It's over between Gabriel and me," Cecily said. "I feel like every bone in my body is broken, it hurts so bad."

"I know what you mean," Mack said.

"I'll tell you about it when I get home. In fact, I really need to talk to Maribel."

Mack could tell her about Maribel, and about Lacey, but they were subjects that required face time. Cecily thought she hurt now, and she was in for more.

"Listen, do you want me to put you through to your house? I know your parents are anxious to hear your voice."

"I'm leaving in a few hours," she said. "I should be back on the island tomorrow morning. I want to surprise them, Mack, okay? So don't tell."

"Okay," Mack said. "I won't tell." He remembered Bill's weak heart, but a heart wouldn't fail from too much good news, or relief.

"I missed you, Mack," Cecily said.

"I missed you too, kid."

"I'm not a kid," she said.

"Come home and prove it."

"Okay, fine, I will!" Mack heard her old spunk and he knew just how she was standing, with her hip thrown out like an attitude. The slouchy, bright-haired princess of the Beach Club kingdom was coming home.

"So I'll see you tomorrow, then?" she said.

What was home, really, but the place where a space just your shape and just your size waited for you. Here, on this island, at this Beach Club, a space for Mack, a space for Cecily.

"I'll be here," he said.

Summer People

In loving, loving memory of my father,

Robert H. Hilderbrand, Jr.

(1944–1985)

chapter 1

Driving off the ferry, they looked like any other family coming to spend the summer on Nantucket—or almost. The car was a 1998 Range Rover in flat forest green, its rear section packed to within inches of the roof with Pierre Deux weekend duffels, boxes of kitchen equipment, four shopping bags from Zabar's, and a plastic trash bag of linens. (The summer house, Horizon, had its own linens, of course, but Beth remembered those sheets and towels from her childhood—the towels, for example, were chocolate brown and patterned with leaves. Threadbare. Beth wanted plush towels; she took comfort now wherever she could find it.)

Three out of the four passengers in the car were related, as any one of the people milling around Steamship Wharf could tell. Beth, the mother, was forty-four years old and at the end of pretty with blond hair pulled back in a clip, a light tan already (from running in Central Park in the mornings), and green eyes flecked with yellow, which made one think of a meadow. White linen blouse, wrinkled now. A diamond ring, too big to be over-looked. One of Beth's seventeen-year-old twins, her daughter, Winnie, slumped in the front seat, and the other twin, her son, Garrett, sat in back. That there was no father in the car was hardly unusual—lots of women Beth knew took their kids away for the summer while their husbands toiled on Wall Street or in law firms. So it wasn't Arch's absence that set their family apart from the others on this clear, hot day. Rather it was the dark-skinned boy, also seventeen, who shared the backseat with Gar-rett: Marcus Tyler, living proof of their larger, sadder story.

Beth lifted her ass off the driver's seat. She'd driven the whole way, even though the twins had their learner's permits and might have helped. She'd been awake since five o'clock that morning, and after four hours on the highway and two on the ferry, her mind stalled in inconvenient places, like a car dying in a busy intersection. In her side-view mirror, Beth checked on the two mountain bikes hanging off the back of the car. (It had always been Arch's job to secure them, and this year she did it herself. Miraculously, they were both intact.) When she brought her at-tention forward again—she couldn't *wait* to get off this boat!— her gaze stuck on her diamond ring, perched as it was on top of the steering wheel. This wasn't the ring that Arch gave her twenty years ago when he proposed, but a really extravagant ring that he presented to her last summer. He called it the "We Made It" ring, because they *had* made it, financially, at least. They had enough money that a not-insignificant amount could be wasted on this diamond ring. "Wasted" was Beth's word; she was the frugal one, always worrying that they had two kids headed for college, and what if the car got stolen, what if there were a fire. What if there were some kind of accident.

You worry too much, Arch said.

A rotund man wearing a Day-Glo vest, long pants, and a long-sleeved shirt in industrial blue, even on this sweltering day in June, motioned for Beth to drive off the ramp, following, though not too closely, the car in front of her. Seconds later Beth was not on the ferry anymore—not on the ferry, not on I-95, not in a parking garage on East Eighty-second Street. She was on Nantucket Island. The rotund steamship man waved at her (she could see him mouthing, "Come on, lady, come on," as if she were just another elegant housewife from Chappaqua), but he didn't know what had happened to her. He didn't know that, along with the Pierre Deux bags and the expensive mountain bikes, they'd brought along the urn that held her husband's ashes.

Beth's forehead grew hot, her nose tingled. Here, again, were the tears. It was the new way she evaluated her day: On a good day she cried only twice, in the morning shower and before her Valium kicked in at night. On a bad day, a *stressful* day, it was like this—without warning, in front of the kids, while she was *driving*, in *traffic*. Tears assaulting her like a migraine.

"Mom," Winnie said. She'd slept for most of the drive and the ferry ride, and now she gazed out the window as they cruised past the bike shops, the ice cream parlor, the Sunken Ship on the corner. The whaling museum. The Dreamland Theater. People were everywhere—on the sidewalks, in the stores, riding bikes, eating ice cream cones. As if nothing bad could happen. As if nothing could hurt them. Meanwhile, Beth negotiated the traffic surprisingly well at full sob.

"Mom," Winnie said again, touching her mother's leg. But what else could she say? Winnie pulled the neck of her sweatshirt up over her nose and inhaled. It was her father's old, raggedy

Princeton sweatshirt, which he'd worn often, sometimes to the gym in their building, and it smelled like him. Of all their father's clothes, the sweatshirt had smelled the most like him and so that was what Winnie took. She'd worn it every day since he died, ninety-three days ago. Winnie tried to convince herself that it still smelled like him, but his smell was fading, much the way her father's vivid, everyday presence in her mind was fading. She couldn't remember the whole of him, only bits and pieces: the way he loosened his tie when he walked into the apartment at the end of the day, the way he ate a piece of pizza folded in half, the way he'd fidgeted with a twig when he told her and Garrett the facts of life one warm and very embarrassing autumn afternoon in Strawberry Fields. (Why hadn't her mother done "the talk?" Winnie had asked her mother that question a few weeks after the memorial service—now that Daddy was dead, certain topics could be broached—and Beth said simply, "Your father wanted to do it. He considered it one of the joys of parenting.") A whole life lived and all Winnie would be left with were snippets, a box of snapshots. She breathed in, listening to the atonality of her mother's sobs as if it were bad music. The sweatshirt no longer smelled like her father. Now it smelled like Winnie.

The Rover bounced up Main Street, which was paved with cobblestones. Garrett shifted uneasily in his seat and checked for the hundredth time on the urn, which was a solid, silent presence between him and Marcus. It was embarrassing to have his mom losing it with a stranger in the car. Beth kept Garrett awake at night with her crying and he had a weird sense of role reversal, like she was the kid and he was the parent. The Man of the House, now. And Winnie—well, Winnie was even worse than his mother, wearing that sweatshirt every day since March six-teenth—every day: to school over her uniform, to sleep, even. And Winnie refused to eat. She looked like a Holocaust victim, a person with anorexia. And yet these two loonies were far pref-erable company to the individual sitting next to him. Garrett couldn't believe their bad luck. The last thing Arch had done, practically, before his plane went down, was to invite Marcus Tyler to Nantucket—not for a week, not for a month—but for the entire summer. And since a dead man's words were as good as law, they were stuck with Marcus.

Your father invited him to come along, Beth said. *We can't exactly back out.*

Yeah, Winnie said. *Daddy invited him.*

Garrett tried to talk to his mother about it, using the most powerful words he had at his disposal, the words of their ther-apist, Dr. Schau, whom they all saw together and separately.

We need to heal this summer, Garrett said. *As a family.*

Your father invited him for a reason, Beth said, though Garrett could tell even she wasn't sure what the reason was, and Garrett called her on it.

We need to help those less fortunate, his mother responded lamely.

Why is Marcus less fortunate? Garrett said. *He has a father.*

You know why, his mother said.

Because Marcus was the son of a murderer. Even as the Range Rover jostled up Main Street, Marcus's mother, Constance Ben-nett Tyler, was locked up in Bedford Hills Correctional Facility because she had killed two people. Arch had been Constance's defense attorney, and he'd gotten to know Marcus and like him. That was why Garrett shared the backseat with this huge black kid, this refugee from one of the most talked-about court cases in New York City in years. And because Marcus was the same age as Winnie and Garrett they had to be friends. Because of the tragedies in life that had converged on the four people sitting in this car, they had to join together. Empathize. It was the most twisted, unfair situation Garrett could imagine, and yet it was happening to him this summer.

Garrett glanced sideways at Marcus. Marcus was wearing an expensive-looking white dress shirt with his initials—"MGT"— embroidered on the pocket. It was the kind of shirt one wore to brunch or a college interview, though it was inappropriate for seven hours of car travel. Marcus had been sweating the whole ride and now the shirt looked like it'd been plucked from the bottom of a laundry hamper. Marcus had shown up at their apartment that morning wearing a squeaky new pair of dock shoes, which looked so unlikely on Marcus's feet that Garrett wondered if he'd worn the shoes to mock them somehow, to mock this trip to Nantucket. He'd taken the shoes off before they even hit Connecticut and his enormous bare feet gave off an odor that nearly caused Garrett to gag. Before Garrett could dwell on the other aspects of Marcus's appearance that bothered him—his closely-shaved head, his heavy-lidded eyes that made it seem like he was always half asleep—Garrett realized that Marcus had his elbow on the urn. He was using the urn as an *armrest*. Garrett held no fantasies about the contents of the urn—it was only ashes, another form of matter. There had been a few weak attempts at levity since the urn arrived from the crematorium— one night, Garrett set the urn at their father's place at the dining room table—but Garrett didn't believe the urn in any way contained his father. Only the remains of the body that once belonged to his father. Still, using the urn as an armrest was *not*

okay. Garrett glared at Marcus, but refrained from saying anything. They'd made it all the way from New York City without
incident and Garrett didn't want to start trouble now, when they
were almost at the house. An instant later, as if reading Garrett's
mind, Marcus lifted his oxford-clad elbow and Garrett moved
the urn into his lap, where it would be safe from further indig-
nities.

❀

Marcus was the only one who thought to offer Beth a tissue. She
seemed genuinely grateful, turning her head so that he could see
her try to smile. "Thanks, Marcus," she said. She stopped crying
long enough to blot her eyes and wipe the runny stuff from her
nose. "Here it is your first time on Nantucket and I'm blubbering
so hard I can't point things out. I'm sorry."

"S'okay," he said. He'd gotten the gist of the place already:
the gray shingled houses, the cobblestone streets, the shops with
expensive clothes and brass lanterns and antique rocking horses
in the windows. White people everywhere all excited about summer.

Beth stopped crying and put on her sunglasses. Marcus wasn't
sure what to make of the woman. He couldn't tell if she was
being nice to him because she wanted to, or because she felt she
had to—if pressed, he would lean toward the latter. She spoke
to him like he was in nursery school. (At McDonald's that morning for breakfast, with a pinched smile, "And, Marcus, what
would *you* like? How about some pancakes?" As if he was too
simple to navigate his way around the menu.)

Marcus had met the twins twice before. The first time was
when Arch brought them along to visit Marcus and his family in

Queens. The twins had stood in the apartment looking around like they were on a field trip about poverty; he could almost hear them thinking, "So this is where it happened." The second time Marcus met them was at Trinity Episcopal Church on East Eighty-eighth Street, at the memorial service for Arch. The twins' father, Arch Newton, had been the gold standard of human beings (Marcus intended to use this phrase in the book he was writing), the only white person in all of America who was willing to help save his mother's life. And for free—an expensive Manhattan lawyer who offered to defend Constance Bennett Tyler against the death penalty, even though everyone knew she was guilty as sin.

I'm going to help your mom, Arch told Marcus. *I'm going to see that she gets the best possible defense.*

Arch was there through the worst of it: the hot hours in the courtroom, the cold visits to Rikers, the reporters, the TV cameras, the disturbing photographs in the *New York Times,* especially the one of Candy's body being carried from the building, all of her covered by a sheet except for her patent leather shoes, the shoes that, ironically, Constance had bought for her. They reprinted this photo a lot; it became the icon for the case. Every time Arch saw the photo, he tore it in half. *They love it because it screams, "Baby killer!"* he said. If it weren't for Arch's powerful, steadying presence—his defense less a legal term and more like a physical shield that he held over Marcus and his family—Marcus never would have made it. But then, on the evening of March fifteenth, flying back from Albany, where Arch had traveled to meet with an attorney he knew who was close to the governor and might be able to speak out on Constance's behalf, Arch's plane crashed into Long Island Sound. Ice on the wings. It was a week before the trial was to start, and bizarrely, Arch's death added an element of humanity that had been missing from the defense's case; the media softened, hailing Arch as a hero for the common man, specifically, for a woman facing death row with no resources to fight it. Another attorney from Arch's firm took the case to trial, which lasted only three days. The jury convicted Constance of one count of first-degree murder and one count of second-degree murder, but the judge spared her the death penalty and nobody protested. It was as if Arch had taken the punishment for her.

Offering Beth a tissue was the least Marcus could do. Because what all four people in the car knew but nobody acknowledged out loud was that if Arch hadn't been defending Constance, he wouldn't have died. And so, Marcus *would* be a slave to these people if that was what they wanted. He'd haul out the garbage cans, he'd sweep sand off the porch, he'd rub oil onto their backs so they didn't burn in the sun. Yes, he would. Before Marcus left New York, his father, Bo, said, *These people didn't have to invite you, son. So be a big help, and make me proud.*

As they drove out of town, the houses grew farther apart. Then Beth signaled left and they turned onto a dirt road. Bumpy. Dirt and sand filled the air, gravel crunched under the tires.

Marcus would offer to wash the car.

He saw the ocean—it was in front of them suddenly, glinting in the sun like a big silver platter. Beth shut off the air-conditioning and put down all four windows.

"We're here," she said. She pulled into a white shell driveway that led to a house—a big, old, gray-shingled house—which sat on a ledge overlooking the water.

"Whoa," Marcus said.

Beth shut off the engine and climbed out of the car, raising her hands to the sky. "It takes my breath away every time. I feel better. Kids, I feel better already."

Marcus stuffed his feet into his very uncomfortable white-person shoes, wondering if he should help unload the car, but before he could make a move, Winnie took his hand and pulled him to the edge of the bluff. "Look, Marcus. What do you think?"

Marcus thought he might be experiencing some kind of reverse claustrophobia. Because he felt queasy, unsettled, unable to place himself. He was used to the Elmhurst section of Queens, and Main Street, Flushing. He was used to dirty streets and bodegas that smelled like too many cats and the long line outside the yellow brick public health building on Junction Boulevard. He was used to Shea Stadium and LaGuardia Airport—obnoxious Mets fans in their blue and orange hats crowding the subway cars, jumbo jets overhead at any given moment. He was used to sitting in the back row of the classrooms at Benjamin N. Cardozo High School so nobody could stare him down. He was used to a dark, low-ceilinged apartment that he shared with his father, his sister LaTisha, and the belongings of his mother—her head scarves, her record albums, her knock-off Prada bag—things that now simply took up space because she would never be back to reclaim them. He was *not* used to this—a Range Rover with leather seats, a white shell driveway, a golden beach, the Atlantic fucking Ocean, not to mention people who were civil to him even though they knew his mother was a murderer.

"It's cool," he said.

Winnie steered him toward the front door. "Come inside," she said.

Beth pulled the key out from under the welcome mat.

"Has that been there all winter?" Marcus asked.

"It has," she said. "And this is the last time we'll use the key until we leave in September."

"You're kidding," Marcus said. "What if somebody steals your stuff?"

Beth laughed. "That's the beauty of this place. Nobody's going to steal our stuff."

When Marcus got inside, he realized there wasn't much worth stealing. He followed Beth through the rooms, nervously thinking of Garrett behind him carrying bags. He should be helping Garrett. But Winnie had taken his hand and now he was sandwiched between Beth and Winnie both asking him, *Didn't he just love it? Didn't he think it was magnificent?*

The house was big. Marcus could say that with confidence. There was a hallway where you walked in with a living room on the right. A flight of stairs on the left. Past the stairs were a kitchen and dining room that had a row of windows and glass doors looking out over the water, and a deck beyond the kitchen with a green plastic table and chairs. The house was big but not fancy. The furniture was white wicker, except for one nasty-looking recliner the color of a dead mouse. The pictures on the walls were faded watercolors of the beach; the curtains were a creepy filmy material. The floorboards creaked and the house had a smell. An old, grandmother smell. Marcus wasn't sure what he'd expected—he guessed he pictured something like a fashion magazine, something more like the Newtons' apartment on Park Avenue which he'd seen for the first time that morning—with real antiques and Oriental carpets and brass candlesticks and sculpture. This house didn't feel like poverty, just like a house owned by white people who'd stopped caring. How had Arch described it? *A funky old summer cottage*—and Marcus had pretended to understand what that meant. Now he knew, it meant this. This was how white people lived when they relaxed at the beach.

Marcus checked out the view from the deck and then wandered back through the first floor. Garrett brought in a second load of stuff and dropped it at Marcus's feet in the living room. Marcus was looking for the TV; he didn't see one anywhere.

"Is there TV?" Marcus asked.

"No," Garrett said. "Sorry, man, you're going to have to do without *Bernie Mac* for the summer."

"Hey," Marcus said, straightening his shoulders in his new white shirt that was so fine it felt like money on his back. *Fuck you* was on the tip of his tongue. What the fuck was that supposed to mean? Was that a racial comment already? Well, why not? Why not put him in his slave's place right away? Before Marcus could prepare a response, Garrett was headed out the door again, aiming for load number three. Marcus followed him out.

"I don't appreciate your tone," Marcus said. He sounded, ridiculously, like a homeroom teacher. Garrett didn't even turn around. "I'm sorry I'm bumming you out. I don't want to ruin your summer with your family." Marcus couldn't believe he was talking like this. What he'd learned in the past nine months was that the easiest response to other people's shit was silence. Let his eyes drop to half mast, pretend like he hadn't heard. Pretend like nothing they said could bother him. Marcus would get his revenge on everyone later, once his book was published.

"Why did you come then?" Garrett said. "I know my mother offered. But you could have said no. You could have spent the summer at home. Closer to . . . your own family. Why did you come with us?"

Marcus felt guilt rising in his throat along with his long-ago-eaten breakfast. He *should* be at home. His father was going through a very stressful time trying to live without Mama. But things at home had gotten so horrible that Marcus needed to escape. At home, the phone was always ringing, the press calling, or people who had somehow gotten their number who wanted to share their feelings about what a monster Constance was. Marcus had lost all his friends, he suffered cold-eyed glares from his neighbors and teachers and people he didn't even know. He couldn't get an aspirin from the medicine chest without seeing all of Constance's half-used make-up, the tubes of lipstick, the skin stuff she loved that made her smell like apricots. He couldn't walk in or out of the apartment without thinking of Angela and Candy's bodies bleeding onto the floorboards. The worst had passed—the weeks after the murders when they were forced to stay in that fleabag motel, the humiliating afternoon in the swim team locker room—but Marcus's life in Queens, his new identity as the *murderer's son*, suffocated him. His mother was gone forever but at the same time she was everywhere, tainting every moment. He wanted out. On the whiter, brighter side, there was Marcus's book deal, Mr. Zachary Celtic, true crime editor at Dome Books, the thirty thousand dollar advance that no one knew a thing about except for Marcus and his English teacher. At home, Marcus would have had to get a job. Here, he had the luxury of a summer without work—long days of quiet hours to write the truth about his mother, whatever that was.

But he couldn't say any of that to Garrett. He reached past Garrett into the car for his own bag—a black leather duffel that had cost him nearly two hundred dollars. He'd bought it to impress these people, but in the Nantucket sun, Marcus saw it was all wrong. It looked like a drug dealer's bag with garish brass buckles and a strong smell of leather.

"I don't know," Marcus said. "But here I am. A nigger boy on your turf."

Garrett glared at him. "That's a low blow. You're calling me a racist, and that's not what this is about."

"What's it about, then?" Marcus said. He felt himself sweating and worried about the expense of dry-cleaning his new shirt. It was at least ninety degrees out.

"It's about us losing our father," Garrett said. "That's what this summer is about. That's what every day has been about since his plane crashed. That's the only thing anything's going to be about ever again, okay?" Garrett got tears in his eyes, but because his hands were full, he wiped his face on his shoulder.

"Okay," Marcus said. He was proud of himself because he understood not only what Garrett was saying, but what he hadn't said. *Our father is dead because of your mama. If he hadn't been defending her, he wouldn't have gone to Albany. If he hadn't gone to Albany, his plane wouldn't have crashed.* Arch was another victim of the day Connie Tyler lost her mind. Marcus wanted to apologize on his mother's behalf, but apologizing wouldn't help. If Garrett hated him, Marcus would have to live with it. It wouldn't be worse than the other stuff Marcus was living with.

Suddenly Winnie appeared, tugging on Marcus's arm in an eager, excited way, like a little kid. All three of them were seventeen, but Winnie seemed younger. Maybe because she was a girl. Or because she was so skinny. She had no body to speak of, certainly not the way some of the girls at Cardozo had bodies—with huge tits like balloons under their sweaters and curvy asses. Winnie was a stick person—right now she was wearing jean shorts that showed two Popsicle-stick legs, and her torso was swimming in her sweatshirt. She had blond hair like her mother and she was cute in a way that elves are cute. But not womanly. Even Marcus's twelve-year-old sister LaTisha had more action going on than Winnie.

"Come on," she said. "I'll show you your bedroom."

"In a minute," Marcus said. He wanted to finish with Garrett, although he could see that the moment had passed. Garrett walked by them with his load of luggage and Marcus slung his bag over his shoulder and reached for another box. He needed to catch up.

"Come on," Winnie said. "Please?"

Marcus managed to stave her off until he and Garrett had unloaded most of the car. In silence, except for the squeaky complaints of Marcus's shoes.

"Come on, Marcus," Winnie said.

Marcus picked up his leather duffel, which looked nothing but ugly compared to the Newtons' luggage, and followed Winnie up the stairs.

❦

"This is your room," Winnie announced. She could feel herself gushing but she didn't know how to stop. Ever since Marcus appeared at their apartment at, like, five that morning, it was as if Winnie were wearing some kind of electric bracelet that sent shocks up her arm to her heart. She'd had a crush on him since the minute she knew of his existence. More than six months ago now, since the morning that Arch took her to EJ's Luncheonette to have breakfast (she and her father both loved the red flannel hash). They were supposed to be talking about grades, school, her prospects for college (he wanted her to apply to Princeton; she wanted to stay in the city—NYU, Barnard), but instead they got on the topic of Constance Tyler's case and once Arch was on that topic, he couldn't stop.

He'd read about the murders in the *New York Times* the day after they were committed. That was a second morning emblazoned in Winnie's memory. Her father so engrossed in the front-page story and the photograph of the dead girl wearing black party shoes, that he held his hand up for quiet when Beth asked him what his schedule looked like that day. He drank the story in, and then hurried with the newspaper into the living room where he plucked his Princeton face book off the shelf and rifled through it, holding up the paper for comparison—because next to the picture of the dead girl in the Mary Janes was a picture of the suspected murderer, Constance Bennett Tyler, a public school teacher.

"Bingo!" Arch shouted. "Constance Bennett, Queens, New York. I went to school with this woman." He held the face book up. "Nineteen-seventy-five freshman class, Princeton University." Then his expression crumbled. "Well, she killed someone."

"That's Dad for you," Garrett said. "He loves all things Princeton. Even the murderers."

"Did you know her, Dad?" Winnie asked.

"Never seen her before in my life," Arch said. He tucked the paper into his briefcase and Winnie forgot all about it.

But not Arch. Although he didn't generally handle criminal cases, he made a few phone calls that day, and discovered that the woman's case had been taken by a P.D.—no real surprise—

and the D.A.'s office had already announced it was seeking the death penalty. They wanted Constance Bennett Tyler to be the first woman to die of lethal injection in the state of New York. Arch decided to go to Rikers where Connie was being held and talk to her. She had been indicted for the murder of her sister-in-law and her sister-in-law's nine-year-old daughter. She explained the whole story to Arch, and he was so intrigued by the circumstances and by Connie herself that he took the case and refused to be paid a penny.

Arch told Winnie all this as he sat across from her in EJ's, moving hash around his plate, but not eating because he was too nervous to eat. *If I save this woman,* he said *my life will have been worthwhile.* Trent Trammelman, the managing partner at Arch's firm, discouraged Arch from taking the case. It would bring too much unwanted publicity—every time the damn case was written up in the papers, the name of their firm would be mentioned. Arch countered that no publicity was unwanted, that the majority of New Yorkers were against the death penalty anyway. He was taking the case and that was final. *Trent knows that when I say final, I mean final,* Arch had said. Winnie understood that her father had power. He was a full partner and a top earner, and yet when he was with her, he was just a dad, motioning to the waitress for more coffee for both of them. Then he said, *Connie has a son, you know. A son your age.*

Does she?

She does, and that's another reason I took her case. She has a son who's on the swim team at Cardozo High School. You'd like him, Winnie. You two have a lot in common.

Winnie wasn't sure what sparked her interest. It was everything, probably, in combination. She liked swimmers. Her last and, truth be told, only boyfriend, Charlie Hess, was on the swim team with her at Danforth. Charlie was all arms and legs, lean, muscular, pale. She liked the way he looked when his goggles were on top of his head and his wet eyelashes stuck together. But she hadn't been serious about Charlie Hess. When swim season ended, they broke up.

Winnie also saw Marcus as her ticket into her father's new, consuming passion. She championed this boy whose circumstances were so dire. When her father got home from work at night, she asked about Marcus as though he were an old, dear friend.

Winnie had loved him before she ever laid eyes on him.

His actual person won her over permanently. Marcus was six feet tall with gorgeous brown skin and hair shaved close to his head. He was a man, not at all like the boys she went to school with. He had dimples when he smiled, although Winnie had only seen him smile once—when Winnie and Garrett went with their father to Marcus's apartment. As they were leaving, Arch made a joke and Marcus smiled, thus the dimples, which had now taken on the fleeting, mystical properties of, say, a rainbow. One of the reasons Winnie was thrilled to learn that Arch had invited Marcus for the summer was that she might, with good luck, get to see his dimples again. And yet every time she was around him she felt stupid and talked too much and couldn't locate her sense of humor.

Not only was Marcus beautiful, but he was kind. He escorted his younger sister to the memorial service and they sat in the row behind Winnie and her family. Winnie heard Marcus crying. When she turned around to peek, she saw Marcus with his arm around his sister, wiping his sister's tears. She decided right then that Marcus was a person to whom goodness came naturally. Unlike Winnie herself, who was selfish and mean-spirited at times, and petty. She tried to be good, but again and again she failed. There was a nagging part of her that suspected these flaws had caused her father's death. That she somehow deserved it.

Marcus dropped his black bag on the floor. That was all he'd brought, just one bag. "The room's fine," he said. "It's good."

"You have your own bathroom," Winnie said. "Well, toilet and sink. The bathroom with the shower's down the hall. And there's a shower outside. Actually, this used to be my room."

"Did it?" Marcus sat on the edge of the double bed and bounced a little, testing the mattress. The room, just like the family and the population of the island, was white. White walls, white furniture, white curtains, white bed. He tried to imagine writing a memoir of darkness and death in this room; it wasn't ideal.

Winnie noticed Marcus's eyes falling closed, like she was boring him to death. He looked way too big for the bed with its white chenille spread. The bed, and the room in general, were too dainty. But all the other bedrooms had two singles, except for the master bedroom which had a queen. Winnie thought she was being generous by giving Marcus her room, but now she wasn't sure. He didn't look happy.

"Aren't you happy?" she asked.

Marcus sat perfectly still, his hands resting on his knees. He wasn't sure yet what kind of responses these people expected of him. *Happy?* There was a word that had lost its meaning. All he could think about was setting his feet free from these damn shoes and putting on his pool flip-flops with a pair of tube socks. "I'm just getting used to it here," he said.

"Yeah, it's different from where you grew up, huh? Different from New York, I mean. That's why Mom likes it. It's quiet. There isn't even a phone in the house. Which is going to be a problem, I guess, if you want to call your family? Your dad? Or . . . do they let you call your mom?"

"They let me," Marcus said. "But I don't call." His voice was dead; he had no desire to talk about his mother. He liked the idea, though, of no telephone, no TV, no papers, no connection to the outside world. He liked the idea of three months isolated at the edge of the water. He needed it. Arch had known he needed it, and that was why Arch invited him here.

The room, Winnie realized, was stifling hot. "Maybe we should open the window," she said. "Maybe you'd like some air, for, you know, breathing purposes." She checked for the dimples but Marcus just stared at her.

"I can do it," he said.

"Right," Winnie said. She could make a pest of herself no longer. Her mother always referred to the things "any self-respecting woman" would or would not do. In this case, any self-respecting woman would leave Marcus alone for half a second so he could get adjusted.

Winnie backed out of the room. "Okay," she said. "I'll see you, I guess? I mean, obviously, we both live here. Want to swim later? I'm on the swim team at Danforth, you know."

"I know," Marcus said. "Your dad told me."

Winnie's mouth fell open. She was filled with an incredible emotion that she couldn't name: her father talked about her to Marcus. Bragged about her, maybe. "Did he?"

"He said I'd like you," Marcus answered, truthfully, because Arch was always telling him that. *My daughter, Winnie, you'd like her.*

"That's what he said to me about you," Winnie said. "Those were his exact words."

Marcus didn't respond except to nod almost imperceptibly.

"Do you?" Winnie asked.

"Do I what?"

She almost said, *Do you like me?* But she felt her self-respect about to fly away forever, so she made herself leave the room. "Oh, nothing," she said. "Never mind."

⁂

Beth did feel better although she'd planned on saying so regardless, for the kids' sake. Was it possible that Arch's spirit resided here, that his soul had slogged through the icy waters of Long Island Sound to wait for them on Miacomet Beach in Nantucket? When Beth looked out over the water she felt a sense of peace, she heard Arch sending her a distinct message, *It's going to be okay, honey. It's all going to be okay.* That was, perhaps, just the healing property of water, of clean air, of open space. Of being, finally, in the place that she loved more than anywhere on earth. Her family's house on Nantucket.

The house, the house. The house was named Horizon by Beth's grandfather, her mother's father, who bought the land and built the house in 1927. Beth had been coming to the island every summer since she was in utero, but her memories started at age five, the summer of 1963, when her grandfather bought a cherry red Volkswagen bug convertible and drove her around the island with the top down, while she ate lollipops in the backseat. She remembered sitting on Horizon's upper deck with her grandmother at night, looking at stars, her grandmother singing, "Mister Moon." Ordering take-out fried shrimp dinners from Sayle's and eating them on the beach at sunset. The summers lined up in Beth's mind like the scallop shells that she and her younger brothers collected and left to fade on the windowsill all winter. Starry nights, shrimp dinners, long days at the beach, outdoor showers, rides in a convertible with a fresh lollipop, bonfires, her first cold beer, falling in love, blueberry pie, riding the waves all the way back to shore, cool white sheets against sunburned skin—every detail that defined an American summer— that was what this island meant to Beth.

In honesty, Beth wasn't certain that either of her kids felt the magic of Nantucket the way she did. Arch never understood it: he joined them every weekend, and for two weeks at the end of August, but even then he set up camp at the dining room table and worked. Even then the FedEx truck rumbled out to their spot on West Miacomet Road every day but Sunday. No, this was Beth's place.

If they could just make it through the first day, Beth thought, things would be all right. If they could just settle into a routine. But that wasn't going to happen instantly. Beth wanted to dive right in, she wanted to be in her bathing suit lying on the beach with a sandwich and a cold Coca-Cola five minutes from now, listening to the pound and rush of the surf, listening to the twins and Marcus, poor Marcus, playing Frisbee, laughing, getting along. But there had to be process first: pulling the cushions for the furniture from the dank basement and airing them out on the deck (she could ask Marcus to do that; she needed to start treating him like one of the other kids, and less like a charity case that Arch had left her to handle). They had to unpack—put the kitchen supplies away, move their shorts and T-shirts and sandals from their suitcases into the empty dresser drawers and closets that smelled like old shelf paper and mothballs. They had to let

the hot and cold water run in all of the spigots to clear the
residue out of the pipes. Beth would clean—dust the bookshelves
that were crammed with bloated and rippled paperbacks, vacuum
the floors, and convince Winnie to beat the braided rugs with
the long-handled brush that hung in the outdoor shower.

Before Beth could organize her thoughts—new ones kept ma-
terializing like clowns popping out of a car—Garrett collapsed
in one of the wooden chairs at the kitchen table. The chair
groaned like it was an inch away from breaking.

"Mom," he said.

Mom, Beth thought. The one-word sentence that both Garrett
and Winnie used all the time now. It had so many meanings and
it was up to Beth to decipher which one was relevant at any
given time. *Mom, I'm angry. Mom, I'm bored. Mom, please make the pain
go away. Mom, stop harassing me. Mom, please stop crying, you're embarrassing me. Mom, why aren't you Dad?* Beth twisted her diamond ring.
The "We Made It" ring. A constant reminder of how sadly ironic
the world could be.

"You have to be careful with this furniture," Beth said. "It's old
and you're big. You're the man of the house now, don't forget."

"I'm hungry," he said.

"Me, too," she said. The McDonald's in Devon, Connecticut,
where they stopped for breakfast, seemed like another lifetime
ago. She had to shop for food, cleaning supplies, paper towels.
She had to go to the store. That would be first. "There's cheese
and stuff in the Zabar's bags. Some bagels. Can you just make
do for now? I'll go to the store. You should really unpack. It
would make me happy. Has anyone shown Marcus his room?"

"Why are you so worried about Marcus?" Garrett asked.

"Because he's our *guest,*" Beth said.

"He's not my guest," Garrett said.

"He's your father's guest," Beth said. "And we have to respect that." The subject of Marcus made Beth anxious. As if, she thought, as if we didn't have enough to deal with. Now there was Marcus, a casualty of a complicated and excruciating murder case. But Arch adored the kid, and Beth suspected that he used Marcus's merits to justify taking Connie Tyler's case at all. Certainly a woman with such a fine son was worth spending months of unpaid time saving. Arch bragged about the kid—how he won second place in the All-Queens Invitational in the two hundred meter butterfly, how his grades hadn't faltered since the murders and he hadn't missed a day of school except to attend Connie's important court dates. This was all leading up to the big announcement—only a week before the plane crash—that Arch had invited Marcus to Nantucket for the summer. Arch was glowing when he told Beth, so happy was he to be able to give yet more to this poor family. Beth, however, was not happy. First of all, Arch hadn't asked her. Not only had they agreed long ago to confer about all important family decisions, but the house on Nantucket was *her house.* Furthermore, she was the one who spent the summer there while Arch worked; she wasn't exactly thrilled at the idea of a third teenager to keep track of—fine young man or not. But Beth bit her tongue and said nothing, which was how she'd handled the Constance Tyler matter since the beginning. She let Arch fight Connie's fight since it inspired him the way his regular work did not. Then, after Arch died, Beth felt obligated to re-extend the invitation to Marcus for the summer since it definitely fell under the category of "What Arch Would Have Wanted."

The twins knew this as well as she did. *Marcus is here out of respect to your father.* She hoped she didn't have to repeat this phrase too many more times.

"Now, are you okay with lunch?" Beth asked Garrett. "The bagels and stuff?"

"Yes."

"Okay," she said. "I'm off to the store."

※

At the Stop & Shop, Beth was so caught up in her thoughts—Arch, the twins, Marcus, would this summer be okay?—that she didn't even see David until he touched her shoulder.

"Beth?"

Her nipples hardened. Because it was chilly; they were standing in the produce section in front of the hydroponic lettuce.

"Oh, God. David." Beth put her hands to her face in such a way that her elbows shielded her chest. She felt like she was going to cry, but no, she was just overwhelmed. Why him? Why now? She'd been in the store, what? thirty seconds, only long enough to chastise herself for not making a list, and here was David Ronan, her first love. Her first love and more. David fucking Ronan.

She peeked through her fingers. Yes, he was still standing there. Staring at her like she was from outer space. Of course—who acted this way upon bumping into an old friend at the store? Who hid like this? Well, he was still as handsome as ever—dark blond hair, a great tan. Wearing a red button-down shirt turned back at the cuffs, khaki shorts, and black flip-flops. Holding a head of lettuce. David Ronan, owner of Island Painting, year-round resident of Nantucket, father of two daughters, husband of Rosie Ronan who was a gourmet cook and threw notorious cocktail parties (Beth and Arch went to one, years ago). He had every right to be here at the Stop & Shop, and yet Beth felt taken by surprise. Affronted, even. Like he planned this somehow, to fuck her up.

"I heard about Arch," David said softly. "I read about it in the *New York Times*. I wanted to call, or write, or something to let you know how incredibly sorry I am for your loss."

"I can't talk about it," Beth said. She still hadn't moved her hands. David reached out, circled her wrist and gently pulled it away from her face.

"It's okay," he said.

She blinked away her tears, was it the second time she'd cried today, or the third?—and then, because it was David Ronan standing before her, she began to worry what she looked like. Her hair, her wrinkled blouse. The bags under her eyes.

"I'm fine," she said finally. "I am fine. Thank you for your condolences. How are you?"

"Surviving," he said.

"That's all we can hope for," Beth said. "I want to ask about Rosie and the girls, but I can't right now, David. I'm too . . . I'm too frazzled. We just got on-island an hour ago. Will you forgive me if I just shop?"

"I forgive you," he said. "We can catch up later. I'll stop by the house sometime."

"Good idea," Beth said. He was being polite, just like every time she happened into him. He wouldn't come by the house; he never did. He was busy in the summer. If she bumped into him again in a few weeks, or a month, he would explain how busy he'd been.

David made haste in dumping his lettuce into a plastic bag and headed for the deli. Then around the corner, out of sight.

Beth took a head of lettuce herself and breathed out a long stream of anxious air. David Ronan. Of all people.

Beth lingered in the produce section trying to transfer her angst into concentration on the mundane task at hand: Did she want strawberries? Yes. Grapes and bananas? Yes. What else? What kind of fruit would Marcus eat? The same as everybody else, she assumed. He was, after all, just a person. No different because he was black, because he was poor, because he was sad. David Ronan, too, was just a person. Why then did he seem like so much more? Beth was afraid to leave the produce section. She bought red and yellow peppers and some button mushrooms. It was too early in the season yet for really good zucchini or corn. She was afraid that David Ronan would be standing at the cheese case or in front of the cereal. She couldn't bear to see him again. She would have to stay by the produce until she was certain he'd left the store.

The produce section, however, was freezing. Beth had to move on. Besides, she was an adult. That was one of Dr. Schau's favorite refrains: *You're an adult, Beth. You have years of experience in how to cope. Use that experience.* Okay, Beth thought. She saw David every summer, sometimes several times a summer, and that one year they'd even socialized at the cocktail party. (Arch was the one who'd wanted to go. Beth pleaded to stay home until Arch insinuated that her reluctance meant that she still felt something for David. So they went to the party and Beth drank too much.)

She'd never been this alarmed to see David Ronan before, so why now? Because Arch was gone? Yes, that was it. She was no longer happily married. Her fairy tale had come to an end, and so she felt vulnerable, somehow, to David Ronan and the memories of pain and love that came with him.

As she moved carefully into the next aisle, her insides filled with an awful, heavy guilt. She remembered Arch, years earlier, in the hour before they left for the Ronan cocktail party. Arch teased her because she stood in the closet in her bra and panties with a glass of white wine debating what to wear. She put on a sundress, then declared it too matronly and went with silk pants and a skimpy halter. Arch whistled in such a way that let her know the outfit was too sexy. She poured herself another glass of wine and changed her top.

You're making a big deal out of this, Beth, Arch said.

No, I'm not.

The guy's crazy about you. He always has been. He'll think you look beautiful whatever you wear.

Shut up, she said. *Why aren't you jealous?*

Why should I be jealous? I got you in the end, didn't I? I'm happy to go. I want to gloat.

That was Arch through and through. Never jealous, only proud. That was the perfect way in which he loved her. At the party, Beth drank too much, laughed too loudly in conversation with Rosie Ronan, and stumbled on her way out, catching the heel of her sandal between the flagstones of the walk. The ride home was the closest she had ever come to telling Arch the truth about David, but blessedly, she'd kept her mouth shut. Back at Horizon, Arch put her to bed with two aspirin and a glass of ice water, kissed her forehead and deemed the night an enormous success.

Long ago, Beth had decided that every man, woman, and child had the right to one secret. One piece of private history, and hers was David Ronan.

But what did she care about David Ronan now? The way she reacted probably made him think she was still in love with him.

She should find him and try to act like a normal person. Set things straight.

Beth abandoned her cart and hurried through the store until she spotted the red of David's shirt in the dairy section. She stopped. He was buying—What? Milk, half-and-half, two packages of Philadelphia cream cheese. She moved in front of him.

"Oh," he said. "Hi."

"I'm sorry I acted strangely back there," she said. "I don't know what's wrong with me."

"You've been through a lot," David said. "I was just thinking how awful it must be for you. And the kids."

"And Arch's mother, and Arch's partners, and his clients, one of whom narrowly escaped death row. It amazes me. He was just one person but he left behind such a big hole."

"He was a good man," David said. "I feel lucky to have met him."

"That's nice of you to say."

"I mean it, Beth."

She looked at him and realized that she'd been avoiding his eyes this whole time. He smiled. His face was as familiar to her as the faces of her own brothers. She'd devoted so many hours to studying it when she was younger.

"Okay, listen, let's not make excuses. Will you bring your family for dinner on Friday?"

He frowned. "Friday?"

"Are you busy? It would be great if Winnie and Garrett could meet your girls and we have another boy their age staying with us this summer. It'll be fun. We'll cook out?"

"Thanks for the offer, Beth, but I . . ."

"You won't come?"

"Well, you haven't let me explain."

"Okay, explain."

He put his hand over his mouth and wiped at his lips. "I'll explain on Friday, I guess. It's too much to go into here. What time would you like us?"

"How about seven?"

"Fine. We'll see you then. Friday at seven."

"You remember the house?"

"You're kidding, right?" David asked.

"Right," Beth said. How could he forget Horizon, the house her father threw him out of so many years ago? David left her with a little dance step, a wave and a half-turn in which he gathered up a dozen eggs and disappeared around a display of meringue cookies. Beth took a minute to regroup. The Ronan family was coming for dinner. Perfect. Right? Beth hoped she hadn't made things worse by trying to make them better.

She found her cart and resumed shopping. She went back to produce and selected eight russet potatoes and three pounds of asparagus. An additional head of lettuce. Rib-eye steaks, butter, sour cream. Some Ben & Jerry's. She wasn't a gourmet cook like Rosie Ronan, but that was okay. She wouldn't go to any great lengths; she would wear jeans and flip-flops. Having old friends for a cookout was no big deal. It was just one of the things you did in the summertime.

As soon as his mother got home, Garrett realized something had happened at the store. Or maybe it was just the effect of Nantucket on his mother's brain. He heard the car swing into the driveway and then the car horn and his mother proclaiming, "Kids, I'm home!"

Garrett was the only one around. Marcus and Winnie were swimming together and Garrett watched them from the deck, the two of them trying to do the butterfly against the tough surf. Garrett wouldn't admit to any racist feelings except for when it came to Marcus and his sister. Winnie fawned all over the guy, which wasn't surprising considering how mentally unstable she'd become, but Garrett was damned if he were going to stand by and let Marcus fuck his sister. He was the man of the house, now. He'd kill Marcus before allowing that to happen.

Garrett walked through the house and out the front door to help his mother with the groceries. She looked different. She looked manic, overexcited, like a kid who'd eaten too much Halloween candy.

"Thanks, sweetie. Thanks a million. You've been such a big help today. Really, I mean it. You've been an angel."

"Mom?"

Beth sailed into the kitchen and flung open all of the cabinet doors. "I forget, every year, where we put things. I guess it doesn't matter. We can make it up as we go along!"

It occurred to Garrett that his mother had been drinking. Or maybe she'd popped the pills that Dr. Schau gave her (their mother was the only one to get pills). Garrett unloaded the bags and handed groceries to his mother. She was moving around the kitchen like she'd been shot out of a pinball machine. Bouncing around with all this extra energy.

Garrett is very sensitive to other people's moods, Mrs. Marshall had written on his end-of-the-year student evaluation. *He is tuned in to their needs, desires, and intentions.* It was true, he thought. He could read other people in a matter of seconds. Some people might call it intuition, but that word sounded too feminine. Garrett preferred the word "perceptive." Like a detective. Or a writer. Or like Dr. Schau, who could tell what you were thinking before you even opened your mouth. Right now, watching his mother, Garrett knew something had happened at the store. He pulled out the steaks.

"Why so many steaks?" Garrett said.

"Steaks?" his mother cried out. She knit her brow as though she didn't know what he was referring to, as though it was easy to forget what must have been a hundred dollars worth of steaks in one of the bags. Just repeating that word, "steaks," was as good as lying.

"Why so many?" Garrett asked.

"Well, because," his mother said. "There are four of us and we're having four dinner guests on Friday."

Garrett dropped his ass into a kitchen chair. It squealed, but thankfully did not break. *"Dinner guests?"*

"Before you get all worked up, let me tell you who it is," his mother said. "It's my friend David from growing up, his wife, and their two *teenage daughters*. You know, girls, girls, girls. I thought you'd thank me. It seems like all your friends here are either at camp or their parents moved to the Hamptons."

Garrett closed his eyes. More teenagers he was supposed to connect with. He couldn't believe his mother. She barely kept it together in front of her family; what made her think she might make it through an evening with other people? The topic of Garrett's father would inevitably come up. His mother would drink too much wine and start to cry. Maybe Winnie, too. The guests would sit dumbfounded and uncomfortable, the *teenage daughters* wishing they were anywhere but trapped in this house.

"No one's moved to the Hamptons," Garrett said irritably.

"The Alishes," Beth said. "Carson Alish's parents moved to the Hamptons."

"That is so beside the point," Garrett said.

"What point?"

"We're supposed to be healing as a *family*," Garrett said. "It's bad enough you invited Marcus, and now we're having some strange people over?"

"Just for dinner," she said. "Besides, they're not strange. David and I have known each other since we were sixteen years old. For six or seven summers, he was the best friend I had."

The way his mother said the word "friend" tipped Garrett off immediately.

"So this is an old boyfriend, then?"

"He's a friend. From a hundred years ago, Garrett. And he's coming with his wife and kids."

"Dad's only been dead for three months," Garrett said.

Beth fell into the chair next to him. "I know you're having a hard time, sweetie. We all are. But I worry about you especially because you're putting up such a strong front. You're being tough for all of us. I'm sorry I keep telling you you're the man of the house. That isn't fair. I want you to know it's okay to grieve— to cry, to scream, to be angry. But don't misdirect your anger at me."

"Except I *am* angry at you," he said. "You invited your old boyfriend here for dinner. You invited Marcus here for the whole summer. We're never going to have time alone, just our family."

"We'll make time," she said, patting his hand. "We'll take bike rides, we'll walk on the beach, and we'll find the right time and place to scatter Daddy's ashes. Just you, me, and Winnie. I promise."

Beth returned to the groceries and Garrett watched for a minute. Then he heard Winnie blabbering and he turned to see her and Marcus trudging up the steps from the beach. Winnie's blond ponytail was dripping wet; she wore the sweatshirt over her bikini. Unbelievable. But she had taken it off before she went into the water. Garrett wondered if she felt lighter, freer, without it. It was an interesting concept: grief as something she could take off every once in a while, like when she wanted to enjoy the first swim of the summer. Garrett was almost envious of his sister and the way she'd appropriated their father's sweatshirt and made it her own symbol: *I'm sad.* Garrett's sadness churned inside of him like food that was impossible to digest.

Marcus wore a pair of cut-off jeans as his swimsuit. He looked like a kid who should be getting wet under a fire hydrant.

"Are you two hungry?" Beth asked. "I went shopping."

"I'm not hungry," Winnie said.

Garrett gauged Beth's response to this, which was no response at all. She was definitely distracted. Winnie never ate anymore, and this was a manifestation of her grief that Garrett didn't envy. Food made Winnie sick. If she was eating and accidentally thought about their father, she threw up. Every day at Danforth she bought lunch in the cafeteria and then walked it right out the front door and down half a block to where three homeless men in turbans camped out under some scaffolding. Every day Winnie gave them her lunch then walked back to school with the empty tray.

"Do you want anything, Marcus?" Beth asked. "A sandwich or something? We have smoked turkey here, and some cheese. Or I could fry you an egg."

"Turkey's fine," Marcus said.

"I'll make his sandwich," Winnie said.

"I'll make it," Beth said. "You kids dry off."

Garrett watched his mother make Marcus's sandwich. It was as if she were entered in a sandwich-making contest. She'd bought three loaves of Something Natural herb bread, unsliced, so she brandished her serrated knife and cut two thick slices. Then mayonnaise, mustard, three leaves of lettuce that she washed and dried first, two pieces of Swiss Lorraine, and finally the smoked turkey that she draped over the cheese one slice at a time. She put the top on the sandwich, cut it in half diagonally. Arranged it on a plate with two handfuls of Cape Cod potato chips.

"Marcus, what would you like to drink?" she called out.

Garrett had seen enough. He'd made do with an untoasted bagel with cream cheese that had traveled with them in the warm car all the way from New York. But that wasn't what got him mad. It was something else. Winnie and his mother fighting over who got to make Marcus's sandwich, for starters. Garrett found the urn on the mantel in the living room and he carried it upstairs to his room. They'd been here all of three hours, and already he could tell this summer was going to suck.

꙰

Garrett's room was on the side of the house that faced the ocean. The room had been built for Garrett's great-great-uncle Burton, his great-grandfather's brother. Burton had been a world traveler and insisted on a room where he could see the horizon. The room had two single beds with a nightstand between them. The lamp on the nightstand had a fringed shade. On the wall was a map of the world from 1932—no Israel, Garrett noticed, and the names and boundaries of the nations in Africa were different. The map was marked with multicolored pushpins, showing all the places across the planet where Uncle Burton had laid his head for the night. Singapore, Guatemala, Marrakech. Katmandu, the Fiji Islands, Santiago, Cape Town. Underneath the bed that Garrett didn't use was Uncle Burton's traveling trunk. Garrett and his father had sifted through it once, examining the masks, the kris knife from Malaysia, a ladle made out of a coconut, the postcards and cocktail napkins from fancy hotels in Europe.

Garrett placed the urn on top of the dresser. He wanted to convince his mother to let him take a year off before he went to college. He wanted to go to Perth, Australia. Garrett stepped out onto his one-person balcony, dreaming about a flat in Cottlesloe Beach, long drives into the Outback, sightings of emus and crocodiles and kangaroos, which he'd heard were as plentiful as rabbits. Arch had spent a year in Perth between college and law school, and he told Garrett all about the Fremantle Doctor, which was the name of a breeze that came off the water in January, and about the sheilas, a term for gorgeous Australian women with *Baywatch* bodies.

Garrett wanted to live a life exactly like his father's—Australia, college, law school. A career as a Manhattan attorney, a wife and two kids, including a son of his own. He could then pick up where his father's life tragically ended. Arch's plane crash was, quite simply, the worst disaster imaginable. The plane was a Cessna Skylark. It had been gassed up at the Albany airport, and checked by mechanics. The flight pattern was cleared by the FAA, by the tower in Albany, by the tower in LaGuardia. The pilot had over two thousand hours of flight time. But he was only twenty-five years old, and the plane had propellers, like the toy planes Garrett used to play with as a kid.

When they recovered the body, and the black box, two days after the crash, Garrett had wanted to see both. He wanted to see his father's body; he wanted to listen to the flight recorder. But no one was willing to let him do either. The managing partner at his father's firm, Trent Trammelman, identified the body. Garrett summoned the courage to ask Trent, *What did he look like? Please tell me.*

He looked fine, Trent said. *Peaceful.* That word, "peaceful," clued Garrett right in: Trent was lying. And so Garrett was left to imagine his father's body. Blue, bloated, broken. Garrett's father, his dad, whom he knew so well and had seen happy and healthy and handily in control of every situation that arose since Garrett had been born, was altered forever in a matter of seconds. Killed. Boom, just like that.

The cause of the crash was ruled as ice on the wings. There had been a driving freezing rain and it was dark—the worst possible flying conditions. There was a mechanical failure—something called a "boot" on one of the wings was supposed to expand and crack off the ice, but it malfunctioned, and one wing grew heavier than the other. The pilot changed altitudes several times, but nothing worked. The pilot couldn't recover. The plane went into a spin and crashed. The thing that Garrett hated to think of even more than the condition of his father's body after the crash was those seconds or minute when the plane spun toward earth. What could those seconds possibly have been like for his father? Did his father scream? Did his father think about Garrett, Winnie, their mother? He must have. The only reaction Garrett wanted to imagine from his father was anger. His father would have been yelling at the pilot to regain control. *I have kids!* he would have said. *I have a beautiful wife!* Garrett chose to believe his father was too angry to be scared, too furious to cry out in fear for his life. But those images slid into Garrett's brain despite his best efforts to push them away: his father crying, stricken with terror.

Better to watch your parent die of cancer, Garrett thought. Like Katie Corrigan's mother who got breast cancer and died a year later. Then, at least, you could prepare yourself. You could say good-bye. But Garrett's father had been ripped from their lives suddenly, leaving behind a hole that was ragged and bloody, smoking.

Garrett stayed in his room until the sun sank into the water. His walls turned a shade of dark pink; the urn was a silhouette against the wall. There was a knock at the door.

"Who is it?" Only one answer would be acceptable.

"Mom. Can I come in?"

"Okay," he said.

She stood in the doorway. "We miss you downstairs. I'm about to start dinner. What are you doing up here?"

"Sleeping," he said. "Thinking."

"What are you thinking about?" she asked. She glanced at the urn.

I'm a seventeen-year old boy. I need my father. As if there were anything else to think about. "Nothing," he said.

chapter 2

Three days later, Marcus felt like the main character in that Disney movie where the little boy is adopted by wild animals and lives among them in the jungle. Here it was, two o'clock in the afternoon, and he was lying on a beach. There was no one else for miles, except Winnie, who lay in a chaise next to him wearing purple bikini bottoms and her Princeton sweatshirt. She seemed intent on getting a tan—all shiny with baby oil—but she refused to take off the sweatshirt. Except for when she swam, which she and Marcus did whenever they got too warm. This, Marcus thought, was what people meant by "the good life." Sitting on a deserted beach in the hot sun—no bugs, no trash, no other people kicking sand onto his blanket or blaring Top 40 stations on the boom box like at Jones Beach—and he could swim in the cool water whenever he wanted. Plus, he had a handmaiden. Winnie made lunch for both of them—smoked turkey sandwiches and tall glasses of Coca-Cola that she spiked with Malibu rum. At first, when Marcus tasted the rum in his drink, he balked. Because he did *not* want to have his summer over before it even began for getting caught drinking. He said so to Winnie and she promised him that they would just have this one cocktail—he loved how she called it a "cocktail"—and that her mother was out doing a two-hour jog and would never know. The Malibu rum had been sitting in the liquor cabinet for a couple of years; she and Garrett dipped into it all the time, even with her father around, she said, and they had never gotten caught.

The mention of Garrett made Marcus uneasy. Garrett was lying up on the deck, presumably because he never swam and didn't like to get all sandy, but Marcus suspected it was because he wanted to keep his distance. And up on the deck he could watch everything Marcus and Winnie were doing. Like Big Brother. Like God.

Marcus squinted at Winnie. "If you're so concerned about getting tan, you should take your sweatshirt off."

"You just want a better look at my body," Winnie said.

Marcus found that funny enough to laugh, but he didn't want to piss her off. "Why do you always wear it?"

"It was Daddy's."

Immediately, Marcus's reality kicked back in. Despite the hot day, he felt the chill of humiliation as he recalled the worst personal shame of his life. At the beginning of swim season, he'd come out of the showers to find the locker room abandoned, to find his locker jimmied open, to find all of his clothes missing, even his wet bathing suit. He stood in his towel, shivering, not because he was cold, but because he'd thought the guys on the swim team, at least, would cut him some slack about his mother. But no: they, too, wanted to expose him. Marcus sat for a long while on the wooden bench by his empty locker, too mortified to wander the school's hallways for help, too ashamed to contact his father, before he thought to call Arch, collect, at his office. Arch came all the way out to Queens with a gym bag and Marcus got dressed in Arch's sweats. The very same Princeton sweatshirt that Winnie was wearing. If Arch had asked a single question, Marcus probably would have broken down. But Arch just offered him the gym bag and said, *Put these on and let's get you home.*

Winnie, it seemed, was trying to get his attention. "Marcus?" she said.

"Huh?"

"Now can I ask you something?"

"What?" he said, warily.

"Why do you lie out in the sun when you're already black?" She giggled.

Marcus tried to relax. If she was going to wear the damn sweatshirt all summer, there was nothing he could do about it except let it be a reminder of how far he'd come. How he didn't let other people get to him anymore. How he'd shown the jackasses on the swim team something by placing second in every single meet all season. Placing second *on purpose* so his name wouldn't make it into any headlines. "Black people get tans, too, you know. Look." He lowered the waistband of his shorts a fraction of an inch so that Winnie could see his tan line. "In winter I get kind of ashy. Besides, I like the feel of the sun on my skin."

"Me, too," Winnie said. She pushed up her sleeves and rolled up the bottom of her sweatshirt so that her stomach showed. "You're right," she said. "That's better." She picked up the bottle of baby oil and squirted some on her stomach and rubbed it in with slow, downward strokes that made Marcus think she was trying to be all sexy for him. The poor child, as his mother used to say.

Winnie had a crush on him. Anyone could see it. The past two nights she'd enticed Marcus into playing board games after dinner. Marcus asked if there were anything to do in town, and Beth offered to drive them in for an ice cream or the movies, but there were only two movie theaters showing one movie apiece that all of them had already seen, and Winnie turned down the ice cream without a reason. Not going into town left them with what Marcus's mother used to call Nothing to Do but Stand on Your Head and Spit in Your Shoe Syndrome. So Winnie pulled a stack of board games out of a closet. The boxes of the games were disintegrating and some games were missing pieces and dice, and the bank in Monopoly only had three one-dollar bills but Winnie cut some more out of blank typing paper. They made do. Marcus and Winnie spent two long evenings building pretend real estate fortunes and getting out of jail free.

It was as different from his life in Queens as anything could be. Winnie kept apologizing because *There's practically nothing to do here at night, not until I get my license, anyway.* She had some notion that Marcus went out every night at home, clubbing, or hanging out on the streets. But in fact, at home, Marcus stayed off the streets. He couldn't afford to get into any trouble, and the best way to stay out of it was to stay home. Last summer, he'd worked all day on the maintenance crew at Queens College—mowing lawns, trimming hedges, recindering the running track—and by the time he got home, his ass was kicked. He ate dinner with his family and then either watched TV or went over to Vanessa Lydecker's apartment and drank a beer with Vanessa's brother and fooled around with Vanessa in her bedroom.

Before the murders, Marcus's family was nothing special. His father worked at the printing press for the *New York Times* as a supervisor, and his mother, with one year of Ivy League education and three years of city college, was a reading specialist who split her time between I.S. 224 and P.S. 136. She tutored kids on weekends for extra money, which she tucked into Marcus's college account. And then, on October seventh, Constance murdered her sister-in-law Angela Bennett and Angela's nine-year-old daughter, Candy Cohut. Constance stabbed Angela to death, and in the process fatally wounded Candy. Even now, when Marcus thought about the murders, it seemed so incredible it was as if it had happened to somebody else.

"I'm going to eat my sandwich," Marcus said. He'd drained his cocktail and the ocean began to take on a wavy shimmer. He needed food.

"Okay," Winnie said. "Enjoy."

"Aren't you going to eat?" he asked.

"I'll wait until later."

In just three days, Marcus had learned what this meant: Winnie would let her sandwich sit for another hour or two, then throw it away, claiming the mayonnaise had gone bad.

"You know why you're so skinny, don't you?"

Winnie didn't respond.

"Because you don't eat. If my father had to sit here and watch you waste a sandwich with turkey on it that costs, like, ten dollars a pound, he'd throw a French fit on your ass." Marcus took a lusty bite of his sandwich. Even the food here tasted better. These sandwiches he'd been eating, for example. The bread was homemade, the smoked turkey was real turkey, not some white meat paste that was processed to taste like turkey, the lettuce was crisp, the tomato ripe. Beth used gourmet mustard. It was so superior to any sandwich that could be purchased in Marcus's neighborhood or in his school cafeteria, that it was as if he'd been eating cardboard and ashes all these years and only now had stumbled upon actual food. "I mean, really," Marcus said. "Why don't you eat? Do you have some kind of problem? There was a girl at my school who had anorexia. She walked around looking like she had AIDS or something."

"I don't have anorexia," Winnie said. "And I don't have AIDS."

"But you look like a skeleton. I haven't seen you eat the whole time you've been here."

"I eat when I'm hungry," she said.

Marcus finished the first half of his sandwich, then wished he'd saved some of his cocktail to wash it down with. He eyed Winnie's cocktail. She'd give it to him if he asked her for it. Then he remembered that Beth had slipped two bottles of Evian into their beach bag. That woman was improving in his eyes. Marcus drank one of the bottles down to the bottom. He felt much, much better.

"There are people in Queens, you know, and the rest of New York City, who don't eat because they can't afford to."

"I'm well aware of that, thanks," Winnie said. "I do my part to feed the homeless."

"Do you?"

She sat bolt upright. "For your information, I gave my lunch to homeless people every day this spring."

"Good for you," Marcus said. He believed her. Although he'd only known Winnie for three days, he could tell that was exactly the kind of thing she would do. She loved charity cases. Him, for example. "But you should take care of yourself while you're at it."

Winnie stood up and her sweatshirt dropped to her waist. She put on her sunglasses, snapped up her towel and headed up the stairs without a word. Marcus had pissed off his handmaiden by telling her the truth. She looked like a skeleton. If she didn't start eating soon, she was going to make herself sick.

Well, fine then. Marcus concentrated on his sandwich. Actually, it tasted better now that he was alone. He noticed that Winnie had left her sandwich behind, and since there was no hope that she'd ever eat it, and since the rum made him extra hungry, he finished that one, too, and drank the second bottle of Evian, and while he was at it, polished off the remains of Winnie's cocktail. Then he lay back on his blanket and listened to the sound of the ocean. It was almost pleasant enough for him to forget about his worries. His mother. The photo of Candy, all covered up except for her shiny black shoes. The unwritten book. The tactile memory of five crisp hundred dollar bills that his editor, Zachary Celtic, handed him on the day they sealed the book deal with a handshake. Zachary gave him the cash with the understanding that at the end of the summer Marcus would have fifty pages to show him, and an outline for the remainder of the book. Marcus spent the money in less than a week, buying items for his trip to Nantucket that he'd hoped would convince the Newtons that he wasn't a charity case after all: the all-wrong leather bag, the uncomfortable dock shoes, the portable CD player. The best thing Marcus bought was his white shirt. He'd taken the subway into Manhattan to buy it—at Paul Stuart, where a young German woman waited on him as though he might pull a gun on her at any moment. He charmed her, though, and by the end of the transaction, she suggested the monogram and threw it in for free.

Now that the money was gone (there had been some idiot-

spending, too: two or three meals at Roy Rogers, a ten-dollar
scratch ticket, a bouquet of red roses for his sister LaTisha as an
apology for leaving her alone with their father all summer), Marcus felt an urgent pressure to write. But yesterday afternoon when
he'd closed the door of his white bedroom and sat on the bed
to write, he couldn't think of how to start. Zachary Celtic had
spewed forth all sorts of garbagy ideas when he pitched the
book, but Marcus pushed those phrases from his mind, leaving
a blank slate. And so instead of writing, he'd spent ninety minutes
doing a line drawing of what he saw out his window—low lying
brush, a rutted dirt road, the pond in the distance.

Zachary Celtic was a friend of Nick Last Name Unknown.
Nick was the boyfriend of Marcus's English teacher, Ms. Marchese. Nick showed up at school a lot wearing gold rings and suits
paired with shiny ties, and since no kid at Benjamin N. Cardozo
High School was truly stupid, it was agreed upon that Nick was
in the mob. For this reason, everyone behaved in Ms. Marchese's
class and everyone, even the absolute lowlifes and basketball
players, turned in the assignments. Marcus liked English class
anyway, and he liked Ms. Marchese, because she was the only
teacher whose attitude toward Marcus didn't change after the
murders, and plus, she was always telling him he was a gifted
writer. So his guard wasn't up like it should have been, maybe,
when Nick stopped by at the end of class one day with a better-
looking guy in a better-looking suit and Ms. Marchese said that
the second guy was a book editor from Manhattan and he was
there to talk to Marcus.

Since October seventh, Marcus had fielded hundreds of
phone calls from reporters, producers, publicists—from New
York One, the *New York Post*, the *Daily News*, *The Geraldo Rivera*

Show. Everyone wanted the inside scoop on his mother. She was a black inner-city woman who had made it as far as the Ivy League—how did she end up a baby killer? In response to all publicity, Marcus's father had issued these directives. *Politely decline, then hang up!* If photographers come to the door, tell them through the chain that they will never get a picture inside the apartment. But something about the phrase "book editor in Manhattan" got past Marcus's radar. He thought, stupidly, that this guy was interested in him for a reason other than that he was a *murderer's son*. He thought the editor had shown up at their high school in Queens wearing a thousand-dollar suit (which, when Marcus asked, Zachary told him he'd gotten at Paul Stuart) because Marcus was a *gifted writer*.

Nick and Zachary Celtic invited Marcus to lunch. Although it was two-thirty and Marcus had already eaten lunch in the cafeteria at noon, he agreed to go along. They went to a diner down the street from the school, and after Nick made it clear that Zachary was picking up the check, Marcus went crazy ordering a roast beef club, fries with gravy, chocolate milkshake, lemon chiffon pie. Zachary asked Marcus all kinds of questions about how he liked school (*fine*), why he liked English class (*liked to read*), who his favorite writers were (*Salinger, Faulkner, John Edgar Wideman*). It was as Marcus was slipping into a food coma induced by this second lunch that Zachary announced that he was the true crime editor at Dome Books and that he wanted to offer Marcus thirty thousand dollars to write a first-person account of life with his mother, before and after the murders.

Marcus dropped his fork. He worried he might be sick—not because he was disgusted at this man for suggesting such a thing or disgusted at himself for falling for it—but because he'd eaten too much and the whole idea of a *first-person account* and *thirty thousand dollars* overwhelmed him.

"There are a lot of people who will pay to read your story," Zachary said. "I'm thinking of a real insider's view. Your mother as, like, an educated woman, a teacher and everything, and Princeton in her background, and then one day she just . . . you know . . . snaps." Zachary snapped his fingers with such force that both Marcus and Nick flinched. "Goes totally haywire on members of her own family. I'm thinking . . . you know . . . the blood-splattered sheet and how that made you feel. The dead bodies in your own apartment. The little girl in the shoes. God, everybody's going to want to read this. And there was sex involved, too, right? I mean, in your mother's testimony . . ."

Marcus belched, loudly, then worried once again that he might be sick. Zachary moved his hand like he was clearing smoke and said, "The mere *mention* of death row is going to have the citizens of this great city flocking to Barnes & Noble to buy your book. What it felt like to have your own mother, a pretty woman, too, facing the strap-down on the gurney, the long needle . . ."

It was Nick who finally stopped him. "You get to tell the story in your own words, kid. I'll bet that's something you've been itching to do."

Marcus wondered if Ms. Marchese told Nick about Marcus's isolation, his status as the class pariah. How he switched seats from the front row, where he could stretch out his legs, to the back row, where nobody could see him, throw shit at him, or mouth dirty words at the back of his head.

Marcus asked for time to think about it. Zachary held up his palms in agreement, saying, "Take as much time as you want. My offer stands." He slid a business card across the table towards

Marcus and an American Express Platinum card toward the check.

There was no one to ask for advice. Marcus couldn't ask his father because his father would say no, absolutely no. And Arch was dead, he'd been dead for five weeks by that point, and all of the protection and hope that Arch provided had vanished. As awful as Zachary Celtic was, Marcus sensed this book deal was a way out. It was thirty thousand dollars which, Zachary promised, he wouldn't have to pay back even if the book tanked. Thirty thousand dollars would buy a lot more college than Marcus could afford without writing a book. He'd seen the bank statement of the account his mother stashed her tutoring money in, Marcus's "college" fund. The balance was $1,204.82.

Finally, Nick's comment stuck with him. *You get to tell the story in your own words, kid.* That appealed to Marcus, even though he didn't know *how* he felt. It was possible that he still loved his mother, but that love was buried under a huge, crushing anger. Marcus was furious. Constance had murdered their way of life that, although not luxurious, had at least been tolerable. If he was coerced into write terrible things about her, she probably deserved it.

The following morning, Marcus called Zachary Celtic from a pay phone outside the school cafeteria and agreed to write the book. That day after English class, Zachary appeared with Nick, and Zachary handed Marcus an envelope containing the five hundred dollars.

"An advance on the advance," Zachary said. "You get me the first fifty pages and a complete synopsis by the end of the summer. I show it to my people. If they like it, the big money rolls your way."

Marcus accepted the envelope. Ms. Marchese looked away,

just like other teachers did when they saw a drug deal.

Now, Marcus lay on the beach, filled with turkey sandwich, buzzed on pilfered rum, and toasty in the sun—a better set of circumstances than he ever could have imagined for himself— except he should be up in his room *writing*. And now there was this problem of Winnie being mad at him. He should go up to the house and apologize before Garrett and Winnie formed a coalition and kicked Marcus off the island, like on that dumb-ass TV show. Or, worse, Winnie might tell Beth that Marcus was drinking. Frame him, then turn him in. That was the kind of thing that happened to black people all over America, getting blamed and busted for things that weren't their fault. Marcus could write a whole book on that topic alone. He could write a book about a lot of things, once he found his groove. He decided to nap, take a swim, and think about everything else in a little while.

Beth left the house for a run at noon. This was her new way of torturing her body, by running ten miles in the heat of the day. She put on a white hat, tucked a bottle of Evian into her fanny pack, and kicked off down the dusty road. Tonight was her dinner party and she'd spent the morning cleaning every nook and cranny of the house with a giant sponge from the car wash and a bucket of bleach and water. Garrett had looked at her stonily and she read his mind—she was going to a lot of trouble for her old boyfriend.

"The house needed to be cleaned anyway," she said, sounding more defensive than she intended. "It's been sitting here all winter collecting dust and mouse droppings."

Garrett shook his head and retreated to the deck. When had he gotten so *judgmental?* Well, she knew when. And he wasn't judgmental so much as protective. He was the man of the house, now, and thus it was his job to protect his women. Fine. She would let it go.

Since Arch died, running had become Beth's only pleasure. The motion placated her anxieties, the symbolism of it quenched her secret desire to run away. At home in New York, she ran four, five, six times around the Reservoir, or tackled the long, hilly route around Central Park. Both were cathartic, but nothing in the world was like running on Nantucket in the summertime. Beth ran past Miacomet Pond, which today was the deepest blue, bordered by tall dune grass that sheltered a clump of wild iris and red-winged blackbirds. It was beautiful here, and even in the heat, the air was fresh and clean. For the hour or two that she was gone, she didn't have to be a mother. She didn't have to be the problem-solver or the ultimate authority. Beth had discussed this sense of relief with Dr. Schau. It was wrong and unnatural, wasn't it, for a mother to want to escape her kids? And especially Beth. Beth loved her children to distraction. When they were born, she felt she was the luckiest person on the planet—she'd hit the birthing jackpot—a boy and a girl. Two perfect healthy babies, one of each. The entire first year of the kids' lives she and Arch would take a second every so often and marvel. How had they gotten so lucky? Why had they of all people been so blessed?

Beth adored the trappings of motherhood: the pacifiers, the wooden blocks, the Cheerios underfoot, the darling outfits (always matching boy/girl outfits until the twins went off to kindergarten.) She loved *Sesame Street* and playgrounds and *Pat the Bunny* and even nursing the kids when they had earaches and the chicken pox. Other mothers complained, secretly, that kids took up so much time, that they left the house a mess—fingerprints on the TV screen, and yes, Cheerios underfoot—that they sucked the intelligence out of everyday life. These complaints baffled Beth. She didn't have a job outside of the home, maybe that was it, but she never expected Winnie and Garrett to appreciate Chagall or Bizet at age three. She didn't care that they took all her time—what, she wondered, could she possibly be doing that would be more worthwhile?

As the kids grew, life got more interesting. There were friends and multiplication tables and soccer. Trips to the dentist, to the Bronx Zoo, to Wollman Rink for ice skating every Christmas Eve. Then high school—advance placement classes, soccer team (Garrett), swim team (Winnie), phone calls, proms, learner's permits.

Beth loved it all. Yes, she did.

But when Arch died, one of the many, many things that changed was the way she felt about her children. It wasn't that she loved them less—if anything, she loved them more. Especially since they were dangerously close to leaving home; a year from now, they'd be headed for college. What Beth felt was just an occasional sense of relief—when they walked out the door in the morning to go to school, for example. Dr. Schau assured her it was perfectly normal: Beth was alone now, her job was doubly hard. She'd lost not only her husband but her coparent, and so all the duties she once shared with Arch now fell to her alone. It was perfectly normal to feel relief at escaping the pressure, if only for a little while.

Beth ran all the way to Madaket, the hamlet at the western

tip of the island. She stopped at the drawbridge that looked out over Madaket Harbor and drank her bottle of water, slowly, cautiously, to avoid getting cramps. There were sailboats and red-and-white buoys bouncing gently in the breeze. Beth was dripping with sweat. She worried that she'd come too far and wouldn't make it home.

But the way home was into the wind and that cooled Beth off somewhat, and the water helped, and she allowed herself to think about the dinner that night. David Ronan was going to set foot in her house for the first time since August 31, 1979, when Beth's father threw him out. That morning was such ancient history, such a drop in the ocean by now, and yet it caused Beth's chest to contract with guilt. The best thing was to have this dinner and put the past behind them.

Beth made it all the way back to where the road turned to dirt before she had to stop and walk. She judged it to be almost two o'clock and she was parched. The Evian bottle had a quarter inch of water left, enough to get the dusty film out of her mouth. She'd run eleven or twelve miles. She felt light, clean, and completely spent.

A car rumbled up behind her, a horn beeped. She stepped into the tall grass to let the car pass, but when she turned around, she saw it wasn't a car and it wasn't passing. It was David Ronan in his Island Painting van idling there in the road, window down.

"Hi," he said.

"Hi." Beth wiped her forehead. Well, here was the worst possible luck. She was slick with sweat and coated with dirt and certainly she stank to high heaven. Not to mention her hair. "Are you . . . working out here? You have a job out here?" Her teeth were gritty.

"No, actually, I was headed to your house. I need to talk to you."

"Oh, really? Why?" Though Beth feared she knew: Rosie didn't want to come to dinner. And who could blame her? Especially with Arch gone. It would be a sadly uneven equation; Beth had considered this numerous times since leaving the Stop & Shop on Tuesday.

"I didn't think it was fair to show up tonight without telling you something first," David said. "There's something I have to explain."

Beth looked nervously in both directions. No one was coming. She remembered from their conversation at the store that there was something David wanted to explain, but she hadn't even let herself venture a guess. And now here was David tracking her down because clearly whatever it was couldn't wait.

David motioned for her to come closer, which was not something she was particularly anxious to do. But she obeyed and stood only inches from his open window. She glanced into his van: it was messy with clipboards and newspapers and a couple of wadded-up bags from Henry's. He was listening to NPR. Then Beth caught sight of something on the dashboard—a yellow stick-'em on which a single word was written "Beth." Her name was stuck to his dashboard right where he could see it. Her name.

"Rosie's not coming to dinner," David said.

As Beth suspected. A host of indignations rose in her chest: Rosie was being childish, jealous, unreasonable. But she said, simply, "Oh?"

David turned down the radio and squinted out the windshield. His sunglasses hung around his neck on a Croakie. He wore a blue chambray shirt and navy blue shorts, the same black flip-flops. Beth was amazed at how clean he looked even though he was in the painting business. He was the owner, of course; Beth was pretty sure he didn't go near any actual paint.

"Rosie left," he said.

"What?"

"Rosie left. She left me and the girls."

Beth pushed the lock button of David's door down, then pulled it back up again. She heard an approaching engine and saw a car coming toward them.

"Oh, shit," she said.

The other car slowed to a stop, waiting for Beth to move, but she could do nothing more than grind the soles of her Nikes into the dirt and will the road to swallow her up. She should never have asked David for dinner. She should have let him go on his merry way and forgotten all about him. She should have kept him safely in her past where he belonged—yet now, here he was, most definitely occupying her present. Right now—and tonight, without a wife.

"Shit," Beth said again. The driver of the other car hit his horn then shrugged at Beth as if to say, *What, exactly, would you like me to do?*

"Will you get in?" David said. "Please? So we can talk?"

"Get into your van?" She tried to swallow but the inside of her mouth was like crumbling plaster. "Don't you have work?"

"Work can wait. Hop in."

Beth saw she had no choice. She ran around and climbed in the passenger side. She discovered a bottle of water hidden underneath *The Inquirer & Mirror.* This was a very small positive.

"Mind if I have a swig?" she asked. "I'm dying of thirst."

"Help yourself." David said. "Sorry I don't have anything stronger." He started to drive. "Shall we go to your house?"

"No," Beth said. "No, no. Let's . . . well, let's drive around or park somewhere." She was sorry as soon as she said "park somewhere," because it brought back memories of when she and David had parked at the beach right up the road and made love in the sand. "Let's drive around."

He stepped on the gas and Beth appreciated the cool wind through her window. She finished the entire bottle of water, trying not to panic. Trying not to think of Garrett. Trying not to bombard David with questions, the most obvious being, *Why didn't you just tell me at the store?*

"So," David said.

"So," Beth said. "So Rosie left. Are you going to tell me what happened?"

"She moved to the Cape after Christmas. She said the island was suffocating her. It was too small, too limited, and suddenly after eighteen years of living here, not at all what she wanted. And she said I was emotionally cruel."

"Emotionally cruel?"

"That's what she said."

"What about the girls?"

"Rosie didn't want to take the girls. She said they were happy in school and that she could be an equally effective mother from the Cape. If not more so." David spoke the words like a robot, like he'd committed them to memory then spoken them on a hundred separate occasions. "She rented a house in Wellfleet, which is to say, *I* rented a house, and she started a catering company, which is to say, *I* started the catering company, and I fly the girls over whenever their hearts desire. The three of them have a fine time, shopping and going to movies and spending my money in any other way they can find."

"A catering company," Beth said. "That makes sense. So the girls are all right with this, then?"

"They appear to be. Piper just turned seventeen, and she's developed a very independent, very empowered personality. She's thrilled that her mother has broken free of male domination."

"Oh," Beth said. "What about the younger one?"

"Peyton still loves me the best, thank God," David said. "But she wouldn't admit it in front of her mother or her sister. She's not brave enough. She's not brave at all."

"How old is Peyton?"

"Thirteen."

"I can't believe you and Rosie split," Beth said. "I just can't believe it." This was dangerous news. Beth stared at the stick 'em on the dashboard, wishing for clarity. David Ronan had split from his wife, and now he was driving around Nantucket with Beth's name on his dashboard. "How are you doing?" she asked. "Are you . . . are you angry?"

"Shit, yeah, I'm angry," David said. "And heartbroken and discouraged and deeply incredulous. I loved Rosie. She saved my life."

This comment, Beth knew, was aimed at her. What David really meant was: *Rosie saved me from you.* Beth heard the old pain, the old intensity in David's voice and she knew where the conversation was headed if she didn't stop it—blame for Rosie that was really blame for Beth. The first woman who'd left him.

"We'll have to cancel dinner," Beth said, cringing at how hardhearted, not to mention *rude*, that sounded. But the whole point had been to invite the Ronan *family*. To prove to the kids and Beth herself, and Arch, wherever he was, that this was just a normal friendship.

"I already told the girls. They're excited to come. But I guess you don't want us now? I hope you don't think I'm on the prowl."

"No, I never—"

"My girls," he said. "They think this is a date, even though I *assured* them it's not. I mean, I told them about your husband. But I haven't been out, anywhere, well, in six months, so they're hopeful." He smiled. "They want me to move on. I explained to them that I'm not ready to move on, and that even if I were, *you* weren't ready to move on." He glanced at her. "I'm embarrassed telling you all this. I came to find you because I knew it was unfair to spring it on you tonight. So we won't come."

The world's most awkward situation. What should she *do*? If she disinvited David, what did *that* say? That she didn't trust herself? That it wasn't okay for two old friends to have dinner together? "Forgive me," Beth said. "It's just that this took me by surprise. You could have told me at the store."

David tucked his chin guiltily. "You seemed upset at the store," he said. "About Arch, I mean. I didn't want to burden you with my problems."

"It wouldn't have been a burden," Beth said. "It would have been useful information."

"I guess subconsciously I wanted to come to dinner, and so that's why I didn't tell you," David said. "Since Rosie left, the whole island has treated me like an untouchable."

"You're not an untouchable."

David held out his hand. "Prove it."

Beth stared at his hand, the knobby knuckles, the golden

hairs, the clean, clipped nails. How many years had passed since she'd noticed David's hands?

She squeezed David's pinky. "I'm sorry Rosie left."

"Thanks. It makes me feel better to hear that opinion expressed, even by a summer person."

Beth smirked. She'd only spent ten minutes in David's presence and already they'd resumed their old roles. Year-rounder versus summer person. How old would they have to be before they rose above. "I hereby cancel my cancellation," she said. "Please come to dinner. I'd like to meet your girls and it'll be good for Winnie and Garrett. Just come at seven and we'll have a good time." *A good time.* It sounded so refreshing that Beth almost believed it was possible. "But don't bring me flowers or anything."

"No purple cosmos?" he said.

That hit too close to home. Beth shut her eyes, remembering the flowers wilting in her hand because she held them so tightly. They left golden dust on her skin.

"I'm sorry, Beth," he said.

"You don't know what I'm like these days," she said. "Boiled turnips can make me cry." She wiped her eyes. "Just take me home. I need to shower. Take a nap. And I don't want the kids worrying about where I am."

They drove to her house in silence, and then Beth leapt from the van. She needed David to drive away before anyone saw him. "I'll expect you at seven," she said.

"You're sure about this?" he said.

"I'm sure."

He waved. "Looking forward to it."

As Beth headed inside, she noticed the mail basket was full.

Already, some of her mail had been forwarded from New York. There were two bills, a credit card solicitation addressed to Archer Newton, and a letter for Marcus. The return address was 247 Harris Road, Bedford Hills, New York. It was a letter from Constance Tyler.

※

Garrett watched his mother closely from the minute she walked in the door from her run. The first thing she did was to look in the hallway mirror—the one that she and Uncle Danny and Uncle Scott had decorated with scallop shells in their youth—and groan.

"I look like a dirt sandwich," she said.

Although she hadn't acknowledged him, Garrett assumed the comment was for his benefit, and that he was expected to refute it.

"What do you care what you look like?" he said.

She turned, apparently surprised to see him there, sitting at the kitchen table, eating a lunch that he'd made himself. It might seem a small detail, but Garrett was keeping track of the fact that three days into the summer, neither his mother nor Winnie had offered to make him lunch, although they both fell over themselves to prepare food for Marcus.

"Garrett," she said. "It's two-thirty."

"So?"

"So, don't you think it's a little late to be eating such a big lunch? We're having dinner at seven."

As if he were likely to forget "the dinner," which, judging by the way his mother cleaned this morning, was a bigger event than she originally promised.

"I'll manage," he said.

As his mother walked toward him, he saw that she was holding some envelopes. She waved one in the air. "Where's Marcus?"

"I have no idea," Garrett said, though he had every idea. Marcus was on the beach. Alone. Winnie had come running up about
forty-five minutes earlier in a state. It seemed Marcus had given
Winnie some flak about not eating. *As if my digestive tract is his
concern,* Winnie said in this bitchy, conspiratorial way, nudging
Garrett to agree with her. Although Garrett wanted nothing
more than to gang up on Marcus, it wasn't going to be for that
reason. In this instance, Marcus was right: Winnie needed to eat.
Garrett said as much to Winnie and she stomped up the stairs,
her empty stomach clenched in fury against him.

"Well, can you find him for me, please?" Beth said. "There's a
letter for him."

"I think he's on the beach," Garrett said. "He can read it when
he comes up."

"It's a letter from Constance," Beth said. "It can't wait."

There was faulty logic there somewhere, but clearly this letter
had put ants in his mother's pants and so Garrett walked out
onto the deck and was about to yell down to the beach when
he saw Marcus marching up the rickety stairs, loaded down like
a pack mule with all the beach stuff—towels, beach bag, and
Winnie's chaise lounge. Once Marcus reached the deck, he
dropped the stuff and rubbed his eyes.

"Whoa," he said. "I fell asleep down there."

Garrett studied him. He heard the clink of glasses in the
beach bag and realized that Marcus and Winnie had been drinking. The Malibu, probably. How easy it would be to bust this
kid, Garrett thought. He shook his head. "Mom has a letter for
you. From Constance."

Not even the faintest glimmer of interest crossed Marcus's

face. "Okay, man, thanks." He headed for the outdoor shower and Garrett watched him step in and close the door. Then he heard the water. Garrett returned to the kitchen where his mother was drinking straight from the big bottle of purple Gatorade.

"Marcus is in the shower," Garrett said.

Beth paused in her drinking. "Did you tell him about the letter?"

"Of course. I guess it can wait after all."

"Hmmpf," Beth said. Garrett noticed her staring at the envelope, and he moved closer to inspect it. A regular number ten business envelope addressed in blue ink. The return address said, "247 Harris Road, Bedford Hills, New York," as if this were a domestic street address and not the address of the largest women's correctional facility in the state. The penmanship was neat, pretty even, and European, like the handwriting of Garrett's French teacher, Mr. Alevain. Of course, Constance Tyler was no dummy. She'd gone to Princeton, and that was how Garrett's father got involved in all this in the first place.

Although the envelope was unremarkable in every way, it had power, and Garrett found himself wondering what the letter might say. On the one hand, there was so much to explain, but on the other, how could mere language convey the range of emotions Constance Tyler might be experiencing when she knew she would never be free again? She would never lie on a beach, ride a bike, dip her foot in the ocean. Garrett picked up the envelope and held it to the window trying to make out a word or two, and naturally, as soon as he gave in to this temptation, Marcus stepped into the kitchen, one beach towel wrapped around his waist, one wrapped around his head like a turban.

Except for these two towels, Marcus was naked—dark and muscular and imposing, like some two-hundred-year-old tree.

He nodded. "That my letter?"

Beth spoke up. She, too, had an impulse to scrutinize the letter, though it was none of hers or Garrett's business. "It's from Constance."

Marcus snatched the letter from Garrett's fingers. "All right, then," he said, and he disappeared upstairs.

❧

At five o'clock, Garrett was slumped in the only comfortable chair in the house, reading. The chair was a bona fide La-Z-Boy recliner upholstered with worn fawn-colored velour; Garrett's grandfather had brought it home one summer from the dump, and although all the women complained that it was an eyesore and smelled like mildew, they kept it around because it was so comfortable. Garrett was reading *Franny and Zooey*, the first book on his required summer reading list. He'd reached the part where Zooey was soaking in the bathtub reading a letter wishing that his mother would leave him alone. Garrett paused for a minute, identifying with Zooey's frustration with Bessie Glass, except Garrett was frustrated by too little attention from his mother, or the wrong kind of attention. Something about his mother was really bugging him, although Garrett couldn't put it into words. If Garrett were the one taking a two-hour bath, for example, Beth would knock on the door and explain that since Garrett was the man of the house now, it was his responsibility to offer the same hot bath to Marcus. Garrett honestly couldn't believe that Marcus was here this summer. After all, if it weren't for Marcus's mother, Arch would still be alive. Garrett mentioned this glaring fact at one of their family therapy sessions, but Dr. Schau told him that was a small person's point of view. Constance Tyler didn't kill Arch, she said, he died by accident. It was nobody's fault.

Garrett rested the open book on his chest and closed his eyes. It was embarrassing that he'd even found time to start his required reading. He needed to get a life.

Suddenly, he heard his mother. "This is *going* to be a low-key affair." She said this as if trying to convince someone—herself, he supposed, or anyone else who might be listening. The ghost of his father, maybe. Garrett opened his eyes to see Beth come down the stairs wearing jeans, a pale pink T-shirt, and a pair of flip-flops. Her hair was still wet, and as she grew closer to him he caught the scent of her lotion. "I am *not* going to a lot of trouble."

"Okay," Garrett mumbled. "Whatever you say."

"Oh, *Garrett*," she said. She stopped at the hall mirror and inspected her face closely, much the way Garrett himself did when he was worried about acne. "Will you please just participate here? Will you play along?"

He dog-eared the page of his book and climbed out of the recliner. "Sure," he said. "What can I do?"

Beth turned to him with narrowed eyes, suspicious of his sudden willingness. "Well," she said. "You can help me in the kitchen."

It was on the tip of Garrett's tongue to ask *Where's Winnie? Where's Marcus? Why can't they help?* But he kept quiet and followed his mother.

Garrett had helped with his parents' dinner parties for years, and he knew from looking at the raw ingredients that tonight was a big deal disguised to look like no big deal. His mother pulled a bag of jumbo shrimp out of the fridge—all peeled and deveined and steamed to a lurid pink. At least fifty dollars worth of shrimp, which his mother shook out of the bag onto a hand painted platter that one of Garrett's cousins had made on a rainy day. She took a bottle of cocktail sauce out of the fridge, then grinned at Garrett sheepishly and said, "I think I'll doctor this a little." She proceeded to mix in mayonnaise, horseradish, lemon juice, and a generous splash from the vodka bottle she kept in the freezer. "We have chives, I think," she said. "For a garnish."

"What do you want me to do?" Garrett asked. "You need help, right? When did you go to the fish store?"

"This morning before you got up," she admitted. "Why don't you set the table."

"Okay," he said. "How many of us are there again?"

Beth paused. "Eight, right? Isn't that right? Set the table for eight people. The dining room table."

"Do we have eight of everything?" he asked.

"If not, make do," Beth said. "This is no big deal. The world won't end if someone is short a steak knife."

"Obviously not," Garrett said. He checked a few drawers and found five disintegrating straw place mats and three green plastic place mats that were meant to resemble large cabbage roses. He laid these out on the dining room table, pleased by how awful they looked. As he headed back to the kitchen to find napkins, he bumped into Beth. She eyed the table over his shoulder.

"No, Garrett, sorry," she said. "Those are hideous. I brought the place mats from home, the blue ones, and the napkins. They're in one of the plastic bags in the pantry."

"But you said—"

"Thanks, sweetie." She collected the place mats quickly, like a poker player who didn't want anyone to see her losing hand. "These are going right into the trash."

For the next hour, Garrett watched Beth break all her promises. The blue linen place mats and matching floral napkins went on the table along with the "good," meaning unchipped, china, three balloon wineglasses for the adults, and a bouquet of daisies and bachelor buttons that Beth had somehow found time to purchase at Bartlett Farm. Beth asked him to wash the silverware before he put it on the table, even though it was already clean. As Garrett stood at the sink, he catalogued all the effort that went into the dinner. The thick steaks seasoned with salt and pepper, the baking potatoes scrubbed and nestled in foil, the asparagus trimmed and drizzled with the special olive oil from Zabar's. The butter brought to room temperature, the sour cream garnished with chives, and while his mother was at it, a little crumbled bacon.

It was the smell of bacon, maybe, that lured Marcus down from his room.

"What's going on in here?" he asked.

"Don't you remember, Marcus?" Beth said. "We're having dinner guests."

"Who?"

"Old friends of mine," Beth said. "And their kids. Two girls. A little younger than you."

"Okay," Marcus said. "Can I help?"

"Where's Winnie?" Beth said. "It's five minutes to seven. They'll be here soon."

"Her door was closed," Marcus said. "She must be napping."

Beth let out a very long stream of air and Garrett knew this meant she was trying to hold back her tears. He wanted to yell at her. It was a terrible idea to throw this dinner party, what was she trying to prove, anyway? What made her think she could act like a happy, normal person? But as angry as Garrett was with Beth, he felt sorry for her, too. Her pain was as real as his own and Winnie's; it was immense and unwieldy and it had a deeper element—she had lost the man she was in love with. Dr. Schau had gone over this with Garrett many times: losing a spouse was different, and yes, worse, than losing a parent.

"I'll go get her," Garrett conceded.

"Thank you," Beth said. "Marcus, would you like a Coke?"

Garrett marched upstairs and tapped lightly on Winnie's door.

"Go away," she said.

"Winnifred!" Garrett said in his most playful falsetto. "Winnifred, open the door this instant!"

"Fuck off, Garrett," she said.

Garrett cracked open the door. It was a much-disdained fact that none of the doors in Horizon had a working lock. Winnie was curled up on her narrow bed wearing her sweatshirt and a pair of jean shorts.

"You have to come downstairs," he said. He paused, then decided to try one of their father's favorite jokes. "We're having people for dinner."

Winnie sat up. She'd been crying, of course, but she gave him a tiny smile. "I hope they taste good," she said.

For the first time in a long time, Garrett felt a connection with his sister. No matter what happened with their mother, the two of them could keep their father's spirit alive. "I'm serious. Mom wants you to come down."

"Not a chance," Winnie said. "I'm not hungry and I don't want to meet anyone new."

"Me either," Garrett admitted.

"Teenage girls. Yuck. Marcus will probably fall in love with one of them."

This was something Garrett hadn't considered. He figured the daughters would be awkward and gangly, with braces and zits. But maybe Marcus would have the hots for one of them and then Garrett could stop worrying about Marcus and Winnie.

"Okay," he said. "I'll tell Mom you don't feel well."

"Thanks," Winnie said, snuggling back down into her pillow. "You're my best friend, you know that?"

"Yeah," Garrett said. This little bit of affirmation from his sister made him happier than it should have. He really needed to get a life.

The doorbell rang as Garrett was coming down the stairs. Beth shouted, "Garrett, would you let our guests in, please?" He cursed to himself and considered running back upstairs to hide with Winnie in her room. His newly discovered sense of optimism dissolved. He dreaded opening the door.

But open it he did, to find a man and two girls.

"You must be Garrett," the man said. He thrust a bottle in a brown paper bag into Garrett's hands, then stepped aside and ushered the girls in. "I'm David Ronan, and these are my daughters, Piper and Peyton."

"Hi," Garrett heard himself say. His mind was grappling with two equally alarming facts. The first was that the mother, the wife, Mrs. Whomever, didn't seem to be present—Garrett glanced out toward their car, a silver Dodge Dakota pickup, but no, she wasn't lagging behind carrying a pie or anything. This was it: just the man and two girls. Garrett had been duped. This was a date for his mother, after all. But before he could deal with that thought, he needed to contend with the other pressing fact, which was that one of the girls, the older, taller one, was a complete knockout. As in, one of the hottest chicks Garrett had ever seen. "Hi," he said, right into the girl's face. "I'm Garrett Newton."

"Piper," she said. She had long light brown hair and green eyes and what looked to be an incredible body. She wore a tank top and tight white shorts and sandals with cork heels. She had two silver hoops in her right ear, and a diamond stud in her nose. She was a goddess. Beth appeared in the hallway and gushed, "Welcome to Horizon, let's go out on the deck, we'll watch the sun set, can I get you all something to drink?" Garrett nearly hugged his mother, despite the fact that she'd been lying to him about the purpose of this dinner for days.

Thank you, he thought, thank you for inviting this beautiful person to our house. He loved the way Piper moved down the hall, flipping back her hair, shaking Beth's hand, saying "Thanks for inviting us, Beth. It was about time Daddy got out of the house."

"I'm glad you could come," Beth said. She felt Garrett's judgmental gaze boring into her back and she tried to keep her voice light and steady. "It's no big deal tonight. Just a casual cookout."

Garrett remained in the hallway holding the bottle of wine while everyone else moved out to the deck. He needed a minute alone. He watched Marcus shake hands with Piper, then the other girl, who was also pretty, but younger. He watched Marcus and David shake hands. Then he watched Beth and David shake hands and kiss on the sides of their mouths. These greetings took a few minutes, then everyone seemed to appreciate the view, and

Garrett heard Beth taking drink orders. The shrimp was on the table outside and Piper was the first to help herself.

"I'm absolutely *famished*," Garrett heard her say, and he thought how that word, "famished," would have sounded phony if anyone else had said it, but when Piper said it, it sounded retro and cool. Famished.

Beth stepped into the kitchen and Garrett moved toward her holding out the bottle of wine.

"They brought this," he said.

"David just told me he lets Piper have a glass of wine at dinner parties," Beth said. "Would *you* like a glass of wine?"

"Yeah," Garrett said.

Beth took the bottle from him and brought another bottle out of the fridge. The Ronans had only been here two minutes and already she'd resorted to bribery. Arch had never approved of the twins drinking—not even watered-down wine at a fancy dinner. "We won't overdo it though, okay?"

"Okay."

Then, suddenly, Beth sensed something wrong. She checked her jeans pockets as though she'd misplaced her wallet. "Where's your sister?"

"Upstairs. She's sick."

"Sick?"

"Yeah."

They both paused for a minute, thinking the same thing: Winnie was sick, very sick, but not in a way that should keep her from this dinner party. Garrett could tell by the liberal way his mother poured the wine that she was going to let it go. She handed Garrett two glasses to carry out. "Let's go socialize," she said.

The world was treating him fairly again. That was what Garrett thought as he sat on the end of a chaise lounge at Piper Ronan's feet, drinking wine, watching the sun set from the deck of his family's summer home. The party had split up into three conversations: David chatted with Marcus, Beth talked to the younger daughter, Peyton, and that left Garrett to hang out with Piper, who immediately started asking him what it was like to live in Manhattan. It must be cool, she said, to actually *live* in the same city with the Empire State Building and Greenwich Village. The Metropolitan Museum of Art and the Guggenheim *and* Soho. Garrett felt like a rock star. The wine went right to his head.

"Yeah, it's okay," he said. "I mean, I was born there so I don't know what's it's like to live anywhere else. Except here, I guess, in the summer."

"Do you take cabs all the time?" Piper asked. "Do you take a cab to school?"

"I walk to school," Garrett said. "Danforth's on the Upper East Side, where I live."

"Upper East Side," Piper said. "God, I just *love* the way that sounds! I can't wait until I graduate from college. I'm moving to Manhattan. What about clubbing? Do you go clubbing?"

"Sometimes," Garrett said. "But that scene gets old pretty quick. There are long lines and the people are fake, and you come home smelling like smoke."

"Oh," she said. She sounded crestfallen. "Really?"

He took a long moment to drink some wine. "Yeah. But some great bands play in the city. At Roseland and Irving Plaza. I saw Dave Matthews last year, and Fishbone."

Piper lay back in the chaise and waved her wineglass in the direction of her father. "Save your money, Daddy!" she said. "I'm headed for the Big Apple!"

David groaned. Garrett looked at Piper's ankles and let his eyes glide up her legs, over her tight shorts, the six inches of exposed midriff to her breasts, which he knew better than to stare at for too long, to her face. She was smiling at him.

"Want to go for a walk on the beach later?" she asked.

"Yeah," he said. The wine made him feel like he was levitating. "Definitely, yeah."

"There it goes!" Beth cried out. She leaned over the railing and pointed at the sun, which was just about to sink into the ocean. Beth led them in a round of applause. "Garrett, will you light the grill?" she asked. "It's getting time to eat."

❧

Beth controlled the dinner conversation like it was a big, un-wieldy bus that she had to keep on safe roads: What was it like to live on Nantucket year-round? How did Peyton like school? Where was Piper applying to college? Every time Piper opened her mouth, Garrett stopped chewing and listened.

"I'm only applying to three schools," she said. "BU is my safety, BC is my probable, and Harvard is my reach."

"Boston schools," Beth said.

"I'm a city person. I wanted to apply in Manhattan, but Dad said no."

Garrett looked at David Ronan. He was busy digging every last bit of potato out of the skin. He took a sip of wine and cleared his throat. "I have to keep the girls close otherwise they'll never come see me and I'll be left alone."

"Where's your wife?"

Everyone at the table stopped eating, or maybe it just seemed that way to Garrett who sat in utter confusion. The words had been right there in his brain, in his mouth, but he never would have had the guts to speak them aloud. No, it was Marcus who'd asked. Marcus who had already finished every bite of food on his plate and who was reaching for more salad had asked the question. *Where's your wife?*

Quietly, David said, "She's on the Cape."

Marcus loaded his plate with salad. "The Cape?"

"Cape Cod," Beth said.

"We're separated," David said.

"My mom is a caterer now." This came from Peyton, the younger girl, who, Garrett noticed, had a piece of meat stuck in the front of her braces. It was the first thing Peyton had said at dinner other than "please" and "thank you." "She makes little quiches."

"She makes a lot more than just quiches, Peyton," Piper said. "She's chosen to pursue her life's dream, and that's one of the beauties of living in this country. Freedom to change your life if you don't like the way it's going."

"Freedom to leave your husband and children if that's what your heart desires," David said. Garrett watched him empty the contents of the wine bottle into his glass and then carry the empty bottle into the kitchen. "Shall we open the bottle I brought?" he asked Beth.

Beth was cutting her steak into tiny pieces and moving them around her plate, a trick she'd learned from Winnie, to make it look like she'd been eating. She turned her head in David's direction; her cheeks were hot. "It's on the counter."

"Maybe you shouldn't drink any more, Dad," Piper said.

"Maybe you should keep your opinions to yourself, young lady," David said.

"God, you're being so confrontational, I can't believe you." Piper touched the diamond stud in her nose with her pinky finger. "You're angry at Mom and it's causing you to drink too much. Or maybe," she said, "maybe you're drinking too much because you're nervous about seeing Beth."

Garrett's stomach flipped. He put down his knife and fork with a clang. "May I be excused?"

Piper's eyebrows shot up. "Did my saying that *upset* you?"

David came back into the dining room, pulling the cork from his bottle of wine. "This is a Bordeaux," David said to Beth as he filled her empty glass. "I hope you like it." He threw a killer look at Piper. "You, my dear, aren't making many friends at this table."

Peyton, too, dropped her utensils abruptly and held her face in her hands. "She does this all the time."

"I do *what* all the time?" Piper demanded.

"Make trouble for Daddy."

"I wasn't making any trouble," Piper said. "I was merely defending our mother and her choices. She's running her own *business*, for God's sake."

Suddenly, Marcus spoke up. "It's my fault," he said. "I shouldn't have asked."

"It's not your fault, Marcus," Beth said, and this made Garrett angrier than anything else that had been said all evening. Of course his mother would jump to Marcus's aid, and *of course* nothing was Marcus's fault, even when it was.

Beth tried to change the subject. The bus was swerving. "We have ice cream for dessert," she said. "Ben & Jerry's."

"I've lost my appetite," Piper said.

"You're being rude," David said. "I expected more from you."

Piper flipped her hair in response. "I'm only playing the role you cast me in," she said. "The difficult child? I hear you say so all the time."

"That's enough, Piper," David said and Garrett could tell he meant business. Garrett's own father never raised his voice; when Arch got angry he became cool and polite in a way that let you know you'd disappointed him, and then you'd be willing to cut off your left hand to make him talk and joke with you again.

Piper stood. "Garrett and I are going for a walk on the beach," she said, and with that, she stormed through the kitchen and out onto the deck.

Garrett remained in his chair, returning the stares of the other people at the table: Peyton, Marcus, David, his mother.

"Go ahead," Beth said.

He almost stayed put just to spite her—he didn't need his mother's permission to walk on the beach—but his desire to be outside with Piper overwhelmed him. He went.

She was smoking a cigarette and he wondered where she'd gotten it until he noticed a jean jacket lying across a chair and he figured there must be cigarettes and a lighter in the pocket. She was sucking on the cigarette in an angry way, like the young, jilted, male lover in an old movie, and Garrett understood it was high drama for his benefit.

"I can't stand it when people smoke," he said.

"Why should I care what you think?"

"You shouldn't care," he said.

"I don't."

"Fine. Do you really want to go for a walk or were you just using me as an excuse to leave the house?"

"I'll walk."

"If you're walking with me, please put out the cigarette."

She stabbed it on the sole of her sandal and flicked it down into the dune grass. "There."

"Yeah, except you littered."

"So call the police."

"You *are* difficult," Garrett said.

"As advertised," she said.

⁂

At home, in New York, Garrett had success with girls, mostly because they weren't important to him. Soccer was important, his grades were important, and his friends were important—and by putting these things first, Garrett found he could have any girlfriend he wanted. Girls loved to sit on the sidelines at Van Cortland Park watching him play striker, they loved it when he left beer parties early because he had a math quiz the next day. Morgan, Priscilla, Brooke—they all went out with him whenever he asked and allowed him to touch their bodies in various ways. He'd lost his virginity the previous Christmas to a girl named Anna, who was a freshman at Columbia. He met her at Lowe Library while he was doing special research for a paper on Blaise Pascal; she showed Garrett how to access the university computer system, then later invited him back to her room and once they started making out, Garrett discovered he couldn't stop and she didn't force him to. His father had given him condoms for his sixteenth birthday and made Garrett promise to always use them. "I don't want anything to happen to you or anyone you're close to," he said.

Garrett didn't see Anna again—she went home to Pough-keepsie for Christmas break and never resurfaced.

Garrett didn't tell his father that he lost his virginity; he was too embarrassed.

He got an A on the Pascal paper.

❧

As Garrett led Piper down the steep staircase to the beach, he felt his attitude about girls changing. Maybe because this girl was so beautiful and spoke to her father with exactly the same rage that Garrett felt for his mother. He wanted this girl. That was what he thought as they took their shoes off and stepped on the cold sand.

There was no moon, but there were millions of stars. Garrett craned his neck to get a good look.

"I never see stars like this," he said. "In New York, the sky is pink at night."

Piper pulled her jean jacket close to her body. "I can't wait to go away to college. I can't wait to get off this rock."

"You were hard on your dad," Garrett said.

"He drives me nuts."

"Which way do you want to walk?" Garrett asked.

She pointed to the left. The beach was dark—only a couple of houses along the bluff had lights on—and the ocean pounded to their right. Garrett felt pleasantly buzzed from the wine, pleasantly buzzed from the way Piper had managed to set them free from the dinner party. He felt bold and confident—he took Piper's hand, and she let him. They walked, but the only part of his body that Garrett could feel was his hand. He was so consumed by it that he couldn't think of a single thing to say.

"Do you have a girlfriend?" Piper asked him.

"Not right now," he said. "What about you?"

"I have lots of girlfriends." She giggled.

He tightened his grip on her fingers. "Boyfriend?"

"Sort of."

"Oh."

"I'm breaking up with him tomorrow."

"How come?" Garrett said.

"Because I met you," she said.

Garrett sent a message to his father, whom he sometimes thought of as a satellite dish in the sky, always there to receive information. *Are you listening to this?*

"He's just a stupid football player, anyway," Piper said. "He's never been anywhere."

Garrett imagined the hulking, unsophisticated brute who was currently Piper's boyfriend. Garrett knew the type—the kind of guy who would pound Garrett into the sand like a horseshoe stake if he knew Garrett was holding Piper's hand right now.

"If you could go anywhere in the world," he asked. "where would you go?"

"I already said, New York City."

Garrett had been hoping for a more imaginative answer. "I want to go to Australia. I've wanted to go there ever since I was, like, six years old. I'm going to ask my mom to let me travel after I graduate from high school. I might not go to college right away."

"Really?" she said.

Garrett could tell she thought that was crazy. "I'm different," he said. "My father used to tell me I thought outside the box."

She coughed a hacky, smoker's cough. "Your dad died, right?"

The question took Garrett by surprise and he seized up with

panic. He hadn't encountered very many kids his age who wanted to talk about what happened to his father. Everyone knew, of course. Practically the entire student body of Danforth attended the memorial service. But no one wanted to talk to Garrett about the loss, not even his good friends. The other kids were afraid to talk about it and that made Garrett afraid. He felt that losing his father, that being *fatherless*, was something to be ashamed of.

"Right. My dad died."

"In a plane crash?"

"Yep."

Piper raised her face to the night sky, giving Garrett a view of her beautiful throat. "I can't imagine how awful that would be. Even though I get angry at my dad, I want him alive. If anything ever happened to him or my mom, I'd go crazy."

"Yeah," Garrett said. "My sister's pretty much gone crazy. That's why she wasn't at dinner. We have to keep her locked in her room."

Piper stopped. "Oh, God," she said. "You're kidding."

"Yeah," he said. "I am."

She swatted his arm and walked on. "How has it changed you? Losing a parent, I mean."

It was an insightful question, and one he'd never been asked. How to explain? It was as if his seventeenth year were a bridge that had broken in half. His old life, his life before his father died, was on one side of the bridge, and now he found himself standing on the other side, with no choice but to move forward. What else could he say? He felt jaded now, hardened. The things that other kids worried about—grades, for example, or clothes, or the score of a soccer game—seemed inconsequential. In some

sense, losing his father allowed Garrett to see what was important. This moment, right now, was important. Garrett stopped
and slipped his hands inside of Piper's jean jacket so that he was
touching the bare skin under her rib cage. Her skin was warm;
she was radiating heat. Garrett had no clue where he was finding
the courage to touch Piper.

"I'm a difficult child, too," he said. "That's how my dad dying
changed me."

"So we're two difficult children," Piper said. She locked her
hands behind Garrett's back and pressed her hips against his.
"However, I notice you haven't pierced your nose."

"Not yet," he said. "But maybe I will."

"You have such a pretty nose," she said. "Don't ruin it."

"*You* have a pretty nose," Garrett said. He leaned forward
and kissed the tip of her nose, then lifted her chin and kissed
her lips. She tasted smoky, but smoky like charcoal, not cigarettes. He kissed her again, parting her lips with his tongue.
She kissed him back for a second or two, enough time for
Garrett to marvel at his good fortune, but then she pushed him
gently away.

"I'm difficult, as in, not easy," she said.

"Oh," Garrett said. He was dying, *dying*, to kiss her, but he
liked it that she had boundaries. And he had all summer to knock
them down, so he gave up without asking for more. He took her
hand and led her down the beach.

⁂

At ten o'clock, Beth found herself sitting alone at the table with
David. The candles were burnt down to nubs, and two quarts of
Ben & Jerry's Phish Food had been decimated—Marcus finished

one quart single-handedly before he excused himself and headed upstairs. Garrett and Piper were still on their walk—they'd been gone for over an hour, a fact which embarrassed Beth—and Peyton had wandered into the living room, plucked a paperback off the shelf and fell asleep reading in the recliner. Her soft snoring was audible in the dining room where Beth and David nursed the last two glasses of wine.

"Was dinner a success?" Beth asked. Her words came out slurred. It had been a long time since she drank this much. Across the table, David had taken on a mystical aura. Was that really David Ronan in this house after so many years?

"Huge success," David said. "If only because we managed to get rid of all the kids."

"Winnie never even showed her face," Beth said.

"I'd like to meet her sometime," David said. "Is she beautiful like her mother?"

"She's beautiful like Winnie," Beth said. "But she's very sad. I don't know what to do to help her."

"She needs time," David said. He lowered his voice. "What's the deal with Marcus? I asked him if he was a friend of the kids' from school, and he said no."

Beth dropped her head into her hands. "It's a long story. I don't want to get into it."

David stood up. "Come on. Let's go out onto the deck."

"I don't think we should."

"Why not?"

"Because," Beth said. Her voice was louder than she meant it to be, and she noticed a snag in Peyton's breathing, but then the gentle snoring resumed. "Because," Beth said again, "I'm drunk and I can't help the things I'm thinking."

"Such as?"

"Such as, what are you *doing* here?"

"Aside from drinking myself silly?"

"Why did I bump into you at the grocery store my first day here? Why did I ask you to dinner? Why did you have my name stuck to your dashboard?"

David extended his hand. "Let's go out to the deck. Your grandfather built that deck for nights like this one."

Beth rose but she didn't take David's hand. Instead she carried her wineglass forward carefully, solemnly, like a chalice. Out onto the deck they went.

The beach was dark below them. "Should we be worried about the kids?" Beth asked.

"Garrett seemed trustworthy."

"Is Piper trustworthy?"

"With everyone but me."

"She's a lot angrier about you and Rosie splitting up than you realize."

"She's not angry about us splitting. She's angry at me, alone, because I won't give Rosie my blessing."

Beth lay back in the chaise lounge and David pulled a chair up next to her. Beth closed her eyes. Six summers she'd spent with this man—from ages sixteen to twenty-one. That last summer was the most magical summer of her life, until it ended. Ended with Beth's father throwing David out of this house, and Beth watching the whole scene from up in her room, like a princess locked in a tower. She was twenty-one, an adult, with only a year left at Sarah Lawrence; she could have defied her father. That was what David wrote later in the letters that arrived at her college post office box. *You could have defied your father. You could have honored our commitment.*

Beth thought fleetingly of the purple cosmos.

"I never told my kids about us," she said. She took a deep breath. "And I never told Arch."

"You never told Arch?" David asked.

"No," she said, the guilt souring the back of her throat. On top of everything else, the guilt. "I decided to keep that part of my past private. What about your girls?"

"I'm not sure how much they know. Rosie might have said something. She was always jealous of you, because you were first."

"Arch wasn't jealous of anyone," Beth said. "He wouldn't have been jealous of you, even if I had told him the truth. Arch was a man who was perfectly confident in who he was and content with all he'd been given. He never looked sideways, only forward." Just speaking this way about Arch revived Beth. She sat up. "I'm glad you came tonight, David Ronan," she said. "It was good to see you. And to meet your girls. They're beautiful."

"Why does it feel like I'm getting thrown out?" David said. He leaned closer to her and lowered his voice. "The reason why your name was on my dashboard was because I wanted it there."

It was chilly out, but Beth flushed. Heat bloomed in her chest. He wanted her name there.

"Where I could see it." He let his hand fall onto her thigh, as lightly as a leaf.

"This is not okay," she said, lifting his hand. "I'm not yours to touch."

"But you were."

"Yes, I was. Twenty-five years ago. In the interim, though, I married Arch and had two children and lived a very happy and fulfilled life that came to an end three months ago."

"I understand," he said. "You're not ready."

"I may never be ready."

"Well, if and when you are . . ."

"David . . ."

"You don't have to say anything else. I'm sorry I'm being forward. Is it okay if we see each other again?"

"See each other, how?"

"Can I take you to breakfast in the morning?"

"No."

"Lunch?"

"No."

"How about the sunset, then, in Madaket?"

"I can watch the sun set from here."

"Fine," he said. "Be that way."

"You can call me," Beth said.

He seemed placated by that, but only for a second. "This
house has no phone," he said.

"That's right."

"Do you have a cell phone?" he asked.

"In New York," Beth said. "I didn't bring it. I didn't anticipate
having suitors."

"So how will I call you?"

"I guess you won't. But we'll bump into each other. It's a small
island, David. Right now, though, you must go."

"Well, I'm not leaving without my daughter."

"No, I guess you're not," Beth said. She felt guilty because she
was the mother of the boy. If it were Winnie out there, she'd
feel panicked. But before she could wonder too long about where
Garrett had taken Piper, she heard voices, and a minute later,
the kids ascended the stairs holding hands. Beth smiled. When
Beth and David were seventeen, they'd been dating for a year

already. They'd had sex already. They'd said "I love you" already and meant it with all their hearts.

And now here were Garrett and Piper, their children: Beth and David a generation removed. It touched Beth in a way she couldn't name.

"We're going to see each other tomorrow night," Garrett announced.

"Fine," Beth said, as if he'd been asking permission.

"Can you drop me off here tomorrow night around seven, Dad?" Piper asked her father. "If you say no, I'll ride my bike. I don't care if it's dark."

"I'd prefer you not hand me any ultimatums," David said. "But, yes, I'd be happy to bring you here tomorrow." He winked at Beth. Victory for him. Then he woke Peyton and directed his girls out to the car.

Beth and Garrett stood at the screen door until the Ronans pulled away.

"Piper seems nice," Beth said. "She's very pretty."

"You told me his wife was coming," Garrett said.

Beth closed the front door and turned off the porch light. The house was quiet. That was perhaps the most noticeable difference between Nantucket and New York. The absence of noise. "I thought she was coming. I didn't realize they had split up." A little background noise—some cars honking, people yelling or singing or hailing cabs—might disguise the lie in her voice. Here, the lie was naked, exposed. Garrett would hear it.

"Piper told me her dad considered this to be a date."

"David might have considered this a date," Beth said. "But I didn't."

Garrett looked at her in a way that let her know he could see right through her. She hoped and prayed that Piper didn't know about her and David. Every man, woman, and child was entitled to a secret and Beth had hers; she didn't want to fear its disclosure if Garrett and Piper started dating. She grew angry at the unfairness of it—it was *her* past, her secret, her history, years before she met Arch and had these children. It was not mandatory for her to share it—not even with Arch. Her husband and kids did not automatically own everything that happened in her life.

Beth sighed. This summer was going to be even harder than she'd initially thought. And she could blame nobody but herself. *She'd* invited David for dinner. Disinvited him, then invited him again.

"What are you and Piper doing tomorrow?" she asked.

"Don't know yet."

"But you had a good time tonight?"

Garrett's stare softened into a smile. He looked at the floor. "Yeah."

Beth hugged her son, who was rigid and unyielding in her arms. This was what it felt like to hold an angry teenager.

"Okay," she said. "Sweet dreams."

꧁

Winnie woke up in the middle of the night, hungrier than she'd ever been in her life. A voice in her head screamed out for food. She waited until her eyes adjusted to the dark and then she padded downstairs to the kitchen. Her mother, of course, had cleaned everything up. (Winnie's father used to say, "Mom can't sleep at night if there's an unwashed dish in the house.") All of the leftovers were in the fridge, covered with plastic wrap. Sliced steak, two baked potatoes, some sour cream. Winnie fixed herself a plate, poured a glass of milk and sat down at the kitchen table. The trick was to keep from thinking about her father. Thinking about her father made eating impossible. Even thinking that one stupid thing: her father lingering in the kitchen after a dinner party while Beth cleaned up. Wearing his blue pajamas and his tortoiseshell glasses because he would have taken out his contacts, the top of his head grazing the copper pots that hung from the ceiling. Drinking ice water from the Yankees mug he'd gotten as a kid that he kept by his bed every night. Saying, "Mom can't sleep at night if there's an unwashed dish in the house." That was Winnie's father in one of his simple, human moments, a moment she never would have given a second thought, except now he was dead and every memory seemed unspeakably precious. It made Winnie upset enough that she stared at her plate of food. Yes, it looked delicious, yes, she was hungry, but no, she couldn't eat.

Then she heard a whisper. "A-ha! Caught you."

It was Marcus. Wearing boxer shorts and a gray Benjamin N. Cardozo swim team T-shirt. Holding an envelope in one hand and his CD player in the other. He opened the fridge and brought out the platter of leftover steak. Popped open a Coke, found utensils, and sat next to her. Winnie felt so happy that she managed to poke open the top of her potato and stuff it full of sour cream. It wasn't eating, exactly, but it was close.

Marcus started in on the steak, eating right off the platter. He noticed her staring at him. "I didn't get myself another plate because I plan to finish all this."

"You eat a lot," she said.

"I'm hungry a lot."

"Me, too," she said.

"You don't eat in front of other people?" he said. "Is that it? Because if I'm keeping you from eating, I'll go into the other room. You need to eat, Winnie."

"I have a problem," she said. She wished she'd just been able to say those words that afternoon at the beach instead of getting angry at him. Sustaining anger at Marcus was not something that made her happy. She loved Marcus! "I have an eating problem." She expected him to say, *Yeah, no shit,* but he didn't. He just chewed his steak, waiting for her to say more.

"What's that envelope?" she asked.

"A letter from my mother."

"Really?"

"Yep."

She paused, hoping he would offer more information. He downed half the Coke, then he belched.

"Excuse me."

Winnie stared at her cold, cream-filled potato. She reached for the salt and pepper. "What does it say?"

"I have no idea," Marcus said.

"You haven't read it?" Winnie asked.

"Nope."

"How come?"

Marcus chewed his steak and drank some more Coke. Winnie trembled internally. She wanted to have a real conversation with Marcus. If they couldn't talk here, in the dark kitchen in the middle of the night, intimacy would be hopeless.

Finally Marcus said, "I don't read my mother's letters."

"Why not?" Winnie asked.

"Because I don't want to," Marcus said.

"But you brought it down here with you," Winnie said.

"To throw it away." He pointed the tines of his fork at her. "Are you going to eat or what?"

Winnie picked up her knife and fork, cut a piece of steak and deposited it into her mouth. Chewed. Swallowed.

It was delicious.

"Good job," Marcus said.

She ate another piece of steak, then some potato, which was good even cold, and she felt her body thanking her. She drank some milk; the screaming in her head quieted.

"Why don't you want to read her letters?" she asked.

Marcus put down his utensils and sank back into his chair, which squeaked. "Girls just have to know everything."

"Your mother's in jail for the rest of her life," Winnie said. "I'd think you'd want to read her letters and maybe write some back."

"My mother's in jail for the rest of her life because she killed two people, one of whom was only nine years old. You know the story."

"I know what I read in the papers," Winnie said, though this was a lie. Arch had asked both Winnie and Garrett not to read the papers, and out of respect for him, they didn't. All Winnie knew about the case were the most basic facts. She'd seen the photographs, naturally, the one they showed again and again of the little girl in black Mary Janes covered with a bloody sheet. Winnie had also caught a clip on TV of Constance Tyler, hands cuffed behind her back, being led from the courthouse in Queens. Winnie was surprised by how pretty she was. No one expected a murderer to be pretty. "My dad said that Constance didn't deserve the death penalty. He said killing the little girl was an accident."

"You don't know what you're talking about."

"Tell me then," Winnie said. She stared at her plate, then to prove to Marcus that she could do it, she devoured her potato until the empty brown skin sagged like an old shoe.

Marcus dragged the last slice of steak through the juices and popped it into his mouth. When he'd left the dinner table earlier that evening, he'd gone up to his room, pulled out his legal pad and tried to write, but nothing happened. He groaned at the memory of the five hundred squandered dollars and the items he now owned in their place. The spent money was a shackle on his creative spirit. Now the writing felt like a job at McDonald's—he had to do it to earn money! He closed his eyes and conjured the face of Ms. Marchese, her full Italian lips painted dark purple. *You're a gifted writer, Marcus.* He'd even considered opening his mother's letter, thinking it might give him a place to start other than with *the blood-splattered sheet, dead bodies in your own apartment.* There was far more to the story than Zachary Celtic knew. But just looking at his mother's handwriting on the envelope pissed Marcus off. *How could you? You killed them!* Before he went to bed, he wrote one line at the top of his tablet: "My mother is a murderer."

Now here he was being egged on to write the next sentence. Only this time by Winnie, and she wasn't paying him thirty thousand dollars. The murders: How? When? Why? He felt his eyes drooping closed in defense, even though the reason he came downstairs was because he couldn't sleep. Maybe if he started slowly, it would come to him. "My mother killed her sister-in-law, Angela Bennett, and Angela's daughter Candy. My uncle Leon has basically killed himself, but you could hold Mama responsible for that one, too."

"Why did she kill them?" Winnie said. "Do you know why?"

"Well, the newspapers made it sound like she woke up one

morning and decided to kidnap and kill people, but it wasn't like that."

This much Winnie knew. Her father *hated* the newspapers. He even went so far as to suspend their delivery of the *New York Times*; Winnie hadn't seen a single edition the whole time leading up to the trial—until the day her father's obituary came out. Arch used to rant, *They're making her out to be a monster! The most esteemed paper in the country and they aren't reporting the facts!* Thankfully, Danforth was a liberal school. Most teachers and kids thought Arch was doing the right thing. *The death penalty is abominable, inhumane,* everyone said out loud. Still, Winnie sensed a lack of understanding because murder was also abominable and inhumane and Constance Tyler was guilty of murder. She could almost hear everyone's unspoken thoughts: *How did Arch Newton get involved in this mess?*

"What was it like?" Winnie asked. She wanted details so badly, but she was embarrassed to pry. She turned her attention to finishing what was left on her plate.

Because Winnie wasn't looking right at him, demanding an explanation, Marcus felt okay to speak. "First you need to know who Angela Bennett is. Angela Bennett was married to my uncle Leon, my mother's older brother."

Winnie nodded, head down. She had only two bites of steak remaining.

"Uncle Leon and Angela were married for twenty years."

"I didn't know that," Winnie said. She was mortified to find this surprised her. But why? Lots of black people were married for that long and longer. She needed to get in touch with reality. As Arch used to say, *The world includes more than Park Avenue and Nantucket.*

"They met in the seventies. At a party somewhere. Angela

was white, Italian, and her parents had some money. Not a lot of money . . . not like you people . . . but some money. Except Angela's father disowned her when he found out she was marrying Leon."

"Because he was black?" Winnie asked. "That is so backwater."

Marcus waited until Winnie finished her last two bites and then he cleared their dishes. Doing something with his hands made talking easier.

"It was the seventies," he said. "Everyone was supposed to be in tune with civil rights, but nobody was."

"So what happened next? The father disowned her . . ."

"And she moved into my grandmother's apartment with Leon. My mother was a senior in high school."

"Our age," Winnie said.

"Yeah. And she told me about the weird stuff that happened when they all lived together. Like one time my mother woke up in the middle of the night and Angela was sitting on the end of her bed staring at her."

"What do you mean, 'staring at her'?"

"She was just staring at her. It really freaked my mother out. She thought from the beginning that Angela was bad news. But then, a while later, my mother found out that Angela was into drugs and the reason she was in my mother's room was because she had lifted money and jewelry and stuff from my mother's dresser. Angela and Leon basically robbed my grandmother of everything she had and spent it on smack. Somehow Angela accessed my grandmother's savings account and emptied it. My mother's college money. That was why she only stayed a year at Princeton. Angela spent Mama's college money on drugs for her and Uncle Leon."

"Your mother must have been angry," Winnie said.

"That was only the beginning," Marcus said. Oh, was it ever. He washed the plates and left them to dry in the rack, then he turned off the light over the sink and came back to the table and sat next to Winnie. The kitchen was dark now and they could hear the sound of the waves through the open window. Marcus lowered his voice.

"Angela was like a disease in the house, my mother said. She basically caused my grandmother to die of a heart attack, and once my grandmother was dead, Angela and Uncle Leon kicked Mama out of the apartment. But she said she was glad to go. She married my father a little while later and then I was born."

"It must have been the proudest day of your mother's life," Winnie said.

Marcus smiled sadly. "Except my mother never wanted to be young and married with a child. She wanted a career, you know, something better." This was easy for Marcus to understand but difficult to swallow. What his mother had dreamed of her whole life was something other than Bo Tyler, Marcus, and LaTisha. Constance was the smartest person Marcus knew—she had a near-perfect score on her SATs, a fact she'd reminded Marcus of since he was in the ninth grade. She used words like "egregious" and "polemic." She did the puzzle in the back of the *Times* magazine. Once Marcus was old enough to understand how smart she was, he began to wonder what she was doing still living in Queens. In his earliest memories, Constance's favorite topic of conversation was what her life *could* have been like. Her year at Princeton had taken on a romantic shimmer that Marcus was pretty sure hadn't existed at the time—the tailgate parties, the eating clubs, the fireplaces in the living suites that they kept lit as they studied for finals. One of Constance's English professors reading aloud from a paper Constance had written on James Baldwin. Constance had sung madrigals in Latin and Italian and French. She ran the one-hundred-meter hurdles for the track team in the spring.

From his father, Marcus also knew a few of the less glamorous details. His mother had a work-study job in the dining hall that required her to wear high rubber boots and long rubber gloves and spend fifteen hours a week scraping trays and loading an industrial dishwasher with a crew of university-employed food service workers, all of whom were black women from Trenton. Marcus learned that Constance had initially been assigned to a living suite with a girl from Hattiesburg, Mississippi, who pitched such a fit about having a *Negro* roommate that Constance was moved, for her own good, the dean of students said, to a living suite with twin girls from Pakistan. But to hear Constance tell it, if it hadn't been for Angela and Leon, her life would have been a cake walk. It would have meant a real career as a college professor; it would have meant a brownstone apartment in Manhattan filled with books and leather furniture. It would have meant a husband, possibly even a white husband, who sat on boards and took her to the symphony.

Instead, Constance's whole slumping, resentful demeanor suggested she had gotten stuck with Bo, Marcus, LaTisha, a job working for the New York Board of Education, and an apartment in the same neighborhood she grew up in.

Marcus noticed Winnie staring at him, waiting for more.

"Angela and Leon got hooked on smack," he said. He cringed at how typically urban, how typically *black* this sounded. "Then Angela disappeared for a while. She ran off with another man for two years, and my mother managed to get Leon into rehab. But Angela turned up again with this baby girl, Candy. My uncle went right back to her."

"Why?" Winnie asked. "If she had a baby with another man. Wasn't your uncle angry about that?"

"Some people like what's bad for them," Marcus said, parroting his mother's words on the topic. "Leon was under this woman's spell. She asked him to do all this crazy stuff. Do drugs, steal money from his friends." Marcus paused for air. He didn't want to tell the story anymore. It was too gruesome. But this was the point Zachary Celtic had tried to make during their lunch: the grislier the content of the book, the more people would flock to buy it. Marcus eyed Winnie; he thought of the five hundred dollar bills slipping through his fingers like water.

"When Candy got older, and I'm talking, like, eight and nine years old, Angela used to pimp her out. Let men come to their apartment and have sex with her daughter for money. Because neither she nor Leon worked that was, like, their source of income."

"I think I'm going to be sick," Winnie said. Her stomach was churning in an unpleasant way and she concentrated on her breathing. Her science teacher, Mr. Halperin, told their class once that nearly all pain could be managed by deep breathing.

"I should stop," Marcus said. He knew, though, that even if he stopped talking, he wouldn't be able to stop the images: how Angela used to dress Candy up like a woman, in nylon stockings and high heels. Marcus and LaTisha joked about it—the way Candy teetered around in the heels, the nylons bunching around her skinny, eight-year-old ankles. They had no idea what was going on, that Angela was offering Candy up to the low-life men who hung around their apartment building. Marcus had no idea that this was why Constance bought Candy the pair of black patent leather shoes and thick white cotton tights—so that she would look like a little girl and not a prostitute.

"I'll be okay," Winnie said. "Go ahead."

"When my mother found out what Angela was doing—when she found out how *bad* it all was—she demanded that Angela let Candy live at our house. She told Angela if she didn't let Candy come to our house to live, she'd call the police. But it was tricky, see, because *then* Angela told my mother that Leon had been having sex with Candy, too, and so he'd be the first person to go to jail."

Winnie felt herself shaking on the inside. Marcus took her hand, and this surprised her. His hand was huge and warm, which made Winnie realize how small and cold and brittle her own hand was. She stared at their interlocking hands. He stared, too, confused by his own gesture. He'd taken Winnie's hand instinctively, like he was reaching out to steady himself.

"My mother decided she didn't care about Leon and she didn't think Angela would turn him in anyway since he did all the dirty work scoring their drugs. Angela never left the house; she just laid in bed all day, got high and ate Hostess cakes." Marcus emptied the last few drops from his Coke can into his mouth, then with his free hand he pried off the tab and dropped it into the can. "My mother was a teacher so she planned it." There it was, the premeditation. "On October seventh Candy had a half day of school because of in-service. My mother waited for Candy on the street at noon and brought her home. Like, to live with us." *Intent to abduct*, the D.A. said. "Mama gave her some lunch and told her, you know, that Angela and Leon were sick and needed time to get better so Candy was going to move in with us. Candy nodded and said she understood but she was crying. Mama gave her a glass of milk and let her watch cartoons on PBS." Marcus rattled the Coke can, a sound effect—his jittery nerves, his dried-out brain rattling in his skull. "Angela wasn't as clueless as my mother thought. When Candy didn't make it home from school she knew where to look. She came over to take Candy back."

Here was where the story got convoluted—for the judge, for the jury, and for Marcus. Why did Constance let the woman in? In his mind, Marcus reconfigured the end of the story so that Mama just bolted the door shut and waited for someone else to get home—Bo, Marcus, even LaTisha. Or waited for one of the neighbors to call the police. There might have been an ugly scene, but no one would have been killed.

꙼

Marcus was in the room the first time Arch met with Connie at Riker's. Bo and LaTisha had walked out—Marcus could tell his father was nervous about having a private attorney show up because how would they ever pay for it? Connie asked Marcus to stay. The public defender was a milky-skinned woman named Fiona Dobbs who got bright pink spots on her cheeks when she spoke to Constance. She was twenty-seven years old, eighteen months out of Pace Law School, and although there was no way her defense would be effective, Constance felt comfortable around her. Arch was another story—a tall, successful-looking man with such a cheerful demeanor that Marcus wondered if he realized the reason they were here was *murder*. Arch introduced himself, shook hands with both Connie and Marcus, smiling right into their eyes. To Connie, he said, "We were freshmen together at Princeton. 1975, right?"

"Right," Connie answered warily, as if it were some kind of trap. "Did I know you?"

"No," Arch said. "But that's why I'm here. I looked you up in the facebook. I thought maybe I could help you."

"I can't afford your help," Connie said.

Arch sat down and pulled a yellow pad out of his briefcase. "Free of charge," he said. "Let me ask you a couple of questions."

A couple of questions turned into her whole life history up until the murders. Marcus fell asleep, his head resting against the cinder block wall behind his chair, his arms crossed in front of him. When Arch started asking about October seventh, Marcus opened his eyes. Arch's voice was much more serious.

You were holding the knife when you opened the door?

I was trying to scare her.

That doesn't answer my question.

Yes, I was holding the knife. She was there to take the child, and I wasn't about to let that happen. I hated the woman. I'd always hated her.

That's not something you're ever going to tell a jury. What happened, exactly, when you opened the door? What did you say? What kind of movements did you make?

I can't remember.

You're going to have to remember. They want to execute you, Connie.

My life was over a long time ago.

That's not true. What about your family?

Connie glanced in Marcus's direction, her eyes like a couple of closed doors. Marcus stood up to leave. His father and sister had the right idea. He didn't want to listen to this. *Poor child. It's not his fault. My life was over before he was even born.*

Arch nodded at Marcus, as if giving him permission to go. He leaned forward, elbows on his knees. *Can you tell me what happened with Candy?*

Connie started to cry. *She's dead. God, she's dead.*

⚜

In Constance's official testimony, there was a fight, a struggle, just like in the movies—a duel between herself, Candy's savior, and Angela, who wanted her nine-year-old daughter to have sex with grown men for money. But in this day and age, you can't lie about something like that. The forensic expert found no evidence of a struggle. Connie opened the door. Angela stepped in and Connie stabbed her.

⚜

"Whatever," Marcus said now to Winnie, shaking the vision out of his head. "Mama stabbed her to death."

Winnie swallowed sour saliva. "What about Candy?"

What *about* Candy? Marcus might someday forgive Mama for killing Angela—the woman was strung out every time Marcus saw her, with her dark hair wild and frizzy, her skin pasty, track marks like the red eyes of rats running up the inside of both arms. But the worst thing about Angela was her foul mouth, the trashy language she threw around even the youngest children. Words that the worst kid at Benjamin N. Cardozo High School wouldn't dream of using. Angela, in Marcus's opinion, could barely be considered human. But Marcus would never forgive his mother for killing Candy, nor understand how the sweet little girl his mother had tried to look out for—the tights, the patent leather shoes!—and had taken into her home to *save* ended up dead. Stabbed, just once, in the neck. Constance claimed all along that it was a "tragic mistake," that Candy got in the middle of things, that when she saw her mother at the door she ran to her then started shrieking and kicking and lashing out at Constance. "Like she didn't know I was trying to save her," Constance had testified. "Like she didn't understand the sacrifice I was making. I was trying to save the girl's life and she starts fighting me and calling me a bitch." The next thing Constance knew, Candy was bleeding from a dark spot at the base of her neck. Constance called 911 then pressed a bath towel over Candy's wound, but Candy bled right through it.

"Candy got mixed up in it," Marcus said. "Mama cut her, maybe accidentally, maybe on purpose. She bled to death." Marcus squeezed Winnie's hand. "My uncle Leon shot himself when he found out. He blew half his head off, but he lived. He's retarded now. In a state hospital." Head permanently tilted to one side, tongue hanging out like a thirsty dog. Marcus had been forced to visit him once, but would never go back.

Winnie leaned against Marcus's shoulder and closed her eyes. It was the most horrible story she had ever heard, worse than a movie or TV. And it was true. It happened in the life of this person right here. Winnie was impressed by Marcus in a way she knew she'd never be impressed by anybody again. Because he'd survived. Because he'd just had the courage to tell her the truth, instead of making excuses. She was impressed by him because he had the courage to spend the summer with three people he barely knew when he had this nightmare to contend with.

"It's going to be okay," Winnie said.

"No, it won't," Marcus said. "My mother is a murderer, Winnie. She killed a *third grader*. Do you hear what I'm telling you?"

"Yes," Winnie said.

"She's a bad person. Everyone thinks so."

"I don't believe that," Winnie said. "My father would not have died defending a bad person. He didn't think Connie was bad."

"No, he didn't," Marcus said. In fact, Arch's confidence in Constance was the only thing that kept Marcus from drowning. Arch, for whatever reason, was able to see the good in Connie. He was able to make Marcus recall the admirable things about his mother—her beautiful singing voice (she was always a soloist with the church choir) and the way, when she tutored kids at the kitchen table, she would give them as much milk as they wanted, many times sending Marcus or LaTisha to the store for more. "But he was the only person in New York City who thought she deserved to live. Everyone else called her a monster. And they think I'm a monster because I'm her son. At my school . . . whatever, its like I have this permanent stink following me around." He ran a hand over his hair. It needed to be trimmed already—it felt like a pilled-up vinyl rug. "If Arch hadn't taken my mother's case, he would still be alive. Have you ever considered that? Of course you have. Your brother knows it well enough."

Winnie sat with this awhile. True, Garrett blamed Constance Tyler for their father's death. But what Garrett didn't understand was how strongly Arch felt about the case. If Arch had known he was going to die saving Constance Bennett Tyler, he probably would have done it anyway. *If I save this woman*, he told Winnie at EJ's, *my life will have been worthwhile.* And he'd saved her.

"It was an accident that killed my father," Winnie said. "Pilot error."

"I guess we'll all believe what we want," Marcus said.

"I guess we will." Winnie sighed. She waited to see if there was anything else Marcus wanted to say, but she could tell by the way his eyelids flagged that he was shutting down. Their conversation was over. Winnie wanted to talk to Marcus all night long for the rest of the summer. "Want to go up?" she asked.

"Sure."

They ascended the stairs and when they reached Winnie's room, she took Marcus's hand and realized he was holding his mother's letter. "I don't want to go to bed now," she said. "I'm scared."

"Me, too," he said. "I'm scared all the time." He stood close to her in the dark. Winnie thought he might kiss her. She lifted her face and closed her eyes, but then she heard him whisper, "Good night, Winnie," and by the time she opened her eyes, he had disappeared down the hallway to his room.

chapter 3

I can't believe I'm not going to see you for three whole days," Garrett said. He was at the airport terminal sitting on a bench with Piper until her plane was called. She was flying to Hyannis to visit her mom. Beth was parked outside, waiting in the car.

"Ssshh, don't even say it." Piper kissed him slowly with tongue. She tasted like the blueberry pie they'd shared at Hutch's for lunch. Whenever Garrett kissed Piper, he felt like he was falling. A rush went to his head. He shifted on the bench and looked around the terminal: lots of people and dogs and guys carrying toolboxes who stole glances at Piper. Because she was gorgeous, sexy, a knockout. Looking especially hot today in a pink string halter and a little jean skirt. When she bent over earlier at the Nantucket Air counter to hoist her bag onto the scale, he caught a glimpse of her white panties.

"For God's sake," he said, blushing. "Bend at the knees."

Now Garrett held her around the waist, trying to memorize

how her skin felt against his fingertips. He couldn't wait for three days to pass. By the time Piper got back, he was going to have his driver's license. He'd convinced his mother that getting a Massachusetts license was the right thing to do. He could use the Nantucket address, and he might end up going to college in Boston anyway. He and Piper had already talked about applying to the same schools.

"That way," Piper had said, "we'll only have to be apart for one school year."

The thought of nine months away from Piper was too much to bear. The thought of the next three days without her was nearly as bad, since the last two weeks she and Garrett had been inseparable. But she had to leave, she said. This was the longest she'd gone without seeing her mother since Rosie moved off-island in December, and Rosie called to complain, saying a new boyfriend was no excuse for staying away. Piper didn't tell her mother Garrett's name, and she wasn't going to any time soon. David had asked her not to.

"He doesn't want Mom to know that Beth's around," Piper said. "Don't ask me why. Those were strict orders, punishable by a very long grounding, he said."

"I think you should go ahead and tell your mom about me," Garrett said. "If she gets angry at your dad maybe he'll stop chasing after my mom." One bad side effect to Garrett and Piper dating, and Garrett not having his license, was that every time they saw each other, David stopped in to talk to Beth. Or if Beth were the one driving, David came out into the driveway. One night he'd gone so far as to climb into the front seat and ride with them into town. He popped a cassette tape into the stereo without even *asking*, and he sang to Beth. Old-fashioned stuff, like Elton John. It made Garrett want to puke.

"I promised Daddy I wouldn't," Piper said.

"Since when do you keep promises to your dad?"

"Since now," Piper said. "I'd die if I got grounded and couldn't see you. Besides, I'm not ready to tell Mom your name yet. First you have to prove yourself."

He kissed her and bit her lip. "I intend to." As soon as Garrett got his license, they were going to drive out to the beach and have sex. They'd decided this together, last night, when they'd made out on the beach and Garrett's shorts were down to his knees and Piper's tank top was pushed up. She made him stop. She said she wanted to wait until they had a car.

She was a virgin, she said.

A voice came over the loudspeaker: "Anyone holding a green boarding card please proceed to the gate." Piper's plane. She stood to go, her purse hitched over her shoulder. She blinked rapidly.

"I'll have Daddy bring me over the second I get back," she said. "Tuesday at four. Or four-thirty. Okay? Promise you'll be home waiting for me?"

"Promise," he said. He kissed her again until he knew if he didn't stop, he'd never let her go. "Be good."

She skipped out onto the tarmac, waving to him the whole way.

Outside, it was hot. Beth sat at the wheel of the Range Rover reading the *New Yorker*. She smiled when Garrett opened the door.

"Piper got off okay?" she asked.

"I guess," he said. "Can I drive home? I have to practice for my test."

"Sure," his mother said. They passed each other in front of the car, switching seats. Garrett got himself buckled in behind

the wheel and started the engine. Shifted into drive and eased
out of the parking space.

"You're going to miss her," Beth said. "But you're probably
ready for some time alone. You kids have spent every waking
second together. That's not usually your style."

"My style's changing," Garrett said. He and Piper had been
together so much that he felt weird now, without her. He
checked the air for her plane, wishing she could see him driving.
As he turned onto the main road, he thought about the past two
weeks. He and Piper sat out on the deck in the afternoons drinking Malibu and Coke, they swam, they walked the beach at night
and made out in the sand. They rode their bikes to Sconset one
day and had lunch at Claudette's. They walked to Bartlett Farm
to get Beth the first zucchini of the summer. They went to two
movies. They played Monopoly with Winnie and Marcus—with
Piper there even that was fun.

There had been only one bad night, the beginnings of an
argument. Piper took Garrett to a bonfire on Cisco Beach where
kids from her high school were having a keg. They walked there
from Garrett's house—a long walk in the dark—and Garrett
stepped in a shallow hole and twisted his ankle. Piper stopped
to inspect his injury. *A little tender,* she said, *but nothing you can't
handle, right? You don't want to turn back?*

No, he said, *it's fine.*

He limped along, enjoying the way Piper held him closer,
cooing in his ear, rubbing his lower back. Then they saw the
distant flash of the fire and the silhouette of bodies. Piper hurried
him along. Her friend Jenna was going to be at the party and
her friend Kyle. Garrett was uncomfortable as he hobbled toward
the group. The fire was in a pit; it was smoky and a couple of
people fed it newspapers and paper bags.

"All the guys at my high school have a car," Piper had told him earlier. Garrett saw the vehicles lined up on the beach: Jeep Wranglers, a rusty old Bronco, and one brand new canary yellow Land Rover Defender series with all the bars.

"We're here," Piper announced to the party in general. There were high-pitched screams and girls came running up to her, kissing her, touching her hair. Just the way the girls at Danforth acted when they saw each other outside of the classroom—freaking out like they'd been separated by continents and decades.

Everyone was looking at Garrett; he could tell even in the dark. So many orange glowing faces. Garrett nodded in the direction of the male population who were either feeding the fire or standing around the keg. He took a deep breath. His science teacher had once told the class that nearly all pain could be managed by deep breathing. His ankle swelled.

"I need a drink," he said.

A kid with a shaved head wearing a fisherman's sweater held up a plastic cup. "Beck's."

"Nice," Garrett said. Piper was completely encircled by friends, and so Garrett made his way over to the keg, found the sleeve of cups lying in the sand and poured two beers. He drank his down right away. His ankle really hurt and he could tell already he was going to have a sucky time at this party. He tried to remind himself that these kids weren't as smart or sophisticated as the kids at Danforth. They drove their Wranglers on the beach, but Garrett was pretty sure they'd get lost taking the cross-town bus.

Piper tugged on his arm. "My friends think you're cute," she whispered. "Jenna actually said '*gorgeous.*' "

Garrett couldn't hide his smile. "Am I going to meet them?"

"Later," she said. "Right now I want you to meet my friend Kyle. He's definitely here. That's his Rover."

"Okay," Garrett said. "Let me fill up." He topped off his beer. It was warm, but it did lighten his mood. "I'm not sure how long I want to stay."

"We just got here."

"What time is your dad picking you up?"

"Not until eleven," she said. "Come on, there's Kyle."

They found Kyle on the far side of the Rover, lying in the sand, smoking a cigarette. A girl sat on either side of him. Kyle wore jeans and a gray tank top. He, too, had a shaved head.

"You guys all use the same barber?" Garrett said.

"Football team," Kyle said. "Who the fuck are you?"

Garrett stepped forward on his good leg. "Garrett Newton. I'm a friend of Piper's. Nice to meet you."

"Garrett's a summer person," Piper said. "From Manhattan, New York City."

Kyle regarded Garrett and blew smoke out his nose. " 'Manhattan, New York City,' " he mimicked in a high voice.

Garrett swallowed half his beer. He looked up into the sky and heard, despite his wishes, words from his father. *These are her friends. This is her life. She wants to show it to you. Yes, it's difficult, life is difficult. If you want easy, date a girl from Danforth. Date Tracy Hayes whom you've known since Montessori.*

"I like your car," Garrett said.

Kyle nodded, then he touched Piper's leg. "Ronan," he said. "Where've you been lately?"

"With Garrett," she said.

"You were supposed to meet us at Ego's on Tuesday."

Piper swatted Kyle's hand away, like it was a fly on her food. "I was busy Tuesday. With Garrett."

Garrett laughed nervously. "You actually know someone named Ego?"

"Nickname," Piper said. "My old boyfriend. They call him that because he's so full of himself."

One of Kyle's girls stood up to get Kyle another beer and Kyle pulled Piper down into her place. Then he passed her his cigarette and she took a drag. Garrett shifted his weight. He couldn't believe she was smoking. He was about to say something when Kyle slid his arm around Piper's waist and pressed his face against her stomach to make a farting sound. The girl on the far side of Kyle, who looked completely stoned, burst out in giggles, and Piper pushed Kyle's head away. "Gross," she said. "You need to grow up."

"I thought you loved my boyish charm," Kyle said.

"I'm out of beer," Garrett said.

He limped back to the keg and filled his cup, taking the tap from Kyle's minion, then decided he was angry. Piper was smoking, she was letting this asshole Kyle touch her, she wasn't introducing him to her girlfriends which was the reason he came. She didn't seem to care that his ankle hurt. Hurt so much that he dreaded walking home, except that home meant an ice pack.

He left the party without her, trying not to think about how uneasy he'd felt around Kyle or about the ex-boyfriend named Ego, or about how pissed Piper would be when she realized he was gone. He concentrated only on making the dark stretch of beach before him disappear.

She caught up with him an hour later. He was very slowly climbing the stairs to his house. Wishing he'd kicked sand in Kyle's face, thinking he might be better off with Tracy Hayes or Brooke Casserhill or some girl whose idea of a good time did not include smoking Marlboros and fawning over someone who looked like Mr. Clean's delinquent son.

But then he heard her calling his name and when he turned around he saw that she was close to tears.

"Thank God I found you," she said. "I can't believe you just *left.*"

"My ankle hurts," he said. "I need to ice it."

"You should have told me."

"It looked like you were having fun."

"Fun?" she said. "With those bozos? I can see them whenever I want. My time with you is precious." She linked her arm through his and helped him up to the deck where Beth and David were playing cards. Garrett realized that David hadn't gone home and come back; he'd been here all along.

"How was the party?" Beth asked.

"Fine," Garrett said.

"Terrible," Piper said. "I need to get out of this place."

❧

Now that Piper was gone, the memory of the party was even more painful to Garrett. Later, Piper had accused him of not liking her friends and Garrett pointed out that he hadn't even met her friends, only Kyle. Kyle was her friend, she said, and Garrett admitted that Kyle seemed like a jerk. *Yeah,* Piper said, *Kyle is a jerk.* They'd left it at that, but somehow Garrett understood that he'd failed in her eyes. The people at that party were her real life, and he hadn't fit in. He was a "summer person." Now, in the car, a turn was coming up and Garrett signaled. He hit the brake kind of hard and the car bucked a little. His turn was tight. If there had been another car at the intersection, he would have smashed it. He sighed.

"What's wrong?" Beth asked. "You're doing fine."

"Nothing," he said. He never talked to his mother about girls, although truth be told, he felt differently this time. Maybe because his mother was connected to Piper through David. Maybe because Beth seemed different now that she was unmarried. Garrett couldn't believe he was thinking such things. He checked his rearview mirror. The road was deserted, ahead and behind. He gave the Rover some gas. It surged forward.

"How did you and Dad meet?" Garrett asked.

"You know the story," Beth said.

"I know the Disney version," Garrett said. "Tell me the real story."

Beth leaned her head back and closed her eyes. "I had just graduated from Sarah Lawrence. I was twenty-two. We met in July. I spent that summer in New York—it was the only summer of my whole life when I wasn't here on Nantucket. Your father was in law school at NYU and he says he was studying on the subway platform when he got distracted by a pair of legs coming down the stairway."

Garrett said, "And he vowed to himself, 'I am going to marry the woman attached to those beautiful legs.'"

"See," Beth said. "You already know."

"But what was it *like*?" Garrett said. "When you first started dating? Did you know you were in love with him?"

"No," Beth said. "I'd sworn off men at that point in my life. I wanted to make some money so I could pay my rent. But your father was persistent. Once a week he took me on what he called 'Date Package A,' which was a fancy restaurant and drinks at a club. Sometimes dancing. Then once a week we went on 'Date Package B,' which was the movies, and beers afterwards. Some nights we walked in Central Park or the Village or Chinatown. We went to the Frick or the MOMA on Sunday afternoons. We ate at the Turkish restaurants on Eightieth Street. Your father knew the city inside and out. I always teased him that he had the subway maps tattooed on the inside of his eyelids."

"He knew every stop on every train," Garrett said.

"He lived with Gram and Grandad on Sutton Place, so he had no rent to pay. They gave him plenty of money to take me out. They wanted him to get married."

"What about you? Did you want to get married?"

"No."

"Why did you, then?"

"Well, because. We dated for almost two years and then it was time."

A stop sign up ahead. Garrett touched his foot to the brake gently. "You married Dad because it was *time?*" he said. "What about being madly in love?"

Beth pointed out the windshield, indicating that it was safe to proceed. "Why are you asking me this?"

"Because I want to know."

"You and Piper just met, sweetheart. It's infatuation. Puppy love."

Garrett clenched his teeth. "Don't tell me what it is."

Beth bit her lower lip. "Okay, sorry. You're right. Yes, I married your father because he was smart and funny and I knew he'd take care of me. I'll tell you something now that I've never told anyone else. I didn't fall in love with your father until after we were married, and even then I can't pinpoint a moment. It was a process—the process of shedding the cells of Beth Eyler and growing the cells of Beth Newton. I very slowly became a woman who was deeply in love with your father. That is the real story."

Garrett turned onto their dirt road and his heart crumbled at the thought of three days in their house without Piper. He reviewed his mother's story. It was funny to think of his mother as a single woman who at one time could have decided to resist his father's advances. Who, in fact, had married his father without loving him.

"So you gambled on him, then?" Garrett said.

"I trusted myself," Beth said. "I had a gut feeling that marrying Arch was the right thing to do."

"If you'd married someone else, you wouldn't be a widow," Garrett said. He pulled into the driveway and shut off the car, hoping his mother wouldn't cry. He wasn't sure why he'd just said that.

"True enough," Beth said. "But I don't regret being married to your father for one second. If I'd known he was going to die at the age of forty-five, I would have married him anyway."

"Really?" Garrett said.

"Really," Beth said. "Because that's what unconditional love is all about. The 'no-matter-what's.'"

Garrett walked into the house. It was quiet; Winnie and Marcus were probably at the beach. He would join them; he felt too lonely to hang out in his room by himself, although he needed to finish *Franny and Zooey*. He wondered, would he love Piper no matter what? Not yet, but Garrett felt the possibility growing. As he changed into his swim trunks, he eyed the urn of ashes on his dresser.

"I never thought I'd say this," he said. "But you were a lucky man."

With Piper gone, Beth figured she would finally get a break from David. She had seen him every day since the dinner party. When he came to pick Garrett up, he showed up early and knocked on the screen door, and just seeing his silhouette on the other side of the front door brought back a host of memories—David knocking on that door when he was still a teenager. His very presence in her life now was so astonishing that Beth couldn't help herself from inviting him in for a beer. They talked about everyday things—his work on huge summer homes owned by twenty-eight-year-old millionaires, traffic, taxes, the new recycling laws. Every so often, he called Beth by her old nickname, "Bethie," pronounced in a drawn-out New York accent, and as their conversations deepened, he unearthed a memory or two from their summers together: watching the meteor shower from First Point on Coatue, the time they went blackberry picking at Lily Pond and David got stung by a bee, fell into the prickly bushes and ended up the next day not only with awful scratches, but a bad case of poison ivy.

"I can honestly, say, Bethie, I haven't eaten a blackberry since then."

For the first time since Arch died, she found herself able to laugh.

Although she relished the companionship, she was still steeped in the morass of her sorrow. She still half expected to be picking up Arch at the airport on Friday afternoons. She still took a Valium in order to sleep. One night, when Garrett and Piper went to a party, David enticed her into a game of cards on the deck, and she made a point of telling David about her marriage to Arch.

"It wasn't perfect by any means," Beth said. "But it was good."

She and Arch had laughed together. They enjoyed the kids. They took a vacation each winter by themselves, to exciting places—Tahiti, the Seychelles, Venezuela. Of course, it went deeper than that. Beth and Arch had understood each other on every level. They occupied each other's psychic lives. They were each other, to the extent that this was possible in a marriage. Yes, Arch worked long hours in his office downtown; yes, Beth administered every detail of their domestic life. No, they didn't have a lot in common in the way people understood that phrase. Rather, they were opposite sides of the same coin. They complemented each other, completed each other. They'd created a life that glowed.

"I just can't get over him and move on," Beth said. "He was my husband for twenty years."

David appeared to be listening but it was as if he didn't understand her language, or chose to ignore the meaning of her words. Beth grew close to screaming out, *Yes. I loved you but that was years ago and now I need you to leave me alone!*

Yes, I loved you, she thought.

Beth was grateful when Piper went away. She needed time to regroup. To strengthen her resolve.

Horizon had no telephone on principle. Living without a phone was the ultimate nod to a Nantucket summer, which in the mind of Beth's grandfather, was reserved for long hours of undisturbed reading or beach time, leisurely meals. Interaction should be conducted as in the old days: in person. Or by mail. It was outdated, yes, but Beth respected it. She never considered putting in a phone line.

Once Piper flew to the Cape and Beth had a respite from David, she hunted down a phone booth in town. She wanted to call Kara Schau, her therapist. First to set up an appointment, and then, the next day, to talk. It was more than inconvenient to talk to her therapist in the booth outside of Visitor Services; it was embarrassing. She turned her body so that she faced the building. She would keep her voice low.

Kara Schau came on the line sounding chipper and enthusiastic, and Beth pictured her wearing a beige linen blouse and black skirt, her dark curly hair escaping its bun. Kara was a dream—the kindest, most perceptive woman Beth knew. In the months since Arch died, she'd become a friend, which Beth viewed as a problem. She wanted Kara to like her; she wanted Kara to praise her. She didn't want to delve into the messy emotional situation at hand, but Beth needed to talk to someone, and Kara was a professional.

"How's Nantucket?" Kara asked. "I'm terrifically envious, you know."

"It's fine," Beth said. "Therapeutic."

"As long as it's not putting me out of business," Kara said. "And since you called, I gather it's not. How's everything going?"

"Fine," Beth said. "The kids seem to be coping okay. Marcus is adjusting. He and Winnie spend a lot of time together."

"Good," Kara said. "They both need peer support. Garrett, too, but he's not as forthcoming. I would have been surprised to hear that Garrett and Marcus were close. That bond, if it forms at all, is going to take some time."

"They're not close," Beth said. "At first I worried that they would, you know, *fight*, but that problem has been headed off, for the time being, anyway."

"How?"

"Garrett found a girlfriend."

"Already?" Kara said. "Someone he knew before?"

"Someone he just met," Beth said. "Her name is Piper Ronan. Her father and I are old friends."

"Is it serious?" Kara asked. "Are there sexual issues?"

"Oh, God," Beth said. She took a breath and turned to inspect the street scene. Thankfully, it was a gorgeous day and town was deserted. Everyone was at the beach. "I haven't given the nature of their relationship that much thought. They've only been dating a couple of weeks."

"Fair enough," Kara said. "So it sounds like the kids have found peer support. Winnie and Marcus with each other and Garrett with the new girlfriend. That's excellent. They need it. But what about you? How are *you* doing, Beth?"

"I'm confused," Beth said. Her nose tingled. She couldn't believe the way crying had become such a natural instinct for her, like blinking or yawning. "I miss Arch."

"Yes, you do," Kara said.

Tears fell and Beth pulled a tissue out of her purse. "I really, really miss him."

"It's perfectly natural," Kara said.

"But this thing has happened," Beth said. "This man I mentioned? Piper's father? He's sort of . . . well, he's put himself in my life."

Silence. Beth knew this meant she was to explain further, but she was ashamed to say more. Arch had only been gone for three and a half months and here she was on the phone to her therapist talking about another man. Kara would think she was a terrible person, a cheap, insincere person. But Kara didn't know David Ronan.

"Listen, there are some things I can share with you about this man, and some things I can't. He was my first love. We were together for six summers, from age sixteen to twenty-one. We were . . . very serious. Very. And then we split up and I haven't really seen him since. Oh, once, maybe twice a summer. Arch and I went to his house for a party a million years ago. Then, my first day here, I bumped into him at the grocery store and later I found out he'd separated from his wife, and next thing I know, my son is dating his daughter and he's started pursuing me."

"Pursuing you?" Kara's tone of voice was neutral.

"Well, it's not as if he sends flowers every day," Beth said. In fact, Beth half expected David to produce a big handful of purple cosmos from behind his back every time she saw him, but thank God he hadn't gone that far. "He's just always around. Wanting to talk, wanting to have a beer together. That kind of thing."

"Any physical contact?" Kara asked.

"Minimal," Beth said. This was true, thank God. David hadn't touched her in any significant way. But the way he looked at her—the way his eyes ran up and down her body—made Beth feel like she was standing there naked. He made her feel self-conscious about her appearance. She had actually bought a hair dryer and mascara at the pharmacy last week. How to explain *that?*

"And yet you feel confused?" Kara said.

"Part of me feels drawn to this man," Beth admitted. Okay, there, she'd said it. Part of her was *flattered* by David's attention; if it suddenly stopped, she might miss it. But the guilt—God, the guilt was enough to weigh her to the ocean floor. "But it hasn't been long enough. My grief for Arch is so raw, so consuming—it's exhausting. And I feel disloyal because being with David makes me less unhappy."

"Frequently, one sees a couple who is married for a long time, and then, let's say, the wife dies, and the husband remarries right away. It causes confusion and anger in the people close to him because of the very issue of loyalty. One way to explain this behavior is that he believes in marriage. The second marriage as a tribute, of sorts, to the first. Now, I'm not saying this example applies in your case. But it might. You were married to Arch for a long time. This man fills needs that have been unattended since Arch died."

"Maybe," Beth said. Naturally, she and Arch had talked over the years about what would happen if the other one died. Beth had said she would not want Arch to remarry, mostly because she didn't want another woman raising her children. It was a selfish response, but honest. It made her sick to think of Arch married to someone else. When Beth asked Arch if he would want her to remarry, he said, *Oh, Beth, I would want you to be happy. As happy as you could be without me.*

"What do the kids think?" Kara asked.

"They have no idea," Beth said.

"It's interesting, isn't it, that your relationship with this man . . . what's his name again?"

"David," Beth said, her voice practically a whisper. "David Ronan."

"That your relationship with David is directly tied to Garrett's relationship with his new girlfriend. You can expect some conflicting emotions regarding that."

"I do," Beth said. She waited a beat. "So what do you think? It's wrong, isn't it? I have to stop this before it goes any further." She laughed at her own absurdity. "It's wrong to give him any hope."

"It sounds like you want me to tell you it's wrong," Kara said. "And I'm not going to do that."

There was more to it than just David's advances. There was the whole problem of David himself, their shared past. Beth remembered the ride home from the Ronan cocktail party. She could have told Arch then; she could have come clean. But she clung to her privacy. *Every man, woman, and child is entitled to one secret.* Even from her therapist. Kara Schau was the wrong person to talk to about this. Beth was looking for absolution where there was none. Arch was dead. There was nothing Beth could do now except live with her decision. "I can remember when David was the only person who mattered to me," she said. "His voice was the only voice I wanted to hear."

"Couldn't you pursue a friendship with this man?" Kara asked. "You need more friends, Beth. I've been telling you that for months."

"We're 'just friends' right now," Beth said. "The reason I called is because I sense that David wants the relationship to head in another direction."

"Do *you* want the relationship to turn into a romance?" Kara said.

"I can't believe you're asking me that."

"But that's the question here. That's why you called me. You want me to ask you because you're afraid to ask yourself. Do you want a romantic relationship with this man?"

"Arch just died."

"That's right," Kara said. "I'm not going to tell you what to do, Beth. But I will tell you this one thing. It is very difficult, if not impossible, to relinquish and attach at the same time. Do you understand what I'm saying?"

Did Beth understand? The words brought up a series of perplexing images. She pictured herself relinquishing Arch, like he was a security blanket she was clinging to. Relinquishing Arch like he was a heavy suitcase she could put down. Relinquishing Arch like he was the string of a balloon she could just let go. She thought of her kids: Garrett with the urn of ashes on his dresser, Winnie in the raggedy Princeton sweatshirt. But was it that simple? When the ashes were scattered and the sweatshirt doffed, would the pain go away? Would Arch be gone, finally? And what about the word *attach*? Would she attach to David like a barnacle on his boat? Like they were two subway cars hooked together? Relinquish and attach; what Kara was talking about was the flow of energy in opposite directions. Beth twisted her diamond ring, then realized she was keeping Kara waiting.

"I'm not sure," Beth said.

"You have mourning yet to do," Kara said. "Grief to process. You've been through a lot, Beth."

"I know. I think about it all the time."

"Well, don't do too much thinking," Kara said. "Remember what I told you before you left: less thinking and more doing. Hug your kids. Walk the beach. Pick flowers. Appreciate the moment."

"Pick flowers," Beth repeated. Those damn purple cosmos! "Thanks, Kara."

"Call me whenever you need me," Kara said. "The kids, too."

"Okay," Beth said. " 'Bye."

She hung up and hurried across Federal Street to her car. She felt vaguely criminal, like she'd smoked marijuana or trespassed on private property, and she had to remind herself that what she'd done was perfectly legal. She'd just made a phone call.

At noon, Beth left the house for a run. It was hot outside, which suited her just fine. She wanted to sweat, she wanted to punish herself. She couldn't believe she'd had the guts to tell Kara Schau about David. She thought again about Kara's words: *It is very difficult, if not impossible, to relinquish and attach at the same time.* Like trying to drink wine while standing on her head. Like trying to raise a flag in a hurricane. The next time she saw David, she would repeat Kara's line. And what would David say? That they had beaten odds before. They kept their love alive over six long winters. Every year at the end of August when Beth left Nantucket, she cried all the way back to her family's house in New Jersey. Her mother was kind, offering new clothes for school, reciting the names of Beth's friends whom she would see again after three months away. *We'll have a party!* Beth's father said. *You'll forget about that boy before you know it.* But Beth never forgot. She and David wrote letters, they talked on the telephone at Christmas, and once they were at college—he at UMass/Amherst and she at Sarah Lawrence— they visited each other.

Nothing was like the summertime, though. The warm days at the beach, driving David's Jeep to Coatue, getting munched by mosquitoes when they sailed his Sunfish on Coskata Pond. Spending rainy days reading magazines at the Athenuem, skinny-dipping at the Sankaty Beach Club late at night. Dancing at the Chicken Box, back when it still had a dirt floor. Once a summer splurging on dinner at the Galley at Cliffside Beach where everyone applauded when the sun went down. Standing on Horizon's deck looking at the stars while Beth's brothers whistled out their bedroom windows. Driving to the beach at night to kiss, grope, and finally make love in the sand.

They had loved each other so completely. The last summer they were together, David rented a cottage on Bear Street, and everything grew more serious. They practically lived together. Beth invented a fictional friend from Sarah Lawrence—Olivia Marsh—whose parents owned a summer house. Several times a week, Beth told her parents she was spending the night at Olivia's house, and because there was no phone at Horizon, and no phone at Olivia's parents' cottage, her mother never checked on her. Beth and David cooked meals, they lit a fire if it was chilly, they made love in the bed and fell asleep intertwined.

Beth didn't want to think any further. She couldn't. She was running down Hummock Pond Road towards Cisco Beach and she decided to take a left onto Ahab Drive, the road where David lived. This was a very stupid move, Beth knew. This was counterproductive. She wanted to stay away from David! But David wouldn't be home. He was at work, and he ate lunch on the job. The last place she would be likely to see David was here on Ahab Drive. Peyton had camp until four; Piper was away.

Beth had been to the house the one time for the cocktail party, and then several times these past two weeks, but only as far as the driveway. As she ran past the house, she waved. *Hello, David's house.* She glimpsed the manicured front lawn and the flagstone walk where she'd caught the heel of her sandal as she was leaving the cocktail party.

Beth jogged to the end of the street. The roads in this development all wound back into each other somehow, but Beth wasn't sure exactly how, and so she returned past David's house. It was a nice property, she thought. An actual house rather than a summer cottage like Horizon. It had heat, insulation, a garage.

Without thinking, Beth ran into the gravel driveway. It was as if her feet weren't connected to her brain. All Beth could do was narrate to Kara Schau in her mind.

I went inside David's house when he wasn't home. The door was open. I knew it would be. I wanted to look around.

The house was neat. The kitchen was painted bright blue and there was a package of hamburger defrosting on the counter. There were photographs on the refrigerator—of the girls and David mostly, but some of Rosie. I wasn't surprised because Rosie is still the girls' mother, she's still part of their life as a family. It bugged me a little that Rosie was so beautiful in the pictures—the long hair and the long legs like Piper. And the stomach and ass like she never gave birth to one child, much less two. I spent a fair amount of time studying the pictures of Rosie. Then I went upstairs to David's bedroom. His bed was made. He had a copy of the New Yorker on the nightstand. That caught my eye because I was reading the same issue, and then I wondered if he'd bought it because he knew I had read it.

I went into his bathroom, and this was when I began to wonder if I was losing my mind. What was I doing snooping around David's house? I found a framed picture of Rosie and David on their wedding day. The picture was sitting on top of a small bureau and a reflection of the picture was in the bathroom mirror, which was how I noticed it. David looked so young. He was my David, but he had his arm wrapped around Rosie's tiny waist. They both looked very tan and very happy. The picture made me strangely jealous. I was in Manhattan the summer they got married, the summer after David and I split, and I felt as if Rosie had somehow snatched away what was mine—though of course that wasn't the case. Without thinking twice, I flipped the picture down.

Then I heard a noise downstairs and I nearly leapt out the window. A man yelled out, "UPS!" So I jogged down the stairs and there was the nice UPS boy holding out a manila envelope. He said, "Mrs. Ronan?" And I nodded. He showed me where to sign. Elizabeth Ronan.

Beth left shortly thereafter and ran home thinking, *Forgive me, Arch. I am sicker than I thought.*

⚜

That night, she bought lobsters for dinner. She lugged the big cooking pot up from the basement, she melted a pound of butter, quartered lemons, and shucked some early corn.

"We're going to do it right," she said to Marcus and Winnie when they came up the stairs from the beach. "Lobster dinner."

Marcus eyed the dark creatures suspiciously as they lumbered across the counter. "They're still alive."

Winnie's forehead crinkled. "She's going to boil them alive. They scream. I've heard them."

"They do not scream," Beth said. "This is a treat. A luxury. Where's your brother?"

"Upstairs in his room, moping," Winnie said. "He spent the afternoon writing Piper a letter. I told him that by the time he mailed it, she'd be home. He said it's for her to read when she gets back."

"You shouldn't give your brother a hard time," Beth said. "It's nice that he found a friend."

"He said you're taking him to get his license tomorrow," Winnie said. "True?"

"True," Beth said. "Does that bother you? Do you want to take your driver's test, too? You haven't practiced much."

"I'm not ready yet," Winnie said. "I'd fail."

"Dinner's in thirty minutes," Beth said. As she set the table with the lobster crackers and plastic bibs and butter warmers, she thought about how, at heart, she didn't want Garrett to get his driver's license. Once the word "accident" popped into her brain, it was impossible to stop worrying. Another horrible accident. But the good news was that when Garrett got his license, Beth wouldn't have to see David as often. In fact, she might not see him at all.

I'm sicker than I thought.

Beth dropped the lobsters into the boiling water, then left the kitchen, in case they did scream.

⚘

There was something festive about the way the table looked with a scarlet lobster sitting on each plate, but Beth seemed to be the only one who was excited about it. Garrett slouched miserably in his chair, and Winnie picked her lobster up by the claw and plopped it into the bowl meant for empty shells.

"I'm not eating that."

Marcus was inspecting his plastic bib. "Weird," he said. "This is a bib like a baby wears."

Garrett and Winnie hadn't even deigned to acknowledge their bibs. "It's to keep the melted butter off your shirt," Beth said.

Marcus frowned, but tied the bib behind his neck anyway. "If you say so."

Beth secured her own bib in solidarity, then she lifted her glass of white wine. "Cheers, everyone! Happy summer."

"What do I do with this thing?" Marcus asked, wielding his lobster cracker.

Garrett rolled his eyes and huffed a little.

"Sorry," Marcus said. "We don't eat a lot of boiled lobster in Queens."

Beth showed Marcus how to crack open the claws, and she

separated the meat of the tail from the shell. This, she knew, was the kind of scene Arch had in mind when he invited Marcus to Nantucket. "You're going to love this," she said. "When you get the meat free, you dip it in the melted butter."

Garrett cracked his lobster. Winnie helped herself to a roll, which she tore into pieces. Once Marcus tasted the lobster, his face brightened. "This is great!" he said. "This is delicious." He picked up the extra lobster. "I'll eat Winnie's if she doesn't want it."

"Go ahead," Winnie said.

Beth sipped her wine. She felt empty, scooped out. As a kid, lobster night was magical. It was symbolic of a good, rich life. Her parents always drank too much wine on lobster night; they sang the old songs. *Falling in love again . . . I can't help it.* Now here she sat, alone, with her recalcitrant twins and this boy whose life was anything but good and rich. Beth felt tears coming, but no, she wouldn't ruin it. She was going to work with what she had. Garrett and Marcus were both eating. Winnie had torn up her roll and was now tentatively considering an ear of corn. Beth picked the snowy flesh out of her lobster claw, dunked it in butter and let the taste fill her mouth. She was doing the best she could.

"Piper comes home tomorrow?" she asked Garrett.

"Friday."

"It's nice to have you around for a change. We haven't sat down to dinner like this in a while."

"We should go out more," Winnie said. "When Daddy was here, we used to go out more."

"What do you care if we go out or stay in?" Garrett asked. "You never eat."

"Shut up, man," Marcus said. "I've seen Winnie eat plenty."

"Thank you," Winnie said.

"Maybe we should go out," Beth said. "Maybe all of us should go out when Piper gets back."

"Who cares about Piper?" Winnie said.

"I'll take Piper out alone, thanks," Garrett said. "And if you want to go out with David alone, then just go. Don't use me as an excuse to see him."

"Who said anything about wanting to go out with David?" Beth asked. She ripped off one of the lobster's legs and sucked the juice out of it. "Are you ready for your driver's test tomorrow?"

"You're changing the subject, Mom," Winnie said.

"What subject is that?"

"The subject of David," Winnie said. "I think we should talk about it."

"There's nothing to talk about."

"He likes you."

"He's an old friend. I've known David since I was sixteen years old."

"If you want to date him, I think it's okay," Winnie said. "You don't have to keep blowing him off because of us."

Garrett gagged on his food, sending a shower of corn kernels across the table.

"Spare me," Winnie said to Garrett. "It's okay for you to be happy with Piper, but it's not okay for Mom to be happy?"

Garrett reddened. "These are personal matters," he said. "Family matters."

"Oh, what?" Winnie said. "Now you're going to blast me for bringing this up in front of Marcus? You suck. You really suck."

"I love you, too," Garrett said.

"I'll leave," Marcus said. "I can eat outside."

"You'll do no such thing," Beth said. "This summer, you're part of the family. You're going to have to tolerate our squabbles."

"I like David," Marcus said. "He seems straight up and down. But he's not Arch. Arch was one in a million."

Everyone at the table was silent at those words. Beth put a finger under her nose. *Don't cry,* she told herself.

"Thank you for saying that, Marcus," she said. "That means a lot."

Marcus shrugged and dug meat out of a lobster claw. "It's true," he said. "Arch will never be replaced. He died trying to save my mother."

"Arch's death had nothing to do with your mother," Beth said. "It was an accident."

"He wouldn't have been on that plane if it weren't for my mother," Marcus said.

"That's true," Garrett said. He looked defiantly around the table. "I mean, no one can really deny that."

Winnie glared at Garrett, then rolled the ear of corn away from her on the plate. "Let's get back to the subject at hand. We won't think you're trying to replace Daddy if you want to date David, Mom."

"I will not be dating David," Beth said. Her voice sounded unusually firm. She wanted to set the record straight, for the kids and for herself. "We're just friends. But thank you for your permission. It's nice to know you realize I'm a person, too. I get lonely, too. In fact, sometimes it's very lonely being the mom."

"But you have us," Winnie said.

Beth tried to smile. "Of course," she said. "I have you."

⚘

Beth sat on the wicker sofa drinking wine long after the kids went to bed, thinking about how unfair it was that David Ronan should reappear to haunt her *this* summer, which was already so painful. She couldn't believe she had gone to his house. She had signed her name as "Elizabeth *Ronan*." Beth cringed, thinking that in a million years she would never have the guts to admit that one to Kara Schau, much less anyone else.

She didn't want to waste her time thinking about David Ronan. She should be thinking of Arch, remembering him. Remembering what was the freshest in her mind—their last day together. It was early March, not a romantic time of the year in anyone's book, but Arch had called mid-morning from the office.

"Lunch at Le Refuge?" he said. "I can get out of here in ten minutes and meet you at quarter to one if traffic's not too bad."

"Sure," she said. "What's the occasion?"

"I have to go to Albany in the morning," Arch said.

"For how long?"

"Just the day," Arch said. "But for a good reason. Alex Benson has agreed to meet with me about Connie."

Alex Benson was an old law school friend of Arch's. He was close to the governor, politically and personally, and Beth knew Arch had been trying for months to set up this meeting. "Anything promising?" she asked.

"Oh, who knows," Arch said. "To be honest, honey, the most

promising thing in my life right now is our lunch date. I'll see you in a little while."

Beth could remember thinking, as she hung up the phone, that she wished Constance Tyler's trial would start and finish, if only because the gravity of it sapped Arch of his usual sunny disposition. Since Arch had started working on the case, he'd become preoccupied, and less tolerant of frivolity. He'd snapped at Winnie the week before for complaining about her SAT prep course.

"Thank God you don't have any real problems," Arch said. "You could be sitting on Riker's Island facing lethal injection or life in prison."

He was impossible now, too, at cocktail parties. He took legal research to the gym and read on the StairMaster.

Taking on the case and taking it on for free made Arch feel righteous. He earned lots of money defending corporate Manhattan against charges of fraud, false advertising, sexual harassment, and general bad faith, but with the Constance Tyler case he felt he was helping someone who needed help. He knew she was guilty, but he was so opposed to the death penalty that to be able to fight it and win just once would make his career worthwhile. His partners at the law firm frowned on all the time the case was eating up, and the enormous expense, but this didn't phase Arch in the slightest. He brought in twice as much business as any other partner—he'd earned the right to take this case, a point he made quietly at the monthly partners' meeting. Constance Tyler was his top priority, period. At times, Beth actually felt *jealous* of Connie, so thoroughly did she consume Arch's thoughts.

❧

At lunch, Arch was in a surprisingly good mood. He arrived before Beth and was waiting at their favorite table with a bouquet of flame-colored roses.

"Look at you," Beth said. "Look what you've done."

"Orange roses," he said, presenting them to her. "They seemed right somehow for a dreary day in March." He kissed her. "I love dating my wife."

"This is a great surprise," Beth said. "I was just at home thinking about how I might clean out the china cabinet."

"Let the china cabinet go uncleaned!" he said. He called the waiter over and ordered a bottle of Sancerre. "I'm not going back to the office today."

"You're not?"

"No, I'm not. Once the trial starts next week I'm going to be slammed. So today I'm going to have a long, leisurely, wine-soaked lunch with my wife and then I'm going to walk her home in the rain and spend the afternoon in bed with her."

What Beth remembered now was how fortunate she felt that afternoon. They drank not one, but two bottles of wine, they ate goat cheese and wild mushrooms and garlic-studded lamb and lemon tart. They talked about all of the things they never had time to talk about at home—trips they wanted to take once the kids went to college, the books they were reading, current events. After Arch paid the bill, Beth floated to the door inhaling the scent of her roses. She was certainly the luckiest woman on earth.

They walked home in the cold drizzle, giggling and falling against each other. Arch pulled Beth past their apartment building, up to Madison Avenue.

"I want to buy shoes," he said.

They went into Giovanni Bellini's, which was hushed and smelled of expensive leather. The sumptuous pairs of hand-crafted loafers were lined up on the shelves. The first pair Arch reached for were an outlandish electric blue.

"To go with my seersucker suit," he said. To the salesman, whose mouth was a grim line, he said, "Ten and a half, *por favor*. Oops, wait a minute, that's Spanish. Beth, how do you say 'please' in Italian?"

She sat on the plush bench in the middle of the room. "*Prego*, I think."

"Like the spaghetti sauce?"

They started giggling and the salesman disappeared and returned with a box. Arch tried the shoes on. He looked adorably clownish—his dark suit and the blue shoes.

"The thing is," Arch said, "some people actually buy these. Europeans."

Beth urged him to be quiet.

"You know," Arch said to the salesman, "these are a little flamboyant for me. May I see the black tasseled loafers in a ten and a half?"

Arch bought two pairs of shoes and three pairs of dress socks. This improved the salesman's humor. When they left the store, he bid them farewell with an authentic sounding "*Ciao!*"

Beth and Arch returned to the apartment and showered together, something they hadn't done in years. They made love on the bathroom floor, then wrapped themselves in towels and fell into bed.

It was dark when Beth woke up. Arch lay next to her, snoring. She was confused for a minute, thinking it was the middle of the night, but then she remembered the lunch. It was still afternoon.

Five minutes to five. Winnie had swimming until six, and what was today? Monday. Garrett had floor hockey on Monday. He'd also be home around six. Beth snuggled up to Arch. She loved to watch him sleep. He slept so devotedly, like he was giving sleep everything he had.

She switched on the TV and caught the last half hour of *Love Story* on TNT. Oliver buys plane tickets to Paris, but no, it's too late. Jennifer has leukemia. She dies, Oliver sits alone in the snowy park. Beth was sniffling when Arch finally opened his eyes.

"Jennifer's dead," she said. She turned off the TV and sank back into the pillows. "I love that movie but I always hope that it will end differently. Of course it never does. We should get up. The kids'll be home soon. They'll need to eat."

"Jade Palace?" Arch said. "Pu-pu platter for four?"

"After that lunch, I thought I'd skip dinner," Beth said. "But I could go for a pu-pu platter."

Now, at Horizon, Beth poured herself the last of the wine. She remembered that dinner, the four of them at Jade Palace eating potstickers and spare ribs and crab rangoons. She remembered Arch and her sitting in the backseat of the cab with Winnie on the way home—Arch in the middle with his arms around both of them, saying, "I love my girls." She remembered getting home and listening to the phone messages—one message from Arch's secretary, Polly, with his travel arrangements for the next day, and one message from Caroline Margolis inviting them to a dinner party on Saturday.

"Tell her we'll come if she makes her key lime pie," Arch said.

The day ended with Beth calling Caroline to accept, the kids going to their rooms to do homework, and Arch disappearing into his office to prepare for his trip to Albany. Later, Beth and Arch climbed into bed and read for a while.

"This was the perfect day," Beth said. "Thank you."

Arch kissed her. "If I could, Beth, I'd spend every day with you just like I did today."

He was gone in the morning before she woke up, but when she rolled over she found one of the flame-colored roses on his pillow.

The painful part about remembering all the details from her last day with Arch was that these same details were cruelly present two days later—she didn't find out Arch's plane had crashed until very early on the morning of March 16th. Beth was wakened by the phone at quarter to six in the morning, and when she noticed Arch wasn't in bed, she yelled to him to answer it. She didn't realize he wasn't home. He'd called the night before to say his flight was delayed because of weather and he'd be home late, and Beth assumed he came to bed then got up early to work in his study. When the phone didn't get answered and the machine picked up, Beth groaned and reached for the phone through the fog of her sleep. That groan, that action of reaching, was the last innocent moment before learning the awful truth. At times, she wished she could freeze time and stay there, half asleep, in the not-knowing.

It was Trent Trammelman on the phone, the managing partner of Arch's firm. The authorities had called him first because it was the law firm's plane.

Beth screamed like she was falling into a hole she knew she would never escape from. And then, the absolute worst thing she'd ever had to do in her life: tell Winnie and Garrett, who were in their rooms getting ready for school, that their father was dead. Winnie was in her bra and panties, shrieking with embarrassment when Beth opened her bedroom door. Beth didn't remember speaking any words, but she must have conveyed the news in some way because Winnie crumpled to the ground like she'd been hit by a bullet, and Beth sank to her knees and covered Winnie's body with her own, the two of them moaning. Garrett found them there and he, too, started wailing, which really pushed Beth over the edge: her strong teenage son crying like a baby.

Before she knew it, the apartment was filled with people. People from the law firm, friends, Arch's mother, kids from Danforth. In Beth's mind, this happened instantly. The apartment was filled with people and the smell of coffee and cell phones ringing and talk of the black box, and there was Beth still in her nightgown, like one of those bad dreams where she was throwing a party but had forgotten to get dressed. The buzzer from downstairs rang again and again—the florist with sickly-sweet arrangements, her neighbor with a ham, Caroline Margolis with a key lime pie. Was she imagining this? It was all happening so fast, so soon, these condolences, that Beth grew confused. She was waiting for Arch to walk through the door to the apartment and send everyone else home. By evening, hysteria set in. Arch was never coming home. She would never see him again.

One of the people who came that first day was Dr. Schau, who was Trent's wife's therapist. She showed up after office hours and gave Beth a shot and finally everything slowed down. Beth was able to see the horrible things in the apartment that no one else could see: the eleven orange roses, the boxes with two brand new pairs of men's shoes, the leftover moo shu pork in the refrigerator.

The vision, when she closed her eyes, of Oliver sitting alone in the snowy park.

※

By midnight, Beth had finished the wine but she was still wide awake. She would be forced to take a Valium, but first she stood up and went to the screen door. It frightened her to remember how raw her grief had been. Now, after four months, she had coping mechanisms in place. The thing that helped the most was that she was here on Nantucket. Not only was Nantucket quieter than New York, it was darker. All she could see were the stars and a couple of tiny lights from her neighbors' houses in the distance. Then, a pair of headlights approached. Kids headed to the beach. Drunk, probably. Beth shuddered: when she woke up, she would have to take Garrett to get his license. As the car drew closer to Beth's house, it slowed down. Beth switched on the porch light. David's truck. She blinked twice, certain she was hallucinating. Too much wine. But no—it was David, driving by her house in the middle of the night. Beth's first instinct was indignation, until she realized it was no worse than her walking through his house that afternoon. She opened the door as quietly as she could and tiptoed down the shell driveway in her bare feet. She climbed into the truck.

David was in a T-shirt and shorts. His hair was mussed. Without a word, he drove toward the water. When all that was in front of them was ocean and night sky, he stopped. He undid his seatbelt and slumped against his door. "I couldn't sleep."

"Me, either."

"I missed you so much. I managed twenty years without you, but the last three days almost killed me."

Beth had no idea how to respond to this. Part of her felt the same way—she had gone to his *house!* But, as ever, there was her guilt and longing for Arch. She remembered back to March sixteenth. At night, after all the people went home, she and Winnie and Garrett slept in the same bed. They did that for two weeks.

"David, we have to stop this."

"I feel like a teenager," he said. "I used to do this all the time after you left for the summer. I'd drive by your house and imagine you standing inside the screen door, just like you were doing a few seconds ago. It used to make me feel better to look at your house because I knew you'd always come back to it."

Beth put her hands over her eyes; he was so handsome she was afraid to look at him. The smart thing, she realized, would have been to stay safely inside her house. "We can't recreate those days, David. Too much has happened in our lives."

David rubbed his stubbly chin. "We were in love."

"Yes, we were."

"Were, Bethie?"

"Were," she said.

"I'm in love with you now," David said. "When I split with Rosie . . . when I read about Arch in the paper . . . when I saw you at the store . . . actually, no. Forget all that. I never stopped loving you. I had to *live* here, Beth. I had to live each day with all of our memories. It made getting over you impossible."

"You managed fine without me," Beth said. "You married Rosie the next year. You had kids."

"It was never quite right," David said. "Rosie finally realized it and left."

"You're not blaming me for your separation?" Beth said. "That's absurd."

"It's only your fault in the larger sense," David said. "In the sense that during all those years with Rosie, a part of my heart was missing."

"Don't tell me that, David," Beth said. "Your problems with Rosie are between the two of you. They have nothing to do with me." She remembered the wedding picture she found in David's bathroom. Something about how it was placed so that there were actually two pictures in the bathroom—the picture itself and its reflection—made Beth understand that the picture was important to David. What it represented was important. After all, Rosie was still alive; her marriage to David was still viable. Maybe he'd go back to her. That would be for the best.

"The past two weeks have been the happiest weeks I've had in ages," David said. "Just knowing I would see you, even for a few minutes." He leaned over the console that separated the two seats and took her chin. He held her face and hooked her eyes, making her look at him. Making her see him. What did he want from her? Maybe he wanted her to admit the truth—that she felt the same way, that she, too, looked forward, a little bit, to seeing him, that he made her feel less sad, that he provided hope, a glimpse into what might someday lie beyond all this heavy grief. But a second later, Beth understood that what David wanted was beyond words. His face grew closer; he kept his fingers on her chin. He was going to kiss her.

He was kissing her; they were kissing.

Beth forgot herself for a second. She was tired, she'd had a lot of wine, and surely just one second wasn't going to hurt anyone, one second of David's lips, which tasted like the best young love imaginable, which tasted like summer, which tasted like home. One second then one second more. David's tongue touched her bottom lip lightly, and that was enough. Beth opened her eyes.

"Whoa," she said, pulling away. "Whoa. Wait."

David stared at her. Her cover was blown, her lie exposed. She wasn't a woman in mourning after all. She had kissed him back. A hideous blackness gathered behind her eyes and she gazed out the window at the water. She had kissed him back.

"There," he whispered.

There? As in, *take that?* Beth wasn't sure what he meant by "there," but it didn't make her feel any better. "Okay," she said, fresh out of words herself.

"You can pretend that never happened," David said. "I, of course, won't be able to."

Beth's mind raced around in search of something to say. A kiss! What a perfect ending for today—she had walked through David's empty house, she had signed her name Elizabeth Ronan, *and for my final trick, ladies and gentlemen . . .* the kiss. Only months after the death of her husband, she had kissed David Ronan.

"I'm taking Garrett to get his license tomorrow," she said. "Once he can drive, the kids won't need us to chauffeur them around."

"So we'll go out alone," David said.

"We will not," Beth said. "I know I'm sending mixed messages—and not only to you, but to myself. But I just lost my husband, and unlike you, a piece of my heart *wasn't* missing. I loved Arch Newton with my whole heart. I loved him with my mind and soul and spirit."

David straightened his arms to the steering wheel. "Because you left me with your heart intact," he said. "*You* left *me*. I was the one who got his heart broken. I was the one who had to face your father at the front door of that house back there and listen to him tell me that you never wanted to see me again and that I'd be hearing from his lawyer."

"I won't talk about that," Beth said. "And I don't want you to talk about it either."

"You do remember what happened, don't you?"

"*Of course* I remember what happened," Beth said. "But guess what? Splitting with you wasn't the worst thing that ever happened to me. The worst thing was—"

"Losing your husband," David said. "I know, I know."

"You do *not* know," Beth said. "I'm offended that you pretend to know."

"I know about losing the person I loved most in the world," David said. "That's what it was for me when you left."

Beth was quiet. She deserved this and worse, even twenty-five years after the fact. But she felt she needed to address the kiss; she had to let him know that there would be no more kisses and certainly no dating.

"I'm going to ask you to give up," Beth said. "I'm going to ask you to leave me alone."

"I will not give up," David said. "Because some day you'll recover. And when you do, I'm going to be here. I'm going to be waiting for you."

Beth bumped her head against the passenger window. She felt sixteen, as emotionally inept as her children. "I'm tired," Beth said. "Will you please take me home?"

They drove back to Horizon in silence. David let her out at the end of the driveway, but as she walked past his window, he grabbed her arm.

"You never once said you were sorry," he said. "You broke a solemn vow without explaining why. I figured it out eventually—you were too young, you were scared—but you didn't even apologize."

When she looked at him, she saw the past in his eyes. She recognized the look of loss on his face as he stood at the front door of Horizon confronting her father. It was too painful to remember. Beth turned away.

"Good night, David," she said.

chapter 4

He'd been on Nantucket for three weeks but it felt like three months. Or three years. His reality had changed. He was now a person who ate steak and lobsters, he was a person who lounged on the beach and took outdoor showers. He was a person who read Robert Ludlum novels and played Monopoly, amassing paper fortunes.

Now that Garrett was dating Piper, Marcus spent a lot of time alone with Winnie. Since the night he found her eating in the kitchen, they'd grown closer. Marcus saw that Winnie was like Arch—beneath her little-girl, noneating, self-pitying facade lay a decent heart. She listened, she asked questions, and she moved through her days utterly devoted to him, Marcus, a black kid from Queens with a now awful-looking Afro. Not because she felt sorry for him, but because she thought he was special. Marcus could tell she was genuine in this.

After nine months of losing people in his life, he had found a friend.

They spent practically every day at the beach together. Swimming in the waves—almost always the butterfly, which was Marcus's stroke. He was teaching Winnie how to improve her form; he wanted her to be a kick-ass flyer in time for her senior year. When the tide was right, they swam out past the breaking waves where Marcus could still stand on the sandy bottom and he held Winnie—one hand under her stomach, one hand on the back of her thighs—and showed her how to strengthen her kick. He only touched her when they were in the water, and he had to admit, he was starting to like the way she felt weightless in his arms. He liked to watch her body do the stroke, her ass bucking through the water. He liked how she tried so hard to do exactly what he said, *keep your head down, lengthen your reach*.

One day when they were drying off, she said, "So what do you think? Are Garrett and Piper having sex?"

Marcus fell face-first onto his striped beach towel. This wasn't a conversation he wanted to have. Especially since he knew the answer was yes; he'd seen a Trojan wrapper in the bathroom trash when he emptied the can three days before. "What do you care?" he said.

"He's my twin brother."

"I'd think that would make you not want to know."

"Of course I want to know. I mean, I guess it's no big deal if he has sex before I do. He *is* a boy."

"Whatever that means."

Winnie rested back in her chaise. "I just worry about getting left behind."

"It's not a race," Marcus said.

Winnie rolled her sweatshirt up under her bikini top. "Piper is so pretty. Don't you think she's pretty?"

"She's pretty," Marcus said. "But not as pretty as you."

Winnie whipped her head around. "Really?"

"Relax," he said.

"You just implied that I'm prettier than Piper. You think that? Really, Marcus?"

"The correct response was 'thank you.' I never say stuff unless I mean it, but I'm not going to repeat it a hundred times so you can feel all wonderful about yourself."

"How about repeating it once?"

"You're prettier than Piper," Marcus said. Winnie beamed and lay back in her chaise, smiling at the sun. Yes, she was prettier. Piper was good-looking, but she knew it. She wore outfits that put her commodities on display for the world to see. Winnie was pretty in a quiet, natural way, like Beth. Half the time, she looked terrible—hair wet, eyes red and puffy from crying, and always wearing that god-awful, misshapen sweatshirt—and yet her humanity made her beautiful.

As July approached, Marcus found himself with two new worries. The first was that twenty-one days had passed and he'd gotten nowhere with his writing. His legal pad was blank but for the one sentence: *My mother is a murderer.* The five hundred dollars, gone forever, took on *Alice in Wonderland*–like proportions in his mind. He now had three unopened letters from his mother, which he'd stuffed into his left dock shoe. His dock shoes were in the back corner of his closet where he didn't have to think about them. He would only open his mother's letters if he got really desperate. Marcus tried to banish the memory of Zachary Celtic (*your own mother, pretty woman, too, facing the strap-down on the gurney, the long needle . . .*) and concentrated instead on Nick's sole comment, "You get to tell the story in your own words, kid." It was beginning to seem that Marcus had no words. Not on this topic, anyway.

Marcus's other worry was that he was attracted to Winnie. Maybe because she had brought up sex, or because Garrett was having sex, sex became an invisible third party hanging around whenever Winnie and Marcus were together. And sex was out of the question. If it ever happened, Garrett would kill him and Beth would send him home immediately.

Marcus was supposed to call his father every two weeks, but since Horizon had no phone, Marcus only called when he got the chance. At the beginning of July, he called from a phone booth in town. Too anxious to sit, Marcus stood in the booth and stared at the street, all the white people in their fancy clothes shopping for scented candles and needlepoint pillows. The first question his father asked was, "Why haven't you answered your mother's letters?"

"How do you know I haven't answered them?"

"I know," Bo Tyler said, "because your sister and I visited her last week and she told me she's written to you three times and hasn't heard back."

"I don't feel like writing," Marcus said. Man, was that the truth!

Bo made one of his *hmmph*ing noises. Then he said, "Your mother needs our support."

Here was the thing Marcus couldn't get his mind around. Constance had committed murder—she was responsible for two deaths, three if you included Uncle Leon, four if you included Arch—and now she needed their support? The Newtons all went to see some kind of therapist to help them deal with their loss, and that sounded like what Marcus needed—someone to help him with his loss. He had lost his mother. She woke up on the morning of October seventh, and without warning, changed their lives forever.

On that day, Marcus was sitting in trigonometry class trying to file away what he would have to remember about sine, cosine, tangent, and cotangent for the next quiz, when the intercom buzzed and the secretary asked for Marcus to be sent to the office. The kids in his class all *ooohed* and *uh-oh*ed, because a student generally got sent to the office for bad things, although Marcus was one of the least likely people in the class to be in trouble. Marcus himself thought uneasily of how, the month before, his friend Eriq had been called to the office because Eriq's girlfriend had given birth to twin girls. And that was it for Eriq and Benjamin N. Cardozo High School. He dropped out the following week and Marcus hadn't seen him since.

Whatever Marcus was preparing himself for as he loped down the hall to the main office, it certainly wasn't the sight of his father, Bo, in brown pants, yellow shirt, brown sweater vest, his face twisted into an unrecognizable, sobbing mess. What could Marcus think but that his mother or sister had died? Without a word, Bo led Marcus out of the school and into a waiting police car. Marcus's sister, LaTisha, was sitting in the back screaming and crying like her limbs had been severed, and so, Marcus concluded, *My mother is dead.*

And really, Marcus thought now, wasn't that the truth of the matter? With her incredible act of violence, Constance had ended her life. She had ripped herself from the family. Marcus and LaTisha no longer had a mother, Bo no longer had a wife. And yet here was Bo on the other end of the phone telling Marcus that they needed to support his mother. Marcus loved his father—Bo was a sturdy, hard-working man who went to church and put food on the table. But Bo had moments of ignorance and weakness and it took effort for Marcus not to feel sorry for his father. Bo worked at the printing press of the *New York Times* and so he had been one of the first people to read the incriminating articles, to see the ghoulish photographs. Right there in the newspaper that he himself printed! Marcus asked Bo why he didn't quit on the spot, and Bo said, "I've had the job for seventeen years, son. It's not something I would just walk out on." The same was true for their apartment. The blood damage in the apartment was so bad that Marcus, Bo and LaTisha spent the subsequent twenty days in the Sunday Sermon Motel while disaster specialists cleaned up. Marcus and LaTisha had to share a room; the hotel had roaches and intermittent hot water, and it took Marcus an extra 40 minutes to get to school. The whole time, Marcus begged his father to consider moving. He couldn't stomach the idea of living on the place where "it" happened.

"Where would we go?" Bo said. "Our apartment is rent-controlled. We'll stick it out, and eventually people will forget. They'll move on to the next thing. I've seen enough news pass before my eyes to know this to be true."

Bo had remained loyal to Connie through it all, but Marcus felt differently. He was going to write this book, take the money, and leave his old life behind.

"Okay," Marcus said to his father, just to say something. "I'll give it some thought."

"See that you do," Bo said. "Are you having fun up there?"

"Yep."

"Helping out?"

"Yes, Pop."

"All right, then. We miss you, son."

"I miss you, too, Pop," Marcus said, feeling like he'd eaten nothing but guilt for breakfast.

"We'll talk to you. Please write to your mother."

" 'Bye," Marcus said. He hated to admit it, but he was relieved to hang up the phone.

⚘

That night, Marcus woke up when Garrett came home from his date with Piper. Marcus checked his clock: one-fifteen. He waited until Garrett used the bathroom, brushed his teeth, and returned to his room, then he went to the door and peered down the hallway. Dark. The door to Winnie's room was a few yards away. It was hung crooked and didn't close properly and something about that door, slightly ajar, was irresistible. But Marcus knew what would happen if he went into her room. Just the way Mama knew what would happen when she opened the door to see Angela. Marcus tried to steady his breathing; he should go back to sleep. But his throat ached with the need to talk to someone and Winnie was the best friend he had now.

The house made some eerie creaking noises beneath his feet. He stood at Winnie's door and held onto the frame on either side, steadying himself. He was afraid that if he knocked, the door might swing open and she would be frightened and yell. So he knocked on the frame. The wood was dense and the sound of knocking was hard to hear, even to Marcus's own ears. Three tough knocks, indistinguishable from the house's other settling noises. Marcus was terrified that Garrett or Beth would come out into the hallway. He figured Garrett had stayed up late many nights trying to catch Marcus in this very act: going after his sister. And then Marcus remembered the horrible scene from *Native Son* where Bigger Thomas goes in to the rich white girl's room—she asks him to—and he's so afraid of getting caught that he kills her. Marcus shook his head. When they'd read the book in Ms. Marchese's English class, Marcus never imagined he'd be involved with a white girl. But here he was, scaring himself. He would go back to bed.

Right then the door opened and Marcus saw a very narrow slice of Winnie. One eye, a sliver of gray sweatshirt, one toenail painted pink.

"I'm sorry to bother you," Marcus whispered. Already, he felt like a fool. He hadn't considered what he would say if Winnie actually answered the door, and now that she had, he sounded like a Jehovah's Witness. "Do you mind if we talk?"

She opened the door a little wider. He could see most of her mouth. "You want to come in?"

He noticed she was wearing only the sweatshirt and some underwear. He looked beyond her to her rumpled bed. He was making a huge mistake. He should wait and talk to her in the morning, on the beach. But he couldn't make himself move away. He was sucked into Winnie's gravitational pull.

Winnie took his hand. She had prayed to God every night since they got here that this would happen, and now she was so elated she practically pushed Marcus into her bed. She'd made out with Charlie Hess in the humid, chlorine-smelling corridors outside the pool, but that was the extent of her sex life. She was ready for more.

Kissing her, really kissing her, lying down on the bed, Marcus almost cried. Winnie fit in his arms perfectly, like a child would have. She was so small, so slender. He wanted to go slowly. He wanted to kiss her until sleep carried them both off. But Winnie was going crazy. Her hands were all over him, and she was warm. He was overwhelmed by having her so close, and he willed his body to relax. He had a sense that sex would change things, possibly even ruin them, and yet he was so turned on, he was rigid, pulsing, and utterly confused. He should have stayed in his own bed, in his own room! He pulled away from her and tried to get his bearings—they were falling off the bed. Talking—what was the right posture for talking? He sat against the headboard and gathered the covers into his lap to hide himself from her.

Winnie sat up next to him. She knew she'd gotten him worked up and it made her proud. "So," she said, teasing him. "What do you want to talk about?"

He tasted different words: "my mother," "Mama," "Constance." But he couldn't bring himself to speak. There were so many things he wanted to tell her. About the sweatshirt for starters— how his own teammates had left him without a stitch of clothing and how Arch had come all the way to Queens with the sweatshirt, and how that afternoon proved to Marcus that Arch was one person in the world that he could trust. Everyone else had abandoned him—his friends, his teachers, his cowardly father. His mother. Marcus also wanted to explain to Winnie how dealing with all that made him stronger. How he knew he could have won every race of the swim season, but he held himself to second each time, so that Marcus's swim coach seemed to forget that Marcus was the murderer's son and presented him with the most consistent swimmer trophy at the end-of-the-season banquet. He wanted to tell Winnie about how he was going to write a book and with the money, put himself through college. Marcus was afraid that just saying the words, "book deal," would sound like bragging and quite possibly the magic attached to those words would vanish.

Marcus felt badly because he came here with noble intentions—of talking—but now he found his body in stiff revolt. His body wanted to be kissing Winnie and rubbing her right up against him.

"I like you," he said, finally. Because this seemed like a truth that had to be acknowledged.

"I like you, too," she said, snaking a hand under the covers.

He banged his head lightly against the wooden headboard of her bed and moved her hand away. He remembered when Arch invited him to Nantucket. It was only a few days before his trip to Albany, it was early March—cold, wet, and miserable. Arch called Marcus at home, ostensibly to see how Marcus had fared in the All-Queens Invitational (second place) but really just to check in, take Marcus's temperature, as it were.

Only ten days before the trial. How are you hanging in?

My life sucks, Marcus said. *I can't wait for this thing to be over.*

Arch was quiet for a minute, then he cleared his throat and said, *What are your plans for this summer?*

This summer?

You like to swim, right? Do you like the beach?

Yeah, Marcus said. *I guess so, yeah.*

How about you join my family and me on Nantucket this summer? We stay in a funky old summer cottage that my wife inherited. It's right on the ocean.

I don't know, Marcus said. At the time, it seemed like Arch was offering too much and Marcus had the sinking feeling that Arch knew something Marcus didn't. Like they were going to lose the trial and Constance was going to die.

I want you to consider it, Arch said. *Seriously. It would be good for you to get away. It would be good for my family, too.*

Marcus had doubted that, even at the time. The Newtons needed him around like they needed bugs in their beds.

"I shouldn't be here this summer," Marcus said now, to Winnie.

"What?" Winnie said. "You don't know what you're talking about. I love it that you're here."

"Garrett hates me," Marcus said. "He looks at me funny."

"He looks at everybody funny," Winnie said.

This was true. As many times as Arch had said, *My daughter, Winnie, you'll like her*, he'd never said anything similar about Garrett.

"There was something else I wanted to tell you," Marcus said. "Something you should know."

"What is it?" Winnie said.

"I miss him, too."

"Who?"

"Your father," Marcus said. "Arch . . ." He didn't know how to continue. What to say about Arch that Winnie didn't already know or that hadn't already been said by somebody else? In the *New York Times* a city councilman was quoted as saying "New York has lost not only a good attorney, but a good citizen, a hero for the common man." A hero, Marcus thought, for one family on the verge of imploding. "Your dad. Arch. I miss him just like the rest of you do."

Winnie covered her eyes with her hand. "Will you please stay here with me tonight?"

"I can't," Marcus said, though sex, that tangible presence, seemed to be standing next to the bed, egging Marcus on. "What if we get caught?"

"We won't get caught," Winnie said.

"Not tonight," Marcus said.

"Tomorrow night?"

"Another night," he said. Talking, too, would have to wait for another night. Real talking—telling Winnie all the secrets that were crowded into his heart. He couldn't go into any of it while he was in Winnie's bed with Winnie half naked and all over him. With enormous effort, he moved away from Winnie and put his feet on the cool wood floor. When he stood up, the floorboards squeaked. He pushed sex out of the way and tiptoed into the hall, closing Winnie's door behind him. Arch was dead, Constance was alive. It was wrong and yet with all his anger and confusion, Marcus also felt gratitude, an enormous gratitude because he was *here*. Suddenly the summer seemed short and precious; he wanted it to last forever.

⚘

In the Elmhurst section of Queens, the Fourth of July was a huge, multicultural block party. Whole streets were closed off and the half-barrel bar-b-q pits appeared for jerk chicken and pork shoulder—the Laotian women passed around hand-rolled lumpia. Kids set off bottle rockets and adults drank beer on the front stoops. The music was loud; there was a fist fight or two. Constance had always disdained the chaos—year after year she stayed inside with the air-conditioning cranked, drinking from a cold bottle of white wine while she prepared coleslaw for a hundred people. At dinnertime, she sent Marcus down to the street with the coleslaw mounded in her one good wooden salad bowl with more or less the same sentence: "Make sure nobody walks off with that bowl, child!" No one would confuse Connie for a patriot.

This year things were going to be different. Beth had gotten up at six in the morning to beat the rush to the grocery store, where she bought red, white, and blue napkins, plates, cups, miniature flags, and bags and bags of food. When Marcus woke up and went downstairs, he helped Beth put the groceries away.

"Are you, like, a member of the D.A.R. or something?" he asked.

"No," Beth said. "But we're taking a picnic to Jetties Beach tonight. We do it every year. And this year's special because you're here. And Piper and Peyton are coming."

"And David?" Marcus asked.

"No, not David." Beth didn't explain why, and Marcus knew enough to keep his foot out of that mud puddle.

Every day on Nantucket was summer, but the Fourth of July was especially summer. Beth made blueberry pancakes for breakfast and then Marcus and Winnie rode their bikes into town to watch the small parade up Main Street, the water fight between the Fire Department and the elementary school kids, and the pie-eating contest. Marcus and Winnie held hands—which started as Winnie grabbing Marcus's hand so that he wouldn't get lost in the crowd, and ended up as just plain holding hands. They went into some shops, looking for a suitable souvenir to send home to Marcus's sister. Marcus found nothing suitable, although he wasn't really concentrating. He was too aware of Winnie's hand in his, how good it felt, and yet he was concerned about what they must look like, a black boy and a white girl. Marcus felt as if he had a flashing red light on his head, announcing, INTERRACIAL COUPLE! But nobody even glanced at them sideways until they rounded the corner onto Federal Street and bumped smack into Garrett and Piper.

Marcus dropped Winnie's hand immediately but she made things worse by putting her arm around his waist and squeezing him. He moved away. He'd told her that one of the conditions of their being together was that they had to conceal it from Beth and Garrett. Winnie didn't understand why he felt this way; she didn't like hiding things from her mom and brother, but she agreed. She had said, *Okay, I promise,* and yet now here she was, in Garrett's face, hugging Marcus.

Garrett frowned. Marcus couldn't believe they'd run into him. He had still been asleep when Marcus and Winnie left the house on their bikes.

"What's up?" Marcus said.

"Nothing," Garrett said.

"We're shopping for LaTisha," Winnie said. Winnie pronounced the name like it belonged to a white person: "Leticia." "We watched the pie-eating contest. This skinny girl won. She ate a whole pie in, like, thirty seconds."

"You should have entered, Winnie," Garrett said. "You could use a whole pie."

"Okay, we're going," Winnie said, taking Marcus's unwilling hand. "Hi, good-bye."

"I'll see you tonight," Piper said. "I think my dad might join us even though he's technically not invited."

Winnie pulled Marcus down the street, like he was a stubborn dog. "See ya!"

Marcus said, "I thought we agreed to keep this a secret."

"We all live in the same house," Winnie said. "It's been a secret for two days. You think they don't know something's changed between us?"

"They didn't know until now."

"Who cares what Garrett thinks anyway. He's turned into such a jerk since Daddy died."

"He'll try to kill me."

"He doesn't care about you and me. All he cares about is having sex with Piper." Winnie stopped in front of another souvenir shop. "What about pot holders? Do you think LaTisha would like some pot holders?"

When they got home, the Range Rover was in the driveway; Garrett had beaten them back. Marcus wanted to go up to his room and give writing a try, but Beth had made a special Fourth of July lunch. Grilled hotdogs, pasta salad, homemade lemonade. Marcus ate three hotdogs sitting next to Winnie at the picnic table. Garrett sat across from them, scowling. Even Beth seemed impatient. She snapped at Winnie for cutting her hotdog into pieces.

"I went to a lot of trouble to make this lunch, young lady," Beth said. "You *will* eat it."

This was so unlike Beth that everyone at the table stopped eating, except for Winnie, who actually put a piece of hotdog into her mouth.

When, after lunch, Winnie asked him if he wanted to swim, Marcus said no. He was going upstairs to his room. He wanted to let things cool off, then make Winnie come to her senses.

She knocked on his door later that afternoon. It was four-thirty; he had fallen asleep over his still-blank legal pad, which he shoved into the drawer of his nightstand.

"Come in," he said.

Her hair was wet—from a shower, not the ocean. She wore

the sweatshirt and a white tennis skirt with blue and red piping.

"A skirt," he said. "That looks nice."

She shrugged. "Fourth of July. Mom gets a big kick out of it."

"I noticed."

"No one cares about us being together, Marcus," she said. "Trust me, I know."

"Garrett cares. And your mother cares. She yelled at you at lunch. She's never done that before."

"She's upset about something else. She's upset about David."

"What about him?"

"He's coming with us tonight and I guess she doesn't want him to."

"Oh."

Winnie closed the door and climbed on top of him. She lay her head on his chest and he could feel his heart pounding into her ear.

"Mom and Garrett don't have time to worry about us," Winnie said. "They have their own lives to worry about. So let's just be ourselves, okay?"

Marcus looked around the room, which over the past four weeks had become as familiar to him as his own room: the wainscoted walls, the ceiling fan that didn't work, his bed with the white cover. He wasn't sure who he was anymore. He'd changed so much, he'd lost track. Last year everyone in his neighborhood stayed on the street until the fireworks over Shea Stadium ended. When Marcus and LaTisha went upstairs they found Constance asleep in front of the television; she liked to watch the Boston Pops. This year he applauded as little kids with streamers on their bikes rode up a cobblestone street in a procession. He had grilled hotdogs and homemade lemonade for lunch. And now he had a white girl lying across his body.

Sex grinned at Marcus from its post by the door. "You have to go," Marcus said. "You're driving me crazy."

Winnie pressed her hips against his. "In a good way or a bad way?"

Marcus lifted her off of him. "Good way," he said, knowing how this would thrill her. "Now *go*."

꙳

Later, Marcus helped Beth pack the picnic into coolers: fried chicken, potato salad, cucumbers in vinaigrette, deviled eggs, oatmeal cookies, iced tea, beer. She had a special red, white, and blue tablecloth, and all of the matching plates and napkins.

"This looks great," Marcus said. And then, before he could stop himself, he said, "My mom always made coleslaw. With horseradish in it. It was a big hit."

Beth stopped what she was doing and stared at him, and Marcus got the awful feeling that followed whenever Constance was mentioned. Marcus wished Winnie would come down and rescue him—but she was napping, and Garrett had taken the car to pick up Piper and Peyton. Marcus tucked a sleeve of plastic cups into the picnic basket.

"Oh, Marcus, I'm sorry," Beth said. She got an unsteady vibe in her voice, like she might start to cry. "I didn't even *think* what this would feel like for you. With your mother in jail, you probably don't want to celebrate Independence Day."

"Uh . . ." Marcus was caught off-guard. "No, don't worry about it. It's fine."

"It's *not* fine," Beth said. "It was insensitive of me. But we do this whole rigmarole every year, and I just thought that if I kept things normal they might start to *feel* normal."

"I'm excited about a picnic," Marcus said. "I've never been on an actual picnic, with a picnic basket and everything."

Beth sank into one of the kitchen chairs, thinking that this was another thing Arch would have loved: taking Marcus on his first picnic. "You're sure you don't mind? Maybe we should just forget it."

"I want to go," he said.

Beth threw her hands into the air. "I don't want to see David!" she said. "I should never have invited the girls, but I thought a big group of kids would be fun. Plus, David goes to the same party every year, at this huge house on the Cliff. But no! This year as soon as he hears the girls are coming with us, he decides to forget the party. He's only coming along because he knows I don't want him to."

Marcus began to wonder if what Winnie said were true. Maybe Beth and Garrett were too consumed with their own lives to give their little romance a second thought. But before Marcus could pursue this reasoning further, he heard Beth whisper something under her breath.

"I'm sorry?" Marcus said. "I didn't hear you."

"I said, I'm keeping a big secret from my children."

She was crying now. Marcus handed her a red, white, and blue napkin. He sat quietly, wondering if she was going to tell him the secret. He felt extremely interested, but also ashamed at this interest. If she told him the secret, he might have to keep it from Winnie.

Beth crumpled her napkin and tossed it lamely in the direction of the trash can. Marcus had an urge to pick it up and throw it away, but he was rooted to his chair.

"It's about David."

Marcus let his eyelids droop, his standard defense when he heard something he didn't like. "Please," he said. He stalled, unsure of what to say. He liked Beth; he could see the woman was in pain, the kind of pain you felt when you had something to admit and couldn't wait to get it off your chest. The kind of pain Mama had been in right after the murders. She had called the police and turned herself in. "Please don't tell me."

Beth looked crestfallen, and he felt bad. Beth was the reason he was here. She'd given him the great gift of this summer, with picnics and fireworks and everything.

"I wouldn't be able to keep it from Winnie," he explained.

Beth smiled. "You like Winnie."

Marcus squeezed his eyes shut. "Yeah."

"Just promise me that you'll be there for her this summer when she needs you."

"I'm here for her," Marcus said.

"She's so fragile, and your friendship is important to her."

Marcus felt embarrassed and proud, and relieved, because it sounded like she was going to let him off the hook. He opened his eyes.

Beth lifted herself out of her chair and stood by him. She put her hand on his shoulder and left it there a second. Marcus's throat ached. For the first time all summer, he missed his own mother, the way she used to be, when she put her hands on either side of his face if she couldn't find the words to express herself.

Marcus heard a car pull into the driveway. Beth walked out into the hall.

"There they are," she said. "Marcus, will you go up and wake Winnie? We have to get ready to leave."

The screen door opened and Garrett walked in, followed by Piper, Peyton, and David. David was carrying a six-pack of Heineken.

"I hope someone made deviled eggs," he said jovially.

As Marcus headed up the stairs he tried to imagine what the secret might be, and he figured it had to do with sex. An affair, maybe. Marcus was irritated; he could tell he'd be thinking about this all the time now, although he was interested to know that sex was plaguing people other than him. He knocked on Winnie's door.

"Come on," he said. "We're going."

Her hair was mussed and she was rubbing her eyes. "I'm grouchy," she said.

Marcus felt a rush of emotion. She was so childlike, so funny and adorable that he flashed her his dimples. That worked. Her face brightened and she hugged him.

⁂

Walking down the cliff toward Jetties Beach, Beth noticed that Peyton was the only one without something to carry. In front, leading the way, were Garrett and Piper holding hands, each lugging a thermos in the other hand. Behind them were Winnie and Marcus holding either side of the big cooler. Beth had the picnic basket and two blankets and David was loaded down with folding chairs. Peyton slunk along at David's side, empty-handed.

"Why don't you catch up to your sister?" David asked her.

"I don't want to. She's with Garrett."

"Well, go anyway. I need you to scout out a good spot for us."

"I'm hungry," Peyton said.

"Exactly why we need you up front. We can't eat until we've found a place to sit."

In her mind, Beth willed Peyton to stay right where she was, next to her father, but Peyton succumbed to her hunger. She ran ahead, if you could call stumbling forward in clunky sandals running, leaving Beth and David to bring up the rear alone, if you could call walking with four thousand strangers alone.

"You don't want me here," David said.

"I thought you had the Swifts' party."

"I wanted to be with my girls," David said.

"Maybe," Beth said. "Or maybe you wanted to be with me."

"You have a high opinion of yourself."

"The kiss was an accident, David."

"An accident?"

That was the wrong word. An accident was breaking a glass in the kitchen sink, a fender bender; an accident was what had happened to Arch. The kiss was something more intentional— it was a mistake.

"It didn't mean anything," she said, cringing at how cruel that sounded. But didn't he see? It *couldn't* mean anything. "I was kind of drunk."

"Drunk," David said flatly. "That's original. You kissed me because you were drunk."

Beth pressed her lips together. She liked the way Winnie and Marcus were carrying the cooler. They made it seem effortless. Piper and Garrett, on the other hand, appeared lopsided, and a second later they stopped in their tracks. Piper had to set down her thermos and rest.

"I need you to respect my wishes," Beth said. "I'm not interested in a relationship with anyone right now."

"You sound ridiculous."

"Why is it so ridiculous?" Beth said. Winnie turned around with raised eyebrows. Beth smiled at her reassuringly, then lowered her voice. "I need time and space to grieve for my husband."

"I understand that, Beth."

"You don't understand. If you understood, you wouldn't be here. You would be giving me space."

"Don't you ever ask yourself why it's *me* you don't want around? I'll tell you why. Because you still have feelings for me and you're afraid of those feelings."

"I don't have feelings for you."

"You love me."

Beth looked to see if he was being funny. But his eyes gave off a searing heat. He was serious; he was challenging her to deny that preposterous statement.

"I loved you twenty-five years ago," she said. "Trust me when I say things have changed."

"It didn't seem that way the other night," he said.

Beth didn't have to respond because seconds later, Peyton found a spot on the beach large enough to accommodate all of them, and then there was the welcome distraction of setting up camp: spreading out the blankets, unfolding the chairs, taking out the food and pouring drinks. David opened a beer and hovered at the far edge of the blanket while Beth took charge of doling out fried chicken, spooning mounds of potato salad onto paper plates, and trying to keep pieces of plastic wrap from flying into the water. This time last year it was the same menu, but there was only four of them: Beth, Arch, and the twins. Arch loved drumsticks. He ate them all—a total of seven—then joked about the poor one-legged chicken that was limping around some-

where. Stupid, maybe, but the kids thought he was the funniest
man on the planet, and so did Beth. She put a drumstick on
Garrett's plate, hoping he would remember, but he was too absorbed with rubbing Piper's arms. She was chilly, it seemed. Well,
yeah, Beth thought, that's what you got when you wore a halter
top to the beach at night. When Garrett finally did notice the
drumstick, he ate it in three bites without comment. Beth almost
said, *Hey, Garrett, remember when Dad* . . . but she knew she wouldn't
be able to pull off the happy nostalgia she intended.

As she ate her dinner, she thought about how one day Garrett
and Winnie would get married and have families of their own,
and Beth would be left to remember all of the funny jokes alone.
She watched as David wandered away to talk to some people he
knew, waving his beer around in defiance of the open container
law. Maybe she should listen to him, otherwise she might end
up old and alone, still clinging to her grief.

It grew dark. Beth collected the paper plates and the wadded
napkins and passed around oatmeal cookies. David appeared back
at the blanket with a box of sparklers and he gave one to everybody, including Beth, and lit them with a Bic he borrowed from
Piper. He watched Beth's face as he held the lighter to the tip
of her sparkler and when the sparkler came to life, bright stars
dancing and hissing, he said, "There you go, my dear. Now you
can write your name."

Garrett and Piper wrote their names in a heart, as did Winnie
and Marcus. Beth turned her back to the group and wrote her
name in the dark air over Nantucket Sound. *Beth*. She hoped that
Arch would see it, from wherever he was watching her.

❧

Beth collected everyone's spent sparklers and the rest of the trash and settled back in her chair in time for the first burst of fireworks. Red, gold, purple. David sat in the chair next to hers and opened another beer. Beth loved fireworks, the whistle and crackle in the air, the smell of cordite, the *oohs* and *aahs*. When the sky was all lit up, she watched the silhouettes of her kids—both of them obviously paired up now. Marcus was leaning back on his hands and Winnie sat close to him, resting her head on his shoulder. Piper lay on her back and Garrett lounged on his side right behind her. They were kissing. Beth studied them for a minute, enough time to dispel any illusions about their innocence. They were having sex. Beth glanced at David to see if he saw what she saw: the tongues when they kissed, the way Garrett's fingers tugged insistently on Piper's belt loops. Beth didn't know how to feel about the situation. She and Arch had always vowed to be honest with the twins about sex and the responsibility that came with it. Arch gave Garrett condoms, and, Beth assumed, informed him how and when they should be used. Beth herself had lost her virginity at sixteen with the man sitting next to her, but somehow she had seemed older then, at sixteen, than Garrett did now, at seventeen. She would have to say something to Garrett about the sex this week—and to Winnie, too, if this thing with Marcus developed. It would embarrass all three of them—really, Arch had been much better at dealing with the kids' emerging sexuality—yet what could she do? Let her kids go wild in the sack without a few words of caution?

Blue spirals shot through the air, enhanced by a bunch of silver flashes that sounded like very loud popcorn. David applauded for that one. Beth was bothered by everything David had said earlier. Okay, maybe she did have feelings for him, but any fool could see that the feelings made her so uncomfortable that all she wanted to do was push them away.

The finale started and the sky was a messy artists' palette of color, one bright burst inside another. The great thing about the finale was that just when Beth thought the sky was saturated, just when she thought it must be the end, they shot off more. It kept going and going. Beth leaned her head back against the webbing of her chair. She tried to conjure Kara Schau's words: *Don't think. Smell the flowers.* Don't worry about packing up and fighting the crowds all the way back to the car. Don't worry about David Ronan in the chair next to yours. Just enjoy.

Beth couldn't help herself from doing a visual sweep of their area, mentally calculating how long it would take them to break camp. It was then that she noticed Peyton was gone.

She looked at David. He was grinning like a boy, his face catching light from the sky.

"Did Peyton go to the bathroom?" Beth asked.

David checked the blanket. His smile faded and he sat up straighter in his chair. "Piper," he said. "Where's your sister?"

Asking this was pointless. Piper couldn't hear David over the noise of the fireworks. No one could hear him but Beth. Piper was so absorbed with tasting the inside of Garrett's mouth that anyone could see the whereabouts of her younger sister was the furthest thing from her mind. David concluded as much after a few seconds, and he picked his way across the blanket, over the cooler and between thermoses, to ask Piper again. Piper sat up and looked around. Shrugged. David asked something of Winnie and Marcus, who mimicked Piper's actions. *We don't know.*

Beth stood up. She felt sorry for David—a missing child was a parent's worst nightmare. Even when the child was thirteen. Even in a place as safe as Nantucket.

"They don't know where she went?" Beth asked.

"No," David said. He scanned the patchwork of blankets around them. "How long has she been gone? And how did she leave without my noticing?"

"You went to talk to some people," Beth said. "Maybe she met up with friends."

"Maybe," David said. "Or maybe she just went to the bathroom."

"That's probably it," Beth said. She, too, wondered how long Peyton had been gone. Beth remembered handing her two oatmeal cookies and then offering to refill her lemonade, but that was before the fireworks started. Beth tried to remember if she'd seen Peyton with a sparkler. The sparklers were a long time ago, certainly allowing enough time to go to the bathroom and come back. Unless there was a horrendous line.

As if reading her mind, David said, "I'm going to check the bathrooms. Will you stay here?"

"Of course," Beth said. "She'll probably make it back before you do."

Beth's optimism flagged once the fireworks ended, because at that point, chaos broke out. Children started to whine and everyone and his brother tried to jam their way through the narrow passageway between the dunes that led to the parking lot. People poured past them, like a stream moving around a rock. Beth stood on her chair and waved her arms so that Peyton might be able to locate them. Marcus followed suit, standing on the cooler, waving the flashlight that Beth had packed. Winnie folded the blankets and the unused chairs while Garrett and Piper clung to one another—Piper suddenly so concerned about her sister that she needed constant petting from Garrett. Beth almost snapped at them to separate and help, but what kind of help was needed? They simply had to stay put until Peyton materialized out of the crowd, and Garrett and Piper were doing just that—staying put with their hands all over each other.

David returned, his eyes darting everywhere. The key, he said, was not to panic because Peyton had a good head on her shoulders and she could find her way to the police station once she got to the road.

"It's not like she's a tourist," he said. "This island is her home."

They waited until the last stragglers left the beach. At this point, Beth was tired and had to go to the bathroom herself. She walked through the cold sand toward the now-abandoned portable toilets. Because she was from New York, she couldn't help thinking of how the fingers of evil could touch anyone, even here. Beth eyed the dark ocean. With a missing child on the brain, it looked sinister.

On the way back she was more hopeful. But from a hundred yards away she could see David standing on the cooler; as she neared, she heard him calling out Peyton's name. Beth joined Winnie and Marcus who were huddled nearby. They told her that Garrett and Piper had gone to the lost child tent, or whatever it was, that the police had set up.

Beth helped David down from the cooler. Even touching his hand made her feel conflicted.

"She'll turn up," Beth said.

"Oh, I know," he said. "I'm not worried."

"Of course you're worried," Beth said. "She's your baby girl.

You don't have to play tough guy with me, not under these circumstances. Maybe she went home."

"There's no way she would have gone home without telling me. It's too far to walk. It's four miles in the dark."

Garrett and Piper approached; Piper's face looked ready to crumble. "The police haven't seen her," she said. "Your friend was there, Dad, Lieutenant Egan, and he said he'd send his guys out to scan the area. He said if she doesn't turn up in the next twenty minutes, you should go talk to him."

"Twenty minutes, my ass," David said. "I'm going to talk to him now." David charged through the sand toward the parking lot, calling Peyton's name along the way. Beth stayed with the other kids.

"None of you saw her leave?" Beth asked. "Who spoke to her last?"

"I told her I liked her shoes," Winnie said. "But that was during dinner."

Piper nuzzled Garrett's neck and ran a hand inside the collar of his polo shirt. Something about Piper touching Garrett made Beth uncomfortable. She wondered if this were a typical mother-son-girlfriend dynamic at work, or if there was actually something about Piper that was unlikable, which only Beth discerned.

"This isn't like my sister," Piper said. "Peyton is such a goody-goody. It's not like she ran off to smoke and drink with her friends. She never does anything on her own unless she asks Dad, like, six times if it's okay. So I don't know what to think. Maybe she was abducted?"

"She wasn't abducted," Beth said. "But she may be lost."

Piper sniffed. "We used to play on this beach when we were kids. If she got lost, she'd wait for us in the parking lot. Plus, the police tent is in the parking lot and she wasn't there." Piper's tone was condescending—it was the tone of voice she normally reserved for David, and Beth was about to let her know that it wasn't an okay tone to use with her boyfriend's mother when David jogged toward them through the sand.

"They're going to start a real search," he said. "I'll stay here. Beth, you take the kids home. To my house. Keep your eyes peeled for her on the way. The police seem to think she got bored, or angry, and decided to walk home. They said they see it every year. Also, check the machine, Piper, when you get in. Maybe she left a message. I'll call you later to see if she's turned up."

❧

Beth and the kids trudged back to the car, everyone so loaded down with stuff that there was no opportunity for kissing or hand-holding. It was a silent march out to North Beach Street and then up the Cobblestone Hill. They piled into the Range Rover and drove to David's house, slowing to check the identity of each person walking on the side of the road along the way. No Peyton. The house was dark except for the onion lamp by the front door.

"She's not home," Piper said. "God, I hope she left a message."

The kids trooped into the house while Beth stood at the back of the car and separated out David's belongings from her own— his chairs, his thermos, his blanket. She knew there wouldn't be a message. No one had spoken to the girl, no one noticed her missing until she was long gone. Peyton had been ignored, so she ran away. It didn't take a brain surgeon to figure it out, only a mother.

When Beth walked into the kitchen, the kids were sitting on barstools around the island.

"No message?" she said.

Garrett shook his head. Piper started to cry quietly. Beth put a hand on her back.

"And you checked the whole house?"

Piper nodded, then moved into Garrett's arms where she collapsed.

"Maybe she went to our house," Winnie said. "It's closer. Maybe she got tired and decided to wait for us there. She knows we don't lock it."

"Okay, we'll check," Beth said. "Piper, you stay here and wait for your father's phone call. Tell him our plans."

Piper clung to Garrett with a ferocity Beth had only previously seen in two year olds. "Can Garrett stay with me? Please? I'm freaked out to be here by myself."

Beth hesitated. Garrett staying here meant only one thing: sex. In a bed, probably, which would have irresistible appeal. Beth fought off images of the cottage on Bear Street with David. All summer long, sex on a bed, sex every which way.

"I don't think that's a good idea," Beth said. "Because how will he get home?"

"I'll have Dad run him home when he gets back."

"David shouldn't have to do that," Beth said. "It's late. Garrett will see you tomorrow."

Garrett threw Beth a dirty look. "I'm not ten years old, Mom. I'll stay here with Piper and if David won't take me home then I'll walk."

"In the dark?"

"Yes," Garrett said.

Beth heard the challenge in his voice and decided she wasn't up for it. "Well, if Peyton's at our house, we'll come back. Obviously. And if she's not there, I guess we'll come back anyway and wait to hear what David says. Or I will. Marcus and Winnie may want to go to sleep." Beth closed her eyes. Teenagers were going to be alone in a house full of beds no matter what she decided, that much was clear. "So I'll be back in a short while, then. A couple of minutes."

Beth drove to Horizon saying a prayer to God and Arch and anyone else who would listen. *Please bring the girl home safely.* Horizon, too, was dark, except for the porch light.

"She's not here," Marcus said. "Man, this is getting weird."

The three of them went in, Beth and Marcus each carrying a load of picnic stuff.

Winnie said, "Mom doesn't care who's dead or missing as long as the dishes get done."

"Winnie, that's not fair."

Winnie acknowledged as much with a pat to Beth's head. "Sorry, Mom."

Beth turned on some lights and checked all the rooms on the first floor. She checked the deck then went upstairs and poked her head into the bedrooms, hoping to find Peyton asleep, like Goldilocks. No such luck. Beth returned to the kitchen. "Listen, you two stay here. I'm going back to the Ronans' house in case another vehicle or another set of hands is needed. You guys get some sleep." She wanted to get back to Garrett and Piper as soon as possible.

"We'll clean up," Marcus said.

"If you want," Beth said, so grateful for this offer that she wondered if Winnie's statement weren't right on the money. "Garrett and I will be home shortly."

"Okay, Mom, good luck," Winnie said, and Beth could tell

Winnie was anxious for her to leave. *Are you watching this?* she asked Arch on her way out to the car. *Everyone wants me to leave so they can fool around!* Somehow the prospect of Winnie and Marcus didn't worry her nearly as much as Garrett and Piper, and so she hurried back to David's house.

The house was as she left it, with the front light on and a light in the kitchen. Beth slammed the car door to warn of her impending arrival. But no one was in the kitchen. Beth called out, "Hey, I'm back!" and was met with silence. She listened to the hum of the refrigerator and the drip of the sink, her heart racing. She twisted the spigots of the sink and the dripping stopped.

"I'm back!" Beth shouted.

Silence.

"Garrett!" she hollered. "Garrett Newton, get down here this instant!" She marveled at how much like a typical mother she could sound.

Still nothing. Either the house was remarkably well built or they, too, had disappeared. Beth was faced with having to go upstairs and check on them. She was starting to boil inside. How dare they put her through this! She stormed up the stairs, only partially cowed by the fact that she'd been up these stairs two weeks earlier when she was snooping around. She heard noises coming from the bathroom. Beth moved toward the door. She heard a groan, her own son's distinctly sexual groan. Okay, that was it. Beth couldn't stand to hear anything more. She pounded on the door.

"Meet me downstairs, Garrett," Beth said. "We're going home."

There was silence, then some shuffling, then an, "Okay, Mom, give me a minute?" As though she was supposed to believe he was in there alone.

Beth returned to the kitchen, furious. She started rehearsing a lecture for the drive back to their house—God, what was she going to say? She should have stayed at home in blissful ignorance. They were upstairs in the bathroom. Unbelievable. No parent would tolerate this! Beth studied the pictures on the refrigerator, but only for a second. The pictures of David, whom she had kissed! The pictures of Piper who was having sex with her son upstairs! Suddenly, Beth was distracted by flashing lights. A police car pulled into the driveway. Beth went to the door. David and Peyton stepped out of the car.

"Oh, thank God," Beth said. The girl looked defiant—arms welded across her chest—but fine, otherwise. David chatted with the officer at the wheel for a second, clapping him on the arm, and then the police car drove off. Beth opened the door for them.

"What happened?" she said.

Peyton glared at Beth, a look so hateful that it startled her.

"I'm going to bed," she spat.

When she disappeared, Beth looked to David. "Where was she?"

"One of the cops found her sitting by herself on Steamship Wharf," David said. "She was waiting for the early boat so she could sail to Hyannis to see her mother."

"Why?" Beth said, though of course, she knew why. "What's wrong?"

"She thinks everyone is paired up but her. The other kids, and you and me. She felt left out, so she ran away."

"Ouch," Beth said.

"I reminded her that she was my date tonight," he said.

"You didn't treat her like your date," Beth said. "You kept trying to get rid of her so you could talk to me."

"Ouch," David said.

"It's true," Beth said. "And I hate to open your eyes to other unpleasant realities, but when I got here a few minutes ago I found Garrett and Piper locked in the upstairs bathroom together. One doesn't have to be a Rhodes scholar to figure out what was going on in there."

David's face fell. "I guess not."

"We have to keep our families separated. Maybe the girls *should* go visit their mother." Beth put a hand up to stop his objections. "I'm not telling you what to do with Piper—"

"Yes, you are."

"I just want you to know that the Newtons will be keeping a low profile at Horizon for a while."

Garrett appeared then, eyes cast to the floor.

"We're going," Beth said. Garrett was already headed toward the door, which David held open for them.

"At least everyone's safe," David said. "Happy Fourth of July."

"And *don't* drive by my house tonight," Beth said.

"I wouldn't dream of it, Bethie," he said.

chapter 5

Just like that, Piper was getting shipped off to her mother's house—not for a long weekend, not for a week, but for ten whole days. Garrett was grounded from the car to boot, because his mother had caught him and Piper in the bathroom together.

"What were you two doing up there?" Beth had asked him as they drove home from the Ronans' house.

He couldn't believe she was embarrassing him like this. He'd held out hope that she would be cooler, that she would just let the issue drop. "It's none of your business what we were doing," he said. This, he suspected, was the answer Piper would give, and she was a master at handling her father. "If you want details of somebody's sex life, get your own."

Beth slammed the brakes of the car and they both pitched forward. "Out," she said. "You're walking home."

"What?"

"I do not want you in this car. Get out."

Garrett opened his door and the light came on. Beth's face was a block of ice. "I'm going back to Piper's," he said.

"You can try," Beth said. "But David won't let you set foot in that house."

Garrett stepped out onto the gravel road and slammed the door. "Bitch," he muttered. The Rover took off sending a spray of stones and dust from its tires. "We were having sex!" Garrett called out after the car. He stood where he was, waiting to see if his mother would stop, but she didn't. She kept on going, leaving him there.

"Well," he said, to nobody except his father, he supposed. "What do you think of that?"

He headed home because he suspected his mother was right about David. It had been Piper's idea to fool around upstairs, to hurry up and do it before his mother returned. Garrett was nervous and it took him a while to relax and concentrate on her body. Then, when his mother knocked, he was so startled that he pushed Piper away and made a mess of the condom and everything. Piper laughed at his nervousness, then she got angry. "God, Garrett, calm down. We're practically adults. Anyway, this is *my house.* Your mother is trespassing." Garrett felt ashamed at himself for acting so flustered. Piper was right. His mother *was* trespassing, trespassing on his life.

As he walked, Garrett thought back to the previous autumn when Arch had taken him and Winnie to Central Park to give them the "sex talk." Arch warned them in advance that this was going to be the topic of discussion and so they should think up all the questions they had and Arch would do his best to answer them. Winnie was nervous about it—she did everything in her power to get out of going along—but it ended up being the best conversation Garrett could have dreamed of. Arch was funny and honest and realistic. *You two will probably have sex in the next few years. Enjoy it. Use condoms. Be considerate. And, most importantly, don't mistake sex for love. They are two different things that feel the same in the heat of the moment.*

Reviewing this advice, Garrett felt a little better. He'd followed it to a "T." He wasn't sure what his mother's problem was. He'd done nothing wrong.

⚘

He wasn't surprised, though, when all hell broke loose the next day. Marcus went to the beach early to swim in the waves, and as soon as he left, Beth began to lecture Garrett and Winnie about sexual responsibility.

"It's a private thing, an *intimate* thing between two people," she said. "It's not something you flaunt in front of your mother or anyone else."

"I hear you, Mom," Garrett said. "But you walked into Piper's house. You were, technically, trespassing."

This sent Beth into a flurry of expletives, at the end of which she grounded him from the car. Two weeks.

"Good," Winnie said. "Because I want to go for my license and I can't practice with Garrett hogging the car."

"What about Winnie?" Garrett challenged. "Not flaunting sex in front of Mom's face means Winnie can't have sex with Marcus."

"We're not having sex," Winnie said. "Why don't you figure out what you're talking about before you open your big mouth, lover boy."

"This is bullshit," Garrett said. He walked out the front door and considered taking the car—but that was a line even he wouldn't cross—so he hopped on a bike and pedaled to Piper's. Garrett rode as hard as he could, over the dirt road, hitting all the bumps on purpose. He hadn't ridden a bike since the year before, and it felt good to get the exercise. He'd have to be in shape for soccer in September. He should start jogging, like his mother. But Garrett didn't want to think about his mother or September, when he would be separated from Piper. Nor did he want to think about the sex in the bathroom, although his mind kept returning to the subject, as he tried to gauge how much of an ass he'd made of himself. Pushing Piper away, disengaging, fumbling with the condom, trying to hide the evidence as he heard his mother pounding on the door. At the time he hadn't thought of Beth as trespassing; he'd thought of his *mother* catching him having sex with his girlfriend. That was enough to make anyone act like a moron.

He reached Piper's house in less than ten minutes, but when he arrived, he was chagrined to see that both David's pickup and the painting van were in the driveway. Meaning, David was home.

And not only home, but right there in the kitchen, sitting at the island with Piper and Peyton, the three of them drinking coffee. Garrett knocked on the frame of the screen door, although he had an urge to eavesdrop on the conversation. It looked serious—it was serious, definitely, if David stayed home from work.

All three of the Ronans looked up at the knock. Garrett expected Piper to run to the door, but seeing him seemed to cause her physical pain. She winced.

David was the first to speak. "Come on in here for a second, Garrett."

Garrett sensed that his timing was bad. "I'm interrupting?"

"Not at all," David said. "Because we have something to tell you. Both girls are leaving this morning to see their mom in Wellfleet. They'll be gone until the fifteenth."

"The fifteenth?" Garrett repeated. He tried to locate himself in the month. Yesterday was the fourth, today the fifth. The fifteenth was ten days away—ten precious summer days that he would not be spending with Piper. He gazed at her, asking her with his eyes if this was anything she had control over, but her face was deep in her coffee cup. So he guessed not. This was more parenting gone haywire.

"You and Piper may talk for five minutes in the driveway, alone," David said. "And then she's going upstairs to pack and I'm taking her and Peyton to the airport." He checked his watch and carried his coffee cup to the sink. "Understood?"

Garrett, speechless, was already outside. He kicked at the pebbles of the driveway and waited for Piper to follow him out. Instinctively, they walked to the very end of the driveway, which was shielded from the house by a Spanish olive tree. Garrett took her in his arms and noticed for the first time that she'd taken the diamond stud out of her nose, revealing a sore-looking divot.

"What happened?" he said.

"I have to go. He's seriously pissed this time. Because you and I were upstairs, but also because of Peyton. He thinks you and I, whatever, our *behavior* was one of the reasons Peyton ran away last night. He called Mom and they talked for, like, two hours. They both think this is the best thing."

"You don't think it's the best thing, do you?"

She dropped her chin to her chest. "I don't know, Garrett."

"What do you mean you don't know?" he said. "Do you *want* to be separated for ten days?"

"Not really."

Not really? Garrett felt like his heart was going to explode. He wondered if she thought less of him because he acted like such a buffoon in the bathroom.

"I love you," he said, and his father's words popped into his mind: *Don't mistake sex for love.* But Garrett wasn't mistaken here. He did love Piper. Just the thought of not seeing her for ten days made him want to do something drastic.

She didn't respond to his declaration. He'd always been good at reading other people's thoughts, but here he was drawing a blank.

"You love me, too, don't you?" he asked.

She touched her nose. "Yes."

Garrett let out a long stream of highly relieved air. Then, he felt buoyant. They were in love!

"Five minutes is up!" David yelled from the house, though clearly it had only been three or four minutes. "Inside, Piper. Pronto!"

Piper kissed Garrett on the mouth, but chastely. "I'll see you when I get back," she said.

"Wait," he said. "Give me your mom's phone number. I'll call you from town. I'll call every day."

She took a few steps backward, shaking her head. "I don't think you should," she said. "I'll see you when I get back." She waved, but in a way that looked like shooing.

Garrett watched her retreat to the house. His lungs ached; he felt like a scuba diver descending deeper and deeper where the pressure of the water was unbearable and there wasn't enough oxygen to survive. Ten days! He waited until Piper reached the door, hoping she would turn and wave, but she didn't. She

stepped into the house—or was pulled in, Garrett couldn't tell—
and the door closed very tightly behind her, leaving him with
nothing to do but climb on his bike and pedal morosely away.

※

Under certain circumstances, ten days could seem like a very
long time. For example, Garrett imagined that ten days in prison
would seem like a long time. Ten days of hard manual labor
would seem like a long time. The first ten days after Garrett's
father died had seemed like an eternity. But even that didn't drag
on quite as long as ten days without Piper. Especially when Garrett's favorite pastime became reviewing those minutes with her
in the driveway in his mind.

On the bright side, Piper had told him she loved him. On
the dark side was her response of *not really*, when asked if she
wanted to be separated for ten days, and the fact that she didn't
want him to call her, and the more awful fact that when she left
she didn't kiss him with any kind of passion. The conclusion
Garrett drew—the only conclusion he could live with for ten
days—was that David had said or done something to scare Piper
right out of her normal personality. She was sheepish, she was
timid. Without the diamond in her nose she hadn't even looked
like herself; she was Wonder Woman without her magic bracelets. The only part of the conversation Garrett could really take
to heart was the part when Piper said she loved him—because
that one word, "yes," had sounded completely sincere.

Garrett called up a favorite saying of his father's: *It's fruitless to
speculate*. Garrett would simply have to wait until the fifteenth.
There would still be plenty of summer left. In the meantime, he
tried to make it through the hours. The mornings dragged, even

when he managed to sleep until nine, which wasn't often now that he was falling asleep shortly after nine at night. The sun rose at five and a stripe of light fell across his face around six-thirty, and that usually woke him. He figured he might actually knock a couple of books off his summer reading list. He finished *Franny and Zooey*, which he liked, even if he didn't fully understand it, but then he got bogged down in *A River Runs Through It.* Talk about a boring book! Ten days would seem like a very long time if you were standing knee-deep in cold water trying to catch a fish without any bait.

The worst punishment for Garrett was having to spend time with Winnie and Marcus. They were so happy, so obviously a couple now, that it turned Garrett's stomach. Winnie practiced driving the Rover with Beth in the passenger seat and Marcus in the back; he went along for moral support, Winnie said. Garrett thought meanly that Marcus would probably never get his driver's license; he would never own a car, and could probably count on one hand the number of times he'd taken a cab. Still, Marcus joined the driving lessons, leaving Garrett alone in the house to contemplate the injustices in his life.

On the fourth day without Piper, Beth asked where she was. Garrett was shocked by the question. Although he hadn't told anyone about Piper being banished to Cape Cod, he counted on Beth, at least, to intuit it. Why else would he be moping around the house?

"She went to see Rosie," Garrett said. "She'll be back next week."

His mother raised her eyebrows. "She went to see Rosie," she repeated. "How about that."

On the seventh day, it rained. Winnie and Marcus started a Monopoly marathon at the kitchen table. The wind was out of the southwest and the house shook. Garrett helped Beth close all of the shutters and the storm windows, while Marcus and Winnie rolled the dice. Garrett watched them, stupidly wishing that he could play, but resenting them too much to ask. Beth, probably taking pity on him, asked him to build a fire while she went to work making a vat of clam chowder. Garrett got the fire roaring, then helped his mother by peeling potatoes and dicing onions. Once the soup was simmering, he crashed in the recliner in front of the fire and vowed not to get up until he'd finished *A River Runs Through It.*

He was eighteen pages from the end when the electricity went out. He heard a cry from the kitchen—"Oh, no! Our game!"—and he knew Beth would be rummaging through the utility drawer for candles and matches. Garrett put down his book and leaned back in the recliner.

You love me, too, don't you?

Yes.

A few minutes later, Beth brought him a candle. "How're you doing?" she asked.

"Fine."

Garrett was surprisingly grateful when she sat down next to him.

"I don't like being angry at one another," she said. "This thing with you and Piper . . ."

"I love her," he said. It felt brilliant to admit it. "I'm in love with her."

His mother searched his face. "Okay."

"You think we're getting too serious too fast," he said. "I know you think it. But you're not me and you're not Piper."

"That's true," she said. "Do twenty-five years of experience count for anything?"

"You don't remember what it feels like to be young," he said. "You don't know what I feel like. She's only gone for ten days, right? But it feels like *forever*."

"I do remember what it feels like," Beth said. "I was in love at your age."

Garrett felt a split second of connection with his mother, until he realized what she was referring to. "With David?" he sneered.

"Yes, with David. I was in love with him. We were having sex."

"I don't want to hear about it," Garrett said.

Beth faced the fire. *I know what I'm talking about!* she wanted to shout. *Please believe me!* Instead, she said, "You're so young, Garrett. Piper is just one in a long line of girls."

Garrett held his book up so that it blocked Beth's face. "See, you don't know what I feel like. Because if you knew, you wouldn't say that."

"Summer does something to the brain," Beth said. "It's intoxicating. Everything shimmers. And when you fall in love in the summer, it's the best love you can possibly imagine. Especially here. Because there are sunsets and walks on the beach and fireworks. But summer loves aren't meant to last. They burn very hot and bright, and then they go out. Eventually, Garrett, they always go out."

"You're not making me feel any better," Garrett said. "You're making me feel worse."

"If I never split with David, honey, I wouldn't have married your father."

He felt a different kind of sadness then, a sadness because the ease with which he used to talk to his mother was gone. Now, every conversation was unpleasant for him. "Please don't say anything else," he said.

Garrett waited for Beth to leave the room, but she remained next to him in the candlelight, lost in thought. After a minute of listening to the howling wind and the *rat-tat-tat* of rain against the shutters, Garrett returned to his book. He wasn't really reading, he was skimming, because damn it, he wanted to finish. And more important, he wanted Beth to understand that his relationship with Piper was *his;* it wasn't some reincarnation of her and David. She couldn't predict the ending based on something that happened a generation ago.

Garrett finished the book and set it victoriously on the side table. Beth was asleep, thank God, and since there was nothing else to do, Garrett blew out the candle, eased back in the recliner and closed his eyes. *You love me, too, don't you? Yes.*

❧

That night, a gust of wind pushed open Garrett's bedroom door. Garrett was tired, and he contemplated leaving the door open, but he felt oddly exposed, so he got up. Then he saw something move in the hallway. Somebody: Marcus slipping into Winnie's room.

Garrett's first instinct was to sound an alarm. *Hey! Stop! You can't go in there! This isn't allowed!* If Marcus were sneaking around in the middle of the night then he must be having sex with Winnie. So Winnie had lied to Garrett and Beth, lied right to their faces. Garrett was suddenly wide awake. He crept down the hallway toward Winnie's room.

He stood outside Winnie's door and suspended his breathing, thinking of his mother banging on the bathroom door while he was inside with Piper. Winnie's door didn't close properly, and when Garrett pressed his forehead against the door frame and squinted, he could see in. He was a despicable person after all, a Peeping Tom, a pervert. *If you want details of someone's sex life, get your own.* He was a hypocrite! But he was propelled forward by his desire for justice. It was bad enough that Marcus was here for the summer, but having sex with Winnie! Garrett would turn them in; Beth would be forced to send Marcus home, and she would have to admit she never should have invited the kid here in the first place.

When Garrett peered in, what he saw was this: Marcus and Winnie lying in bed, fully clothed. Winnie was wearing her sweatshirt and Marcus had on a T-shirt and shorts. Marcus was holding Winnie from behind, spooning her, his chin resting on top of her head. They appeared to be sleeping. Garrett stood there for several minutes, waiting for more to happen, but nothing did. They slept. Like an old, married couple. Garrett stepped into the room and yanked Marcus out of bed. Marcus hit the floor, ass first. Winnie sat up, confused. She nearly screamed because she saw *Garrett* in her room. Garrett stood over Marcus with his fists in the air. He'd never fought anybody in his life, but he was going to fight Marcus now.

"Get up," Garrett growled. "Get *up*, motherfucker."

Marcus blinked, rubbing his backside. He squinted at Garrett. Here it was, his biggest fear realized, but Marcus found he wasn't scared. He was merely annoyed. "What are you doing here, man?"

"Garrett, *get out*," Winnie hissed. She climbed out of bed, pulling the bottom of her sweatshirt down over her rear end.

"No," Garrett said, in a loud voice that he hoped would wake Beth. "I'm not getting out until Marcus tells me what the hell he's doing in your bedroom."

Marcus held his palms up. "We were sleeping, man."

And though he knew this was the truth, Garrett kicked Marcus in the chest as hard as he would have kicked a soccer ball if he had an open shot on goal. His adrenaline surged. He *hated* the guy.

Marcus took the blow with a sharp release of air, and fell over his knees, guarding his chest with crossed arms. His breath was gone and he flashed back to a time, years earlier—before he became a master at holding his breath underwater—when a cousin had dunked him in the municipal pool and Marcus thought he was going to die. *Where was the air?* Marcus's vision turned red, and when it cleared, he saw Garrett dancing in place, waving his fists. "First your mother causes our father's death," Garrett said. "And now you're trying to screw my sister."

Garrett's leg shot out again, and Marcus felt like a dog being kicked by a cruel child. It felt like every mean word and deed of the past nine months was contained in that second blow, which caught Marcus in the windpipe. He fell over backward. Thinking of the hour and a half he'd sat, all alone and completely naked, in the swim team locker room as he waited for Arch; the way his father sprayed the baseboards of their room at the Sunday Sermon Motel with Raid to get rid of the roaches; how not one of their neighbors had spoken to them since the murders, and Vanessa Lydecker wouldn't even open the door to her apartment when she saw it was Marcus through the peephole.

All Marcus could do was wheeze. It occurred to Garrett that Marcus was really hurt, possibly even dying. Winnie picked up the lamp by her bed. She wanted to bash Garrett over the head, but she was afraid of showering Marcus with broken glass.

"You asshole! You jerk!" she screamed. "How dare you! You kicked him! You hurt him!"

"It's not fair!" Garrett said. "He doesn't belong here, Winnie. He doesn't belong in this house and he doesn't belong in your *bed*."

With slow deliberation, Marcus sat up, then got to his feet. His chest and throat throbbed with a red, glowing pain, and from that pain came a power, monstrous and terrifying, a sudden knowledge that he was capable of really bad things. Marcus's lungs felt like they were bleeding and he couldn't swallow, but that hardly mattered. He grabbed the front of Garrett's T-shirt and threw Garrett onto the bed. He had four inches and thirty pounds on the kid, and Marcus marveled that Garrett had had the guts to come after him in the first place. But it incensed him, too. Garrett thought he was superior because he was *white*, because he was *rich*. Marcus punched Garrett right across his pretty face and instantly there was blood everywhere. Marcus backed away. He coughed a loogie up into his hand. The room spun. Winnie shrieked and dropped the lamp onto the floor, where it shattered. She was screaming now, screaming for Beth.

Marcus cut his foot on a shard of glass from the lamp. Now his foot was bleeding and maybe his lungs, and certainly Garrett's face. There was blood everywhere and Winnie was going hoarse in her upper registers trying to wake Beth. Marcus stumbled forward and looked at Garrett who had his arms up now, shielding his face. Marcus wanted to call him a baby, a sissy, a *pussy*, but what he said was, "I'm not going after your sister, not like that anyway. We're friends."

Garrett tried to spit at Marcus, but he only managed to dribble some bloody saliva.

"Do you want me to hit you again?" Marcus asked. Wondering if fighting back all along would have been this easy, this gratifying to the dark side of his psyche.

"No!" Winnie said. "Look at him, Marcus! God, he's *covered* with blood."

The bedroom door swung open and the light came on. Beth entered the room in her seersucker bathrobe.

"What," she said, her voice hoarse and murderous, "is going on?" She saw the blood and gasped. "Garrett!" she said. "What *happened?*" She spun on her heels and pinned Marcus with her eyes. "What have you *done?*"

It was the blood that was the problem, Marcus realized. Garrett was covered with blood and Marcus wasn't. His mind skipped beyond explaining the course of events, beyond being sent home, beyond being found guilty of assault, and sent to a juvenile detention center until his eighteenth birthday. It skipped to this: *They all think I'm just like her.*

"Marcus," Beth said. "What have you done?"

"I punched him," Marcus said.

"Mom, you don't know what happened . . ." Winnie said.

Beth didn't seem to hear. She helped Garrett up and led him to the bathroom where she dabbed at his face with a wet towel. So much blood, but thankfully not much actual damage—a swollen nose, maybe, and by the morning, a black eye. Winnie crowded into the bathroom with Beth and Garrett, crying now, because this was all her fault.

"We were just *sleeping*," Winnie said. "And Garrett barged into my room and started beating Marcus up."

"Garrett beat *Marcus* up?" Beth said. "Looks to me like it was the other way around. Just look at your brother! Look at his *face.*"

Back in Winnie's room, Marcus sat on a clean part of Winnie's bed holding a wad of Kleenex to the gash on his foot. *They all think I'm just like her.*

"Garrett started it," Winnie said. "He kicked Marcus in the

chest, twice, really hard. He came into my room, he pulled Marcus onto the floor and then he kicked him!"

There were splotches of blood now on Beth's bathrobe. "Garrett?"

Garrett inspected his face in the mirror. It looked like someone else's face.

"Garrett attacked Marcus in his sleep, like a *coward*," Winnie said. "So Marcus hit him back. Marcus only hit him once." Winnie had seen in Marcus's eyes, though, the possibility of more, and it frightened her. She ripped off a long piece of toilet paper and blew her nose. This was all her fault.

Garrett touched his eyelid. He had a sharp headache.

"Garrett should mind his own fucking business!" Winnie said. She wasn't sure yet if her mother realized she had broken a lamp. Every piece of furniture in Horizon had, like, seventy-five years of history behind it, and so her mother would blame that on her, too.

Garrett raised his eyes to meet Beth's gaze. He had no words.

"I don't know what to do," Beth said. "I don't know how to fix this." She wasn't crying but her voice was so defeated that it was worse than crying.

Marcus stood in the doorway of the bathroom. His voice was gravelly. "You've been wanting to kick me like that since the first day here," he said to Garrett. "And I've been wanting to punch you for wanting to kick me. Because I, myself, have done nothing wrong. I am not a criminal. All I did was show up. Because your father invited me. *Arch Newton* invited me."

Everyone was quiet. Beth opened the medicine cabinet and hunted for bandages. God, how she wished she could just keep the kids separated—locked in their own rooms like jail cells, like cages at the zoo. *This is too much!* she wanted to shout, loud enough so that Arch could hear her. *This is too much for me to deal with alone!*

"It doesn't matter what happened," she said. "I want you kids to get along. For my sake. This is the hardest summer any of us will ever have. The name-calling has to stop. The fighting is unacceptable. If Arch were here . . . frankly, I can't imagine what he would think."

"If Dad were here," Garrett said, "none of this would be happening."

"Well, he's *not* here," Beth said. "He's not here and so we have to deal as best we can without him. We *have to deal.*"

Winnie glared at Garrett. "Why can't you just leave us alone? God, I could kill you!"

"Winnie!" Beth said.

"I'm sorry," Garrett said. He was suddenly exhausted, and his longing for Piper was worse than ever. He wouldn't be surprised if she never wanted to see him again. He was a mean, evil person and his head hurt. And his foot hurt from where he'd kicked Marcus, like maybe he'd broken a toe against Marcus's chest.

"I'm sorry, too," Marcus said. He snatched a bandage for his foot. *They all think I'm just like her.* He limped back to his room, thinking what he was really sorry about was that he would never get to touch Winnie again, never get to hold her while she slept.

Winnie went back to her room to sweep up the pieces of the lamp. Sniffling, because this was her fault.

Beth put ointment and a small bandage on the cut under Garrett's eye. "Oh, Garrett," she said. When she first walked into Winnie's bedroom and saw Garrett bleeding and Marcus looming over him, she thought . . . well, she thought Marcus had attacked him, and her instincts were to protect her son. But now, she faced a feeling ten times worse: her son was the bully. Her own child was bringing this pain down on his own head.

Garrett missed his girlfriend. Then he missed his father. Then he missed himself—the happy, good-natured person he used to be. He couldn't even thank his mother for nursing his wounds. He hobbled back to his bedroom; outside, the wind groaned. He deserved to die in his sleep.

᪣

Garrett spent the next few days hiding in his room, emerging only for meals. His right eye was swollen shut and mottled purple and green, and his mother, taking pity on him, bought him a bottle of extra-strength Tylenol for the pain. Marcus had a lump on his windpipe and a bruise the size of an egg on his chest. Winnie had broken an antique lamp—the only valuable thing in the whole house if you believed what Beth said. Horizon took on a cautious hush, like a hospital where everyone suffered from hurt feelings.

By the time Garrett's face resumed its normal shape and color, it was the fifteenth. He woke up on that morning in a panic. He didn't know when or how Piper was arriving on-island, and he certainly couldn't ask David. He considered staking out the house on his bike, but that was psycho, and since he was finished with psycho behavior, he decided his only alternative was to sit home and wait.

Which was pure torture, a hell unimaginable—far, far worse than waiting for Piper when she was off-island was waiting for Piper when she was on-island, or might be. The key was to keep busy, and so Garrett joined Marcus and Winnie at the beach.

They looked surprised to see him, but they didn't get up and leave, though he wouldn't have blamed them if they did. He swam for the first time all summer and the water felt great. He bodysurfed in the waves until his nose stung and his lungs ached and then he headed up to the house and made sandwiches for everyone, including Marcus, who said it was delicious after the first bite.

After lunch, Garrett started to read the third book on his summer reading list, *Animal Dreams*, by Barbara Kingsolver. A *chick* book, he realized after twenty pages, something added to the list to appease all of the neo-feminist girls in Garrett's class. He put the book down, incredulous that the reading list should be so ill-suited to his tastes, and he checked the clock for the very first time that day. Two-thirty. Garrett went to the front door and looked down the long stretch of dirt road that led to their house. No Piper. He tried to be rational. She would either ride her bike or have David drop her off as soon as she got home. And it was Sunday, so David wouldn't be working. Garrett stood at the door for a long time, long enough to feel desperation seeping into his skin. Garrett hopped on his bike and rode to Piper's house, just as he promised himself he wouldn't.

He cruised by the house, checking for clues. The yard was empty, thank God, since the worst thing, which Garrett hadn't considered until he sailed past, would have been David out mowing the lawn. But no, the house looked quiet; both of David's vehicles were in the driveway. Which meant what? Either Piper was already home or not home yet.

It's fruitless to speculate.

Garrett rode out to Cisco Beach, then back home. It was 3:30.

When she still hadn't appeared at seven o'clock, he began to feel sick. Sick like he had stomach cancer and was dying. He told Beth he wanted to skip dinner—they were going out for dinner, she said, to Bluefin for sushi, didn't Garrett remember? No, he answered, he didn't recall hearing anything about it, and besides sushi would make him hurl. His mother and Winnie and Marcus left without him, which was just as well. He wanted to die in peace.

At eight o'clock, he stood on the small deck of his room and prayed: *Please let her still love me. Please.*

At nine o'clock, there was a noise downstairs and Garrett, who was lying in bed listlessly reading his chick book, jumped to his feet. But it was his mom and Winnie and Marcus, back from dinner.

"We brought you some food!" Beth called out.

Despite his deep agitation, he was hungry, and solitude had proved to be more excruciating than company, so he decided to go down and eat. It was fruitless to speculate, he told himself. Maybe Piper had been forced into staying another day, maybe she missed her flight or lost her ticket and was stranded in Hyannis. Maybe she decided she didn't love him after all.

When he reached the bottom of the stairs, his mother was standing there, and then the front door opened and Piper stepped in. For a second, Garrett didn't know what to do or think. He was transported to a state of elation and relief that was beyond anything he'd ever felt. Tears blurred his eyes.

"Mrs. Newton?" Piper said. "I know it's late, but is it okay if Garrett and I go for a walk on the beach?"

Garrett wondered why Piper was calling his mother "Mrs. Newton," when before she'd always just called her Beth. Beth may have been asking herself the same thing, but she just said, "Sure. Of course."

Piper walked down the hallway, through the kitchen, and out onto the deck without acknowledging Garrett in any way. Garrett spied the plastic container of jewel-colored sushi on the kitchen table, but his hunger had vanished. All he wanted was to be at the beach, alone, with Piper.

Piper descended the stairs to the beach in a hurry. She was practically running, and because it was so dark, Garrett worried she might trip. But he understood her instincts—to get to the beach as quickly as possible, where they could be alone.

When they reached the beach, Piper jogged to the left. Garrett ran after her.

"Hey, where are you going?"

Finally, she looked at him. Her nose ring was back in place, and Garrett took this as a positive sign. "I want to get away from the house," she said. "Far away."

She wanted to make love, then, on the beach. Garrett allowed himself a joyful yelp as he raced after her. And then she stopped, and he was able to gather her up in his arms.

"I love you," he said.

She raised her eyes to him. Her long hair spilled over the shoulders of her jean jacket.

"Let's sit down, Garrett." Her breath smelled like cigarettes; she'd gone back to smoking, then, while she was away. But Garrett decided not to say anything about it. *You love me, too, right?* he wanted to ask.

"I missed you so much," he said. "It damn near killed me to be without you for so long."

She sighed. "I have something to tell you," she said. "Something big and you're not going to like it." She plopped down in the sand and pulled him down next to her.

She was going to break up with him. She went away and

decided that she didn't love him after all. Here, then, was his punishment for attacking Marcus, for being a person so unlike his father that it was hard to believe they were related. Garrett took her hand. "What's going on?"

Piper fell back onto her elbows as if the weight of her news was too much to bear sitting up. "My mother and I had a long talk while I was over there. A lot of long talks. I told her all about you. I told her your name."

"Yeah?" Garrett said. "That's good, right?"

"She knows you're Beth Newton's son, Beth Eyler's son."

"That pisses her off?"

Piper squeezed his hand so hard he thought she might break his fingers. "There was a reason why my dad didn't want me to tell my mom your name."

"What reason is that?" Garrett asked.

"They were married."

"Who?"

"Our parents."

Garrett was confused. Piper sounded so grave, and well, so horrified.

"Of course our parents were married," he said. "They're our parents."

"No, Garrett," she said. "My father, David Ronan, was married to your mother, Beth Eyler. In 1979. They were married for two weeks before your mother filed for divorce. They were *married*, Garrett. This is a huge secret they've been keeping from us our whole lives."

Garrett wanted to tell Piper she was nuts, off her rocker. There was no way that what she said was true. "Did you . . . ask . . . your dad?"

She nodded. "Affirmative."

"Did he have an explanation?"

"An explanation that took three hours and kept us from eating dinner. Do you want to hear it?"

"No," Garrett said. Could it be true? he thought. His own mother married to David.

"Not only did they keep it from us," Piper said. "But my dad said, he *said*, Beth told him that your father didn't even know."

"My father didn't know?"

"That's what Dad said."

Garrett felt heavy and cold, like a piece of petrified wood. His mother had been married before, married to David, and nobody knew. Arch had been kept in the dark with Garrett and Winnie, dragged along to Nantucket each and every summer, oblivious to what had happened in their mother's youth.

"What are you going to do?" Piper said.

"I don't know. What are you going to do?"

"Aside from never trust my father again, you mean?"

"Yeah, aside from that."

"I don't know," she admitted.

"Maybe we should run away and get married ourselves," Garrett said. "They couldn't stop us."

"No," Piper said. "They couldn't."

※

In the middle of the night, there was a knock on Winnie's bedroom door, and she assumed it was Marcus, although he swore that after the scene with Garrett, he'd never, ever come to her room in the middle of the night again.

"Come in?" she whispered.

The door opened. Winnie was crushed and indignant when she saw that the person staring at her through the darkness was not Marcus, but her twin brother, who these days ranked right up there with the biggest jerks she'd ever met.

"What do you want?" she demanded. "He's not here, as you can see, though it wouldn't be any of your damn business if he were."

Garrett sat at the foot of the bed. Winnie rolled away to give him room, though she didn't summon the energy to sit up.

"I have some really bad news," he said.

Winnie doubted this was true. One of the consequences of her father's death was that *really bad news* no longer existed. For Winnie, the really bad news was that her father had been killed in a plane crash—all other news was only bad news, or usually, not-so-bad news.

"You broke up with Piper?" she guessed.

"No!" Garrett hopped to his feet and lunged like he was going to sock her for even suggesting such a thing.

"Calm down," Winnie said. She liked saying this. So often it was she who was hysterical and Garrett who was the cool customer. Recently, the tables had turned. Her brother was a nut case. He thought he was so much older than Winnie—getting his license, having sex—but what he didn't realize was that Winnie was maturing this summer, too. Her friendship with Marcus was helping her to deal with her grief and move on. He was helping her to grow on the inside, as a person.

"Don't you want to know what the news is?" Garrett asked.

"If you want to tell me," Winnie said.

Garrett eased back down onto the bed. Winnie yawned, looked at the clock. 1:30. Her heart cried out. The usual time for Marcus.

"I found out something about Mom," Garrett said. "Something big."

He was baiting her. He wanted her to jump up and down, begging, "Oh, please, Garrett, please tell me!" But first Winnie considered the possibilities. Something big about Mom. The words had the unmistakable scent of gossip about them. And gossip meant sex, right? So Beth was having sex with David. Winnie had to admit she didn't love the idea. She wanted her mother to be happy, true, but she wished that happiness would be found in a place that did not involve any man other than Winnie's father. However, this was childish, and since Winnie now eschewed all childish thoughts and emotions, like the ones Garrett so grossly displayed the other night, she figured she would have to be happy for her mother. She would have to celebrate this relationship with David.

"God, Garrett, grow up," Winnie said. "Mom is an adult. She can do whatever she wants."

"She lied to us," Garrett said.

"Didn't you listen to what she told us a few weeks ago?" Winnie asked. "That sex is a private thing?"

"Sex?" Garrett said. "You don't even know what I'm talking about. I'm talking about a lot more than just sex."

"Okay, fine, tell me. What is it then?"

Garrett paused. Of course, now that she'd asked, he was going to make her wait.

"Mom was married to David," he said. "The summer between her junior and senior year in college, 1979. They got married at the Town Building here on Nantucket." He leaned forward and whispered viciously. "They were *married*, Winnie, and she never told us. And worse than that, she never told Dad."

Winnie felt the bottom of her stomach swoop out. This *was*

really bad news because this news altered the way the whole world appeared. Everything shifted, reconfigured. Winnie recognized the reaction in her gut. Her father dead? Of course not. Her mother married before? Impossible.

"Where," Winnie said, "did you hear this?"

"From Piper."

"Oh, please," Winnie said. "Piper is *lying*. Or she has bad information. Like, if David told her that, he's the one who's lying. He probably *wishes* he was married to Mom."

"I thought the same thing," Garrett said. "Except Piper heard this from her mom, Rosie."

"So Rosie's lying."

"It's a matter of public record," Garrett said. "It's registered at the town clerk's office. David told Piper this. Anyone can go check."

"So tomorrow," Winnie said. "We'll check."

"I don't need to check," Garrett said. "I know it's true."

"I'm going to check," Winnie said, "in the morning." She paused. "And Dad didn't know?"

"That's right. Mom told David that Dad didn't know."

"He died without knowing," Winnie said.

Garrett stood up. "I can't believe her! I can't believe she'd keep a secret like that from her own family! I want to wake her up right now and make her admit it to our faces."

Winnie thought about this idea. She wasn't ready for another big, messy middle-of-the night scene. Besides, Winnie didn't want to hear her mother admit it. It would be too heartbreaking for everybody. Winnie felt betrayed—of course she felt betrayed!—but she also felt deeply ashamed for her mother. Who kept a huge secret like that? Lots of people, probably, all over the world, every day. But Winnie didn't like lumping her mother into a category with other secret-keepers and cover-uppers: the Bill Clintons, the Richard Nixons. It made her mother seem too fallible, too human.

"How long were they married for?" she asked.

"Two weeks."

"Only two weeks?" Winnie tried to decide if this made things any better. She decided not; getting married was an unalterable fact, like having a baby. You were either married or you weren't; duration didn't matter. Beth had been married before. "Un-fucking-believable." Garrett probably thought she was cursing to show off, but truly, that was the only phrase that came to mind. Beth had been married before, to David Ronan. For two weeks. She never told Winnie and Garrett, and, even worse, she never told Arch. This was like a brick wall Winnie had to scale without a rope; she had no idea where to find a fingerhold of understanding. Her own mother. Among other emotions was a raw hurt, because Winnie and Beth were friends. They were the female half of the family, comrades, confidantes, or so Winnie thought. Aside from Marcus, Winnie considered Beth to be her closest friend. And not only a friend, of course, but her *mother*. The first and last person she went to with everything. Her safe place, her absolute, final refuge. And yet what Garrett just told her changed all this. Beth was now someone Winnie barely knew, a woman capable of hiding a huge secret.

Winnie stared at Garrett's shadowy figure at the foot of the bed. He was waiting patiently while she processed the news. Reality settled over Winnie: there was no one left in her family that she could trust.

"What should we do?" she asked.

"I have an idea," he said.

Garrett's plan of action was drastic and mean, the kind of get-even scheme that only the mind of a teenager could conjure. But Winnie immediately recognized that in this instance he was right. The twins would exercise the only power they had left, and they would do it secretly, the following night. The plan was so awful and so irrevocable that Winnie insisted they be positive of their mother's guilt before going through with it. She would check in town the next day.

⚘

The morning was as bright and beautiful as any morning on Nantucket had been so far that summer, and yet for Winnie it was the start of a day of subterfuge, and that cast a gloomy pall on her spirit. She climbed out of bed as soon as she heard the water for Marcus's shower, pulled on her jean shorts, which she wore almost as frequently as her poor sweatshirt, and padded downstairs. She stopped and stared at herself in the hallway mirror. Her face was tan, her hair practically white. Although she and Garrett were twins, it was much commented that Garrett resembled Arch, and Winnie was a dead-ringer for Beth. This had always made Winnie pleased and proud to hear. Her mother was no super model but she had a kind of clean beauty that made people think of good diet and good breeding and lots of time spent in the fresh air. Now, Winnie was appalled at the features she shared with her mother. Would she do something awful like Beth had done?

No.

Winnie sat out on the deck with a bowl of Cheerios, gazing at the water. This news about Beth had at least restored Winnie's appetite; she hadn't voluntarily fixed herself breakfast in four months. Winnie heard noises in the kitchen and dread clutched her heart. She could *not* face Beth this morning, and maybe not ever again. She wished fervently that she and Garrett were leaving for college in the fall. But unfortunately there was still an entire year of living at home with their mother before their escape into adulthood.

Winnie listened to the rustlings in the kitchen until she was certain it was Marcus, and then she relaxed somewhat. When she finished her cereal, she propped her legs on a second chair and lay back, basking in the early morning sun. It was far too warm for the sweatshirt, but she wouldn't take it off, especially not now. Not unless she replaced it with a T-shirt that said MY MOTHER IS A LIAR.

Marcus joined her at the table with his breakfast: two peanut butter and beach plum jam sandwiches on raisin bread, a hardboiled egg, a nectarine, and a giant glass of Gatorade.

"Hi," he said. "You're up early. Did you *eat?*"

Winnie didn't answer except to move her hand indicating, *Hi, so what, of course.*

Marcus took a huge bite out of one of his sandwiches.

"I'm going into town this morning," Winnie said.

Marcus swallowed and took a long pull of his Gatorade. "Really? Why?"

One of the things that made today so painful was that Winnie and Garrett had agreed to keep this a secret, at least until their plan was executed. This meant no telling Marcus, even though Marcus would understand. He was angry at his own mother; he practically hated her.

"I have to buy some books for school," she said.

Marcus nodded, unimpressed. The best kind of lie, Winnie
realized, was a boring one.

🜏

The worst kind of lie was the kind that Winnie uncovered at the
town clerk's office less than an hour later. Winnie was nervous
as she entered the Town Building—it was air-conditioned and
hushed with polished concrete floors. It had long corridors like
a high school. The building felt different from the rest of Nantucket—this was an office building, where people *worked*. Winnie
stood for a minute outside of the town clerk's office. A brunette
woman wearing a melon-colored dress and stockings and heels
sat typing at a desk. When she looked up, Winnie walked away,
the soles of her running shoes squeaking against the polished
floor. Now she felt like an idiot, but she didn't know what to
say. What if the woman asked her for ID? She didn't even have
a driver's license! She should have insisted Garrett come with
her; he was better at dealing with adults than she was, but Garrett
hadn't wanted to come. He was certain of their mother's guilt;
he didn't need proof.

Winnie decided to walk around for a few minutes. She
climbed the stairs and the first office she came to was the DMV.
How ironic it would be if she took her driving test now and
returned home with her license. Even that would be enough to
hurt her mother's feelings. Beth was excited about waiting in the
awful DMV room while Winnie took her test. She wanted to be
the first passenger that Winnie drove legally on her own. Winnie
hesitated; maybe she *should* take the test. That would be enough
punishment for Beth, and then she and Garrett could forget
about their horrible plan for tonight. Winnie closed her eyes and

tried to picture herself parallel parking, but when she did, she saw herself hitting the granite curb and popping a tire. Winnie moved on: past the court rooms, past the passport office, all the way to the stairs at the opposite end of the building. Then, without options other than leaving or finding out the truth, she marched back to the town clerk's office. The woman in the melon-colored dress looked up and smiled in such a friendly way that Winnie decided it was okay to speak.

"I want to check and see if my mother was married in 1979," Winnie said. "Is that something you can help me with?"

Melon stood up and walked over to a large gray filing cabinet. "Name?"

Deep breath. "Winnie Newton."

"We're looking in 1979," Melon said. "What month?"

"Summer?" Winnie said. "July, August?"

"And you said the last name is Newton?"

"That's my last name," Winnie said.

Melon smiled at her as though Winnie were telling a joke and she was waiting for the punch line. "Is that the last name I'm looking for?"

"No," Winnie said. *Oh, God, Garrett!* "I'm sorry. My mother's last name at that time was Eyler. Elizabeth Eyler. E-Y-L-E-R."

Melon nodded definitively as if this made much more sense. She started flipping through the cards in the filing cabinet. "Nope, nope, nope," she whispered. "Nope, nope, nope."

Winnie didn't know what to do with her hands. Putting them in the back pockets of her jean shorts seemed too casual, too teenagerly. She decided it would be more reverent to clasp them in front of her.

"Nope, nope, nope."

A very small part of Winnie held out hope that this was all
a hoax, a mistake, even a lie concocted by the Ronan family.
How Winnie would relish telling Garrett he was wrong. If there
were no record of the marriage here, then she would never believe it was true.

"Here it is!" Melon said brightly. "Eyler and Ronan. Oh." Her
forehead crinkled. "David Ronan? Your mother was married to
David Ronan?" She put a hand up. "Don't answer that. It is *none*
of my business." She handed the card to Winnie. "It's fifty cents
for a Xerox copy, and a certified copy costs five dollars and takes
three business days."

Winnie pulled a dollar out of her pocket. Thank God she
thought to bring money! "Just one copy, please."

"My pleasure." Melon took the dollar bill from Winnie, and
removed fifty cents from her desk drawer. Five seconds at the
copier and a bright flash of light later, Melon handed Winnie
the change and the proof of her mother's betrayal. Melon smiled
again, in an intimate way, and Winnie felt her face turn red.
Melon obviously knew David Ronan, and now the news of his
secret first marriage would leak out. But, really, what did Winnie
care?

When she gazed down at the marriage certificate, the first
thing she noticed was the word "Divorced," stamped in large
black letters across the top. Winnie scanned the paper, line by
line. Bride's name: *Elizabeth Celia Eyler;* Bride's D.O.B.: *May 2, 1958;*
Groom's name: *David Arthur Ronan;* Groom's D.O.B: *September 18,
1957;* Date of marriage: *August 16, 1979;* Officiant: *Judge Leon Macy;*
Witnesses: *Kenneth Edwards, James Seamus, Kelly Wilcox.* The marriage certificate was all signed, sealed, and official-looking. It was
real. Winnie felt like she might vomit up her Cheerios right into
Melon's typewriter. She pressed the paper to her chest, whispered, "Thank you," and ran from the building.

She sat outside on a park bench with her head between her knees. Okay, this was really bad. This was—not the worst—but the second-to-worst. Her mother and David all signed, sealed, and official on a card in the Town Building where anyone could look, where anybody could get a copy for only fifty cents! Well, she and Garrett had been betrayed, that was all there was to it. Winnie tried to imagine what her father would do if he were still alive and he'd found out this sickening news. She tried to imagine him getting angry, except he didn't get angry at Beth. He would probably say he was disappointed—not because Beth had been married before, but because she chose to conceal it. Deeper down, he might be sad and maybe even a little jealous. Arch, though, had a way of understanding and then forgiving other people's flaws—Constance Tyler's, for example. Arch might even say it wasn't any of their business—but that thought evaporated immediately. Beth was his wife, their mother! This was their business!

Winnie climbed on her bike. She would go home and lay low until nightfall, when she and Garrett would inflict their revenge. What they planned to do would break their mother's heart, but Winnie no longer cared. She had a copy of the marriage certificate in her pocket, made official by a younger version of her mother's signature. Now it was Beth's turn to learn what it felt like to be shut out, to be excluded from life's most important knowledge.

⚘

Beth was out for a run when Winnie got home. Winnie wrote a note and left it on the kitchen table. "Don't feel well! Please do not disturb!!!—W." But of course Beth knocked on her door as soon as she got home. Winnie had anticipated this very situation and moved her small dresser in front of the door as a blockade.

"Winnie," Beth said gently. "Honey, what's wrong?"

"Period!" Winnie spat out. How she loathed even the sound of her mother's voice!

"Did you take any Midol?" Beth asked. "Can I make you some chamomile tea?"

"Go away!" This in the most venomous voice Winnie could muster.

"You're not acting like yourself," Beth said. "Are you sure there's nothing else wrong?"

"*I* am a self-respecting woman," Winnie said. Her point being that the woman on the other side of the door could not be described as such. The bigger point being that her own mother, who heretofore had been a paragon of virtue, was now someone else entirely.

Beth tried the door and found herself stymied by the dresser. Winnie couldn't help smiling with self-satisfaction. There was something about a house with no locking doors—everyone felt justified to barge in on everyone else. But not this time.

"Winnie, what have you done?"

"I said, 'go away!' "

Silence. Then, "Fine, fine, fine. If that's the way you want it. I'll be out on the deck eating lunch. Let me know if you need anything."

When her mother was safely down the stairs, Winnie whispered, "Liar."

🌿

Later, there was a distinctive knock on the door. A Marcus knock.

"Hey," he said. "Open up."

For him—yes. But only him. Winnie didn't even want to see Garrett until later. Winnie shoved the dresser aside and it scraped some green paint off the floor. *Oh, well!* Winnie didn't care; it was her mother's house. She'd finally stopped feeling guilty about breaking the valuable lamp. She couldn't be bothered anymore about her mother's heirlooms.

She opened the door to find Marcus holding out a plate: a BLT on toasted Portuguese bread with a handful of Cape Cod chips. Winnie's stomach reared up. She hadn't realized she was hungry.

"Your mother told me to tell you that these are Bartlett tomatoes," he said. "Also, she didn't put on too much mayonnaise."

"Mom made the sandwich?" Winnie asked dejectedly. She'd entertained a brief fantasy that Marcus made it.

"Yep."

"I'm not eating it."

Marcus walked past Winnie into the room and sat on the bed. Winnie closed the door behind him and slid the dresser against it.

"Well, then, I'm going to eat it," Marcus said. He took a huge bite out of the corner and tomato seeds slipped down his chin.

"I'll have half," Winnie conceded. She was hungry and had no intention of going down for dinner. She and Marcus sat side-by-side on the bed eating the sandwich and all of the chips, using a couple of Kleenex as napkins.

When they finished, Marcus said, "You've been up here all day."

"Yeah."

"Girl stuff?"

Winnie sighed and lay back against her pillows. "Let me ask you something," she said. "What if one of your parents did something really bad—"

"Like commit murder, you mean?"

Okay, she deserved that. She thought about how to start over.

"What if one of your parents kept a secret from you your whole life. Like, oh, I don't know . . . like they flunked out of college or had a child out of wedlock. Would you be pissed?"

Marcus shifted on the bed and glanced up at the ceiling. Winnie followed his eyes—there was a light water stain and a tiny black spider. Without a word, Marcus stood up, collected the spider in a tissue, and let it go out the window. Winnie marveled. Any other guy would have squished the thing to death. When Marcus sat down again, his eyelids drooped. After two months together, Winnie knew what this meant: he was shutting her out!

"Wake up!" she said impatiently.

"What's going on, Winnie?"

Winnie chewed her thumbnail. Garrett had sworn her to secrecy, but that wasn't fair. After all, *Piper* knew about Beth and David. Winnie motioned for Marcus to come closer. He rolled his eyes—she was being silly—but he leaned in.

"What is it, Winnie?"

"Mom was married before," Winnie said. "She was married to David."

Marcus straightened. *Married* to David. Well.

Winnie studied Marcus's face; she was interested to know how someone else would react. He seemed nonplussed, like he didn't get it.

"When was this?"

"When she was twenty-one years old," Winnie said. "They were married for two weeks. And she never told us."

"How'd you find out?"

"Piper's mother, Rosie, told her and Piper told Garrett. I checked it out this morning when I was in town. I made a copy of the marriage certificate." She pulled it out of her pocket, unfolded it and presented it to him. "Here. This is it."

That explained why she'd acted so strangely at breakfast. Marcus *knew* she wasn't going into town for books. He looked over the marriage certificate. "Did you talk to your mom?" he asked.

"Hell, no. I'm never talking to her again."

Marcus guffawed. "What, over *this*?"

"Yes, over this. She lied to us, Marcus."

"Maybe she had her reasons. Maybe she was embarrassed."

"That's no excuse."

"Why? You can't tell me you've never kept a secret from your mother."

Winnie thought for a minute. She couldn't think of a single thing she had ever kept from anyone. "I don't keep secrets."

"Some people do," Marcus said, thinking uneasily of the still-blank legal pad in his room. "It's called privacy."

"Privacy isn't okay under these circumstances," Winnie said. "Besides, there's worse news."

"What's that?"

"She never told my dad," Winnie whispered. In her mind, this was such a horrible fact that it couldn't even be spoken aloud. Her dear, departed father deceived by the woman he loved.

Marcus set the marriage certificate down on the bed. Here was Beth's secret, then—the one she kept from her whole family but almost told *him* on the Fourth of July.

"You need to talk to your mom, Winnie," he said. "You need to work this out."

"No way," Winnie said. "Mom is going to pay."

"Pay? What do you mean, *pay*? You're being ridiculous."

Winnie bristled at this. "Shut up! You don't talk to your mother. I don't see you 'working things out' with her! She's sent you at least three letters that I know of, and you haven't opened one of them."

"First of all, my letters are none of your business," Marcus said. "Secondly, *my* mother did something really bad. She *killed* a woman and a nine-year-old girl. She killed them inside our home with a knife from our kitchen. I have a reason to be angry."

"I have a reason to be angry, too," Winnie said. "This changes my whole life. I've been deceived, my brother has been deceived, and worst of all, my father! I feel like my whole life is a sham. Anyway, Garrett and I have planned some revenge."

"*Revenge?*" Marcus said. Winnie kicked herself mentally—she shouldn't have said anything about the revenge. "You want revenge because your mother was married to David for two weeks twenty years ago? That's the stupidest thing I've ever heard." Marcus felt a wave of exhaustion roll over him. He closed his eyes and lay back on the bed.

"Don't pretend like you're falling asleep!" Winnie said. "You do that all the time when you don't want to deal with reality."

"Oh, do I?" Marcus asked, his eyes still closed.

"Yes, you do. Anyway, why are you taking Mom's side? You're my friend. You have to take my side. My side is the *right* side."

Marcus stood up and studied the dresser in front of the door. "You're crazy, you know that?" He moved the dresser with enormous ease and stepped out into the hallway. "You need to put your shit into perspective. You wouldn't know a problem if one bit you in the ass." He sounded truly pissed and Winnie groped for words to reel him back in, but then she told herself she didn't care what he thought. Marcus was the person who was supposed to *understand*. Okay, maybe Beth wasn't a murderer but that didn't mean Winnie's feelings weren't hurt.

"You know what you are?" Winnie said. "You're self-absorbed."

"*I'm* self-absorbed?" Marcus said. "Sister, look in the mirror."

"Fuck you," Winnie flung out. "I wish I hadn't told you."

"I wish you hadn't told me either," Marcus said. "Because I used to respect you. I used to think you had a decent heart."

"I do have a decent heart," she said. "And this *is* a real problem."

"Don't get me going," Marcus said. "If you want to hear about real problems, I'll tell you sometime. But what I'm hearing now is you judging something you don't understand. You need to talk to your mother."

"I told you, I'm never talking to her again," Winnie said.

"Well, then," Marcus said. "It sounds like you've made up your mind."

"I can't believe you're being such a *hypocrite*," she hissed. "You don't talk to Constance."

"This isn't about me," Marcus said.

Winnie was so furious—here was Marcus making *her* feel like the bad guy!—that she slammed the door, but it bounced back in her face. Marcus walked down the hall to his room without another word. Winnie closed the door as best she could and moved the dresser in front of it. Then she flopped face-first on her bed. She *didn't* understand. That much was true. She didn't understand anything anymore.

※

The plan was scheduled for one in the morning, to be completed by three. Garrett had read that these were the hours that the average person—one who went to sleep at ten-thirty and woke at seven—slept most soundly. Before one A.M. a person was in light REM sleep, and after three the average person woke at least once to use the bathroom. Garrett sounded convincing on this point and Winnie conceded. After all, she didn't want to get caught. She found it impossible to fall asleep, and thus lay awake in a state of fearful agitation, replaying her conversation with Marcus. After she skipped dinner, she thought he might realize that she was depressed and come up to check on her, but he didn't. On top of everything else she had to deal with, now she and Marcus were fighting.

At exactly one o'clock there was the lightest of taps on her door. Winnie stood up. Her body felt tingly and numb; she was shaking. She pulled on a pair of jeans and picked up her flip-flops; they would be too noisy to wear down the stairs. When she opened the door, she found Garrett standing there with a strange, peaceful expression on his face. He, too, was wearing jeans, and his Danforth wind breaker. He held the urn in both his hands.

They slipped downstairs. The house made noises, but these didn't phase Winnie. She was used to being awake in the middle of the night because of Marcus, and had learned that the house creaked, as though complaining about growing older. There was a little bit of light cast through the living room windows by the stars and a crescent moon. Garrett eased open the front door.

Winnie said, "I think I'm going to eat something."

Garrett whipped around. "What?"

"I'm hungry."

"Tough."

"Tough for you." Winnie went into the kitchen and opened the refrigerator. There were always leftovers when Beth cooked, the remnants of dinner, all wrapped up: BBQ ribs, Beth's macaroni salad, and three buttermilk biscuits. Winnie had smelled the biscuits baking earlier.

"I'm taking the biscuits," she said.

Garrett narrowed his eyes. "You went three months without eating and now you can't wait two hours for biscuits?"

"No," she said. "I can't. And they have to be warm."

"What?"

"Or the butter won't melt." She put the plate of biscuits in the microwave and set it for one minute. Every time she pressed a button there was a loud, electronic beep. Garrett lowered himself gingerly into a kitchen chair, the urn in his lap.

"I can't believe you," he said. "Do you *want* to get caught?"

Winnie didn't answer. She watched her biscuits, bathed in light, as they circled around inside the microwave. She took the butter dish from the fridge. Maybe she did want to get caught. Maybe she did want her mother to come down and find them both there, with the urn.

The microwave beeped five loud times to let her know the biscuits were finished. Garrett said, "I'll wait for you in the driveway." Winnie got a knife from the drawer, sliced open the hot biscuits, and put a pat of butter inside each one. Then she wrapped them in plastic; she could eat them on the way. But she needed a drink. She opened the fridge again and took out a Coke. Popped it open right there in the kitchen; it sounded like a cap gun. Winnie waited, willing her mother out of sleep. *If you wake up, you can say good-bye!* But there were no stirrings from upstairs. Whatever Garrett read about human sleep patterns must have been correct.

She walked out to the driveway carrying her snack. She took a swill of her Coke, then followed Garrett to the car.

The hardest part had been deciding where. Winnie wanted to scatter the ashes right off the deck—that way their father's remains would become one with their property, one with Horizon. Garrett disagreed; he wanted to really hurt their mother by scattering the ashes somewhere she would never think of. After they'd bandied about several possibilities—the cornfields of Bartlett Farm, the marshes around Miacomet Pond, the Easy Street boat basin—Garrett claimed he had the perfect place in mind. But they needed the car. Winnie was going to drive because technically Garrett was still grounded from the car. Winnie was nervous about driving in the dark but Garrett said he'd be right there in the passenger seat, helping. It would be easier, he said, without so many cars on the road.

They climbed in the Rover, just barely clicking their doors shut. Winnie held the keys. They felt foreign in her hand and Winnie was reminded of the only time she ever smoked a cigarette and she wasn't sure how to hold it. She wiggled the key into the ignition and took a breath. This was the biggest risk: that Beth would hear the car. But, as Garrett pointed out, even if she did hear it, it would be too late. They'd be gone and she would have no way to follow them.

Winnie backed out of the driveway. Garrett peered through the windshield at the house and Winnie nervously glanced at her mother's bedroom window. Nothing. Winnie pulled onto the dirt road, and when she was a safe distance from the house, she switched on the headlights.

Garrett leaned back in his seat, the urn in his lap. "Home free," he said.

"Now will you please tell me where we're going?" Winnie said. She resented the fact that Garrett got to choose their father's final resting place. Winnie had also suggested scattering the ashes into the ocean—maybe because she was a swimmer, and felt more at home in the water than she did on dry land. But Garrett protested. *No way,* he'd said. *Not the water.* He'd referred to the map on his bedroom wall. *Dad will end up in Portugal. Or the Canary Islands.*

"We're going to Quidnet," Garrett said.

"*Quid*-net?" This was a part of the island Winnie had heard of but she couldn't remember ever going there, and she certainly wouldn't be able to find it on her own. "Why Quidnet?"

"Dad and I went there once, a few years ago. A secret road. A meadow surrounded by trees on one side and water on the other. It was a cool place, and I don't know, it was like the two of us discovered it."

"Where was I?" Winnie wanted to know.

"At home," Garrett said. "With Mom."

At home with Mom, the liar, while Garrett and Arch explored the island together. Winnie liked the sound of this less and less. Garrett was commandeering the mission.

"You know, Garrett," Winnie said. "It's not like it's *Daddy* in that urn. It's just the remains of the body that belonged to Daddy."

"I know," Garrett said defensively, but Winnie saw him clench the urn. Of all of them, Garrett was the most protective of the ashes—after all, they'd sat in his room all summer. To be perfectly honest, Winnie didn't like to think about the ashes. Her father's burned remains. She wanted to scatter them so they'd be gone. So she could be left with the memories of her father that lived in her mind. Dr. Schau, however, had reminded them in the final therapy session before they left for Nantucket, that scattering the ashes was an important symbolic act. It was one tangible way to say good-bye. Winnie felt a pang in her chest at the thought of Dr. Schau. After they did this, how would they ever be able to face Dr. Schau again? She would think they were evil children—stealing a coping mechanism, an avenue of healing away from their mother. And then there was Marcus: *You wouldn't know a problem if one bit you in the ass.* It wasn't as if Beth had committed a crime. She hadn't hurt anyone physically, and she hadn't broken any laws except for one that Winnie and Garrett held in their heart: *We should know everything about our mother.*

"I'm having second thoughts," Winnie said. She clenched the wheel as they rumbled over the ruts in the dirt road, and yearned for her biscuits. She wanted one, now. She pulled over to the side of the road, located the biscuits in the console, and stuffed one in her mouth over Garrett's protests. She drank some of her Coke. "Remember how Dad always said, if you have a choice between the right thing to do and the easy thing to do, choose the right thing?"

"Well, what about Mom?" Garrett said. "She chose the easy thing by lying to us for seventeen years."

"It probably wasn't easy," Winnie said. "It's never easy to lie because you're always so afraid someone will find out."

"Trust me, Winnie," Garrett said. "We're doing the right thing. She lied to Dad, too, don't forget."

"I guess," Winnie said. Garrett was older than her by four minutes, and he had put himself in charge. But, in a brilliant twist of fate, *she* was driving the car. She could turn around and go back to the house; she could foil this plan. Winnie ate the second biscuit. The butter greased her lips. "I don't know, Garrett."

"Come on," he said. "You're the one with the marriage certificate."

True, true. The marriage certificate was in the back pocket of her jeans. Winnie thought of Melon smiling at her with such compassion, as if to say, *You poor girl. Your mother and David Ronan.*

"You're right," Winnie said. She finished the second biscuit, drank some more Coke, and signaled left, even though there wasn't another car for miles. "Let's go."

Nantucket was bigger than Winnie realized. She'd been coming here every summer since she was born and yet her experience of Nantucket consisted of the south shore from Cisco Beach to Surfside, and the roads that led into town. Once or twice a summer they drove out Milestone Road to get ice cream from the 'Sconset Market, and two or three times they'd done the Milestone–Polpis bike path as a family. But driving through the moonlight with Garrett and her father's ashes, Winnie saw whole sections of Nantucket she never even knew existed. The winding dirt roads between Monomoy and Shimmo, for example. There were whole neighborhoods—lots of people lived here. How did Garrett find these roads? He went exploring with Piper, he said. He directed Winnie back to the Polpis Road and they cruised past Quaise, Shawkemo Hills, and Wauwinet.

Winnie put her window down and the night air rushed in. They had the radio on, the oldies station, hoping they would hear a song that reminded them of their father, and as it turned out, every song that played reminded them of Arch. "Here Comes the Sun," by the Beatles, "Red Rubber Ball," by Cyrkle, even "Puff, the Magic Dragon," which he used to sing to them as kids. Winnie started to feel like they were doing the right thing. It was a perfect night, the island was as beautiful as she'd ever seen it, and their father's spirit was filling the car.

Garrett gave her plenty of warning before her left hand turn on to Quidnet Road; she put on her blinker.

"You're doing a good job driving," he said.

This pleased her. "Thanks."

He told her to take another left onto a dirt road. The road was bordered on both sides by tall trees that arched above them. A tunnel of trees, and every so often through a break in the leaves and branches, Winnie spied the crescent moon.

"We're almost there," Garrett said.

After a while, the trees on the left hand side opened up to a meadow, and beyond the meadow was the flat, calm water of Nantucket Sound. Winnie caught her breath. "This is it?" she said.

"Yeah," Garrett said. "It's cool, isn't it?"

"You came here with Daddy?"

"That one time he and I went surf casting out at Great Point?" Garrett said. "We explored on our way home and found this place. He said he wanted to bring you and Mom here for a picnic."

"Really?" Winnie said. "Where should we stop?"

"Up here," Garrett said.

Winnie pulled onto the shoulder. The radio was playing Linda Ronstadt singing "Long, Long Time." Garrett opened his door and they both blinked at the dome light. "Let's do it," he said.

Winnie's heart pounded in her ears. She was unable to move. "Garrett?" she said.

He came to the driver's side and helped her out of the car. He kept his arm around her as he steered her into the meadow. There were Queen Anne's lace, black-eyed Susans, and a thicket of low blueberry bushes.

Garrett opened the urn. He put the top of the urn by his feet, and when he straightened, he reached into the urn, but then he withdrew his hand.

"You first," he said. "You throw first."

"Why?"

"Because you were his little girl," Garrett said. "He loved you best."

Immediately Winnie's eyes were blurred by tears. She sniffled. "Oh, Garrett, you know he loved us exactly the same."

"He loved us a lot," Garrett said. He was crying, too, and this made Winnie cry harder. She knew she would never forget this moment as long as she lived. Her twin brother, this hidden meadow, and the water beyond it, the music in her head, her mother's secret in her heart. Winnie slipped her hand into the urn. The ash was fine and silky with a few chunks. The remains of her beloved father, the man she loved first, the man she would always love beyond any other man, even Marcus. Winnie called up the memories she had left: her father across the table from her at EJ's Luncheonette eating his red flannel hash; her father in the balcony of Danforth's indoor pool, whooping like a rodeo cowboy as a signal to her to give the last lap of the race all she had, her father on any one of five thousand nights coming in to kiss her good night on the forehead, never shutting the door without saying, "I love you, Winnie. You're my only little girl." He had been a great lawyer—that was why his obituary ran in all of the New York papers, including the *Times*—but he'd been an even greater father. This, she realized, was the highest compliment anyone could give a man.

With a wide, circling motion of her arm, Winnie scattered him, set him free, let him go.

chapter 6

Just like that, Marcus's summer was falling apart. He wished he'd never heard the secret news about Beth and David—it was family business and he'd been dragged in, first by Beth, then by Winnie. Marcus had promised Beth he would support Winnie, but her reaction to the news was so overblown, so immature, that Marcus could feel nothing but disappointment in her. Their relationship, whatever it was—boyfriend/girlfriend or just friends—was turning to rags faster than Winnie's sweatshirt.

Marcus couldn't figure out what the twins' so-called revenge was, but there was a definite change in their behavior. They spoke very little to Beth, and when they did speak, it was in a cool, formal tone, the way you would talk to a stranger at a bus stop. One-word sentences, short, tired phrases, crisp and distant. Beth tolerated it for about a day and a half, then she confronted them at dinner. "All right, kids. What's going on?" Garrett and Winnie didn't blink, didn't crack a smile; they simply looked at each other meaningfully and retreated into themselves, like a set of twins Marcus read about once in a magazine article who had their own spooky form of communication.

Winnie had also stopped talking to Marcus. When they occupied the same space—the kitchen, for example, while making breakfast or lunch—Winnie smiled at him benignly, like Marcus was someone she'd met once before but whose name she couldn't recall. He wanted to shake her—*this is not how you treat people when you're angry!* But Marcus didn't want to give Winnie the satisfaction of knowing how much her behavior bugged him. After all, he had his own life. He had, he reminded himself with increasing guilt each day, a *book* to write.

He couldn't stop himself from thinking of her, though, from listening to every word that came out of her mouth (mostly words directed to Garrett, or to Piper, if she was around). He couldn't help himself from listening for her in the middle of the night; he knew her footsteps, and when they were in the house together, he kept track of her. One afternoon, as he hung out in his room, he heard her march up the stairs and stop just outside his door. He tried to steady his breathing as he waited for her to knock. Marcus was ready to forgive her—even to apologize.

Strangely, no knock came. Instead, there was a whooshing sound as an envelope skated across the wood floor. Marcus shook his head. It was just like a woman to write a note.

When he bent over to retrieve the envelope, however, he saw that it wasn't a note and it wasn't from Winnie. It was a Western Union telegram and that, he realized with a surge of fear, meant only one thing: Zachary Celtic. Zachary had bugged Marcus for a phone number, a fax number, an e-mail address—he wanted a way to contact Marcus to check on the progress of the book.

When Marcus reported that there was no computer at the house where he was staying, no fax machine, *not even a phone,*—*That's right*, Marcus had said, *I guess these people I'm staying with are old-fashioned or something*—Zachary Celtic had grudgingly written down the address, saying he would send telegrams.

So here was a telegram, delivered by a person so angry with him that she couldn't even knock on the door and hand it to him. Marcus slit the envelope with his pinky nail.

> 21 July
>
> *Dear Marcus,*
>
> *How is the book coming along? No pressure, man, just checking in. September will be here before you know it! Call if you need guidance—that's what editors are for! (And to rip the shit out of your first three drafts, of course—only kidding, man!)*
>
> *Best regards,*
>
> Z

Marcus winced. Zachary Celtic wasn't used to writing to black people if he thought the only name they related to was "man."

The telegram reignited the panic that lay in the bottom of his stomach like cold kindling. With trembling hands, Marcus took the legal pad from his bureau drawer. *My mother is a murderer.* Even that was more than Marcus wanted to say. He tossed the legal pad onto his bed and opened the louvered folding door of his closet. His beautiful white shirt was the only thing hanging. Marcus's black leather duffel lay across the closet floor, as hideous as a body bag. The only thing that made Marcus feel worse than the duffel was the pair of dock shoes, the left shoe stuffed with Constance's unread letters. Those three things—the shirt, the duffel, and the shoes—were physical proof of the five hundred dollars he would never be able to pay back and thirty thousand dollars he would never see unless he could figure out how he wanted to tell his story.

Marcus lay back on his white bed. *The dead bodies in your own apartment . . . your mother, pretty woman, too, strapped to the gurney, facing the long needle . . . the blood-splattered sheet . . . You get to tell the story in your own words, kid. I'll bet that's something you've been itching to do . . . Your mother as, like, an educated woman, a teacher and everything, and one day she just . . . snaps.*

Yes, Marcus thought, she just snapped.

He didn't know why his mother had killed Angela and Candy; he didn't *have* an explanation and it wasn't fair—to his readers or to his mother—to make one up.

❧

Winnie and Marcus didn't sit together at the beach anymore. Instead, Winnie sat on the deck with Garrett and sometimes Piper, and Marcus went to the beach alone. He swam the butterfly, some of his strongest swimming, because he knew Winnie was watching. He thought about how he could have won first place in every meet last season. He'd held himself back on purpose. Now *that* took skill, because nobody suspected he was throwing his races. Or maybe his coach did suspect and decided to keep quiet because he didn't want Marcus to win. He didn't want to face the headlines any more than Marcus did. MURDERER'S SON WINS ALL-QUEENS INVITATIONAL.

Marcus grew lonely, especially in the hours after dinner when he and Winnie normally played games. Now he stayed in his room, listening to his portable CD player, reading about spies, thinking about his mother.

For the first time all summer, he missed TV. And with utter dismay, Marcus realized that he wouldn't be able to write a word while he was so agitated about Winnie.

He considered going home. It was nearly the end of July; he'd had six good weeks. The atmosphere in his white room wasn't conducive to writing, that was a big problem, so the best thing was to get home—away from so much whiteness. Away from the Newtons.

He called home on a Tuesday night, enjoying the unconcealed intrigue on Winnie's face when he stood up from the dinner table and announced that he was riding one of the mountain bikes into town. She didn't say anything, but her eyebrows moved a fraction of an inch, belying her thoughts: *What is he doing in town at night?* It was likely she also had questions about the telegram—Marcus had checked the envelope and was relieved to discover there was no return address to give him away. Let her wonder. Let her wonder, too, when he disappeared for good.

It cost two dollars and fifty cents in quarters to get a line to Queens on the pay phone, and at first the answering machine picked up. Marcus listened for a few seconds to his father's melancholy intonation, "We're not in at the moment, please—"

Then, the voice was cut off, replaced by the breathless alto of Marcus's sister, LaTisha. "Yeah? What?"

"Or 'hello,'" Marcus said, thinking despite himself that even if the Newtons had a phone they would never answer by saying "Yeah? What?" "You could say hello."

"*Marcus?*" LaTisha said, her voice interested, if not apologetic. "Is this Marcus?"

"Yes."

"How are you?" LaTisha asked. "How's Nantucket? Is it incredible? Dad says you never describe it."

Marcus looked out at the darkened street. The shops were lit up and people strolled by eating ice cream cones. A Lincoln Navigator rumbled down the cobblestones and stopped in front of Twenty-one Federal. Two women climbed out wearing brightly colored sundresses, followed by a man wearing a navy blazer over what Marcus guessed was a Paul Stuart shirt. The man escorted both women up the steps of the restaurant while the driver of the Navigator—whom Marcus could only identify as a madras-clad elbow—called out, "Order my drink while I park this beast! Mount Gay and tonic!" How to describe such a place to his father or LaTisha? All Marcus could think was that *this* was the life Constance had visualized for herself—a life of glamour and privilege and ease.

"It's fine," he said.

"*Fine?*" LaTisha repeated. "That doesn't help me any. What's the beach like? And the house. Is it really, really huge? Is it a mansion?"

"It's not a mansion," Marcus said. "It's just a house."

"On the beach, right?"

"On a bluff overlooking the beach."

"A *bluff?* That sounds cool. And the family—is the family okay, or are they, you know, snotty?"

"Snotty" was the wrong word, though Marcus understood why it was the word that came to LaTisha's mind. Because that was what Marcus had feared, too, before he got here—that the Newtons would be snotty, snobby, that they would look down on him. That was the reason for buying the props—the shirt, the deck shoes, the leather bag. He had thought, before he spent any time with these people, that it would be about money. But it was ten times as complicated as that. The Newtons were just so very sad—as sad as Marcus was—and they kept getting sadder. Marcus cleared his throat and shook his head. He didn't want to start feeling sorry for them now.

"The family is fine," Marcus said. A blatant lie. "Listen, is Dad there?"

"It's Tuesday," LaTisha said. "He's at support group until nine-thirty."

"Oh," Marcus said. He'd forgotten about the support group. The details of his life in Queens had all but vanished from his mind. "What are you doing?"

"Nothing," LaTisha said. "Watching TV with Ernestine."

Ernestine was a girl with learning disabilities from down the hall who had remained LaTisha's steadfast friend through everything. Marcus suspected Ernestine lacked a full understanding of what had happened with their mother, but he was glad LaTisha had her for company, even if all they ever did together was watch TV.

"The house here doesn't have a TV," Marcus said.

"What?" LaTisha said. "You're kidding, right? They don't have TV? God, Marcus, what do you do all day? And at night?"

"I swim during the day, and you know, sit on the beach. I read. Listen to music. Hang out . . ." He almost said, *Hang out with Winnie,* but he caught himself. "I relax."

Suddenly, LaTisha's voice grew suspicious. "You're calling Dad because you want to come home, right? Geez, Marcus, I don't blame you. You must be bored to death. Well, I'll be happy if you come home. I miss you. This place *sucks* when you're not here. Pop is practically never home and I have this ridiculous curfew. Eight o'clock. It's not even dark at eight o'clock. And if he's not here he has Mrs. Demetrios check on me. I'm almost thirteen, for God's sake!" She paused to catch her breath and Marcus pictured her young face and her skimpy braids. When Constance first went to jail, LaTisha cried all the time because Mama wasn't there to do her hair. "I thought I might make a little money this summer, but nobody calls me to baby-sit anymore. They probably think . . . well, who knows what they think."

"They probably think you're going to kill their children," Marcus said.

"Yeah," LaTisha said, as though this were something she had realized and accepted long ago. "Anyway, things would be better if you came home."

"I'm not coming home," Marcus said. As bad as shit was, at least he wasn't frying on the griddle of hot city blocks, or worse, trapped inside, supervising his sister, watching reruns of *Three's Company* and begging the air conditioner to do a better job. He felt sad about this—*home* should be a place you wanted to run to no matter what. It should be a refuge. "I just wanted to check in is all."

"Well, as much as I told you I was glad to get rid of your ass this summer, I'm really not. It feels like everyone is dropping out of this family."

"I'm not dropping out," Marcus said.

"I know," LaTisha said. "It just feels that way."

"You should . . . read more," Marcus said. "Go to the library."

"*Library?*" LaTisha said. "Now you sound like Mama." Before Marcus could assert his obvious difference from their mother, LaTisha added, "I'll tell Pop you called. You'll call back—when?"

"Soon," Marcus promised. "I'll talk to you later, sis. Okay? Tell Ernestine I said hello."

He hung up the phone then looked out at the charming Nantucket street. He was a person who belonged nowhere.

⚜

A few days later, there was a knock on Marcus's bedroom door. Marcus had his legal pad out and was jotting down notes, if not actual sentences. It hardly mattered to Marcus—he was so relieved to have words on the page, even if those words had no more meaning than entries in a dictionary: "Princeton University," "smack," "petty theft," "child prostitution," "anger," "social services," "intent to kill???" Now that the ball was rolling, or if not rolling than at least moving, *of course* there would be an interruption. Marcus tucked the legal pad under his white pillows and grumbled, "Come in."

It was Beth, a fact that both relieved and disappointed him. She looked awful—thin and desiccated like a plant that needed watering. She gave him a smile, though, and held out an envelope. Marcus's first thought was, *Another telegram. Leave me alone, man.*

"From Constance," she said.

Even worse! A fourth letter from Mama.

"Okay," he said. "Thanks." He took the envelope from Beth and dropped it on the bed in front of him as though he planned to read it once Beth left. Beth, however, remained in the doorway smiling at him. Then her friendly smile turned into a worried smile and she said, "Can I talk to you for a minute?"

This was the last thing he wanted, though he was surprised it had taken her so long to confront him. Garrett and Winnie had joined forces and so it only made sense that Beth and Marcus would do the same. Except neither of them wanted to. Marcus was used to being cast out on his own—that, after all, was what he'd expected from the summer: the twins wrapped up in their own exclusive cocoon, Beth lost hopelessly in the outer space of her grief. As for Beth, well, she believed she understood her kids well enough to know that whatever was bugging them would pass. But now their bizarre aloofness had lasted more than a week and showed no signs of abating. She needed help.

Beth closed the door to Marcus's bedroom and sat on his bed. The letter from Constance lay between them, a boundary.

"I was just wondering," she said, "if maybe you knew what was going on. In this house, I mean. With the kids. Winnie and Garrett. Their behavior. This isn't like them."

Marcus lowered his eyelids, an involuntary sign for her to stop. Obviously he knew what she was talking about; he wasn't an idiot. The question was whether Marcus was going to tell her the bad news. He considered the consequences. If he told Beth the truth—that her secret was out—Winnie would *never* forgive him. Furthermore, the workings of this family were none of his business. He felt badly for Beth—yes, he did—but he couldn't speak.

He shrugged.

Beth hooked his gaze, trying to pry him open with her eyes. "Winnie hasn't *said* anything to you?"

"Winnie hasn't said anything to me," he repeated. "In about ten days."

"They're pushing us away," Beth said. "It's not like they're openly hostile, but I'm beginning to feel like their butler. Know what I mean? I've been thinking of inviting our therapist to come for the weekend. Kara Schau—you'd like her."

The therapist. Marcus supposed that's what rich people did

when they had family troubles—invited the therapist for the weekend. He shook his head, then eyed the letter.

"I'd like to be alone now," Marcus said. "I don't mean to kick you out of a room of your own house, but I really do want to be alone."

What could Beth do but respect his wishes? She stood up to go.

"You'll let me know if you learn anything?" she said.

The woman was just begging him to lie to her. Sometimes, he supposed, that was what people needed.

"Sure," he said.

❦

That night, Winnie went to the movies with Garrett and Piper. They didn't invite Marcus along, and it took Beth to ask, "Isn't Marcus going with you?"

They didn't answer her, and Marcus quickly stated that he wanted to stay home. He went upstairs to his bedroom, listening through his open window to Winnie's voice, her laughter, the sound of the car doors slamming. He felt so angry with her, and yet their separation didn't seem to bother her at all. As the Rover drove off, Marcus pulled Constance's most recent letter from the inside of his dock shoe and opened it. He decided he would read it, then throw it in the trash.

July 24

Dear Marcus,

> *Through everything I have never stopped loving you. I will wait as long as it takes.*

Mama

Marcus crumpled the letter and threw it at the mirror. "It's bullshit!" he said, louder than he meant to. "Bullshit!"

The fury in his voice bounced back at him from the white walls of his room. Beth was somewhere in the house but she didn't call up to him. He opened the other letters; they all said basically the same thing: *I love you, child . . . I think of you every day . . . I pray to hear the sound of your voice . . .*

"It's bullshit!" Marcus shouted. God, it felt good to yell. It felt good to let go for once. At home, his father and sister would have been frightened, not to mention baffled, by his anger. He ripped the letters in half, though he yearned to destroy them more permanently—with fire or water. He stuffed the pieces of paper back into his dock shoe then threw the shoe at the door of his room, a fast ball. He pulled his notebook out of the drawer, tore out the single page that constituted the sum of his work this summer and started a fresh page.

Dear Mama, he wrote. *If you loved me, you wouldn't have done it.*

※

Later, there was a thunderstorm. Marcus woke up to a loud crashing, loud enough to make him think lightning had hit the chimney. The house shuddered. Marcus lay in bed, listening to the deep rolls and sharp cracks of thunder. He'd never heard a storm like this before. He looked out his window—the sky flashed with light, bolts of lightning hit the pond in the distance, and rain poured down in sheets. Out in the driveway, he noticed the windows of the Rover were down. Winnie and Garrett had forgotten to roll them up when they got back from the movies. They deserved to have a ruined car—they were spoiled brats, both of them. But then Beth entered his mind. He'd already disappointed her once that day and so Marcus threw on a T-shirt and ran downstairs and out the front door. The rain pummeled his back. He dashed for the car. They always left the keys in the ignition, even when they parked in town. *Any idea how fast this car would be gone in Queens?* Marcus asked once. He turned the key in the ignition and put up the windows. Then he leaned back in the driver's seat, straightening his arms to the steering wheel. He thought of driving away. But there was no escaping this island in the middle of the night. Marcus relaxed against the leather seat until it sounded like the rain was abating a little. But three seconds outside—from the car to the front door—left him soaked. He peeled his shirt off as he climbed the stairs, cursing himself for being such a slave. When he got into his room, he tossed the wet shirt onto his chair, missing Winnie by a few inches. She was standing there, in his room.

"What the hell?" he said.

She looked different. He switched on the night-light that Beth gave him the first day of their vacation so he could find his way to the bathroom. It was a scallop shell night-light and it glowed pink; this was the only time he'd ever used it. It gave off just enough light for him to study Winnie. She was staring at him. It occurred to Marcus that maybe she was sleepwalking. Then he pinpointed what was different—she wasn't wearing the sweatshirt. She was wearing a short pink nightgown. Marcus felt his body temperature rise. He dug through his dresser drawer for a dry shirt.

"If your brother catches you in here, I'm dead meat."

"He doesn't care anymore, Marcus."

"Yeah, right."

"No, really, we talked about it."

"I'm sure you did," Marcus said. He imagined some elaborate trap—sending Winnie in here to give Garrett a reason to attack him again. "Where's your sweatshirt?"

"I'm finished wearing it," she said.

"How come?"

She moved closer to him. "I can't explain it, really. I just don't feel the need to wear it anymore. I might wear it once in a while, if I get cold."

"Oh," he said. Along with everything else, he felt betrayed that the shedding of the sweatshirt took place without his knowledge. Because Marcus knew that meant something bigger had happened, a change in Winnie's brain or heart. He thought the retiring of the sweatshirt deserved some kind of ceremony, the sweatshirt that Marcus had worn once himself. He still hadn't told Winnie about that, and now he figured he never would. "Well, congratulations." Although he meant it, his voice was laced with sarcasm.

"Thanks," she said. "It's a good thing."

The pink nightgown was sheer and through it, Marcus could see the outline of Winnie's white panties. He was afraid to go near his bed, but there wasn't anywhere else to sit, aside from the chair where his soggy shirt lay in a puddle. "Do you mind telling me what you're doing here?"

"I came to apologize."

"Did you?"

She lowered herself onto the bed next to him, and Marcus glared at the floor, allowing only the side of Winnie's foot in his view. "I acted badly. I said mean things."

"Yeah, and there was a lot you didn't say."

"I know."

"You haven't said shit to me in over a week, Winnie. You cut me out."

"I'm sorry—"

"You can't treat people like that. You've been horrible to your mother."

"She was horrible to us."

"She *wasn't* horrible," Marcus said. "She just kept a part of her past private."

"An *important* part."

"Fine, an important part. There's no law saying that parents have to explain themselves to their children, Winnie." He raised his head and looked at the brown smudge on the door where his shoe had hit. "My mother hasn't explained herself. I don't know why she killed those people and I probably never will. Everyone has their secrets."

"I don't," Winnie said.

"Well, I do," Marcus said. "I have a big secret that nobody knows about, but if I told you, you'd probably be mad at me for keeping it, even though it's mine to keep."

"I won't be mad at you," Winnie said. "What is it?"

"Why should I tell you?" he said. The nightgown left her shoulders bare—bare shoulders, bare arms, bare legs to midthigh. And her neck. For ten days there had been no Winnie, and now there was all this. "When you and I first became friends, I thought I wanted to be a part of this family. Now I don't want to. You know the other night, when I went into town? It was to call my pop and tell him I wanted to come home early. Do you know how bad things must be for me to want to go back to *Queens?*"

Winnie touched his leg, and Marcus jumped up. This was a terrible room for confrontation because there was practically nothing in it. He crossed the room in three steps and sat on top of the wobbly dresser. His shirt was dripping, making a puddle on the floor under the chair.

"Please don't go home," Winnie said. "I didn't mean to hurt you."

"What about the last ten days? What about not one kind word in ten days?"

"I was confused. And angry. And I thought you were angry at me. And Garrett—"

"Don't even mention his name," Marcus said, rocking the dresser back and forth. "I should have beat him blind when I had the chance."

"Garrett and I have to confront my mother," Winnie said. "We have to get this out in the open."

"I told you that before."

"I wasn't *ready* before. I had a lot to think about."

"Whatever," he said.

"I'm sorry I slammed the door in your face," she said.

"I'm used to people treating me that way," he said. "I'm used to being shunned. That's all I get at home. But here everything was different. Everything was better."

"I was feeling better, too," Winnie said. "Until."

"Until."

"My mother," Winnie said.

"Your mother? What about my mother?" Marcus said. "Can't you tell the difference between a misdemeanor and a felony?"

"No," said Winnie. She rubbed her arms as if she were cold. "Anyway, I'm sorry I didn't sit on the beach with you. That was mean."

"I managed."

"You looked good swimming."

"Thanks."

"Did you miss me?" she asked.

He shook his head. "I had other things to worry about."

"I want you to forgive me."

"What do you care if I forgive you or not?"

"I came here tonight because I want you to know how I feel." She stood up and held her arms out like she was handing him something very heavy. "I feel like I'm in love with you. I'm in love with you, Marcus."

It wasn't until that moment that Marcus noticed the thunder was growing fainter, and so Winnie's words seemed very loud to Marcus, so loud he felt the entire world could hear. His throat ached in the same place where Garrett had kicked him, and he realized he might cry.

"You're in love with me?"

"Yes," Winnie said.

"I don't see why I should believe you," he said.

"I guess you should believe me because it's true," Winnie said, nodding at the bed. "I want to be with you. Really *with* you. We've been waiting all summer for this. You know it as well as I do."

Did he know it? He was too aware of Winnie in her pink nightie to answer. What would happen if he got his ass off this fragile heirloom dresser and went to her? Winnie pulled him across the room and pushed him into the bed, her skinny arms surprisingly strong from so much swim practice. He wondered again if this were some kind of trap, the big trap, the one that would get him sent away. Winnie ran her hand up the inside of his T-shirt and suddenly Marcus didn't care who came barging in. He felt vulnerable, but the swirling tornado of anger inside of him was stilled, just from having her in his arms. He had missed her, this blond girl from Manhattan with all her quirks and flaws and rays of light.

"All right," he said, thinking that the best life would be one where they could exist in an alternate universe, without their families.

She kissed him very softly on the lips, and slid out of her nightgown. Marcus remembered again of all those swim meets where he'd held himself back. Now, Winnie had given him the green light; she was waving him on toward the finish. Tonight, he was going to win.

⚘

Beth couldn't believe she'd been so dumb, so blind, so naive. For nearly two weeks the twins' behavior had been so inexplicable that she'd called Kara Schau's office twice, only to learn that Kara was on vacation in the Hamptons. It was by chance that Beth went to the liquor cabinet for vermouth for a recipe and found the nearly empty bottle of Malibu rum. She knew for certain that neither she nor Arch had touched the rum in years, and so the culprits had to be the kids. They were drinking! Beth was chagrined that she hadn't guessed the problem sooner and yet relieved that the answer might be so simple. They were raiding the liquor cabinet. She decided not to say anything about the Malibu until she figured out exactly what was going on. She wanted to check the twins' rooms, which she did under the auspices of dusting one incredibly hot and muggy August morning. If they were going to be sneaky, well, then, so was she.

Winnie's room was an organized mess. She'd started wearing clothes again, instead of just the Princeton sweatshirt. Beth wondered at this development but didn't dare question it. She found the sweatshirt folded neatly on a chair in Winnie's room. There were other clothes on the floor, some books, a journal. A glass of brown liquid on the night table. Beth sniffed it, then took a sip: warm, flat Coke. Okay. She made a few cursory swipes over the dresser and mirror, over the bedposts, and over the windowsill with her soft yellow cloth. Her spirit balked at the thought that in three short weeks, she'd be dusting this room for real—the final clean before closing the house for the winter. Although it had been a difficult summer, Beth hated the idea of leaving. The only way she'd made it through the spring was by thinking of Nantucket. New York was beautiful in autumn, and crackling with excitement—new theater, new restaurants, getting the kids back to school, the leaves changing in Central Park— but this year none of it held any appeal. New York was funereal, depressing, the site of tragedy. Beth understood that after the kids graduated from Danforth, she may have to sell their apartment and move somewhere less painful.

She walked down the hallway to Garrett's room, wiping the frames of the watercolors that hung on the walls. Garrett was out with Piper, and Marcus and Winnie were at the beach. Beth was relieved to see that Marcus and Winnie had worked things out, although neither of the twins had spoken to Beth in a normal way in almost two weeks. She confronted them several times, but this only made things worse, and so Beth forced herself to let it go—it was just some awful, weird phase—but now there was the alcohol to explain it, and possibly worse things: marijuana, ecstasy, LSD.

Beth poked around Garrett's room until she found a box of Trojans in his nightstand drawer. This stopped her cold, and she sat on his bed with the box—a huge box—in her lap. Well, it wasn't exactly shocking, and she supposed she should be relieved he was using protection, but it made her sick-hearted to be holding physical evidence of her son's sexual life. She returned the box to the drawer and checked in the closet and under the bed. There she found the trunk of her uncle Burton's traveling artifacts. No six-packs, no baggies of weed.

Beth dusted the bedposts and the top of Garrett's dresser. The urn of Arch's ashes was sitting on the dresser and Beth spoke to him in her mind. *I'm in way over my head here, babe. Sex, alcohol— God knows what else. You're supposed to be here to help me. This is the heavy lifting. I can't do it on my own.* It didn't help that it was now August, the part of the summer when Beth would begin to anticipate Arch's two-week vacation. He didn't love Nantucket the way she did, but she adored having him on the island for those two weeks, even if he did spend too much time at the dining room table working.

Last year, on the night he'd arrived, he was the most relaxed she had ever seen him. He'd come off the plane wearing his Nantucket red shorts and his Yankees cap backward, his white polo shirt untucked. He convinced Beth to take a walk on the beach with him after the kids went to bed. There was a half-moon hanging low and phosphorescence in the water. They held hands and caught up on what had happened the previous week— this time last year Arch was defending a major magazine conglomerate against charges of lifestyle discrimination, a case he eventually won. They talked about what they wanted to do with the kids over the next two weeks—picnics and outings and lob-

ster night. Amid all this happy chatter, Arch stopped and presented her with a velvet box—but shyly, nervously, like he was
about to propose. Beth took the box, knowing that whatever was
inside of it was way too expensive and absolutely unnecessary,
but marveling, too, at the butterflies in her stomach—even after
twenty years. Romance!

The diamond ring. The "We Made It" ring. Because it was a
moonlit August night on the beach below their Nantucket cottage. Because Garrett and Winnie were healthy, bright, well-
adjusted kids. Because Arch had a successful career. Because after
twenty years they were still in love.

"We made it," Arch said as he slipped the ring on her finger.
"It's easy sailing from here."

Beth wondered if she was remembering wrong. She didn't think
so. Everything had been that perfect, momentarily. It would be
two months later that Arch took Connie's case. It would be seven
months later that his plane crashed.

Tears blurred Beth's eyes as she lifted the urn off the dresser.
It was lighter than she remembered; it was light enough to make
her pry off the top and check inside.

The ashes were gone, and in their place was a piece of paper.
Beth set the urn down on Garrett's dresser and unfolded the
paper. It took her a minute to realize what she was looking at,
but then the names and dates, typed in their little boxes, came
together. It was a marriage certificate. Hers and David's.

The room was very hot and close and Beth felt like she was
going to faint. She flung open the door to Garrett's small balcony
and stepped outside, sucking in the fresh air and the sight of the
ocean. Beth considered hurling the urn off the balcony onto the
deck below. But instead she clung to the empty urn, the urn that

once contained the remains of her husband, and she carried it downstairs. A glass vase of zinnias sat on the kitchen table, and Beth removed the flowers and carried the vase outside to the deck. It wasn't a particularly good vase, but it had been in the house for as long as Beth could remember. It was a vase that Beth's grandmother used for her favorite New Dawn roses, which had climbed up the north side of Horizon until Gran died and the roses withered from lack of care. It was a vase that Beth's mother used for the flowers Beth's father always brought on weekends from their garden in New Jersey. Beth lifted the vase over her head and flung it against the deck. It was satisfying, the honest sound of breaking glass.

Let them cut their feet to ribbons, she thought. She then filled the urn with water and arranged the zinnias inside, placed the urn on the kitchen table, where they couldn't miss it. She thought about ripping the marriage certificate to shreds and leaving that on the table, too, but instead she just crumpled it up and threw it in the kitchen trash with the coffee grounds and eggshells.

They knew about David and they had scattered the ashes without her.

Her instincts told her to get out of the house. She couldn't see the twins; she would kill them. Strike them, at the very least. Garrett had the Rover, and so Beth changed quickly into running clothes, tucked two bottles of water into her fanny pack, and took off down the dirt road.

It was hot, and before Beth even reached the end of Miacomet Pond, she stopped to drink. How dare they—that was all she could think. How dare they delve into her past, how dare they unearth her secret, and how dare they punish her for it. They never thought what it might be like for her. They never considered how difficult each day was, each night alone.

She had visualized scattering the ashes at sunrise on the morning of their last day—out in front of Horizon, into the sand and the dune grass. She had planned to say something meaningful; she had wanted to write a prayer. Well, it hardly mattered now. The twins had stolen Arch from her.

Beth reached a section of dense woods on Hummock Pond Road. She wanted to disappear among the cool trees. Let the kids raise themselves since they thought living was so easy. Let them get from age seventeen to middle age without making any mistakes. Then Beth heard Arch's voice in her head: *Your mistake isn't the problem, honey. It's that you concealed it.* She had hidden the truth from him, too, her own husband, dead now. On the ride home from the Ronans' cocktail party six years ago, she had almost told him. Her joints were loose from too much wine, and just the fact that they'd spent three hours in the same house with David made Beth want to confess.

There's something I want to tell you about David, Beth had said to Arch, as they sped through the night toward home. *Something you should know.*

Arch chuckled. *I liked the guy well enough. You'd better not say anything or you might change my mind.*

Even though she was drunk, those words registered. There was no reason for Beth to bring up the unfortunate, unchangeable past. There was no reason to upset Arch or herself. For years, she had felt her brief marriage to David Ronan was too private to share, and that was how it would stay. Her private history.

꽃

When she got home she was dismayed to find the Rover in the driveway. She had downed both bottles of water, she was slick with sweat and her vision was blotchy. She needed to eat, she needed rest. She couldn't bring herself to face her children. What would she say? Where could she possibly start?

When she walked inside, the house was quiet and Beth removed her socks and shoes on the bottom step of the stairs. She might be able to forego lunch and just pull her shades and climb into bed. She was so overwhelmingly tired that she knew she could sleep until morning. But then she heard whispering and she forced herself to tiptoe down the hallway and poke her head into the kitchen.

Garrett and Winnie were sitting alone at the kitchen table staring at the urn now filled with flowers. The broom and dustpan were out, and beyond the twins, Beth could see the deck had been swept clean. When the kids looked up and saw her, Beth had a hundred simultaneous memories of their faces. She remembered seeing them for the very first time, when they were an hour old, sleeping in their incubators in the hospital nursery. She pictured them on their second birthday, their mouths smeared with chocolate icing. She saw them at age ten, the first time they ever took the subway alone—the six line down to Union Square where Arch was going to meet them. She visualized them in the future, walking down the aisle at Winnie's wedding—Garrett in a tuxedo and Winnie in a pearl-colored slip dress, arm-in-arm, Garrett giving Winnie away. More times than Beth could count in the last five months, she had thought, It should have been me who died. But now, gazing at her children and the urn of flowers, that sense of guilt, guilt at *surviving*, vanished. She was their mother. They needed her more than they needed anyone else. Including Arch.

Beth poured herself a Gatorade. The only sounds in the kitchen were the cracking of ice, and the distant pound and rush of the waves outside. Beth drank the entire glass of liquid, then poured herself another. The silence was helpful. This was going to be the most important conversation she ever had with her children and she wanted to pick her words carefully. She couldn't help herself from asking, "You scattered the ashes without me?"

Winnie traced a scar in the table. Garrett said, "Yes."

Beth sat down; her legs felt weak. "Why?"

"We were angry," he said.

Beth imagined Kara Schau as an invisible fourth party at the table. She would praise Garrett for identifying his emotions. Beth wasn't as pleased. What she thought was: When you're angry you break a vase, you yell, you resort to sarcasm. You do not deceive your mother in the cruelest possible way.

"Angry about what?" she asked.

"You were married," Winnie whispered. "And you never told us."

"That's right," Beth said. "I was married and I never told you."

"And you never told Dad," Winnie said.

"And I never told Dad."

"You lied to all three of us," Garrett said. "Your family."

"I did not lie."

"You lied by omission," Garrett said. This was a legal premise that he'd learned from his father. What you didn't say could be just as damaging as what you did.

"It happened a long time ago," Beth said. "Before your father, before you. It has no bearing on your lives." She swallowed some more Gatorade. "It is none of your business."

"Except you're our mother," Winnie said. "We thought we knew you."

"You do know me."

"It doesn't feel like it," Garrett said.

"We want to know the whole story," Winnie said. "We want to know what happened."

"Oh," Beth said. This she wasn't ready for. She had devoted so much energy to not thinking about the details of August 1979 that to conjure them up would be like calling a voice or spirit back from the dead. "I'd like you to respect that it's my private past. It's not something I want to share—with you or anyone else."

"Piper knows the whole story," Garrett said. "But I wouldn't let her tell me about it. I wanted to hear it from you."

"Piper heard the story from David?"

"From Rosie, actually," Garrett said, knowing that this detail, beyond all others, would prod his mother to speak. "So I wasn't sure how accurate it'd be."

"It wouldn't be accurate at all," Beth said. She was livid at the thought of *Rosie* giving away her secret. Rosie!

"Just tell us, Mom," Winnie said.

Beth leaned back in the chair; it whined. "Where did you put Daddy's ashes?"

They were both quiet and Beth watched them exchange a quick look. She wanted to tread carefully here because she wanted the truth.

"In Quidnet," Garrett said. "We'll show you where. Later."

Later, meaning after Beth explained herself. It was blackmail, but what did she expect? These were teenagers.

"Where's Marcus?" Beth asked.

"He's in town," Winnie said. When Winnie saw the broken glass on the deck and then the urn right there on the *kitchen table*, she'd warned Marcus that there was going to be a confrontation, and without hesitation, Marcus said he would make himself scarce.

"Go ahead, Mom," Garrett said. "Tell us."

❧

It was nearly impossible to explain the romance of that sixth and final summer of Beth and David. But maybe not—because here were her twins, each experiencing love for the first time. Still, Beth feared she wouldn't be able to convey the heat and light, the depth and weight of her love for David. It was their sixth summer together; they were each twenty-one. When they rejoined in late May they realized that they had grown into adults, or almost. David had moved out of his parents' house and he rented the cottage on Bear Street. Beth was given full use of her grandfather's Volkswagen bug, which still ran, though barely. It was the perfect summer. David worked as a painter six days a week from seven until three; Beth didn't work at all. While David painted, Beth ran errands for her mother, helped out around the house, and sat on the beach in front of Horizon. Then at three o'clock, she disappeared. Beth's mother was preoccupied with Scott and Danny, who, at fourteen and sixteen, were turning her hair white. Beth's father flew in from the city every other weekend. And so Beth was free—she met David at his cottage at 3:15 and for her, the day began. They swam, they sailed, they went to the nude beach, and they raked for clams that they cooked up later with pasta for dinner. They went to bonfires and drank too much beer and fell into bed in the wee hours giddy and spinning. They made love.

David asked Beth to marry him in August. It was his day off, a Wednesday. Beth heard David rise early, before the sun was up, and when she opened her eyes, he was sitting on the edge of the bed holding a tray. A blue hydrangea in a drinking glass, a slice of cantaloupe, a bowl of strawberries. A bottle of Taittinger champagne.

"Whoa," she said, sitting up. "What's this?"

"Will you marry me?"

Beth laughed. She remembered wanting to open the champagne. She remembered David wrapping his hand around the back of her neck.

"I'm serious. I want to marry you."

"I want to marry you, too."

"Today."

"What?"

"We'll get dressed, we'll go to the Town Building."

"You're a nut."

"Next week, then. Next Wednesday. Will you marry me next Wednesday?"

"You're serious?"

"Yes," David said. "Bethie, I love you."

Beth never actually said yes, but she never said no either. She got swept along by David's enthusiasm and by her own desire to have the summer last forever. They were going to get married.

But Beth couldn't bring herself to inform her parents. She didn't dare breathe the word "marriage" under Horizon's roof.

Beth and David went to the hospital to have their blood tested. Beth bought a white sundress in town. She savored the tingly, secret excitement, the outlandish daring of it—she was getting married! They bought rings, inexpensive ones, plain gold bands, a hundred dollars for both.

The morning they were to be married, David rose early again. He returned with a huge handful of purple cosmos.

"Your bouquet," he said.

Only when Beth saw the flowers did she have her first pang of regret for what had yet to happen. This was her bridal bouquet. The white crinkled cotton sundress hanging in the closet was her wedding dress. She and David were going to climb into the bug, bounce down the cobblestone street to the Nantucket Town Building and get married. David was absolutely *glowing*— he looked the way she always thought she would look on her wedding day. But it was a different wedding day that she'd dreamed of: six bridesmaids in pink linen dresses and six groomsmen in navy blazers. Her father walking her down the aisle. She hesitated. The trappings of a wedding didn't matter. Who cared about a cocktail hour, a nine-piece band, chicken Kiev, and chocolate wedding cake? She took the flowers from David.

"They're perfect," she said.

❦

Winnie and Garrett stared at her. Not in many years had she held them in this kind of rapt attention.

"Are you saying you knew you were about to make a mistake?" Winnie said.

"I had mixed feelings," Beth said. "But you hear about cold feet all the time—a bride and groom are *supposed* to have cold feet. And I loved David. I was twenty-one years old. If I'd wanted to back out, I would have."

⚘

When she emerged from the tiny bathroom in her white dress and rope sandals with the cork heels, David fell back on the sofa with his hand over his heart. "You look so beautiful you scare me," he said. "God, Beth . . ." His eyes filled and Beth felt a swell of pride. This was exactly the kind of reaction she wanted from her husband on her wedding day. She wanted to bowl David over; she wanted to bring him to tears. Beth was pleased with how she looked—young and blond and very tan. The dress, while not a wedding dress, was perfect for a girl like her on a summer day. Her spirits lifted.

David drove into town but had trouble finding a parking space. It was overcast, and the town was filled with people lunching and shopping. Beth remembered being terrified that her mother would see her, or a friend of her mother's. She squeezed the purple cosmos; they left gold dust all over her hands, and she had to wash up in the public restroom of the Town Building before the ceremony.

The wedding itself was unremarkable. A judge wearing Bermuda shorts married them in a room without windows. The room was empty except for a conference table and three folding chairs. The judge stood on the far side of the table, looking not so much like a judge as one of Beth's father's golf partners. Two male law students who were working in the probate court for the summer were brought in to witness, along with a secretary from the selectmen's office. Those three strangers sat next to Beth and David in the folding chairs. The law students were just kids not much older than Beth and David, and they looked put upon for being asked to watch for ten minutes in the name of legality. The secretary was older, with kids of her own probably. She dabbed her eyes with a tissue as Beth and David said their vows. Before Beth knew it, it was over. She signed the marriage certificate, the judge in the Bermuda shorts kissed her cheek and said, "Congratulations, Mrs. Ronan." He left shortly thereafter to meet his wife at the Yacht Club.

David and Beth went for lunch at the Mad Hatter, a place they went when David got a cash bonus for a painting job or when Beth's father slipped her extra spending money before returning to New Jersey.

Their table, Beth noticed right away, had a centerpiece of purple cosmos, and there was a bottle of Taittinger chilling on ice. For reasons beyond her understanding, these details, arranged by David ahead of time, made her heart sink. He was trying so hard and yet it didn't seem like enough. That was what Beth thought as she sat down. The two of them, alone for their wedding reception, didn't seem like enough.

Beth drank nearly the whole bottle of champagne herself. Throughout lunch, David talked nonstop about plans: getting her things moved into the cottage, her finding a job, the fall and winter on Nantucket, a vacation in March—a belated honeymoon—to Hawaii or Palm Beach. Kids. (Kids! At the mention of kids, Beth laughed. She was a kid herself.) Beth ate a plate of fried calamari, then a lobster roll, then a hot fudge sundae since the restaurant didn't have cake. A glob of hot fudge sauce hit the front of her white dress and she blotted it with a wet napkin, but to no avail. There was a spot; she was sullied. She reached for the champagne bottle, and finding it empty, waved their waiter over and ordered a gin and tonic. She felt David watching her. When she met his eyes, she saw so much love there it frightened her. She urged him to get the bill while she bolted her drink. When it was time to go, she had to grab onto the table in order to stand up. The ring irritated her finger. David led her out to the car, and when they got home they made love. Beth fell asleep before the sun even set.

In the morning, David left for work. It was lying in bed, alone and dreadfully hungover, that Beth confronted the gravity of what she had done. She had eloped with David. She went into the bathroom and looked in the mirror, which was still foggy from David's shower, and she held her hand up alongside her face. The ring told the truth: she was a married woman. She took three aspirin then went to the kitchen for coffee and found the bouquet of purple cosmos limp and wilting on the counter. It was enough to bring tears to her eyes, but she didn't cry. She was too scared to cry—scared because she was going to have to tell her parents.

She got dressed in the same shorts and T-shirt she had left the house in two days earlier and drove home. Never had Horizon seemed so imposing. Beth understood as she walked into the house that her parents might be angry enough to disown her and ban her from both Horizon and their home in New Jersey forever.

Beth found her mother sitting at the kitchen table—the very same table where Beth sat with Garrett and Winnie now—smoking a cigarette and drinking coffee, sick with worry because Beth had spent two nights away from home.

"You've been with David, haven't you?" her mother said.

Beth nodded and then held out her hand to show her mother her wedding ring and her mother dropped her cigarette on the floor and cried out, "You've gone and done it! Oh, dear child, I have to call your father!" Beth's mother flew out the front door in her housecoat, and drove their woody wagon to town where she could use the telephone. Beth picked the cigarette up off the floor—it left a burn mark, which she pointed out now to Garrett and Winnie—then went upstairs and packed her things and left the house, in her mind, for the final time.

⁊

A few days later, Beth had a job as a teller at Pacific National Bank, a bank where her parents, pointedly, did not have an account. Her hours were similar to David's and they resumed the rhythm of their summer. Swimming, sailing, dancing at the Chicken Box. David called her "Mrs. Ronan." Beth scanned the streets for her parents before she stepped outside. She expected her father to show up on their doorstep any second, but he never came. This made Beth feel even worse. Her father was finished with her. She began to worry that she would never see either of her parents again.

What Beth remembered most about the two weeks that she and David were married was that David was so happy. Seeing him so happy made Beth realize that she wasn't as happy as he was. In fact, she was miserable. As she took deposits and cashed checks at the bank, she thought longingly of returning to Sarah Lawrence. She'd already registered for courses—courses she knew David would find elitist and useless: Discourses on Gender and Ethnicity, History of the American Musical Theater, The

Literature of the Lost Generation, Etruscan Art. Beth wanted to finish college and then move to Manhattan and get a real job in publishing or advertising. She didn't want to be a bank teller living in a rented cottage on Bear Street, estranged from her parents who had provided her with every possible advantage in life. One evening at dinner, which Beth now felt a wifely responsibility to prepare, she broached the topic of returning to Sarah Lawrence.

"I won't live apart for another winter," David said.

She took his hand; his wedding ring was already flecked with paint. "You can come with me," she said.

"To *New York*?" As if she had suggested Mongolia, or the moon.

"You'll like it."

He withdrew his hand. "There's no way I'm leaving the island. I have a job here. I want to save money for our future."

"I want to finish college," Beth said.

"We wouldn't be able to afford a year of your college," he said. "Plus a place to live, plus food. Your daddy's not taking care of you anymore, okay? It's me." His voice softened. "I love you, Mrs. Ronan."

"Stop calling me that."

"What?"

" 'Mrs. Ronan.' It makes it sound like you own me. You don't own me." She started to cry.

"Hey, hey," he said. "I know you want to finish your degree. I'll help you make some calls. There's a community college in Harwich. You could take the boat over a couple days a week, maybe."

Beth pushed her plate away. They had been married thirteen days.

꽃

That night, she lay awake watching him sleep. She remembered back to the evening she met him, six years earlier. David had just inherited a dirt bike from an older cousin and he was giving it a whirl up and down West Miacomet Road. Beth was sitting on Horizon's front stoop, shucking corn with a paper bag between her legs. She watched this boy zip past then back again. He was shirtless and barefoot, his hair glinted gold in the last of the day's sunlight. Eventually Beth became so entranced that she stood up and watched him unabashedly. He stopped at the end of the driveway.

"Want to go for a ride?"

Up close, the bike looked hardly sturdy enough to support him, much less the two of them. But Beth nodded—she abandoned the pot of corn and the bag of husks and silks and climbed onto the back of this strange boy's dirt bike. By necessity, she linked her arms around his bare torso and with a sensation like a rocket launching, they took off. Beth was sixteen years old, flying over the bumpy roads at a speed she'd never imagined. The wind tossed her hair. It was the first time she'd tasted freedom.

In the morning, after David left for work, Beth packed her things. She left her wedding ring on top of a white piece of paper on the kitchen table, where he would be sure to see it.

꽃

Winnie's eyes were wide. "Then what happened?"

"I drove home," Beth said. "My parents were sitting right here at this table eating breakfast with Danny and Scott. Grandpa was eating shredded wheat, Gramma was having a cigarette and coffee, and the boys had scrambled eggs with ketchup."

"You can remember that?" Garrett asked.

"Like it happened this morning," Beth said.

The house had grown silent as soon as the front screen door clapped shut behind her. By the time Beth made it to the kitchen, all eyes were on her.

"I'm back," she said brightly, as though she'd just returned from a semester abroad.

Her mother shooed the boys out of the kitchen. Her father methodically finished his shredded wheat—it was well known that even a fire couldn't keep Garrett Eyler from his shredded wheat—and then he approached Beth, kissed her on the forehead, and grasping her upper arm said, "You did the right thing."

At these words, Beth broke down. Her mother took over—leading Beth upstairs to her bed, which was freshly made, lowering the shades and saying, "You stay right here until the worst has passed." As though they were expecting a storm.

What her mother was referring to, of course, was David, who screeched into the driveway in his painting truck at half past three. He pounded on the front door. Beth sat up in bed, petrified. She heard him yelling, "Let me see her! I love her! Let me talk to her!" And then Beth heard the low, calm tones of her father. "I've contacted my lawyer. It will all be taken care of." The conversation continued—David's voice growing so hysterical that Beth had to peek out the window. She saw her father and David standing just outside the door. David's expression was so anguished, his voice so desperate that Beth collapsed and pulled her two feather pillows over her head. She didn't listen to another word; she didn't even hear him drive away.

❦

"And that's it?" Garrett said.

"That's it," Beth said. "That's the whole story. My father's attorney took care of the divorce. I didn't see David again for several years, and by that point, we were both married to other people. And I made the conscious decision never to think or speak of it again. To anyone, including your father. I'm sorry if you feel betrayed, and I'm even sorrier if you feel I betrayed your father. But that was my decision. It was an event from my past. *Mine*. Do you understand?"

The twins nodded mechanically, like marionettes.

Beth felt drained. There were other things she wanted to discuss with the kids—the Malibu rum, the whereabouts of the ashes—but those things hardly mattered to her at this moment. The only thing that mattered now was that she had told the one story she'd tried with all her might to forget. The reason she'd tried to forget was because of the expression on David's face that final morning. It was the look of a man whose dream had been crushed without warning. It was the look of a man who *would* have loved her forever, who would have taken her for a ride on the back of his dirt bike into infinity.

Beth stood up. She made herself a piece of toast at the counter, ate it in four bites, then went upstairs to her room. Her business with the twins was finished for the time being; they would have to process all they'd heard. What Beth realized before she took a Valium and fell into bed for a nap was that there was one more person she needed to talk to about all of this before she put it to rest for good, and that person was David.

𝒥ℰ

Beth thought of biking or driving out to David's house that evening before dinner (it grew dark at seven o'clock now, a sign that August had arrived), but Beth didn't want to talk with David in front of his girls. She let a few days pass. Her relationship with the twins returned to almost normal, however they seemed to bestow upon her a new kind of respect—maybe because she had finally owned up to the truth, or maybe because they had never before imagined her as a person capable of getting married on a whim by a judge wearing Bermuda shorts. When Beth saw Piper, she, too, treated Beth differently, more formally, always calling her "Mrs. Newton." One night, Beth screwed up the courage to ask Piper where David was working.

"This week, Cliff Road," Piper said. And then, as if she knew what Beth was planning, she added, "One of the new houses on the left just before you reach Madaket Road."

Beth decided to go see him the following morning, climbing into the Rover at the ungodly hour of seven o'clock. She wanted to catch him early, say her piece, and leave. Unfortunately, there was a blanket of fog so thick that Beth couldn't see any of the houses from the road and she worried that she wouldn't be able to find the right one. But then she spied two huge homes with fresh yellow cedar shingles on the left, and she took a chance and chose the first of the two driveways. There were a number of vans and trucks—one of them David's.

Beth parked in a spot well out of everyone's way and climbed out of the car. She began to feel nervous about this plan—after all, David was working. He had a business to run, contracts to fulfill, he didn't need his old girlfriend showing up to rehash something that happened back in the Ice Age. Beth glanced at her car and considered leaving, but what if he saw her? That would only make things worse.

The house was so new that there was no front door, only an extra-wide arched opening. The floors were plywood, but all of the drywall was hung, and a boy of about eighteen knelt in the hall sticking a screwdriver into an outlet, which seemed to Beth a perilous undertaking. When the boy saw her, he stared for a second—clearly there weren't many women on these work sites— and Beth was able to ask for David.

"They're painting on the third floor," the boy said, finally blinking. Beth wondered if something was wrong with the way she looked—she'd taken extreme care in appearing casual. Khaki shorts, white T-shirt, flip-flops, her hair in a clip. Beth thanked the boy and proceeded up the stairs, two flights, to the third floor, which was comprised of a long hallway with many doors— bedrooms, bathrooms, a big closet. Beth found each one being painted a tasteful color—buttercream, pearl gray, periwinkle— but she did not see David. The kids painting were all teenagers, too. Beth asked one of them if he knew where David was.

"On the deck at the end of the hall, drinking his java," the young man said. This kid was very pale and had black hair to his shoulders. "You his wife?"

Beth walked away without answering.

At the end of the hall were French doors, one of which was propped open with a gallon can of primer. The doors led to a huge deck that overlooked Maxcy's Pond, which through the fog, had a dull silver glint, like a pewter plate. David sat in a

teak chair, drinking his coffee, reading the newspaper. Beth
watched him for a second, his right ankle was propped on his
left knee and the paper rested on his legs. His sipped his coffee,
turned the page, whistled a few bars from the music inside. Beth
realized how enraged she was. At him, at Rosie—God, Rosie—
and at herself.

"This is quite a view," she said.

He swung around so quickly he spilled his coffee. When he
stood up, the paper slid off his lap onto the deck.

"Beth," he said. "What are you doing here?"

"I had a sneaking suspicion you didn't actually work," Beth
said. "And I see now that I was correct."

David wiped the coffee off his arm with a napkin, then he
folded the paper up, but seemed at a loss for what to do with it,
so he tucked it between the rails of the deck. It slipped through
the rails and fluttered to the ground, three stories below. Beth
took the chair next to his.

David gazed glumly at the newspaper below. "I've been here
since five-thirty getting my guys set up," he said. "I was taking
my coffee break."

"Not a bad life," Beth said.

"Why are you here?" David asked. "You certainly didn't come
to praise my choice of career."

"You know why I came."

He looked at her in that old, intense way that made the bottom of Beth's stomach swoop out. "I had nothing to do with it,"
David said. "Rosie told them."

"Oh, I know," Beth said. "That only makes it worse."

"She's been wanting to tell the girls for years," David said.
"She was just waiting for the opportunity to present itself." David

sank into his seat. "Finding out that Piper was dating your son was irresistible."

"It's none of her business," Beth said in a tight voice. She felt herself losing control and she reached for her mental reins. She breathed in through her nose; her ears were ringing with the injustice of it. Rosie kept the secret for twenty-five years only to let it splash at the worst possible time. "It's nobody's business but ours. Yours and mine."

"We were *married*, Beth." David looked at her, as if for confirmation, and she nodded. "It's a part of your past you have to face."

"But that's what I mean," Beth said. "Why shouldn't I be able to face it when I want, or not at all? It belongs to me. But no one else thinks that way. You don't believe I have a right to my own past, and neither do my kids. So I was forced to tell them the story about you and me and that summer, the cottage, the blood tests, the cosmos, the judge. I told them everything. Okay? I hope you're happy."

David was quiet for a moment. "How did you explain the part where you left me?"

"I explained it like it happened."

"And how, exactly, *did* it happen?" David asked. He raised his palms and showed them to her, then he placed them on the sides of her face. She pulled back—this was already too much contact—but his hands held her steady. In her mind, she saw a struggle, she sailed over the deck's railing to the ground where the newspaper lay in the mud.

"Let go of me," she said, as calmly as she could.

"I loved you," he said. "And you left me."

"Yes," she said.

He dropped his hands from her face and stuffed them into
the pockets of his gray canvas shorts. Beth gazed at his tan legs
fleeced with golden hairs, his crooked toes. His person was so
familiar to her and yet he had changed. They were both different
people now from the characters in the story she had told the
twins. She noticed for the first time some gray hairs around his
ears.

"I've thought about it so much this summer," David said. "I
haven't seen you in what—three weeks? four?—and yet I've
thought about you every day. I thought about kissing you."

"David."

"I thought about making love to you."

"David!"

"And I asked myself over and over, *What do you really want from
this woman?* She just lost her husband. What do you really expect?"
He grabbed onto the rail and leaned forward as though he were
the one contemplating a headlong dive. "Do you know what I
decided?"

"What?"

"I want to know why you left me."

Beth bounced on her toes. She felt the bike path calling her.
She didn't want to explain herself; she wanted to run away, just
as she had twenty-five years ago.

"There were a lot of reasons," Beth said. "Mostly, I wanted to
finish college."

"You could have finished on the Cape."

"I wanted to finish at Sarah Lawrence."

"You have no idea how snotty you sound," he said.

"Maybe that is snotty, or maybe I just like to finish what I
start."

"Except in the case of our marriage," David said.

Beth stared at the pond, which was a shade darker now. It was going to rain. "I couldn't stand to disappoint my parents."

"Now we're getting somewhere."

"I wanted to live my life the right way, David. Graduate, get a job, get married in a church with my parents' blessing."

"You were a coward," David said. "You weren't brave enough to follow your heart. When you actually agreed to marry me, I thought I had changed you into the kind of person who took risks. But when you left I saw that you were the same scared little girl you were at sixteen. Afraid of doing anything wrong, afraid of being your own person."

He was trying to hurt her and she couldn't blame him. At the time, Beth felt she had a choice between pleasing her parents and pleasing David, and, in the end, she chose her parents. But deep down, Beth also knew she was doing what was *right*. Thinking about that lunch at the Mad Hatter made her cringe inside, even now. She wouldn't have lasted eighteen years as David's wife. She would have taken off long before Rosie had. This, however, wasn't a sentiment that ever needed to be spoken out loud, even if David was prodding her to admit it.

"I acted as my own person," she declared. "I left of my own free will, because I knew it would be better for both of us."

"Well, it wasn't better for me."

Beth stood up. "What is it you want me to say? That I'm sorry? Of course I'm sorry! Of course I remember what happened. When I was telling the story to the kids, I remembered every single detail down to what Danny and Scott were eating for *breakfast* the morning I went back home." She glanced at David and was dismayed to see that there were tears in his eyes. Why was he ripping the scab off this old wound? *Leave it alone!* she pleaded silently. *We're old now. We have gray hair.* "I was wrong for the way I left you. I was wrong not to tell you to your face, but I simply couldn't. I was afraid. I knew I was going to hurt you and I didn't have the courage to sit and watch. I loved you, David, in that blind way that teenagers love each other. But I was smart enough to realize that it wasn't love for the long haul. When I left, I did us both a favor. That doesn't make it right. I'm sorry. Even now, I'm sorry."

"You didn't do me a favor by leaving," David said. He lay across the chair like he'd been shot. His neck was exposed, and his Adam's apple; she could see his pulse. Beth imagined her young self climbing onto the back of his dirt bike, and holding on to him for dear life. Kicking up dust into the sunset. That was how this all started, and this was how it was going to end, here on the deck of a complete stranger's house.

"I *am* sorry, David."

"So am I."

They remained silent until the first raindrops fell, and then Beth announced that she should let him get back to work.

"I'll see you out," he said.

They walked down the hall, past the rooms with their heavy smells of paint and blaring music and the teenage boys who would ask one another on their lunch break if Beth was David's estranged wife. A few of the kids would say yes, a few would say no, and nobody, Beth realized, would be completely wrong.

chapter 7

*G*arrett's days with Piper were dwindling. The Newtons were scheduled to leave the day after Labor Day, and when Garrett checked the calendar, he found himself staring at the fourteenth of August. They had less than three weeks left.

That night, Garrett and Piper went to the Gaslight Theater to see a heist movie. Piper knew a guy who worked there and so they were able to buy beers at the bar and take the beers into the theater with them. Piper took one sip of her beer and excused herself for the bathroom. She was gone a long time—she missed all of the trailers. When she returned, she took Garrett's hand and squeezed it so hard that Garrett winced and looked over, even though as a rule, he disliked it when people talked in movies.

"I threw up," she whispered.

Garrett moved his arm around her shoulders. "Do you want me to take you home?" he asked.

She shook her head and slumped in her seat toward him.

Garrett hoped she wasn't getting sick; the thought of even a day without Piper disheartened him. He drank his beer and the rest of Piper's as well.

After the movie, Garrett drove to the beach. No matter what they did at night, they always parked at the beach on the way home. But when Garrett pulled up to the water, shut off the engine and made a move to kiss Piper, she raised her hands to shield her face.

"Hey," Garrett said. "What's wrong?"

"I don't feel well," Piper said.

"Still?"

"Still."

Garrett rested his hands on the steering wheel and looked helplessly out the window. Even though they had more than two weeks left, everything had started to take on a sheen of nostalgia. The ocean at night, for example. Garrett soaked in the sight so that when he went back to New York he might remember what it was like—the waves, the reflection of the moon on the water, the way it felt to have Piper next to him.

"Do you want me to take you home?" he asked.

Piper didn't respond. A few seconds later when Garrett looked at her, he saw she was crying again. Piper had cried three nights in the past week because she was so upset about his leaving. That was probably why she threw up earlier. Garrett knew from his experiences with Winnie that girls threw up when they got upset. He didn't like the fact that he was causing Piper to cry and vomit, although he was glad she was going to miss him.

"It's only a year," Garrett said. "Not even a year. Nine months—September to June."

"That's not it," Piper said.

"I'm *not* going to find another girlfriend," Garrett reassured her. "I already told you, there isn't a girl in New York City as pretty as you."

"Garrett."

"We'll talk on Sundays when the rates are low, and we'll e-mail every day. God," he said. "I wonder what people did before they had e-mail?"

"I'm late for my period," Piper said.

This took Garrett so by surprise that at first he couldn't decipher what she meant. "What?"

"But I'm, like, super erratic. My cycle can be twenty-eight days for six months and then I'll skip a cycle all together. It's happened before. A bunch of times. At least twice."

"Are you telling me you might be pregnant?" Garrett asked. He couldn't believe this. They had used condoms every single time they had sex. He'd made sure of that. He'd been so, so careful—well, except for the time his mother caught them, when he hurried, when he fumbled while disengaging. But that was so long ago, the Fourth of July. He leaned his head back. *Oh, please, God, no.*

"Might," Piper said.

"How late are you?"

"Pretty late." She burst into a fresh round of tears.

"Okay, okay," Garrett said. He had to keep her from getting hysterical. What was it his father had always said? *It's fruitless to speculate.* There was no need to jump ahead and consider how neither of them was prepared to become a parent at seventeen. Not with a year of high school and four of college and three of law school for Garrett. No need to jump ahead to where Piper might get an abortion—it certainly couldn't be done on Nantucket—or how to pay for it or what their parents would say.

"You need to take a test," he said.

"Where am I going to get a test?"

Garrett wrinkled his brow. "At the store? I don't know. The pharmacy?"

"I *live* here, Garrett," Piper said. "I know at least three people who work at the Stop & Shop and my father is friends with the couple who own the pharmacy. He paints it every year. I can't go buy a pregnancy test. Everyone knows me."

Garrett felt like Piper had thrown a huge blanket over his head and he was having a hard time shaking it off. "So what are you going to do?" he asked.

"*Me?*" she said. "It's not *my* problem, Garrett. It's *our* problem. If I am pregnant, it's half your fault."

"I know," Garrett said defensively.

"*You* should buy the pregnancy test," Piper said. "Nobody knows you."

She had a point; he knew practically no one on the island other than his family. Still, the idea of buying a pregnancy test was humiliating. Buying a box of condoms had been bad enough. The condoms—Garrett couldn't even think about the condoms without shrinking inside.

"Okay," he said. "I'll do it."

Piper seemed to relax a little at this promise. She fell across the front seat and lay her head in his lap. A few seconds later, she fiddled with the zipper of his jeans, but Garrett took her hand and held it tightly. His body was filled with nervous tension that would be impossible to battle. He held Piper close and after several minutes he felt her body melt into his. She was falling asleep.

"Piper," he said. "I'm taking you home."

When they pulled into the Ronans' driveway, Piper roused herself enough to undo her seatbelt. "So you'll get it?" she asked. "Tomorrow?"

"Yeah," he said. He pulled Piper toward him and kissed her. "Do you think you are?"

Her eyes were only half open. She was, as Garrett's mother would say, falling asleep in her soup.

"No," she said dreamily. "Probably not."

Garrett felt a rush of relief. It was, after all, her body.

"Okay," he said. "I'll see you tomorrow. I love you."

"I love you, too, Garrett."

The next morning, Garrett rose early and drove to the Stop & Shop. He bought a pint of raspberries for his mother, who loved them, a bag of Doritos, a package of bacon, a jar of olives, a six-pack of root beer, and the pregnancy test. He dashed for the checkout line. The cashier, an older Jamaican woman, rang up the groceries without even glancing at him. Garrett paid with cash, refused his receipt, and hurried from the store.

Once in the car, he transferred the pregnancy test from the shopping bag into the backpack that he normally used for school—he'd brought it to Nantucket filled with the books on his summer reading list, but now it was going to serve as the place where he would hide the pregnancy test until that evening when Piper would take it. They were going to meet early, while it was still light out, and head someplace private.

At home, his mother was the only one awake. Garrett sauntered into the kitchen holding the bag of groceries—the backpack was already tucked into the dark recesses of the front hall closet. Beth stared at him as he put the shopping bag on the table and began emptying its contents.

"I bought you some raspberries," he said.

"You went to the store?" she asked. "What on earth for? Was there something special you wanted? You should have just told me, honey."

"And olives," Garrett said, holding up the jar. "You do like olives, don't you?"

At six o'clock, Garrett and Piper picked up sandwiches from Henry's and drove out to Smith's Point to catch the sunset. This was one of the things Garrett wanted to do before he left the island for the summer. In previous years, Garrett's father had arrived for the last two weeks of August and they did stuff as a family every night, including a sandwich picnic at Smith's Point. As Garrett drove over the rickety wooden bridge at Madaket Harbor, he noted how vastly different this year was from last year. This year he was the one driving the car with his girlfriend in the seat beside him, his girlfriend who thought she might be pregnant. His father was dead; his mother had been married before. Garrett reeled at the enormity of it. He glanced at Piper. She looked pale, and nervous. He took her hand.

Garrett lowered the air in his tires at the gatehouse, and then he and Piper drove over the huge, bumpy dune to the beach. Piper groaned and clenched her abdomen. Garrett's heart sank.

"Are you *okay*?" he asked.

"Just get there," she said.

They drove out the beach to the westernmost tip of the island. Across the water, Garrett could see the next island over, Tuckernuck. Piping plovers scuttled along the shoreline; the air smelled of fish, and in fact, the only other people on the beach were a couple of surf casters in the distance. Garrett spread out a blanket and unloaded the bag of sandwiches and the shopping bag that contained the Doritos and the root beer. It was a clear night; the sun was a pinkish-orange ball dropping toward the blue horizon. Piper sat resolutely in the Rover.

"Aren't you getting out?" he asked.

She moved in slow motion, like she was running out of batteries.

"Do you want to take the test before or after we eat?" he asked.

She shrugged. "Before, I guess. While it's still light. I have to pee anyway."

"Okay," he said. He double-checked their surroundings; they were shielded from the fishermen's view. He took the test out of his backpack and studied the instructions. "You pee in this cup, and then you put the stick in. If a second line shows up, it's positive. If not, it's negative." He handed Piper the cup and with the lethargic movements of an amoeba, she disappeared into the nearby dunes.

Garrett tapped the plastic stick against his palm. *Dad?* he beckoned. But this moment was too monumental and too scary to share with his father. Garrett tried to clear his mind. He could smell his meatball sub and his stomach growled. He'd been too nervous to eat anything all day, and now he was starving.

After an eternity, Piper popped out of the dunes, holding the cup discreetly at her side, blocked from Garrett's view. "Give me the stick," she said.

He handed it to her and she opened the back door of the car and moved inside. Garrett's pulse was screaming along like a race car. He was too nervous to pray.

"How long does it say to wait?" she asked.

Garrett didn't have to check the instructions; he had them memorized. "Three minutes, but no longer than ten."

Piper checked her watch. Garrett lost all control. He tore open the bag of Doritos and stuffed a handful into his face. He felt like an ogre, a glutton, but he couldn't help himself. Piper didn't even seem to notice. Nearly half the bag was gone when Piper stepped from the car. Garrett paused in his eating; his lips burned with spicy salt. Piper emptied the contents of the cup behind the Rover's back tire.

She smiled at him. The diamond stud in her nose caught the last rays of the setting sun. She waved the stick over him like it was a magic wand, changing his life forever.

"It's positive," she said.

⚜

The summer was fading fast. It got dark earlier, and there was a chill in the air at night. Garrett read the last two books on his summer reading list; he started running three miles each morning to get ready for soccer. Anything to lend normality to the very abnormal set of circumstances that bore down on him as surely as the impending autumn. Piper wanted to have the baby.

"But why?"

This was the question Garrett had asked over and again for the past three days. Garrett realized he should stop asking, because every time he asked, Piper came up with a more convincing answer. She valued the life inside her, she believed in a woman's right to choose and her choice was to have the baby, she couldn't bring herself to destroy a life that had been formed out of her love for Garrett.

Garrett countered with the predictable arguments—they had high school to finish, college to attend, years and years of life experience to acquire before either of them would be remotely capable of raising a child.

"Who said anything about raising a child?" Piper asked.

She wanted to have the child and put it up for adoption. There were thousands of good people in the world who were aching for a baby, she said.

"What about your senior year?" Garrett asked.

"What about it?" she said. "The baby isn't due until April. I can accelerate my course work, take my exams early and graduate."

"Yeah," Garrett said. "But you'll be pregnant."

Piper stared at him like he was the stupidest person on earth. "That's right," she said.

Being pregnant empowered Piper. From the second she saw the positive result at Smith's Point, she had transformed before Garrett's eyes. She stopped being his girlfriend and became someone's mother. She scared Garrett now, the way religious fanatics scared him. Only Piper's religion was her body. Her body was changing, producing a hundred thousand new cells every hour, she said. She was desperate to see a doctor, to have an ultrasound and blood tests—but to do this, she needed access to her father's insurance.

They had to tell their parents, she said and soon. There were only two weeks before Garrett returned to New York.

Garrett read and ran and moped, avoiding Beth and Winnie and Marcus. He moaned internally over his bad luck. He threw the remnants of his box of condoms into the trash. They were doubly useless—Piper didn't want to have sex anymore. She didn't want anything to harm the baby. She quit smoking for good, she said, and she began eating a lot of red meat and vegetables, although she was having a hard time keeping food down. Piper was going to have the baby and that was that. Garrett couldn't believe he had no say in the matter. For the rest of his life, Garrett would have to live with the fact that his child was walking the earth.

Piper insisted on presenting a unified front. She wanted to tell their families together, in one large group. She stopped by one day at lunch, and Garrett entered the kitchen to find her and Beth sitting at the table planning an end-of-the-summer barbecue. Beth seemed energized by the idea. His mother was so predictable—she wanted to keep the last bits of summer alive by filling the house with people.

"You don't mind that David is coming?" Garrett asked his mother later.

"I cleared the air with David," Beth said. "I think he should come. He's been an integral part of the summer."

There was an understatement. Garrett felt just as he had at the beginning of the summer when his mother announced that she had invited the Ronans for dinner. He didn't want them to come! If Beth hadn't invited them in the first place, Garrett wouldn't be in this gut-wrenching position. They might have had a peaceful summer.

Over the next few days, Garrett watched Beth pull out all the stops. She ordered clams and lobster tails from East Coast Fish, and beer from Cisco Brewery; she bought New York strip steaks; she bought French cheese and summer sausage and baguettes, and a jar of mustard that cost sixteen dollars; she made potato salad and coleslaw and corn pudding. She bought red and yellow tomatoes and made her own pesto. She made peach pie and homemade ice cream. She baked a chocolate cake. She decorated the house with zinnias and gladiolas and huge black-eyed Susans.

"I wish it could always be summer," Beth said wistfully.

Garrett wondered what Beth would say when she heard the news. He was surprised to find he didn't care what she thought— there was no way that she could be more distraught about Piper's pregnancy than he was. He couldn't wait to get back to New York. In less than a week, his feelings for Piper had changed. His love for her had evaporated, and in its place was fear of her and her plans.

On the evening of the barbecue, the Ronans arrived at six o'clock, the three of them unpiling from the front seat of David's truck. Winnie and Marcus were already out on the deck drinking Coke and holding hands. Winnie was trying to convince Marcus to eat a clam. Garrett eyed them enviously. They hadn't been stupid enough to let themselves get pregnant; they had made it through the summer intact. It wasn't fair—except that Garrett knew they would both be supportive when they heard the news, far more supportive than Garrett would have been under the reverse circumstances. First Garrett shuddered at the idea of Winnie bearing Marcus's child, then he shuddered at his own flawed character. He deserved a life of nasty surprises, he decided, and he steeled himself for what was to come.

The dinner went smoothly. David and Beth shared a big bottle of Whale's Tale Ale, Winnie talked to Peyton about what it was like to start high school. Piper held on to Garrett's hand and beamed benignly at everyone, in a fantastic imitation of the Virgin Mary. She said very little and ate even less—just a tomato and a tiny piece of steak. Beth noticed right away. Garrett wasn't surprised; his mother always noticed when someone wasn't eating.

"Are you okay, Piper?" Beth asked, as she began to clear the table. "You barely ate a thing and you've been so quiet. This isn't like you."

Piper squeezed Garrett's hand under the table. Here it comes, he thought. All hell is about to break loose. He wished for a final time that God would step in and save him.

"Thank you for noticing, Mrs. Newton," Piper said, in a loud, attention-seeking voice. "I didn't eat very much because I feel sick."

"I didn't realize you were sick," Beth said. "That's too bad."

"No, it's good," Piper said. "I feel sick because I'm pregnant."

Winnie let out a shriek. Everyone else was silent. Garrett stared at his plate—a mixed pool of juices from the steak and tomatoes, a few kernels of corn, a smudge of pesto. After what he considered to be a reasonable amount of time for this bombshell to detonate in each diner's mind, he glanced up. Someone was going to have to say something. One of the adults? Beth had retaken her seat without so much as a creak or a whisper, and now she sat with a stack of dirty plates in front of her, a totally blank look on her face, the way she must look, Garrett thought, when she first wakes up in the morning and she can't quite place where she is or where she's been. David was inspecting his glass of wine as though an insect or a small piece of cork were floating on the surface. He was so intent on this task that Garrett thought he hadn't heard; however, a few seconds later, he was the first to speak. When he did, it wasn't to Piper at all, but to Beth, across the table.

"How about that?" he said, raising his glass. "We're going to be grandparents."

"*What?*" Beth said. "Are you kidding me? Surely she's not keeping this baby?"

Garrett turned to watch Piper. Her face was unwavering in its calm repose. "That depends on what you mean by 'keep,' Mrs. Newton."

"You'll have an abortion," Beth said. "You're still just a child."

"I will not have an abortion," Piper said. "I've given it a lot of thought and I've decided that I want to have the baby and put it up for adoption."

"*Adoption?*" Beth said.

"Adoption," Piper said.

"What you want may not matter," Beth said. "You have to do what's best for everybody involved."

"I'm the mother," Piper said. "I have to do what's right for me and for the baby. Maybe you're not aware of the law. It's the mother's right to choose."

"That's a very self-centered attitude," Beth said.

"I think what's *self-centered* is wanting me to get an abortion so the matter is taken care of and you don't have to worry about it."

"She's got a point," David said.

Piper glanced at her father, and as if strengthened by this confirmation, continued. "I don't want to terminate the pregnancy. I want to give the baby life, then share that life with another family. That's the choice I've made. It's one I can live with."

David stood up and moved to Piper's chair. He knelt in front of her and she fell into his arms in a way that made her seem like a very young girl to Garrett. He got a lump in his throat.

Peyton started to cry. "You always do things like this," she said to her sister. "You do it for attention. But you never think of anyone else. Me, for example. Everyone at school is going to make fun of me."

Winnie rubbed Peyton's arm. "No one will make fun of you."

"They'll say my sister is a slut."

"They'll think Piper is brave for sticking to her principles," Winnie said. "I think you're brave, Piper."

Piper couldn't respond. Her face was hidden in David's shoulder.

Garrett looked around the table. He was both relieved and offended that no one was paying attention to him. Everyone was focused on Piper. This moment was all about her.

"I think you should take some time before you make a final decision," Beth said. "Even if you don't plan on keeping the baby, simply giving birth can be traumatic, physically and emotionally. And then there's your schoolwork, applying to colleges—"

"Don't try to talk her out of it, Mom," Winnie said. "After all, we're talking about a human being here. A human being who is related to everyone at this table—well, except for Marcus."

Marcus held up his palms as if relinquishing all claims of being related to the baby.

"We're talking about a cluster of cells," Beth said. "A microscopic organism. Not a human being, not yet."

"It's a human being," Winnie insisted.

Piper separated from David. "I'm having the baby. You should take as much time as you need to absorb that fact. I'm going to see a doctor and I'm going to research adoption agencies so that I'm sure the baby ends up in the best possible home. They've made it so that you can practically handpick the family that takes your child."

Peyton shook her head. "You are such an alien," she said. "I can't believe you're my sister."

David returned to his seat, only now he gripped the table and lowered himself gingerly into the chair, as if he were an old man. "Honey, we need to show your sister support. We have to rally around her."

"What about me?"

These words came from Garrett. He waited a beat to see if anyone had heard—yes, everyone at the table turned to him.

"I guess the question for you, young man, is why weren't you more careful?" David said.

"I was careful," Garrett said. He'd used condoms every time, and it was just the one time when his mother startled him when he wasn't paying full attention. But he couldn't explain that. "We had some bad luck."

"Good luck," Piper said, rubbing her still-flat stomach. "I consider this good luck."

"You consider this good luck," Garrett said to Piper. "So I guess what I think doesn't matter. And this is my child, too."

"I care what you think," Beth said.

"So do I," said Winnie.

"So do I," said Marcus. "What do you think?"

Garrett's eyes blurred with tears. What he thought was that if he had to sustain any more growing pains, any more major changes in life or death, he would explode. What he thought was, *thank you* to his mother and his twin sister and yes, even Marcus, for caring about him despite the fact that he possessed a despicable character. What he thought was, *I am sorry, I am so, so sorry* to the child that Piper carried within her. *I want to do better by you, but right now, I just can't.*

When Garrett spoke, his voice was thick with confusion. His normal voice had abandoned him.

"Let's just do what Piper wants," he said. "She's the mother. It's her decision."

Beth sighed. David clapped Garrett's shoulder. Winnie said, "Well, congratulations, then!" Marcus saluted Garrett. Peyton went over and touched the top of her sister's hair, as if checking for a halo. Garrett fell back in his chair, he was exhausted.

"Is there dessert?" he asked. He was grateful when Beth said, "Of course! Yes!" and bounded into the kitchen to serve it. Anything predictable, to Garrett, was now unspeakably precious.

⚜

Winnie couldn't believe it, but she was jealous. For years she had heard of girls her own age having babies—once even a girl at Danforth—and it was always spoken of with distaste. It was called "getting in trouble." But why? As Winnie lay in bed with Marcus that night, she longed to be filled with another human life, a life that could miraculously be created out of thin air and passion.

"It would be romantic, wouldn't it?" Winnie asked. "To have a baby?"

"Don't talk that way," Marcus said. "It won't be romantic for Garrett and Piper. Those two didn't even kiss good-bye tonight."

Winnie had noticed. The relationship between Garrett and Piper was different now, and not in a good way. Garrett kept talking about going back to New York like there was nothing he'd rather do. Meanwhile, Winnie wanted to stay on Nantucket forever. Once she got back to New York, everything would change. She would go back to living on Park Avenue, Marcus would go back to Queens. They could still see each other; it was thirty-five minutes on the subway. But it wouldn't be the same. They wouldn't be living together; they wouldn't spend every afternoon on the beach swimming; they wouldn't eat breakfast, lunch, and dinner together on the deck. Instead, Winnie imagined herself stepping off the train in an unfamiliar neighborhood where all the other girls her age were black or Hispanic and *tough*. Smoking cigarettes, chewing gum, dishing out attitude when they saw Winnie and Marcus walking down the street holding hands. Winnie had been to Marcus's apartment once before with her father and Garrett—the building was shabby, and although Marcus's apartment was nice on the inside, it looked like an apartment where the mother was absent. There had been dishes in the sink—lots of them—and there were two TVs blaring in different rooms. Marcus's sister, LaTisha, he said, came home from school and plunked herself in front of the set until bedtime. She did her homework in front of *Oprah* and ate her dinner in front of *Jeopardy!* Winnie didn't want to place herself in that apartment or on the street in Queens, but she was afraid the trip to Manhattan would intimidate Marcus just as much, and that he wouldn't come. New York, Winnie was certain, would stink. They wouldn't be safe from the rest of the world like they were here.

𝓎

A few days later, the Western Union truck pulled up in front of the house. Winnie was the only one around. Garrett and Beth had gone running together and Marcus had fallen asleep down on the beach. Winnie was in the kitchen making sandwiches when she heard the crunch of tires on the shell driveway and she reached the front door in time to meet the driver and sign for an envelope. Winnie became sore with the memories of previous summers—the FedEx truck came nearly every day with documents for her father.

The Western Union man tipped his hat at Winnie in an old-fashioned way that made her smile. She looked at the envelope and saw it was addressed to Marcus. It was a telegram, she realized, another telegram for Marcus. There had been one a few weeks earlier, back when they were angry at one another, and she had forgotten to ask him about it. From one of his parents, his father probably, telling him it was time to come home. She wanted to throw the envelope away, or else she wanted it to contain happy news, like Marcus had been offered a college scholarship. Like his father had found a great new job and they were moving to Manhattan.

Winnie took the envelope down to the beach along with their lunch. Marcus was still asleep, face down, on his beach towel. He was so tall and solid; at night, when he held her, she wanted to melt into him and disappear.

She nudged the bottom of his foot with her big toe. "Turkey sandwiches," she said. The days of Malibu and Coke were over, but she'd brought a thermos of icy lemonade. She laid out lunch as Marcus rubbed his eyes and sat up.

"I'm really going to miss this," he said. "You know?"

Winnie squinted at the ocean. A seagull stopped at the edge of their blanket and squawked for some of their lunch. Winnie threw a piece of bread crust. Finally she understood the heartache her mother felt every year when she left this island. It was falling in love here that did it, Winnie guessed. It was falling in love here that made you never want to leave.

"A telegram came for you," Winnie said. She pulled the envelope out of her jean shorts. "Just now. Western Union."

Marcus looked at the envelope but didn't reach for it right away. Winnie's heart dropped. It was bad news. She remembered the morning of March sixteenth, her mother coming into her bedroom while Winnie was getting dressed for school. Her mother didn't have to say a single word; Winnie knew in her gut that her father was dead.

"Is everything okay?" Winnie whispered.

The seagull returned, begging for more. Throw the telegram to the seagull, Winnie thought. Throw it into the ocean. It seemed plausible on such a gorgeous day that bad news could simply be tossed away.

Marcus opened the envelope, shaking his head all the while. Maybe it was from Constance. Could a person send telegrams from prison?

"What does it say?" Winnie asked.

He fell back onto his towel. "There's something I have to tell you. Remember back a couple of weeks ago when I got that other telegram? I know you were the one who slid it under my door."

Winnie nodded. It was awful of her to slide the telegram under the door like Marcus was some kind of leper, but at the time she'd been too indignant to knock.

"And remember when I told you that I had a secret?"

Of course she remembered! She felt like shaking him. Didn't he understand that his every word printed indelibly on her brain?

"Yes," she said. "But you don't have to tell me what it is if you don't want to."

"I want to," Marcus said. "These telegrams? Are you ready?"

Winnie was pretty sure she wasn't ready, but she nodded.

"They're from my editor."

Winnie smiled at him. She thought he'd said "editor."

"I don't understand," she said.

"I have an editor," Marcus said. "At Dome Books in New York. His name is Zachary Celtic."

Winnie felt like the butt of some kind of joke, though she

wasn't sure yet if she was supposed to be angry or laugh along.

"I still don't understand."

Marcus squinted at the ocean. The sun seemed to have gotten brighter in the past few minutes. So Winnie was skeptical. She believed in him, but not that much.

"I have a book deal with Dome," Marcus said. "This guy, this editor, Zachary Celtic, offered me thirty thousand dollars to write a book about what happened with my mother."

"You're kidding," Winnie said. "Thirty *thousand* dollars?"

Those three words had power, Marcus realized, even over someone with plenty of money like Winnie. They'd held so much power over him that he'd agreed to write a book he didn't want to write. There, he'd admitted it.

He didn't want to write the book.

"They gave me five hundred dollars already," Marcus said. It sounded like such a paltry sum when compared to thirty thousand, but since Marcus now knew he had to pay it back, it seemed like a lot. "But I spent it. And what this telegram says is that the first fifty pages and a complete synopsis are due next week, September first. 'Per our agreement.'"

"You've written fifty pages?" Winnie said.

"No," Marcus said. "I've only written one page. I had writer's block this summer."

"Maybe they'll give you more time," Winnie said. "Like an extension on a term paper?"

"More time won't help," Marcus said. "I'm not going to write it at all."

"Really?" Winnie said. Now she was having a hard time processing what he was telling her. He had a book deal for thirty thousand dollars but he was giving it up? Turning it down?

She felt compelled to push him toward greatness. Marcus could be a writer, a real writer, before he even turned eighteen. "Why not?"

"I don't have it in my heart," Marcus said. "I'm furious with my mother and I know better than anyone else that what she did was wrong, but that's not stuff I want to explain to the rest of the world. I want to work it out privately."

"But you don't talk to your mother," Winnie said.

"Yeah, I know," Marcus said. He felt like crumpling up the telegram and tossing it into the water, but it had the phone number of Dome Books on it and now he had to call. "Don't get me wrong. I want to be a writer. And I will be someday. But I'm not writing this story. I kept thinking of your dad, too. He wouldn't have wanted me to write this book."

"Yeah," Winnie said. "He wasn't into exploiting his cases."

That word, "exploiting," was the one that made Marcus squirm. Along with the horrible things Zachary Celtic had said at lunch, and the way the five hundred dollars was handed to him—cash in an envelope—so seedy, so underhanded. They were buying Marcus's betrayal. "Anyway, that's my secret. I have a book deal with this big publishing house for all this money but I'm not going through with it."

"Well, okay, then," Winnie said. She poured two cups of lemonade and handed one to Marcus. They clicked cups in a toast, though they had different ideas about what they were drinking to. Winnie thought they were drinking to Marcus's future career as a writer, if not with this book then with another. Marcus thought they were drinking to his freedom.

Winnie was thrilled to accompany Marcus on even the smallest errand; standing in line at the post office to get stamps with him was a delight. But this—going with him in the morning to call his editor and turn down the book deal—was monumental. Marcus was so nervous about the prospect of contacting this man, Zachary Celtic, that he said he wouldn't come to Winnie's room at all that night, even though she begged him to as they sat on the deck looking at the stars. She reminded him that their nights together were dwindling in number.

"I can't," he said. "My guts are bound up about this call tomorrow. I just want tomorrow to come so I can do it."

"What are you going to say?" Winnie asked.

"I'll just tell him I'm not writing it. I'll tell him I'll return the five hundred bucks."

Even though Marcus and Winnie were in love, there were certain things she was afraid to ask. Like where he was going to get that kind of money.

"And what about your mother?" Winnie said.

"What about her?"

"Will you go see her when you get home?"

He squeezed her hand so tightly she nearly cried out in pain. "I don't know what to do about my mother," he said.

※

In the morning, they rode their bikes into town and called Zachary Celtic from a phone booth. Marcus had brought the telegram along with him. He dialed the number, then pumped the payphone full of quarters; his pockets were heavy with them. Winnie stood at Marcus's back, outside of the booth. She was afraid she wouldn't be able to hear the conversation, and for a moment she wondered why he'd invited her along when clearly this was something he wanted to do by himself. She looked up and down the street at the people walking their dogs, drinking coffee, waiting for the shops to open. A man on a bench nearby read the *Wall Street Journal* and talked on his cell phone about the upcoming football season. Marcus had two fingers plugged in his ear and his head bent forward. Winnie heard him say, "Zachary Celtic, please. True crime. It's Marcus Tyler calling." His voice was strange. Winnie wanted to touch him in some reassuring way, but she was scared to. The man on the bench blabbed into his cell phone, bragging now about the dinner reservations he'd managed to "score" at the Pearl and American Seasons. Winnie nearly shushed him. Marcus pumped more change into the phone. He turned around and smiled weakly at her, saying, "They're seeing if he's available."

"Do you have enough money?" Winnie asked.

He patted his pockets for confirmation, then he yanked Winnie into the booth with him. She was relieved. The two of them wedged themselves on either side of the telephone, and Marcus managed to squeeze the door shut. He held the receiver in one hand and Winnie's wrist with the other. Then he swallowed, and when he spoke, his voice sounded like that of a nine-year-old boy.

"Mr. Celtic? Yeah, this is Marcus Tyler? Yes, I got it yesterday. Listen, I have some bad news."

Winnie squeezed his fingers.

"No, more time isn't going to help. When you first asked this spring, I thought I could write it. I definitely wanted the money, and I understand it was, like, a huge leap of faith to offer that kind of cash to a kid. But I tried all summer, and I can't seem to get any decent sentences on paper. At first I thought it was writer's block, but then, I don't know . . ." Marcus took a huge breath, sucking all of the remaining oxygen out of the phone booth, then said in his normal voice, "I don't want to write it."

There was silence, then the frantic, faraway voice of Zachary Celtic talking. Marcus listened with his eyes squeezed shut, like he was enduring some awful pain. He took a breath to speak, but was shut out. Winnie hated to see him like this—trying to say his piece, but failing. She felt as badly as she would have at a racial slur—standing with Marcus on Second Avenue, say, while cab after cab passed by Marcus's outstretched hand.

"Mr. Celtic?" Marcus finally said. It sounded like he was interrupting. "I'll pay you back the five hundred dollars. No, really, I want to. And I'll pay you back whatever it cost you to take me to lunch that day. Just please don't say anything bad about me to Ms. Marchese because I need her to write me a college recommendation, you know?" He paused for a minute then dove back in. "Except, see, I don't think I'm going to change my mind. What's done is done. Angela and Candy are dead, my mother is in prison for the rest of her life, my uncle only has half a brain, and I don't have any explanations for that. I've made up excuses on my mother's behalf, I've tried to justify her actions, I've tried to understand every possible reason why she killed two people but I don't have the answers. I'm not even sure my mother has the answers. But it doesn't matter. *I'm not going to write this book.*" Marcus hung up the phone on Zachary Celtic, saying, "I'll send you that money, sir."

The receiver hit the cradle so hard there was a residual

metallic ring. Marcus stared at himself in the front of the phone.

"Well," he said.

"You did a good job. You said all the right things."

"Think so?" Marcus asked. He touched the receiver as though he wanted to call back and start over. "He said in true crime hot topics go cold real quick, but that he thought my mother's story would always have appeal, in case I ever changed my mind." Marcus wiped sweat off his forehead. "I'm not going to change my mind."

"I know you won't," Winnie said.

"I'm determined to pay the guy back, even though he said I should hold on to the five hundred bucks. He said that was money he was willing to gamble with. But I don't take money for nothing."

"Do you feel better?" Winnie asked. "Now that it's over?"

Now that its over. Marcus feared that this thing with his mother would never be over; it would be a part of him for the rest of his life. However, the dread about the phone call was gone, leaving Marcus feeling empty, in a clean way, like a vessel that had been washed out. "Yes," he said. "I guess I do." He took Winnie in his arms and hugged her, and then they opened the door and stepped out into the fresh air.

✿

Piper scheduled her first ultrasound appointment before Garrett left because she wanted him to come with her.

"I don't think that's a good idea," he said.

They were sitting side by side on Horizon's deck in upright chairs like an elderly couple—not sunbathing, not reading—just staring at the ocean and thinking. They still hung out together in the afternoons, though evening dates were over; Piper was too tired and Garrett had no desire to pursue her. He figured his reluctance to go to the appointment would just be one more thing that pissed her off, but instead she took both his hands and looked him dead in the eye. "I know there's a person inside you who wants to do the right thing."

But how, he wondered, was going to the ultrasound appointment the right thing? It wasn't a baby he was ever going to know.

"Right now this baby is in our care," Piper said. "It's our responsibility to make sure it enters the world healthy."

The appointment was the following day at two. Garrett drove Piper to the hospital. They sat in the waiting room watching the action in the adjoining ER—a man had fallen off his moped and done something unnatural to his arm, followed minutes later by a little girl who had been stung by a jellyfish—until Piper's name was called.

A nurse led them down the white hallway to the X-ray room. Garrett's heart was thudding like a bowling ball hitting the gutter. He thought of that first walk on the beach with Piper, then the bonfire where he met her awful friend Kyle, then buying the box of condoms, the first time they made love, then the Fourth of July, the long stretch of days while she was at Rosie's, the summer evenings they spent parked at the beach. It all seemed like it happened eons ago, with another person.

Garrett had expected a doctor, but the woman who entered the room to do the ultrasound was young, with a ponytail and thick Boston accent. She patted the exam table, indicating that Piper should sit down on it.

"My name's Marie," she said.

Then she asked Piper questions: *Bladder full? Date of birth? Date of last menstrual period?* If Marie was surprised that Piper was only seventeen, she didn't let on.

"Go ahead and lift your shirt, hon," she said.

Piper did so—the days of halter tops were over—and Marie squirted a clear jelly onto Piper's abdomen. Garrett was embarrassed; he stared at his feet in his Sambas and wished he were running across the soccer field in Van Cortland Park right now. Only four days left until their ferry.

Marie switched on a monitor and a blank computer screen lit up. Then she moved a thick wand over Piper's belly. The screen came alive with blobs and swirls.

"Where's our baby?" Piper asked. She propped herself up on her elbows and studied the screen.

"Patient, hon," Marie said. "We're looking for something the size of a pea." Garrett noted that Marie had yet to acknowledge his presence in the room, although he was growing used to being ignored where Piper's pregnancy was concerned.

"Here we go," Marie said. A white peanut appeared on the screen. Marie zoomed in. "There's your baby."

Garrett gazed at the screen with interest. The peanut, he could see, was moving. The peanut had tiny arms and legs.

"See this dark spot?" Marie said. "This is the baby's heart. Here, wait a sec."

Marie fiddled with a knob on the computer. Suddenly, a rhythmic whooshing sound filled the air.

"What's that?" Garrett croaked.

"What's *that?*" Marie said, as if she couldn't believe anyone would be brave or stupid enough to ask. "Why, that's your baby's heartbeat."

The baby, Marie said, was due March twenty-seventh. "But frequently first pregnancies are late."

"Good," Garrett said. "Maybe the baby won't be born until April. March is a terrible month."

Piper glared at him. "What do you care?"

"My father died in March," Garrett explained to Marie.

"Sorry to hear it," Marie said. "Well, look at it this way, if your baby is born in March, it will become a good month."

Garrett rolled his eyes. The woman didn't know what the hell she was talking about.

"I'm going to take a few pictures for your doctor," Marie said. "And for you, if you want one."

"Of course I want one!" Piper said. "Can you tell if it's a boy or a girl?"

"Nawp, not yet," Marie said. "Another eight weeks or so and you'll come back for a second round of this. They can tell you then."

"I feel in my heart that it's a girl," Piper said.

Garrett shut his eyes. He needed to sit down. A girl, a boy— the baby would be one or the other. God, it was all too much. He managed to stay on his feet while Marie took pictures of the white peanut from different angles.

"I just need to develop these," she said. She handed Piper a couple of tissues for her belly. "You clean up. I'll be back in a sec."

Once Marie left the room, there was an awkward silence. Piper swabbed the gunk off her skin, then handed the tissues to Garrett.

"What am I supposed to do with these?" he asked.

"Throw them away." She nodded to a trash can near his feet.

He slammed the wad into the can with all his strength.

"You're angry," she said.

s u m m e r   p e o p l e

"What?"

"You're furious with me. You think this is my fault."

"I don't think that."

"Of course you do." Piper stood up from the table and tucked
in her shirt. "You think it's my fault I'm pregnant. But I have
news for you, Garrett. You have to accept fifty percent responsibility."

"Fifty percent responsibility but not fifty percent say in what
happens."

"You saw the baby floating around on that screen," Piper said.
"Do you honestly want to kill it?"

"I don't know what I want."

"I'll tell you what you want. You want to be back in New
York where you can pretend none of this ever happened. Where
you can pretend I don't exist."

"That's not true."

"It *is* true. But you know what's funny? I don't care. I don't
care that you knocked me up and now you don't love me anymore. It doesn't bother me! All I care about is doing the responsible thing here, the adult thing, and I'm doing it! I'm taking
responsibility for this child without compromising my future.
You never would have made this decision because it's too hard
and you're not strong enough. This doesn't fit into the life plan
you concocted for yourself. Well, guess what, Garrett? Part of
being an adult is learning that sometimes in life, pieces don't fit."

"We're not adults, though," Garrett said. "We're kids. We're
kids having kids."

"You're a real summer person," Piper said. "I realized that when
this whole thing started."

"What's that supposed to mean?"

"You show up here for three months of the year when the weather is nice and the water is warm and you use the island. You use it up. Then in September you go back to wherever you came from and forget all about this place. Because you don't really care about Nantucket or the people who live here." Piper's voice was high and shrill; her face was flushed. "You probably won't even come back here for the birth."

Garrett stared at her. "Of course I'm coming back for the birth."

"You are?"

"Yes." He actually hadn't given it a moment of consideration, but he would not stand here and have this girl call him a coward and be right. If his child was going to be born here, he would be here. And his mother and Winnie, too. They would all get a chance to see the baby, to hold him or her, then say good-bye.

"Well, fine, then," Piper said. "But you're not going to be my labor coach. Peyton has already offered."

"You're going to have a thirteen-year-old labor coach?" Garrett said.

"By March, she'll be fourteen," Piper said.

The door swung open and Marie stepped in, holding an envelope. She looked between them. "Everything okay in here?" she asked.

"Sure," Piper said.

"Here are the pictures. I got two for you—" She handed two to Piper. "And one for you." She handed one to Garrett.

Garrett scrutinized his picture, grateful that he had gotten a good shot, where the arms and legs were visible and he could see the dark spot where the baby's heart was.

He looked at Marie. "This is my baby," he said.

She clapped him on the shoulder. "You're a lucky man."

⚜

At home, Garrett found Beth in the kitchen packing up the place mats and napkins, the coffee grinder, the food processor. She had saved the Zabar's shopping bags and was filling them with the things they couldn't get in New York: loaves of Something Natural herb bread, containers of smoked bluefish pâté and clam chowder, huge beefsteak tomatoes from Bartlett's.

She smiled indulgently as he walked into the kitchen. "How'd the appointment go?"

He shrugged. "Okay." The picture was in his shirt pocket—he'd pulled it out twice after dropping Piper off to look at it. "Here, want to see?" He handed the photo to his mother.

Beth held it up to the light.

"These are the arms and legs," Garrett said. "And this dark spot? That's the heart."

His mother turned the picture and squinted. Despite her most fervent wishes, a few tears leaked from her eyes.

"I know you're disappointed in me," he said.

She wiped her tears away quickly. "I wasn't thinking that at all. I was just thinking of all of the things your father is going to miss."

"Can we come back for the birth?" Garrett asked. "The baby is due March twenty-seventh."

"This house doesn't have heat," Beth said. "And it's going to be tricky with school. I don't even know when your spring break is."

"Please?" Garrett said.

Beth handed him back the picture. "I guess we'll figure something out," she said.

※

With only two days before they were to leave, Beth became very busy. First, there was packing—and when Beth looked around the house, she saw things everywhere that had to be put into boxes. It overwhelmed her. She got up before dawn and made herself a pot of coffee. When Arch had come at the end of August, they used to awaken early all the time and watch the sun rise, brightening the water. It was Arch's favorite time of day, the time when Nantucket, to him, seemed its most at ease.

Beth poured a cup of coffee and sat down at the kitchen table. She heard a groan, followed by the splintering noise she'd been fearing all summer, but before she could steady herself, the chair she was sitting on crashed to the ground. Beth hit the floor with a tremendous wallop—her whole body vibrated and there was a sharp pain in her right wrist. The surprise and the pain of it was enough to make her cry, but all Beth could think was that the ancient chair finally breaking was some kind of message from Arch. Things can fall out right from under you and you will survive. Beth picked herself up. Brilliantly, her coffee remained intact on the kitchen table. She took a long sip, then rotated her wrist a few times. It still worked.

She inspected the chair, wondering if it could be salvaged, but decided, in the end, it should go into the trash. Furniture was one of those things that could be replaced.

※

She left the house for a run before any of the kids got up, inhaling the air like she might never breathe again. She ingested the sight of the land—the flat blue pond, the green dunes, the gold sand, the ocean.

She didn't want to leave.

Of course, she felt this way every August—but in previous Augusts, Arch had been around to help, and he was very matter-of-fact about packing up. He washed and vacuumed the car—three months of accumulated sand and grime from driving on these dirt roads—then he brought the empty boxes up from the basement and he packed while Beth cleaned. It took them twenty-four hours. Arch double-checked their reservation at the Steamship. They gave all of their perishables to Mrs. Colchester three houses down who stayed until Columbus Day; they ate their final dinner at the Brotherhood, locked the house, tucked the key under the mat, and left. Beth had been sad to leave since she was five years old, old enough to realize that the island had a soul that she loved as much as she loved a real, living person.

Why were they going back to New York? What waited for them there? The kids had another year of school, the most critical year. Beth had the apartment, her position on Danforth's advisory board, a few friends who would allow her to be a third or fifth wheel at dinner parties. She had Kara Schau. She had her gym, her hairdresser, the best Chinese food in the world at the Jade Palace, the museums, which she rarely visited anymore, though she felt encouraged by their stately presence in her neighborhood. There was Arch's mother, Vivian, on Fifty-ninth and Sutton Place, whom they would see once a month for a lunch of roast beef and watercress sandwiches. It was a bleak picture.

And then there was the matter of the baby. Beth marveled that she and David hadn't ended up in the same pickle so many years ago—thinking back, she couldn't remember what they had used for birth control. Beth felt sorry for Garrett and disappointed in both him and Piper, although she had to admit, Piper's decision was mature and responsible. David and Rosie had raised her right, and Beth was mortified to discover that she herself felt much like Garrett—hoping for an abortion, hoping that the whole mess could just be swept under the rug. But no—there was to be a baby in March. Now that it was an undeniable fact, now that Beth had seen the ultrasound photo, her feelings changed. That baby was her grandchild. The mere word made her gasp with disbelief—she was far too young!—but it was true. The baby belonged to all of them. It whispered in Beth's ear, begging her to stay.

⚘

She packed the kitchen and the dining room, leaving only breakfast things. They got sandwiches from Something Natural for lunch and ate strange combinations of leftovers for dinner. The kids were good about helping—they gave Beth their clothes for one final wash and she did all of the beach towels except for two, since Winnie and Marcus wanted to swim right up until the final morning. Beth packed up her room and started cleaning. She dusted every surface in the house with a rag, then bleach and water. She vacuumed all the floors and had Winnie beat the rugs. As long as there were tasks still ahead of her, she had time left. And so she took out all of the screens and sprayed them down with the hose; she rinsed all of the deck furniture. She went into town and bought an approximate match of the kitchen chair she had broken. She delivered a big bag of perishables to Mrs. Colchester, and because the woman wasn't home, Beth left the bag on the front porch with a note that said, "Another summer ending!"

Then, with less than a day left—they were leaving on the 9:30 boat the next morning—Beth decided to broach the topic with the twins that gnawed at her insides. She couldn't leave the island without doing so.

She found Garrett in his room neatly folding shirts and shorts and putting them in his suitcase, but Winnie had to be called up from the beach. Beth promised Marcus, "I'll only borrow her for a few minutes." Once she had the twins in the same place, the upstairs hallway, as it happened, she took a deep breath.

"I need you to show me the place where you put Daddy's ashes," she said.

They nodded, as though this request were long overdue. Garrett abandoned his packing and Winnie yelled from the edge of the deck to Marcus. "I have this thing to do. I'll be back in a little while."

The three of them walked silently out to the Rover, where Beth climbed into the backseat. It was late afternoon, sunny, a gorgeous day in early September. Garrett sailed up the Polpis Road, a section of Nantucket Beth had always found beautiful, with handsome homes along the road, and winding dirt roads that led to either the harbor or the moors. She studied the backs of the twins' heads. There was something odd about sitting in the backseat while they drove. It was the role reversal—years and years had passed with Arch and Beth up front and the kids in the back. Beth supposed she should be sad, but what she felt was freedom. She didn't have to be responsible; she could let them lead the way.

With them facing forward, it was also easier for her to bring up the crazy idea that had been festering in her head the past few days.

"What if we stayed?" she said.

Garrett reached for the volume knob of the radio and turned it down. "Did you say something, Mom?"

Beth cleared her throat. "I did. I asked you, What if we stayed?"

Winnie turned her head, though not far enough to meet Beth's eyes. "Stayed where?"

"Stayed on Nantucket. This year. What would you think?"

"No way," Garrett said.

"You could go to Nantucket High School," Beth said. "We could get heat for the house. A furnace! And we'll put in a phone. When the baby is born, I could take care of him or her. Piper wouldn't have to put the baby up for adoption. I mean, you guys will be going to college next year, anyway, and I could, you know, live on Nantucket and raise the baby." Her voice gained strength and conviction, like the plan was a dream she was remembering more vividly as she kept talking. Raise the baby herself, of course! With occasional help from David. Piper and Garrett could visit all the time, whenever they wanted, but their baby would be like a much younger sibling instead of their child. It would be a real Nantucket baby, who would grow up in Horizon, the fifth generation of Beth's family to sleep under its roof. The idea of the baby, the bassinet, the stroller Beth would push while jogging, the outfits she still had from when Winnie and Garrett were young, the wooden toys, the silver spoon that would deliver pureed pears and sweet potatoes into the tiny pink mouth—it all sounded so superior to returning to New York that Beth was crushed when Winnie snapped her fingers and said, "Mom! Earth to Mom! Return to reality!"

"The baby is going to be put up for adoption," Garrett said.

"And we're going back to New York," Winnie said. "That's where we live."

"But your father—"

"Dad would want us to go back to New York," Garrett said. "And finish at Danforth."

"Is *here*," Beth said. "Your father is here."

As if on cue, Garrett hit the turn signal and directed the car down the road to Quidnet. Beth sealed her mouth. She was losing her mind. Stay on Nantucket? Keep the baby? She was talking nonsense. She was trying to make these minutes in the car be about something other than what they were really about. They were really about going to see the place where Arch's ashes were scattered. Thinking about the ashes meant thinking about the decision to cremate, those wretched days in the apartment with all the people drinking coffee and preparing Beth sandwiches that she couldn't possibly eat. It meant thinking about the day the doorman called up to say she'd received a package and opening the box that contained the urn, sent to her via UPS like it was something she'd ordered from a catalog.

Garrett drove through a thicket of trees and then Beth saw a meadow and on the far side of the meadow, the harbor. The water shimmered in the late afternoon sun. Garrett pulled over. He opened the door and helped Beth out like she was an invalid.

"This is it," Garrett said.

She couldn't have wished for a more beautiful spot. It was flat and calm and quiet. It was everything a final resting place should be.

"All these years on Nantucket," she said. "And I've never been here."

"Dad and I discovered it," Garrett said proudly.

Winnie and Garrett each took one of Beth's hands and the three of them stepped out into the meadow. Beth bowed her head. *Thank you*, she said—to God or to Arch, she wasn't sure—

thank you for this, the most awful summer of our lives. As crazy and gut-wrenching as it was, we made it. We are stronger. We are closer. We are still standing here, together, a family.

To her children, she said, "When I die, will you bring my remains here? Will you put me here with Daddy?"

Winnie rested her head on Beth's shoulder. "We don't want you to die."

"But when I do . . ."

"We'll bring you here," Garrett promised.

❧

The next morning, Beth woke at six and went downstairs to tend to the last details of leaving: a note for Carl Drake, the caretaker, breakfast for the kids, all of the trash taken out. Beth looked at the ocean as often as she could. Impossible to believe that to-morrow it would be Park Avenue. But that, really, was the story of her life.

Marcus was the first one to come down.

"Is there anything I can do to help?" he whispered. He was wearing the same white oxford cloth shirt he'd worn the day they arrived—Beth didn't recall seeing it at any other time this summer. She closed her eyes and remembered opening the door to their apartment in New York and finding Marcus there, wear-ing this shirt, carrying his black leather duffel bag, which now was packed and waiting at the bottom of the stairs. The son of Constance Bennett Tyler, convicted murderer. But he was more than that, as Arch had promised. This was a fine young man—smart, considerate, good in a way that so few people were good anymore. When Beth opened her eyes, she realized how much she would miss him. He had become like a third child to her.

"Is there anything *I* can do to help?" Beth asked. She wasn't quite sure what she meant by that—all she knew was that she wanted to make the rest of Marcus's life easier for him, as easy as his days on the beach here had been.

Marcus wondered if Winnie had said anything to Beth about the five hundred dollars, because her words sounded like an offer of money. But he'd already made up his mind to get a job as soon as he returned to Queens. He sat down at the kitchen table and let Beth pour milk on his cereal. "There's no way I can thank you for this summer," he said. "This summer saved me."

"Oh, Marcus."

"It gave me peace. And it gave me love."

"Well, you gave us things, too, you know," Beth said. "You gave us yourself."

"That doesn't seem like much in comparison," he said.

Except it was. At that moment, Beth understood that Arch hadn't invited Marcus to Nantucket for only Marcus's sake. Arch had invited Marcus to Nantucket for all their sakes—Beth's, Garrett's, Winnie's—so they could learn from him about character. About how to rise above.

"You have to promise to come see us," Beth said. "You have to promise to let us know how you're doing."

"I will." He dug into his cereal with gusto. All summer, Beth had loved to watch him eat because he was so enthusiastic about the food she put in front of him. She remembered with an ache in her throat the way he'd tied the bib around his neck before eating his first lobster. It was going to be a huge loss to have him leave their midst. She would wonder about him all the time; she would worry.

"We're coming back here in March or April, when the baby

is born," she said. "Just for a week or so. Will you come back with us then?"

"I don't know if Garrett wants me here," Marcus said. "He might just want family."

"Marcus," Beth said. "You are family."

Marcus smiled, gracing the room with his dimples. Beth could tell he felt as she did—that as long as there was a bright spot on the horizon, they might make it successfully through today.

"Sure," he said.

※

And so they went: out to the car, which was packed to the top, once again. Garrett sat up front and Winnie and Marcus climbed in the back. Beth stood in the front door—first looking at the car and then turning and looking at the empty house.

"See you in the spring," she said.

She locked the door and tucked the key under the mat.

The scene at Steamship Wharf was as chaotic as one would expect for Labor Day weekend. The standby line was twenty cars deep. Beth was grateful for her reservation. She pulled into a spot for ticketed cars and let the engine idle. They still had a few minutes before boarding.

"Do any of you want to use the bathroom before we get on the boat?" she asked.

No response. In her rearview mirror, she saw Winnie asleep on Marcus's shoulder. Garrett was in outer space somewhere, and who could blame him?

A few minutes later, the car in front of theirs inched forward in anticipation. Beth herself was exhausted—she wanted to get the car onto the boat, then pull a pillow out of the back and sleep for an hour. The drive home was always so draining, followed by the torturous business of delivering Marcus to Queens, then unloading all of the stuff from the back of the car and hauling it onto the freight elevator of their building. How would she ever make it through the day?

Finally it was her turn to go. A steamship worker with a grizzled beard motioned her forward. Just before Beth drove up the ramp onto the boat, she saw David's van and then David himself sitting on the bumper. Wearing khaki shorts, a green polo shirt, the flip-flops, sunglasses. Grinning at her, he lifted his coffee cup in her direction—a toast.

There was no point in analyzing why she felt so happy to see him or how touched she was that he found time in his day to see them off, or how safe she suddenly knew she was—there was someone in the world who cared for her, who probably even loved her, and who would be here on island, waiting, the next time she returned. For now, David was what she needed most: he was her friend.

She decided not to wave; she didn't want the kids to notice him. He wasn't there for the kids, anyway; he was there for her. Beth did put down her window and turn her face in his direction. She wanted to give him something to hold on to while she was gone—the memory of her smile, warmed by the summer sun.

chapter 8

The most amazing aspect of life, Beth thought, was the way that time passed—the days, the months, one following the next without slowing down or stopping for tragedy or triumph.

They returned to New York and—how else could she say it?—resumed their lives. It took two weeks for Beth to readjust to New York, but then one day she woke up and realized everything was back to normal. The laundry was done, the apartment had been cleaned, the last of the Nantucket bread and tomatoes had been consumed—now the kids were devouring bags of apples and gallons of cider, almost faster than Beth could buy them. Winnie had her first physics quiz and she rattled off formulas in a cheerleader's chant. Garrett had his first soccer game at the end of the week, plus his application for Princeton was due soon, if he wanted to qualify for early admission. One night, Beth found him in Arch's study on the phone—odd, because he normally took calls on the cordless in the kitchen. He was sitting at Arch's desk doodling on a legal pad, and with his head bent, he looked so much like Arch that Beth caught her breath, inadvertently announcing her presence—she had planned to slip out of the room unnoticed. But Garrett looked up and saw her and she asked, "Who are you on the phone with, honey?" The typical response whenever she asked either of the kids this was, "None of your business," but this time Garrett moved his mouth away from the receiver and whispered, "Piper."

Beth stood in the doorway for a beat. She wanted to ask, *How's she feeling? How's the baby? What does the doctor say?* She wanted to talk to David. The phone line led directly to Nantucket, and although she was now back in New York, Beth yearned to transmit herself there. Instead, she nodded and closed the door.

⚘

Winnie started her senior year at Danforth a changed woman. She was no longer the naive goody-goody spoiled brat child of privilege whose life had been torn apart by the untimely death of her father, she was no longer a girl who thought it was okay to wear her father's Princeton sweatshirt as though it were a mourning band or torture her body by denying it food. And she was no longer a virgin, physically or emotionally.

While it was true that her relationship with Marcus changed—there was no way to keep up the intensity of their friendship when they lived apart—it ended up being okay for both of them. Winnie's time was occupied by school. She nurtured the friendships that she'd all but ignored as of March sixteenth, and she tried to foster friendships with one or two of the African American kids at her school, although she soon realized that just because these people were black did not mean they had an

excellent character like Marcus. Winnie did her best to eat as
much as she could and three afternoons a week she worked out
in Danforth's weight room as she prepared for the upcoming
swim season. She was going to surprise everyone on her team
by trying the butterfly this year.

Marcus's life got incrementally better. During the summer his
father had cleared the apartment of most of Constance's things,
which helped. Marcus had school which he took seriously; he
studied hard. He, too, went to the gym three afternoons a week,
and he got a job working two evenings plus Saturdays at a pizza
shop in the student union at Queens College. It was a job that
could easily have gone to a work-study student, but Marcus's old
boss at the grounds department put in a good word for him,
even though he knew about Marcus's mother. Marcus didn't actually make pizza—no tossing or spinning of dough, no painting
of sauce or collage of toppings—but he did become proficient
with the pizza peel, the pizza cutter, and the cash register. He
made $6.75 an hour and by mid-October had saved almost two
hundred dollars toward his debt to Dome Books.

On Sundays, Marcus took the seven line into Manhattan to
watch the Giants game at Winnie's apartment. Those afternoons
on the leather sofa were a quiet fantasy. They snuggled under a
fleece blanket, and although there was no opportunity for sex—
Beth was always around—they reveled in the warmth of each
other's body, just as they had on those nights in Horizon when
they'd done nothing but sleep. Beth served them Cokes from a
silver tray and made delicious pub food—potato skins, chicken
fingers, mushrooms stuffed with sausage and Parmesan cheese.
Sundays that autumn made Marcus glad to be alive.

Thanks to Beth, he'd met four times with Kara Schau, who

actually traveled to Benjamin N. Cardozo High School to speak with him during his study hall. Mostly, he talked and she listened, but she left him with a few helpful sentences: *You can be related to someone who's done a bad thing and not be a bad person. You can love someone who's done a bad thing and not be a bad person. You can even be someone who's done a bad thing and not be a bad person.* It helped Marcus to think this way, and he cut a deal with his father— sometime before the holidays he would go up to Bedford Hills to see Constance. He refused to partake in the weekly phone calls with Bo and LaTisha. When he was ready to talk to Mama, he told himself, he would do so face to face.

The first Saturday in November he rescheduled his work shift and he and Winnie went to the prison together, on the train. They were as solemn as they would have been at a funeral, holding hands and gazing out the window as the last of the fall leaves in Westchester County passed them by. Since Marcus had never been to the prison before, Bo told him what stop to get off at and how to catch the free bus to the prison grounds.

"It's not a pretty place," Bo said. "You know that, right?"

Marcus knew it intellectually, but that was different from actually *seeing* the Bedford Hills Correctional Institute—the barbed wire, the armed guards, the stench of lost hope, the absolute concrete and metal desolation of the place. It was hell on earth. When Marcus and Winnie stepped down from the bus, they were herded into a huge waiting room filled with other visitors. Marcus gripped Winnie's arm and led her to a space on a vinyl couch. There were glass-topped coffee tables with torn magazines and coloring books and broken crayons—because the waiting room was filled with little kids. It could have been a pediatrician's office except for the edgy way the adults acted, sneaking glances, both shameful and interested, at one another. Everyone in the room loved someone who had done a bad thing.

During the wait, Marcus nearly fell asleep. He felt his body wanting to check out, shut down. Because it was too much to handle—the prospect of seeing his mother. Winnie was reading her English assignment, *Macbeth,* and Marcus wished he'd brought something to read, though he doubted anything would distract him. Finally, over the buzz of the room, Marcus heard his name. He helped Winnie up and walked toward the heavy black woman who was waiting for him. He tried to clear his mind as he would before a swim meet.

Constance, when he saw her, was behind glass, but Marcus marveled at how familiar she was. His *mother.* Mama. He'd expected her to look sad or tired; he'd expected her to look older. But, in fact, she looked much the way she had his entire life— with smooth brown skin, wide brown eyes, and the hair she always claimed she could do nothing with. At home, she wore silk scarves over her head, but here she made do with a navy blue bandana.

In those initial moments of studying her face—and yes, she looked as terrified and unmoored as he did—he waited for his anger to surface. This was what he was worried about—his anger. But instead he felt a profound sadness—his mother had ruined her life. Marcus's life—as the summer had taught him and as his father had promised—would move on past the murders. But for Constance this prison was the last stop.

Constance sat and Marcus sat and they both picked up the phone.

Her voice was the same soft-and-scratchy tone, forever irritated by constantly explaining the basic tenets of the English language to kids who didn't want to learn.

"Hello, child," she said. "I'm glad you came."

When she spoke, Marcus remembered one of the words Kara Schau had given him: "acceptance." He didn't have to forgive, he didn't have to understand. All he had to do was show up. And here he was.

"Hello, Mama," he said.

Winnie was standing a foot or so behind Marcus, a mere observer to the proceedings, but she teared up as she watched Marcus and Constance. She wondered what it would be like to see her father again for fifteen minutes. She would be tempted to give him news—about falling in love with Marcus, or about Beth being married before, or about Garrett becoming a father himself—but then she realized that she would do what Marcus was now doing: telling his mother he loved her.

Winnie couldn't hear Constance's voice, but she read her lips: *I know, child, I know.* Just the way Arch knew, wherever he was, that Winnie loved him and would keep him alive every way that she could.

It might have been the sound of Winnie crying that brought Marcus back to himself. He pulled Winnie forward, closer to the glass.

"Mama," he said. "This is Winnie Newton, Arch's daughter."

Winnie had imagined this introduction twenty times the night before as she tried to fall asleep. She imagined Constance falling to her knees in gratitude, waxing on and on about what a great man Arch was. But now, in the actual moment, when Marcus handed Winnie the phone so that Constance could speak to her, what Constance said was, "I would have known you anywhere. You look just like your father."

And this, of course, endeared Constance Tyler to Winnie forever.

❧

By holiday time, Piper was six months pregnant. As Garrett moved through the days of his life—classes, the end of soccer, the beginning of intramural floor hockey, weekends with friends at the movies, even the occasional date (which he kept secret from his mother and sister)—it was easy enough to forget that the first girl Garrett had ever loved and might still love a little was suffering physically and emotionally as Garrett's child grew inside her on an island thirty miles out to sea. At times—when Garrett took Brooke Casserhill out to dinner at a Peruvian chicken place, for example, where they were able to smuggle in a bottle of wine lifted from Brooke's father's wine *cave*—Piper seemed far away and less than real. She seemed like folklore. But at other times, mostly in the dark hours when Garrett should have been sleeping, Piper and her plight took on a gravity that nailed Garrett to his bed.

He tried to figure out what she expected from him. She accused him of being a kid. Well, yeah—he was seventeen years old, a senior in high school, just like she was. Had she wanted him to marry her? Raise the child? If that was the adult thing, and maybe it was, then Garrett conceded: it was out of his reach. He couldn't do it.

He called her every month after her doctor's appointment, and their conversations consisted almost entirely of the clinical: how much weight had she gained? (Fifteen pounds.) What was she measuring? (Twenty-four centimeters.) Did the AFP screen come back normal? (Yes.) Did she test positive for gestational diabetes? (No.) When would she sign up for Lamaze classes? (After the first of the year.) The baby kicked all the time now, Piper said, and the girlfriends who'd shunned her when they found out she'd let that *summer kid* impregnate her were now the ones who were most eager to lay their hands on the firm sphere of Piper's belly and feel the baby drum from the inside.

Garrett had had no idea that a single baby could consume so much mental energy; always, in these conversations with Piper, it seemed like there were a hundred small points of discussion all revolving around the baby. In history class, Mr. Rapinski spoke of women in Third World countries who excused themselves from the assembly line of whatever factory they worked at, gave birth in the restroom and handed the infant off to a family member to care for at home. But it was nowhere close to that easy for a couple of white American upper-middle-class teenagers.

Garrett didn't tell anyone in New York about Piper or the baby, and he forbade Beth and Winnie to mention it to anyone but Kara Schau. His mother understood. "Every man, woman, and child is entitled to one secret," she said. "I had mine, now you have yours." Garrett hated putting himself in a similar situation to his mother, and he wondered if the adult thing to do was to come clean, confessing to everyone he knew that he had impregnated his summer girlfriend and then left her to deal with it by herself. Then he could accept blame; he could wear the scarlet letter. *You want to be back in New York where you can pretend none of this ever happened*, Piper had said. She was right! Garrett didn't want to be whispered about; he didn't want the information fermenting his teachers' opinion of him as they wrote his college recommendations. He didn't want to lose any friends. He couldn't wait until March when Piper

would birth the baby, then give it away, and the ordeal
would be ended.

※

The holidays came, and because they were the first holidays
without Arch, they could only be described as bearable. In January, Beth took the twins to Hunter Mountain to ski, and for
the break in February, the three of them flew to Palm Beach and
stayed at the Breakers. Garrett praised his mother for these trips,
these *distractions*, and helped out as much as he could—carrying
luggage, arranging the limo to and from the airport, and being
as amiable as possible.

While they traveled, he found himself thinking about the
baby more often. He'd never realized how many children inhab-
ited the world. Babies in car seats and strollers clogged the train
station and airline terminals. Garrett heard their cries during
takeoff and landing. He noticed, in every public bathroom he
used now, the beige Koala changing station bolted to the wall.
These had been there all along—they hadn't been installed to
torment him—and yet he never remembered seeing one before.
At Hunter Mountain, Garrett, Beth, and Winnie ate dinner at a
Mexican restaurant and Garrett became so preoccupied with a
blond two-year-old boy at the next table who did a fire engine
puzzle over and over, shrieking with delight each time he completed it, that Garrett barely touched his fajitas. At the Breakers,
he separated from his mother and sister and lay on a lounge by
the baby pool where he watched the little ones cavorting in their
water wings. A baby, an actual baby, lived inside of Piper and
this time next year that baby would be crawling or walking or
swimming. His child. His little boy or girl. It hurt him in a way

he couldn't name. It was worse than heartbreak. It was worse, in a way, than losing his father.

❧

Beth thought that March would never arrive, but then, of course, it did. They marked the one-year anniversary of Arch's death quietly—dinner in the apartment with Arch's mother. Trent Trammelman called Beth in the morning to say that the law firm was donating money in Arch's name to establish a scholarship fund at Danforth. Arch's secretary, now the secretary for a new attorney, sent flowers, and a bunch of thoughtful souls sent cards. Beth hated the idea of a death day as an anniversary, and yet once it was past, she felt relieved. A milestone survived. Since Christmas, friends had been inviting Beth over to meet men—single, divorced, widowed—and once Beth caught on, she always begged off, saying, "Please, it hasn't even been a year." Now that the anniversary had come and gone, her excuse vanished. And yet, Beth couldn't bring herself to think about dating. All she could think about was their impending trip to Nantucket.

Beth spoke to the headmaster at Danforth: this was a very important family trip (she did not call it a vacation), and for reasons she couldn't specify, she didn't know how long they'd be gone.

Everyone at Danforth accommodated them. Winnie and Garrett both had excellent grades and they'd both been accepted to college. Garrett got into Princeton on early admission, and Winnie had been accepted at NYU, though she was still waiting to hear from Columbia, Williams, and Brown.

They were free to stay on Nantucket as long as they cared to.

Marcus was coming along for the week of his spring break. He, too, had been accepted to college—Queens College, a short bus ride from his apartment, and Colgate University, upstate. Colgate was a white person's school, but his English teacher, Ms. Marchese, encouraged him to apply. He wrote an essay about his mother. The admissions committee was so impressed by the essay that they offered him a full ride for all four years, giving Marcus an opportunity worth much more than thirty thousand dollars. Marcus spoke to the swim coach and the head of the black student union, both of whom encouraged him to come. But the deciding factor was the enthusiastic call from one of the English professors who'd read his essay. *You have a way of turning words on a page into pure emotion,* the professor had said. *You have the makings of a fine, fine writer.*

Beth had never been to Nantucket in March, and as soon as she stepped out of the Rover onto Horizon's shell driveway, she understood why. The wind was brutal, whipping across Miacomet Pond in cold, wet sheets. The sky was low and gray and the ocean was a roiling black. The town had been practically deserted—less than half of the businesses showed any signs of life. In New York, trees had already started to bud; crocuses were up. But not here.

This time, Beth had brought her cell phone, and as soon as she sent the kids to the Stop & Shop for firewood and groceries, she called David. He'd sent a Christmas card—no picture, no note—just the three names signed in his handwriting at the bottom. She was nervous dialing his number and not because of Piper. A couple of times over the winter she caught herself repeating his words of the previous summer. *I thought about kissing you. I thought about making love to you.* When she got very lonely—weekend nights at home when the kids were out and she could hear New York frolicking outside without her—she entertained the possibility of her and David together. Not married again, but together. As companions—that's what she wanted as she grew older—someone to spend time with once the twins left. Would it be so crazy if that person was David? She went so far as to wonder if he would ever visit her in the city. He'd never been there to her knowledge. She could show him the city the way everyone should experience it.

When David answered the phone, she said, "Hi, it's me."

"Me?"

"Bethie," she said. Flirting with him already. "How's Piper?"

"Two centimeters dilated, ninety percent effaced," David said, sounding like a doctor himself. "She's as big as a house. I mean, huge. I can't believe this is my little girl. I just can't believe it."

"Yeah," Beth said. They were silent a minute, listening to the static of the cell phone. "You'll call us as soon as . . ."

"As soon as," David said. "The doctor said any time now. How long are you staying?"

"We're staying until Piper has the baby," Beth said. "That's why we came, after all."

"Right," David said.

"Has she . . . changed her mind about adoption?" Beth asked.

"No."

"So, how will it work, then? Will they come get the baby? Take the baby away?"

"There's a procedure, yes. The people from the agency are professionals, Beth. They've met with Piper and gone over the range of emotions she can expect. They give her twenty-four hours with the baby, then she signs a document and the baby goes. Piper made it clear that she and Garrett want to name the baby, and that's allowed."

"She and Garrett want to *name* the baby?" Beth asked.

"Yes."

Beth took a deep breath of the shockingly cold air inside Horizon. The house felt stingy without any heat. They were all going to spend the night on air mattresses and sleeping bags in front of the fire. Roast hot dogs, that kind of thing. It would be fun for about three hours.

"I don't know if I'm going to be able to handle this, David. Watching some stranger carry away my grandchild. How about you?"

He sighed. "Oh, Beth. I've lived with this decision every day for the last nine months. I've had to deal with people coming up to me on the street, telling me how irresponsible I am as a parent and Piper is as a person. She lost two of her closest friends, she says the kids at school stare at her all the time, and her teachers treat her differently, too. They treat her like she's stupid. But she's not, of course. She got into BU and BC, and was wait-listed at Harvard. Her grades are the best they've ever been and she's going to college, just like she said she was going to. But it's been hard. I guess you haven't had to give it much thought while you were in New York."

There he was, using the same old refrain—*I had to live with the pain while you were away*. God, this was a bitter man. But no, that wasn't quite right. He had a point; she was lucky. She had always been able to lead a double life; she had always been able to escape.

"I gave it a lot of thought," she said. "I thought of it every day."

"Did you," David said. "Well, I bet Garrett didn't tell his buddies. And I'll bet you didn't report it to his teachers. In fact, I'll bet no one in New York knows why you're mysteriously off to Nantucket this week."

Where was all this anger *coming* from? "Not true," Beth countered. "My therapist knows."

"Your therapist," David said. He breathed forcefully into the phone, then chuckled. "God, I need a therapist. We'll see you at the hospital then, Bethie?"

She was grateful that he used the nickname. "Okay."

She hung up the phone and stared at it for a moment, wishing that the conversation had gone better, that there had been some kind of connection between the two of them. This was the man she fantasized taking to brunch in Soho?

It was true that none of the kids had acknowledged the real reason they were here. On the ride up, Marcus and Winnie perused the Colgate catalog and admission packet line by line, trying to figure out what Marcus's freshman year might be like. ("It sounds cool," Winnie concluded. "It sounds cold," Marcus corrected her.) Garrett drove the entire way and didn't take his eyes off the road except to collect money for tolls. Now, all three kids stampeded into the house with bags of groceries—a pile of Duraflame logs and every kind of junk food imaginable. This was a camping trip for them. Winnie and Marcus braved the icy staircase to the beach because they wanted to check out the ocean, and Beth sent Garrett to the basement to switch on the water heater. When he came back upstairs, she said, "I just spoke with David on the phone. He said any day now. He said he's going to call us." God, even she couldn't say it: Piper *is due* any day now. He's going to call us *when the baby is born.*

Garrett's face was wooden, expressionless. "Okay, thanks."

Beth touched his shoulder. He pulled away. He was so foreign to her. In six months, he would leave for Princeton and she would never know him again, not really. Such was the sadness of sons.

⚘

That night in Horizon was unlike any Beth had spent there. Because of the cold, she supposed—the cold changed things. For a few years, when Beth was in college, she had arrived in early May, when the house was chilly and damp. She kept the fireplace lit and walked around in her grandfather's Irish fisherman's sweater and jeans and thick socks. But those days didn't come close to this kind of cold—a cold that required the Newtons to sleep in fleece jackets inside their flannel-lined sleeping bags in front of the fire. Winnie and Garrett brought the same gear they wore to Hunter Mountain—Bodnar ski jackets and Patagonia microfiber pants. Marcus had to make do with layers—T-shirt, long-sleeved T-shirt, sweatshirt, a fleece that he borrowed from Beth when the leather jacket he brought grew stiff and almost cracked.

They got a fire blazing, and when the sun went down they roasted hotdogs, made popcorn in an old-fashioned popcorn maker, and Beth got the stovetop working where she warmed up cider. They all took showers—Beth was the last one in and her hot water conked halfway through. She dried off as quickly as she ever had in her life and jumped back into her clothes.

They arranged their sleeping bags lengthwise so that everyone's head faced the fire. Winnie and Marcus were in the middle, Beth and Garrett on either side. The kids talked about school mostly, and college. Beth drifted in and out of the conversation; her mind was consumed with her conversation with David and with her own discomfort. She interrupted them.

"Tomorrow," she said, "we're checking into the Jared Coffin."

Before they could protest or cheer (Garrett and Marcus were all for it; Winnie liked things just as they were, cozy like this), the phone rang.

Piper was in labor.

"Her water broke right in the middle of *The West Wing*, and now her contractions are a minute and a half apart," David said. "We just got to the hospital a few minutes ago. You can either come now—it might mean a long time waiting—or I can call you when the baby is born."

Beth looked at the kids. Even Marcus's expression was that of the keenest interest. They would never sleep, that much was clear.

"We'll come now," she said.

Compared to Horizon, the hospital was positively tropical. Beth shed a layer of clothing before they reached the admitting desk.

"Which way is labor and delivery?" she asked.

A nurse directed them upstairs. Standing in the elevator, Beth squeezed Garrett's hand. He squeezed back.

"It's going to be okay, honey," she said. "Babies are born all the time, every day, all over the world."

"I know, Mom," he said.

The elevator opened on the second floor and they followed signs. Beth was hurrying, though she, who had been in labor for eighteen hours with the twins, knew how long it could take. They came upon a pastel-colored waiting room filled with over-stuffed sofas and chairs. The kids flung themselves all over the furniture—yes, it was more appealing than sleeping on the floor of that icebox. There was a woman on one of the couches read-ing a copy of *Martha Stewart Living*, and she looked up, alarmed at the invasion. She was very attractive, with honey-colored hair tied back in a braid. The woman looked them over, no doubt wondering what they were doing there—this was a maternity ward, not the common space of a college dorm. The woman opened her mouth to speak.

"Beth?" she said.

Beth smiled, politely at first, flipping through her mental Ro-lodex. Who was this? Then a quiet panic infiltrated and she fought to keep her smile steady. She really *had* been out of touch in New York. Because although she had given the impending birth of this baby hours and hours of thought, *never once* had it occurred to her that she would have to see Rosie. But here she was—of course—Rosie Ronan, Piper's mother. The other grandmother.

"Oh, God, Rosie," Beth said. In her mind, Beth realized, she had filed Rosie away as "absent." Like Arch. Not there. Beth went to the woman and took both her hands, even went so far as to kiss her on the corner of the mouth. This was *so* awkward. More awkward than the cocktail party so many years ago when Rosie introduced Beth to a friend as "David's old flame," right in front of Arch. At the time, Beth had swilled deeply off her glass of Chardonnay, and Rosie laughed and said, "Well, we're all adults, right? What's passed is past!" Now here she was—hadn't aged a day in six years—if anything, she was prettier than ever. Beth turned Rosie toward the kids who were halfway to sleep—who could blame them? it was eleven o'clock and the day had been long—and said, "Winnie, Marcus, *Garrett*, this is Rosie Ronan, Piper and Peyton's mother."

Her kids, always polite with other adults, took a few seconds to process what Beth was telling them. Garrett groaned under his breath; he knew he should be the first one to his feet, knew it by the way his mother hit his name the hardest—this woman was, after all, sort of like his mother-in-law. Before Garrett could summon energy to stand, Marcus jumped up. Garrett was grateful for this; it gave him a few seconds to think.

"Marcus Tyler," he said. "Congratulations on your impending good news."

"Thank you," Rosie said, with such a sense of entitlement that one might have thought it was *Rosie* who was having this baby. Beth wondered what she was doing out here in the waiting room, but before she could ask, she watched Garrett rise from the love seat. With a gallantry Beth rarely saw in him anymore, he introduced himself and then he introduced Winnie. "Garrett Newton, Mrs. Ronan, and this is my twin sister, Winnifred Newton."

"It's nice to finally meet you," Rosie said. "Piper and Peyton and David are down the hall in a labor room. I've been banished for making too many suggestions." She smiled sheepishly at Beth, and Beth, against her will, sympathized with her. It *was* always the mother who took the brunt of a teenager's anger.

"Is Piper making any progress?" Beth asked. Just standing so close to the maternity ward brought it all back to her—how delivering a baby was a fight for ground, a struggle for centimeters, one painful contraction at a time.

"Some," Rosie said. "She wants to wait for as long as she can before she takes the epidural. She read somewhere that it slows labor. She was moaning pretty loudly in there and she lost her dinner. The nurses here are outstanding. There's a nurse back there with Piper now who was here when I had both Piper and Peyton. Of course, it wasn't that long ago."

"Only seventeen years," Beth said, then felt like she had stated the unstatable. She removed her layers until she wore only a turtleneck and jeans. The hospital's heating system blew hot, dry air out of a vent directly under Beth's feet. "So I guess we'll just wait then."

"Is it okay if we drift off, Mom?" Winnie asked. She was curled up in a large armchair and Garrett and Marcus were each spread out on a love seat. That left a space on the sofa next to Rosie, who had returned to her magazine—perhaps hearing the blunt declaration of her daughter's age upset her. Beth sat down, then said, "Garrett, do you want to at least tell Piper you're here? In case she wants to see you?"

Garrett opened his eyes and stared at the acoustic tiles of the ceiling. He was so tired, this all seemed like a dream. He looked to Rosie Ronan, and she nodded at him. "That might be a good idea," she said.

Garrett rose.

"You can ask one of the nurses where she is," Beth suggested.

"I'll find it," Garrett said, walking away.

Beth removed her boots and propped her stocking feet on the glass coffee table. She fell asleep before Garrett returned.

When she woke, the waiting area was dark, though the lights in the adjoining hallway were on. All three kids snored shamelessly, and when Beth glanced next to her, she saw Rosie Ronan sitting right there, legs crossed at the ankle, eyes closed. Then, suddenly, Rosie's eyes opened and the two women gazed at each other.

"Beth," Rosie whispered, as though she were seeing Beth for the first time. "Beth Eyler."

"Beth Newton," Beth said. "I haven't been Beth Eyler for twenty years."

"In our house," Rosie said, "you're always called Beth Eyler."

Beth didn't like anything about that statement, and she sensed she wasn't supposed to.

"Any news about Piper?"

"They gave her the shot," Rosie said. "She's sleeping."

Beth nodded slowly, then tried to close her eyes, as though drifting off to sleep. Rosie allowed it for a few seconds before she spoke again.

"I was very sorry to hear about your husband."

Beth opened her eyes. "Thank you."

"David told me what a difficult time you had this summer."

Beth resented this even more: the thought of the bereaved Newton family as a topic of conversation between the Ronans.

"We're doing okay now, thanks."

Rosie uttered what sounded like a soft laugh, egging Beth to look her way. "I was just thinking about the circumstances that led the two of us to be sitting here together," Rosie said. "It's extraordinary."

"I guess it is."

"To think your son impregnated our daughter."

Beth thought about telling Rosie that Piper was hardly an innocent in all this. Those halter tops, the way she clung to Garrett—but she had no desire to fight. Instead, she stood up and turned toward the lighted hallway, thinking she would grab a cup of tea if she could find a vending machine—anything to get away!

"You're leaving?" Rosie asked. A challenge.

"I'd like something to drink," Beth said, and then to be gracious, "Would you like anything?"

Rosie rested her head against the back of the sofa, her eyes at half mast. "I'm all set," she said. "But you might ask my poor husband if he wants a Coke or some coffee. We've been here since nine-thirty."

Beth blinked; the heat was drying out her eyes. "Your poor husband?" she said. "You mean, David?"

Rosie answered with her eyes closed. "I mean David."

It wasn't the woman's words, but her tone of voice that informed Beth. It was the slight smile of victory on her closed lips. David and Rosie were back together. Beth was shocked, incredulous, and crushed, a part of her. It wasn't fair, was it? For them to reunite just as Beth was beginning to glimpse the possibility of moving on, and the desire, if only nascent, to want to move on with David. She brought her hand to her mouth and bit down on the diamond of her "We Made It" ring. It wasn't fair because Beth was, once again, left alone.

A hand touched her shoulder. Beth turned to see a nurse. Gray-haired, big-bosomed, with the kind of weary and wise face that seemed to answer Beth's thoughts by saying, *You're right. It's not fair. But you'll manage. Everyone does.*

What the nurse actually said was, "She's pushing. We're very close. Would you ladies like to come watch the birth of your grandchild?"

Rosie followed the nurse down the hall.

The thought of being in the same room with Rosie and David addled Beth, but that baby was the reason she was here. She walked alongside Rosie, love for this new child rising to heat her skin like a fever. Halfway down the hall, she remembered Garrett and she hurried back to the waiting room to wake her son. Her son who, due to the miracle of life, was about to become a father.

Epilogue

One person dying is like a single drop rejoining the ocean. If Arch could tell his wife and children—and the grandchild who is about to emerge into the world—anything, it would be this: *It's all going to be okay, even in death, especially in death.* But he lacks the power to communicate; he isn't a ghost, only energy crackling in the air.

At a quarter to three on the morning of March twenty-fourth, he is in a delivery room of Nantucket Cottage Hospital. Piper Ronan is in the birthing chair, Peyton Ronan is moving a wooden rolling pin over Piper's lower back, David Ronan is sitting in a straight-backed chair borrowed from the cafeteria with his hands covering his eyes because Piper has forbidden him from watching. Carla Hughes, labor and delivery nurse, has been on this ward for twenty-one years and has helped to deliver twelve hundred babies, though this is her first second-generation child. She helped deliver Piper nearly eighteen years ago. Carla isn't one to pass judgment on the mess kids get themselves into. She has

three teenaged sons herself—one of whom makes honor roll
every report card, one of whom was arrested for taking a baseball
bat to their neighbor's mailbox, and one of whom has yet to
distinguish himself as saint or sinner. Carla will say that this
particular seventeen-year-old girl is a model patient. She doesn't
complain, and doesn't make demands, although she did send her
mother out of the room, but this is to be expected from even
the most seasoned patient. So far the delivery is going smoothly.
Carla imagines it has something to do with the youth of Piper's
body—the muscles are loose and flexible. A teenager's tolerance
for pain is high; just look, for example, at her pierced nose.

The doctor monitors Piper's progress.

"Three more pushes," he says to everyone in the room.

Outside the door wait Beth, Rosie Ronan and a barely conscious Garrett. Arch focuses on his son. If he had a body, he
would give Garrett a hug. The birth of this baby is confusing
him; he doesn't know how to cope with it. Despite all of his
conflicting emotions, Garrett is looking forward to holding his
child, if only for a few minutes. Arch remembers holding his own
children for the first time. What he remembers most vividly is
how grateful he was that God gave him two arms: one for a baby
boy, one for a baby girl.

Beth and Rosie Ronan are doing everything in their power to
suppress their eagerness. Both are afraid to even poke their heads
in. They can hear through the crack in the door the sounds of
Piper struggling: the breathing, the moaning. Rosie is ashamed
that she has been banished from the room, but that, she figures,
is the price she pays for leaving the girls to their father. It will
take a while for either of the girls to trust her again, to trust her
and David together.

Beth is afraid to enter the room because David waits on the other side. Arch understands the complexity of her feelings. Another thing he would like to tell her is this: *Every man, woman and child is entitled to one secret.* Arch's secret is that he knew about Beth's first marriage from the beginning. During their engagement, Arch clerked for a judge and one day during a lull he checked to see if his future wife had ever appeared on public record. In death, all is forgiven, but in this case, Arch forgave Beth long ago. He hopes that someday she will forgive herself.

Piper bears down, remembering the first time she laid eyes on Garrett Newton, when she went to his house last June for a cookout. He'd looked so sad. Handsome and sad—an irresistible combination. Now she's the one who's sad, because twenty-four hours after the birth, this child will be handed into the waiting arms of a couple from South Hadley, Massachusetts, a philosophy professor and her husband. Her own baby whom she's felt kick and squirm inside of her every hour for months, who stepped on her bladder last week, causing her to leak in her maternity overalls during calculus class. Her baby—for nobody knows this baby yet but Piper—will be carried out the front door of this hospital, leaving Piper alone with an aching body and bleeding psyche. She imagines meeting the child again someday and being asked to explain: *Why did you give me up?*

I am so very young, Piper thinks.

Another contraction on the horizon, like a Mack truck, and Piper knows it's headed right for her.

Peyton is proud of the job she's doing as birthing coach. She's the only family member who hasn't made Piper cross. But Peyton is tired. It's nearly three o'clock in the morning and she's starving. Her parents promised her a huge Downyflake breakfast as soon as Piper and the baby went into recovery, and so that's what Peyton thinks about: blueberry pancakes with blueberry syrup, a plate of crisp bacon, a glass of fresh OJ.

"Here comes the head," the doctor says. "Give me one more big push."

Piper grits her teeth. The epidural has all but worn off. Nothing in the world prepared her for how this feels.

"One more," the doctor says.

"I can't!" she screams.

"I have the baby's head," the doctor says. "I need one more big push."

Arch sends her a surge of energy. This is, after all, his grandchild.

Piper takes a deep breath and thinks, though she's not sure why, of Nantucket as a baby, floating in an amniotic ocean. Then, even stranger, of Nantucket as her mother.

She hears her baby cry. Feels a hot, wet weight on her belly.

Piper grasps for the child and it is brought up to her, close, where she can smell the tang of blood and fluids from her own body.

"It's a boy," the doctor says.

A boy, Arch thinks.

A boy? Piper is confused. She'd been so sure . . .

"A boy!" David cries. He kisses Piper's forehead and hugs Peyton. He has never been so proud of his daughters. Then he's out the door and nearly knocks over Beth and Rosie and Garrett. "It's a boy!" he proclaims, so elated by the news that he doesn't have time to wonder if Beth knows that he and Rosie are back together and that he has finally let what's passed be the past. He kisses both women.

There is laughter and crying. Beth hurries down the hall to wake Winnie and Marcus. Garrett slides down the wall until his ass hits the floor. *A boy.* A son of his own, just like he always thought he wanted.

They name the baby Archer Newton. The adoptive parents will add their own last name—they may even change his first and middle names—but for the next twenty-four hours when the baby is in the arms of the people around him, the people who loved him first, he will be Archer Newton.

No one is surprised by the name except, perhaps, Arch himself. The way that life continues, the way that human beings persevere, regenerate, *keep going*, summer after summer, season after season, generation after generation, amazes him. Even now.

New York City, June 2016

Winnie's roommate and best friend from Brown, Alison Marsh, is getting married. To Winnie's ex-boyfriend. On Winnie's thirtieth birthday. On Nantucket Island. And Winnie doesn't have a date. It's a set of circumstances that makes Winnie want to sing the blues. She will celebrate the close of her third decade by serving as maid of honor—again. She has already done maid of honor twice before—for Garrett's first wife, Riley (because Riley had no sisters and *no close girlfriends*, a warning sign if ever there was one) and for her mother, Beth, when Beth married David Ronan (for the second time).

Beth describes Winnie as "a bit adrift," which is a romantic way of saying Winnie has nothing meaningful anchoring her to the earth: no job, no significant other, no plan. It is only thanks to the trust fund set up when Winnie's father, Arch, died that Winnie isn't an indigent living in an alley in Alphabet City. But because Arch was thoughtful with his estate planning, Winnie has plenty of money and owns a two-bedroom condo (with one exposed-brick wall and built-in bookshelves) on East 89th Street, a scant block from Danforth, her former high school. Unfortunately, her apartment's proximity to Danforth underscores how little Winnie has achieved since she graduated.

Things started out okay. She graduated with honors from Brown and scored a 170 on her LSAT, which gained her admission to law school at both Yale and Georgetown. She chose Georgetown because Washington had been popular with her friends that year. Alison got a job at the NIH, and Winnie's boyfriend, Tag, was offered an entry-level position in the front office of the Washington Redskins. Winnie rented a charming row house right on M Street and she shared it with both Tag and Alison.

But law school had been a disaster and the dreams of following in her father's footsteps as a corporate attorney fizzled. Winnie dropped out after her first year and she broke up with Tag, whom, Winnie suspected, would be far happier with Alison.

This had proved to be true: Alison and Tag are now getting married in the backyard of Alison's grandparents' house, High Tide, in Sconset. Winnie harbors no hard feelings about Alison and Tag; she all but set them up when she moved out. Winnie is jealous only of their coupledom, the way they seem to so thoroughly enjoy and respect each other and the way they bring out each other's best qualities. Winnie's relationship with Tag had been adversarial from the start; when they were getting along, they bickered, and when they weren't getting along, they fought loudly, often in public.

After dropping out of law school and breaking up with Tag, Winnie moved back to New York City. For many people, New York was a dream realized—if you can make it there, you'll make it anywhere—but for Winnie, it was capitulation. New York was home base; the Upper East Side was as comfortable and familiar as Winnie's beat-up Converse sneakers. She bought the apartment and people congratulated her, which she found odd. She hadn't *done* anything except spent her trust fund, and she wasn't even sure she'd gotten a good deal.

She took an evening bartending course in Brooklyn, then got a job mixing artisanal cocktails at a new place called Jett in Williamsburg. She started dating the bouncer at a seedy bar down the street. Chuck was big and intimidating-looking: shaved head, tattoos, earrings, a long beard dyed electric blue. Winnie couldn't bring Chuck to meet her mother; she couldn't bring Chuck to Manhattan, period. Theirs was a borough-specific romance that lasted for nine months, which was how long it took for Jett to go bankrupt and close.

Thankfully, Winnie had been dating Erik Chambers in the period following her Brooklyn phase because that was when Garrett met and married Riley Dillon. Riley worked with Garrett on the trading floor at Merrill Lynch. She was beautiful and sharp with an encyclopedic knowledge of swear words, football, and punk bands. Garrett had to fight off every other single guy in the company for Riley's affections. It was the chase and the competition that had been enticing for Garrett, rather than any deep, meaningful bond with the girl herself. Both Winnie and Beth tried to tell Garrett this, but he wouldn't listen. Winnie, who at that time was working as a salesgirl at Intermix, was nearly as thin as she had been after her father died. She was also employed and dating appropriately WASPy Erik Chambers, who was a marketing executive at Colgate-Palmolive. Winnie had worn a size-zero bridesmaid dress in the palest yellow silk, to fill the honor spot because although Riley had forty men she could ask to stand up for her, there wasn't a female she knew except Winnie who would be willing to fill the position.

Garrett and Riley's marriage lasted nearly a year, then it was revealed that Riley was and had been sleeping with her (and Garrett's) boss. By that time, Winnie had broken up with Erik Chambers and quit her job at Intermix.

She and Garrett had started hanging out together. They went to dinner; they drank at bars. Winnie realized that people mistook them for a couple, which was disturbing, but Winnie relished the time spent reconnecting with her twin.

She said, "I think there's something wrong with me."

"There's nothing wrong with you, Win," Garrett said.

"The only man I've loved, in my entire life, other than Daddy . . . is Marcus."

"There is something wrong with you," Garrett said.

It was eight years later, and Winnie still found herself in love with Marcus Tyler, the boy she had lost her virginity to on Nantucket the summer after her father died.

Marcus had attended Colgate University. He and Winnie had exchanged emails throughout their freshman year, but immersion in their separate college experiences broke them up. Through her mother, Winnie had heard that Marcus graduated from Colgate, then moved to London with his girlfriend. A few years later, Beth told Winnie that Marcus was attending the graduate fiction workshop at the University of Iowa. Then, he'd been awarded a Stegner Fellowship at Stanford. His first novel, *Infamous*, had been sold to Alfred E. Knopf after a heated auction, and Marcus had received a high six-figure advance. Fox Searchlight had optioned the film rights and signed Michael B. Jordan to play the lead— who was, of course, a thinly disguised version of Marcus himself.

When the novel hit shelves, the details of Constance Bennett Tyler's trial were brought back into the spotlight, including her defense by Archer Newton. Beth emailed Winnie the links to every article that mentioned Arch, but by that time, Winnie was living in Santa Teresa, Costa Rica, with Paolo and the events that had led up to her father's death seemed extremely removed from her present life—long ago and far away.

What she thought was that she was happy for Marcus. She hoped writing the book had helped him exorcise his demons. She wondered how he was handling all the fortune and fame; Winnie had always known Marcus would be successful. She had believed in him far more than she had ever believed in herself.

Had Marcus gotten married? Winnie was tempted to check at one of the Internet cafes in town, but she was afraid that if she found out he had gotten married, the delicate equilibrium she had achieved might crumble.

Winnie had gone to Costa Rica on vacation; she was drawn to the beaches and the jungles. After traveling through the usual tourist spots—Monteverde Cloud Forest, Arenal Volcano, Jaco, Manuel Antonio National Park—she had ended up in the sleepy, hippie surf town of Santa Teresa and it had felt like home. She got a job as a barista at the one upscale French bakery and soon after, she met Paolo. Eventually, Winnie got a better job as a property manager for a German couple who owned six rental villas in Santa Teresa. This allowed Winnie to lie on the beach watching Paolo surf until four o'clock, at which point she climbed onto the back of Paolo's motorbike. They would meet the renters—nearly all Americans—at the Super Hacienda. Paolo and Winnie—and often their pit bull named Quidnet, splayed across Winnie's lap—would lead the tenants to the villas. Winnie would explain the Internet, the laundry, the security system, and the air-conditioning, and then she would leave the exhausted, overwhelmed Americans to have a happy vacation. It was a cupcake of a job, but "property manager" had more cachet than "bartender," "barista," or "salesgirl." And Winnie had a year-round tan.

Costa Rica lasted four years, until the German couple hit

financial hard times and all six villas went into foreclosure. Winnie had considered buying one of the villas herself using part of her trust fund, but she suspected it was time to end her Costa Rica phase. She was sick of the dust and the *amigas* in the kitchen and the girls in teensy bikini bottoms bending over to pick up their surfboards right in front of Paolo. She was also sick of Paolo, sick of translating to him and for him; she was sick of empanadas, sick of the mangy, three-legged dogs that growled at Quidnet. She wanted to go home.

✄

And so, at the age of twenty-nine years, eleven months old, Winnie finds herself waiting for her life to begin.

It's June and the city is beastly hot. Winnie is heading up to Nantucket for Tag and Alison's wedding in a week. It's tempting to simply stay there for the summer. She could get a job bartending at the Miacomet Golf Club down the road from the house; Winnie saw they were advertising when she checked the classified ads. But to stay on Nantucket would mean delaying adulthood for another three months and Winnie just can't wait that long. She wants to create something *real*, something *lasting*.

✄

A few days before Alison's wedding—the strapless floral silk dress Winnie will be wearing as M.O.H. is already tucked neatly into her garment bag—Winnie plans to have dinner with Garrett and his second wife, Joanie. Joanie is sweet and pretty, a schoolteacher at the Little Red Schoolhouse. Joanie is also five months pregnant. Winnie wonders if Joanie minds being Garrett's second wife and then she wonders if Joanie knows that she will bear Garrett's second child. His first child, a son, Archer Newton Messier, is being raised by a couple in South Hadley, Massachusetts. "Archie" is thirteen years old, play soccer, excels at math, and has two younger brothers because after Archie was adopted, Mrs. Messier got pregnant, then got pregnant again. Garrett hasn't seen his biological son since the day after he was born, but Mrs. Messier sends Beth a card and letter with photographs of Archie every year at Christmas. Winnie studies the photographs like a fiend. She can't get over how much Archie looks like her father. She longs to hug Archie, to talk to him, to tell him what a fine human being the first Archer Newton was. She wants to express how amazing she finds it that Arch's genes live on through Archie. But Winnie understands that any communication with his birth family can be confusing, especially in adolescence.

Winnie meets Garrett and Joanie at the Cleveland in Soho. She kisses Joanie and puts a gentle hand on her swelling midsection. Winnie wonders if she will ever be pregnant; it seems like a far-away dream.

The three of them are seated in the back garden, a hidden treasure of the city, especially at this time of year. The air is so hot and close—even now, at nearly eight o'clock at night—that Winnie reconsiders Nantucket. She would have Horizon to herself; Beth and David had sold David's house and bought a three-bedroom condo on Cliff Road. Beth loves being able to walk to town. She and David only hang out at Horizon on the hottest beach days.

Winnie decides she will not succumb to temptation. Big things are coming her way; she feels it strongly in that instant. Her life is about to change, finally, for the better.

After Winnie and Garrett order cocktails, and an expensive bottle of water for Joanie, Garrett says, "You're not going to believe who's reading at the Barnes & Noble on 86th Street tomorrow night."

Winnie's mouth falls open.

❧

She spends the next day in trembling anticipation. She is going to see Marcus Tyler for the first time since she was a freshman in college. She double-checked what Garrett said. Marcus will be reading from his second novel, *Darkstep*, about a racially motivated murder at a predominantly white liberal arts college in upstate New York, that evening at the bookstore on East 86th Street. Winnie calls the store to see if she needs a ticket and the store clerk says, "No, but I would get here early. We're expecting quite a crowd."

Winnie finds the phrase "quite a crowd" both awe-inspiring and intimidating. She has done nothing with her life that would cause "quite a crowd" to gather. But Marcus has! Is it wrong to think, even for a second, that Winnie and her family played a part in setting Marcus on the road to success? Is it possible they *saved* him? Or is that a typical white-person perspective? Marcus is talented. Marcus would have succeeded with or without the Newton family.

Winnie switches gears. Did she teach Marcus anything about *love*? She knows that she did, but that doesn't mean someone else hasn't taught him more—or better.

❧

Winnie wears one of the flimsy, flowered surf dresses she favored in Santa Teresa; it's too hot for anything else. She still has a tan and her hair has been sun-bleached to a shining white-blonde. Will Marcus recognize her? She feels bad taking him by surprise. She doesn't want to sabotage his concentration. How can he possibly focus on reading when a significant person from his past is sitting in the front row? And yet, a part of Winnie worries that he will be unaffected by her presence, or that he will act like it's no big deal. If he has a wife or girlfriend with him, he may just awkwardly introduce Winnie as—how does the song go?—"somebody that I used to know."

Even so, Winnie is excited. She arrives at the reading forty minutes early and snaps a seat front and center. For a few minutes she's completely alone, wondering if maybe the sales clerk was mistaken. Maybe there won't be "quite a crowd," maybe Winnie will be the only person in the audience. Whereas Winnie would feel embarrassed for Marcus, she would also be elated to have him to herself. They could skip the reading and go right to the Drunken Munkey.

But no sooner does Winnie fantasize about this than the chairs around her fill up. Winnie looks discreetly around. The crowd is half black, half white and nearly everyone wears glasses. Are there any women who might be attached to Marcus? Winnie doesn't think so. Her heart is walking a tightrope toward hope and elation one wobbling step at a time. She has never been this nervous in all her life. She has never felt so alive.

✿

Marcus sees the blonde in the front row right away. It's a bad habit left over from his days of loving Winnie Newton: He always notices blonde women first. It used to drive Saneika crazy and, probably, was one of the things that led to their breakup. *You like white women,* she said accusingly. *The whiter the better.* What Marcus had been unable to explain is that he liked, or more accurately loved, one white woman. But that was a long time ago, and he hasn't dated a white woman since.

Marcus tears his eyes off the blonde and tries to focus on the flurry of nervous questions being asked him by the bookstore events manager, Kai. *Anything to drink?* Cold water. *Any special kind of pen for signing?* Ballpoint. *Anything else you need?* A copy of the book, marked at pages forty-two and seventy. *Are pictures okay at the signing?*

Yes, Marcus says. In honesty, he hates pictures and would like to refuse them but his publicist, Otto, extols the benefit of Facebook. When Marcus's picture gets posted by Molly Maybe, Molly's two hundred "friends" see it. Pictures sell books, Otto says.

Kai takes Marcus to a very small green room where they wait for the crowd to assemble and settle. This is Marcus's one and only event in Manhattan. He's at Books & Things in Bergen County tomorrow night; he has the weekend free and then next week he hits the Boston area stores: Wellesley Booksmith, Porter Square, the Harvard Coop.

It feels peculiar to be back in the city. Last night, Marcus had dinner at Windies with his father and LaTisha, who now teaches English at I.S. 227 in Queens. Queens felt less like home and more like the place he escaped from. His father looked old and his sister, tired. They talked about Constance only briefly. Apparently, she has started a literacy program within the prison—no surprise there. Marcus's father seemed about ready to suggest that Marcus go visit his mother, but Marcus headed him off by saying, "I'll go next time I'm in New York. I'll go when I'm not on tour."

It's impossible for Marcus to be on the Upper East Side of Manhattan and not think about the Newtons. The last time Marcus spent any real time here was his senior year in high school when he used to come visit Winnie every Sunday. He still remembers the building and the apartment number. He thought about stopping by but the last he heard, Beth was spending half the year on Nantucket. She had married David Ronan in 2010 after David's wife, Rosie, left him for good, this time moving across the country to Portland, Oregon. And Winnie was living in Costa Rica, apparently. Marcus doesn't know where Garrett is and, frankly, he doesn't care.

Events Manager Kai checks in with him. "Great crowd out there. Ready to start?"

Marcus nods. He double-checks that the marked pages are correct and bows his head as Kai strides out of the green room to the podium to introduce Marcus.

"The *New York Times* book reviewer Michiko Kakutani said of Marcus Tyler's *Darkstep* . . ."

Marcus tunes out. This tour is comprised of twenty-seven events; tonight is number sixteen. It's hard to provide a unique, dynamic, memorable experience every night. Marcus sometimes motivates himself by imagining Winnie Newton in the audience. She is, quite honestly, the only person he cares about impressing.

". . . it is my distinct pleasure to introduce . . . Marcus Tyler!"

Applause, a lot of it. Marcus strides out to the podium. The audience is a sea of faces, more white than black, although the more Marcus writes about race issues, the less race seems to matter in real life. There aren't enough Oscar nominees of color, but our president is an African American. Marcus is sometimes referred to as a "black novelist," but more often he's just referred to as "a novelist."

Marcus sets his novel down on the podium and gives the audience a smile, revealing his dimples. He doesn't zoom in on one face until he succumbs to the magnetic pull of the blonde in the front row.

❧

Winnie can't believe what happens next.

Marcus looks at her. He sees her. Her recognizes her. His face opens up, it blooms, like a flower. He is happy to see her! Then, just as quickly, his eyes mist. He is overcome.

"Winnie?" he whispers into the microphone. "Is that you?"

She nods. When she blinks, tears fall. *She* is overcome. Marcus holds out his hand. She floats to the podium and he squeezes her.

The crowd, confused at first, must soon sense that something important is happening. Important and good. They start to clap.

Winnie wonders if her father is pulling marionette strings from up on his heavenly perch—because how else can she explain the turn of events? She and Marcus go to dinner at the Drunken Munkey after his event and then, Marcus comes back to Winnie's apartment on 89th Street and they make love like it's their second first time. It's so beautiful and tender that Winnie cries and Marcus wipes her tears and says, "I forgot this about you. You cry."

Marcus has the weekend free. He can come to Nantucket with Winnie on Friday and stay until Monday morning. He can escort her to Tag and Alison's wedding; he has a suitcase filled with dress clothes, including one festive pink shirt that matches Winnie's dress.

She will not be alone on her thirtieth birthday. She will be with Marcus.

❦

They are back at Horizon together, thirteen years later. The house, Marcus is pleased to see, looks exactly the same. It smells the same, the front screen door still smacks the frame, and there is still no phone (and no Wi-Fi and no cell service).

Beth and David are out on the porch when Winnie and Marcus arrive. They look older. Beth's blonde hair is streaked with gray and David's hair is nearly white. Beth practically runs to Marcus. She gives him a hug and a kiss on each cheek.

"I didn't realize how much I missed you until just now, when I saw your face," she says. "I have missed you, Marcus Tyler."

Marcus and David shake hands. Marcus last saw David the night that Garrett and Piper's baby was born—and Marcus was pretty sure then that he would never set eyes on David Ronan again.

But here he is. Here they both are.

❧

That evening, Winnie takes Marcus to the Nantucket Yacht Club, where the rehearsal dinner is being held. First things first. Winnie pulls Marcus through the crowd and introduces him to the bride-to-be, Alison.

"This," Winnie says, "is Marcus."

Alison's eyes grow round and her irises start to spin. "*Marcus* Marcus? *The* Marcus? Marcus, your one and only true love?"

When they get back to Horizon after an evening of cocktails, dinner, and dancing—which Marcus enjoyed more than just about anything in his life—Beth is upstairs reading in bed and David is finishing a beer out on the deck. Winnie runs upstairs to tell her mother the details of the evening and Marcus takes a bottle of beer from the fridge and joins David outside.

The two men stare at the ocean in silence. Marcus is now something of a wordsmith, but in this instance, he feels words might ruin the moment. He's pretty sure that David Ronan feels as Marcus does: that they are the luckiest men in the world.

As if reading his mind, David turns to Marcus and raises his beer bottle. "Here's to waiting it out," he says. "And ending up with the right woman in the end."

❧

Winnie's thirtieth birthday is bright, sunny, sparkling. Days don't get any more picturesque than this. It's a good sign, Winnie thinks.

Alison's grandparents' house is a large, gray-shingled cottage with immaculate white trim. It has big gabled windows and a plethora of decks and porches. The front lawn is lush and green, the flower beds pop like fireworks—blue and lavender hydrangea bushes, cosmos, snapdragons. The flower boxes are bursting with candy-striped petunias.

A sign over the front door reads: HIGH TIDE.

"That's funny," Marcus says. "This house isn't even on the water."

❧

Marcus takes a seat among the rows and rows of white folding chairs. He sits on the bride's side, although Winnie has admitted she also has "history" with the groom.

The string quartet begins to play Pachelbel's Canon in D, softly at first, though with each note they grow a little louder. The assembled guests pivot in their seats as the bridesmaids process down the aisle. They are pretty girls wearing short, strapless flowered dresses, identical to the one that Winnie is wearing. But Winnie, last in line, sets herself apart, merely by the magnitude of her smile.

She looks the same way that Marcus feels: like a cup that is brimming over. His love for Winnie swells with the strains of the music—the sublimely beautiful progression of chords, the ecstatic sweetness of the top note. Marcus is experiencing his own personal high tide. He can't imagine getting any happier than he is at this moment.

But then, as Winnie walks by, she turns to Marcus and blows him a kiss, proving him wrong.

❧

Winnie Newton is thirty years old and she is shining like a bright new penny. She stands one step behind the bride, who is marrying Winnie's former boyfriend. The minister raises his hands.

"Dearly beloved," he says.

Winnie holds her breath.

This is it, she thinks. *The beginning.*

Acknowledgments

Thank you—

To the professionals: Michael Carlisle, Jennifer Weis, Jennifer Reeve, Sally Richardson, George Witte.

To Becca Evans, Lauren and Mara Rosenwald, Julia Chumak, Amanda Congdon, Margie Holahan and Sally Hilderbrand, life-savers all.

To Clarissa!

To Congdon & Coleman Insurance, Wendy Hudson at Book-works, Roberta White at Mitchell's Book Corner—and Wendy Rouillard of *Barnaby* fame, because everyone should have a friend in the business.

To my inner, inner circle—Eric, Randy, Heather, and Doug—and to Judith Hilderbrand Thurman, for keeping the spirit of our shared childhood with Dad alive.

Finally, a big hug and kiss to my steadfast cheering section, my source of endless sunshine and encouragement and love, my very own "boys' club": my husband, Chip Cunningham, and our sons, Max and Dawson.

Sun-drenched reading with soul from
ELIN HILDERBRAND